Look for More Titles by Cassandra Chandler

The Blades of Janus
PACK
PROGENITOR

The Department of Homeworld Security
Gray Card
Resident Alien
Business or Pleasure
Tied up in Customs
Entry Visa
Duration of Stay
Duel Citizenship
Invasive Species
Export Duty
COALITION RECKONING
Import Quarantine
Homeworld for the Holidays
Nothing to Declare
THE DEPARTMENT OF HOMEWORLD SECURITY OMNIBUS 1
THE DEPARTMENT OF HOMEWORLD SECURITY OMNIBUS 2

The Forbidden Knights
FORBIDDEN INSTINCT

The Summer Park Psychics
WANDERING SOUL
WHISPERING HEARTS
LINGERING TOUCH
THE SUMMER PARK PSYCHICS OMNIBUS

Other Works
CRAFTING A WRITER'S LIFE: Building a Foundation

Coming Soon

The Blades of Janus
PERIHELION

The Summer Park Psychics Omnibus

Wandering Soul
Whispering Hearts
Lingering Touch

Cassandra Chandler

Copyright Page

Wandering Soul

USA TODAY BESTSELLING AUTHOR
CASSANDRA CHANDLER

Wandering Soul

The Summer Park Psychics
Book One

Cassandra Chandler

Dedication

For those who don't give up on love.

Chapter One

London, England—1881

Flames fell from the rafters as Dante and Edgar staggered toward the door, Mary's limp form held between them. Dante blinked his watering eyes to clear them of smoke. Each breath burned its way into his lungs. A timber crashed to the ground close enough to singe the hairs on the back of his neck.

Only a few more steps and Mary would be safe.

When they stumbled onto the cobblestone street, Dante gasped in the chill, damp air. The evening breeze cooled the left side of his face. If he could have torn off the mask that covered the right side without horrifying Edgar, he would have. The scarred skin beneath was slick with perspiration.

They did not stop until they had carried Mary to the other side of the street, where she would be safe from the horses of the Fire Brigade. Edgar took her weight so Dante could remove his jacket. Dante laid it on the pavement to provide a comfortable place for Mary to rest, then helped Edgar sit with her.

"Mary? Mary!" Edgar cradled her head in his lap, growing more hysterical by the moment.

"She needs you to be calm," Dante said, lightly touching Mary's throat. Her pulse was fast, but strong. Her breathing was not labored.

Dante rose, pulling off his vest. He ran to a nearby rain barrel and submerged the dark fabric till it was soaked through. He wrung it out and brought it back to Edgar, then knelt at Mary's side.

"Take it," Dante said. "She will be fine. You both will."

Edgar took the sodden vest and used it to dab Mary's forehead. His face was pinched with concern. Dante did not have time for further reassurances.

He slid his mother's wedding ring from his little finger. The metal was warm, gold gleaming in the light of the fire.

He passed the ring to Edgar and said, "Sell this to start your lives together. Consider it a dowry."

Edgar grabbed Dante's arm as he started to rise, but quickly pulled away. Dante did not miss how Edgar paled as he stared at Dante's mask. Giselle's lies had wormed their way even into Edgar's mind.

"You cannot be considering going back in there," Edgar said. "Leave it to the Fire Brigade."

"Klaus and Giselle are still inside."

"You would risk your life for them? They tormented you."

"That does not mean they deserve this fate." There was no time for Dante to explain. "I do not wish to die, but I could not live with myself if I did not try to save them."

Edgar's mouth pulled down in a grim line. "What do I tell Mary?"

Apparently, Edgar held little faith that Dante would survive. Dante looked down at Mary and dusted a lock of hair from her forehead. She looked so frail and young.

With a sudden certainty, he knew he would never see her again. Even if he survived, he would not return. Mary considered Dante family. She would want them all to stay together, though she and Edgar and even their children would be judged and shunned for their association with Dante, as his own mother had been. He would not allow that to happen.

"Tell her I want her to be happy."

As Dante stood, Edgar handed back his vest.

"Take this. It might help."

Dante gratefully accepted the wet garment. "Take care of each other. Love each other."

Edgar nodded briefly, then lowered his gaze to Mary once more. Dante turned to face the theatre. The fire had spread since they escaped. Smoke rose thickly from the building, blacking out the stars. There was no time to waste.

Though the main door had not yet succumbed to the fire, it was worse than he had imagined inside. Rafters were falling throughout the building, distant crashes mingling with roaring flames that licked across the ceiling and poured down the walls.

He crouched low to keep his head beneath the smoke as he made his way to the office where Klaus and Giselle spent most of their time poring over ledgers for the failing theatre. Nearing the room, he saw Klaus lying on the floor. Dante leapt over a timber to reach his brother's still form, praying he was not too late.

"Klaus..." Dante's throat seized, the loss overwhelming him. Klaus stared at the ceiling with glassy eyes that reflected the inferno surrounding them.

Dante had only known they were brothers for a week, yet the pain of Klaus's loss brought Dante to his knees. He would never know why his brother hated him so much. Or why their father had waited until the very moment of his death to tell Dante they were kin. He would never understand why Heinrich had abandoned him. He could only guess it was due to his disfigurement.

The last moments of their father's life played through Dante's mind once more. Heinrich's revelation that he was Dante's father. The pained expression that swept across his face as he clutched his chest and fell from the catwalk where they had been speaking. The memory was so vivid, he could almost feel Heinrich's grip going lax as he tried to hold on.

His most cherished dream, being part of a family, had literally slipped through his fingers. It had driven him somewhat mad at the time. He had even thought he had seen an apparition floating near him, a glowing angel whose gaze held a sadness and longing that matched his own.

Dante gently closed Klaus's eyes. He could indulge in self-pity later, if he survived. Giselle was still in the theatre. There was a chance to save his brother's wife. Dante was not sure she would deign to let him touch her, even if it was to carry her from a burning building.

He found Giselle not far from Klaus, a timber resting on her back where it had struck her down. She seemed to sneer at Dante, her lips curled up from her teeth. The lockbox for the theatre's proceeds was clutched against her chest, scuff marks on the floor showing where she had dragged it back toward herself after falling.

How could someone be so filled with greed, even in the face of death? Dante left Giselle and the lockbox where he found them.

He headed for the side door that led to the carriage house, hoping the fire had not yet consumed that part of the building. Above the crackling flames, he could hear men shouting and the cries of frightened horses. The Fire Brigade must have arrived.

He started back the way he had come, only to find a wall of fire. The ceiling groaned in agony, moments from collapsing. Flames surrounded him. At every turn, smoke and heat assaulted his senses.

He was going to die, and for nothing. He had not been able to save Klaus or Giselle. His home was being consumed around him. Everything was turning to ash. Tiny particles made their way through the now dry vest he held to his mouth.

Dante spun in circles, looking for a way out—any way out—but there was none.

If his mother had known he would die this way, perhaps she would have given him a different name. Adding to that dark irony, the only part of his person not roasting in the blaze was the scarred skin beneath the mask covering the right half of his face. It seemed the porcelain protected him from more than the shrieks of startled people. If he had breath to spare, he might have laughed.

Until one of the rafters came crashing toward him.

He curled into a ball, though he knew it was futile. Instinct overpowered reason. Clenching his eyes shut, he waited for the impact, the searing heat and pain it was sure to bring.

Instead, he felt someone's arms wrap around him, their chest pressed against his back as if they were trying to shield him from his fate. The heat that had been baking him vanished. He opened his eyes to see the rafter resting on the floor, somehow occupying the same space as his feet. Flames whose heat he could not feel rose from the wood.

His body was glowing with a soft golden light. He had seen this light the day Heinrich died, emanating from the apparition. Dante's benefactor gripped him more tightly, pressing her body against his.

He glanced over his shoulder to see the apparition's face. He could not quite make out her features through the light she exuded, but he knew the deep chestnut of her eyes.

He had died then, and this was the angel sent to take his soul to the afterlife. He would gladly go with her. Perhaps he would see Heinrich again.

She placed her hand on his shoulder, and said, "Trust me."

Dante did not think he could speak. Instead, he nodded. She helped him rise, then shifted to stand before him, keeping her arms around his chest the entire time. She squeezed him tightly enough that his sore lungs protested.

How could he still feel discomfort when he had moved beyond his body? But more pleasant sensations quickly followed.

She pressed her face against his chest, her cheek smooth upon his skin where his shirt had fallen open. Her hair was as golden as the light surrounding her, stray strands tickling Dante's chin. She clung to him as if her life depended upon it.

The thought unsettled him somewhat, as did her next words.

"Hold on tight."

Dante had no idea what to expect. He wrapped his arms around her, marveling at the slightness of her form. He had never dared to hold another person so closely. He felt her body tense, her grip on him tightening even more, and then a great force whipped him from his feet.

The building around them disappeared, replaced with a frozen void. The contrast from the recent heat of the theatre would have robbed him of breath, except he found that he could neither inhale nor exhale. Even the light of the angel vanished, though he still felt her arms around him. He clung to her desperately.

Light returned along with a sudden sensation of thousands of needles pricking him over his entire body. His knees folded beneath him, and he dropped to the floor.

"Dante? Dante, are you all right?"

He could not speak, his body trembling violently from the icy darkness she had pulled him through. Was this what death felt like?

"I'm so sorry," the angel said. "I didn't think it would be this bad."

She cast a dark cloak over him and joined Dante on the floor, molding her body against his back. She was warm, and as she rubbed his arms and chest, some of the chill receded. The pins-and-needles sensation slowly left his skin, and his breath began to even.

"Stay with me."

The warmth of the room seeped into him and his tremors subsided. He felt the strength return to his limbs, yet was reluctant to rise. With how tightly the angel held him, he wondered if she would even let him should he try. He was content to further collect himself, resting in her arms.

The afterlife was not what he had expected. It looked surprisingly like a private box in a theatre. Two chairs rested in the center of the room, facing a closed curtain of rich purple. Beyond, Dante heard voices and music paired in the unmistakable cadence of a performance.

His afterlife was to be in a theatre? He had hoped for something a bit more varied from his mortal existence.

"Please stay with me," the angel said, still rubbing Dante's arms and chest.

He gently clasped the angel's wrist to halt her efforts to warm him. Though his teeth still chattered slightly, he managed, "I assure you, I have no plans to go elsewhere."

She did not speak, but wrapped her arms around his shoulders, holding him close. Dante could not stop his smile. She was certainly affectionate, this angel of his.

Though he was loathe to leave her embrace, he did not want to spend eternity on the floor. He pushed himself up so he was sitting.

Questions began queueing up in his mind. About the afterlife, the angel, even the play beyond the curtain. He felt her rise to her knees, and turned to make the first of many inquiries, but his voice caught in his throat at his first true sight of her.

Her hair was a halo of gold floating around her face in soft waves. Her eyes were a rich shade of brown and so full of warmth that the last of Dante's chill fled at once. Her lips were pink and full, slightly parted as she gazed at him. Though she no longer glowed, her flawless skin was lightly sun-kissed.

Dante could see a great deal of it. The dress she wore had no sleeves and nothing covered her chest down to the top of her bosom. The black fabric ended just above her knees and was pulled so tightly around her figure that it left little to the imagination.

Well, perhaps that was not entirely accurate. Shocking thoughts filled his mind from the way she leaned toward him, seemingly oblivious to the view that provided. She was kneeling right at his side, and for a moment, Dante wondered what would happen if he closed the small distance between them.

She would most likely scream. At the very least push him away. He snapped his gaze to hers, pushing the fevered thoughts from his mind.

"How do you feel?" she asked.

"I scarcely know where to begin."

"Are you hurt?"

While the prickling sensation that had greeted him upon his arrival had hardly been pleasant, Dante found himself feeling quite well. "I do not believe so. For the most part, I am confused."

"That's understandable," she said. "I'll explain everything as soon as I can. But right now, we have to go."

Perhaps this was merely a way station and his journey had not yet ended. It made sense to take him to a familiar place, a theatre, while shepherding him to the next stage of his existence.

The angel rose and offered him her hand. He took it in his as he stood, though he had recovered enough to stand on his own. He could not resist the chance to touch her again.

"Where is it that we are going?"

She smiled softly. "Home."

Chapter Two

Closing night for the play had brought in a full house. The performers were pouring everything they had into their lines, the crew backstage following their prompts with laser focus. Elsa could still feel the pull of it, all those artists in the act of creation, the emotions of the audience heightening the energy in the theatre.

She had used that energy to bring Dante back with her to her time. She couldn't believe it had worked, even with him standing right in front of her.

She kept a tight grip on his hand, his skin rough from crafting sets for the theatre. He'd been cold when he first arrived, but now she could feel the warmth of his body. Elsa leaned into it, staring up at him.

His eyes were a shade of hazel she'd never encountered before, the color seeming to shift as she watched. She could only see one of his eyebrows, gracefully echoing the shape of his eyes. His face was a perfect balance of strong lines and elegant angles. There was a slight cleft in his chin, and his nose was straight, neatly bisected by the porcelain mask that covered the right side of his face.

One of the actors on stage shouted a line loudly enough to snap Elsa out of her reverie. The play would be over soon, and they needed to leave before the audience filled the hallways of the theatre.

Elsa had consulted on the modern adaptation of *The Phantom of the Opera* now being performed outside her private box. If anyone saw her walking out of the theatre with a man dressed as a more classic version of the character, they would have questions she didn't want to answer.

She glanced at the door, and a flash of gold shining against the dark charcoal of the carpet caught her eye. She released Dante's hand and stooped down to pick up her ring. Well, not really *her* ring.

"This is yours." She placed the ring in Dante's palm.

"My mother's ring. How is it that you possess this?"

"It's a very long story, and we really do need to leave."

Elsa walked to the door and opened it a crack. She peered down the hallway in both directions. It was empty. When she turned back to him, he was sliding his mother's ring onto his pinky finger.

From Dante's perspective, he'd only been without the ring for a few minutes. Elsa had been wearing it for years.

Ironically, she, the time traveler, didn't have time to think about that at the moment. She bent down again to pick up the velvet cloak pooled at his feet. Standing on her tiptoes, she threw it around his shoulders, then fastened it at his neck.

The cloak was much shorter on him, but it would cover his face well enough. It was the mask she needed to hide. He frowned as she lifted the hood into place, tilting his head away from her so his face was even more hidden.

"People will ask questions if they see your mask," she said, resting her hands on his shoulders for a moment. They were firm and warm, even through the layers of fabric. She pulled her hands away before she did something stupid, like lean in and kiss him. "I hope you understand."

"I understand all too well."

She threaded her arm through his elbow, then led him from the box and through the hallways of the theatre. She kept her pace as brisk as she could without being too conspicuous, hoping he wouldn't see anything too modern.

Elsa had funded the production in part so she had a say in what theatre they used. She had selected this one for its Victorian-inspired décor. Dark carpeting covered the floor, and ornate moldings offset floral designs painted on the walls. The light fixtures were made to look like candles, even down to the flame-shaped light bulbs.

They walked down the stairs to the lobby without encountering anyone. She let out a breath of relief and guided Dante toward the side exit.

The night air was muggy after the chill of the air-conditioning inside. A Dumpster in the alley added a faint smell of garbage to the humidity. It wasn't the best first impression for Dante of the modern world, but the front exit wasn't an option. She couldn't risk him seeing cars driving by. She had things to explain first.

They walked around to the back of the theatre, where she had instructed the driver she'd hired for the night to wait. He was standing dutifully by the rear door of the limo, which he opened when he saw them.

She nodded at the driver, then slid into the back seat, pulling Dante in after her. Once the door was closed, she gave Dante the back bench seat to himself and took the one closest to the driver. She wanted to be sure the partition separating the front and back compartments of the limo remained closed. With what she and Dante had to discuss, Elsa didn't want anyone listening in.

"This is a carriage," he said.

"Yes. I'm a little surprised you realized that."

"It has a seating compartment set on four wheels, though they appear quite thick and heavy. I confess it more closely resembles a train car than any carriage I have seen, but there are no tracks for it to ride upon."

She had planned to expose him to the modern world slowly, to give him time to adjust. She knew he had a keen intellect, but she hadn't known how observant he was.

They pulled away from the curb and he placed his hands on either side of the seat. Elsa had traveled to enough times before cars were invented to know it was second nature for those used to the jostling rides of a horse-drawn carriage. In the dim light, she could see Dante's head move from side to side as he looked around the compartment.

"A horseless carriage," he said.

"Another astute observation."

"Not so. It is apparent that we are moving, yet the coachman had not time to harness horses to the carriage. Also, there were no horses in the alley."

She smiled, wishing she could see Dante's expression. She could almost hear the hint of a smile in his voice, as if he was joking with her.

"Have you seen a horseless carriage before?"

"Designs only. But promising work on many aspects of the invention is under way in several countries. I am sure we are on the brink of a great advancement. That is to say, those we have left behind."

Elsa wasn't sure what he meant by that. Was it possible he had already figured out that she had brought him to another time?

She was counting on him being able to adapt, but this seemed a little fast. Then again, she'd only really observed Dante during the biggest ups and downs of his life, moments when his emotions had been strong enough to leave an imprint on the ring he wore.

Even after a century had passed, she felt the energy of those moments stirring in his ring when she bought it. She had been able to use their pull to travel back in time and witness his life.

As powerful as that pull had always been, it was nothing compared to being in Dante's actual physical presence. His touch was intoxicating. Addictive.

Elsa needed to keep her distance. She was supposed to be helping him. Dante would be relying on her to guide him through his new life, his new world. It was her job to protect him, and the weight of that responsibility was only just settling on her shoulders.

For a floundering moment, she wondered if she was completely out of her depth.

"I do not know whether to feel obliged to you or fearful," he said.

"I prefer neither. I'm here to help you, Dante."

"You know my name. I am afraid you have me at a disadvantage."

"I'm Elsa. Elsa Sinclair."

"Dante Lucerne," he said.

"I know."

After a brief silence, he said, "May I ask you some questions, Miss Sinclair?"

"Please, call me Elsa."

"Very well, Elsa."

Hearing him say her name sent a shiver down her spine. She rubbed her arms to tame the goose bumps running wild along her skin.

"Please, take this." He took off the cloak and handed it to her.

"Thanks." She folded the cloak on her lap.

She could see him better now, though not as well as she would like. He was staring at her, and her stomach started doing flip-flops. Riding backward in the limo turned the sensation from pleasant to nauseating. At this rate, she'd wind up getting sick on the side of the road.

"I'm sorry, I can't ride backward like this."

She crossed to the other side of the limo, sitting as close to the window opposite him as she could. She put the cloak on the seat between them as a reminder to stop touching him. She wanted to reassure herself that he was okay, that he was really here with her.

"Are you all right?" he asked.

"It's just a little motion sickness."

"I can hardly feel that we are moving, yet we seem to be passing the lamps at quite a speed."

He was reacting well to the things he'd already figured out. Elsa hoped he would react as well to what she was about to tell him next. It was one thing to make the leap from horse-drawn carriages to cars. It was quite another to hear someone talk about time travel.

The nausea returned full-force as she recalled the last time she'd told someone about her ability. She shoved the memory ruthlessly into the back of her mind. This wouldn't end that way. Dante would understand.

She let herself put her hand on his arm, drawing his attention from the view out the window. His skin was so warm.

"I understand this is confusing. Please trust me. I think eventually you'll be very happy here. It just might take some getting used to."

"I imagine so," he said.

"I have something that will help."

Elsa glanced around the seat, searching for the book she'd brought along on the development of automobiles. Since they'd be starting off in a car and he had seen carriages, she thought it was a good way to ease him into believing that she'd taken him forward in time.

The limo's interior was too dark to see properly, so she reached up and switched on the overhead light. Electricity might have been a better place to start.

"What on earth is this?" Dante reached up and cautiously pressed his fingers against the glass.

Elsa was stunned for a moment by the wonder unfolding on his face. The corners of his lips lifted slightly in an almost-smile. He gently traced his long fingers over the surface of the light fixture.

When he turned back to her, his eyes were a roiling blue-green. Elsa's heart seemed to stop. She couldn't catch her breath.

His smile faded, and Dante sat back against his seat, turning his face away from her. "I apologize. I did not mean to startle you. Perhaps you should extinguish the light."

"I wasn't startled."

"There is no need to preserve my feelings in this matter." The smile he gave her then was rueful. "I assure you, I am quite accustomed to this reaction."

"What reaction?"

"I know that my appearance is…troublesome."

Only in that it made Elsa want to do things that she really shouldn't be thinking about. She couldn't suppress a short laugh.

Dante angled his face a bit toward her, watching her from the corner of his eye. If only he knew how ridiculous that was.

"There is nothing about you that troubles me." Except perhaps that he felt the need to wear his mask at all.

His gaze softened, but he didn't say anything in response. She knew better than to push on this issue so soon. In his time, the mask had been necessary. Elsa would do everything she could to make him feel comfortable enough to show his face to the world. She would start by taking his mind off the matter.

"And the answer to your question is, that is an incandescent light bulb." She dropped her voice to a whisper, remembering the driver. The barrier between the front and back of the limo might be closed, but Elsa was still paranoid. She leaned closer to Dante. "I think those were pretty close to development in 1881 as well, but we'll cover those later."

She saw the book she'd been looking for tucked between the seat and the side of the limo next to him, and reached across to grab it. At that moment, the limo hit a pothole, throwing her off-balance. She might have fallen off the seat, but Dante reached out and grabbed her, pulling her against him.

Elsa's hands landed on his broad shoulders, her breasts pressed against his chest. She thought that time might have stopped entirely, Dante was holding so still. He wasn't even breathing.

He was warm, or maybe she was cold. She couldn't tell. All Elsa knew was that she wanted to be closer, wanted more of them to touch. Parts of her body that she had neglected for years responded to him.

Finally, he asked, "Are you all right?"

"Yes, of course," she said, laughing a little as she pried herself off of him. "Sorry about that. I was just trying to reach this."

She stretched past him and picked up the book. Her heart was still thundering from the contact. It was making her lightheaded.

"Please, look through this." She handed him the book, then leaned back in her seat.

"Carriage schematics?" he asked, leafing through the first pages.

"Just keep going."

Dante skimmed through page after page. "This is quite extraordinary," he said. The more he read, the more creases appeared in his brow. He also began to frown. Elsa hadn't expected that.

"What is it?"

"This is possible," he said.

"Absolutely."

"That is not what I mean."

He closed the book and set it on top of the cloak, his gaze roving over the limo's interior. His hands followed, touching the glass of the windows, the stitching of the seats, the hard plastics and treated wood. He even lifted Elsa's cloak, rubbing the fabric between his thumb and forefinger.

"Talk to me. What's bothering you?"

"The things in this book, though extremely advanced, are within the realm of possibility. There is a logical progression, an evolution of technology, as it were, that cannot be denied. But it is impossible that I should be witnessing them."

"Not everything that is possible can be explained." Her heart picked up again and, for a change, it wasn't because of his closeness.

Dante stared at her for a very long time. She could practically see the thoughts churning in his mind like the waters of a stormy sea.

"Miss Sinclair," he said. "Where exactly am I?"

Elsa glanced to the front of the limo to make sure the partition was still closed. It did little to reassure her. She scooted closer to him and leaned in close.

"You're in America," she said, her voice as low as she could manage. That part wasn't so hard to share. "Florida, precisely."

"Florida…"

Dante looked out the window, though at this time of night, nothing was visible except a dark horizon and stars overhead muted by the tinted glass. Elsa could see his mask reflected back at her. It was surreal.

She had been working for years on bringing him to her time and still had trouble believing he was here. How hard must it be for Dante?

He picked up the book, holding it up as he faced her again. "That does not explain this."

Elsa took the book from him and opened it to the imprint page. She traced down the printing information until she reached the copyright date. Her hands trembled as she lifted it for Dante to see.

It was right there for him in black and white, but apparently he needed to hear the words to believe them. In a hushed voice, he said, "Copyright 2015."

Chapter Three

"You cannot be suggesting that the year is two thousand and fifteen."

Dante might have laughed, if not for the way Elsa clutched his arm, her gaze darting to the front of the cabin. She shifted toward him in her seat, till there was no space left between them. His breath quickened as he felt the softness of her breast pressing against his arm.

"Please keep your voice down," she whispered in his ear. Her entire body trembled.

He lowered his voice to match hers. "Are we in danger?"

She stared at the front of the cabin, though all he saw was a solid wall. A solid wall in a vehicle more advanced than any from his time. Was he actually considering that what she said might be true?

"Not exactly," she said. "But it's important that no one finds out about where you're from. I mean, *when* you're from."

He found neither her tone nor her demeanor reassuring. "I take it that I am not supposed to be here?"

"You *are* supposed to be here, Dante." She turned to him at last, all traces of her uncertainty vanishing. She took his hand in hers once more. "I wouldn't have been able to bring you forward if it wasn't meant to be."

The tremor in her slight frame ceased, as if punctuating her words. Dante was certain she absolutely believed this to be true. But could he believe the rest of it?

His mind was still full of the images from the book she had shown him. Automobiles of all manner were described and pictured within, a variety so great and complex, it was staggering in its implications. If he dared to trust its contents, cars were common. Even a century seemed not long enough for such advancements to have taken place.

If he believed what the book contained, what his own senses told him, what of the rest of it? It would mean that Elsa had somehow transported him through time. She had pulled him from a fire that would certainly have killed him and carried him through that icy void of darkness. And now they were in America and the year was two thousand and fifteen.

"This is a bit difficult to believe."

Elsa let out a short laugh. "I'm having a little trouble with it, myself. I wasn't sure I'd be able to get you here. I'm so glad it worked."

"Given the alternative, I find myself in agreement."

She paled and turned her face away from him. "I couldn't..." Her voice came out low and stilted. "I couldn't let you die like that."

"I was not the only one who perished in the fire."

"You were the only one I could save. I'm sorry I couldn't do more. I'm sorry about the others."

Dante's throat constricted as he thought of Klaus and Heinrich, even Giselle. He turned his face so that his mask was toward Elsa and closed his eyes, shielding him from her view while he collected himself. He felt her touch his shoulder, her skin cold through the thin fabric of his shirt.

She slid her hand behind his back and pulled him closer. Though it seemed he was taking liberties, he could not resist her offer of comfort. He wrapped his arms around her, resting his head in the nape of her neck.

"This is a new start for you. A new world. I'm right here with you and will help you through it."

A new world. Yet he was still himself. Being in a different time did not alter his appearance. He doubted people had changed so much.

And yet, there was Elsa. He had yet to see fear or revulsion or pity in her gaze when she looked upon him. She did not shun his touch or avoid touching him, as if she thought his scars were catching.

"I am forever in your debt," Dante said.

Apparently, that was not the best turn of phrase. Elsa stiffened, slowly releasing her hold on Dante as she slid toward the other side of the carriage. She smiled politely, but it held sadness instead of warmth. Somehow, his words had pushed her away.

"You aren't in my debt. You never will be."

"I apologize. I merely meant—"

"It's okay. I just don't want you to feel like you owe me anything." Elsa brushed her fingers against the ceiling of the compartment, extinguishing the light.

How could he not feel indebted to her after she had saved his life? And she seemed to be taking a great risk by bringing him to her time. The journey had been harrowing enough for Dante. He could not imagine it had been any more pleasant for Elsa.

"We're here." She lifted the cloak and turned to him. "I hate to ask this of you, but could you wear this until we're inside?"

"Of course." He fastened the cloak around his neck, then pulled up the hood. She handed him the book, chewing fretfully on her lower lip as she stared past him out the window.

The carriage—*automobile*—turned onto a narrow lane lined with palms. The trees' dark silhouettes blotted out the stars in fingerlike patterns that spread only from the very tops of their trunks. Dante felt the vehicle stop, and glanced through the window to see a large mansion.

Bright lights flowed out from the latticed windows, painting stripes of green on the otherwise darkened lawn. The walls were stone, the design reminiscent of many buildings Dante had seen in London in his time. He was a bit disappointed at the familiarity of its appearance.

The coachman—no, driver—came around to open the door and stepped aside as Dante exited the automobile. Dante turned back to help Elsa emerge into the balmy night. She thanked the driver, then threaded her arm through Dante's as they walked the stone path to her doorstep.

She opened the door and ushered Dante into a large foyer. Two rooms flanked them—a dining room and a library, from what he could see. A large staircase wrapped around the wall to their left, ending in a landing on the next floor.

A long hallway straight ahead ended in a dark room, its black and white tile flooring only visible from the light of a beautiful crystal chandelier above. Dante could hear the sound of running water and dishes banging against the sides of a sink from the unlit room.

"Winston," Elsa hissed.

Dante was uncertain who Winston might be, but from Elsa's deportment, he assumed the man was in some sort of trouble.

She shook her head and sighed, then turned to Dante. "I'll take your cloak."

Before he could act, she reached up and unfastened the cloak. Her hands slid along his arms, following the descent of the fabric. Having more of his wits about him, and with the benefit of the bright lights above, the effect of her proximity was much more immediate.

His heart quickened, his skin tingling where her hands had paused just above his wrists. He could well imagine those delicate hands removing more of his clothing in a similar fashion. Dante tried to think of something else, anything besides the sweet smell of roses that surrounded her.

He cleared his throat, and said, "Thank you."

Elsa stared up at him, her eyes wide as if she was feeling something akin to wonder. His imagination must be running wild again, projecting his own emotions onto her.

Her lips parted slightly, and he had a strange impulse to run his thumb along their satin surface. Her chest stilled as his gaze strayed to her décolletage. The black fabric of her dress accentuated the golden tint of her skin, which gleamed with a pearl-like cast. Dante was certain if he kissed her neck, she would taste of honey.

She finally stepped back, folding the cloak over her arm. "I should hang this up."

A flush rose to his cheeks. At least she could only perceive half of it. He willed his body back under control, holding the book about automobiles before him to hide his state. Dante was relieved when she walked away, and used the opportunity to take a deep breath and calm himself.

Where were these errant thoughts coming from? He had long since given up on having a physical relationship with a woman. But Elsa was awakening longings and desires he had no right to direct toward her.

"Winston!"

Elsa called out sharply enough that Dante started. There was a commanding edge to her tone that he had not heard before. She hung the cloak in a closet near the front door, then returned across the foyer, her heels clicking on the floor.

A man stooped with age appeared in the darkened doorway. "I thought I heard you come in."

Elsa crossed her arms and let out a sigh. Winston shuffled toward them, one hand tracing the wood paneling along the stairs.

"Now, don't be starting with that." A thick cockney accent slurred his words. "If I decide to wait up for you to be home safe, that's my business."

"And if you're so tired in the morning that you burn the toast, that's mine." There remained an edge to her tone, but she was smiling playfully now.

"I can always make more toast, and the squirrels won't fault me for the mistake."

She laughed and stepped forward, uncrossing her arms so she could hug the old man. If he was a servant, she was certainly not treating him as such. She kissed his cheek, bringing a rosy flush to Winston's face.

"I suppose you've forgiven me, then?" He patted her arms and laughed as well. "But what's this? Smells like you stood too close to a campfire." He started sniffing the air, then said, "Elsa, what on earth have you brought home with you?"

"Not what, Winston. *Who*."

Winston stared blankly at the door, seeming to look right through Dante. Only then did Dante realize that Winston's pale gray eyes had the unfocused stare of the blind.

"I believe I am the one who requires forgiveness," Dante said. "I am in a bit of disarray."

Winston stiffened when Dante spoke, his arm tightening around Elsa.

"Winston, this is Dante. He's the guest we've been preparing for."

"Oh. Well, then." Winston scowled in Dante's direction. "You've got an accent on you there. I can't quite place it."

"Dante was born in London and raised abroad. And that is the end of the interrogation for tonight." She kissed Winston's cheek again, softening the scowl on his face.

Apparently it was not merely with Dante that Elsa was affectionate. He struggled to suppress a strange surge of jealousy.

She had rescued Dante in London, but how did she know of his other travels? He added that to the list of questions he must eventually ask.

"We'll just get cleaned up and then go to bed," Elsa said. "I mean, he'll be in his room, of course."

She corrected herself so quickly that she stumbled over the words. Her gaze darted toward Dante briefly, and her face turned bright red, the flush spreading down her neck and chest.

Winston's mouth twitched into a grin. It must be for Winston's benefit that she had reacted that way. Winston could not see Dante, and might consider the worst—Elsa bringing a man home in the middle of the night.

Winston patted her arm. "I'll bring up a pot of chamomile tea after a bit."

"Only if it's no trouble," she said.

"How's this trouble? It's my job." Winston laughed and waved his hand behind him as he headed down the hall, leaving them alone once more.

Elsa's smile was more subdued when she turned back to Dante. It was just as riveting.

"Come on. I'll show you your room."

She led him to the stairs, the light gleaming off her bare shoulders where her hair fell aside. He was too distracted to notice the flash of black fur that darted in front of him until the very last minute.

"Leo!" Elsa stopped abruptly.

Dante was only able to avoid stepping on it by throwing off his own footing. The book went tumbling onto the stairs.

Elsa ducked beneath his arm, catching enough of his weight that he did not fall. His shirt was still open more than was proper, and her palm landed directly upon his chest. The chill of her skin took his breath away.

"You are so cold."

"Am I? I didn't notice."

Dante grasped her hand, lifting it to his lips to breathe upon. After a moment, he pressed it back against his chest to warm it further. He watched her reaction carefully, looking for signs of revulsion. Instead, her eyes darkened like smoldering embers.

Once more, his body responded to her closeness, only this time, he did not know if he had the strength to pull himself away.

What would she do if he lowered his lips to hers? If he tilted his face to the right, she would not even have to gaze upon his mask.

His mask.

Picturing it felt like being doused in an icy stream. What was he thinking? She was beautiful, intelligent, kind and obviously well off. All of time was at her disposal. She could have her pick of lovers. Why would she ever choose him?

Dante stepped away, releasing his hold on Elsa's hand. A delicate crease appeared between her brows, but only for a moment.

"There is a cat in your house," Dante said.

"Yes. That's Leonardo."

She clicked her fingers at the sleek black cat licking its paw at the top of the stairs. It looked up as she said its name, sitting straight and gazing down upon them. Its eyelids lowered after a moment, and the little creature sighed as if they were beneath its notice.

"Leonardo, mind your manners." Elsa walked up the stairs and picked up the cat, then began scratching under its chin and along its neck. It purred loudly as she cuddled it to her chest. "You'll have to forgive Leonardo. He likes to try to trip people. Winston treats it like some kind of game, but I worry."

Dante thought of suggesting she keep the cat outside, but something in the way she was holding it made him think better of that. He stooped to pick up the book he had dropped. As he rose, he inspected it for damage and was relieved to find none. He followed Elsa up the stairs, watching her carry Leonardo along with her as she led Dante down a hallway that continued from the landing.

"I'll be close in case you need anything." She stopped at the first door on their right. It was carved of a deep walnut that matched the rest of the house. "My room is right here."

She gestured to the partly open door with the cat. Leonardo twisted in her grasp, then slipped to the floor. Dante watched it dart inside the room, his curiosity roused at the thought of seeing where Elsa slept.

The light that spilled forth from the hall revealed a canopy bed set against the far wall, covered with pale golden fabrics. A row of windows with gauzelike curtains stood behind it. Stacks of books occupied every surface, even creeping along the floor around the bed.

"I like to read too," Elsa said.

The way she shrugged her shoulder brought Dante's attention back to her sleeveless dress. He looked away quickly to quell any fantasies the sight might provoke, but his gaze landed upon her bed. The golden sheets would accent her skin perfectly.

He turned around, hoping that would be more effective. It seemed since this flame had been lit, it was difficult to control.

"You're just next door." She took a few steps farther down the hall before stopping in front of another intricately carved door.

This was an even better distraction. She opened the door, then reached into the room to turn on a light. She stepped aside so he could enter first. Dante wondered what sort of new wonders awaited him.

He was glad his back was to her, so she could not see the shock that was no doubt on his face as he peered inside.

A dark four-poster bed took up most of the far wall, which was covered by heavy curtains. He could only surmise there were windows behind them, though they were completely concealed by the thick red fabric. The bed was similarly smothered in red and gold.

Dante had used those colors in his room in the basement of Heinrich's theatre, taking worn curtains from the stage to make his bedding and add some semblance of warmth to the cold stone walls. The place had still felt like a dungeon, though it was better than trying to live in the rooms above with the others.

He pulled himself from his morose thoughts and surveyed the rest of the room. There was a settee to his right, along with a heavy wooden desk. Intricate scrollwork adorned its sides, as well as the chair before it. An armoire in a matching style dominated the left wall, dwarfing the open door that led to a dark room beyond.

He stepped over the threshold, feeling like a ghost. If anything, the furnishings were more old-fashioned than those to which he was accustomed. He turned to see a dormant fireplace set in a wall of bookshelves, completely filled with volumes of a similar design to the one in his hand.

Dante swallowed hard and spun in a slow circle. His skin prickled from the familiar nuances of the place. If he did not know better, he would have thought that all of what had come before was a dream, and he had simply found his way to some aristocrat's home.

The thought made him shiver. He did not want to be reminded of where he had come from. He wanted a fresh start. Dante could well imagine waking in that bed, the night pressing on his confused mind and planting doubts of his sanity.

Time travel? A beautiful woman whose touch stoked desire deeper than any he had ever imagined? It was difficult enough for him to believe while fully awake.

He would simply need to avoid sleep...

"What do you think?" Elsa asked, a vulnerable cast to her smile.

"It is not what I expected."

"What did you expect?"

Dante searched his mind for something that would not make him seem ungrateful. He truly appreciated everything she had done, despite the eerie ambiance of the room. He noticed a small carved ship sitting atop the desk near the settee, and said the first thing that came to mind.

"Hammocks."

"Hammocks?"

"They are quite efficient, really. I had thought perhaps their use would have expanded over time." He smiled at her, hoping she would realize he was making light of his circumstance.

Elsa gave him a puzzled grin, but she laughed, the sound like music.

"We can see about installing some. But I wanted it to feel like home for you, at least at first. To help you adjust."

"I appreciate you going to such efforts."

"This is the best part." She took the book from him and placed it in the single empty spot on the bookshelf. Her gaze roved over the orderly rows. When she found what she was looking for, she pulled out another volume. "Here's a good place to start."

She handed him the book, the broadest smile yet gracing her lips. He reluctantly looked at the cover of the book, wanting to stare at that smile until he could call it to mind at will in perfect detail.

On the solid green cover of the book, gold letters were etched on a dark brown square.

"This is a book about plumbing." Dante read the title again. He could hardly think she believed he would be more interested in this than her smile.

"That is book one of a history of plumbing all the way up to the present. I commissioned this encyclopedia set for you." She gestured at the wall once more, then stared at the books with reverence. "By the time you've read all of these, you should understand more than most people about modern technology, including me."

"You commissioned them?"

She turned back to him with that radiant smile. "I knew you'd have questions that I wouldn't be able to answer. And plumbing is a good place to start, since you'll probably be wanting a shower soon."

He looked down at his shirt, stained with his sweat and soot from the fire. He had not realized how dreadful his appearance was until that moment.

"Of course. I apologize."

"For what?" Elsa's smile dimmed and she shook her head, as if she could not see anything wrong with him.

Dante's heart began pounding. That was what truly mesmerized him about this woman, even more than what she could do, what she had done for him. From the very beginning, she had looked upon Dante in the same manner that she might any other man. Elsa barely even seemed to notice his mask.

"Is something wrong, Dante?"

"No." He smiled at her and shook his head. "Nothing is wrong at all."

Chapter Four

After showing Dante around his bathroom, Elsa indulged in a shower of her own. Spanish mosaics in vibrant reds, blues and yellows brightened the walls of the room. Beneath a wide window in an alcove, a huge bathtub beckoned, but she could feel the exhaustion of her journey catching up with her.

She still lingered for a while, sitting on the edge of the tub and enjoying the fresh scent of roses from her soaps as she dried her hair. She knew her obsession with decadent bathrooms was strange, but hiding in them so often as a child had left its mark on her.

She shook her head, refusing to let bad memories intrude on this space. She had much better things to think about. Like Dante.

He was in her time, in her home. He was right next door.

Elsa couldn't believe her plan had worked. The play was the perfect boost to bring Dante back with her. She had traveled through time using art before, but never as it was being made, using the very moment the powerful emotions that charged the piece were being experienced. She had never felt anything like it.

Everything was coming together just as she'd hoped. Well, except that she couldn't seem to keep her hands off of him. And it was only getting worse.

While she showered, she kept thinking of Dante doing the same. She shivered again at the thought of his pale skin slick with soap, imagining his hands roving over his body, following rivulets of hot water.

"What is wrong with me?" she muttered, drying her hair more vigorously as she stood and walked to her bedroom.

It made sense that she'd be fantasizing about the naked man in the shower next door, since her baths were the most sensual thing she'd experienced in the past three years. Aside from writing her novels.

The mental list of things she needed to tell Dante grew. She was writing a novel about him. For him, really. Before she told him that, she needed to work up the courage to explain the stories that had stemmed from his life, even though they bore little resemblance to it.

Elsa threw on the first pajamas her fingers encountered in the drawer of her armoire—a matching tank top and pants in a soft shade of pink—then ruffled her hair once more with the towel. The room was starting to spin a little, and Elsa knew she didn't have long before she would have to pay the price of ferrying Dante to her time. She still folded the towel before hanging it up to dry on the rack in her bathroom.

When she brought back Leonardo, she had passed out for a few hours. She hadn't meant to bring the cat with her, but when he could somehow see her and had followed her into a busy street, she'd grabbed him out of the way of a horse to keep him from being trampled. She hadn't been thinking at the moment, just reacting. And then they were both back in her time, sitting in front of the painting she had used to travel.

That painting only held one moment with enough emotional resonance for Elsa to connect with. Dante's ring, on the other hand, held dozens of moments she'd been able to view. And that was after the many times she had visited his mother, which was yet another awkward thing Elsa had to tell him.

If she hadn't stumbled onto the first of his mother's paintings, Elsa wouldn't have discovered Dante. She wouldn't have been able to save him from the fire or bring him to her time. And she was certain she was meant to bring him forward.

Like Leonardo, Dante had seen her while she was traveling. It was the day his father, Heinrich, had died. Her heart had nearly broken at how distraught Dante was, and she had longed to be able to do something to help. When his gaze locked on hers, she knew she could.

Passing out for a while was nothing. Elsa would have done anything to save him. She just needed to get him settled before it happened. She leaned against the bathroom door until the dizziness subsided, then went to his room.

Winston was there when she arrived, setting up tea and some cookies at the small table near the fireplace. Leonardo had followed him in and was curled on the settee, flicking his tail back and forth.

"Thanks for the tea, Winston." She wrapped one arm around him and hugged him tight.

"You're quite welcome." He leaned into her a bit. "What's this? You're cold as ice."

Elsa ran her hands up and down her arms. Now that he mentioned it, she was a bit cold. Pushing the thought away, she said, "My hair is wet."

"That'll cool you off. A spot of tea will fix you right up, as soon as that friend of yours is ready to join you."

"He's a good man, Winston. Give him a chance."

Winston made a harrumphing noise and started pouring the tea.

Elsa realized she hadn't shown Dante his wardrobe. Most of the clothes inside the armoire were in the style of his time, again, to help him gradually adjust. But she'd bought him some comfortable pajama pants, not knowing what he usually slept in.

Her imagination started up again, and she pushed away the thought of Dante naked between his sheets. She needed to rein this in. She also needed to leave before he came out of the bathroom.

The dizziness returned with a vengeance, the walls spinning around her like she was at the center of a carousel. Elsa gripped the door to the armoire until the room stopped moving.

Only a little longer, and Dante would be safely in bed. Then she could collapse in hers. She could make it.

She grabbed a pair of pajama bottoms from the armoire's drawer and tossed them on the bed where he would see them. She could wait in the hall until he was dressed, and then…

Then the world tilted and the floor rushed up at her. She heard Winston yelling her name as if he was far away.

This was not part of the plan. Dante needed her. There were still things she had to tell him. Elsa felt as if she was swimming against a strong current. She slipped further away from Winston's voice, sinking into darkness.

Chapter Five

Dante had never been so clean in his life. His shower was nothing less than luxurious. Elsa had left typeset notes on thin rectangular tiles placed throughout the bathroom explaining the purpose and use of the various items in amusing detail.

The tiles themselves were even more intriguing than their content. They looked like small pieces of paper that had been encased in a smooth, transparent material that left them impervious to water. He would certainly ask her about them as soon as he had a chance.

His mask rested on the back of the sink. Dante picked it up and turned it over in his hands, not wanting to put it on quite yet. He wasn't sure why. The lighting in the room was bright, much brighter than he was used to. He set down his mask and placed his hands on either side of the cool surface of the sink.

Morbid curiosity. That was all this was. He should not indulge it. And yet, he knew he would.

Dante ran his hand over the fogged surface of the mirror and looked at himself.

If anything, the lighting made the scars look worse. He could see each bright red welt rising from the surface of his skin in greater detail, the shadows highlighting his disfigurement like some sadistic bas-relief. His mother had never told him what happened, though she bore similar marks on her hands.

Why had Elsa brought him here? What had she seen in him that could possibly overpower this?

He would wake up soon, and find this all to have been a dream. Or perhaps his mind had finally snapped from the persecution and oppressive loneliness he suffered. He wasn't sure which was the better alternative. At least if he was mad, he could stay in this wonderful delusion.

"Help! Help!"

He jumped at the sound of Winston's frantic voice. Dante ran to the door and flung it open to find the old man huddled on the floor over Elsa's prone form. There was a pair of pants at the foot of the bed, barely more than leggings, but Dante pulled them on as he approached.

"What happened?"

"I don't know! One minute we were talking, then I heard her sort of sigh and then thump to the floor. I was afraid to move her. I can't see how bad it is."

"Calm yourself," Dante said.

"Calm nothing! How is she? Is she hurt?"

Dante turned his attention to Elsa. She was pale, her lips bloodless and her brow furrowed. Her breathing was quick and labored. He gently touched her shoulder. Her skin was much cooler than it had been earlier in the evening. He could not rouse her.

Dante's heart seemed to wish to crawl out of his body, but his throat would not accommodate it.

"It's bad, isn't it?" Winston said.

"I do not know. Could it be a fainting spell?"

"Fainting spell?" Winston sputtered. "I'll give you a fainting spell. She's cold as ice. Come on. Let's get her to the bed."

Winston rose, leaving Dante to carry Elsa. He slid his arms beneath her and lifted her from the floor, his heart still in his throat. Winston hobbled to the bed, then turned down the covers.

As Dante set Elsa upon the bed, Winston said, "I'm calling Garrett."

"Garrett?"

"He's a doctor. Lives right next door. You get in there and keep her warm." Winston started for the door at a pace that was possibly too quick to be safe.

"I beg your pardon?" Dante said.

"You heard me. Get in there and pull the covers up and keep her warm till I can get us help."

Dante looked down at Elsa's still form, his mouth suddenly dry. "I am uncertain if—"

Winston turned sharply at the door. "Listen, you! Elsa trusts you enough to have you live with her, so I'll trust you too. Now get in there before I knock your teeth in!"

Dante nodded foolishly, too flustered to recall Winston's blindness for a moment. "Of course."

"And if I find out you tried something with her while I'm gone, I'll really give you a walloping." Winston disappeared through the doorway before Dante could say any more.

Elsa shuddered, a crease appearing at the center of her forehead. Could he really be contemplating following Winston's instruction? Perhaps the covers would be sufficient. Dante pulled them up to her chin, tucking them in around her shoulders. Her brow smoothed somewhat, and she sighed his name.

Dante froze, uncertain if he had heard correctly. It could have been his imagination, fueled by the extraordinary events of the evening. Regardless, it gave him the courage to lift the covers and slide into the bed behind her.

He slid one arm under her neck and the other over her waist, pulling her as close as he dared. Her body fit snugly against his.

She was terribly cold. Dante reached up to brush a few strands of hair away from her face. He was intent upon her to the point that he nearly cried out when some small thing leapt upon his back.

Elsa's cat crept over him as if he was no more than a pillow. It sniffed at her lips, then crawled under the covers and curled up against her chest, purring loudly. At least it could lend its warmth to her.

Winston entered the room, murmuring to himself. Dante craned his head over his shoulder and saw that Winston was carrying a great burden of blankets.

"Allow me to help you," Dante said. He started to rise, but Winston stopped Dante with a look so piercing, he wondered for a moment if Winston's blindness was a charade.

"Don't you dare. You just keep her warm."

Winston dropped the blankets on the foot of the bed, then started spreading them atop the pair. Dante adjusted them so they were covering Elsa, yet not burying her cat so deeply that it would be smothered. She seemed rather fond of it.

Winston paused for a moment, then threw the final blanket over them. "I hear Garrett's car. I'll be right back."

As he left, Dante's stomach lurched. His mask was in the other room. Winston was blind. There was no harm in him being near Dante without his mask. But this Garrett fellow… Who knew how he'd react?

The man was a doctor, so hopefully Dante's face would not send him screaming from the room. The lighting was dim, and Dante's right side was toward the pillows. There was that, at least. But what would Dr. Garrett think of finding Dante in bed with Elsa, barely dressed as they were?

He was spared from his racing thoughts as Winston entered the room again, followed by a man so tall his head nearly brushed the top of the doorframe. He was blond, his skin richly bronzed by the sun, and he had the flawless features of a leading man. A perfect match for Elsa.

He was dressed in a thin gray shirt with sleeves that did not reach his elbows. His pants were similar to the ones Dante currently wore. Perhaps this was the fashion of the tropics.

"You must be Dante," Garrett said, surprising Dante with a genial smile.

"And you must be Dr. Garrett."

"Dr. Wolfstrom, actually, but I'd prefer you call me Garrett."

Despite Dante's misgivings, he found himself liking the man. Garrett's smile came easily, and his tone lacked any hint of condescension. There was a lilt to his voice, an accent Dante did not recognize.

Dante started to move away from Elsa, but Garrett motioned for him to stay.

"Winston said she's cold, and body heat's all we have at the moment." Garrett glanced at the empty fireplace, then crossed to the opposite side of the bed. "There's not much call for furnaces in Florida. If it's all the same, I'd rather you stay where you are."

"Of course," Dante said.

Garrett set his black doctor's bag down near the pillows and pulled out what looked like a stethoscope. Dante's theory was confirmed as Garrett clipped its listening tubes onto his ears, then crawled across the bed toward Elsa and placed the chestpiece above her heart.

Garrett listened for a moment before shifting the device to check a few other places. Finally, he opened each of her eyes, shining a tiny light into them.

Dante angled his head more toward the pillows. Garrett must be able to see Dante's face, but Garrett's gaze never strayed to his, and Garrett made no mention of it. He seemed barely aware of Dante's presence until handing Dante the smallest thermometer he had ever seen.

"Put this under her arm, if you would." Garrett smiled, and said, "I like to do things old-school."

Dante nodded as if that statement did not confuse him, then lifted Elsa's arm gingerly to place the thermometer. He fought the flush trying to creep up his neck as the scent of roses flooded his senses. Elsa melted against his body as if they were meant to fit together. He reminded himself to remain focused on assisting her and not think of how right it felt to have her in his arms.

"How is she?" Winston's worried voice cut through Dante's thoughts.

Garrett shook his head and said, "It looks to me like she's just passed out."

"Passed out?" Winston said. "That's not like her."

"This isn't the first time." Garrett scratched Leonardo's head as the cat purred even louder. Garrett winked at Dante and said, "She slept right through our second date. I came over to pick her up for dinner and she passed out before we made it to the car. She was fine in a couple of hours, but it damn near broke my heart."

Dante felt as if the floor had dropped out from under him. An invitation to dinner was unmistakably courting behavior. And Elsa had accepted.

Garrett and Elsa were involved. It made sense. He was a doctor, handsome and charismatic. Why Garrett had not trounced Dante for being in bed with Elsa was the mystery.

"I apologize." Dante thought to rise, but he was trapped. If he sat up, Garrett would see his face fully before Dante had a chance to cover himself.

"Don't worry about it," Garrett said. His smile broadened and he slapped Dante on the arm. "That ended years ago. This little guy stole her right out from under me."

Garrett scratched Leonardo's head once more, then pulled the thermometer from beneath Elsa's arm. His brow furrowed slightly as he examined it, but then he shook his head and slid to the side of the bed. He placed his tools back in his bag, which he sat on the bedside table.

"Her temperature is a little low, but not dangerously so. We'll keep an eye on that. Winston, did you turn off the AC?"

"Yes sir," Winston said, shuffling toward the fireplace.

"Ugh, don't call me 'sir'. You know I can't stand that."

Garrett walked over to Winston and put his hands on the older man's shoulders and squeezed, then patted him on the back. Dante's heart warmed toward them both. The whole group treated each other as family. It was a beautiful thing to behold.

"I keep forgetting." Winston chuckled roughly.

"I'll keep reminding you. Now sit down before I wind up with two patients. I've got this."

Dante risked lifting his head to watch as Garrett built up a raging fire. The doctor seemed as confident with menial tasks as with his examination of Elsa. Again, Dante found himself liking Garrett.

Winston sat at the small table before the fire, his face drawn with worry. "She never mentioned fainting spells. What could have brought it on?"

"Any number of things," Garrett said, adjusting the blazing logs a final time before rising and putting the poker back in place. "Overexertion is at the top of my list of suspects."

"She does like to do that," Winston said. "She went to that play again tonight."

Garrett laughed. "Of course she did, Winston. It's Saturday."

"Is it?" Dante asked. He immediately regretted letting the question slip from his lips.

Garrett glanced at Dante without flinching. He felt his cheeks heat, but held Garrett's gaze. Dante had never felt more exposed in his life. Garrett looked at the scars on Dante's face briefly, then turned back to Winston. That was all.

"I'll stay at least through the night," Garrett said. "But I'm sure she'll be fine after she gets some rest."

"Thank goodness," Winston said. He was still wringing his hands. "Do you think you could make us some coffee?"

"Of course. It's the least I can do." Winston stood, the ghost of a smile crossing his face, and headed out the door.

Garrett walked back to the bed and sat opposite Dante. "I didn't want to say this in front of Winston, but she actually warned me that something like this might happen again. How she knew is the mystery. The last time was just after Leonardo came to live with her." He laughed, and said, "Maybe it's the excitement of new roommates."

"I do not wish to be a burden to her." Dante could scarcely think that Elsa's bringing him here was unrelated to her collapse.

"Come on," Garrett said, the easy smile returning to his face as he leaned against the headboard. "If we weren't burdens for Elsa, what would she do with her time?"

Elsa shivered, and Dante pulled her closer without even thinking. He could not believe how soft she felt against him. He did not miss the shadow that crossed Garrett's face before the man looked away.

"What is she to you?" Dante asked. He hadn't meant to give voice to his thought.

"We're friends."

"Friends."

"Good friends." Garrett shrugged, his smile becoming a bit strained. "We've known each other for years. We tried dating at first, but it didn't work out."

"I cannot imagine why." Dante tried to keep any bitterness from his tone. A handsome man like Garrett would surely find his company in high demand.

"I worked in the ER when we met. My hours were crazy back then. I'm mostly retired now, but I think that ship has sailed."

The look Garrett gave Dante was one he'd never seen before. At least, not directed at him. Something akin to anger flashed across Garrett's gaze, followed quickly by resignation.

"I am sorry." Dante understood little of what Garrett had said, but it seemed appropriate to apologize.

Garrett shrugged, his smile returning. He crossed his legs before him on the bed and folded his hands over his chest.

"My theory's that she doesn't like blonds." Garrett winked at Dante and continued. "Jazz tried to set her up with an artist from the gallery a while back, but Elsa didn't take the bait. Jazz said Elsa didn't even realize it was a blind date. Which is probably good, because if Elsa knew, she would've killed Jazz."

Dante took a moment as his mind pored over Garrett's words. *Setting Elsa up* with someone in conjunction with speaking of dates helped his understanding. However, the idea of a *blind* date puzzled him. He dismissed the idea of actual blindfolds and presumed they merely had not met previously. This Jazz person was making the introduction.

"I am unfamiliar with that name. Where is he from?"

"*She* is from Kansas City." Garrett's smile faded, one eyebrow rising on his forehead. "Elsa didn't tell you about Jazz?"

Dante scrambled to provide an explanation that would not rouse Garrett's suspicions, determined to keep Elsa's secret safe.

"We have not known each other for terribly long. I am eager to learn more about her friends."

"I bet," Garrett said, a smirk deepening the dimples on either side of his face. "Jazz is Elsa's best friend from college. They met at some arty school up in Virginia. Her real name is Ling, but since she's from Kansas City, people called her Jazz. It really suits her, so it stuck."

"Does it have something to do with the cattle trade?"

"What?"

"The word *jazz*. I am unfamiliar with it."

Garrett stared at Dante, his jaw slack. Dante must have made some dire mistake, given away his ignorance of this time. His fears were realized when Garrett said, "Where the hell did Elsa find you that you don't know what jazz is?"

Not wanting to lie to the man, Dante came up with a palatable truth. "I fear where I am from is quite behind the times."

Garrett laughed. "Well, my friend, you are in for a treat. Jazz is only the best form of music ever invented. I know all the best jazz bars around. Once Elsa's back on her feet, you and I can hit the town and paint it red."

Dante wondered if any of the books in the encyclopedia set covered the common vernacular. He could tell there was quite a bit he needed to catch up on. But it was clear that Garrett meant his words as a sincere invitation. He was not concerned to be seen with Dante in public. Garrett did not even know that Dante had the good manners to wear a mask.

His throat constricted at the thought. Could people truly have changed so much that he could walk the streets without hearing gasps or screams?

"Thank you," Dante said.

"For an excuse to go to the clubs? I'm looking forward to it already."

The conversation was strangely intimate. It was hard not to feel comfortable in Garrett's company. Dante could not recall ever having such a discussion with another. He had been lured into similar conversations briefly, but those had always taken cruel turns.

Garrett seemed genuine, accepting. Already, by bringing Dante to her home, Elsa had given him an opportunity he had never encountered before. Friendship. He was not used to being with someone who treated him as an equal. His closest experiences had been mentoring Mary and being mentored by Heinrich.

Grief pierced Dante's heart at the memory of his father, sharp and deep. The weight of Klaus's loss pushed the knife in further.

Without his mask, Dante could not hide his distress. He was more exposed than he had ever been. Vulnerable. Visible. It was too much.

"Might I trouble you to bring me my mask?" Dante's voice took on a rough sound, like waves breaking on a rocky shore.

"Your mask?"

"It is just beyond in the other room. When Winston cried out, there was no time for me to put it on."

"Sure."

Garrett rose from the bed, and Dante took the moment of semi-privacy to close his eyes and try to regain his composure. He took a deep breath, but that merely filled his lungs with the sweet fragrance of Elsa's hair. While it brought to mind more pleasant thoughts, they did nothing to help calm him.

The light was still on in the bathroom. Garrett picked up Dante's mask, slowly turning it over in his hands. He took a few steps toward the bed, but paused in the doorway. His gaze never left the mask.

"What the hell?" Garrett said, lifting the mask. "Did Elsa put you up to this?"

"I beg your pardon?"

"This mask. It feels like porcelain. And the design is just too much. There is a line, man."

"I fear I am still at a loss."

Garrett shook his head and said, "I don't know what you guys have going, but this is a little messed up."

Garrett's lip twitched up, as if Dante's mask offended him. The irony of the idea nearly made Dante laugh aloud, until Garrett looked up at them, the same expression of distaste on his features. He walked around the bed, then set the mask on the bedside table nearest Dante.

"Look, if you guys want to dress up and play *Phantom of the Opera*, that's your business. But I think it's a little weird and more than a little unhealthy. Tell me you at least have some more practical masks you use out in public."

"That is the only mask I possess."

In fact, it was *all* Dante possessed, aside from his mother's ring and the clothes he'd been wearing when Elsa brought him to this time. Dante was used to having little, though this brought the matter to extremes.

"Well, if you ever want something more comfortable, come see me." Garrett pointed over his shoulder. "I'm just next door."

Dante could not fathom what had upset Garrett so, but it was troublesome enough to end their conversation. Strangely, even after such a short time, Dante missed talking with him. Garrett sat by the fire, a grim set to his lips as he stared at Dante. Exhausted as he was, he doubted he would sleep under Garrett's watchful gaze.

Chapter Six

Gravity was crushing every molecule of Elsa's body. The mattress couldn't possibly keep supporting her. She envisioned it collapsing as she sank into the earth.

Panic chewed at the edges of her mind. She pushed it away by focusing all of her energy on waking up. Gradually, the weight lifted until she felt strong enough to force open her eyelids.

Dante was lying on the settee, a book splayed open in his hand as he slept. Most of his face was concealed behind his mask. With each gentle rise and fall of his chest, Elsa's panic was replaced with wonder. She might have thought she was dreaming, except for the bone-deep exhaustion. She was too tired to be asleep.

He had pulled the settee right next to the bed, close enough for her to reach out and touch him—if she could lift her arm. He was wearing black slacks and one of the white linen shirts from his wardrobe. His shirt had fallen open a bit, revealing his pale skin.

She noticed he wasn't wearing any shoes or socks. A warm feeling spread through her at seeing him dressed so casually in her home. He looked comfortable, like he belonged. Several dozen books from the encyclopedia set were stacked around him, forming a miniature city.

Dante must have sensed her watching him, because his eyes slowly opened, an earthy jade today.

"Elsa?"

She shivered at the velvet sound of his voice.

"Has your chill returned?" He put his book next to him as he rose from the settee. He sat next to her on the bed, then lifted one of her hands in his and pressed it against his left cheek for a moment. He didn't release her hand when he lowered it from his face. "You seem warm enough. How do you feel?"

When Elsa tried to speak, her throat was dry and raw. She half expected sand to come out instead.

"I'm fine," she croaked.

Dante frowned. "Let me get you some water."

She wanted to stay in that perfect moment for a while longer, to tell him not to go, but her mouth wouldn't cooperate. Instead, she tried to gauge how much time had passed.

Light peeked around the edges of the curtains, so it was at least morning. She was still in Dante's room. Other than the relocated settee and stacks of books around it, nothing had changed.

Dante set the glass of water on the bedside table. Without hesitating, he wrapped his arms around her and pulled her against his chest. Elsa's heart started pounding. She was vividly aware of every place their bodies touched.

All too soon, he released her, having propped her up against some pillows. He sat next to her on the bed, then brought the glass of water to her lips.

Being coddled was strange and seemed inappropriate. She was supposed to be helping him, not the other way around. Her arms trembled as she reached for the glass. She wasn't sure if it was from fatigue or his proximity.

"Please, allow me to assist," he said.

She didn't have the strength to argue. Instead, she nodded, then drank half the glass with his help. Finally able to speak again, she said, "I'm sorry I slept late."

"You may sleep as long as you like. I am merely relieved to see you so much better."

Better than what? Her brain felt like it was made of cotton. She struggled to put words together in a way that made sense. The last thing she remembered was being in his room and laying out some pajamas for him. She must have passed out.

"I was just tired. I didn't mean to leave you alone so long."

"Winston and Leonardo have been excellent company. And Garrett has been visiting twice a day."

"Garrett?"

A surge of adrenaline scattered the fog in her mind. Garrett had been there while she slept? How had Dante explained his presence? What had he told Garrett?

Action seemed imperative. Elsa leaned forward, but Dante gripped her shoulders, then gently pushed her back against the pillows. It was a good thing too, because the room was starting to spin again.

"You must not let yourself get overexcited."

"How long was I asleep?"

"A little over two days."

"Two days?" she nearly shouted. Her mind reeled. How could she have left him alone for two days? And right after bringing him to her time. He must have been so lost. "I'm sorry."

"It is I who must apologize. Bringing me here appears to have taxed you greatly."

"You didn't tell them, did you?" The question slipped out before she could stop herself, but once it was spoken, she couldn't think of anything except his answer.

"I have kept your confidences. You can trust me."

If only she could. But trust was something that had died in her long ago.

Winston arrived before she could say anything else. His eyes had dark shadows under them, and his shoulders were slumped.

"Any change?" Winston asked, shuffling toward them.

"Indeed." Dante stood, pushing stacks of books out of Winston's way to clear a path to the bed.

"Good morning, Winston," Elsa said.

Winston's eyes widened and a broad smile spread across his face. "Oh thank God."

He stumbled over to her, hands outstretched. Elsa grasped them, leading Winston toward her so he could sit on the bed at her side.

"Are you all right?" Winston asked.

"I think so."

Winston leaned forward and pulled her into a hug. "I was so

worried."

"Um, Winston, could you not squeeze me so hard?"

"Oh dear." He pulled back. "I didn't hurt you, did I?"

"No, I just need to use…" She glanced over at Dante, trying not to blush.

"Yeah, I bet you do. Sleeping for days. A grown woman!" Winston stood, but didn't let go of Elsa's hands. "I'll help you up."

Dante was lingering nearby, and said, "Perhaps you would allow me?"

"That's a good idea." Winston turned to Dante and said, "You get her comfortable while I make lunch. She must be famished!"

Winston patted Elsa's hand, then hobbled out of the room. Before she could argue, Dante stepped forward and lifted her from the bed. He did it with practiced ease, and she wondered if he had been the one to carry her to bed in the first place.

The image brought on another shiver, which she tried to ignore. It wasn't easy, feeling his chest pressed against her side. The scent of sandalwood enveloped her.

"Are you certain that you are not cold?" he asked as he headed toward the bathroom.

"I'm fine. Why do you keep asking about that?"

He tilted his head away, but she could see the red flush creeping over his skin even with his mask.

"You were quite cold the night I arrived," he said. He stopped at the door to the bathroom, then set her on her feet. "Are you certain you can manage on your own?"

"I'll be fine."

From the way his jaw tightened, he seemed to disagree. "I shall be close. If you need anything, you have only to call for me."

He spoke with such intensity, almost protectiveness. But again, that was backward. Elsa was supposed to be in that role. Before she could take care of anyone else, though, she really needed to take care of herself.

"Thanks." She slipped through the door.

She rushed through her most basic bodily needs, eager to get back to him. When she opened the door to the bedroom again, Dante was standing by the armoire, tracing the carvings with his fingertips. He paused when he saw her.

Determined to show him she was fine, Elsa started toward him, but after two steps she wasn't sure which way was up again. It didn't matter, because he was there to catch her. He gathered her against his chest as if it was the most natural thing in the world.

Her heart felt strangely full. Leaning into him, she felt warmth suffuse her body. No one had ever carried her so tenderly before.

She couldn't let herself enjoy it. If she did, it would be that much more painful when she finally had to let him go.

"Are you all right?"

"Yes, I'm just still a bit dizzy. And I'm not used to being carried around."

"Until you are recovered, perhaps you should strive to become accustomed to it." Dante said, heading to the door. Her stomach did a happy little flip. "I presume there is a kitchen elsewhere in the house?"

She had to clear her throat to reply. "Downstairs."

He nodded, but paused at the open doorway. In a soft voice, he said, "I have not left this room since you brought me here."

"Not once in two days?"

"That would have meant leaving your side and I could not bring myself to do so." He drew in a quick breath, as if trying to pull the words back into his mouth. "That is to say…"

"Thank you."

The smile he gave her was gentle, and he held her a little closer to his chest. She wondered if he was even aware of it. He took another deep breath, his arms stiffening around her, then stepped over the threshold. He paused again on the other side and let out a brief laugh. Elsa felt his arms relax, and he bowed his head as if relieved.

"I half expected to be transported back to my time."

"I would bring you back again."

"I—" Whatever he'd been about to say, he seemed to think better of it. "I appreciate that."

"I don't think it'll be necessary, though. Leonardo's been with me for years now."

Elsa had never told anyone about Leonardo. The only person she had ever spoken with about her power... Well, it was best not to think about that.

The conversation felt even stranger with Dante carrying her. As much as she loved being close to him, the idea of needing someone to take care of her was unnerving. She was literally burdening him.

Her weakness would pass. She was certain of it. And then she could be the one taking care of him. She just had to make sure she didn't enjoy herself too much in the meantime. With a sinking feeling, she realized she could get used to feeling his arms around her all too quickly.

Dante glanced at his feet while walking to the stairs, as if checking to make sure Leonardo wasn't trying to run between them. That was probably a good idea.

"You brought the cat from another time?" he asked.

"Yes. It was an accident, though."

"How so?"

They'd reached the bottom of the stairs, which meant Winston was much too close for them to be talking about time travel.

Lowering her voice, she said, "Could I tell you about it later? I'd rather not discuss this around Winston."

"Of course."

Dante carried her down the hallway to the kitchen. A plate of sandwiches was already on the table, and Winston was standing near the stove, the kettle just beginning to whistle.

"Is that an electric range?" Dante asked, an edge of excitement to his voice.

"Yes, it is." Elsa hadn't thought this through. Dante was going to have questions. Strange questions that she'd have trouble answering in front of Winston.

As if on cue, Winston chuckled and said, "You don't have stoves in your hometown, either?"

Dante must have faced this sort of thing during the days that Elsa was sleeping. She wondered how he had managed.

"I have never seen a stove of this variety," he said, glancing down at her. She smiled, hoping that his other conversations had gone as well.

"I think I'm strong enough to sit up." She nodded toward the table. Dante crossed the room and gingerly set her in a chair. "Thanks."

Within moments of Elsa having a lap, Leonardo ran into the room and jumped onto it. He purred loudly, hitting her in the face with his tail as he pranced around on her legs. Winston turned toward them, carrying a tray with the teapot and three cups.

"Allow me," Dante said, taking the tray and setting it on the table. He poured the tea and added milk and sugar to each of the cups, then handed one to Elsa and one to Winston before sitting down himself.

The moment was completely surreal. She was having tea with Winston and a man who, three days ago, had been in the late 1800s.

"I called Garrett to let him know you're awake," Winston said. "He left strict orders that you're not to overdo and to keep getting plenty of rest."

"I think I can manage that." She took a bite of her sandwich and found that she was absolutely starving. She tried to pace herself in front of Dante, but wondered if the stack of food in front of her would be enough.

"Can you now?" Winston snorted, then turned to Dante. "This is on you, Dante. Turn your back on her for a minute, and she'll be doing all kinds of things she oughtn't. Laundry and dishes."

"I assure you, Elsa's well-being is the very highest of my priorities," Dante said. His words sent a thrill through Elsa, and she felt herself blushing.

Winston made a "hmph" sound, but he was smiling. "Garrett will be by this evening. I'll make a special dinner."

"I would be happy to assist," Dante said.

"Your job is to look after Elsa." Winston laughed and said, "Trust me, I have the easier task."

Elsa was too tired to be offended. Plus, she was enjoying the conversation too much, watching Dante and Winston smile as they talked to one another.

They finished eating and, exhausted though she was, she couldn't stand the thought of going back to bed. There was so much she wanted to show Dante, so much to tell him.

"Let me show you around the house," she said.

"I would like that a great deal." Dante pushed his chair back from the table and stood. He began gathering up dishes, but Winston reached out and swatted at his hands, landing a few pretty good thwacks.

"You're as bad as she is. That's for me to do. Go on now."

Dante looked like he might object, but was distracted as Elsa nudged Leonardo from her lap, then tried to stand and fell right back in her chair. Her legs wouldn't support her.

"Allow me." Dante swooped her up again.

She couldn't resist leaning against his chest. His arms were strong around her, lifting her with ease. She had never enjoyed someone's touch so much.

"Where shall we begin?"

Elsa had been staring again. He was polite enough not to mention it, so neither did she. She had to get herself under control.

"How about the library?"

Some rooms hadn't changed much in a century. Her library was full of books and the dining room held a table and chairs. They spent a long time in the entertainment room, talking about movies and television shows and the technology that brought entertainment so effortlessly into people's homes. Dante seemed willing to stand there holding Elsa while she explained everything, but she insisted he at least set her on the couch for that part of the tour.

He was particularly interested in how the remotes worked and asked for a demonstration. His eyes widened in wonder as the first images appeared on the screen. She convinced him to wait to actually start watching something until after they'd gone through the rest of the house. She was eager to show him the studio and the gardens outside, wondering if he'd love them as much as she did.

She steeled her resolve before he picked her up this time. She would not lean into him, no matter how strong his chest felt. She would not melt into his arms, even though they gave her the first glimmer of what it might be to feel safe.

The French double doors that led into the converted solarium were just down the hall. She waited for Dante to pause in front of the doors before saying, "I saved the best for last. This is the studio."

It was more than a studio, though. It was her sanctuary, her most holy ground. She reached down and opened the doors, watching Dante's face as he took in the room for the first time.

It was her deepest dream that the two of them would eventually spend many hours here together, whether working on a shared project or on their own. The openness of the room might be too much for Dante at first after spending so much time in the basement of his father's theatre. She didn't want to push him too far too fast.

The exterior walls and the ceiling of the studio were made up of windows. In the bright afternoon sun, every inch of the room was illuminated with natural light. Flowers and greenery pressed against the steamy glass on the far wall.

Dante walked to the center of the room, spinning in a slow circle. His gaze rested first on the easels in the painting corner, then passed to the workbenches where sculpting tools were set up. Against the interior wall, there was a sewing corner with a dress form and shelves filled with fabrics, paints, clays and every kind of tool for creativity that Elsa could think of. Her writing desk was nestled against the wall of windows.

"Do you like it?" she asked, unable to contain her curiosity.

A soft smile played at his lips, and his eyes were wide with wonder. "In the past few days, I have managed to convince myself that I had not died and moved to the afterlife." His voice was low and reverent. "In this room, I find myself questioning that once again, for I can hardly conceive of a more lovely paradise than this."

Elsa's heart seemed to explode in her chest. Visions of them spending time together in this room played out in her mind like a kaleidoscope. They would leave the second set of doors open to the patio to enjoy the breeze and have tea outside when they needed to let their creative energies replenish.

She imagined them walking through the garden, arm in arm. They would pause beneath the climbing roses. Dante would take the opportunity to lean down to kiss her...

She shook her head to clear it of the last part of her fantasy. He was relying on her to introduce him to this new world. She couldn't— wouldn't—let herself cloud his experiences with her own selfish desires. Besides, if she let herself fall in love with him, she would ruin any chance they had of being friends. She wanted him in her life forever. Passion had a way of burning out, leaving only ash and destruction behind.

"Are you all right?" He frowned down at her, his brow furrowed. His eyes were almost gray against the robin's-egg blue of the afternoon sky behind him.

She forced herself to smile and shook her head. "I'm fine."

Dante didn't seem appeased. He carried her to the nearest chair, at her writing desk, and finally set her down.

"If you would please indulge me," Dante said. "It would not do for you to have a relapse of your earlier condition. Neither Winston nor Garrett would forgive me if I let that happen while you were in my care."

He knelt in front of her so she didn't have to crane her neck to look up at him.

"I'm supposed to be taking care of you," she said.

"You have already done more for me than anyone in my life."

"I don't think that's true."

"My life has not been filled with kindness, apart from the blessing of my mother." There was no bitterness to his tone, only a sad resignation.

"What about Heinrich?" Elsa realized her mistake just as the words slipped from her lips, but it was too late. She couldn't take them back.

Dante paused for a beat too long. Suspicion clouded his eyes. "What do you know of Heinrich?"

Elsa knew more about Heinrich than Dante could imagine. She'd only stumbled across Dante because of her fascination with his parents. She had never seen two people more in love.

It took years and a considerable amount of money, but Elsa had collected all the art that she knew touched their lives just in the hopes of seeing a couple who were kind to one another rather than violent. It was so drastically different from her parents and all the men that came after her father.

How could she possibly explain all that without driving Dante away? She figured she didn't have to worry about him leaving. Dante had nowhere to go. He was trapped with her.

She was too familiar with what that felt like. She vowed once more to help him establish himself in her world, to achieve independence. Knowledge was easy to provide for him. A legal identity was another matter.

He stood and took a step back, but she grabbed his hands and said, "There's more I need to tell you."

What would he say if she bared her soul to him and told him everything? The only other time she'd confided with someone, things had gone horribly wrong, and Dante had much more reason to be upset. Elsa had never felt like a voyeur before, but she'd also never spoken to anyone she observed during her travels. Her entire body was trembling, reminding her that the wounds she had suffered as a child weren't just to her heart.

"You should rest," Dante said. "We can discuss this later."

She let out a huge sigh, grateful for the temporary reprieve. She still felt like she might be sick, but it was passing. Closing her eyes, she rested her forehead against the backs of his hands.

"Perhaps I should call Garrett," Dante said.

"No, I want you." Elsa's face tingled with embarrassment. "I mean, I want us to be alone so I can answer your questions. About this time, not... Not how I brought you here."

She glanced up at him, hoping she had covered for letting that slip out. He regarded her silently for a few moments.

"If you are certain you are well enough." His voice softened. "I would like that as well."

Chapter Seven

If Elsa had not explained herself, Dante would have thought he misheard. As it was, the haste with which she spoke, coupled with the way she clung to him, conveyed her desire more clearly than any words. She wanted him near her, though he still had not determined why.

"There's a lounge chair outside." She gestured to the thick foliage beyond the windows. "Maybe we could sit in the garden for a bit?"

An urge that he could not suppress overcame him, and he reached forward, scooping her up into his arms again. She gasped, but smiled as she wrapped her arms around his neck. He was growing accustomed to having her next to him, feeling her embrace. He found himself smiling back at her.

The fact that she seemed not only to not mind his proximity, but perhaps even enjoy it was one of the most novel things of all about this new world. Dante doubted anything in his previous life could have been as satisfying as Elsa's soft exhalation as she leaned against his chest. Her tremors subsided as he held her.

Another double set of doors led to the garden, much like the ones between the house and solarium. A key rested in the lock of the right-hand door. Elsa reached down to turn it, then pressed the handle. The door swung open onto a stone patio surrounded by lush green plants adorned with brightly colored flowers.

The studio seemed like Heaven, with resources to dabble in so many of the creative arts. But if the studio was paradise, then surely this was the Garden of Eden. Dante stepped out into the bright afternoon light.

Warm gray bricks spread out in a path before him that opened up into a circle like a stone sun. He could see several paths trailing out from that center, with vivid greens and beautiful flowers embracing them. Everywhere he turned, Dante saw color. Beautiful, glorious color. All spectacularly illuminated by the sun.

He lifted his face to the cerulean sky, watching clouds as thick as cotton drift lazily across the horizon. Emerald grass stretched out beyond the garden, ending in copses of bizarrely shaped trees.

Even while traveling with the circus with his mother, Dante had never left the cities where they performed. He'd never been to the country, had never even dared to venture to a park. But here, there was quite literally an entirely new vista.

"It's beautiful, isn't it?" Elsa said, drawing his attention back to her.

He wondered how even that magnificent view could have distracted him from the beautiful woman in his arms. The light caught every strand of her hair, making it shine more brightly than any gold he had ever seen. Her eyes were honey-brown in the sun. The color had returned to her lips, a rich heliotrope.

Once more, he had the urge to gently trace his thumb across her lips. They parted as he stared at her, and the desire flared, quickly spreading to other parts of his body. His hands were busy holding Elsa. Perhaps he could brush her lips with his own...

She cleared her throat and said, "The chairs are right over there."

"Of course." Dante's voice came out a bit breathless.

He walked into the sunburst pattern of stone. Just across from the patio doors, several chairs flanked a table with an enormous umbrella sprouting from its center. He gently placed her in the lounge chair and then set about adjusting the umbrella to make sure that she was protected from the afternoon sun. When he was satisfied, he sat in a chair opposite her, hoping to marshal his thoughts with the help of some distance.

"If you sit in the sun, you'll burn." She reached to the nearest chair and weakly pulled it toward her in the shade. "Come sit next to me."

His theory that she enjoyed being close to him was gaining strength by the moment. Dante sought to test it further, watching her expression as he pushed the chair nearer, turning it so they would face each other.

As he sat, her smile deepened, her eyes crinkling up at the corners.

She enjoyed his company. He still had no idea as to why. She had all of time from which to choose companions. Why him?

She drew him from his musings. "How is the encyclopedia set working for you?"

"Quite well, thank you. The knowledge within them is beyond remarkable." This was an excellent topic. Focusing on his learning would distract him from the fullness of her lips, the thin fabric of the revealing shirt she wore.

"What's your favorite thing you've read about so far?"

"It is difficult to choose."

"Well, what stands out to you?"

Dante looked over the grounds, soaking in the rich scent of earth and the heat from the patio stones. The sensations relaxed him as he tried to formulate his thoughts.

"I read the books covering transportation. I could scarcely believe the section on airplanes, though the physics behind them was clearly explained. However, there was nothing regarding…"

Elsa's face had paled, her forehead pinched above the delicate slope of her nose. Though he would feel better once he understood how she had brought him here, he could not bring himself to strain her further.

"Forgive me. We were not to speak of this."

"No, it's okay." She began chewing on her lower lip—an unconscious habit he'd noticed the night before when she was worried. "You won't find time travel in those books."

Dante kept his voice as gentle as he could. He did not wish to frighten her away now that she seemed willing to broach the topic. "I take it the occurrence is uncommon?"

"I'm the only person alive that I know of who can do it."

"But you keep your ability secret, so how can you be sure?"

"If anyone else can do it, they're smart to keep it to themselves."

He reflected on her words, the vehemence and utter hopelessness with which she spoke. As advanced as this time was, the instinct to persecute others was deeply ingrained in the human psyche. Dante was well acquainted with this. Nothing would inspire fear in people's hearts faster than something they did not understand.

"You have not even told your friends?"

"No one else can know. Please."

"I will keep your secrets."

She let out a deep sigh, her smile returning. "Thank you."

She shifted the conversation back to the encyclopedia set and how well he was assimilating the information. Apparently, the subject of time travel was closed once more.

Dante barely minded. He settled back in his chair to enjoy the conversation and the beautiful view. His gaze did not stray from Elsa.

Chapter Eight

The shadow of the umbrella slowly drifted across the patio while Elsa and Dante talked. She watched him rearrange it several times to keep them in the shade. The third time, she said, "It must be getting close to tea time. We should go help Winston."

"I will assist him," Dante said. "You need to rest."

"I can at least come along."

"The sun and fresh air seem to be doing you good. We should make use of them while we can."

"If we're out too much longer, we'll have to light the citronella candles and turn on the box fan in the studio to keep the mosquitoes away."

"I promise, I will only be a moment."

She smiled and nodded, even though she didn't like the idea of him leaving her behind. Who knew what kind of questions Winston would ask. It made her heart beat faster to contemplate, but she knew she would have to trust Dante not to tell people her secret.

They were still in the honeymoon period of their relationship, getting to know each other. Eventually, the novelty would wear off and they would need more time to themselves. Time with others. She couldn't be with him constantly. But she could enjoy their time together now.

The afternoon had passed with a dreamlike quality. They didn't just talk about what he was learning, but about art and creativity itself. He was turning out to be even more amazing than she had expected. Considerate, kind, intelligent, artistic. He was everything she wanted and couldn't let herself have.

Dante stood, but paused before he left. His lips parted as if he was about to say something, but instead, he gently lifted Elsa's hand and kissed her knuckles so softly she barely felt his lips.

Fire flooded her body. His warm breath on her skin was like a spark set to kindling longing for a flame. Dante released her hand as he stood, and she had to stifle the urge to reach out to him. He bowed, then walked briskly through the studio doors, as if he was as eager to return as she was to see him again.

Elsa couldn't take her eyes off of him as he left. His broad shoulders perfectly offset his tapered waist. His legs were long, his backside... She should not be thinking about his backside. Or any side of him. Not while drooling, anyway.

Closing her eyes, she leaned back in the lounge chair, taking deep, steady breaths. She had not brought Dante to her time so that they could have a relationship. Well, other than a lasting friendship she hoped they'd develop. He needed to be free to do as he wished with whomever he wished.

There were plenty of women in her time that would be just as flattered by his attentions. He needed to know he had a choice. He needed to be completely independent if there was ever a chance for something more between him and Elsa. Otherwise, she would never know if what he felt was love or gratitude.

He had already said he felt indebted to her, and a sense of obligation would be the worst of all. Her heart bunched up in her chest, reality crushing her dreams underfoot like an empty tin can.

Dante would never be independent. He had no identification, and Elsa had no idea how to get him any. It was the one part of her plan she hadn't been able to figure out. Ironically, she had run out of time.

She could sense that the moments in his life that she could connect with through the ring were almost used up. She couldn't visit the same moment twice. When she had seen he was about to die, she had to bring him back right then.

She didn't know what to do. Even broaching the topic would raise questions about who Dante was, where he had come from, and most importantly, how he had arrived. If the wrong person found out, they would both wind up in a lab.

If he decided he wanted reconstructive surgery when she told him about it, who knew what his bloodwork would show. Elsa had already tested the waters with Garrett to see if Dante sounded like a good candidate, but even if she paid the bill, Dante would still need identification before anyone would operate on him.

There were too many variables, too many things she couldn't control. She closed her eyes, pushing all the thoughts away. He was here, now. He was safe. She would keep him that way.

Imagining them as a couple was a dangerous dream to have in the first place. She knew firsthand the harsh realities of how relationships could change people—bring out the worst in them. She needed to keep that reality as a shield, to protect herself from wanting too much, from hoping for more.

She could dream up as many "happily ever after" endings involving Dante as she wanted. But he was a real human being, with human failings. A human temper.

"Elsa! Are you okay?"

Elsa jumped at the unexpected voice coming from the side of the house. She glanced over at the path to see Rachel running toward her.

This was a nightmare. Rachel was Elsa's chattiest friend. As Jazz's assistant in the gallery, Rachel's outgoing nature was useful. When trying to keep something private, she was the last person Elsa would want to involve.

The white of Rachel's jeans was blinding in the late afternoon sun. A matching white purse was slung over her shoulder, and she wore a pale blue blouse that was almost the same color as her eyes. With the addition of her perfect features and supermodel height, she was absolutely stunning.

"Garrett said you were sick. Are you sick?" She pulled Dante's chair closer to Elsa and sat.

"I've felt better." Elsa smiled and pulled herself up higher in the lounge chair. Rachel grabbed Elsa's hand and squeezed it, her enthusiastic grip chasing away the last lingering sense of Dante's gentle touch.

The sooner Elsa could get Rachel to go home, the better. Dante would be back any moment, and if Rachel saw him, the questions would be nonstop. Elsa didn't have the answers ready yet.

"Is there anything I can do for you? What do you need?"

Rachel was in full manic mode, her exuberance seeming to suck up all the energy in the area. Normally, her awe of pretty much everything was endearing. At the moment, it was sapping Elsa of what little strength she had recovered.

"I think what I need most right now is rest." She hoped Rachel would get the message and leave.

Elsa should have known better.

"Let me keep you company, then. I haven't seen you in so long."

That much was true. Rachel had been conspicuously absent for a couple of months. Now that she had brought this to Elsa's attention, her curiosity was piqued.

"Why is that?"

"I'm not supposed to say." Rachel looked at the ground, her expression as sad as if she was five and had just dropped her ice cream cone. Then a smile spread across her face, her mood switching so quickly it made Elsa dizzy. "But I can trust you to keep a secret."

If only she knew…

Rachel scooted her chair even closer to Elsa, beaming. Whatever this new secret was, Rachel was over the moon about it.

"I met someone."

"I should have guessed." Elsa smiled and asked, "And who is this new love of yours?"

"I'm not supposed to say." Rachel's gaze once more trailed off toward the ground. This sad look vanished even faster than the first. "He's an artist! He has a new exhibit opening at the gallery soon."

"You know Jazz doesn't like it when you date the artists displaying at her gallery."

"Yes, but all the best artists display there. No one can discover the next hot trend like Jazz can. His career will be spectacular with her help."

"Just remember your own career. You can learn a lot more from Jazz than from one of her clients."

"How can you be so unromantic when you've written a dozen bestselling romance novels?"

Rachel dropped Elsa's hand and leaned back, pouting. Elsa knew men were often devastated by that look. Luckily, she was immune. Arching an eyebrow, she scowled until Rachel looked away.

Rachel's tone was a bit petulant when she said, "I wouldn't have gotten involved with him if I didn't think it was serious."

"Rachel, you always think it's serious. Remember when you dated that bicycle delivery guy for a week and started picking out china patterns?"

"Hello, I'm an interior designer. Anyway, that was different. That guy was totally wrong for me. This one is an artist. An artist!"

Elsa sighed. From the breathy way Rachel said the word, it was obvious he wasn't just an artist. He was what Rachel thought of as *an artist*. Which meant he was probably one of the most sensitive, moody, temperamental men that Elsa would ever have the misfortune to meet. She'd met artists Rachel dated before and hadn't liked any of them. She especially disliked how they treated Rachel.

Torn between encouraging Rachel to leave and making sure she wasn't getting into yet another bad relationship, Elsa said, "Maybe we can have lunch next week and talk about it."

"Oh no. I don't think I can get away with that."

"What do you mean?"

"Well, he's a very private person. No one's supposed to know that we're dating. In fact, he doesn't know that I'm here visiting you." Rachel gave an impish grin. "He thinks I'm running an errand for Jazz. And technically, I am. I just decided to take a little detour on my way to the contractor."

Elsa's stomach gave a sudden sideways lurch, the hair on her arms standing on end like a live wire had passed too close to her skin. "He doesn't want you talking to your friends?"

"He's kind of figured out that I have a little bit of trouble keeping things to myself." She shrugged her slender shoulders as if that made it all right.

"Rachel, that's part of who you are," Elsa said. "Has he ever thought of just not telling you things he doesn't want other people to know?"

"Hey!"

"Well? This guy can't expect to keep you in a cage so you don't ever talk to anyone. You're a people person. If this guy can't appreciate you for who you are, he's not right for you."

"You don't even know him."

"The people who really love you figure out how to let you be you while maintaining the relationship."

At that moment, Dante emerged from the studio doors, carrying a tray with a pitcher of iced tea, two glasses and some cookies.

"I trust you will enjoy…" His voice trailed off as he saw Rachel sitting at Elsa's side.

Elsa couldn't help but wonder what Rachel looked like to him. She was petite, her flaxen hair hanging around her face in waves that seemed as wild as her spirit, yet somehow not at all disheveled. And she had the blue eyes that were supposed to go with blonde hair, along with the creamy complexion and rosy cheeks.

Rachel also knew how to dress, and Elsa realized with a shock of embarrassment that Dante had only seen her in pajamas since that first night at the theatre. She reached up and straightened her tank top self-consciously. Rachel was so much better at being blonde than Elsa was.

Rachel seldom used her looks purposefully, but when she did, it was devastating. She knew just how to pout, just how to veil her eyes, and just how to swish her hips to get any man's complete attention whenever she wanted it. It had never bothered Elsa before, but now, with Dante staring at both of them at the same time, she felt completely outclassed.

Not that it should matter to her. What did matter was Rachel's inevitable reaction to Dante.

Rachel turned around slowly in her chair, her gaze scanning his clothes, his face and his mask. Even the way he stood set him apart from other men. No one's posture was that good anymore.

"Oh my God," Rachel said. "You're finally writing the book!"

Rachel let out a squeal that was closer to a shriek, clapping her hands as she leapt up from her chair and practically skipped across the patio. Dante frowned as she ran in circles around him, like an over-excited terrier.

Elsa started to swing her legs over the side of her seat, but Dante quickly crossed to her, Rachel trailing behind. He set his tray on the table, then lifted Elsa's legs back onto the lounge chair. "Elsa, you know you are supposed to be resting."

Elsa could hear the strain in his voice.

Rachel let out another squeal. "Oh my God. Where did you find this guy? He's perfect!"

"Rachel..." Elsa warned.

But the momentum of Rachel's excitement would not be denied. Dante turned to face Rachel, blocking her path to Elsa almost protectively. Elsa felt a flutter in her stomach at the thought.

"Is he from the theatre?" Rachel asked. "From the play you've been going to every weekend? I bet that's it."

"Rachel!"

Elsa's tone must have snapped Rachel a bit back to reality. She finally tore her eyes away from Dante and glanced at Elsa.

Elsa took a deep breath before speaking. "This is Dante. He's a friend who will be staying with me for a while. And I'm sure he doesn't like being ogled like that."

"Then he shouldn't be so gorgeous!" Rachel said, smiling as she sat back down in one of the chairs at the table.

Dante looked like he'd been slapped. He took in a sharp breath, every vertebra perfectly stacked atop each other, but didn't say anything.

He probably thought Rachel was teasing him, playing a cruel joke, like Giselle often had. But flirting came as naturally to Rachel as breathing, and she really did have a point. Dante was absolutely gorgeous. Elsa's heart sank a little, as she added that to the list of things he needed to realize before she would consider him independent.

"Are you an actor from the play Elsa funded? Are you helping her with her book?"

Elsa stifled a groan. She was going to tell Dante about all of this, but not now. Not like this. Elsa was desperate to make Rachel stop.

"Rachel, please. Leave him be."

"I am here to help Elsa in whatever way I can," Dante said, his voice smooth, but with a cold evenness that Elsa had only heard him use with people from his time. People who had tormented him.

"Wow, you even sound like him."

"Like who?"

Rachel laughed, oblivious to the chaos she was spawning. "The Phantom of the Opera."

Chapter Nine

"You are the second person to speak of this apparition. However, I am at a loss." Dante had not questioned Garrett on the matter, hoping to avoid a topic that seemed quite uncomfortable for him.

"You've never heard of the Phantom of the Opera?" Rachel smiled and lifted one slender shoulder toward her head, inclining it as she gazed at him. "I get it. You're a method actor. Since you're supposed to be the Phantom, you wouldn't know about the character."

"I am afraid I do not follow your meaning."

"Sure." Rachel nodded in an exaggerated manner. "Is Dante your real name or a stage name?"

"It is the name my mother gave me."

The way the woman gawked at him and her coquettish gestures reminded Dante of the actresses in Heinrich's theatre. He would not serve himself up for her amusement.

"It's a great name." Rachel turned to Elsa. "You should totally use that in your book."

"You are a writer, then?" Dante angled his face so that only his mask was toward Elsa, hoping to hide his expression until he had gained better mastery over his emotions. Rachel was Elsa's friend, and Dante did not want Elsa to think him impolite.

"I was going to tell you," she said.

Rachel interjected once more. "I can't wait to read that book! Especially with you going all out and hiring someone to play the part of the Phantom in your house!"

Playing a part. Was this why Elsa had chosen him to be her companion? Was she truly writing a book about him? His life did not seem interesting enough to warrant such attention. Dread mingled with curiosity within him.

"Perhaps you could assist me with my role."

"Sure!" Rachel said.

He sat next to Elsa. "Tell me of this Phantom, as if I knew nothing at all."

"Oh how fun!" Rachel clapped her hands together. "Well, the original story was written like over a hundred years ago, but a ton of other versions have come out since then. Basically, the Phantom is this mad genius who runs around in catacombs or something under an opera house in Paris. He only surfaces to create his music, but he mostly winds up killing people."

"I beg your pardon?" Dante was uncertain if he had heard her correctly. Aside from his living in the basement of Heinrich's theatre, there was nothing in what she said that bore the slightest resemblance to Dante's life, for which he was extremely grateful.

"He's really good at inventions," she said. "He makes all kinds of traps and stuff and uses them to kill anyone who gets in his way."

Dante's heart sank as Rachel's story took on a familiar note. Giselle had seemed to delight in spinning tales about him. She painted him as a deformed monster that lurked in the basement of the theatre, coveting her and using the mechanisms he designed for the theatre's productions to ill effect.

"So," Dante said. "He is a villain."

"I guess he is in most of the stories, but people still sympathize with him. He's an outcast, and everybody wants to be accepted. See, his face was all messed up when he was born, and he was raised in a freak show."

Dante felt his jaw drop. He quickly checked his mask to ensure it was in place. "They believe his disfigurement justified him in murder?"

"Well, not exactly," Rachel said. "But anyway, don't worry. Elsa hates all the horror movie versions of the story. I'm sure in her book, you get to be the good guy."

"Indeed."

Dante glanced briefly toward Elsa. Her face was pale, her eyebrows pinched above her nose. Through parted lips, she pulled in breath after breath, as if drowning. When their eyes met, she leaned forward, clutching his arm.

"I'm sorry…"

Her words hit him like a blow. There was no denial. She was an author writing a book about him. Bringing him to her time was the same as commissioning the encyclopedia set. She had brought him forth for her research.

"Is there more?" he asked.

Elsa's eyes glittered as if she fought back tears. She pulled away from him and, angry as he was, he missed her touch.

Rachel continued, though she spoke a bit haltingly. Perhaps she finally sensed that something was wrong. "There's the love story, of course."

Dante's gaze snapped to Rachel. "Love story?"

"Yeah, that's my favorite part. I've seen movies and plays and read books all based on the same story, and I still wonder whether the young protégé will choose the mentor or the childhood sweetheart." Rachel leaned forward and patted his knee. "I always cheer for you."

"Cheer for…"

Dante shook his head, appalled as he realized what Rachel meant. Mary had been of age when they met, but he was not the sort to take such a young bride. He had been careful to always play the role of mentor with her, though she was the only person in his life who did not seem profoundly disturbed by his appearance.

He looked to Elsa. "I was twice her age."

"Giselle," Elsa said, as if that explained it all.

Truthfully, it did. Giselle's exaggerations at work once more. The thought that Elsa was trying to tell yet another tale surrounding his life made his stomach churn.

"Does he ever break character?" Rachel asked.

Elsa let out a long sigh. "Rachel, I really do need to rest. Could we maybe visit some other time?"

"Sure, now that I know you're okay." Rachel leaned over to give Elsa a quick hug, and said, "You guys are really taking this method acting seriously."

Elsa stared pointedly at Dante. "I've been working on this book for a long time. I want to get it right."

Rachel stood and slung her purse over her shoulder. With a broad grin, she said, "I bet you do. It's no wonder you're so tired with a hottie like this helping you with your 'research'. I'm sure he's being very thorough."

"Rachel!" Elsa gasped, her face reddening instantly.

Dante caught the insinuation and said, "I beg your pardon?" at the same time.

Rachel just laughed. "As much as I'm looking forward to reading the book, you should really let Elsa get some sleep."

She hurried off around the side of the house, waving once over her shoulder. After a long silence, Dante heard what must be the engine of Rachel's car starting. It faded into the distance.

He stood and walked to the greenery at the edge of the patio. Taking a moment to gather his thoughts, he gently traced the white petals of a gardenia with his fingertips.

"I'm sorry," Elsa said at last. "I didn't want you to find out that way."

"Find out what, Elsa?" He could not bring himself to look at her. "That you have brought me to your time merely to assist your efforts to spin more tales around my life? Or that history remembers me as a monster?"

"Giselle's stories took on a life of their own. They merged with other tales, traveling from one person to the next over decades and turned into urban legends. *The Phantom of the Opera* is not your story. That's why I'm writing this book. To tell your story. I'm writing it for you. I'll destroy it right now if you tell me to."

Dante did turn toward her then. He had to see the truth in her eyes. When he spoke, each word was clipped, demanding.

"Why am I here?"

Elsa swung her feet to the ground and stood before he could stop her. She seemed steady enough that he left the distance between them.

He did not trust himself to keep seeking answers if he was distracted by her touch.

"Because I couldn't let you die."

Dante could not help but think she must have had some other motive behind her actions. She had paid such a toll to bring him here. What would she expect of him in return?

She took several quick breaths, as if she was preparing to leap over some hurdle. When she spoke, the words rushed from her lips in a flood.

"I use my ability to go to other times and places to do research for the books I write. I was researching something else when I found you."

"And decided to write this book of which Rachel spoke."

"Yes."

Elsa winced when the word left her lips, as if speaking it pained her. Despite his misgivings, Dante wanted to comfort her, but he would not allow himself to do so.

"If I hadn't made that choice, I would never have discovered that I could save you," she said.

"What do you mean?"

"I was researching the book and I saw Mary and Edgar after the fire." Elsa's voice quieted, though the tension never left her slight frame. "When Edgar gave Mary the ring."

Dante felt as though the ground shuddered beneath him. He had been confident that Mary would be all right. Knowing beyond doubt that she and Edgar had a chance to lead a happy life together removed a weight from Dante's heart he hadn't known he carried.

"Was she well?"

"Physically, she was fine. But she was so upset." Elsa's gaze became unfocused, as if she was seeing something far away. "She kept saying that they didn't find your body. She refused to give up hope that you were still alive. And when I heard her say that, I knew. I knew I could save you. I had to."

Elsa looked at him then, and the raw despair that flooded her features staggered him.

"I would have done anything to save you."

She took a hesitant step toward him, but her legs gave way. He was not close enough to catch her before her knees struck the stone of the patio. She caught herself with her hands, but her arms trembled from holding her weight. Dante ran to her side, then knelt next to her. He drew her against his chest.

"Are you all right?"

"Yes." Elsa shook her head. "I'm just tired of being so...tired." She took a deep breath and leaned against him.

Whatever else he believed, he knew that she had risked herself to bring him here. She was still paying the toll of that journey. He lifted her from the ground and carried her into the studio.

"I can walk."

"I believe we have both seen that is not the case."

The nearest chair was at the desk nestled against the wall of windows just inside the door. Dante set Elsa upon it as gently as he could. He knelt before her, turning over her hands to inspect her injuries. The soft skin of her palms had been roughly lacerated from the stonework of the patio.

"It's nothing."

Dante brushed the grit and pebbles from her hands as delicately as he could. "I am sorry that you fell."

"It wasn't your fault."

"I am not so certain of that. You would not be in this state if you had not brought me here, whatever your reasons. And I am grateful to be here."

"I knew this was going to upset you. That's part of why I was putting off telling you. I don't deal well with conflict."

She had that unfocused look about her again, and Dante wondered what horrible specters of the past she was seeing. He could not leave her there to face them alone.

"I am not of the opinion that ignorance is bliss, but rather, it is dangerous. If I am to adapt to this new world, there are things I need to know. Not the least of which is how others will react to my presence, given the legends that may be associated with me. I would rather you preserve my safety than my feelings."

Elsa nodded. "I'll do my best, but please try to understand, I'm not used to talking about any of this. It's hard for me to share."

"You have been alone with this for a very long time." When Elsa tried to look away, Dante dared to cup her cheek with his hand, his thumb gently stroking the softness of her skin. "I will keep this in mind, so long as you also remember that, no matter what else happens, you are no longer alone."

Her eyes filled with tears. She blinked them away, smiling at Dante, though there were lines of strain at the corners of her lips.

"It'll be hard to forget, since you insist on carrying me everywhere." She lifted her hand to cover his and pressed her cheek into his palm. She tightened her grip for a moment, then pulled his hand away.

He knew she was making light of the situation, and he let her. There were weights she carried deep within her soul. The more time he spent with her, the more obvious they became.

Though he could not bring himself to smile, he did lift her from her chair, preparing to carry her to a more comfortable spot for her to rest. For the first time, she did not melt against him, but instead reached for something on her desk.

"Wait."

Dante lowered her back into her chair and watched as she picked up a strange box. It was shaped somewhat like a book, but had cords coming out of it, which she promptly removed.

"Is that a computer?"

Despite what had just passed between them and the uncertainty he still felt, a surge of excitement flowed through him. He had read of computers and was eager to witness one in use.

"Yes, it is." She picked it up and held it to her chest, then leaned forward as if she intended to stand.

"Elsa, please," Dante said, using a tone more stern than he had ever dared with another. Her eyes widened slightly, but she paused and allowed him to pick her up once more.

Her skin was warm, her body soft against him. Even now, he ached to pull her closer. How could it be that holding her in his arms felt so natural, so right? The scent of roses came to him from her hair. Dante felt a sudden urge to bury his face in it, perhaps trail his fingers down her neck before placing a kiss on the graceful slope of her shoulder.

His voice came out unexpectedly low, with a rough tenor, when he managed to speak. "Where am I to take you?"

Elsa's lips parted, her eyelids lowering briefly. For a moment, Dante wondered if her thoughts, her desire, had mirrored his own. But then, she cleared her throat, and said, "The entertainment room, please."

When they arrived, he gently deposited her on the couch, though he was loathe to let her slip from his embrace.

"The movies you want are in that cabinet there." She pointed to a shelf next to the large television.

"I must first tend to your injuries."

"I'm fine, really."

"Then it should not take long."

Another bathroom adjoined the room. Inside, as expected, he found clean washcloths, which he ran under cold water. An unbidden memory played through his mind, of dousing his vest during the fire. Had it only been days ago? Or decades?

It was too much to consider. At the moment, he needed to focus on Elsa. He wrung out the washcloths and took a towel from the rack above the sink, then returned to her side.

She shifted away from him as he sat next to her on the couch. At first, he thought she was trying to put distance between them, but the sight of her soft smile, the rosy flush creeping up her neck convinced him it was actually an invitation.

The doubts that plagued him faded in the light of her offer, and he found himself sliding even closer to her. He gently dabbed at her hands with the wet cloth. When he had satisfied himself that her wounds were clean, he placed her hands together with the cool cloth held between to help soothe them.

He wondered if he dared to lift the hem of her pants to inspect her knees. Though she seemed to enjoy his touch, surely there were limits he dare not cross. Regardless, it needed to be done. Dante shifted to sit by her feet, turning so that he could see Elsa's face. He needed to watch her expression.

Her eyes were wide as she watched him slide his hands along the sides of her shapely calves. Her skin was like silk. Her lips slowly parted and her breath became uneven. When her legs were exposed up to the tops of her knees, she finally glanced at him.

Her eyes were heavy-lidded, smoldering. They burned like embers, and the heat of her gaze raked Dante down to his soul.

As quickly as the look appeared, it vanished, leaving him to wonder if it had been nothing more than a flight of fancy. Returning his focus to his task, he took two more wet cloths and laid one on each of her knees. They bore red marks from her fall, but the skin had not broken.

He lifted her legs carefully, then placed the towel beneath her knees for support. His hands trailed down her calves, a lingering touch that he could not resist. Elsa never shrank back. She never looked away.

He could feel his heart hammering in his chest. She had brought him to her time, her home, to assist with her book. It made a certain sense that she would want to hear from him what his life had been like, but after Rachel's words, he wondered if it was possible that Elsa wanted more. Could she be seeking to create new moments between them to use as inspiration?

If so, Dante was uncertain he would even try to resist.

Chapter Ten

Telling Dante about the legends surrounding him had always been part of Elsa's plan, but not so soon. He needed to adjust, to adapt to his new world and get to know her. He needed to trust her first.

From his perspective, they had only met a few days ago. She was surprised he was still talking to her after what Rachel had told him.

"Shall we begin, then?" Dante was kneeling right next to her, his hands lingering on the backs of her legs. Her skin felt electrified, tingling heat pooling low in her body.

Before she could respond, Winston wandered into the room, an empty glass in his hand. Dante leapt up, then walked several steps away from Elsa. He cast a guilty look at Winston.

"Not interrupting anything, am I?" Winston asked.

"Winston…" Elsa said.

He chuckled. "I heard a car a bit ago and thought you might need another glass for tea."

"The tea!"

Dante gestured for her to stay in place. "If I may—our unexpected visitor has gone. However, I fear it was quite a distraction. I will go and fetch the tea presently and bring it here. That is, if you will both excuse me?"

"Go on, then." Winston snorted. "You don't have to be so formal about it."

"If you would be so kind as to remain here and ensure that Elsa does not try to leave the couch," Dante said. "I would be much obliged."

"Absolutely. She needs to be resting, and I'll see that she does."

"Don't forget to lock the studio doors when you come back in, please," she said.

"I will take care of it. Do not worry."

In the doorway, Winston stepped aside enough for Dante to pass, but reached out and patted his shoulder. Elsa didn't miss the smile that crossed Dante's face at the gesture.

Winston inclined his head as if listening to Dante's retreat, then joined her on the couch, sitting next to her when she scrunched up against the cushions. Winston was practically beaming.

"I like him."

"That's high praise, coming from you. What did he do to get in your good graces so quickly?"

"Why, he's been taking such good care of you, of course. Don't think I don't know. He's been doting on you for days." Winston leaned in and whispered, "And it's about time too."

"Dante's just a friend, Winston."

Winston shrugged. "For now, perhaps. But he's a fine man. You could do a lot worse."

She was well aware of that. In fact, she didn't think it was possible to do any better. Before she knew that she would be bringing him back to her time, she'd dreamed so many times of living with Dante, of loving him. An idealized love. It was hard to keep those dreams at bay. But he wasn't some weird time-travel mail-order groom.

"And how are you, my love?" Winston asked, reaching over to pat her knee. His hand landed on the wet cloth that Dante had so thoughtfully applied. "What's this?"

"It's nothing. I just took a bit of a tumble in the garden."

Winston puffed out a breath. "That's it. I take back all the nice things I said."

Elsa laughed. "It's too late for that. I know how you really feel about him."

"And what about you?"

She took the dry towel from under her knees and set it on the coffee table, then folded the damp washcloths and placed them on top. They weren't wet enough to soak through and damage the wood.

"It's complicated."

"Pfft. I'll let you in on a secret. Life is a lot simpler than you think. And it's also shorter. If you like him, you need to act on it."

"I don't know that he likes me as much." She wished she hadn't let that slip out, but Winston just laughed and patted her knee again.

"He likes you, all right. He's just too well mannered to let on about it. Why else would he stay by your side all this time?"

Elsa could think of dozens of reasons that had nothing to do with Dante liking her. Fear and uncertainty were at the top of the list. And even if he had been starting to warm up to her, that had been halted by Rachel's untimely information dump.

Dante cleared his throat, appearing in the doorway. How long had he been standing there? Elsa turned scarlet thinking about it.

"You!" Winston turned around. He jerked his thumb over his shoulder toward her. "I expect you to take better care of Elsa from now on."

"It was my fault," she said.

"I fear I must disagree." Dante entered the room and set the tray of tea and cookies on the coffee table. He straightened stiffly. "I should have been more vigilant. For that I apologize. Both to Elsa and to you, Winston."

"Well, you just see to it that it doesn't happen again, or you'll get that walloping I promised you the first night you came."

"I do not doubt it, sir."

"Well, then. I'm off to make dinner. You kids have fun." Winston stood and slowly shuffled down the hallway.

"He threatened to wallop you on your first night here?" That was hardly the welcome she wanted for Dante.

"There were extenuating circumstances."

"I can't imagine what they were. Maybe he was joking."

"I am quite certain he meant every word. It was shortly after your collapse."

"He was probably just upset."

"We both were."

"I didn't mean to scare you."

Dante let out a short chuckle and shook his head. His right side was toward her, and he inclined his body so most of his face was covered with his mask. Elsa couldn't stand when he did that, hiding right in front of her.

"The matter was hardly under your control," Dante said.

"Still, I wanted your first days to be pleasant. That's one of the reasons I was trying to put this off. I want you to be happy here."

"Happiness based on half-truths is seldom lasting."

"Full disclosure, then. Or as close as I can manage."

Elsa held out her hand to seal the agreement. At least, that was what she told herself she was doing. She wasn't just coming up with an excuse to get him closer. The flutter in her chest when he took a step toward her and gently grasped her hand had nothing to do with it.

"I appreciate your efforts."

He let go of her hand, which was just as well since it was already starting to shake. He sat next to her and waited for her to begin. If only she knew where to start.

Going all the way back to the first time she'd time traveled was much too intense. The memories there were dark enough that Elsa never wanted to think of them again. Besides, she didn't want to overwhelm him with too much information. She decided to start with the legend, since Dante was so focused on that at the moment.

"These legends that grew up around you, they have very little to do with who you are or even what Giselle said about you. The story has taken on a life of its own."

"A nefarious one, it would seem."

"There are many versions of the story. Some are frightening, but some are actually quite lovely."

"From what Rachel said, I do not see how that can be so."

Elsa sighed, trying to find the right words. She knew this was a turning point both in their relationship and in Dante's relationship with her time.

"There's something compelling about the notion of an artistic genius working so hard to keep creating his art. It resonates deep within many people's souls."

"Even if he resorts to murder?"

"Not all of the stories say that he did. Some of them say he was blamed unjustly."

"As Giselle blamed me for Heinrich's death."

"I'm so sorry. I couldn't keep her from saying so in your time. But I can write a different story now. Your story."

"Your book?"

"Our book. I won't write it without you. And I will never show it to another person unless you want me to."

Elsa picked up her laptop. She typed in her password and opened her manuscript folder, then turned the computer around so he could see the screen. He shifted closer as he watched her use the track pad to select the document.

"This is the file with everything I've written so far," she said. "It's only a rough outline and notes, really. Tap it twice, and the file will open. Or you can press the key that says 'delete' and the file is gone. I'll promise you I will never try to write it again."

"You identify so strongly with this character who would do anything for his art, yet you would destroy your work so willingly?"

"You're more important." Elsa hadn't meant to speak with such intensity. She tried to cover it up, but only made things worse. "Besides, for most people, it's not about the art. It's about the longing for love and acceptance. That's something everyone can relate to."

Dante watched her silently for a few moments, then he said, "At the very least, I should like to read it first."

"If you tap on the track pad here, you can open the document. Read it whenever you want."

"Thank you."

She thought he might get so distracted by the laptop that he would forget about watching the movie, but she wasn't so lucky.

"I believe I am ready to proceed."

Elsa leaned forward to put the laptop on the coffee table. Dante reached out and took it from her, then set it aside for her.

"If you do not mind, I would like to avoid Winston's ire. I do not doubt he would make good on his threat if you were to injure yourself again. Indeed, I should not resist his punishment."

"He shouldn't have said that. Especially not on your first night here."

Dante ran his fingertips over her laptop, an unconscious habit that sent shivers down Elsa's spine. She couldn't keep herself from imagining those long fingers skimming over her skin.

"There is something else you should know about the night I arrived."

"Okay." When Dante didn't continue, Elsa said, "You can tell me anything."

"You were quite cold when you collapsed. Winston and I were gravely concerned. There were few resources with which to warm you. We resorted to what was most readily available."

"I don't see a problem with that." She remembered stacks of blankets on the bed when she woke up.

He turned, his gaze focusing on her with an intensity that made her shift in her seat.

"The primary heat source for that first night was…me."

"You?"

Elsa's mind immediately filled in everything he hadn't said. Her skin prickled as she could almost feel Dante's arms around her, his body pressed against hers, the heat of his chest at her back, his long legs twining with hers. She'd only had time to set out a pair of pajama bottoms for him. He probably hadn't even been wearing a shirt.

"I assure you, I was a complete gentleman," he said. "Garrett and Winston can attest to this, as they were present as well."

Nothing could dampen the pure desire that flooded through her body. All she could think of was Dante next to her. Dante in bed with her. Dante half-naked with her.

"I think I'd like some tea." She reached toward the glass as he did. He was probably trying to help her again, but their hands collided.

A shock ran up her arms from the contact, lighting her up even more. She had the strongest urge to grab his arm and pull him down on top of her. She took deep, even breaths to try to rein in her libido.

No wonder he seemed so comfortable carrying her around and touching her. That contact was nothing compared to spending an entire night in bed together.

How could she ever look at him again without picturing that night? And how could she ever stop herself from wanting more from him than she had any right to ask?

Chapter Eleven

Any hopes Dante had that Elsa's interest in him went beyond the academic drowned in the darkness of her eyes, the way she gasped for breath. She must be revolted at the thought of sleeping next to him.

"I apologize." His voice was colder than he had expected. "I should have confessed this sooner."

"You didn't do anything wrong." She curled her legs up under her and leaned against the arm of the couch. Pulling away.

He was not surprised by her reaction so much as how disappointed he felt. The dream of Elsa desiring him had taken root within his mind despite his misgivings. He could not even offer to leave. Where would he go?

At the very least, he could ease her discomfort by completing this task as quickly as possible.

"Perhaps we should proceed."

"I suppose so."

She pointed at a shelf she had shown Dante earlier that was full of movies. The bottom half of the shelf was a cabinet with closed doors.

"There's a made-for-TV movie version on the far right inside the cabinet. I think that'll be the best one to start with."

It did not take long for him to follow Elsa's instructions and begin the movie. She had told him to think of it as a theatre in a box. The metaphor was charming, though unnecessary. Dante had already read the texts on video recordings.

Seeing the technology at work was much more exciting. Elsa was inured to it, however. By his reckoning, she was asleep before the second act had even begun. Her head slowly listed to one side, until it was resting on the arm of the couch.

Dante waited until he was certain she was deeply asleep before pausing the movie and shifting her so that she was more comfortable. He gently lowered her arm to her side and covered her with the blanket that was neatly placed over the back of the couch.

It was difficult not to linger, watching her sleep. The rise and fall of her chest and the soft sounds of her breathing soothed him, even in his current state of uncertainty. Perhaps especially so. It reminded him of his first night in this time, when he had held her in his arms as she slept.

Everything had seemed much simpler then, and the absurdity of that nearly caused Dante to laugh aloud. He contained himself, ensuring he did not wake Elsa.

He smoothed down a few errant hairs on the side of her head and was about to return to his seat, but she sighed in her sleep, brushing her cheek against his hand. He let his thumb trail along her warm skin, then down the line of her jaw.

Her breath distinctly quickened, her lips parting, as if waiting to be kissed. Mesmerized, Dante leaned forward, wondering if her lips would feel as lush as they appeared. He felt her warm breath on his face before he marshaled himself.

He stood abruptly, taking a few steps away from her as he collected himself. What was he thinking? Taking advantage of a sleeping woman... Perhaps this legend was not as far from the truth as he would like.

Dante sat back down on the couch, putting as much distance between them as he could. He took a deep breath and pressed the button that would resume the movie.

So much had happened in such a short amount of time, so much progress made. And he himself had somehow become part of the legends of this world, however tangentially. He could scarcely believe it.

Whatever else she was, Giselle was a master storyteller. She had begun to spin her tales as soon as she joined Heinrich's theatre, leading Dante along and using him to invoke Klaus's jealousy and hasten their marriage.

Dante had often overheard Giselle telling admirers about the reclusive savant who dwelled beneath the theatre and built apparatuses for each production. She painted him as a tortured soul that Heinrich had brought into his home out of the kindness of his heart. She also called Dante a deformed monster who coveted her from the shadows.

A dozen people had seen Heinrich's fall, had watched as Dante clung to his father's arm, trying to pull Heinrich back onto the scaffolding. When Giselle first said that Dante pushed Heinrich to his death, the voices of protest were strong. Gradually, they diminished.

Her story had begun to take root even before the fire. Had it only been two short days ago? And yet, it was a century away.

The memory of Heinrich's death spawned a sharp pain in Dante's chest. Dante clutched one hand above his heart, the other covering his eyes, willing himself back under control.

It would not do for Elsa to awaken and find him so distraught. She might think that it was because of the movie, but no. The more he thought of it, the more the legend made sense. His reputation had died along with his father.

Dante did not need to torture himself with more of the tale. He stopped the movie, switching over to the television. The images were equally overwhelming at first, though in a much different manner. They distracted him from the morose train of his thoughts.

He watched for several minutes, listening to the new vernacular. Television would be an excellent tool for adaptation. Perhaps as important as the books she had commissioned for him.

The laptop sat before him, holding yet another book with knowledge that could assist him. Not a view into this time, but into how Elsa herself saw Dante—what she thought of him.

One moment, it would seem she could not be close enough to him. The next, she would pull away. Dante hoped her manuscript might provide some clarity on the matter.

He picked up the laptop, marveling at how light it was. The screen was mostly dark, a moving display of lights that looked like sentient fireworks flying across its surface in mesmerizing patterns. He watched it for some time before finally tracing his fingertip over the track pad's surface, as Elsa had before.

Immediately, the screen flickered to life, the fireworks replaced with a static view of a monochromatic background with a square in the center asking him for a password.

Elsa had not mentioned a password.

He had avidly read all of the books he could on computers and he understood the premise easily enough. He did not want to wake her to have her open the document for him. Not only was she still exhausted, but he preferred to read this in private.

All he had to do was use what he knew of her. Admittedly, that was not much. He first tried Leonardo's name, then Winston and Garrett, hunting out the letters and pressing each in turn. None of them worked. Dante thought for some time before typing in *phantom*, but it also did nothing.

Strangely, that reassured him. He glanced over at Elsa's still form, watching her take slow, even breaths. Fortified by that peaceful sight, he turned back to the computer. He had not exhausted the list of names he could try, but, on a whim, decided to enter his own next.

It worked.

Dante sat back, stunned by this revelation. Elsa had selected his name as her password. Not the Phantom's. Dante's name.

He felt as if a weight had been removed from his chest. She had said that he was more important to her than her book. Knowing this, it was easier for him to believe her. And he wanted to believe her.

But more than that, he wanted her to see the man that he was, not the legend he became.

He opened the document, eager to see what she had done with the myths surrounding his life. Skimming through the outline, he found extensive notes that she had marked as backstory. Rather than dealing with the legend, they primarily focused on his parents.

There was a lengthy section regarding his mother and her "bright and loving spirit". Several examples of her kindness were briefly described, most of which Dante was unaware. Elsa wrote about Dante's mother with such warmth.

Her notes also spoke of Heinrich's relationship with Dante's mother in great detail. Dante had no idea his father had been so loving, but again, Elsa had documented several events where Heinrich had made a special and sometimes stunning effort to convey his feelings.

Elsa also set forth the beginning of Klaus's hatred for Dante, the jealousy Klaus had felt at the birth of his younger brother. There were references to what Elsa called "the event", but those sections were strangely obscure.

When Dante reached the section regarding the fire in the theatre, he read the paragraph over at least a dozen times, refusing to believe. Finally, he set the computer away from him on the table and leaned back from the screen. He covered his eyes with his hands and rested his head on the back of the couch, trying not to think on what he had read.

It was some time later that he felt Elsa shift next to him, her hands on his arm.

"Dante, are you all right?"

He took a few slow breaths, not daring to uncover his eyes until he had composed himself somewhat.

"Is this true?"

"Which part?"

"The fire. That Klaus and Giselle set it on purpose." Saying the words aloud sickened him. Everything Heinrich had worked for, gone. Everything he had wanted to give to his sons, nothing but ash.

"The theatre was bankrupt thanks to Klaus. There was an insurance policy, and Giselle wanted the money."

"But they died." The horror of discovering their bodies returned— the loss and futility. As did the memory of Elsa, pulling Dante from the inferno.

"Things didn't go according to their plan. Klaus was drunk, as usual." Her voice was sharp with a bitterness Dante did not understand. The edge dulled, as she continued. "I'm sorry. I didn't expect you to read this alone."

He finally removed his hands from his face so he could look at her.

She was kneeling next to him, one hand on his shoulder and the other upon his arm. Her color had much improved and she seemed better able to support herself. Still, she chewed on her lower lip, strain pinching the skin around her eyes.

"How do you know all of this?"

"I was there. Klaus couldn't work the lock on Heinrich's safe. By the time he and Giselle loaded up the lockbox, the fire had spread. Klaus succumbed to the smoke and Giselle... Well, you saw what happened to her."

"I had no idea they had sunk so low."

"Not even when they accused you of killing Heinrich?"

"You know of that too?"

"Yes."

How should he be surprised anymore? Dante shook his head. "I could understand their confusion. As you said, Klaus was often inebriated, and with Heinrich's death... It all happened so fast. To this day, I blame myself."

Her hand tightened on Dante's arm and she rose on her knees, her face quite close to his. Her brow furrowed and her lips pulled down at the corners. When she spoke, her voice was like steel and her eyes flashed as hot as the fire from which she had pulled him.

"Heinrich's death was not your fault." She paused, fretting her lower lip. When she spoke again, her voice had softened. "He was dead before he fell off the scaffold."

"You were there that night as well."

"You saw me."

"I was not certain what I saw."

"I am." Her grip loosened on his arm. She sat back on her legs, leaning against the couch as if her outburst had drained her. "I think he had a heart attack. There was nothing you could have done to save him. You almost died trying to pull him back onto the scaffold, but he was already gone when he fell. I could see his face."

She shivered, her eyes staring blankly over Dante's shoulder, as if she was viewing the memory instead of the room around them. Dante impulsively reached for her, cradling her face in his hands so that she looked at him instead.

"Think no more upon it, I beg you. It was a horrible moment, and one that is best left behind the both of us."

In his mind, the memory was blurred. Too many emotions warred within him. Heinrich had only just told Dante that he was Dante's father moments before falling from the scaffold. Dante had learned more by reading Elsa's notes than Heinrich had been able to explain.

Knowing that Dante could not have saved his father was an added balm to his soul. He had so many reasons to be grateful to her, though he dared not express his thanks.

Elsa smiled gently at him and nodded. She let out a sigh, gripping his hands and pulling them from her face, though she did not let them go.

"It must have been strange for you to see me."

"Not so very strange," he said, returning her smile briefly. He was unsure whether to continue, but she was being so open with him. Dante wished to reciprocate. "You glowed with the same light as the night you pulled me from the fire. I thought you were an angel come to take Heinrich to Heaven."

"I wondered why you came with me the night of the fire," she said. "I was afraid when I came back for you that you wouldn't trust me. I guess you thought it was safe to trust an angel with your life."

Dante let out a short laugh and shook his head. "In that moment, I thought my life was already forfeit. I did not trust you with my life. I trusted you with my soul."

Chapter Twelve

The next day, the invisible weights bogging down Elsa's energy were gone. The emotional ones were heavier than ever. Making it through dinner with Garrett hadn't been the gauntlet she feared. It had actually been pleasant, and a much-needed boost after what Dante had confessed.

Putting his life in her hands was bad enough, but his soul?

What he said didn't change anything. The bottom line remained. He was depending on her, and she was going to come through for him. She would help him establish himself, hopefully they would become friends, and that would be enough for her.

She dressed as quickly as she could, then headed to Dante's room. He wasn't there or in the kitchen. Elsa went to check the entertainment room and noticed the doors to the studio were open.

When she reached the doorway, she saw Dante leaning over a canvas on the easel in the painting corner. The doors to the patio beyond were wide open, letting in a cool morning breeze.

"Good morning." He smiled brightly when he saw her, then went to the sink to wash out his brush.

It took Elsa a few moments to recover from that smile, from seeing him in the morning light streaming through the windows, from... everything.

"Good morning," she finally said. "Am I intruding?"

"Not at all. I believe I have finished the piece."

"Finished? Have you been up all night?"

"I was unable to sleep."

"You should have woken me."

"I hardly think so. You need your rest, and I have much to catch up on. When I tired of reading, I came here. I hope that is all right."

He set the brush aside and turned back to her. The sun struck his tousled hair, tiny highlights of lighter brown appearing that she had never noticed before. It was wavier than she'd seen it as well, and his jaw was shadowed from not shaving.

The confidence she'd felt that morning about just being friends vanished. She wanted to touch the rough stubble on his cheek, to curl up next to him as they read together. She wanted to wake up with him beside her every morning and go to sleep in his arms every night.

Elsa shoved down the urgent longing that pressed against her heart. "What did you paint?"

"You are welcome to look. Allow me to help you."

Dante started toward her, but she knew that meant he was planning to carry her. The thought of him holding her was too painful to bear at the moment.

"I'm much better this morning." She briskly walked toward the canvas. His smile faltered, but she tried not to think about that.

Curiosity helped her push aside her melancholy as she neared his work. She wondered what he had chosen as his first subject. The painting surprised her.

Flowers from the garden outside gracefully filled the canvas, captured in breathtaking colors. On one long, green leaf, an emerald lizard sat, staring out at her with inscrutable golden eyes. The brushstrokes were confident and bold, adding movement to an otherwise still scene.

Elsa felt a sense of awe and wonder wash over her like an ocean wave. It lifted her from her body, but set her back down a moment later. The odd sensation happened several times before she realized that his painting was activating her ability, but the only place it could take her was the present moment—the present spot.

She had never felt anything like it. It was beyond contentment, beyond peace. A feeling of home.

Warmth surrounded her. She was being supported by someone, enfolded in that emotion. It wrapped around her like an embrace. Like Dante's arms.

He was holding her up. Her knees had gone weak and she was leaning against his chest. His strong arms were wrapped tightly around her.

The left side of his face was closest to her as she looked up at him. His eyes were as blue as ocean water over white sands.

"Are you all right?"

"Of course."

"You started to fall again."

"Did I?" She felt her body again like waking from a dream. It had been a long time since her power triggered without her controlling it. "I think I need to sit down."

Dante lifted her from the ground and, as lightly tethered as she was to her body, it felt like a dip on a roller coaster ride. She let out a giggle and was mortified. She definitely needed more sleep.

"Sorry."

Dante's concern softened into a smile that quickly grew. "Whatever for?"

His smile didn't fade as he carried her outside onto the patio and set her on the lounge chair. He pulled another chair close, closer than he'd done the day before, and sat next to her, leaning forward with his elbows resting on his knees.

"Here we are again," she said.

"I can think of nowhere else I would rather be."

Elsa laughed, then realized she agreed. No matter what became of the two of them in the future, right now, the present moment, was absolutely perfect.

"Me too. Your painting is amazing."

"Yes, literally stunning, it would seem." His tone was teasing, but then grew serious. "Unless you are having some sort of relapse."

"No, not at all. The painting just triggered my ability unexpectedly."

"I do not understand."

"Right. I haven't explained how it works yet." She took a deep breath and dove right in before she could talk herself out of it. "The way I travel is through works of art. If a piece is especially filled with emotion, either by its creator when it was made or by events that happened around it, I can latch on to that energy and travel to those moments."

"My painting caused you to travel through time?" Dante looked perplexed, his eyebrows furrowing.

"No. Well, yes. I'm not explaining this well. Your painting made my powers activate, but there was nowhere and no...*when* for it to take me."

"And so it made you faint?"

"It made me start to travel, but since I was already at the destination, I didn't go anywhere."

"I'm terribly sorry. I did not mean..."

"Don't worry. It was really pleasant, actually. I've never felt anything like that." She laughed again and clasped his hand. "What do you call the piece?"

"I had not considered a name. But I would think *In the Sun* should do nicely. My little friend seemed to be enjoying herself immensely as I worked."

"It's a beautiful painting."

"I am glad you like it."

He lifted Elsa's hand to his lips and pressed a gentle kiss on her knuckles. The gesture had felt completely natural, but it took them both by surprise. Dante's eyes widened and he quickly lowered her hand again, shifting in his chair.

Elsa couldn't think of anything to say to cover the awkwardness of the moment. He cleared his throat and saved her from having to try.

"If you travel through art, how is it you discovered me? I spent my life in the circus and the theatre. There were no great works of art around me."

Apparently, he wanted to act as if that precious kiss hadn't happened. She could do that. Elsa was becoming well-practiced at denial since Dante had arrived.

"It's more about the emotions that are experienced around the pieces than their greatness, both that go into creating them and that surround them."

Dante was still holding her hand, and she lifted it slightly, keeping her grip on his fingers so he knew she wasn't trying to extricate herself. Sunlight glinted from his ring, highlighting the etchings of vines that coated its surface.

"My mother's ring?"

Elsa nodded. "Did you know that Heinrich made it for her?"

"I did not." Dante looked at the ring as if he was seeing it for the first time.

"This ring has seen so many important moments in people's lives." She ran her thumb over its surface reverently. "I've seen them all. Amazing moments. Painful moments."

She tried not to, but she found herself staring at Dante's mask, remembering that horrible moment when he'd been burned. That was the worst moment she had ever witnessed. She wished she could scrub the memory from her brain.

If he saw her looking, he didn't mention it.

"Would you tell me?"

"Some things are better left in the past."

"I thought I made my opinion on that matter clear."

She shook her head. "But this is bad. Really bad."

"It is knowledge I am strong enough to bear. Can you not have faith in me?"

A glimmer of something bright and possible fluttered in Elsa's chest. She realized that she actually could. The feeling flooded her body with warmth, with hope. She wanted to let it soak in soul-deep, but Dante was waiting.

This would be hard to say and harder yet for him to hear. She tried to get her thoughts in order, to figure out the best way to tell him.

"The first time Heinrich told your mother he loved her, he gave her this ring."

"That does not seem so terrible."

"That part wasn't. But they started off in a bad place, even though they loved each other deeply. Heinrich left his wife for your mother."

Dante's smile vanished, his lips tightening. "It troubles me to think that she would have become involved with a married man."

"You never met Heinrich's wife. She was horrible. Klaus was her son, and she was wealthy enough to have easily supported him. But when Heinrich left, she insisted he take Klaus."

"She abandoned him," Dante said. "That is why Klaus hated me."

"There was more to it." Elsa's stomach was in knots as she went on. "Your mother was Klaus's governess and much more of a mother to him than Heinrich's wife had ever been. In all my travels, I've never seen someone as kind as your mother. She was so cheerful, even in the face of terrible circumstances. She started over with nothing twice, sacrificing everything for the people she loved."

Dante was silent for a few moments, then said, "You were observing my mother when you discovered me."

"Both of your parents, actually. I found your mother first. She painted too. Not just sets and banners for the circus, but actual paintings."

"Did any of her paintings survive?" He leaned a bit closer to Elsa.

She smiled, and shifted toward him as well. "There's one in the library. A landscape."

He looked toward the studio doors, as if he was about to run to the library. Instead, he turned back to her.

"The emotions surrounding it must have been strong. I hope they were happy ones."

"For the most part, they were. I didn't know it was possible for someone to love others the way she did." Elsa's own pain rose up, pinching her throat shut. She had to push away the memories to go on. "I think she would like that you're painting. You definitely have a future in it, if that's what you want to do."

"I would scarcely know how to begin."

"I can help with that. Do you remember Garrett talking about Jazz last night at dinner?"

"Are you referring to the music or your friend?"

Dante grinned at her, and the logical thoughts progressing orderly through Elsa's mind scattered like startled birds at the sight of that playful smile.

Finally collecting herself, she said, "My friend."

"With the art gallery."

"I could arrange an introduction."

"Perhaps when I have a few more pieces to show her."

"Just let me know when you're ready. We can have her over for dinner or something."

He smiled and said, "I must confess, I quite like having you to myself."

Elsa ignored the way her heart danced at his words, the fluttering in her stomach that made her feel as though she could fly. She focused on everything he needed from her.

"You don't really have much choice of company at the moment."

He leaned back a bit, looking perplexed. "What do you mean?"

"I mean that we have to be careful right now. You don't have any form of identification. We can't explain how you're here, where you came from or how you entered the country."

"If it will help, I have been working to learn modern speech patterns and adjust my accent."

"How?"

He cleared his throat and, in a passable American accent, said, "I watched a lot of TV last night before I hit the studio."

Laughter burst from Elsa's chest. She couldn't stop it. Hearing him talk like that was so incongruous.

"Was it that bad?" he asked, reverting to his normal accent.

"No, it was actually really good. I'm just not used to hearing you talk that way."

"Maybe you should get used to it." He once more adopted the accent, making her laugh even harder.

When she had regained control again, she said, "Pretending to be a native is one thing. Proving it is another. I haven't figured out how to manage that yet. And I can't ask anyone about it, because that would lead to questions that could cause problems for us."

"Do not think on it any longer," he said. "We will sort it out, eventually, and should not let it spoil the current moment."

Elsa wished she could push it from her mind, but then Dante brought them back to the subject of the ring. Working out how to get him papers would have been a more comfortable topic.

"You said my mother sacrificed everything twice for those she loved. She never spoke of any hardships with me, though I was quite young when she passed. I had only thought of her as happy."

"She took everything in stride. But she made some hard choices. She left her governess position to be with Heinrich, even though he had no real way of supporting them. Then she left Heinrich after you were born and set out on her own. It was an amazing act of courage."

Dante sat back in his chair. His chest deflated, as if her words had knocked the wind out of him.

"I had always assumed that my father abandoned us. That it was because of…" He finished his sentence by turning his face away from her, for once hiding his mask from her view.

Elsa sat up, sliding her legs over the side of the lounge chair so that she could be closer to him. Their knees touched, but she ignored the pleasant heat that spread through her body from the contact. She tightened her grip on his hand.

"She left because of Klaus. I think he was jealous of the attention you were getting."

Dante stared at her silently, waiting for her to go on. With a deep breath, she plunged forward.

"You were just a baby. Your mother left you alone with Klaus for just a few moments, and he…" Elsa's throat nearly closed up, as if trying to shield Dante from learning the horrible truth. "There was a candle. It had burned down into a pool of molten wax."

She shook her head, closing her eyes to try to shut out the memory, but it only became sharper. Dante's wailing, his mother wiping the hot wax from his face, even though it was burning her, and Klaus standing nearby, glaring at them both.

"Klaus did this." Dante's voice was barely a whisper.

Elsa felt sick. She couldn't imagine what he was feeling, what he was thinking. He stood up and stepped away from her. She couldn't let go of his hand at first, but forced herself to release him.

Straightening his shirt, he said, "If you would not mind terribly, I should like to be by myself for a little while." His voice was rough as he spoke, and he didn't wait for a response before he left.

She thought about following him, but what could she say? His scars had caused him so much hardship.

Based on Elsa's descriptions, Garrett thought Dante might be able to have reconstructive surgery to remove some of his scarring. But it seemed an awful time to broach that topic. She wanted Dante to know that people had changed. He didn't need to alter his appearance to have a happy life. Others would accept him as he was, like she did.

The thought of Dante going through more pain because of his scars, of taking the risk of surgery, terrified her. She covered her eyes, willing herself back under control. He needed her to be strong.

Some of the fatigue from the day before was returning. She leaned back in the lounge chair, thinking she would rest a bit to give Dante time to process what he'd learned, then find him so they could talk.

Not much later, Elsa heard soft footsteps approaching. She opened her eyes and saw a man hovering over her, backlit by the sun. At first, she thought it was Garrett. The man had the same shoulder-length blond hair, but he was too short and slender.

Her stomach lurched as she realized that she didn't know this man. She started to get up, but he was so close that she didn't have room to stand. The table blocked one side and the man blocked the other. Elsa did her best to put on a stony gaze, conveying only disapproval and hiding her fear.

"It's a lovely morning," he said.

"For trespassing?"

The man laughed in response. It was a rich, throaty sound, but made the hair on her arms stand on end. He pulled over one of the chairs from the patio table and she tried to get up again, but he shifted even closer.

"Please, stay comfortable."

"If you really want me to be comfortable, you'll tell me who you are."

He sat next to her, smiling, though the smile didn't make it to his pale blue eyes. "You really don't remember me? Elsa, I'm crushed."

She didn't like that he knew her name. She tried to think of when they might have met. His features were remarkably handsome, but the smile that pursed his full lips seemed cruel, and the lines around his eyes as he squinted in the sun made him look angry.

"I thought our date went so well. I was disappointed when you didn't call." His voice was as smooth as snakeskin.

Elsa suddenly remembered a dinner Jazz had set up a few months back with one of the new artists from the gallery. Jazz called to say she couldn't make it after Elsa had already arrived, so she tried to cover for her friend. Elsa vaguely remembered listening to him talk about art and the gallery, but she had been so distracted with her plans to bring Dante to her time she'd only half paid attention.

Back then, she knew there were only a few events left in Dante's ring with strong enough imprints that she could use them to travel. She could sense the energy dwindling and she was getting desperate.

The random nature of her powers meant that she never knew when or where a piece of art was going to take her. The first time she saw Dante through his ring had been the day Heinrich died. The next trip took her to the day Heinrich offered Dante a job with the theatre—years earlier in Dante's lifetime. The third event took place between the two moments. He was helping with a performance, running around on the catwalks to operate incredible mechanisms he had developed for a play.

She had also visited times when Mary owned the ring—after the fire. Elsa knew Dante would be in the theatre while it burned. That would be the one moment when she could try to save him. And she had no idea when the ring would drop her there.

When she had met this man sitting next to her, whoever he was, she was focused on getting the play off the ground to hopefully boost her power, preparing her house for Dante's arrival, and figuring out how she could help Dante establish himself.

"I didn't know I was supposed to call," Elsa said.

A wave of anger flashed across his face, his lips tightening in a frown and his eyebrows lowering over those cold blue eyes. Elsa had seen that look too many times before. It usually preceded violence.

She couldn't move. Her heart pounded in her chest and her muscles seemed to turn to stone.

Just as quickly, his expression became placid again. He sat forward and smiled. "It's all right. I forgive you."

Elsa felt herself relax just a bit. Enough for her to ask, "How did you find out where I live?"

His smirk made her wonder if she'd find feathers in his mouth. With a shrug, he said, "Friend of a friend."

Elsa's friends would never give someone she didn't know information about where she lived. But he had found her somehow.

"What is it that you want?"

"I want us to be friends. Good friends." He leaned back in his chair. "I was thinking perhaps we could collaborate on a piece. I find you inspiring, and I think you can understand the allure of having someone to inspire you, what with the actor you've hired to live with you."

"I didn't hire Dante." There was more ire in her tone than was probably wise.

"So it isn't a professional relationship, then?" His gaze slowly slid down her body, making her wish she was wearing baggy sweats, even with the temperature starting to climb. "If I had known you liked to play dress up, maybe our date would have ended differently."

Date? As frightening as he was, Elsa was about to let him know precisely what she thought of that. Rachel and Dante walked out from the studio doors before Elsa could let the guy have it.

"There you are, Michael," Rachel said. "Did you get lost?"

"Only a bit." Michael stood and smiled at Elsa. Her stomach churned. "I saw the garden from inside and just had to take a peek. Elsa was keeping me company."

He walked over to Rachel, then gripped her arms and kissed her passionately enough to make Elsa even more uncomfortable. Dante stepped away from the pair, glancing briefly at her before turning his attention to one of the blooming gardenias.

She suddenly needed to be closer to him. She leapt up from the lounge chair and crossed the patio to stand at his side. She tried to hide the way her legs shook.

When Michael finally released Rachel, Elsa asked, "What are you doing here?"

"We were in the neighborhood and stopped by to see how you're doing." Rachel was breathless, a dazed smile on her face. "Plus, I wanted you to meet Michael, since I already told you about him."

"My sweet little thing couldn't keep a secret to save her life." Michael tapped Rachel under the chin with his finger. "But we should go. We don't want to impose."

He didn't wait for Rachel to respond. Turning on his heel, he put his hands in his pockets, then strolled down the pathway that led to the front of the house. Rachel started after him, but Elsa took a few quick steps after her and grabbed her arm.

"Rachel, are you okay?" Elsa kept her voice low so Michael wouldn't hear.

"Of course I am. You're the one who was sick." Rachel laughed, then gave Elsa a quick hug. "I've got to go. Michael hates it when I keep him waiting."

Rachel waved cheerfully, then ran after Michael. Elsa was left standing in the middle of her patio, a knot of dread heavy in her stomach. When she felt a gentle touch on her shoulder, she yelped and jumped away, then whirled around to face the potential threat.

"I did not mean to startle you," Dante said.

Before he could say anything else, Elsa stepped forward and wrapped her arms around his waist. She buried her face against his chest.

She knew she shouldn't. She should be strong. He was undoubtedly still dealing with what she had told him. But Michael had roused her own skeletons, and their rattling bones drowned out the sound of reason.

Elsa wasn't strong enough to resist the comfort of Dante's embrace.

Chapter Thirteen

The remainder of the day passed in what Dante could only think of as bliss. Elsa had been a bit on edge, and he could not say he did not feel the same after the morning's revelation. However, after hours spent in pleasant conversation on the patio and in the studio, he was feeling more at ease than he had perhaps ever been.

Once she had retired for the night, he planned to read more of the encyclopedias. The natural light faded as the sun set, and Elsa yawned with increasing frequency. Still, she made no sign that she was preparing to return to her room.

The insects were singing loudly as she turned off the fan that kept them at bay. Elsa closed and locked the doors to the patio, her gaze scanning the garden as if some menace lurked within the azaleas. When she nearly stumbled in the short distance between her desk and the door, Dante could no longer remain silent.

"Elsa, you must sleep."

"I'm not tired." Her words were distorted by an enormous yawn that she barely managed to cover with the back of her hand.

He'd been able to finish another painting while she postponed her rest. His brushes were already cleaned and put away. Drying his hands with a cloth, he approached her, unable to tame his smile. He stopped only a few inches from her, enjoying the softness of her eyes as sleep crept in around their edges.

"You are quite stubborn." He was close enough to catch her should she fall. The way she was swaying on her feet made that a very real possibility. He tossed his cloth over the back of her chair, and she did not even protest. "You must rest. Winston has tasked me with keeping you well."

"I'm fine," she said, though she yawned once more. "Let's watch a movie. I can make popcorn."

Dante gently caught her arm as she turned toward the hall and she stumbled into him. Rather than move away, she rested against his chest, yawning again. She seemed close to falling asleep on her feet.

"What is troubling you?"

She stared at the ground, then shook her head. "It's ridiculous."

"Are you still upset from your encounter with Michael?"

"I'm probably overreacting. He's Rachel's boyfriend. I know she has bad taste in guys, but really, how dangerous can he be?"

"In matters such as these, it is always best to trust one's instincts."

"The way he showed up on the patio, the things he said... It was unnerving."

Without thought, Dante pulled her close, holding her tightly. "I will not let anyone harm you."

"I keep telling you," she mumbled into his shirt, "I'm supposed to be protecting you. Great job I've done so far."

"You saved my life," he said, but stopped himself from proceeding. She had not reacted well when he expressed gratitude about the matter before. And he respected that she did not wish him to feel indebted to her.

To lead her from the fretful path her thoughts seemed to be taking, he lifted her from her feet using a bit more energy than was strictly required. She was momentarily airborne before landing gently in his arms.

As he had hoped, she let out a brief laugh. Her smile lit the room more brightly than the electric lights. Before she could gather her wits to begin yet another argument, he carried her from the studio.

She nestled against his chest, letting out a contented sigh. She fit so perfectly against him.

When he reached her bedroom, the door was open. Dante barely hesitated before entering.

In his time, it would have been scandalous for him to be in a woman's bedroom at this late hour. He was glad to be free to assist Elsa as much as needed without worrying about her social standing, especially since she was still having some trouble with her *physical* standing.

He chuckled at his unspoken jest, and she made a soft noise in response, like a roosting dove. It was not until he set her down on her bed that she roused.

"Don't go." She gripped his shirt tightly. "Please. Not yet."

"You are perfectly safe." Dante pulled the covers from under her so that she could slide beneath them.

"I know. I just don't want to be alone. Will you stay for a little while?"

Her eyes were pleading. He was not inclined to disappoint her, given how distressed she appeared.

She slid further across the bed, making room for him. The sight of her lying there, waiting for him, brought heady images to his mind. He imagined lifting the covers to join her, sliding his arms around her waist, pulling her close and...

He scolded himself for the wayward nature of his thoughts and sat instead above the covers, then leaned against the pillows. He did grant himself the comfort of stretching his legs out next to her.

As soon as he did, Elsa tucked her body snugly against his, resting her arm across his stomach and her face against his chest. He could not resist wrapping his arms around her. Indeed, there was nowhere else for him to place them.

She made another soft sound, her breath becoming deep and even as she relaxed. For Dante, the opposite was occurring. His breath came quicker as her warmth seeped into him. He could feel the blood pooling low in his body, hardening him with desire. If she were to fully awaken, he would be mortified.

He wished he could secure more modern clothes rather than the thin slacks he wore that did nothing to conceal his current state. He thought perhaps to broach the subject, but she had gone to such lengths to make him feel at home, it seemed ungrateful to ask for more.

He kept wearing the black slacks and linen shirts to show his appreciation for how considerate she had been, but his clothes and his room only served to haunt him with memories best left forgotten.

This moment was another example of his dilemma. Trapped in his clothes from another time, the only thing he could do to conceal his predicament was turn off the lights, which would plunge him back into darkness.

At least Elsa's room had large windows and he could look up and see the stars. He kept the curtains in his room open as wide as possible, yet still, he felt as if he was back in Heinrich's theatre, buried beneath the earth. Dante wanted only the sky, the air, and the beautiful colors of the garden outside.

Each kiss of sunlight peeled away more of the life he had left behind. Perhaps he might eventually become as bronzed as Garrett. The pallor of Dante's skin was already lessening with his time in the solarium and on the patio. All but the skin under his mask, of course. He doubted even the sun would do anything to the reddened flesh beneath.

Suddenly self-conscious for an altogether different reason, he reached over and turned off the lamp. He would lie with Elsa for a little while, until he was certain she was sound asleep, and then he would slip from her room and return to the studio.

The lounge chair on the patio was quite comfortable, and after his morose thoughts, he hated the thought of going back to his room. He would sleep in the studio, the windows giving him an excellent view of the sky and the stars. Until then, he would enjoy her warmth beside him.

In the darkness, he reached up and touched the smooth surface of his mask. If only it didn't stand between them. And yet, without his mask, the mystery that it presented, they most likely never would have met. Dante could not fool himself into believing that history would have remembered him if he had simply been a set designer for a failing theatre.

He removed his mask and held it up so that it caught what little ambient light was in the room. The smooth porcelain appeared as a pool of silver darkness, a bit lighter than the backdrop of the room.

He had tested many materials before settling upon this. Lightweight, durable and comfortable enough that he barely registered its presence.

At first, he had thought to use a flesh-colored glaze to make the mask less obvious, but that only made others' reactions worse. His experiments with decorative enamels had not been met with any less derision. He had finally ceased trying to gain the acceptance of others and left his masks unadorned.

So much of his life had been dominated by his disfigurement. Knowing that his own brother was responsible…

Dante suddenly wanted the mask away from him, even if only for a few moments. He set it on Elsa's nightstand on top of a stack of books. The silence of the room settled over them, the only sound her soft breathing.

Holding her in his arms, he almost felt normal. What if this was truly what his life was now to be? Meals shared in camaraderie with Winston and perhaps at times Garrett, days creating in the studio and gardens, evenings relaxing in Elsa's company, and nights spent like this. It was more than he dared to dream. And yet, his thoughts went further.

She cared for him a great deal. That much was obvious. And though it had only been a matter of days, he could feel his heart reaching toward her, yearning for her. How could he not grow fond of someone who inspired such loyalty in her friends, who helped others so selflessly?

He pressed a gentle kiss to the top of her head, then smoothed her silken hair against her back. She let out a contented sigh and Dante smiled, gratified that she was so at ease in his presence.

It was wrong of him to want more from her. He knew that he could not give her the kind of life that she deserved, a partner who could stand beside her in the light of day without hiding behind a mask.

She was intelligent, kind, beautiful and strong. She could have any man she wanted. Why would she ever want him?

No, the most he could hope for was her friendship. For that

blessing, he would consider himself the luckiest man in the world. But for a little while, he could let himself think about what their lives could have been if circumstances were different. For a little while longer, he let himself dream.

The room was filled with a golden glow when Dante opened his eyes again. It seemed he only blinked, but he must have fallen asleep. Morning light illuminated everything within the room.

He stretched, enjoying the feel of Elsa lying at his side. She had nestled against him even closer during her sleep, the softness of her breasts pressing upon his stomach and her arms folded over his chest. He glanced at her, wanting to see her face illuminated by the morning light and relaxed in sleep, but she was awake.

One of her hands was pressed against the bare skin of Dante's chest, the contact nearly searing him. His heart began to beat frantically beneath her palm, as if striving for her touch. Her chin was resting on the back of her hand and she was smiling at him.

Her eyes were dark in the rich light of dawn, a smoldering, deep sienna. Breathtaking.

"Good morning." She cast a smile upon him broad enough that the skin at the corners of her eyes crinkled.

He had never seen her smile so completely. It took some time for him to bring himself to speak, dazed as he was by her obvious happiness at waking next to him.

"Good morning. I trust you slept well?"

His hand reached out of its own accord, combing through the golden locks of her hair. He did not even have the pretense of tucking it behind her ear. He was just mesmerized by the light in the strands, the silken texture against his fingers. Fortunately, she did not seem to mind. In fact, she closed her eyes for a moment and leaned her head against his palm.

She let out a contented sigh. "I did. And you?"

"I am quite rested." Something was scratching at the back of his mind, a warning that intruded on his ability to enjoy the moment fully.

"I didn't realize you're already this comfortable with me. I'm so glad."

He laughed. "I have been comfortable enough to sleep next to you from the very first night."

"That isn't what I meant." A blush spread across her face that made him smile despite his forebodings.

She rose on one elbow, which brought her lips very close to his. She lifted her hand to his face and, for a moment, he thought that she might kiss him. Instead, she ran her fingertips lightly along his cheek, the gentle touch resounding through his entire body as he realized it was *the right side* of his face.

Dante was halfway across the room before he even had a chance to fully process the horror of what had just happened. Elsa, beautiful Elsa, had been looking at him, smiling at him, chatting with him. All while he was not wearing his mask.

He covered his face with his hand, hiding the scars as best he could, turning so that his right side was away from her. How could she stand to look at him? To touch the marred flesh that had destroyed his chances at a normal life?

He started back to the nightstand to find his mask, but it was not where he thought he placed it the night before. Perhaps it had fallen among the books she kept at her bedside. Or Leonardo could have knocked it off the nightstand during his nightly prowls.

Dante dropped to his knees, reaching under the bed to see if it had fallen below. It was neither under the bed nor the bedside table. He rifled through the stacks of books, knocking them over in his frantic search for his mask. Where was it?

"Dante…" Elsa's voice was quiet and thin. He had never heard that tone from her before. She sounded afraid. The thought tore through his heart, freezing him in place.

He closed his eyes, taking a deep breath and letting it out slowly. His whole body was shaking with the effort to calm himself. But he was frightening her, and why shouldn't she be frightened? He was used to those who saw his face reacting quite worse than Elsa had. At least she had not screamed.

In fact, she had spoken to him, smiled at him, even touched the scarred skin without seeming troubled at all.

The depths of her kindness went beyond what he had realized. Kindness or pity, the one reaction he found even worse than fear.

Dante opened his eyes, keeping his hand over his face. Elsa was on her knees on the bed, clutching the sheets to her chest and staring at him. Her face was bloodless, a deep crease wedged between her brows. Whatever her initial reaction had been, fear had unmistakably taken over.

He stood and turned his back to her, unable to bear her gaze. "I apologize. It was careless of me to sleep without my mask. I will not let it happen again."

He was halfway to the door when he heard her slip from the bed and quickly cross the room to him. She grabbed his shoulders with her slight hands, as if she could hold him in place. He decided to humor her and stopped. Her fingers trembled.

"Dante, look at me."

He did not think he had the strength to turn around. He could not stand to see those eyes, those frightened eyes, staring at him. He wanted to find some dark corner in the house where he could hide.

When he did not turn, she circled to stand in front of him.

"You startled me," she said. "I don't like it when people get angry."

"I was not angry. I was terrified."

She seemed genuinely confused. "Why?"

"You should never have seen me like that. I should not have let you."

"I'm grateful that you let me see you. I want you to be comfortable with me. As comfortable as I am with you." She stepped in closer. "I don't care about what you look like. I care about who you are. You don't have to wear your mask with me. Not ever."

"A noble sentiment, however, I could not subject you to—"

"I've seen you without your mask before today."

He sought through his memory, but could not think of another time he had been without his mask while they were in the same room. "When?"

Her chest stilled, as if she was trying to keep the answers he sought from escaping with her breath. She bit her lower lip to further trap the truth within her.

"Elsa, what are you not telling me?"

"I did tell you. That I had observed you before."

"When Heinrich died. And the night of the fire, of course."

A sick feeling coiled and rattled in Dante's stomach. Elsa had also mentioned seeing Mary when Edgar gave her Dante's ring. And there were the travels where Elsa had observed Dante's parents. Dante hadn't given it much thought beyond that, his mind too filled with all that he had experienced since coming to stay with her.

"How much of my life have you witnessed?"

"My travels were usually brief, since they centered on moments of extreme emotion. Do you remember when you finally figured out the trick with mirrors and pulleys that you used to make Edgar disappear in your first production with Heinrich's theatre?"

"That hardly seems like something important enough to allow you to…"

The dread in his stomach lashed out, striking Dante's heart and pumping stinging venom through his veins. If such a relatively small accomplishment was strong enough for her traveling, what else had she seen?

"How many events in my life did you witness?"

"A few…dozen." She clasped her hands in front of her chest as if she was begging for forgiveness. At the moment, Dante was too shocked to offer any.

"Dozens? Dozens!"

She took a step toward him, but he lurched back. For the first time, he didn't want to feel her touch. What had once been intimate now seemed invasive. He had the most unsettling feeling, as if she was seeing through his clothing and there was nothing he could do to cover himself.

"What all have you seen?" he demanded.

She looked stricken, and a part of his heart went out to her, wanting to give her comfort. He would not let it win.

"Highlights, mostly." Her voice was small, her gaze fixed on the floor as if she could no longer face him. At least she had the decency to seem abashed. "I saw the night when you met Heinrich at the circus. When he offered you a job at his theatre. I saw how filled with hope you were when you arrived."

Dante's jaw began to ache from how tightly he was clenching his teeth. That was a very private moment. Knowing that someone else had been watching, even Elsa, felt like a violation.

"Go on." He kept his voice as cold as he could.

"I saw how they treated you when you arrived. How it drove you to seclusion beneath the theatre."

Elsa looked at him again, a fire blazing in her eyes. There were ample memories for her to have seen to explain her anger. His treatment at the theatre had been quite horrid, especially in the beginning.

The others made it clear that he had no place among them. Even Heinrich had been distant, though Dante now better understood the origins of his behavior.

"Would that I had known the door was not keeping out all prying eyes."

She gasped, her mouth dropping open. Even now, as angry as he was, Dante longed to reach out and stroke the soft flesh of her lips. That fact only angered him further.

Apparently, his comment awoke a similar spark within her. Her eyes narrowed, and she dropped her hands to her sides.

"I know you watched people from the catwalks when they didn't know you were there."

"I had no recourse. I was reviled! The only people who would speak to me were Heinrich and Mary."

"What makes you think it's that different for me?"

"Don't be absurd. You are surrounded by people who care for you. You can go out in a crowd without people staring, without children pointing, without women fainting or screaming."

"Only because they don't know!" The vehemence in her voice was shocking. As was the bleakness of her expression as she spoke. "If people knew what I could do, they would hunt me down and dissect me."

"You cannot believe—"

"I know it," she said, cutting him off.

Dante was silent for a few moments, wondering at how deep her fear ran within her, how very blind she was to the people around her.

"Even Garrett? Even Winston?"

Elsa looked away, grabbing her left arm with her right as she half hugged herself and stood as stiff as a mannequin. She truly believed that even those closest to her were capable of turning on her viciously. Dante wondered what could have happened to make her have so little faith in those who cared for her so very much.

"And what of me, Elsa?"

When she looked up at him, her eyes were shining with tears, but not a one strayed over her lashes. Her voice was small when she spoke.

"I suppose I'm at your mercy."

Even more than her words, the complete and utter lack of hope she expressed shook him to his core. He thought that risking her life was the greatest threat she faced in saving him. Now he knew her act had a much higher price. She had sacrificed her sense of safety. As he had done with her on that first night, she had placed her life in his hands.

His anger evaporated in an instant. Dante took a slow step toward her. Elsa was on the edge of an emotional precipice. If he was ever to truly reach her, he must take a leap of faith himself. And despite what he had learned, he still wanted to reach her, to be with her.

When he was quite close, he took a deep breath and lowered his hand from his face.

Hope slowly seeped back into her expression, and it seemed to him like the morning sun rising over the horizon. Her lips parted on a quick intake of breath.

He reached out to cup her cheek. His voice rasped low from his throat. "I would never do anything to harm you."

Elsa pulled her lower lip between her teeth, biting it firmly enough that he feared she might draw blood. He finally gave in to his desire, gently brushing his thumb along her lower lip, coaxing her to release it. She took a deep, shuddering breath as she did.

Dante continued to trace its satin surface. The entire time, her gaze never strayed to his scars, almost as if she did not notice them.

Grasping his hand, she pressed her cheek into his palm and closed her eyes. "I believe you."

Her skin was soft and warm. He had no doubt her lips would be much warmer, much softer. He dipped his head toward her, unable to resist the temptation to find out.

Before their lips met, a crashing sound downstairs startled him. Both of them jumped, the moment vanishing.

"What was that?" Elsa asked.

Before he could speculate, he heard Winston shouting profanities that made Dante want to cover Elsa's ears. It was too late for that, as she had already fled to the door and disappeared down the hallway. Dante followed.

They found Winston in the kitchen, lying on the floor. Elsa ran to his side, placing her arms on Winston's shoulders. She looked panicked.

"Winston, what happened?"

Winston let out a low grunt. "What's it look like happened? The old geezer fell down."

"Don't talk about yourself that way. Are you hurt?"

"My ego more than anything else."

"This isn't a joke," Elsa said.

Dante could see her pulling herself together, taking control of the situation.

Her voice was low and level when she next spoke. "Take a moment and assess yourself. Do you have pain anywhere?"

"Only on my arse, where I fell."

"Dante, call Garrett," Elsa said. "The phone is on the shelf by the door."

Dante crossed the room and picked up the device, making a quick study of the buttons on the number pad. He had read about phones, but had not used one as of yet. She rattled off a series of numbers, and he pressed each one in turn, then the talk button at her direction. When finished, he held the phone to his ear as he had seen done on the television.

"This is Garrett." Garrett's disembodied voice came through the phone.

Dante wished he had more time to marvel at the technology, but he needed to keep his focus on Winston.

"Garrett, it is Dante."

"Oh hey, Dante. What's up?"

"I fear it is a matter of what's down." Dante heard Winston chuckle, but when Dante looked over his shoulder, Elsa was scowling at him. Clearing his throat, he continued. "Winston has fallen."

"I'll be there in ten minutes. Make sure he stays still and doesn't move around too much."

"I fear that is easier said than done."

"I don't doubt it. Just have Elsa sit on him. That should do the trick."

"Indeed."

Elsa spoke up, saying, "Tell him we're in the kitchen. That way, he'll come to the right door."

Before Dante could relate this to Garrett, Garrett said, "Got it."

Dante pressed the end button and set the phone back in its cradle. He then returned to Elsa's side. "Winston is to remain as still as possible until Garrett arrives."

"Like hell I will," Winston said.

"Like hell you won't." Elsa moved so that she could sit near Winston's head, crossing her legs and pulling him down so he was using her knees as a pillow. "I don't play the boss card very often, but

I'm laying it down right now. You are not moving."

"I'm going to get more stiff lying on this damn floor than I would if you'd help me up to one of the chairs."

"Then I guess Garrett will have to prescribe some painkillers for you. And I'll schedule you a massage or something."

"Hmph."

Dante watched the exchange with a growing sense of tenderness. Elsa had one hand on Winston's shoulder, and the other she used to stroke his hair. Winston would never admit it, but Dante could see the fear on his face. It was mirrored on Elsa's.

"I'll get a blanket," Dante said.

"Thank you." Elsa looked so stricken when she glanced at him. As Dante left the room, he gently touched her shoulder, and Elsa rewarded him with a faint smile.

The closest blanket that Dante knew of was in the entertainment room. He ran to it as quickly as possible and pulled the soft plum-colored throw from the back of the couch. As he turned toward the hall, he noticed one of the doors to the cabinet at the bottom of the movie shelf was open.

Elsa loved for things to be just so. Dante was certain the cabinet door had been closed when last he was in the room. Between that and his mask disappearing, an uneasy feeling stirred in his stomach.

He had no time to contemplate it further. He ran back to the kitchen and spread the blanket over Winston, then knelt at Elsa's side.

"Thanks," Winston said. Lines were etched around his eyes that had little to do with his age. He might profess that he felt fine, but Dante recognized the signs of pain.

"Was it Leonardo?" Elsa asked. "He's always trying to trip people."

"That cat will never get the best of me," Winston said. "I know how to deal with him. No, I stepped on something. Foot flew right out from under me."

Dante scanned the floor as he searched for what could have caused Winston's fall. His gaze lit upon a small object reflecting the morning light from the windows. He reached under the table to pick it up, then stood, holding it so Elsa could see.

"That's the key to the kitchen door," Elsa said. "We always keep it in the lock. How did it get on the floor?"

Dante glanced at the door, thinking back on the cabinet and his missing mask. "How, indeed."

Chapter Fourteen

The minutes that passed between Dante calling Garrett and Garrett's arrival were some of the longest of Elsa's life. Dante stayed at her side, his hand resting on her back.

She was meticulous about keeping everything in place to protect Winston. The key to the kitchen door stayed in the lock, like the one in the studio. Neither had fallen out before. The doors were old-fashioned, with antique keys that were part of the charm of the house. Elsa would install modern deadbolts as soon as possible to make sure this never happened again.

Garrett didn't bother to knock. When he arrived, he opened the door and came right in. Winston must have unlocked it earlier.

But that didn't make sense. If he had, he would've heard the key fall from the door. Elsa would have to figure it out later. Winston needed her full attention.

"Hey, Winston." Garrett smiled as casually as always, joining them on the floor.

"Hey yourself," Winston snapped.

"Garrett is here to help you," Elsa said. "The least you can do is be civil."

"Why start now?" Garrett winked at Elsa, ignoring her scowl. He placed his hands at different points along Winston's body. "How bad is the pain?"

"I'm fine," Winston said. "I tried to tell Elsa."

Winston let out a yelp as Garrett touched a spot on his back. "Fine, huh?"

Elsa hated seeing Winston in pain. She couldn't believe she had let this happen. "Is it bad?"

"Seems like you bruised yourself up pretty good," Garrett said.

"But nothing that won't fix itself with a few days' rest."

"A few days?" Winston chuffed. "We'll all starve."

"We will not." Elsa tried to feign a confidence she didn't feel. "I can cook."

Winston groaned and Garrett said, "Dante, you better make sure you have my number on speed dial."

Laughing, Winston piled on. "The only thing you can cook is a peanut butter and jelly sandwich. And only then if it's not on toast."

"I would be more than happy to take over the cooking duties," Dante said. "It is the least I could do after all your hospitality."

"There. No one is starving." She wasn't sure Dante could make good on his promise, since he'd never even seen an electric range until a few days ago. Elsa was just glad Winston felt well enough to make jokes.

"Let's get him to his room," Garrett said.

"Finally." Winston waved in the general direction of Garrett's voice, pushing away from Elsa's lap. She supported him as best she could while Dante and Garrett lifted Winston to his feet.

They half carried him to his room, then worked as a team to settle him in bed. Garrett gave Winston some painkillers and strict instructions for bed rest and to sleep. Elsa knew she and Dante would have their work cut out for them to keep Winston resting. Winston was stubborn, but outnumbered now that Elsa had Dante to help.

Once Winston was asleep, Elsa returned to the kitchen with Dante and Garrett. Garrett leaned against the counter and Elsa sat at the table. Dante's presence at her side was a welcome comfort.

"Is Winston really going to be okay?" she asked.

"I think so." Garrett's tone was less than convincing. "I'm more concerned with why he fell. It isn't like Winston to be clumsy."

"The fault was not with him." Dante had placed the kitchen key on the table after finding it. He picked it up to show Garrett. "He slipped on this."

"Did it fall out of the lock?" Garrett asked.

Dante hesitated before responding. "I do not think that is the case."

"What do you think happened?" Garrett crossed his arms.

"My mask is missing. And the cabinet door on the shelf in the entertainment room is ajar."

They hadn't watched TV last night, and Elsa was certain Dante shut the door to the cabinet after getting out the movie they watched the night before. Winston never went into that cabinet. But if none of them had done it...

"Maybe Leonardo somehow opened it," she said. "And he probably knocked your mask behind my nightstand."

Dante sucked in a quick breath of air and cast a wary look at Garrett. It took Elsa a moment to realize she'd just basically told Garrett that she and Dante had spent the night together. Honestly, she had other things to worry about at the moment.

If Garrett was surprised, he wasn't letting on. "It seems a bit much mischief for one night, even for Leo."

Elsa didn't want to contemplate the only other possibility, but she forced herself to face it. "You don't think someone was in the house last night, do you?"

"We must not dismiss the possibility," Dante said.

"Why would they only take your mask?" Garrett asked.

Elsa's cheeks tingled and her heart clenched in her chest as she ran through different scenarios. She had valuables out in plain sight. Taking Dante's mask and leaving everything else made this personal, like someone was taunting them. Her stomach churned at the thought.

"And how did they get in?" Garrett nodded toward the door. "Did Winston forget to lock up?"

"He wouldn't do that." Elsa reached for the key. "May I?"

Dante handed her the key, his fingertips lingering a bit as they traced over her palm. Even with the fear, or perhaps because of it, his gentle touch sparked a shiver down her spine. She hoped it wasn't too obvious.

Elsa stood and walked to a drawer that held several sets of chopsticks. She grabbed one, then went to the door and pulled a piece of paper from the shelf under the phone. She put the key in the lock, then opened the door and stepped outside.

She slid the paper under the closed door, then fiddled with the chopstick until she felt the key jiggle loose. It almost bounced off the paper she had ready below, but she was still able to gently pull the paper toward her until the key was in her hand. She opened the door again, stepping back inside and holding up the key.

"Of course," Dante said.

Garrett shook his head. "How do you know this stuff?"

"I'm a writer. It's my job to know this stuff."

"That's it." Garrett pulled out his phone. "I'm calling the cops."

"No!" Elsa was standing close to Garrett now, and she reached out and grabbed his arm.

"Why not?"

That was a good question. Elsa didn't have an answer ready. She blurted out the first thing that came to mind. "We don't know for sure that someone was here."

"You're kidding, right?"

"It's my decision." She wouldn't let him argue with her about this. The police would have too many questions. They'd want to know about Dante and might ask him to prove his identity. She couldn't risk that.

Garrett let out a sigh, and she knew she'd won. She let go of his arm as he put away his phone. She'd never seen him so serious.

"Fine." Garrett picked up his bag, then fished around inside. He pulled out a small piece of black fabric. Brushing past her, he walked over to Dante. "I picked this up for you."

"Thank you." Dante took the item and turned it over in his hands. It was a mask.

Garrett stepped in close. As tall as Dante was, Garrett loomed over him.

"You listen to me." Garrett's voice was a low growl. "Elsa and Winston are very important to me. They get hurt, and I'm coming for you."

"Garrett!"

Neither man reacted to her exclamation. In a quiet and calm voice,

Dante said, "I will protect them both with my life. I promise you."

"See that you do. I'll be back to check on everyone tonight."

Garrett didn't say another word to Elsa. He stalked out the door and slammed it behind him.

"I'm so sorry," she said. "I've never seen Garrett act that way."

"He cares for you a great deal. I am glad for that."

"That doesn't mean he should talk to you that way."

"I believe I would react much the same if our roles were reversed." Dante went to the door and turned the key, then tried the handle to make sure it was locked. He stared out the windows for a few moments before turning to face her again. "Would you have hesitated to contact the authorities if I were not here?"

She couldn't say that she would have. "It doesn't matter what I might have done. You're here and I'm doing what I need to do to protect you."

"This is because I have no way to prove who I am."

"Dante Lucerne died over a hundred years ago. How am I supposed to explain you being here?" She shook her head, all the different ideas she had come up with so far churning through her mind, each with its own challenges. The best idea involved Dante feigning amnesia, and that was pretty weak.

"It is not worth risking your safety."

"It absolutely is." Elsa spoke with more force than she intended. She wanted to cover her outburst, but couldn't think of anything to say.

"I must have been on my best behavior when you observed me to have made such an impression upon you."

Elsa didn't trust herself to respond to that. It wasn't just witnessing his genius or his kindness. His isolation had struck a chord with her. She knew that. But he actually had a chance to form real, honest relationships with people in her time. To be accepted for who he was. She hoped that he was starting to realize that.

Turning his new mask over in his hands, Dante smiled softly. He looked down at it for a moment, then set it on the table.

"Shall we finish breakfast? Winston may be hungry when he

awakens."

Her heart seemed to bloom in her chest. Dante was choosing to let her see him, leaving his mask behind. Even with everything else going on, Elsa couldn't help but smile.

Chapter Fifteen

This was perhaps the happiest that Dante had ever been in his life. It was not just that he had a home, but that he had people who counted on him. He felt a sense of belonging he had not experienced since his mother passed away.

Winston was sleeping comfortably after sharing a dinner with Dante and Elsa. Dante had convinced her to relax and indulge in a bath while he watched over Winston. After rinsing the last dish, Dante set it in the rack to dry. He pulled the plug free and watched the soapy water swirl down the drain, thinking of Elsa in her bath.

The image of her in the large tub in her bathroom sparked a heady warmth in Dante's chest, dropping quickly to lower parts of his body. They had spent the entire day together and she never once stared at him or seemed uncomfortable.

Drying his hands, he walked to the table and picked up his new mask. He had not touched it since Garrett had left.

Even though he'd directed considerable anger and suspicion toward Dante, Garrett had still made this thoughtful gesture. Dante would work to earn Garrett's trust. He truly hoped they would become friends.

Garrett was as nonplussed by Dante's appearance as Elsa. Perhaps no one would have the visceral reactions as those in his time. It seemed impossible.

As impossible as time travel. Dante chuckled.

The bell sounded, and he set down his mask, heading for the front door. Garrett must have arrived to check on Winston. This would be Dante's first chance to regain some of the lost camaraderie he had shared with Garrett on that first night. Showing him that Winston and Elsa were both well would be a good start.

Opening the door, Dante smiled and began a greeting. The words died in his throat as he saw that it was not Garrett who had come calling.

A slender Asian woman stood before him. Her smile vanished when she saw Dante's face. Her eyes grew wide and her mouth dropped open, emitting a brief shriek.

Dante backed away from the door, covering his scars with one hand. He began apologizing, not even certain what words he was using, and raced toward the kitchen.

What had he been thinking? Opening the door without knowing who it was or how they would react. Of course people would still be shocked by his appearance. He pulled his new mask into place. It fit snugly with straps that stretched to conform to the dimensions of his head.

Though it was more comfortable than his previous mask, he was already becoming accustomed to going without. He had never realized how wearing a mask chafed the raised flesh of his scars, or how stifling it was to have half his face covered.

"It's rude to leave visitors alone in your foyer, you know."

Dante jumped at the woman's voice. He turned to find her standing in the center of the kitchen, hands on her hips, one of which was cocked to the side in a cavalier manner.

She wore black leather pants that hugged her legs like a second skin, with boots that rose to her knees. Her thin white shirt dipped down at the neck in a V and fit her thin frame perfectly. Thick black hair trailed down her back and hung about her face in windswept layers. One dark brow was arched at him, and she was frowning.

"I beg your pardon, madam." He tried to maintain as much of a dignified manner as he could. "I did not mean to startle you."

"You're lucky I didn't use my pepper spray on you."

"I beg your pardon?"

"I heard about the break in. Don't worry. I locked the door behind me."

She walked to the sink and took one of the glasses Dante had just washed, filled it with water and took a long drink before turning around again. Her gaze was scrutinizing until a broad smile brightened her face.

"You're the Phantom that Rachel talked about! The actor Elsa hired to help with her book."

"I am Dante Lucerne."

He was eager to separate himself from the character, especially if he was to become part of Elsa's life. She seemed focused on enabling him to move on, but even with a new world to explore, he found he could not bear the thought of leaving her.

"Good name." The woman looked Dante up and down as if she was assessing every part of him.

Her gaze lingered on the exposed skin of his chest for long enough that a blush swept over his face. The woman, oblivious to his discomfort, began a slow circuit around him. She stopped when they were facing once more.

"You are amazing. The mask is all wrong, though. Way too modern."

"It serves its purpose. Had I been wearing it when I answered the door, perhaps you would not have been so surprised." He didn't bother to hide the ire in his tone. He was only grateful that Winston and Elsa had not seemed to hear the disturbance.

"Maybe. Maybe not. I didn't know who you were and someone just broke in."

"Indeed. But was that truly the only origin of your outburst?"

The woman did not seem offended by Dante's bluntness. Her smile turned to a wry smirk.

"Is it makeup?"

"No."

"You're the real thing, then."

Dante did not bother to respond. He held her gaze as she boldly stared at him, her eyes calculating. He wondered if her mind ever stopped turning behind the deep sepia of her irises.

"Okay," she said. "Yeah, I was startled when I saw you. Your face is unusual and I wasn't expecting it. Deal with it. Let's move on."

"I beg your pardon?" He was quite taken aback. He had never heard anyone speak of his disfigurement with such nonchalance.

"Back to begging?" She crossed her arms and smirked.

"Who are you?" Each word came out as a gasp, exasperation winning out over his manners.

"I'm Jazz." She smiled brightly as she held out her hand. Dante took it, bowing curtly and pressing a quick kiss on the backs of her fingers. She arched an eyebrow. "Wow, you really are the real thing."

Perhaps that social custom had changed over the decades. He dropped her hand as he stood, then stepped away from her.

This was Elsa's oldest and dearest friend. He should try to make a good impression, but he was finding her quite overwhelming. Continuing in that vein, she grabbed his wrist with an alarming speed. Closing the space he had created between them, she pulled his arm closer to her face for further scrutiny.

An insect under a microscope might feel similarly exposed while being examined. She ran her finger over paint stains on his sleeve, pale greens and blues from his latest landscape. He had meant to change shirts, but had been too busy enjoying Elsa's company.

"You're a painter," Jazz said.

"Yes. Though I do not know what business that is of yours." He wrested his arm from her grasp as politely as he could.

"It is exactly my business." Her gaze turned almost hungry. She pulled a small card from her back pocket and handed it to him. It read *Jazz Gallery—Cutting Edge Art for the New Millennium.*

"Yes, you own a gallery." He had been so flustered, that fact had slipped his mind.

"This is just too good. You have to let me sell you."

"I assure you, I am not for sale."

"All you artists." Jazz waved her arms at him and made tching noises as she shook her head. "You're so concerned with not selling out. I'm concerned with putting food on your table. Let me represent you and I promise you will become one of the most famous artists of the decade. Not to mention all the money you'll rake in. After my cut, of course."

"You have not even seen any of my work."

"I don't need to see your work. I don't sell art, I sell artists. And the biggest draw for an artist is mystique." She made a point of looking him up and down. "Believe me, you have that covered. This whole Phantom persona is epic. Brilliant marketing. Your paintings could be stick figures and I'd still be able to sell them."

With a revenue stream of his own, Dante would not be reliant on Elsa for things such as a modern wardrobe. She was always so pained when she spoke of helping him to establish himself. With Jazz's help, perhaps he could do so without Elsa's involvement.

The idea was very appealing. He stared at the business card in his hand.

"Don't tell Elsa." He spoke before the thought had even fully formed.

"Why?"

Dante smiled, excitement brewing within him. "I would rather surprise her."

"I like the way you think." Jazz returned his smile.

If only she knew the maelstrom of thoughts circulating through his mind. Beyond his plans for what to do should he be able to support himself, he was beginning to wonder just how much of a hindrance his appearance would, or rather, would not be in this time.

Rachel had complimented how he looked. She had not seen all of his face, of course, but it was still encouraging. Jazz had seen his face, and yet the way she stared at Dante was enough to make him blush.

And then there was Elsa, with her shy looks and soft touches. A thrill passed over his skin, the mere thought of her hands on him causing gooseflesh to spread over his arms.

If he could come to her as an independent man, if he had more to offer her, perhaps the misgivings that always seemed to creep into her gaze would vanish.

Jazz walked to the counter and started to wash the glass she had used. "Now that we have that out of the way, how is Winston? I heard he fell."

"Garrett predicts a full recovery. Winston is sleeping at the moment."

"It is kind of late. I had to wait until I finished up at the gallery before I could stop by."

"Your circle of friends seems to be quite closely knit. I am amazed how quickly news has spread."

Jazz shrugged. "I had lunch with Garrett today. He's one of my best customers and a good friend. I introduced him to Elsa, in fact."

"Another of your dates?" Dante did not mean to say it so harshly, but Elsa had explained that Michael was the man Jazz had attempted to set Elsa up with. Garrett, Dante could understand. Michael had been a woeful error in judgment.

"What can I say? I'm a sucker for the romantic." Jazz set aside the glass and dried her hands. "But don't worry, no more blind dates from me. I can see Elsa's off the market."

"I beg—" He cleared his throat as he decided on a different turn of phrase. "Excuse me?"

If Jazz really thought that Elsa would consider having a romantic relationship with Dante, even after seeing him without his mask... He thought back to his earlier interlude with Elsa in her bedroom, when he'd been overcome with the urge to kiss her. If Winston's fall had not interrupted them, Dante now wondered what would have happened. She had not looked like she was going to pull away.

"Come on. Aside from Winston, Elsa has lived with exactly two other people in her life. Me and you. And the only reason she lived with me was out of financial necessity. The way she doesn't talk about it, I don't even think she ever lived with her family. I swear that woman stepped into this world fully formed."

"You put too much upon her, viewing her in such a manner." He did have to admit that Elsa was the most independent woman he had ever met. And though she spoke freely of his family, she had yet to mention her own.

Jazz shrugged. "All I'm saying is, I've known Elsa longer than anyone and you are the first person other than Winston that she has chosen to live with of her own free will." She leaned in very close. "I will expect an invitation to the wedding."

"Elsa and I are simply friends." Or were they? The excitement growing within him surged through his body, his soul practically thrumming with delight.

"I have a feeling there's nothing simple about this relationship. Anyway, I won't intrude. Please give Winston my regards."

"You do not wish to wait for Elsa?"

Jazz grinned. "I'll leave you lovebirds alone."

"As I said, our relationship is—"

"Yeah, I heard you."

Dante followed Jazz to the front door. She turned to face him once more before leaving.

"It was nice meeting you, Dante. I look forward to doing business with you and getting to know you better."

"And I, you, madam."

"Don't call me madam. It's Jazz."

"Of course. Jazz."

"That's better."

And then she was gone, leaving him alone in the foyer, not quite sure what to do with himself. He locked the door and headed to his room, taking the stairs slowly as he thought over what had just occurred.

He had a potential source of income, and Jazz believed that he had a chance at a romantic relationship with Elsa. It was all quite exhilarating.

Of course, working with Jazz meant the issue of his lack of identity might come up sooner rather than later. Dante felt it was best to deal with the matter right away. Perhaps she would have some contacts who could help him. He would need to acquire funds to assist with his new beginning, but the only thing he had of worth was his mother's ring.

He smiled, knowing exactly what his mother would say on that point. He would call Jazz first thing in the morning while Elsa was tending to Winston, and set up a meeting. That in itself would be a bit difficult, however. He and Elsa were seldom apart.

The realization stopped him in his tracks. Since Dante had arrived, they had spent almost every waking moment together, as well as several nights. He thought back to Jazz's comments about the nature of his relationship with Elsa, and he found he wasn't sure what it truly was.

He happened to have paused just outside the door to Elsa's bedroom. She had left it open a crack. He ran his fingertips lightly down the wood, enjoying the coolness of its surface. Taking it as a good sign, Dante retired to his room to prepare for an evening relaxing in her company.

Chapter Sixteen

Even after her bath, Elsa couldn't relax. She sat at the kitchen table drinking yet another cup of chamomile tea, trying to soothe her frayed nerves. The thought that someone had been in her house was beyond unsettling. She was still hoping that they were wrong, that there was some other explanation.

Maybe they had left the door to the cabinet open themselves. Maybe Leonardo had knocked Dante's mask onto the floor and it bounced under the bed somewhere. Maybe the key had caught on Winston's shirtsleeve as he locked up the night before and it'd fallen to the floor.

None of those scenarios seemed likely. Elsa insisted that everything was just so. She had to admit it wasn't only because she was watching out for Winston. Her friends thought of her as a control freak, and they were right. They just didn't know how much of her life she had felt completely out of control.

She'd crawled under her bed with a flashlight and searched everywhere for Dante's mask with no luck. Winston might be blind, but he had a keen sense of hearing. If he had been in the room when the key hit the floor, he would have heard it.

Elsa couldn't rationalize any of the occurrences away. The most likely explanation was that someone had been in the house the night before, someone who had picked through her things and watched Dante and Elsa as they slept.

Another shudder swept over her body. Elsa held the hot mug closer to her chest. The warmth did little to comfort her, but at least she could distract herself a bit. She focused on the sensation of the steam as it floated around her face, calming herself as she breathed in its earthy scent.

Someone knocked at the kitchen door. She jumped, spilling the tea on her chest. Luckily, she was wearing a baggy T-shirt, and leaned forward quickly enough to avoid being burned.

Garrett was standing outside, rattling the handle. She could see the concern etched in his features through the door's window. Elsa trotted over to let him in.

"Are you okay? I didn't mean to startle you."

"I'm fine." Elsa stepped aside as Garrett entered the kitchen, closing and locking the door behind him. "It was my fault I jumped. I was distracted."

Garrett stared at Elsa's chest, where her T-shirt had plastered itself against her breasts. She pulled the fabric away. The tea on her front was quickly becoming cold, which was just making the situation more embarrassing.

"Sorry." Garrett looked away.

"It's okay. I'll change later."

"How's Winston doing?"

"Grumpy. He says he wants to get up, but I saw him going back to bed from the bathroom and he was walking stiffly."

"That's to be expected. I'm sure he'll shake this off after a couple days of rest. And moving around a bit will be good for him."

"Well, don't worry about us starving. It turns out Dante is a great cook." Which was a good thing, because when he let Elsa make the toast that morning she managed to burn half of it. As in, all of the toast was burned on one side.

"About Dante…" Garrett's mouth was still open, but no words came out.

"What about Dante?"

"I know he's the reason you didn't want to call the police."

"Why would you say that?"

"Listen, this guy isn't who he says he is."

Garrett made his statement with entirely too much conviction. Elsa's cheeks began to tingle, the blood draining from her head and making her dizzy.

"What did you do?"

"My friend Finn is a private investigator. I gave him a call and asked him to do some digging."

"You did what?" Elsa's sense of foreboding blossomed into a full panic attack. Her heart threw itself against her ribs, seeking to flee, while her body felt leaden and rooted to the ground.

What kind of digging? What had he found?

Memories churned through her mind. *"Abomination! Which of my sins was so bad that I was burdened with you?"*

She shoved the pain away. She had to stay focused. Damage control. Assess the threat to herself and Dante.

"How could I not?" Garrett said. "You refused to go to the police after someone broke into your house, and you're shacking up with a guy who is lying to you."

"Dante has never lied to me. Ever."

"Are you sure about that? Because my friend says there is no record of a Dante Lucerne entering the country. In fact, the only Londoner he could find by that name died back in 1881."

"I can't believe you went behind my back and did this."

"What did you expect me to do?"

Rage overwhelmed her fear. "Respect my wishes? Not invade my privacy?"

"I thought you were in danger. I still think so. This guy is conning you. He's playing on your sympathies—"

"Stop. Just, stop." Elsa took a few deep breaths, trying to calm herself down. "If you ever, ever, disparage him like that to me again, you will no longer be welcome in my home. Do you understand me?"

Garrett's mouth went slack, his shoulders slumping. She regretted hurting him, but she couldn't stand by and let Garrett say such things. Especially when Dante was keeping silent to protect her.

Snapping his mouth shut in a frown, Garrett glared at her. Deep furrows formed on his forehead, and she could practically hear his teeth grinding together.

"Yeah, I get it."

Elsa heard a soft voice behind them say, "Am I intruding?"

She turned around to see Dante standing in the hall just outside the kitchen. His eyes were wide and he looked about as stunned as Garrett had a moment before.

"No," Garrett said. "As Winston's doctor, I'm here to check on him."

As angry as she was, Elsa still felt her heart constrict watching Garrett leave the room. He was one of her best friends. She didn't want to lose him over this, but she couldn't think of a way to make him understand without telling him everything.

For a moment, she considered doing just that, but immediately dismissed the idea. Garrett had gone behind her back. He might have been doing what he thought was best, but she had made herself clear and he hadn't respected that. At least he had gone to a private investigator and not the police.

Dante was counting on her. She had to protect him.

Elsa grabbed her mug and stalked to the sink to wash it. Her shirt was still cold and wet, thanks to Garrett as well. Why couldn't he have left it alone?

Dante crossed the room to stand next to her. He spoke in a low voice. "I do not mean to cause rifts between you and your friends."

"You didn't cause this problem. Garrett not respecting my wishes caused this."

She managed to slam her hand against the side of the sink, hitting her thumb just right to make her yelp. She set the mug down a bit more forcefully than was probably wise, shaking her hand to make her thumb stop stinging.

"Did you injure yourself?" Dante reached for Elsa's hand, but she clutched it against her chest.

"It's nothing."

"You must learn to let others help you."

Right, because that had worked out so well for her in the past. Elsa bit her lower lip to keep the sarcastic comment from spilling out. She did let him take her hand and put it under the tap.

Her anger dissipated as he rinsed the soap from her hands, his fingers gliding over her skin. Tingles of pleasure raced up her arms at his gentle touch. Dante turned off the water and held her injured hand close to his chest. He ran his fingertips lightly over her thumb. "Does it still hurt?"

"Not really." Elsa's voice came out a squeak. He stared into her eyes, still lightly caressing her hand with his. She cleared her throat and said, "Thank you."

Dante brought her hand to his lips, pressing a gentle kiss on her thumb. "You are most welcome."

His gaze slid to her lips and he leaned closer, his head bending toward hers. Elsa could feel the heat of his body, as if their skin was already touching. He was going to kiss her—she was sure of it. And suddenly, she couldn't remember any of the reasons she had to stop him.

"Winston is fine, in case you're wondering." Garrett stood in the doorway. His harsh voice scattered the clouds in Elsa's mind.

She couldn't believe she had let that moment go so far. That she and Dante had almost kissed. And here was Garrett, angry because he thought that Dante was trying to take advantage of her. If only Garrett knew the truth.

Dante looked momentarily abashed. "That is welcome news."

"I bet." Garrett scowled at Dante, but didn't even look at Elsa.

She grabbed Garrett's arm as he passed her. "I appreciate you coming to check on Winston."

"It's the least I can do for a friend."

"I know you're only trying to help, and I appreciate that too," she said. "But on the other matter, can you please trust me that I know what I'm doing?"

Garrett shook his head and let out a sharp, low laugh. "Funny. You're so good at asking for trust, but do you ever look at how much you give out? It's a two-way street."

"Garrett, I—"

He didn't let her finish. "I'll call my guy off. Don't worry about it."

How could she not worry? He was asking her to trust him, and she wasn't sure she knew how. His harsh accusation rattled like chains in her mind. But another voice broke into her thoughts. Dante's voice, their conversation from earlier in the day playing through her mind.

"You are surrounded by people who care for you."

"If people knew what I could do, they would hunt me down and dissect me."

"Even Garrett? Even Winston?"

Would they really hurt her? Elsa's mother had been a drunk and a religious fanatic. Winston and Garrett cared for Elsa. They had proven how they felt time and again. But was she brave enough to trust them, too? Like she was learning to trust Dante?

Garrett had only spoken with a private investigator. A friend. He could handle telling the guy to back off. Maybe if she could try to trust Garrett on this one thing, she could mend a little of what had been damaged between them.

"Okay." She loosened her grip on Garrett's arm.

Garrett lingered as if he was waiting for her to say more. He probably expected a long litany of instructions. But she was going to trust him to take care of this, even though it felt sort of like stepping off a cliff.

"Well, all right then."

Garrett's eyebrows scrunched together and he cocked his head to one side as if he was trying to puzzle out what was going on. He hesitantly leaned in to hug her. Elsa stood on her toes to hug him back, which pushed her cold clothing against her skin.

When he let her go, his signature smile was back in place. "Dante, make sure she changes into something dry before she catches a cold. Winston is enough of a handful. I don't think we can stand tending to them both."

The tightness around her heart vanished at Garrett's words. She hadn't lost him. More than that, he had included Dante, as if the two of them were a team. Elsa didn't miss the way Dante's expression relaxed.

"I shall make that the next order of business," Dante said.

"I'm sure." Garrett's smile turned a bit wry, but that seemed to be the end of it.

After Garrett left, Dante locked the door. He put the key on the shelf nearest the door instead of leaving it in the lock. "You should change your shirt."

"I'll just check on Winston first. I think I'll sleep on the couch tonight. I want to be close enough to hear him if he needs anything."

"Garrett was right." Dante grabbed the edge of his shirt, then pulled it over his head and held it out to her. "If you will not take the time to go upstairs and change, at least put this on instead."

Elsa might have if she was able to move, but she was paralyzed at the site of Dante half-naked in her kitchen. The dark hair that lightly covered his chest contrasted against his pale skin, accentuating the broad planes of his muscles and flowing like a waterfall down his flawless stomach. It disappeared beneath the waistband of his pajama pants.

Fireworks exploded through her. Her arms tingled, as if begging her to reach for him. She could barely breathe. The air passing over her parted lips felt like a caress. She longed to touch his chest, to trail kisses along his stomach, to explore every inch of his body…

"Are you all right?"

He took a step toward her, jolting her back to reality. She kept her eyes locked on his, only his eyes, and tried to block out everything she was seeing in her periphery.

"I'm fine, thanks."

She reached for his shirt, but since she wasn't looking, she wound up brushing her hand against his. The physical contact was like touching a live wire. She still managed to grab his shirt and started to pull it over her head.

"Elsa…" Dante stepped closer and grasped her arms to stop her. He was so warm. "You should take off your own shirt first."

She peered at him through the open neck of his shirt, her arms still held above her head. "You want me to…"

A flush spread across his neck and chest, creeping over his face as well.

Elsa would not let this happen. Not until he had met other women, spent time with them, and realized that he had options besides her. If she gave in now, she'd never be sure that he would have chosen her.

She lowered his shirt and backed away from him, forcing a smile. "Of course. I'll change in the laundry room."

She fled from his presence as quickly as she could, heart beating like a frightened rabbit thumping out a warning. The laundry room was just off the kitchen. Elsa closed the door behind her, leaning against it as she brought herself back under control.

This was going to be harder than she thought. Dante was kind, intelligent and beautiful. She loved spending time with him. She was already attracted to him, and that was before what she had just seen. Elsa had never wanted anyone so intensely.

His body was gorgeous, and she had slept right next to *that* not once but twice. She shivered just thinking about it. Her mind filled with images of exploring his chest, her fingers tingling as she imagined trailing them all the way down that dark path.

For once, she was glad for her insane cycles—they had driven her to get an IUD that secreted hormones to lighten her periods. At least if she did give in to her desires, she wouldn't have to worry about birth control.

That was not what she should be thinking about.

She would have to be stronger. With renewed determination, she tore off her shirt and threw it aside, then pulled Dante's over her head. She only realized her mistake after it settled over her shoulders.

The scent of sandalwood enveloped her. His shirt was still warm from his body. His heat seeped into her chilled flesh. She could feel him surrounding her. She moaned and leaned against the wall, unable to make herself take it off.

If it felt this good just to think about touching him, what would it be like if she gave in? But if she did give in, she'd never know if what they had was real.

Changing their relationship would also absolutely change how they behaved toward one another. What if it didn't work out? What if giving in to their attraction brought out dark sides of their personalities? What if they lost what they already had?

Everything would intensify—attraction, passion, rage…

Elsa needed distance. If she kept her hands to herself and tried to avoid physical contact, she could resist the temptation he presented. Clinging to that thought helped as she summoned the courage to open the door to the kitchen again.

He was nowhere in sight. She was both relieved and disappointed. She headed to check on Winston, glancing into the entertainment room as she passed by. Dante wasn't there either.

Winston's door was slightly open. His room was dark, but the light spilling in from the hallway was enough for Elsa to find her way to his bedside. He was sound asleep. The weathered lines around his eyes and mouth had softened.

She watched him sleep for a few moments, reassuring herself that he was okay, then tiptoed back to the door. She left it open a bit to hear him better if he needed anything during the night.

Passing the entertainment room again, Elsa noticed blankets and pillows stacked next to the couch. Dante must have been there, but he had already left. She backtracked to the kitchen, where she found him pouring two glasses of tea. Thankfully, he'd put on another of his shirts.

"I didn't know you were expecting company." She tried to feign a sense of ease she didn't feel.

He set the tea pitcher back in the refrigerator and closed the door. "I thought perhaps we could watch a movie together."

"Okay." The word slipped out before she could stop herself. What was she doing? This wasn't avoiding temptation. This was barreling right into it.

Disgusted with herself, Elsa stormed to the cabinet and pulled out a bag of popcorn. It took her three tries to get it out of the plastic wrap, each more frustrating than the last. She threw the bag in the microwave when she finally managed it, pounding the buttons into obedience.

"Do you need assistance?"

Dante's voice was right at her ear. At least, it felt that way. She spun around to find him standing next to her. She hadn't heard him approach.

"I apologize. I did not mean to startle you."

"It's okay. I guess I'm still jumpy."

He placed his hands on her arms. He was too close for her to step aside. "You do not need to worry. I will not let anything happen to you. Not while it is in my power to protect you."

"I didn't bring you here to protect me. I can take care of myself."

She turned around as the microwave beeped, grateful for the excuse to move away from him. Elsa took out the popcorn and set it on the counter, then opened the bag so it could let off some steam.

"I am well aware of this." There was a bit of an edge to his tone. "As you have repeatedly told me it is so."

She turned to face him again, leaning against the counter. "I'm sorry. I didn't mean to say that so harshly. This is frustrating, though. You aren't supposed to be helping me. That isn't why I brought you here."

"It is no trouble at all."

"But it is. You shouldn't have to worry about any of this. I should've had a plan in place. I should've had paperwork ready. You shouldn't be stuck here with Winston and me, taking care of him and making sure that we're safe. I'm supposed to be doing that for you."

Dante stepped closer, his eyes the rich blue of deep water as he gazed down at her. "It is an honor to be able to care for Winston and to protect you both. I have never had someone to take care of. Not like this. It warms my heart more than you could ever imagine. Please do not begrudge anyone for that, least of all yourself."

How was she supposed to keep herself at a distance when he said things like that?

"I appreciate the sentiment, but there are other people you could be taking care of. You should be free to go wherever you please."

"There is no place in this world that I would rather be than here."

"You've never been anywhere else. How can you possibly know

that?"

"Because this is where you are."

Elsa's heart felt like it had suddenly swollen and was about to burst. It would be so easy to give in. All she had to do was lean forward and kiss him. The way he was staring at her lips, she knew he was thinking it too, just like earlier.

She should've stopped him then, and she knew she should put a stop to it now.

"And this is where I'll always be." She smiled, trying to keep the longing she felt from clouding her tone.

A flash of uncertainty crossed Dante's face. She needed to stop sending him mixed signals. But to do that, she needed to get her heart under control. If only her heart didn't want him so much.

Chapter Seventeen

The studio doors were open as Dante worked on yet another painting. Natural light poured in from above and filtered through the windows facing the gardens and patio. He and Elsa must certainly have tea outside, if he could convince her to leave Winston's side for a little while.

Winston was feeling better, and as such, it grew harder to convince him to rest. She had been with him throughout the morning. Dante felt selfish to admit it, but he missed her.

He knew he would not be without company for long. Precisely on time, Jazz appeared in the patio doorway, peeking her head into the studio. She smiled when she saw him, then glanced around.

"Elsa is not here." Dante touched his mask to be sure it was in place. After Jazz's initial reaction, he thought it best to wear in her presence.

"She's with Winston?"

"Yes. But I do not know how long she will be, and they are just down the hall."

"I know where Winston's room is." Jazz stepped into the studio. "I've been around here a while longer than you."

"Of course. I am a bit distracted at present."

"Let me see." She walked around Dante, nodding as she viewed his latest work. She pursed her lips and tilted her head to the side. Finally, she smiled. "Oh, yes. I definitely see a future for you."

He laughed inwardly at her ironic choice of words. If not for Elsa, he would have no future in so many ways.

Jazz turned to face him. "There are others?"

"Yes. These new acrylics dry so quickly." He pulled out the stack of canvases he'd filled since he arrived.

"What kind of acrylics do you use?" She picked up a tube of paint near his easel.

Dante's heart fluttered nervously as he realized his error. For all he knew, acrylic paints had been available for decades.

"I suppose they are the common kind. However, I have never worked with them before. Hence, they are new to me."

One of her eyebrows rose, but she said nothing more. Eager to distract her further, he began showing her his other paintings.

"These are good, Dante," Jazz said. "Very good. The use of color and the brush strokes..." She leafed through the paintings, pausing occasionally to examine one in more minute detail. "How long have you been here?"

"It will be one week tomorrow."

"And have you slept since you arrived?"

"A bit." The nights he had spent with Elsa curled up beside him rose to the surface of his mind. He would certainly sleep more often if he could spend each night in such a manner.

"Well, I'm impressed. You almost have enough for a show already." She pursed her lips again, no doubt puzzling something out. "I had a last-minute cancellation for an opening show next week. Do you think you could have three more of these by then?"

"At least."

Jazz smiled broadly. "Then, my friend, we are in business."

Dante took her hand when she offered it, having studied interactions more closely on various television programs. She shook his hand vigorously and then released him.

"Since we are now business partners, there are a few other matters I would like to discuss."

"I'm intrigued." Jazz walked over to Elsa's writing desk, then leaned against it and crossed her arms.

"The first is a matter of funding. I do not wish to continue to impose on Elsa's hospitality."

"You want an advance from the show?"

"Not at all. But I assume you have contacts who appreciate fine pieces." He took off his mother's ring and held it out to Jazz. "I should like to find a buyer for this."

"This is Elsa's ring. She gave it to you?"

"It is a bit more complicated than that." He struggled to find a way to explain that would not betray Elsa's confidences. "Elsa returned the ring to me the night I arrived. It was made by—"

"Heinrich Gerhardt." Jazz took the ring. She ran her fingers over the intricate design covering its surface.

"You have heard of him?" Dante was unable to hide his astonishment.

"Who do you think found this ring for Elsa? Heinrich was a German goldsmith who only produced for about a decade around the mid-1800s. Which is a shame, really. The man was a genius."

Dante could hardly believe what he was hearing. It seemed everyone knew more about his family than he did.

"Elsa's been obsessed with Heinrich's mistress, Deirdre Lucerne, for years." She stared at Dante, her eyes slowly widening. "Wait a minute. How could I not have realized? Dante Lucerne. You're descended from them!"

He let out a breath of relief. He could hardly deny what she said, and it enabled him to protect Elsa's secret without lying to Jazz.

"I am."

"Wow, Elsa really is collecting everything she can get her hands on."

"I am not an item to be collected by anyone."

"I'm just teasing. But I get it now. How you guys met and why she's letting you live here. I don't get why you want to sell that ring, though."

"I need to make a fresh start free of debt to anyone. My—" He caught himself before he made another slip. "I believe Deirdre would want me to be able to do so."

"Do you owe someone money?"

"Not as such. However, I am imposing on Elsa's generosity. It is not a position in which I am content to remain."

Jazz grinned. "You know her pretty well."

"I hope to know her better." Of all the confessions he could have made, those words did little more than embarrass him. Jazz only grinned the more.

"I bet you do. And I will help with that."

"You will?"

"Elsa has been alone for a long time. Too long. I think you have a shot with her, so I'm going to back your play."

"I...thank you."

Dante could scarcely believe that Jazz thought he had a chance of a lasting happiness with Elsa. He had suspected that Elsa wanted a relationship with him, perhaps even as much as he wanted one with her. Jazz's words corroborated his theory.

Now that he had an ally in Jazz, he was confident enough to ask his next question. "There is one more thing that would help in that regard."

"Spill it."

"I am truly starting over here. My previous situation was untenable. I broke no laws and owed no money, I assure you. However, I find myself in the position of having utterly nothing aside from this ring."

"You don't need to worry. Once I sell that ring, you'll have plenty of money for canvases."

"My needs go beyond that. Elsa arranged for me to come here and is providing for my needs. As you can imagine, it is not the most favorable position for me to begin courting her."

"You want to come to her on your own two feet."

"Precisely. But that is difficult given my circumstance."

Jazz tucked the ring into the front pocket of her pants. "Just tell me what you need."

"I am not even certain how to ask. Sufficed to say, when Elsa brought me here, I was required to leave everything behind. Including the man I was."

Jazz's brow furrowed, her lips pursing as she pondered his words. Finally, her eyebrows rose and her eyes widened.

"Oh! I get it." A devilish look that made him a bit uncomfortable swept across her face. "I'm going to have some fun with this. You have come to the right person. You don't know how lucky you are."

"I am unsure if—"

She did not let him finish. "No take-backs. It's done. My business is making people. And I have never had a blank canvas before." She looked him up and down again and shrugged. "Well, mostly blank. Dante is good. We'll keep Dante at least. And using your personal circumstances to create this Phantom persona—"

"Was never my intention. Not for my career as a painter."

She let out a sigh. "Well, you let Elsa play with it, so you have to let me have some fun too. No wardrobe changes or anything until I've introduced you around. After your unveiling, you can change your look or let Garrett's doctor friends do whatever they want to you."

Dante wasn't sure what Jazz meant by that. He didn't have a chance to ask, as he heard Elsa's voice behind him.

"Jazz? What are you doing here?"

"Elsa! I'm just here to check on Winston." Jazz walked around Dante, crossing the room to give Elsa a hug.

"In the studio?" One delicate brow was arched on Elsa's forehead.

"Well, it'd be rude not to say hello to Dante."

"I didn't know you'd met." Elsa's tone was terse.

Dante was eager to divert the conversation. "I fear I forgot to mention that Jazz stopped by a few evenings ago."

"That seems an odd thing to forget mentioning." Elsa turned her skeptical gaze upon him.

"I was preoccupied with other matters."

"Such as?" She crossed her arms, curiously like the posture he had seen Jazz adopt.

"He was telling me about Winston." Jazz wrapped her arm around Elsa's shoulders. "Isn't that right, Dante?"

Elsa looked back and forth between them, her eyes narrowing. Finally, she turned to glare at Jazz. "What are you trying to drag him into?"

Jazz lifted her hands, her shoulders creeping toward her ears. "Why is it always me?"

"Because you're always up to something."

Dante did not wish to be the cause of yet another rift between Elsa and her friends. As much as he wanted to surprise her with his plan, he could not in good conscience let Jazz take the blame for something she was not responsible for.

"The truth is—"

Jazz jumped in before he could finish. "You caught me. I am up to something."

"What is it this time?" Elsa asked.

"A dance!" Jazz waved her hands through the air as if calling their attention to an imaginary marquee. "Everyone who's anyone will be there, so of course, you and Dante have to come."

"We can't make it." Elsa's frown would brook no disagreement.

"Aren't you going to ask Dante? I'm sure he wants to go."

He wondered if this was part of what Jazz alluded to when speaking of his unveiling. "By all means."

Elsa said, "Dante, you don't know what you're agreeing to."

"And neither do you," Jazz said. "I haven't told you the best part."

Elsa groaned. "I know I'm going to regret this, but what would that be?"

"It's a masked ball."

"Jazz." Elsa's tone turned foreboding.

"You won't have to worry about anything. I'll take care of your costumes. I'll even send a car. But you both have to come."

Elsa shifted closer to him, her warmth seeping through his shirt. "Absolutely not. Dante just got here, and I'm not going to have you parading him around as part of some marketing ploy."

"If I might interject," Dante said. "Jazz has come up with an idea to introduce me to those in your social circle in a manner that I would be most comfortable with. If others are wearing masks, I will not stand out. It is quite a clever idea."

Very clever. Jazz was both covering for their meeting and attempting to launch his career as an artist.

"Finally someone appreciates me," Jazz said.

Elsa began to chew on her lower lip, her shoulders hunching as if a weight was settling upon them. He could bear her discomfort no easier than causing strain between the two friends.

"Jazz, if you would be so kind as to give Elsa and I a moment."

"Sure, I'll go see Winston."

"I am certain he shall enjoy your company."

Dante waited for Jazz to leave the room before closing the distance between himself and Elsa. "Tell me."

"People will have questions." Elsa's voice was tight.

"And we shall have answers. We met through a mutual love of art. Is that not so?"

Her lips twitched up in a wry grin for a moment. He seized on that. He brushed her hair back past her shoulder, then tucked a few stray strands behind her ear.

"This is a chance for me to meet others in a safe manner. It is an opportunity we dare not let slip by."

Her smile faded. "What if something goes wrong?"

Dante slid his fingers beneath her chin and tilted her head up to him. "What if something doesn't?"

Chapter Eighteen

Two of the best days of Elsa's life passed after Jazz's visit. In the sunlit hours, Dante painted while Elsa wrote in the studio. They spent their evenings relaxing with books or watching movies.

During meals shared with Winston, Dante would teach them about what he was studying. Elsa knew how to drive a car, but had never bothered to learn about engines. The way Dante explained everything was fascinating. If he decided not to be a painter, he'd make a wonderful teacher.

Winston was doing so much better. Watching him ask questions, thoughtfully nodding as he listened to Dante's answers, was quickly becoming one of Elsa's favorite things in the universe. Winston had even started downloading audio books on some of the subjects they discussed, his curiosity piqued by Dante's enthusiasm.

Garrett's visits were encouraging too. He had kept his promise and Elsa was beginning to feel more at ease about letting him call off his friend. Nothing bad had come of the private investigator poking around and she felt like she and Garrett were closer than before. Their friendship was stronger from the trust she finally felt able to give him.

The only cloud hanging over her was the thought of Jazz's dance. It crept ever closer until the dreaded day arrived, along with two large packages. Elsa carried them to her bedroom, hoping to inspect what Jazz had sent before Dante had a chance to see the outfits. He happened past her bedroom door just as she was setting the boxes on her bed.

"Have the costumes arrived?" He joined Elsa by the side of her bed.

"I think so."

"Allow me to assist you." Dante opened the first box, stiffening when he caught a glimpse of what was inside. He lifted a white half-mask from within, then sighed. "I begin to understand what you meant by my not knowing what I was getting myself into."

"She didn't!" Elsa turned back to the box, picking up the top item of clothing. It was a long black jacket with dark burgundy accents in a satiny fabric. She dropped it back in the box, then turned toward the door. "That's it. I'm calling Jazz to tell her we aren't coming."

Dante caught Elsa's arm and spun her in a circle till she was facing him again. Elsa stifled the urge to giggle. When she looked up into his eyes, there were playful crinkles at the edges as he smiled. He hadn't worn a mask since Jazz's visit.

"If Jazz would like me to attend as the Phantom of the Opera, I shall not disappoint her. Besides…" He held the mask up to his face. "It is a role I am well prepared to play."

Elsa laughed and shook her head. "You're taking this all pretty well."

"I have had quite a few opportunities to practice adapting of late. It has become second nature." He put the mask back on top of his costume, then drew his fingertips slowly over the unopened box. "Also, I am quite eager to see what she has prepared for you."

"That makes one of us."

"Do you mind?"

"Go ahead."

Elsa watched as Dante opened the other box. She couldn't suppress a gasp as he pulled out an eye mask covered with pale gold feathers in an intricate design. It was absolutely gorgeous. A bed of rich gold silk with chestnut accents lay beneath the mask.

"Rachel had to be involved," Elsa said. "She's amazing with colors and fabrics."

"Then I am beholden to her."

He set aside the mask and gingerly lifted Elsa's dress from the box. He held it in his arms like he had carried her when he first arrived. His eyes darkened to a blue as rich and deep as an autumn sky at dusk.

In a quiet voice, he said, "I should very much like to see you in this."

"I…" Elsa stammered. "Okay."

Dante placed the dress on her bed, a soft smile on his lips. "In that case, I shall retire to my room to prepare for our evening."

He replaced the lid on the box that held his costume, then tucked it under his arm. He lifted her hand once more and pressed a kiss onto her palm, his gaze locked with hers. There was a spark in his eyes, an intensity that flooded her body with warmth.

And then he was gone, closing the door to her room behind him as he left. Elsa sat on her bed, running her fingers over the smooth fabric of her dress, its coolness seeping into her skin. She lifted the mask and stared into its empty eyes.

Scenarios ran through her mind, each more terrible than the last. Dante was set on going. She knew she couldn't talk him out of it, so she would be at his side to help him.

It was going to be a long night.

Elsa spent more time getting ready for Jazz's dance than she'd spent preparing for every other date of her life combined. Not that this was a date. She was accompanying Dante to help him meet other people in a relatively safe setting. That was all.

Standing in front of her armoire's floor-length mirror, she had to admit her efforts were worthwhile. She'd opted to pull her hair back, leaving a few soft tendrils around her face. The bodice of her dress hugged her chest and waist perfectly, lifting and slimming in all the right places. The skirt flowed around her legs like a pool of sunlight.

Rachel was a genius.

Elsa heard a soft rap on the door. "Come in."

Dante appeared in the mirror behind her. She was so stunned she couldn't turn around. She watched his reflection approach. He hadn't worn such an ornate and flattering outfit in any of the times she observed him.

The tails of the black jacket made him look even taller, the tailored pants showing off his long legs. Only the very edges of a white shirt showed beneath the vest under his jacket, everything offset with that rich burgundy satin. His hair was slicked back with something—all but a stray lock that had fallen over the mask he wore.

He strode up to her, resting his hands on her arms and stopping close enough that she could feel his warmth against her back. Even without the tightness of her dress, Elsa would've had trouble catching her breath just from the sight of him. He looked so serious, a strange energy about him that was new.

He leaned in even closer, his lips hovering just above her neck, and whispered, "Do I look the part?"

Elsa stammered until she saw his lips pull into a broad smile.

"Very funny." She stepped away from him. Her stomach was doing flip-flops, and the skin along her neck was still tingling from the warmth of his breath. "Are you enjoying getting into character?"

"I am making the most of the evening. I must confess, it is an interesting exercise to pretend to be the legend that stemmed in part from my life."

"'Interesting' is one word for it. We can still back out if you want to."

"I wouldn't dream of it. Besides, in all honesty, I fear what Jazz would do if we did not make an appearance at the very least."

"That point I cannot argue."

"And it will also be quite some time before I have had my fill of seeing you like this. You look…" His gaze trailed down her body, leaving a wake of sparks that burned through her. "'Beautiful' is not a strong enough word."

She tried to shake off the effect of that look—the urges that rose in her. She needed to stay focused. Who knew what the evening held?

Not sex. Definitely not sex.

Dante lifted Elsa's hand and threaded it through his elbow. "Shall we?"

She took a deep breath, feeling as if she was about to dive into murky water, then nodded.

"Let's go."

Chapter Nineteen

Dante had thought his logic sound when they left the house, but once they were on their way to the gallery, he found himself plagued with doubts. Even the clear view of other cars in the fading sunlight could not distract him.

It had not escaped his notice that Elsa was in a similar state of mind. She was practically wringing her hands as she stared out the window and chewed on her lower lip. He longed to tell her that everything would be fine, but in honesty, he was uncertain.

Uncertain and uncomfortable.

The mask Jazz had provided was made from some sort of clay. It was quite heavier than he was accustomed and was not fitted to the contours of his face like the porcelain versions he had crafted. Already, he looked forward to returning to Elsa's home, where a mask would not be required.

The car stopped in front of a row of shops and buildings nestled so close, there was barely telling where one began and the next ended. Only the color of the bricks and the architectural accents on the upper stories differentiated them.

On the ground level, the walls were made of glass and metal, allowing passersby to see right into the storefronts. *Jazz Gallery* was emblazoned in red lettering above an open door. Dante could hear faint music from within the gallery.

When the driver opened the car door, Dante exited first, then reached down to help Elsa step onto the sidewalk. She was truly a vision.

The burnished gold of her dress made her hair shine like pale honey. Her eyes fairly glowed. For a moment, he simply stood on the sidewalk, mesmerized by her.

She lifted a hand to her face and touched her cheek, the gesture oddly reminiscent of how he checked the positioning of his mask. "Is everything okay? You're staring."

"I am riveted. There is a difference."

The blush that came to her face buoyed his confidence. Pulling her hand through his elbow again, he led her inside.

The press of bodies was oppressive, especially compared with their quiet existence at Elsa's manor. Dozens of people filled the rooms beyond the foyer, milling about and looking at the art upon the walls or gathering in clusters to converse.

Elsa clung to Dante, staring at everyone as if they were an angry mob merely awaiting a target. He knew she was not just worried for him. If people questioned him about his origins and his answers were anachronistic, her secret would be at risk.

The artwork was another danger. They were contemporary, but Dante's first painting had been enough to trigger her ability outside of her control.

He had not truly considered that before and chided himself for his oversight. His resolve to protect her grew. He slid his arm around her waist as he pulled her closer and walked deeper into the throng.

The central room held no art, but was dominated by an open area being used by several couples for a waltz. Everyone was dressed in costumes that spanned the history Dante knew and some he did not. He and Elsa were hardly the most outlandish couple. There was a pair dressed as Marcus Antonius and Cleopatra.

Dante paused as he realized he thought of himself and Elsa as a couple. He wondered if perhaps she felt the same, with the way she pressed herself ever closer into his embrace. It was becoming easier to believe that there was more to their relationship than friendship.

"You made it!" Jazz navigated the crowd to reach them, wrapped her arms around Elsa's shoulders and gave her a kiss on the cheek. Dante was rather surprised when Jazz greeted him in the same manner.

She was dressed as some sort of sailor, he thought, with a ruffled white shirt under a deep red jacket. A matching bandana was tied over her dark hair. Her leggings were tan, though most of her legs were covered in high black boots adorned with many buckles.

"I have so many people I want to introduce you to."

Elsa sighed. "Isn't it enough that we're here?"

"It's great that you're here, but you hardly ever come out, so I have to show you off when I have the chance. Plus, I want Dante to meet everyone."

A server passed with a tray of tall flute glasses filled with gold liquid and chopped berries. Jazz grabbed a pair and handed one to Dante. Rather than give the other to Elsa, Jazz took a sip herself. Dante offered his glass to Elsa, but she shook her head.

Jazz clicked her tongue at Dante. "See, if you two went out more, you'd know that Elsa doesn't drink."

"It's okay," Elsa said. "Go ahead."

Dante would need to ask later if there was some reason for her abstinence. There was no time at the moment, as Jazz led them through the room. Elsa clutched Dante's hand and cast a nervous glance at him. He forced himself to smile, hoping to ease her nerves.

Jazz had not been exaggerating about the number of people she wanted them to meet. Faces, masked and otherwise, blurred together until at last a pair that were familiar neared them.

Rachel waved, though it was hardly necessary. Both she and Garrett were quite tall. Dante easily saw them through the crowd, even without the people stepping aside as they approached.

Rachel's gown was such a pale blue it was nearly white, with full skirts offset by a corset that seemed tied a bit too tight. Her hair was piled in curls atop her head in an overly intricate manner.

With the gloves she wore and the fan she carried, Dante was reminded a bit too much of his own time. He was glad at least that Elsa's dress was more understated. Dancing with Elsa would be much easier with the slenderness of her skirts. He would be able to hold her close.

Garrett trailed after Rachel, wearing a dark suit and crisp white shirt with a small black tie at his neck. He nodded curtly, but said nothing.

Rachel let out a delighted squeal when she reached them. "Oh my God! You guys look great!"

"Where's your new boyfriend?" There was an edge to Elsa's voice, the strain of the evening no doubt showing through.

"He couldn't make it, but Garrett was nice enough to be my date."

"That's me," Garrett said, his hands in his pockets. "Mr. Nice Guy."

"Doctor Nice Guy." Rachel patted Garrett's arm. "My mother would be so proud."

"Elsa tells me that I have you to thank for the exquisite dress she is wearing tonight," Dante said.

"You caught me." Rachel was smiling, but it did not quite reach her eyes. In fact, there was a haunted look to them, as if something was upsetting her. She grabbed Dante's elbow and pulled him toward the dance floor. "We have to have a dance."

Elsa stiffened, but then she released Dante's arm. "You should go."

"Don't worry." Garrett stepped forward, a polite smile etched on his face. "I'll keep Elsa company."

Dante did not want to dance with Rachel. He wanted to dance with Elsa. But she had already backed away, Garrett following. There was nothing for Dante to do but allow Rachel to usher him onto the dance floor.

The waltz was simple enough that he could proceed through the motions without concentrating overmuch. This was good, because he was preoccupied with thoughts of Elsa. Being taller than most of the crowd himself, he could keep her in his sight as he and Rachel danced. Garrett and Elsa appeared to be having a heated discussion. Dante could only see Garrett's face, but he looked upset. Garrett shook his head and walked away, leaving Elsa alone.

The crowd parted as he left, and Dante caught a glimpse of her. Her gaze met Dante's briefly, and he was uncertain if the longing he detected was her own, or a projection of his feelings upon her. The crowd shifted and he lost sight of her again.

"It's really great that you're helping Elsa with her book," Rachel said. "And you're so into the part. Have you been acting for long?"

With chagrin, Dante realized that Rachel had been speaking for quite some time, but he had not been paying attention. Only at the very end, when she asked her question, had he recognized that she was addressing him.

"I am not an actor."

"Oh come on. You have this character down so perfectly. Are you a specialist that only plays the Phantom? I've heard of that before."

She laughed, a high pitch to the sound that hinted strangely at hysteria. It was enough to call Dante's full attention to her. The lines of strain around her eyes had deepened.

"Is everything all right?"

"Of course it is." Rachel gave another shrill laugh. "It's just that I have a wager going on about whether you're a method actor or not."

"I do not know what you mean."

"You know." She looked pointedly at Dante's mask. "I bet you have makeup on under there. To fully embody the essence of the Phantom."

"I assure you, that is not the case." Dante bristled despite his concerns for her.

"Come on. I can see it around the edges of your mask."

As much as Dante wanted to help Rachel with whatever challenge she faced, he was finding their conversation intolerable. He ceased the waltz and said, "If you would excuse me. I believe I will take my leave of you now."

Rachel looked stricken for a moment, and then she lashed out, grabbing Dante's mask and tearing it from his face. Her grip was precarious, and it slipped from her fingers.

The brittle clay shattered as it hit the floor. Rachel was so intent upon him, she barely seemed to notice.

Gasps and whispers spread out from the two of them like ripples from a pebble dropped in still water. One by one, all of the people around them stopped and turned to stare at him. And first among them was Rachel.

"See! I told you," she said.

Dante was too stunned to step back as she reached out and touched his face. A troubled look crossed her gaze, her fingers exploring the raised, rough flesh. The confusion was soon replaced with shock and then horror. Rachel snatched her hand back—yet another misguided soul who thought scars could be transferred by touch.

He waited for the rest. The repulsion. The screams. But they never came. All he could hear were whispers from the crowd around them.

"Oh my God, Dante," Rachel said. "I'm so sorry. I didn't know."

Tears welled in her eyes, quickly spilling down her cheeks. She dropped to the floor and gathered the pieces of his mask in her trembling hands. Dante cleared his throat, trying to find his voice. When he did, it was rough and tight.

"Leave it."

"But your mask... I broke it." A sob escaped her, her breath uneven and her tears continuing to flow.

He knelt beside her, ignoring the stares of the surrounding crowd, and placed his arm over her shoulder. "I can always get another. But you must not try to gather these pieces when you are so distressed. You might hurt yourself."

Dante pulled out his handkerchief and gave it to her. Rather than using it for herself, she opened it on the floor and started placing the pieces of his mask within. He assisted, eager to end the scene the incident had created.

When the pieces had been collected, he tied the corners of the cloth together and placed the bundle in his pocket. He helped Rachel to her feet as he stood and was shocked when she leaned against his side and wrapped her arm around his waist.

She looked up at him, and Dante saw no hint of discomfort or repulsion in her gaze. Only regret.

Elsa and Jazz appeared among the crowd surrounding them. Garrett was standing nearby. Dante did not know how long Garrett had been there.

"Dante, are you all right?" Elsa looked at the scars on his face for what seemed the first time. Her jaw went slack, but then she snapped her mouth shut and turned to Rachel.

"I didn't mean to." Rachel shrank away from the intensity of Elsa's stare.

"What did you do, Rachel?" Elsa's tone was cold and level, the calm before a gathering storm.

"It was an accident." Dante wrapped his arm around Rachel's shoulders. "She did nothing wrong."

Elsa blinked and jerked her head back as if she had been slapped. Her gaze lingered on Dante's hand resting upon Rachel's arm.

"It was my fault." Rachel's breath came in gulps, her eyes filling with tears once more. "I thought he was just playing a part, you know? Helping you with your—"

Elsa did not allow Rachel to finish her sentence. "You pulled off his mask, didn't you?"

Rachel nodded. She squeezed Dante's waist tightly, and he pulled her closer.

The storm broke, but it was not a blizzard. Flames of rage sprang to life in Elsa's eyes. "Of all the inconsiderate, impulsive acts you've done, this has to be—"

"An accident." Dante summoned his most commanding tone as he cut in. "Rachel had no idea of my disfigurement. You could hardly expect her not to be curious as to what lay beneath my mask."

"But I can expect her to respect your personal boundaries," Elsa said, that fire now directed at him. He did not shrink away from it.

"It is I who decide my own boundaries. And it is I who have the right to offer forgiveness, which I most certainly do."

Elsa's eyes flashed with anger, but she held her tongue. Beside her, Jazz was smiling, as if this spectacle amused her. The thought irked Dante as much as anything else from the evening.

Was this the introduction that Jazz had planned for him? If so, he would most certainly have words for her. To start, he wanted to know if she was the one who had put Rachel up to this. He had seen enough manipulation in the theatre to know when someone had been goaded into action.

In the meantime, Dante found himself at the center of too much attention. A few people turned away when he met their gazes, lips curling in distaste, but most simply seemed curious. Many had already moved on from the matter, going about their own business.

There were whispers and stares, but no screams, no pointing. There was no fear.

Jazz raised her arms over her head and clapped loudly. "Okay, everybody. This isn't performance art. This is a dance. Get back to it and cut the gawking."

She cast one final grin toward him, then whispered something in Elsa's ear. Elsa's eyes widened for a moment before she turned to glare daggers at Jazz as she walked away.

Dante wanted to retreat, to cover his face and find the nearest shadow where he could hide and get his bearings. But that would be letting himself be cowed by the few lingering stares still cast his way.

This was a new world, and he would be a new man in it—a man who was not ashamed or afraid to show his face.

"Are you okay?" Garrett was standing just behind Dante, and he started at hearing Garrett's voice so close.

"Yes, I am fine."

Garrett rewarded Dante with a smile and even briefly placed his hand on Dante's shoulder. Looking to Rachel, Garrett said, "I'll be in the back showroom when you're ready to leave."

"Thanks." Rachel sniffled loudly as Garrett left the dwindling group. She smiled up at Dante. "Jazz is the boss. Can we finish our dance?"

"Of course."

Elsa's head whipped back toward Dante and, for a moment, she looked stricken. He could see her pushing away whatever was paining her, just as she shoved away her fear when Winston had fallen.

This time, her expression became completely blank. No fire, no ice, no warmth. No Elsa.

In that moment, Dante felt that she was more distant than when decades stood between them. She turned away, quickly disappearing through the crowd.

Rachel stepped in front of him, lifting his hand in hers as she pulled them into the dance again. The waltz could not end quickly enough. He kept staring out over the crowd, no longer caring at all that he was without a mask. He only wanted to catch a glimpse of Elsa.

"I really am sorry," Rachel said, drawing him back to his present company. "I had no idea."

"And I truly forgive you." Dante managed to glance at Rachel for long enough to smile at her. Her eyes were red-rimmed, the forget-me-not blue of her irises shining brightly from the contrast.

"How did it happen?" Her voice was soft and timid.

He considered how to respond to her inquiry and found he could not malign his brother. Finally, he settled on saying, "A much more unfortunate accident."

"I'm sorry."

"It was a long time ago." How very long indeed.

"Is Garrett your doctor?"

"I suppose you could say so."

"He's a great doctor. I didn't know he did plastic surgery, though."

"How would one perform surgery on plastic?" Dante had researched the material after it came up so often in his other reading.

Rachel gave a tittering laugh. "Very funny. Is Garrett going to perform the surgery, or is he working with someone else on your case?"

"I have no plans for surgery of any kind in my future, if I can avoid it."

"Oh, I'm sorry. I just assumed he was helping you with…"

"With what?"

"You know. Your scars."

Dante stopped dancing quite suddenly. Their momentum caused Rachel to stumble, but he caught her up against his chest so she did not fall.

"I apologize," he said. "That was careless of me."

"It's okay."

"If you could clarify…" Dante's mind was reeling from the thoughts speeding past.

In his time, he had heard of techniques that were being developed to change peoples' appearance. Nothing showed enough promise to give him hope, but that had been over a hundred years ago. With the advancements in other areas he had seen, he wondered what had been accomplished in this field.

"Are you saying that Garrett could perhaps remove the scarring on my face?"

"I don't know for sure, but you should definitely talk to him if you haven't already. Maybe he can refer you to a specialist. There are plenty of people out there who can do reconstructive surgery. If it's something you want, you should keep looking until you find someone who can help you."

"Reconstructive surgery…"

Dante felt a rush of adrenaline spread through his body at the thought. As he soared on the surge of hope, his stomach suddenly clenched, the leaden weight of it dragging him back to cold reality.

Elsa would know of this. This was her world, after all. She would know that there were surgeons who might be able to help him. But then, why had she not mentioned this yet? Why would she keep this possibility from him?

"Are you okay?" Rachel asked. "You look angry."

"I am quite fine, I assure you." Dante reined in his temper and put forth a placid expression. He might not have ever taken to the stage, but he had spent over a decade in the theatre. He knew how to act. "I do find myself growing tired. It has been quite an eventful evening."

"I suppose I didn't help any."

"On the contrary." He lifted Rachel's hand to his lips and pressed a gentle kiss on her knuckles. "I found your company most illuminating."

Rachel laughed, but some of her nervousness had returned. Perhaps she was not as comfortable with his appearance as he thought.

No matter. He had more important things on his mind. He bowed curtly and then headed through the crowd to find Elsa.

He would have answers. And he would have them now.

Chapter Twenty

The evening was turning into a nightmare. Elsa had planned to eventually have a dinner party where Dante didn't wear his mask. She wanted him to be comfortable with the people she invited, to ease him into the idea. Instead, Rachel had ripped off his mask and thrown it on the floor, leaving him exposed for everyone to see.

And he hadn't minded a bit.

This was what she wanted, wasn't it? He was interacting with people without wearing his mask, and he seemed perfectly comfortable. Aside from a few rude gawkers, no one was paying attention to him.

Well, that wasn't entirely true. A few clusters of women had gathered at the edge of the dance floor, no doubt waiting for their chance to dance with him. They would all have to wait. He was completely absorbed by whatever Rachel was talking about as they danced.

The surge of jealousy that rose up within Elsa was like a tidal wave. It knocked the wind from her, made her dizzy. When Rachel stumbled into Dante's chest and he held her close, Elsa felt like she might be sick. The irony of her situation tore through her.

She had been clinging to her hope that Dante would choose her, even after meeting other women and learning that he had options. She thought maybe after dating some other people he would return to her.

Only now did she realize her mistake. What woman would let him go once they had him? What if Elsa had to stand aside as he fell in love with someone else?

She had a horrifying vision of standing in a church among other bridesmaids as a radiant Rachel glided down the aisle to Dante's waiting arms. Elsa's stomach churned again at the thought. She shook her head, trying to force the image away. It was too much.

She glanced back in their direction, but Dante didn't seem to be dancing anymore. He was striding through the crowd, stopping occasionally to either look down as if someone was speaking to him or to scan the crowd.

The bodies between them parted enough to give her a glimpse of women in sultry outfits circling him like piranha. Elsa could almost hear her heart shattering like Dante's mask. There was no one to help her pick up the pieces.

Desperate for space and air, she made her way to the exit. She sat on a bench seat in the foyer near the front door. When Dante was ready to leave, he would find her. She hoped he would be alone and not escorted by some woman looking to go home with him. Her stomach tightened with dread.

At least now he knew he didn't have to wear a mask to be accepted, to be desired.

Maybe it was time to tell him about reconstructive surgery. The thought of him going through a surgery she felt was unnecessary made her feel half sick. There were always risks. Garrett had been clear on that point. But it wasn't her decision to make.

If Dante wanted reconstructive surgery, she would support him however she could. Unfortunately, the most helpful thing she could do was obtain a legal identity for him. There would be paperwork to fill out and questions that would need to be answered. She still had no idea what to do about that.

Her thoughts were chasing their tails when a smooth voice brought them to a halt. "It's a sin for a beautiful woman to be alone."

A man in a cat mask sat down next to Elsa on the bench, leaning in close enough to make her uneasy, but not so close that she felt justified in doing something about it.

"If I see any I'll let them know."

"So modest."

The cat mask had a mane of dark hair attached with streaks of color running through it like a tomcat. The man's smile revealed two rows of perfect white teeth.

There was something about his eyes that gave Elsa a chill. They were cold blue. Emotionless, even when he smiled. She had longed for solitude when she left the party, but she suddenly found herself wishing there were more people nearby.

He leaned back against the window at an angle that put him even closer. "You're very reclusive, being out here all by yourself."

"I prefer to think of myself as selective."

"How interesting. You'd rather be a snob than a recluse."

"I didn't say—"

Before she could finish her argument, Dante stormed into the room. His eyebrows were lowered over his forehead, his hair in disarray, and his lips pulled down in a deep frown. Something else must have happened, and she had left him alone to deal with it. How could she have been so selfish?

Elsa leapt to her feet, guilt and relief warring within her as she ran away from the man on the bench.

"What's wrong? Are you all right?"

"I am fine, thank you." Dante's voice was cold and tense. He glared at the man sitting on the bench. "I do not mean to intrude."

"You didn't intrude," she said. "I was just waiting for you."

"Well, I am here."

"Are you ready to go home then?" She hoped so.

Before Dante could respond, the stranger from the bench stood and walked over to them. "Leaving so soon? But we were only just getting to know each other."

"Perhaps another time." Elsa stepped closer to Dante, latching onto his arm as if he was a buoy on a stormy sea.

The stranger stared at her hands on Dante's arm, his gaze beyond cold. It almost seemed predatory. Dante must have picked up on it too. He put his arm around her waist and started leading her to the door.

"I'll take you up on that, Elsa." The stranger strolled back toward the rest of the gallery.

Elsa didn't remember giving him her name. Hearing him say it sent a chill down her spine. She couldn't keep herself from casting one last glance over her shoulder. Dante followed suit, pausing at the exit.

The man pointed to the right side of his face and said, "By the way, just because this is a masked ball doesn't mean you can crawl out from under your rock and pretend to be a normal person like the rest of us. Next time, stay home at the freak show." He stepped through the doorway, disappearing into the crowd.

At first, Elsa was so shocked that she simply stared after him. Then, fire flooded her veins.

She wasn't sure what she was going to do to that man. She did know that he wouldn't like it. She took two steps before Dante tightened his grip on her waist, pulling her back against his chest. He spun her around to face him.

"Let it go."

"Didn't you hear what he said?"

"Yes, I did. And it is a sentiment that I am quite familiar with. His words speak more of his character than mine."

"How can anyone be so callous?"

"He seems a man who is very accustomed to getting what he wants. I have met his sort before." Dante brushed a lock of hair behind Elsa's ear, then cupped her cheek and tilted her face toward him. "Think no more of it."

She wasn't sure she could manage that on her own. He must have sensed her need for distraction, because he stepped closer and slid his hand to the small of her back, all but pressing their bodies together. He let his fingertips trail along her skin as he shifted his other hand from her face to her shoulder.

The warm breeze from outside couldn't touch the heat that was rising within her. A hint of a smile lifted the corners of Dante's lips. His full, kissable lips.

She needed to do something quickly before this escalated any further. She looked away from him and pulled back a bit to break the spell of the moment.

"I'm sorry I left you alone. I just needed a minute to get some air." She could use even more of it now. Cold air. Or maybe a cold shower.

"I quite understand." He kissed her forehead so lightly she barely felt the brush of his lips on her skin. "Let us go home."

Chapter Twenty-One

The sky was inky black when they arrived at the manor, pinpricks of light scattered over the darkness above like diamonds. Concern had long since usurped Dante's anger. Elsa had hardly spoken to him after they left the gallery. During the drive home, she sat on the opposite side of the car, never once reaching for his hand.

In the foyer, she placed her feathered mask on a side table and stood with her back to him. Not knowing what else to do, Dante pulled the bundle from his pocket that held the remnants of his own mask and set it next to hers.

Hoping to draw her into conversation, he said, "Your friends are every bit as gracious as I would expect from knowing you."

"You really felt comfortable, even without your mask?"

"Very much so."

Elsa smiled at last, and the light he loved so dearly returned to her eyes for a moment. They were still pinched, as if she were in great pain, but did not wish him to know.

"I'm glad it was such a good experience. I hope that you understand things better now. Your options."

"Options?"

"You've seen that people will accept you as you are."

"You have already shown me that. I do not care what others think, only you."

She winced and her smile vanished. "I'm not the only person who accepts you. I wanted you to know that. You can have other relationships. Other friends."

"Friends." He let the word roll around on his tongue. He did not like the taste of it at all. Not when speaking of himself and Elsa.

"And more, if you'd like."

His gaze snapped back to hers, but she was staring very pointedly at the tile floor. She had gone quite pale. Dante's heart started thundering in his chest. It was a wonder she did not hear it, standing so close at his side.

"Rachel seemed fascinated by you." Elsa's voice was reedy. She cleared her throat before continuing. "So did the other women that approached you after your dance. I wanted you to know that you don't have to change to have relationships with other people."

"I am not certain that I understand."

"That's because I haven't told you about this yet."

Her features were pulled so tight, she looked as though she might shatter at any moment. Her eyes had become glassy, and she had to clear her throat again before continuing.

"I know that this has caused you grief throughout your life." She reached up and gently stroked the right side of his face. Her fingers were as delicate as feathers. "I've heard other people say worse things to you than what that man at the dance tonight said. I know it affects you more than you show."

"Elsa—" Before he could say more, she silenced him, sliding her thumb across his lips with that same maddening touch. She stepped in closer, resting both of her hands on his shoulders.

"We've been focusing on the technological advancements that have occurred since your time, but there have been medical advances too. We haven't talked about them yet. But it's possible that you might be able to have reconstructive surgery to remove some of your scars. We still need to work out your identity issue, but if you want, we can talk to Garrett about whether you're a good candidate."

"Is this what you want for me, then? To change how I look?"

"Absolutely not!" The fierceness of her tone left no doubt she meant what she said. "I don't care what you look like. All I care about is who you are."

Dante stepped closer, leaving very little space between them. He dared to rest his hands on her waist. "I believe you."

"You just have to know that you have options." Her voice was barely above a whisper, yet he could feel the longing in each word.

"And what of you? Are you one of my options?"

She stiffened, but did not pull away. A flush spread across her chest, creeping up from the pale gold silk of her bodice.

Dante was done resisting. He leaned toward her and pressed his lips gently against hers.

Elsa trembled in his arms, her hands sliding up to clutch the back of his neck. He deepened the kiss, and her breath came out in a moan as she pulled him even closer.

Tangling her fingers in his hair to keep him captive, suddenly it was she who kissed him, and with a stunning ardor. Her lips were silken fire, starved for him. When she slid her tongue against his lips, he groaned in response to her invitation.

Elsa, his Elsa, warm and soft in his arms. This is what he had been longing for.

His tongue delved between her lips, a prelude of what was to come. He wrapped his arms around her, pressing their bodies together, desperate to be closer.

She gripped his shoulders and pushed him away, breaking off their kiss. Her chest rose and fell in quick breaths. The same desire he felt was mirrored in her eyes.

He could not form words to express what he was feeling. Hope, joy, expectation. All fell short of the immensity of his emotion.

Dante pulled her against his chest, burying his face in her hair. He breathed her in, the scent of roses making him dizzy, the taste of her still sweet upon his lips.

"No." She shook her head and pushed him more firmly. His arms fell to his sides as she stepped away. "I can't do this."

He did not understand what had happened. She shook her head again, and held out one arm as if to ward him off.

"Elsa, I love you."

Of course. That one small word held everything that he felt for her within it.

"Are you sure?"

His blood was a deafening rush in his ears. He wondered if he had heard her correctly. "That I love you? I am certain of it."

She shook her head again, backing away as if she was afraid of him. His heart lurched in his chest. He had seen a similar look too many times before, but never from Elsa.

"You are my life."

"That's what I'm afraid of." She closed her eyes and pressed her hands to her chest as if to keep her heart from leaping out.

"Tell me." His throat was ready to collapse on itself from the weight of his emotion.

When she opened her eyes, they glistened with unshed tears. Her lip quivered for a moment, and she shook her head.

At first, he thought she was rejecting him, but then she said, "How can you know you love me? How would you ever know for sure? I brought you here and gave you a home, a new life. How will we ever know if it's love or gratitude?"

"Elsa—" Dante took a small step toward her.

"No." She was building up her walls, brick by brick, word by word, putting distance between them. A panicky feeling fluttered up from his stomach. "I know you. You'd stay, even if you realized later that it wasn't love. You'd stay from a sense of honor. I don't want that. I never wanted that."

"What do you want?"

His question seemed to break her.

"I want you! I've always wanted you. For years!" Tears spilled down her cheeks as a torrent of words flew from her lips. "The first time I saw you, you were trying to save Heinrich. I could see the love and the pain and the fear in your eyes. And then I watched you with Mary, how kind you were to her, how encouraging. And I'm sorry that I watched you without you knowing. I never thought that we would meet."

"I have already forgiven that."

She continued as if she had not heard him. "All the torment others heaped on you, the pain you bore, and you never once complained to anyone. You never told anyone, but I saw how it tore at your soul, how it pushed you down to your knees. I know that pain, that weight. I've lived with it every day of my life. But I never knew anyone could be as strong as you."

He knew her powers made her feel isolated, that she felt she could not trust anyone with knowledge of her gift. He did not realize how very much that loneliness was costing her. He had no time to think on it, as she kept on, her voice rising.

"And now you're here and all I can think is that you're only interested in me because I'm the only woman you know who accepts you. I thought if you met someone else, maybe if things didn't work out between you, eventually we could..."

Her voice broke, and she covered her face with her hands. "I knew I had to let you go, but then I watched you dance with Rachel tonight and talk to those other women, and it hurt so much. So much more than I thought it would."

She shook her head as if trying to clear it of a nightmare. Dante could bear no more.

With two strides, he closed the distance between them, wrapping his arms around her again. He held her against his chest as she shuddered and cried.

She had not said that she loved him, but the intensity of her emotion left him with no doubt of how she felt. The depths of her pain were as great as her passion. He had to help her understand that his love was real.

"You are the strongest woman I have ever known. There is no other woman I want to be with. Yes, you have given me much, and your generosity is part of why I love you, but it is so much more than that. I would know a feeling of obligation. I would know if it was gratitude. I am grateful, of course, but that is not the summation of what I feel for you."

He pulled her from him through an act of will, tilting her face up so he could look into her eyes. "Do you think that I have not watched you as well? How tenderly you care for Winston, how passionately you look after your friends? You are kind, intelligent, brave and beautiful. How could I not love you?"

"How can you be sure?" she whispered.

"I know my heart. And I believe I know yours. You defied time to bring me here with you. Let me be with you."

"Bringing you back was nothing compared to this." She backed away once more, shaking her head. "You're wrong about me. I'm not brave."

Without another word, she turned away, then walked up the stairs.

Dante did not know what to do. If Elsa would not trust him, how could they possibly have a life together?

He took the stairs slowly, following her path toward his own room. He paused before her door. For once, it was closed.

This was ludicrous. He loved her and he believed she loved him, whether she would admit it to herself or not. They wanted each other, wanted to be together. Fear should not stand in their way. He would not let it.

He opened the door.

Elsa was curled on her side in bed, the lamp dim beside her. She sat up and stared at him.

He hesitated for a moment on the threshold, then crossed into her room and quietly closed the door behind him. "You are mistaken about me as well."

"About what?"

"You think I am overwhelmed with gratitude for all you have given me." He started to close the space between them.

She stood as he approached, as nervous as a bird trying to decide whether to take flight. He would not let it happen. He would not let her deny them the infinite possibilities of being together.

Dante stopped quite close to her. She had to crane her neck to look up at him. Errant locks of her golden hair spilled over her shoulder as she did. He slid his fingers along her skin, nudging her hair back so that he could see the gooseflesh that followed in the wake of his touch. He let the silence stretch on.

"How was I wrong?"

"I am grateful, yes. You have given me a home, companionship, friendship. But I am the most selfish being on this earth."

"No, you're not. How can you say that?"

"Because it is not enough. You have given me an entire world, and it's not enough. I want you."

Chapter Twenty-Two

Elsa could hardly breathe. The room seemed to disappear around her, until there was nothing left but the two of them. The focus, the purpose of Dante's gaze spread shivers over her entire body.

"I told you, I—"

Dante didn't let her finish her sentence. "You told me you want me. You told me that you have longed for me. I will not let you deny yourself this. Deny us this. All of your fears, all your doubts about us are unfounded, and I will spend the rest of my life proving that to you."

He slid one arm around her waist to the small of her back and placed the other on the side of her neck, lightly dusting her skin with his fingertips. The argument she had been ready to make vanished, the words scattering like sparks from a shorting power line as his touch overwhelmed her senses.

He pulled her closer and bent his head to hers. Just before their lips touched, he whispered, "Elsa…"

The thrill of his kiss was unlike anything she had ever experienced. She felt weightless. She wrapped her arms around his neck to keep herself from floating away. He was her anchor. The warmth of his body flowed into her. The softness of his lips was intoxicating.

His mouth moved on hers gently, tasting her, exploring her. He buried his fingers in her hair as his other hand pressed her to him. He deepened the kiss, his tongue coaxing her mouth open.

She didn't care about resisting him anymore. She wasn't strong enough. He was too warm, too real. How could she have ever thought she could let him go?

Elsa tightened her arms around his shoulders, parting her lips and inviting him in. He tasted like strawberries and champagne.

He trailed his kisses along her chin and neck. Sparks rained down through her body from wherever they touched.

"You are mine." His voice was a soft breath against her ear. "And I am yours. I will never let you forget that."

His words were as dizzying as his kisses. Elsa felt her heart lurch as he stepped back, every fiber of her being protesting the distance between them. But his gaze held hers without wavering.

He slid his jacket from his shoulders, then tossed it onto a nearby chair. Slowly, he removed more of his intricate outfit, never looking away from her. She watched him hungrily, imagining that she was the one removing each article of clothing.

When he was down to just the familiar white shirt and black slacks, he stepped closer. He reached out with one hand, trailing his fingertips along the side of her neck, across her collarbones, and ever so lightly over the tops of her breasts.

He pulled her against him and kissed her deeply. His hands flew over the back and sides of her dress, finding the hooks and zippers and undoing them.

Elsa felt feverish. Every touch of air was like a cool breath as her dress slid over her skin.

Dante drew his hands along her hips, guiding the dress to the floor. He kept his gaze locked on hers, as if he was avoiding looking at her body while she stepped out of her dress, then he placed the golden fabric on the chair with his clothes.

He paused briefly before letting his gaze rove over her body. When he did, he let out an audible gasp.

Doubts sprang to life in Elsa's mind. She wasn't toned enough or thin enough or curvy enough. Her imagination produced a million ways he could be disappointed with her. She lifted her hands to her chest and took a step back, but he gently grasped her wrists and followed her as she retreated.

"Do not cover yourself." There was a rasp to his voice, as if speaking was a struggle. "You are so beautiful. Please let me look at you."

She felt herself blushing, but she lowered her hands. Dante released her and took a step back. His gaze was as intimate as a caress, lingering on her breasts, the antique gold lace of her panties. He ran a shaking hand through his hair, leaving it the tousled mass of soft waves she preferred.

Still staring at her, he pulled his shirt over his head, then threw it on the floor where it was quickly joined by the rest of his clothing.

Elsa couldn't keep herself from staring back. His body was all smooth lines of muscle, his chest tapering down to his narrow waist and hips. He was grace, lithe strength and pure masculine beauty. She tried not to stare at his erection, but it was hard to look away from it.

She knew that she would never be the same after this. She was about to ruin herself for other men, and she didn't care. Reaching up to undo her chignon, she stepped toward him. His lips parted as he watched her hair fall around her shoulders.

He smiled at her, running the backs of his fingers along her stomach, sliding them over her ribs, and finally cupping her breasts. He bent down to kiss her again, deeply, as his hands worked magic on her.

Lowering himself on one knee, he kissed her stomach while sliding her panties down her legs. For a brief moment, Elsa saw a possibility play out. A possibility that she knew would haunt her.

Dante on one knee, proposing with his mother's ring. A life, a future together. Truly together. It was an awful dream that held everything she wanted and everything that terrified her.

He stood and lifted her from the ground. She pushed all thoughts, all dreams, all hope and panic away. Instead, she focused on the feeling of his arms around her, his chest against hers as he lowered them both to her bed.

Everywhere, skin was touching skin, and it still wasn't enough. She wanted more contact. Needed more. As he kissed her, she tentatively slid her leg up his thigh. Dante groaned against Elsa's mouth, rolling her onto her back and pressing her into the bed. She could feel him between her legs, so close.

His whole body shook as he took a deep, shuddering breath and held perfectly still. "I know that I should take my time, but—"

"I don't want you to."

She was desperate to know him in this way. Her body was already begging for him. She slid her arms under his so she could run her hands down his back and over the firm muscles of his backside.

That was all it took.

She gasped as he buried himself in the soft flesh of her core, her back arching from the intensity of him filling her. He slid his hands under her back, holding her shoulders as he nuzzled her neck, pushing himself deeper. He was still trembling.

"Impossible," he whispered against her ear.

She had to agree. The moment was perfect, each sensation a miracle. Dante was here, joined with her. It was bliss.

Slowly, he started to move again, every thrust bringing Elsa closer to a precipice she was wholly prepared to cast herself from. She wrapped her legs around his thighs, urging him on. His pace increased, just like the sparks arcing out through her body from where they were joined.

As she felt the explosion start to cascade within her, Dante let out a deep groan and increased his pace to a near frenzy. She cried out his name, forever branding it on her soul.

He collapsed on top of her, his strength seeming to have left him. He nuzzled her neck, placing gentle kisses along the soft, sensitive skin. His touch echoed all over her body.

"Dear God," he said. "I never imagined..."

Elsa was still basking in the glow of things. Her mind slowly processed his words. What had he never imagined? She felt a heavy dread deep in her stomach.

"That wasn't..." She almost hated to finish the sentence. She wasn't sure she wanted to know. But she had to. "That wasn't your first time, was it?"

He managed to lift himself up on his elbows, smiling down at her and kissing her gently before saying, "I hope it was not too obvious."

The dread transformed to crushing guilt. Elsa knew that she was being weak by giving in to her desire for Dante. She was being selfish, not waiting until he'd had a chance to date other women in her time. But knowing that she'd been his first, and that would mean that if he really did love her, she'd be his only...

"Did I do something wrong?"

"No. I did." She rolled out from underneath him. Sitting up on the side of the bed, she pulled the sheets around her.

He rose to his knees, his hands on her shoulders as he pulled her back against his chest. "What is it? Tell me what is wrong."

She covered her eyes with one hand, trying to figure out how to put her thoughts into words. She knew he was already upset by her reaction and didn't want to make him feel worse. Especially not after something that was supposed to be so special.

"I just... I didn't know that was your first time."

"I am gratified to know I performed so well." He brushed her hair from the side of her neck, then pressed a gentle kiss on her shoulder and wrapped his arms around her. "Was there something you would have done differently had you known?"

Not allowed herself to be so weak? She shook her head.

"Next time, I believe I will be better able to take my time. I want to savor you. I could spend days learning your body."

He pressed another kiss against her neck and she closed her eyes, willing herself not to cry. It was bad enough he had already seen that once this evening.

"I don't think there should be a next time."

His arms loosened around her, and she felt him sitting back, pulling away from her. That was good. They needed more distance between them.

"Did you not enjoy it?"

"I did. It was probably the most amazing thing I've ever experienced."

"I do not understand."

Elsa stood up, pulling the sheets with her so that she could wrap them around herself. She turned back to face him, trying to steel her resolve.

"I told you I was worried that you only think you want me because you don't think you have other options." She kept the focus on their physical attraction. She couldn't talk about love without breaking down. "I assumed at the very least you'd had relationships in your own time. I shouldn't have given in. If I had known it was your first—"

Dante rose from the bed, following as she backed away. Her resolve was already weakening. A sheen of sweat from their lovemaking clung to his skin, highlighting the dips and valleys of his muscles. There was a flash of something in his eyes. Intensity, determination.

"I wanted you." His voice was low and level. "And you wanted me. That is all there is to it."

"It doesn't matter what I want. This is supposed to be a new life for you. What I want shouldn't matter."

"What you want will always matter to me. Always."

She shook her head. "No. This isn't right. What you're feeling isn't —"

"Do not dare tell me what I feel. You do not know what I think and you do not know what is in my heart. Only I know these things."

He stalked up to her. Even without touching her, his towering presence was overwhelming. She could feel the heat from him, catch his scent everywhere. She felt as enveloped in his essence as she had when he had been filling her, holding her as close as he could.

"You say that you want me to make a life of my choosing," he said. "I am. And you are part of that, whether you like it or not. There is no other woman I want. I have never desired a woman as I desire you."

"You'd never met a woman from my time before."

"And now I have met several. What does it matter?" He let out an exasperated sigh. "Has it not occurred to you that I have never wanted a woman as I want you, never loved a woman, because I had not met *you*? Do you think I would want you any less if we had met in my time?"

"I...don't know."

He didn't give her time to consider the idea.

"I do know. You say you do not care how I look, that what you care about is me. Do you not think I feel the same about you? I do not care that you are the one who brought me here, only that you are here with me now."

What could she say to that? But still, how could she let herself believe that everything she ever wanted was right in front of her?

Again, he didn't give her time to think. He gripped her shoulders and pulled her against him, crushing his lips against hers. He released her only long enough to tear the sheet away, then wrapped his arms around her, lifting her off her feet.

Elsa grabbed on to his neck as he stood up to his full height. She instinctively wrapped her legs around his waist, gasping as she felt his shaft nudge against her again. Never releasing her lips, Dante stumbled to the wall, pressing her back against it, as he drove himself into her core.

He shifted one of his arms to cradle her bottom, the other grabbing her thigh and using his grip to push himself even deeper. Elsa had never experienced such intensity. Their passion was consuming her and she didn't care. He was the flame, and she was the candle.

He broke off the kiss, his gaze boring into her. "I traveled across time to be with you. I want no other and will have no other. There is only you."

She clung more tightly to his neck, wanting to believe him, wanting to let go and cast herself into his love. But she was so afraid.

They had crossed the line. There was no turning back.

She pushed away the fear and doubt, again focusing on the union of their bodies. She gave him everything she could, everything except her heart.

Dante trailed his kisses down her neck, suckling the skin beneath her ear. She felt herself building toward another climax, this one looming on the horizon even larger than the first.

He plunged himself deeper into her, faster, pinning her against the smooth wood of the wall with his body. He released his grip on her leg, bringing his hand to her cheek and reclaiming her mouth. His tongue was just as hungry, delving into her mouth relentlessly.

Her climax hit her like an earthquake. Every part of her body seemed alive, singing with sensation. The aftershocks kept going as he threw his head back, crying out from his own release. She could feel him pumping his seed within her, the shockwaves of his pleasure reverberating through her body.

When he finally stopped, his body was pressing her against the wall firmly enough that he didn't even need his hands to support her. He caressed her cheek with his thumb, kissing her again, but gently.

The strange intensity was still in his gaze as he pulled back to look at her. He wasn't smiling, his lips instead set in a grim, determined line. Without saying anything, he carried her to the bed and set her down on it, crawling in behind her.

Even though she still wanted to argue, to run away, the look in his eyes said that he would not be dissuaded. He wrapped his arms around her, pulling her tight against his chest, as if he would never let her go. Elsa knew deep in her heart she never wanted him to.

Chapter Twenty-Three

"Those eggs are done cooking," Winston said. "I can smell them from here."

"I am aware of their state. Now please relax and rest, as your doctor has ordered."

Dante emptied the pan of eggs and diced peppers onto two plates that already held buttered toast with jam. When he picked up the plates and turned toward the table, Elsa was standing in the doorway to the kitchen.

His chest felt full at the sight of her. Her hair framed her face in a mane of chaotic gold and her lips were still swollen from his kisses. She stared at him with unfocused eyes and the deep teal top she wore was on backward.

It had been a delightfully long night.

"Good morning." A crimson flush spread up from her chest.

Dante turned back to the stove to hide his broad smile. He set down the plates and rearranged the toast. "Good morning."

"Oh, there you are," Winston said. "I was wondering if you were ever going to get up."

"I guess Jazz's party wore me out." Her chair squeaked across the floor as she sat at the table with Winston.

Dante picked up the plates again, carrying them to the table. He let Winston know where the food was on his plate using the placement of time on a clock face. "Your eggs are at six o'clock, toast at twelve. The coffee will only be a moment."

Winston nodded at Dante, but was not quite done with Elsa. "Are you feeling all right? It's not like you to sleep in so late."

"I'm fine, Winston, really. But how are you? Are you still feeling better?"

"Fit as a fiddle. I've been trying to tell you both. Coddling me like I'm some kind of baby."

"Winston, we care about you," Elsa said. "We're just trying to make sure you're okay."

Dante did not try to hide his scowl. "But we are aware that you are no longer reliant upon us, and shall proceed accordingly out of respect."

Winston's brow knit and a curious smile lit his features. He laughed and shook his head, then began to eat.

The firm set to Elsa's lips as she frowned at Dante told him that she perceived his point, whether she agreed with it or not. He would simply have to show her the truth of his words.

Dante walked back to the counter and prepared coffee for the pair. He carried the mugs to the table and set them near their plates.

"Aren't you joining us?" Elsa asked.

"I have made other arrangements."

"What kind of arrangements?"

"Rachel will be arriving shortly to take me to the city for the day. I will be back by this evening." He placed the skillet in the sink and began to wash the dishes from preparing breakfast. "I apologize for the short notice, but the opportunity only arose this morning."

Elsa scooted toward the edge of her chair. "Are you sure that's a good idea?"

Winston laughed. "Listen to this one, Dante. That Rachel will wear your feet down to the ankles."

Dante crossed back to the table, then placed his hands on Winston's shoulders and squeezed them gently. "I assure you, everything will be fine."

Winston laughed again, reaching up to pat one of Dante's hands.

Elsa's frown remained. "I hope you two have fun."

"It will certainly be an adventure." Dante could see the lines of strain around Elsa's eyes. She still had so little faith in him—in them. He would prove to her that they could have a future together.

To help her along that path, he said, "Have you made any progress with your book?"

Elsa leaned back, the line between her brows deepening. "Not really."

"If it is not too bold of me to request, perhaps you could give it some thought today. I very much look forward to discovering how it ends."

"Me too."

A horn sounded outside, and Dante said, "I am summoned."

He leaned down as he walked past Elsa, resting his hand on her shoulder. Her eyes widened slightly as he bent his head to hers and kissed her soundly. He lifted his hand to her cheek, then trailed his fingers along her jaw and chin.

"I am still hoping for a happy ending to that story." He did not wait for a response, eager to get underway.

As he walked through the foyer, he reached into his pocket and pulled out Garrett's mask. With the day Dante had planned, he preferred to keep his face covered. He wanted no distractions. The fit was snug as he pulled the mask in place, but not uncomfortable.

Upon reaching the front drive, Dante waved at Rachel, who was sitting in a green automobile that lacked a roof. Dark glasses covered her eyes, and she wore a kerchief over her hair. She returned his wave, smiling broadly.

He hastened to the side of the house, where he had placed several of his paintings earlier. They were already wrapped, prepared for the journey to Jazz's gallery.

Once the canvases were stowed in the back seat of Rachel's car, Dante climbed into the passenger seat. "Shall we?"

"We are going to have so much fun today." Rachel pressed her foot on the gas pedal.

He watched everything she did with keen interest, comparing what he had read with the reality of driving a car. He had only ridden in the back of an automobile, where he could not see their functioning.

"Jazz told me I'm supposed to be your personal assistant today," Rachel said. "So just let me know what you want to do."

"I hope that you are as full of energy as I have been led to believe, for there is quite a list." He was a bit nervous to be venturing out on his own, but the rewards awaiting him overcame his fears.

"Oh, I almost forgot!" Rachel stopped the car at the end of the long drive that led to Elsa's home and handed Dante a plain envelope. "Jazz told me to give you this. Also, before we run your errands, we need to go to the Shady Palms building. It has all these great newly renovated lofts. Do you know why she wants us to go there?"

"I am uncertain." Dante opened the envelope and pulled out a note scrawled on a small piece of paper.

"What does it say?"

"'A little something to start you off'," Dante read. Behind the note was a stack of bills that looked quite unfamiliar.

"Holy crap, Dante! That's a lot of money!"

"Is it? Well, we shall have to hope that it is enough."

"Enough for what?"

"To begin with, several outfits. Jazz and I agree I need to *update my look*, as she put it."

"Oh. My. God. I get to help you buy a new wardrobe?"

"If you are up to the task."

Rachel grinned, turned back to the road, then pressed her foot on the accelerator hard enough that the tires made a horrible screeching sound. Dante clutched his seat as inertia pushed him against the padded surface.

"You might want to fasten your seatbelt," Rachel said. "Because this is going to be the best day ever."

He did as she instructed, though the day ahead could hardly compare at all to the previous night. Gooseflesh rose along his arms just at the thought, his skin alive with the memory of Elsa in his embrace, his mind echoing with her cries of pleasure.

"Are you okay?" Rachel asked.

"Fine." He cleared his throat.

"You looked kind of far away there for a moment."

"Perhaps it would be best if you focused your attention on what lies before us."

She shrugged and looked back to the road. It was advice he himself needed to follow. He did not like being away from Elsa. He already found himself missing her and not only because of the night before.

He missed seeing her smile. He missed watching her at her writing desk, the sunlight casting a soft glow upon her hair. He missed their stimulating conversation, her gentle touch, and, most of all, her laughter.

They could not reach town and complete their tasks quickly enough. His only regret was that he could not both share these experiences with Elsa and also surprise her with his accomplishments.

It was probably for the best. He needed to show her that he was able to stand on his own, to support her just as much as she had been supporting him.

In the meantime, he enjoyed the feel of the wind in his hair and the bright blue of the sky. The land was exceedingly flat, and it gave the feeling of the sky being right upon them. The thin fabric of his shirt did little to shield him from the sun, but he did not care.

The drive did not take as long as he remembered, whether because he could actually see the operations of the vehicle, asking Rachel as many questions as he liked, or that she seemed to be driving at an extraordinary speed. In either case, the town formed around them, emerging from the dense palms and evergreens.

Rachel navigated several streets, then pulled up to the sidewalk before Jazz's gallery. "I thought we should drop off your canvases first."

"A wise plan." He opened his door and stepped out onto the shaded concrete.

She was too quick for him to help her from the car, appearing at his elbow and picking up one of the parcels. Dante carried the rest as they entered the gallery.

Various people bustled about, cleaning up from the dance. Jazz stood in the center, pointing as she gave directions for moving sculpture displays back onto the main floor. She smiled brightly when she saw

Dante and Rachel.

"There you are! I was hoping you'd stop by." She hugged Dante, kissing his left cheek, then stepped back. She looked him up and down and shook her head. "You cannot leave your house like this if you want to change your image."

"Rachel shall be helping me with that today," Dante said.

"Good. And thank you." Jazz smiled at Rachel, then pointed to a side room. "You'll be in there, Dante. Let's see what you've brought me so we can start to plan where to place things."

Once they had set down their burdens, he scanned the room, envisioning his paintings on the walls.

"There is another painting I am currently working on which I should like to be the focus. It is a bit larger than the others, but I think it would go well on the wall opposite the door."

"Is it another landscape?" Jazz was already busily removing the brown paper covering his canvases.

"It is a portrait."

She paused long enough to give him a cryptic smile. "Okay. That'll be good to break up the rest. Also, that reminds me…"

She gripped his arms with surprising strength and swung him around so that his back was to one of the blank walls. She then pulled out a small rectangular object from a holster on her belt and pointed it at his face. He was unsure what to expect, but she merely tapped it, then put it back in place.

"What was that?"

"I just needed a picture," she said.

"That tiny device is a camera?" Dante's voice was louder than he anticipated. He had not read about cameras as of yet. The level of advancement was quite amazing.

Rachel had been standing in the doorway, glancing from one wall to another, but she fixed her attention on him. "They don't have camera phones where you come from?"

It was a phone as well? He wanted to ask so many questions, but he knew he had already piqued people's interest in a dangerous arena once more.

Instead, he cleared his throat and tried to sound more modern. "Where I'm from, the people were much more old-fashioned. This sort of thing wasn't ubiquitous."

Jazz let out a brief laugh. "They *were* old-fashioned? What, did a meteor blow up your home town?"

Scrambling for an explanation, he said, "I merely meant—"

"Relax. I'm just teasing you." Jazz smirked. "I'll be sure to add getting you a phone to my to-do list."

"Thank you. I would like that very much."

They spent the better part of an hour planning which paintings to place on each wall. Rachel had a keen eye for aesthetics, but listened attentively to all of Jazz's advice. When they were done, Jazz pulled a key out of her pocket.

"By the way, this is for you." She tossed the key toward Dante. He plucked it from the air and turned it over in his hand. The number 3B was inscribed upon it. Jazz said, "Hurry up with your business so you can get back to the easel."

"Of course. And Jazz..." He found himself a bit overcome at her generosity. Recalling her penchant for being direct, he simply said, "Thank you."

Jazz smirked at him again and nodded. She headed back to the main room of the gallery, giving out more orders.

He was prepared to leave, but Rachel gripped his hand tightly and pulled him toward a room with a rope stretched across its entryway.

"Before we go, you have to see Michael's exhibit! It hasn't opened yet, but I'm sure he won't mind." She unhooked the rope so that they could enter, then reattached it behind them.

Dante truly wished she had left the exit open. He wanted to leave the instant he saw Michael's paintings—portraits of women in dark reds and grays. They were nudes, though most at least had sheets draped over parts of their bodies. But those bodies...

Each was elongated, hunched, curving in ways that were barely human, yet somehow bespoke of a despair and horror that resonated within him. The women were either covering their faces with their hands or looking away, as if hiding some shameful secret.

Dante had the strangest urge to try to reach into the paintings and pull the subjects out, to save them from having to endure an eternity on such bleak canvases.

"They're powerful, aren't they?" Rachel's voice had taken on a serious cast that Dante had not heard from her before. In the darkness of that room, it was fitting.

"Indeed." He was uncertain what else to say. She had not let go of his hand, and was staring at the paintings with something of a stunned expression. He remembered his concerns from the masked ball. "Rachel, are you all right?"

She shook her head and smiled. "Of course I am. Why wouldn't I be?"

He could think of several reasons, first among them that she was involved with the man who had created such monstrous works. In any case, Rachel did not give Dante a chance to respond.

"Come on! We have a lot to do today." Squeezing his hand, she led him from the room. He followed her quite gladly.

They left the gallery and crossed the street on foot rather than taking Rachel's car. Apparently, their destination was not far. Trees lined the streets, thick leaves casting shadows over the sidewalks.

She paused in front of a whitewashed building with large glass windows set on each story above them. "This is it. Do you have an apartment here?"

He held up the key, sunlight gleaming along its serrated edge. "We shall see."

He opened the door to the building and stood aside so she could enter first, then stepped into what was presumably his new home.

The floor was covered in gray slate tile, just rough enough to give traction. The white walls of the foyer rose three stories above them. Opposite the building's entrance, a staircase climbed the wall, pausing at landings that led deeper into the building. Windows set in the top two floors allowed natural light to pour in from three directions.

Beneath the staircase, stones had been cleverly set together to form a waterfall that ended in a small pool where fish swam among water lilies and other plants. A frog leapt from the side of the pond into the water as Dante watched.

"Mr. Lucerne?"

He turned at the sound of his name. A man approached them, wearing a tailored suit with the name of the building tastefully embroidered on his lapel. Apparently, Jazz hadn't chosen to change Dante's name after all.

"I am Dante Lucerne."

"Ms. Zhou told me that you might be stopping by today." The man extended his hand, and Dante shook it. "I'm Charles Brenner. I run the front desk during the day."

He pointed over his shoulder at a semi-circular desk with a top that perfectly matched the floor. The man continued to shake Dante's hand for a few moments before releasing it. Though his gaze strayed to Dante's mask a few times, he did not make any mention to it or seem uncomfortable.

"I wanted to introduce myself so you know where to come if you have any questions or problems." He handed Dante a large envelope. "Here's a welcome packet for the building. Laundry room, gym and elevator locations are marked on a map inside. Again, please don't hesitate to contact me with any questions. My number is inside."

"Thank you," Dante said.

He was already feeling a bit overwhelmed, so he refrained from opening the envelope immediately. It was just as well, because Rachel grabbed his elbow and started pulling him toward the staircase.

"Come on, Dante! Let's check it out!"

"It was a pleasure meeting you," Dante called over his shoulder.

She practically ran up the stairs. He had to walk briskly to keep up with her. When they reached a door marked as 3B, she smiled and placed the key Jazz had given him in the lock.

Rachel paused, then released her hold on the key. She shifted out of the way. "You should do it. It's your place, after all."

"Indeed."

He took a deep breath, then turned the key. The lock clicked, and he exhaled strongly. Part of him had wondered if it would work. Apparently, this truly was his new home. He would need even more help from Rachel than he had anticipated.

Dante opened the door and stepped inside.

Chapter Twenty-Four

Elsa was miserable. She tried to write, but her thoughts kept circling back to where Dante might be and what he was doing. She tried reading, but that was just as useless. She couldn't even focus on watching TV. She wandered through her house and ended up in the studio.

A large canvas was sitting next to Dante's easel, covered by a tarp. She was curious, but respected that he wanted to wait until it was done to show it to her.

She opened the doors to the patio, imagining him standing in the sun with a fresh canvas, ready to capture another familiar view that she hadn't truly appreciated until seeing it through his eyes.

Now, he was out seeing the world with Rachel. He had left Elsa behind, and she was the one who told him to.

"You miss him."

She nearly jumped at Winston's voice. He was hovering in the hallway just outside the door. The studio and Elsa's bedroom were the two places in the house he wouldn't enter, never knowing what projects were underway and potentially underfoot.

"How…"

Winston laughed. "I can hear you moping all the way in the kitchen. And it's about bloody time."

"For what?"

"You know what," Winston said. "I'm blind and I can see it clear as day. You two are together, aren't you?"

"I…don't know."

"You listen to me. Dante's not the type to take liberties. If he started something with you, he's serious. You don't need to worry about that."

"That's not what I'm worried about."

"Then what's the problem?"

That was the question. And the only answer she could come up with was, "Me."

Winston made a *pfft* noise and waved his hand at her. "I never met anyone wound as tight as you. You work so hard to control everything and everyone, most of all yourself. But life can't be controlled. Not really. You can grab hold of it as tight as you can till you suffocate, or let go and enjoy the ride."

Maybe he was right. Maybe that was what had gone wrong with Elsa's parents. All their fighting was their way of trying to control each other.

"I'm not that great at letting go."

"Oh, my love. You can do anything you set your mind to." Winston smiled. "Just have a little faith."

Some of the fear gripping her heart eased as warmth suffused her. Winston was one of the dearest people in her life. He and Jazz were the closest thing Elsa had to family.

"I'll try."

"Good. Now go outside and quit your moping. Get some sun and relax!" Winston shuffled off down the hallway, leaving her alone with her thoughts.

Going outside wasn't a bad idea. Only a few bright clouds broke up the darkening blue of the sky. She stepped onto the patio, enjoying the fresh air and the breeze. She settled in the lounge chair under the shade of the table's umbrella and watched the flowers in the garden sway with the wind.

What seemed a moment later, she jolted awake. The sun was beginning to set, shadows stretching across the stone of the patio. She wasn't sure what had woken her, but her skin was crawling. Someone pressed down on the back of her lounge chair.

Elsa leapt up from her seat, then spun around to find Michael staring at her.

In a soft voice he said, "You look so peaceful when you sleep."

"What are you doing here?" Her heart was thundering in her chest.

"I keep telling you, Elsa, I want us to be friends." He circled the lounge chair. "We have a chance to get to know each other better with Rachel off carousing with Dante." He sneered as he said Dante's name.

His voice, his mannerisms, and those cold blue eyes... Elsa wondered that she hadn't recognized him earlier. A rush of anger flooded through her.

"You were the one in the cat mask last night, weren't you?"

"See? We're understanding each other better already." He slinked toward the flowers, but didn't take his eyes off of her. "Not even Rachel recognized me."

"Why go to all that trouble?"

"Rachel is so clingy. I wanted a night off." Michael turned back to Elsa and took a few steps toward her. His lips curled up from his teeth for a brief moment. "Is that too much to ask for?"

Elsa eased back to keep the distance between them. With each zigzagging path Michael cut across the patio, he was getting closer.

"You could have just talked to her."

His face resumed its semblance of calm. With a smug laugh, he said, "You underestimate my effect on Rachel. She's so weak. Not like you, Elsa. You're strong."

"Saying bad things about my friends is not the way to get on my good side."

"See? So protective. When I trashed you, Rachel ate it up." He narrowed his eyes as he spoke, grinning.

"I want you to leave. Now."

"You should be nicer to me. We're bound to become close, with how serious things are with Rachel and me. Speaking of..."

Elsa didn't want to take her eyes off of Michael, but she heard footsteps behind her. She glanced over her shoulder to see Rachel and Dante walking down the path that stretched around the side of the house.

"Michael? What are you doing here?" Rachel looked from Elsa to Michael and back again.

"Waiting for you, of course." Michael crossed the patio to meet

Rachel. Without a prelude, he wrapped his arms around her and started kissing her passionately.

Elsa actually took a step toward them, wanting to pull them apart, to get Michael away from her friend. Dante must have noticed, because he came to her side and placed his hand on her shoulder.

He leaned close and whispered, "Are you all right?"

Elsa shook her head briefly, then tucked herself under Dante's arm.

Michael finally ended his kiss, then turned to face them. His arm was around the back of Rachel's neck, holding her close. "I was in the neighborhood and thought I would pay Elsa a visit since we didn't get to talk much last night at the party."

"You were at the party?" Rachel asked, her brow furrowing. Michael ignored her.

Dante stiffened next to Elsa. "Your costume was quite an effective disguise."

"At least I can take mine off." Michael laughed, then looked down at Rachel. "Guess you won that bet, didn't you?"

Rachel glanced at Dante, her face pained. "Dante, I—"

Michael talked over Rachel. "You don't need to explain anything." His features softened when he turned to her, as did his voice. "What happened was an accident. You have nothing to feel guilty about."

Rachel was still staring at Dante, as if she wanted to apologize, but Michael placed his hand on her cheek, turning her to face him. His other arm was still around Rachel's neck. It looked more like a choke-hold to Elsa than an affectionate gesture.

He ran his hand over Rachel's hair, then twined a lock around his finger and tugged on it. "Except that you left me alone for the entire day."

"I'm sorry," Rachel said.

Elsa's stomach churned. How many times had her mother apologized just like that to Elsa's father, or one of the many boyfriends that moved in after Elsa's father left?

At least Elsa didn't see any bruises or cuts on Rachel. Or Michael, for that matter. Yet.

"I was lonely," Michael said. "I thought Elsa might be lonely too, so I stopped by to see how she was doing."

"That's so thoughtful." Rachel was eating up his story. Elsa knew better.

"That reminds me." Michael turned back to Elsa and Dante. "How's that butler of yours? I hear he took a tumble."

"Winston is quite well. Thank you for asking," Dante said.

For the briefest instant, a look of disgust flashed across Michael's features. Elsa couldn't believe that this was Rachel's boyfriend. She had to do something.

"Why don't we go inside and have some coffee?" Maybe Elsa could talk some sense into Rachel if they could get a moment alone.

"That's a lovely idea," Michael said. "Unfortunately, we'll have to take a rain check. I haven't been able to look at Rachel all day, and now that I have her to myself again, I don't really feel like sharing."

Rachel smiled, then actually sighed as Michael ran his fingers along her cheekbone. Her expression was rapt.

"I get it." Elsa had to figure out a way to separate them. She opted for the direct approach. "Only there's something that I wanted to talk to Rachel about. Girl-talk stuff."

Michael looked at Elsa keenly, but he smiled and nodded. "I suppose I could let Rachel go for another few minutes. For you. Since we're on our way to becoming such good friends."

Elsa had always wondered how her parents managed to fall in love and get married. Watching Rachel and Michael was almost like traveling back in time. History was repeating itself. Elsa had to try to help Rachel avoid that fate.

They headed into the studio, leaving the men outside. Elsa didn't like the idea of Dante being alone with Michael, but she kept them both in sight through the window.

"What did you want to talk to me about?" Rachel still had a dreamy look in her eyes and kept gazing out toward the patio.

"How long have you been dating this guy?"

"It's been a couple of months now. Can you believe it? That's like forever. I've never had a relationship last this long. He says I'm his muse."

"How well do you know him, though?"

"Well enough to know I love him."

"Rachel, come on. What do you really know about him?"

Rachel let out a huff of breath. "Not all of us like everything laid out in a neat little line. I don't ever want to be with someone who doesn't have mystery. I'm not like you. I'm not ready to settle down."

"Who said I was—"

"I'm not just some dumb blonde. I notice things."

"I have never said that you're a dumb blonde." Elsa was disturbed Rachel would even think that. Rachel could be absentminded, but she was a brilliant designer and had offered Elsa insight any number of times.

"But you've thought it."

"Rachel, I never thought such a thing. I'm just worried about you. Michael is scaring me."

"I'm not the one dating a guy who's pretending to be the villain from a bunch of horror stories."

"What?" Elsa gasped.

"This is exactly why Michael didn't want you to know about him. About us. He was right."

"What are you talking about?"

"You always do this with my boyfriends. You say they're too reckless and unsettled, or too old and experienced. And with Michael, you think I don't know enough about him?" Rachel shook her head. "This is my life. Stop trying to control it."

"I'm not trying to control your life."

"Of course you are. It's what you do. Normally, I don't care. It's cute, even. But not this time. This is off-limits."

"Rachel, please, I'm worried about you."

"I can take care of myself."

"I know that, but I just think—"

Rachel cut Elsa off before she could finish her statement. Elsa had never seen Rachel so angry.

"You want to know what I think, Elsa? I think you keep yourself busy meddling in other people's lives to avoid living your own."

"I'm just looking out for you."

"Who asked you to?" Rachel snapped.

"Rachel, please."

Before Elsa could say more, Rachel turned around and stalked out the door. Elsa followed, but couldn't speak freely with Michael present. She didn't want to set him off and have Rachel pay the price later.

As Rachel passed Dante, she said, "I had a lot of fun today, Dante. Call me if you need another break."

Is that what Dante's day out had been? Was Elsa driving away the people she cared about by trying to protect them?

"Rachel—" Dante began, but Rachel was well down the path to the front of the house. Michael followed.

Before he strolled out of sight, he turned and waved. "It was lovely to see you, Elsa. We'll pick this up again very soon."

Elsa's mind churned, but she couldn't think of anything she could do to help. She hadn't felt so helpless since she was a child, watching her parents' marriage self-destruct, their violence escalating. Were all relationships doomed?

There was nothing she could do about Rachel and Michael, but Elsa could do something about her relationship with Dante. She would make sure that they didn't fight. She would stop trying to control him. If she did, maybe they stood a chance.

Dante put his hands on Elsa's shoulders. "Are you all right?"

"Yes." She forced herself to smile, her heart constricting with every breath. "Everything is fine."

Chapter Twenty-Five

When they were alone at last, Dante and Elsa stood silently on the patio. She had said that she was fine, but he did not believe her. Something was very wrong. He could feel her trembling, could sense her fear.

"I am sorry I was not here for you."

She slid her arms around his waist and pressed herself against his chest. He had not quite expected this, though he welcomed her seeking comfort from him.

He wrapped his arms around her shoulders, then rested his cheek on the top of her head. "I should never have left you alone. It was selfish of me."

"No, it wasn't." He felt her tense, and she stumbled over her words as she continued. "I mean, you should be able to go out and have fun with your friends. You don't have to stay with me twenty-four hours a day."

"It would hardly be a chore," he said, chuckling.

He had expected a lighthearted retort, but instead, her arms tightened around him. He had never known her to be frightened like this, and his anger toward Michael grew.

Dante did not have time to ask her more of what had passed between the two, as Winston appeared in the doorway on the far side of the studio.

"Dinner's ready. In case anybody cares." At least Winston was his normal self.

When Elsa did not respond, Dante spoke in her stead. "We do, and we appreciate your efforts. We shall join you shortly."

Winston shrugged, then shuffled down the hall. Dante took Elsa's hand and led her inside. He made sure the doors were locked behind them.

In the brighter lights of the indoors, he could see a strange haunted quality to her wide eyes. He wondered what ghosts lingered in her mind and how he could possibly banish them.

"Did you eat?" Elsa asked.

"Some time ago. I waited to dine with you and Winston. I missed having my meals with you."

She gave him a subdued smile as they walked to the kitchen. She had always been so strong, but now she seemed to be made of glass. He was afraid if he said the wrong thing that she might shatter. It did not improve as they sat around the table for their supper.

"Did you have a good day out?" Winston asked.

Dante was grateful that someone was talking. Elsa was methodically eating her food, barely even making eye contact. Perhaps she was disturbed that he was wearing his new mask. He had not yet had a chance to remove it.

"Yes, it was both enlightening and productive."

"What did you do?" Winston asked.

Dante glanced at Elsa, who showed a bit of interest in the conversation for the first time. She opened her mouth as if to say something, but quickly closed it again. Then she folded her hands in her lap and stared at her plate.

"Errands, I would say." He wished that she would speak her mind, would confide in him about whatever had happened.

"You've got to be careful with that Rachel." Winston laughed. "She'll run you ragged. I can't tell you how many times Elsa came back from a day like that and just collapsed in bed, groaning about how much her feet hurt."

"I assure you, my feet are quite fine."

The rest of the meal passed in a mix of silence and subdued conversation between Dante and Winston. Elsa barely spoke, and then only when spoken to. Dante missed the confident woman who had brought him to this time. And yet, his heart went out to the vulnerable Elsa sitting next to him.

After dinner was done and the dishes put away, Dante and Elsa sat at the table sipping tea. Winston had retired for the evening and, aside from Leonardo sitting on the counter, watching them through slitted eyes and twitching his tail, they had the room to themselves.

The silence stretched on for as long as Dante could bear it. "Are you going to tell me?"

"Tell you what?" Her voice was so small he could barely hear her.

"What is troubling you."

She shook her head. "There's nothing troubling me."

"That is twice this evening that you have told me something I do not believe to be true. Have we not always been forthright with each other?"

"Like the way you're being open with me about your day?" She gasped, her eyes widening as she sat up straighter. "I'm sorry. I didn't mean that."

"There is no need to apologize. And I certainly think you meant it."

Her shoulders hunched, her brow knitting together so fiercely that his own head began to ache in sympathy.

"I have reasons for keeping my agenda from you," Dante said. "Can you say the same of whatever is troubling you?"

"Yes."

"Then I shall trust that your reasons are sound." He reached across the table and took her hand in his. "And hope that you will share them with me when you are ready."

She smiled faintly, which he found encouraging. Not knowing what else to do, he carried their empty mugs to the sink, then returned to the table.

"Shall we retire?"

He offered Elsa his hand, but as she rose, she wrapped her arm around his waist instead. He would certainly not complain. He smiled at her, putting his own arm around her shoulders and relishing her warmth as she nestled against his body.

They went upstairs and paused before the door to Elsa's room. She turned to him and grasped his shirt. "Will you stay?"

"Will you tell me what that man did to you?"

"Nothing." She would not meet Dante's gaze. "He just scared me, that's all."

"I am sorry I was not here to protect you as I promised." Dante placed his fingers gently beneath her chin, tilting her face back toward him. "But I promise you, I shall not leave your side again."

"That's not practical." Again, her eyes widened as if she was panicked. "I mean—"

Before she could say more, he leaned down and pressed a tender kiss to her lips. He had meant for it to be no more than that, but her taste was too sweet. The scent of roses blossomed around him.

He slid his hands to her waist, pulling her against him. Elsa wrapped her arms around his neck, her kiss carrying all the passion he had missed. She held on to him as if he was the sole thing that kept her anchored in this world.

Her need left him breathless.

Dante lifted her up, carrying her into the room and closing the door behind them. As soon as he set her on her feet, she grabbed his neck and pulled him down to her.

At least here the odd timidity that shrouded her at dinner was gone. She devoured his lips, running her hands through his hair as she pressed herself against him.

He panted for breath when she finally released him. They paused only long enough for her to pull his shirt over his head. His lips found hers again, his hands sliding beneath her shirt as he explored the smooth skin of her sides.

Elsa pulled back once more, tearing off her own shirt and throwing it aside. The golden skin of her breasts bared before him, Dante bent his head to trail kisses over each in turn as he held their soft fullness in his hands.

Her chest rose and fell with quick breaths, her fingers buried in his hair. She started to lift his mask from his face, but then went suddenly still.

He smiled at her as he straightened. "Do you prefer me not to wear it?"

Elsa nodded haltingly. "I don't want anything between us."

The irony was not lost on him, for he knew there was something keeping her from him—an emotional wall he did not know how to surmount.

"Nor do I." Dante pulled off his mask and tossed it onto a stack of books near her bed.

There were still times when he could barely believe any of this was real, but perhaps the most miraculous thing of all was that she preferred him without his mask. She accepted him as he was, entirely. If only he could make her understand he felt the same about her.

He placed his hand over her heart, feeling the staccato of its beating against his fingertips, like the wings of a bird striving for the sky. He bent his lips to Elsa's once more, vowing that he would find a way to free her from her fears.

The next day greeted Dante with all the hope of a cloudless sky. Sunlight streamed in through the windows, clear and bright, but Elsa was not beside him.

"Elsa?" When she didn't answer, he sat up and glanced around the room. He was alone.

He quickly rose and pulled on his pants, then headed off to find her.

Winston was in the kitchen by himself, sitting with an untouched cup of tea, his brow knit with worry. As Dante entered, Winston sat a bit straighter.

"Is that you, Dante?"

"Yes."

Winston stood up, adjusted his shirt, and then took two steps to the center of the room. "You and me, we're going to have those words now."

"I beg your pardon?"

"What have you done to Elsa?"

Dante felt a flush spread across his face, memories of the previous night playing through his mind. He thought that this time had different sensibilities about a man and woman sharing a bed, but perhaps he was wrong.

"I assure you, my intentions are honorable."

"I don't give a crap about intentions. I want to know what you've done to Elsa that's got her cowed."

He was not sure what to say. That Winston had also noticed the change in Elsa both reassured and distressed Dante. But he could not think of anything he might have done to bring about such a change.

When he did not respond, Winston said, "Don't play like you don't know. Last night at dinner, she hardly said two words. And this morning was the same. It's not like her." His voice rasped into a whisper at the end, as if it was breaking.

"Winston, I assure you, I am as disturbed by this change in her persona as you are. And I am equally mystified."

"You two didn't have a fight?"

"No. I believe she was upset by Rachel's boyfriend visiting unannounced again, but Elsa will not tell me what transpired."

"Then maybe he's the one we should be trouncing. Where does he live?"

"I do not know, nor am I certain that a trouncing is in order." Dante was not a violent man by nature, though circumstances were beginning to tempt him.

"It'd make me feel better to trounce someone." Winston had a dejected look about him.

Dante was just as lost. He sat, then leaned his elbows on the table and rested his head in his hands. "Winston, I do not know what to do."

"Neither do I. But I have an idea who might."

Dante found Elsa in the studio. She was bent over a tall table, so focused on her project that she did not notice his arrival.

It was good to see her working on something. Perhaps this was a sign that things had improved. He would certainly rather that than resort to using the advice Jazz had given him when he and Winston called her moments ago.

"Good morning," he said.

Elsa started at the sound of Dante's voice, bouncing inches off her stool before landing again, eyes wide as she stared at him. Apparently, things had not improved so very much.

"I did not mean to frighten you," Dante said.

"You didn't. I mean, it's fine."

He crossed over to her and set his hands upon her shoulders, then ran them down her arms. She did not pull away, for which he was grateful. At least he could reach her physically, if not emotionally. She had become even more affectionate since her strange fearfulness had manifested.

He glanced at the table, curious about her project. A chill swept over him as he saw the mask he had worn to the ball. She had pieced most of it back together. An open container of glue sat at her elbow.

"What is this?" Dante stepped closer to the table.

"It's your mask. Well, not your mask. It's the one Jazz sent you. I'm fixing it."

"But why? I thought you preferred me to not wear a mask."

"You still wear them sometimes. Now you'll have two options."

The remaining fragments lay on the table like a disjointed puzzle. She picked up one of the pieces and applied glue to the edge, then held it in place against the main body of the mask she had already repaired.

"Always you speak to me of options," he said. "And yet you do not listen when I tell you I have already made my choices."

He brushed her hair back over her shoulder, tucking it behind her ear. The only response he received was a tightening of her lips. She did not even turn to look at him.

"Why will you not talk to me?"

"What do you want me to say?" Her voice was flat when she spoke. Emotionless.

"I want you to say whatever is on your mind, as you have always done."

After a brief pause, she said, "I'm thinking about fixing your mask. How I can make the cracks less apparent when it's done."

"Elsa, please. Talk to me!" He put his hands on her legs, spinning her around on her stool so that she faced him. Her eyes widened again, her breath quickening.

"I don't understand," she said. "I am talking to you."

"Words. These are only words. What is on your mind? What is in your heart?" He leaned forward and kissed her, leaving his forehead resting against hers when he pulled back, his hands on the sides of her neck.

Lightly brushing his thumbs across her cheeks, he said, "I can touch you. I can kiss you. And yet, I feel that you are miles from me. I am bereft of your presence, and it is killing me. Please."

"I don't know what you want." Her voice was tight and thin. "I'm sorry."

Dante closed his eyes, remembering his conversation with Jazz a few moments ago. Apparently, this had happened before between the two friends. When Elsa had been dispirited and distant in the past, Jazz would harangue Elsa using topics she was quite passionate about until she finally fought back. In that way, they had emotionally reengaged.

Jazz's advice was simply to *rattle Elsa's cage.*

It went against everything Dante felt was right, and yet, Jazz was Elsa's oldest friend. He had no other insight with which to work.

"There is no need to apologize." He stepped away from Elsa, forcing his voice to be cold. "I believe I more fully understand the reality of our situation."

"What reality?"

"Your true desires are all too clear. You used your ability to bring the Phantom of the Opera to your time as your companion. Here I am."

He spread his arms wide in a theatrical gesture. That there might once have been some truth to his words pained him, and he let his displeasure show.

"That's not true," Elsa said, but then she snapped her mouth shut. At least she did not try to immediately withdraw her words or apologize.

"The irony is not lost upon me. All my life, I have been so concerned that people would look at me and only see my face. As if somehow the mask could not hide what lay beneath and I would be cursed to forever be reviled for my appearance. Yet with you, I fear that all you can see is the mask."

Her eyes were wide, her lips parted. He could practically see the words she longed to say fighting for their freedom. He pressed on.

"Tell me. When you look at me, do you see Dante, the man holding his heart out to you, or do you see this?" He gestured toward the mask in her hand. "A phantom?"

"You know I don't care about—"

"Don't you? Are you certain?"

He remembered his fear that she saw him as nothing more than research and his relief when he determined her password was his name. She had proven herself to him. He wanted to do the same for her, but she was not giving him a chance.

"If you care so little for the legend, why fix the mask? I have the modern one Garrett provided me. I can make others of new design and with better materials. Yet you fix this mask. Why is that?"

"This is what you're used to. I want you to be comfortable."

"Have you listened to anything I have said these past days? I want this world. I want this time. I do not care about familiarity. Relics from the past have no place with me, and yet you cling to them. You refuse to let go, of your fears, of your doubts, of this!"

He reached for the mask, but she jerked away. The piece she had been newly attaching came loose, and she lost her grip. He tried to catch the mask, but it bounced from his hand and fell, shattering against the floor.

Dante had not intended for the mask to break, though he could not say that he was sorry. Perhaps this time, she would let it go.

"Elsa, I—"

His voice caught in his throat when he saw the look in her eyes. They were wide as a startled dove's, her mouth hanging open and her delicate brows drawn so sharply together they nearly touched. Her chest rose and fell like a bellows.

"Are you hurt?" He reached for her so he could carry her over the debris on the floor.

Elsa ducked beneath his arm, stumbling in her eagerness to get away. Away from him.

"It was an accident."

She let out a mirthless laugh, then spat out, "Right. It's always an accident."

"I don't understand."

He took another step toward her, but she shrank back from him. She was frightened of him. He was trying to push her, yes, but he had never intended to frighten her.

Dante felt his heart shatter, the shards falling through his body, leaving his soul in tatters. He wished he could go back, could take it back, but it was too late for that. He could see it in her eyes. He had somehow gone too far.

"I'm sorry." He kept his voice as gentle as he could while trying to puzzle out what had affected her so greatly.

He knew that he had been expressing his frustration openly, but no more so than he had done in the past. He did not understand the severity of her reaction. She seemed frozen, staring at him with those terrified eyes.

He just wanted to fix it. If only he could fix it.

"Elsa, please. Say something. Do something."

Without a word, she bolted from the room.

It took him a few moments to recover, but when he did, he followed her. He could not let her slip away. He had to make her understand how sorry he was for his mistake. And once he did, he and Jazz were going to have a very long talk.

Chapter Twenty-Six

The last few moments replayed in Elsa's mind over and over again. Dante knocking the mask from her hand—everything seeming to slow down as it fell—the horrible crash as it hit the floor.

The instant the mask had left her grasp, she felt a small part of herself break. It was too familiar.

Once the courting was done, the *real* masks came off. The invisible ones that everyone wore until they had what they wanted. She was a fool to have thought it would be any different with Dante.

And now she was back in her usual hiding place—huddled on the floor in her bathroom, knees pulled to her chest, chewing on a towel to muffle her sobs so that no one would hear her. So that no one would find her.

She had never seen that side of him before. Was this the man that he was? The man he so desperately wanted her to see? If so, she wanted nothing to do with him. Nothing.

He'd never acted like this before, though. He'd been kind and gentle. He'd never made her feel afraid. Not like today. How could she have been so wrong? Maybe this was just what love did to people.

When she heard his soft rap on the door, her heart started beating frantically. Thank God she had remembered to lock it.

"Elsa? Are you all right?" His voice was deceptively gentle. The doorknob jiggled, and she scooted closer to the bathtub, pressing herself against it and hugging the towel to her chest. "I am so sorry. Please, this is all a terrible misunderstanding."

How many times had she heard her parents say that to each other? How many times had they talked their way back into the other's good graces, only to fly off the handle again at some imperceptible slight?

"I did not mean to frighten you." His voice sounded strange, constricted. "Please, let me explain. Winston and I were worried about you. You have been so withdrawn. We didn't know what to do, so we called Jazz. She said we needed to push you until you pushed back. I should have just talked to you, but I have been trying so hard to do things on my own, to show you that I do not need you."

Elsa heard Dante groan, then he said, "That came out wrong. It is not that I do not need you. I do. But not in the way you think I do."

She slowly stood, staring at the door. She could hear soft thumping, as if he was tapping on it or knocking his head against it. Every tap sounded like a threat. They echoed in her mind, taking her back to the child she had been, reminding her that she was trapped. Again.

"I love you," Dante said. "I am afraid I love you somewhat desperately, and that has led me down this errant path. Please forgive me. Please tell me how to fix this. I will do anything..."

And then he tried the doorknob again.

Elsa covered her ears to stop the sound of its rattling, and shrieked, "Go away!"

There was a long pause. She slowly lowered her hands from her ears, wondering if he had done as she asked and left. Strangely, the thought didn't comfort her. In fact, it threw her into a near panic.

She didn't want him to go away. She wanted him to be with her, the way he had been before. Laughing with her, sitting in the sun, spending time together in the studio.

But hadn't she changed first? He was right about her being withdrawn. She had purposefully shut herself away from him, trying to avoid the very situation they were in now.

"I will not trouble you further." There was a rough quality to his voice and it broke over the words, as if he could barely manage to speak them.

If he moved away from the door afterwards, she didn't hear him. Moments ticked away, counting down with her heartbeat. If he actually left, she imagined her heart would just stop. If he left, she'd be alone. Truly alone. She'd never get over it, never move beyond where she was.

It wasn't just Dante that Elsa was keeping out. She didn't let anyone in. Ever. And now, she had yet another excuse to keep everyone at arm's length, to keep them all at a distance. To keep herself safe. And alone.

If she had told Dante about her parents, he never would have listened to Jazz's advice. He would have understood what was bothering Elsa in the first place and helped her through it. She was certain of it.

But she hadn't even told Jazz, her oldest friend. Not even in college, when Elsa went to identify her mother's body after she wrapped her car around a tree during another drinking binge. Elsa told Jazz she was away on family business and refused to answer any questions until Jazz finally gave up.

Elsa kept everyone out. She thought she was leaving her past behind by never mentioning it, but she was stuck there, making herself repeat it. Hiding in a bathroom again.

The result was a crushing loneliness that made her gasp for breath, that made her so desperate for companionship that she had traveled over one hundred years into the past to find a kindred soul. And even still, she couldn't—no, wouldn't—let Dante in.

This wasn't fair to either of them. She wouldn't let things go on this way. Elsa had allowed her fear to keep her isolated for long enough. She wouldn't remain trapped in her past.

Dante was her future, her present moment. Everything she wanted was right in front of her. All she had to do was have the courage to embrace it. And to do that, she had to let go of what she was holding on to.

She took a deep breath and opened the door.

Chapter Twenty-Seven

Panicked, Dante paced in his room, running his fingers through his hair and tugging on the strands as if he could pull ideas from his mind on how to fix the situation. No solutions came.

Elsa wanted him away from her. The very thought made his chest constrict painfully. He had terrified her, and he still did not understand how, what he had done that was so terribly wrong. How could he possibly fix a problem when he had no idea as to its cause?

He slumped down onto his bed, burying his face in his hands. If she wanted him to leave, he would, though it would devastate him.

He did not understand how she could have reacted so viscerally. The raw emotion on her face replayed in his mind, an image he did not think he would ever forget.

Elsa had been afraid of him. Terrified. It was his worst nightmare come true.

Despair was encroaching on his mind as he heard the door to his room swing open. Looking up, he was astonished to see Elsa standing in the doorway.

Dante did not dare move, afraid that she would flee again. So he sat where he was, waiting, praying, for her to come to him.

She lingered in the doorway, as if she was uncertain what she wanted to do. Finally, she took a tentative step over the threshold, and then another. When she was in the room, she turned and closed the door behind her.

Resting her forehead against the wood of the door, she said, "I know you didn't mean to scare me."

Dante longed to agree, but kept himself silent. He could tell she remained at the edge of flight by the tense way that she stood, how her shoulders were bunched so that they nearly brushed her ears.

"When the mask left my grasp, why did you reach for it?" she asked.

Her question baffled him, yet he could sense the importance of his answer. "Whatever your reasons, you had worked diligently to repair it. I was trying to catch it before it fell. I am sorry I failed to do so."

Her body trembled as she let out a huge breath. "That isn't what I thought happened. I'm glad I was wrong."

Eventually, she turned to face him, though her haunted gaze passed through him as if he was a ghost. She slowly crossed the room and sat on the farthest corner from him on the bed.

She looked even more hopeless than he had felt just a few moments ago. Dante wanted to wrap his arms around her, to tell her that everything would be all right, but he fought the impulse.

"My father left when I was ten," Elsa said, her voice having that same dull, emotionless quality as earlier in the studio. "I never talked about it. Not even with my mother when it happened. I'm not sure why he left."

She stared blankly at the floor for some time. Dante held his breath, willing her to continue. She cleared her throat and obliged.

"I was glad, really. That he left." She glanced briefly at him, perhaps to gauge his reaction. He tried to temper his surprise.

Her gaze dropped back to the floor. "When he was around, he and my mom fought. Constantly. Violently. They didn't send each other to the hospital often, but it did happen a few times. Mostly when they threw things."

She wrapped her arms around herself and shivered at some unseen memory. "When I was five, I ran between them, trying to get them to stop. I don't remember what it was that hit me, but they had to go to the hospital then. They grounded me for a month." She let out a sharp burst of air, a hollow specter of a laugh. "They grounded me for not ducking fast enough."

Dante felt his heart grow cold toward these callous people. To treat a child in such a manner was reprehensible. That his Elsa had suffered it made his heart break.

"After my dad left, my mom became an alcoholic. That's why I don't drink. I would go straight to the library or museum after school, stay there till they closed, and then go home and find something in the fridge and go to bed. On good days, she was passed out on the couch. On bad days, she was awake…"

Elsa's voice trailed off again. He waited patiently for her to go on.

"She would get sober every once in a while. Usually when she went back to church. It gave me just enough hope to think that maybe she would change, that she was finally ready to be a real mom." She turned to him and gave him a sad smile. "It's hard to give up on your parents. I think that's why I made my mistake."

Her gaze moved to the wall, as if she could see images, memories playing out across its surface. Dante waited as long as he could, but she seemed so forlorn, he could not bear to let her reverie continue.

As gently as he could, he said, "Your mistake?"

Elsa nodded, still staring at the wall, her eyes wide and unblinking. "I came home one day and she was on the couch, lying so still I thought she was dead. But her eyes were open and moving, as if she was watching something. It took me a while to figure out, but then I realized that she was traveling, like I do. I don't know what would trigger her. There was no art in the room, but I'm sure she was traveling."

"She shared your ability?" His astonishment overcame his caution for a moment, but Elsa seemed not to take note of his outburst.

"I'm pretty sure. I was so excited. She'd been sober for a long time then. I waited for her to come back to herself, and then I told her about what I could do."

Elsa's gaze changed, her eyes glazing over as she seemed to shrink into herself, her arms tightening around her middle.

"How did she respond?" Dante asked.

"Riding the Devil," Elsa said. "That's what she kept saying while she beat me."

His chest swelled with air as he sucked in a breath. He wanted to yell, to rail against the injustice Elsa had suffered, but that would certainly frighten her. At least now he understood the origin of her fear.

His arms twitched with the urge to hold her, to protect her, even from the memory. But he was uncertain if even that would overwhelm her in the face of such raw emotions.

"How could she?" The words slipped out before he could catch them, barely more than a whisper. When Elsa glanced at him, he said, "How could she when she shared your power?"

"Not that she ever admitted." Elsa shrugged, the deadened expression returned, along with that even monotone. She was shutting down, removing herself from emotions too strong to experience. "From then on, when she was sober, I was some kind of demon. When she was drunk, I was just a freak."

Rage built within him. His own experiences fed into his sympathy for her. He knew what it was like to be reviled in such a way. But that her own mother had done so, and for a trait that they shared... He found himself hating the woman.

"That was the worst part," Elsa said. "I thought it would help her to know she wasn't alone. I guess she really hated herself. And when I told her I was like her, she hated me too."

"I am so sorry."

Elsa shrugged again and her hands dropped to her lap. "When I turned sixteen, I became legally emancipated. I changed my name, I applied for early enrollment in college and worked hard to get all the scholarships I needed to get far away."

"Have you not spoken to her since?"

Elsa cleared her throat. When she went on, her voice was raspy. "I got a call from the police during my second year of college telling me that she had died. She was driving under the influence and she hit a tree." Elsa's breath became ragged. "At least she didn't hurt anyone else."

But Elsa had been hurt. All the walls that Dante faced, that he worked to overcome, finally made sense.

If her parents had presented violence masquerading as love, Elsa must have been terrified when Dante began to court her. And he had no idea how much courage she had demonstrated by sharing her secret with him. That her mother had *beaten* her when she did the same…

No wonder Elsa had found it so difficult to trust anyone. Such an early betrayal, and from the one person in the world who was supposed to love her unconditionally, as Dante's mother had loved him.

His heart bled for her.

Elsa had been dealing with so much—alone. He could scarcely believe she kept functioning.

A tear rolled down her cheek, and she quickly wiped it away. She was piecing herself back together from the shattered remnants of her childhood, just as she had pieced together Dante's mask—as she attempted to fix everything for those she cared about.

"I never looked back," she said. "At least, I didn't think so. Not until today. Today, I realized that I never really left." She turned to him, placing one hand on the bed between them. "Dante, I don't want to be there anymore."

He closed the distance between them at last, wrapping his arms around her and pulling her against his chest. "Then let it go. You need not remain in your past. All of this is done. You are here with me now."

She shuddered, then wrapped her arms around him, holding him tight. He kissed the top of her head.

"I don't know how to let go of this. It's clouded everything in my life."

"You have told me that I am free to build a life of my choosing. You have that same freedom. Release yourself from these memories. Put them behind you and do not dwell on them."

"You make it sound easy."

"I know that it is not. But if we want something, we must work toward it. Do you think that you can try?"

She was quiet for a moment, then said, "Yes. But it's going to take time."

"Said the time traveler to the man from the 1800s." He was gratified when she laughed, however briefly.

"I've never told anyone any of that."

"I will keep your secrets, if you wish. But I hope that you will consider sharing at least some of this with your friends. They are all good people. Supportive and caring. You do not need to go through this alone, and more than I will help you."

Elsa looked up at him and smiled. "I think I can actually believe that."

He smiled back at her, brushing stray locks of hair from her forehead and tucking them behind her ear. They sat together in silence for some time, holding each other close. His relief that he had not lost her was so great that he felt almost giddy.

"Sharing that was kind of a big deal," Elsa said. "I'm not sure what to do next."

"Whatever you want. Let us do something to make the present moment fill your mind. We could return to the studio, go for a walk in the garden—"

She lifted her lips to his, melting against him as she pushed him back onto the bed. Dante was delighted by her choice.

There was no pause as her tongue slid into his mouth, her hungry strokes fueling his desire. He tried to roll her over onto the bed, but she straddled him, putting her hands on his shoulders and holding him in place.

She had never taken such initiative, and he was eager to see what she had in mind.

Her hands slid down his chest, over his stomach. She deftly unfastened his pants, then leaned forward to kiss him as she ran her hand along his length. He gasped as waves of pleasure crashed through his body from her touch.

He had thought that she had given herself to him physically before, but this... This was different. There were no reservations as her hands roved his body, and each exploration of her lips, her fingertips, inflamed him more than they ever had before.

Dante finally rolled on top of her, grinding his hips against the warmth of her center, aching to feel her body clench around him. Her groans urged him on.

He sat back on his knees and pulled his shirt over his head, then tossed it aside. Elsa followed him up, raining heated kisses over his chest. She pulled off her own shirt and threw it after his.

Her breasts bared before him, he took a moment to drink in their beauty with his eyes before bending his head to them and covering each with loving kisses. As his lips latched onto one of the dusky buds, she gasped, burying her fingers in his hair and clutching him to her. She breathed his name on a whisper, conjuring streaks of lightning that arced through his body.

Reclaiming her lips, he pressed her back against the pillows. He reached down to rid her of her pajama bottoms with her assistance. She gave him no chance to linger, grabbing his wrist and pushing on his arm as if she thought to roll him onto his back once more. He indulged her, smiling as she straddled him again.

It took every effort of his will, but this was the first time that she had taken the lead in their lovemaking and he was not about to discourage her. He closed his eyes and focused on the sensations flooding his body.

Her kisses moved down his cheek and jaw, along his neck and collarbones. The hunger was still there, apparent in every nip of her teeth on his chest, the strength of her grip on his arms. He opened his eyes as she moved to rid him of his pants. Then she rose to her knees and simply looked at him.

Dante had learned not to be abashed by her gaze. In fact, he was starting to love it, as he loved everything about her. This amazing woman, whose gaze traveled over all of him—even his face—not just without wincing, but with reverence. He had worshipped her body as a temple, and now it seemed she was doing the same for him.

She ran her fingers down his chest again, through the dark trail of hair that led toward his manhood. Without his pants in the way, she gripped him in her hand, languidly stroking him as he gasped from the intensity of her touch. All the while, she kept her chestnut eyes locked on his, watching his reaction, gauging what gave him the greatest pleasure.

She leaned forward to press a kiss against his navel, her mouth moving in a slow line farther down. He was not sure of her intentions until she looked up at him, her tongue running quickly over her kiss-swollen lips. His mouth went dry at the sight.

He managed to swallow and was about to say something, when Elsa dipped her mouth to his shaft, running her tongue over the tip. He nearly came right then. His breath left him in a rush, incredible sensations sparking through his body at this, most intimate kiss. She continued to wet his crown, then wrapped her lips around his shaft, taking him into her mouth.

He pressed his head back against the pillow, trying desperately not to release. He groaned from the effort, which only spurred her on. Her hand kept moving, even as she swirled her tongue around him and sucked him deep within her mouth. It was taking him too close to the edge.

Finally finding his voice, he said, "Elsa," in an urgent, hoarse whisper. He moved his fingers through her hair, tilting her face up so that he could look at her. And still, she did not stop. "Please."

She lifted her head from him, her sultry smile promising pleasures he could scarcely imagine.

"Are you asking me to stop or continue?"

Dante swallowed hard. "I fear that if you continue, I shall not last long."

She simply shrugged. "That's fine. We have all night. And tomorrow. And the next night."

She dipped her head to him once more, running her tongue along the entire length of his shaft. Another groan escaped him before he could stop it, but as much as he was intrigued by the idea of letting her continue her stimulating ministrations, he wanted even more to feel himself inside of her, buried deep. He wanted to know this ravishing Elsa completely.

He had experienced her body, but not her heart. Until now.

Elsa was giving him everything. At last, nothing stood between them.

He reached out for her, then pulled her against his chest and rolled her onto her back so he could lie on top of her. She smiled up at him, eyes crinkling at the corners. The sight of her so joyful took his breath away.

His heart was pounding, along with other parts of his anatomy. This was a true union. He could barely wait to begin, yet knew he was still too aroused to last long if he hurried. He wanted to savor every nuance.

He settled between her legs, letting his shaft rest just at her entrance, but not pressing further, no matter how much he wished to. He kissed her, but kept his kisses slow, his tongue languidly thrusting inside her mouth. He could feel her writhing, trying to pull him closer, deeper, but he kept himself only barely parting the warm flesh of her quim.

Finally, when she seemed to be growing more frustrated than tantalized, he thrust himself deep.

She cried out as he filled her, her fingers digging into his back. He took a deep, shuddering breath as he regained his control once more. She had brought him so close to the edge. It was his turn to do the same for her.

Slowly, he rocked his hips, feeling her clench around him as if her body was reluctant to let him go even a little. He relished the feeling as he moved within her, his lips trailing down her neck, where he suckled her skin till he left his mark on her.

He could feel her passion growing, mirroring his own. Pressure built within him, spurring him on to thrust faster, deeper, until she finally shouted his name, her legs wrapping around his as she pulled him as deep as she could within her.

His body answered hers as if a nova had gone off within him, every atom thrumming as waves of heat rippled out from where they were joined. Spent, he collapsed on top of her, their breaths mingling as they panted from the intensity of their union.

On a gasping breath, she said, "Dante…"

He lifted himself on his elbows, smoothing her hair away from her face. He kissed her, then said, "Yes, Elsa?"

She smiled at him, but the mischievous edge was gone. She simply looked happy.

And then she said, "I love you."

Chapter Twenty-Eight

"Are you ever going to tell me what you and Jazz are up to?"

Elsa was lying with her head on Dante's chest. They had spent more time in bed than out of it over the last few days, and she was still in a bit of a stupor from their most recent activities.

"Whatever are you referring to?" His voice echoed in her ear like the low rumble of thunder.

"Yesterday's visit. I know she wasn't just here to visit Winston."

"No, she was also visiting you."

"And you."

Elsa knew they were planning something, but she actually didn't care too much what it was. She was curious, but she trusted them. She was still getting used to the feeling.

"There is something I wish to show you." Dante stroked her hair away from her shoulder, the strands tickling her back.

She raised an eyebrow. "You know, at some point, we really are going to need to sleep."

"That is not what I meant. Although, now that you mention it…"

He rolled her onto her back, kissing her slowly, as if savoring every touch. He paused, then lifted himself on his elbows. "I thought we might go into town later."

A spike of nervousness shot through her at the thought, but she knew they couldn't hide in their home forever. She wasn't sure when she had started thinking of her home as *theirs*, but realizing it made her happy. It was their home, for as long as he wanted to live there.

She pushed away the doubts that still chewed at the corners of her mind. All she had was this moment, and she was going to enjoy it. "Okay."

"I do suppose our trip could wait a little while longer." Dante nuzzled the side of her neck.

"Only a little?"

Elsa hadn't been able to distract Dante for too long. The afternoon sun beat down on them as she drove her convertible toward town. He seemed to be enjoying the trip. He wasn't even bothering to wear the mask Garrett had given him.

The sight of Dante smiling, his eyes closed and his face tilted up toward the sun, was one of the most beautiful things she had ever seen. His linen shirt was open to the wind, his long legs stretched out before him.

He looked so relaxed. It was all she could do to keep her concentration on the road, but she managed, focusing more intently when they crossed into the city limits.

She had a feeling they were headed for the gallery, and he didn't correct her as she drove in that direction. Elsa found a parking spot as close as she could manage. By the time she stepped onto the street, Dante was there, offering his arm.

He didn't lead her toward the gallery. Instead, they walked across the street, then down a few blocks. She wanted to ask him where they were going, but took a deep breath and used the opportunity to practice giving up control. Hopefully, someday it would be easier.

They headed up the walkway to an apartment building that gleamed brightly in the afternoon sun. White walls, glass and chrome gave it a modern look.

Dante smiled broadly as he opened the door for her and followed her into the lobby. She had never seen him so excited.

"Good afternoon, Mr. Lucerne." A dark-haired man in a suit approached them from across the large open space. He blinked when he saw Dante's face, his smile seeming to stumble for a moment, but it passed quickly. When he reached them, he shook Dante's hand. "Ms. Montgomery has been very busy. I hope you're pleased with the results."

"I'm certain we will be delighted," Dante said. If he had noticed the man's reaction, he wasn't calling attention to it. Gesturing to Elsa, Dante said, "This is Miss Sinclair."

"Ah, yes. Miss Sinclair." The man bowed slightly, then shook her hand. He pulled a key out of his pocket and gave it to her. "Ms. Montgomery let me know to expect you."

She stared at the key, her curiosity reaching a breaking point. Dante covered her hand with his, curling her fingers over the key. He slid his arm around her waist and guided her toward the stairs.

"Thank you, Charles," Dante said.

When they had climbed to the third floor, passing a gorgeous waterfall built into the wall, Elsa said, "Charles?"

"I was able to accomplish a great deal on the day I ran errands with Rachel," Dante said. He led Elsa down a corridor deeper into the building. "As you will soon see."

Her stomach was doing flip-flops. She hadn't decided yet if they were the good kind or the bad. But Dante was still smiling, his expression a mix of pride and happiness. She forced herself to smile back at him.

She kept telling herself everything was going to be fine. Whatever this mysterious surprise was, it was going to be good.

"Are you all right?" he asked.

"Yes. I'm just a little nervous, I guess." That was another thing she was getting used to. Actually telling someone how she felt instead of pushing her emotions aside.

"Please trust me a little longer. I promise, I won't disappoint you."

"You could never disappoint me."

Dante traced his fingertips over her cheek and along her neck. He bent down to kiss her briefly, then smiled as he stepped behind her. She was left staring at the door to an apartment marked 3B.

"Open it," he said.

Her heart was racing as she unlocked the door and opened it. Dante gestured for her to go inside.

"After you."

Elsa stepped into a loft with floors of honey-gold hardwood and bright white walls. All the fixtures were chrome, and the wall facing her was made of windows that climbed two stories. There were no curtains, light streaming in and reflecting off every surface, almost blinding her.

An island counter separated the kitchen area from the rest of the great room she stood within, and a spiral staircase led to a second level that covered half the loft.

"I shall return presently," Dante said. "If you will give me but a few moments."

"Okay…"

He walked up the staircase, leaving Elsa alone. She crossed to the windows, impressed by the spectacular view. Restless, she turned back to the great room and noticed an easel in one corner. There were shelves built into the wall behind it filled with paints, brushes and blank canvases.

A few abstract paintings hung on the walls. Aside from the art, splashes of color were added by a few bright cushions on the white couch. Some dyed glass vases filled with exotic flowers softened what otherwise might have seemed too starkly modern. There were more cushions in hanging mesh chairs suspended from the raised level above.

"Hammock chairs," she murmured.

"Thank you for waiting."

Elsa glanced back to the stairs. As Dante trotted down the spiraling metal, her breath caught in her chest.

Dark brown loafers had replaced his polished shoes, and he wore formfitting jeans that showed off his strong, long legs. His backside looked so good, she couldn't imagine anyone not drooling over the sight. The linen shirt she was so used to was replaced by a comfortable-looking T-shirt, tucked in at the waist and accenting his perfect V-figure.

His hair was still mussed from their ride in the convertible, and he had spent so much time in the sun that it had lightened to a tawny brown. It hung around his face in flowing waves. Elsa wanted nothing more than to bury her fingers in it.

She stammered a bit, then said, "This is yours, isn't it?" She looked around the loft again, tearing her gaze away from him for the briefest of moments.

He smiled as he approached, then leaned down and kissed her, leisurely exploring her, as if they had all the time in the world. Ending the kiss at last, he said, "I prefer to think of it as ours." He paused, some of the enthusiasm leaving his voice. "Do you like it?"

"Dante, this..."

It was completely antithetical to the room that she had made for him in her manor. She had strived to recreate the home that she thought would comfort him, but she'd just been perpetuating a life he'd already decided to leave behind.

"If you do not like it, we can make changes," he said. "I truly want this to be your home as well. I want you to feel welcome here—comfortable, as you made me feel when you opened your home to me."

"I don't understand how you did this."

A sudden thought struck her, as she remembered Jazz and Dante's quiet conversations that ended abruptly when Elsa approached. She glanced at his fingers, searching for what she already knew wouldn't be there.

"Where is your mother's ring?"

He took her hands in his and kissed each of them. "That ring has bound many lives together. My parents, and Mary and Edgar. Now, for us, in its way. Do not be distressed that it has been freed to continue its journey."

Elsa's heart tightened, but she nodded. She had already visited every moment she could connect to through the ring. They were both letting go of the past. This was Dante's choice to make. Still, she would miss having it close.

He drew her into an embrace, kissing the top of her head. "You never answered my question. Do you like it?"

"I love it." She laughed, wiping the back of her hand across her tear-filled eyes. "I knew it was your place as soon as I saw the hammocks."

"They add a certain modern sensibility, don't you think?" He said it deadpan, but then grinned.

She laughed again, and let him lead her farther into the loft. A few feet from his painting area, there was a writing desk with a cushioned chair. The wood was deep chestnut brown and the upholstery a rich gold. The design of the set was a perfect mix of classic and contemporary style.

"I thought perhaps this could be your writing desk," Dante said.

Elsa felt tears on her cheeks. For once, she didn't care. He had built a new life for himself, but had made sure there was a place for her in it, right at his side.

"Do you not like it?" he asked

"I love it." She threw her arms around his neck and pulled him down for a deep kiss.

When she finally released him, he laughed. "Well, I believe you have made your sentiment quite clear."

"Maybe we should go upstairs so I can show you what I really think of the place."

"As appealing as that sounds, there is one more stop on our trip, and I am afraid if I take you upstairs now, we will not leave this place for quite some time."

"True." She grabbed his arm and pulled him toward the door. "Let's go."

"You seem to be in quite a hurry."

She stopped, leaning in and running her hands up his chest, finally burying her fingers in his hair as she pulled him closer and kissed him again. She nibbled her way to his ear, tantalizing the sensitive skin until his hands were clutching the back of her shirt.

"The sooner we go," she whispered in his ear, "the sooner we can come back."

Dante groaned, dropping his forehead to her shoulder. "I am so tempted to stay."

She stepped away from him, then grinned as she took his arm once more. Leading him toward the door, she asked, "Where is this mysterious second stop?"

"The gallery, of course."

"Of course."

They laughed the entire way back to the gallery, though she couldn't remember exactly why. She was just so happy. She had never been so happy in her entire life.

Dante grew quieter when they entered the gallery, but he was still smiling as he led her into one of the back rooms. It was roped off, not ready for public viewing yet.

"If Jazz catches us back here, she's going to be really mad," Elsa said.

"Ah, but new exhibits are only off-limits to the public. They aren't off-limits to the artist." He stood in the center of the room, that same gentle smile on his face.

The artist? Her heart soared as she slowly spun around, taking in all of the paintings hanging on the walls. Dante's landscapes. She was surrounded by his vision of the world.

Elsa had always thought his paintings were inspired, but seeing so many of them at once, seeing them all on display, they were breathtaking.

"Dante, this is—"

"Wait, this is not all of them."

He put his hands on her arms, turning her around and guiding her toward the wall opposite the door. A large canvas covered with a sheet filled her view.

"I waited to let anyone see it until I had your approval," he said. "I wanted to be certain that you are comfortable with it first."

"Comfortable with what?" She looked at the nameplate as he worked the sheet loose. *Portrait of my love.*

Dante whisked the sheet away, revealing a portrait of Elsa sitting at her writing desk and staring off into the distance. There was a softness around her eyes in the painting that made her look vulnerable, a hopefulness in her parted lips, and a glow about her that made her heart catch in her throat.

"Do you like it?" he asked, stepping behind her and sliding his arms around her waist.

His secret painting. It was a portrait of Elsa.

"Is this how you see me?" She could barely speak, her throat was so tight with emotion.

He pressed a kiss to the top of her head and pulled her closer against his chest. "Yes. It is how I have always seen you. But you haven't answered my question."

"I love it."

Dante let out a breath, hugging her more tightly. "I am so glad. But are you comfortable with me displaying it? I rather think it completes the exhibit."

"I'm honored."

She was more than honored. She could feel herself surrounded by Dante's love, and for once, when she felt her soul stirring from the incredibly moving pieces of art around her, she was absolutely content to stay just where she was. She didn't want to disappear. There was nowhere else she would rather be in the world—in the universe, in all of time—than right here in his arms.

He had managed to make a life for himself without her help, a life he wanted to share with her. He'd known her fears about him being dependent on her, and he had proven them baseless. She turned around, staring up at him.

"How did you do all of this?"

"I did not do it alone. Your friends have been incredibly supportive. Rachel took care of decorating our loft, and Jazz has been…" He shook his head, and said, "Amazing."

"I still don't understand—"

Dante leaned down and kissed Elsa before she could say anything else. He kissed her deeply, passionately, until her head spun from lack of oxygen. Or maybe it was just his arms around her, his closeness, the love and trust that was still so new to her.

"You're doing that on purpose, aren't you?" she asked when he let her come up for air.

"Only when necessary."

He kissed her again, this time, presumably without ulterior motive. She let her fingers burrow through his hair, clutching him against her as if she would never let him go. But she would have to for just a little while, until they could get back to their loft.

They walked out of Dante's exhibit room, arms around each other's waists. Nothing stood in their way now. They could have the life together that she had always dreamed of. An even better one, because it was one they were going to create together.

They had almost exited the gallery when a loud crash, followed by swearing, caught their attention. From the stream of Mandarin that followed, Elsa knew Jazz was in her very rare freak-out mode.

Dante took Elsa's hands and led her toward their friend. "We should find out if she needs assistance," he said. Elsa nodded.

They found Jazz kneeling in the middle of another roped-off room. A display stand was on its side on the floor, brochures surrounding it. Jazz was on her knees, gathering them together.

"Let us help you," Elsa said.

She knelt next to Jazz and started gathering brochures. Dante righted the stand, then set it down slightly off to the side so it wasn't in their way.

Jazz said something else in Mandarin that had to be a curse-word. "Thanks. I'm running so far behind, and Rachel hasn't shown up yet. The new exhibits open tonight, and—" Jazz looked up, as if seeing Dante and Elsa for the first time. "Oh, Dante. I'm glad you're here. Is your exhibit ready? I want to open it tonight along with this one. Can you be here?"

"The exhibit is ready to show, however, I believe Elsa may have other plans for me this evening." He gave Elsa a mischievous grin, running his hand down her back as he knelt beside her to help pick up brochures.

"Let me have him for one night." Jazz turned to Elsa, waving brochures. "Honestly, I'm trying to start his career here."

"I'm sure we can work something out," Elsa said. "But you really need to calm down."

"Calm down? Rachel decides to miss work for the first time ever on the opening night of not one, but two brand-new exhibits. And you want me to calm down?"

"She didn't call?"

"No. And she's not answering her phone, either."

Elsa felt a heavy weight in the pit of her stomach. "That's not like her."

"Who knows what she's like anymore. Ever since she started dating this guy." Jazz gestured around the room. Only then did Elsa notice the art hanging on the walls.

A dozen portraits of women surrounded her. There was a brutality in the brush strokes, dark paints and shadows dominating each scene. All of the subjects were hiding their faces, cowering from view.

She stood up slowly, the fine hairs on her body standing on end. The brochures dropped to the floor from her suddenly numb fingers as she turned in a circle.

As expansive and filled with light and hope as Dante's paintings were, these were the exact opposite. Elsa felt the weight of them crushing her. She collapsed into a ball, trying to make herself smaller, to get away from the feeling, but it was everywhere.

Snakes crawling on her skin. Ants in her veins. Sheer, naked terror.

There was no hope in this room. Only despair.

And then she traveled.

It wasn't like any of the times she'd traveled before. She felt herself leave her body, but she moved straight up into the air and could look down and see the city beneath her. It was like she was flying, but she couldn't control where she was going.

She felt herself being pulled away from the city, to an area sparsely housed and overgrown with palms and patches of Evergreen. She plummeted toward the earth so quickly that she screamed, though she knew no one could hear her.

When she landed, it took her a moment to realize that she had stopped. There was no light. She was so disoriented, it seemed she could feel the world spinning.

She heard a faint rattling noise. Chains. And then she heard a whimper. Someone was in the room with her.

A door opened and a light came on, casting the room in a harsh fluorescent glare. Elsa was in a garage completely filled with workbenches and shelves. Mason jars containing nails, broken glass and other bits and pieces sat in meticulous lines on every shelf.

The center of the floor held an easel, with a huge canvas visible above the tops of the workbenches. Two vaguely feminine forms had been outlined in what she thought at first was heavy graphite, but there was a weird reddish cast to it. One of the figures was just starting to be filled in with dark paints.

Michael stepped into the room, his hair tied back and a crimson smear on the front of his white shirt. His lips were pulled in a tight smile. He was wiping something bright and red from his hands with a towel.

"That was really stupid, you know." He rubbed the towel over his shirt. "Now I need to take more."

Elsa followed at a distance as he navigated the labyrinthine room. Chains were bolted to the far wall, ending in manacles around a woman's wrists. She had her arms over her head and her blonde hair was matted and tangled. Her wrists were covered in rough cuts, blood coating the metal. She looked up at Michael, and Elsa felt as if lightning had struck her.

Oh God, she thought. *Rachel.*

"It's a big night for me, Rachel," Michael said. "You're so selfish. This is my night. Mine!"

Rachel flinched as he yelled, hunching closer to the wall. Michael went to a cupboard and took out a mason jar and a length of plastic tubing attached to a needle. He carried them over to Rachel, then set them on the workbench nearest her.

As he bent toward Rachel, Elsa tried to get between them, to shove him away. Her hands passed through him.

"It's okay," he said, smoothing Rachel's hair. "You all think you're so much better than me, but I know the truth. I'm the one that's going to make you immortal. What does that make me, Rachel? Think about what that makes me."

Rachel let out a whimper as Michael stood. "I have to get ready for my opening. I'll be leaving for the gallery soon. Just remember next time you want to throw a fit that I can always take more. And I will take more. Till there's nothing left."

Michael walked away, and Rachel collapsed against the wall, sobbing.

Before Elsa could do anything else, she felt as if a tether connected to her middle had suddenly been pulled taut. She found herself hurtling back over town toward the gallery. With a jarring jolt, she snapped back into her body, arms lashing out at whoever was holding her.

"Elsa! Are you all right?"

Glancing around, Elsa saw that she was in a different room in the gallery. Dante was on the floor next to her, holding her against his chest. Jazz hovered just behind him, one hand holding her phone and the other clasped over her mouth. Dante looked stricken, a deep furrow between his brow and his eyes wide with fear.

"Dante?" Elsa said.

"Thank God. I thought I'd lost you." His arms tightened around her.

"No." Elsa pushed him away, trying to get to her feet.

She didn't have time to be comforted by Dante. Rachel was out there—scared, alone, hurt. Michael said he was going to the gallery, so she might be safe for a while, but what if he went back?

Elsa had to get to Rachel. To save her.

"What the hell, Elsa?" Jazz slid her phone back into its holder at her waist. "Was that some kind of seizure?"

As Dante helped Elsa to her feet, she realized she couldn't save Rachel alone. And no secret was worth Rachel's life.

"You need to call the police and paramedics, right now."

Jazz pulled her phone back out, then paused. "Police?"

Elsa nodded. "Send them to Michael's house."

"What are you talking about?"

"Michael has kidnapped Rachel. He's hurting her." Elsa shook her head, the horror of what she had seen returning. "I think he's going to kill her."

"What are you talking about?" Jazz said. "Michael's a little off, but —"

"Jazz, I'm telling you, I know this. I just saw him."

"You saw him? How?"

Elsa reached down and found Dante's hand, gripping it tightly, as if it was a lifeline. It was time to trust Jazz, to tell her.

"I can't explain everything now, but that wasn't a seizure. It was more like a vision."

Jazz snorted. "What, you're psychic now?"

"No. I mean, yes." Elsa shook her head. "I honestly don't know what I am. I've always been too afraid to research it."

"Research what?"

"I can use art to leave my body and travel to other places and times."

"This is really lame," Jazz said. "You know I'm a believer."

"Then believe me. Michael has Rachel. If you don't want to call the police, fine. But at least tell me where Michael lives so I can go and help her."

Jazz was still scowling. She crossed her arms and glared at Elsa.

She had no idea what to say. She'd spent so much time trying to hide what she could do, she never thought about people not believing her. Elsa had to convince Jazz to help.

"Please, Jazz. He's hurting her."

Chapter Twenty-Nine

Dante's stomach clenched as he thought through the implications of what Elsa had told them. He had sensed that Rachel needed help, but had no idea how far things had gone.

"I know this must be a shock for you, Jazz, but you must believe Elsa."

Whatever Elsa had seen, it terrified her. He and Jazz had watched as Elsa's expression changed from fear to horror, as her body started to convulse, her limbs flailing wildly.

The only thing he could think to do was to get Elsa away from the art in Michael's room. Dante was terrified himself—that it was not the proper course of action, that he might lose her forever.

"You're in on this too?" Jazz said. "I bet this is Rachel's idea. I don't have time for jokes, and this one sure as hell isn't funny."

"Rachel's the one who doesn't have time!" Elsa said. "I can't believe all these years I was so afraid to tell you about what I can do, and you don't even believe me."

"Maybe because it's you. You're the most grounded person I've ever met. We've known each other for a decade. There's no way that you could be into this stuff without me knowing."

"I've been hiding it," Elsa said. "I use art to travel through time to research my books. That's why I had you find all those pieces for me over the years. That's why I always insisted on a private viewing alone in a locked room the first time I saw them. I didn't want anyone else to know."

Jazz remained unmoved. "This is bullshit."

"I'll prove it to you. When I went into that room and saw Michael's paintings, I traveled to his house. Normally, I go to different times, but I traveled over the city instead."

Elsa closed her eyes, her brow furrowed in concentration. Dante wrapped his arms around her to anchor her where she was. He didn't want her to leave again. Not to go to such a horrible place.

"He lives several miles south of town," Elsa said. "Away from the suburbs, in a forested area near swampland."

"You could've looked that up." Some of the harshness left Jazz's features, pensiveness taking its place.

"But I didn't. Rachel is in danger. I'm begging you to help me."

"So all this time, you've been using astral projection for your research?"

"Astral what?"

"Astral projection. The ability of the soul to travel outside the body, unbound by the limits of space or time."

"That is quite an accurate description." Dante wished he could ask Jazz more questions. She seemed to know more about Elsa's ability than anyone.

"Let me guess," Jazz said. "You're a time traveler too."

He could hardly refute it, but now was not the time to open himself up to a line of inquiry regarding his origins. He simply said, "I am Dante Lucerne."

"Yeah, I know." Her forehead creased and her mouth fell open as she stared at him. Her arms dropped to her sides. "Wait a minute—"

"We don't have a minute!" Elsa said. "I swear to you, I will answer all your questions after we've saved Rachel."

Jazz nodded. "Have your phone handy. I'll send you his address, then call the cops. When this is done, we're going to have a long talk."

Elsa grabbed Jazz and hugged her briefly, then practically ran for the door. Dante muttered a hasty, "Thank you," and followed.

The car's engine was already humming when he jumped into the passenger's seat. Elsa accelerated away from the curb so quickly her tires screeched in protest.

"We must be alive in order to help Rachel," he said.

Elsa nodded and slowed down a bit, but did not turn to look at him. Her gaze was intent upon the road, her focus palpable. He wondered if she had been this intense when trying to save him.

One thing he knew for certain. She would do whatever it took to save Rachel. And so would he.

Moments later, he was relaying Michael's address to Elsa from the text message Jazz sent to Elsa's phone.

When they reached Michael's home, Elsa didn't bother trying to be furtive. She drove right down the driveway and stopped close to the house. Dante looked around them, but did not see any other cars. Perhaps they were fortunate and Michael had indeed gone to the gallery as Elsa thought.

The gravel of the drive crunched beneath her feet as she leapt from the car. She ran to the trunk and opened it. Dante wasn't certain what she had in mind until she pulled out a large metal cross. From his research on cars, he knew that it was one of the tools used to change tires. This one had a flattened end that could be used as a crowbar.

He followed her to the house. "Should we not wait for the police?"

"I don't know if we have enough time for that."

She tested the door, but it was locked. With barely a pause, she smashed the glass window that ran alongside it with the tool, then knocked out all the loose shards. She reached in to unlock the door and let them in.

They passed through a small foyer. She led him toward the right side of the house, where the garage was situated. A door with a heavy padlock blocked their way. She struck at the lock with her tool to no avail.

"Allow me." He took the tool and placed the flat end between the door and the metal that held the lock in place. Prying the mounting loose took much less force than trying to break the lock itself.

Elsa pushed open the door when he was done, then turned on a light as she stepped into the garage. She did not even have to look at the switch to find it.

The room was completely filled with neat rows of shelves and workbenches. There were narrow aisles between them, but it was impossible to see the entire area at once. The shelves were metal and filled with jars. Some held screws and nails, some pencils or bits of broken glass. Some held liquid with things floating in them that Dante refused to examine too closely.

One of the jars contained fragments of porcelain. Dante halted for a moment, drawn to the familiar material, the shape of the larger pieces... A chill swept over him as he realized it had once been his original mask.

Michael had been the one who broke into their home. The very idea made Dante's skin crawl. They must leave as quickly as possible.

Elsa ignored the shelves and ran along the rows of workbenches toward the far wall. She disappeared from view as she dropped to the floor. Dante heard her say, "Rachel? Rachel, it's Elsa."

He ran to assist them, but froze in horror when the women came into view. Rachel was chained to the wall, her arms outstretched like a butterfly pinned in a collector's case. She was deathly pale, dark circles standing out under her eyes like welts. The hopelessness and despair on her face was worse than any he had ever seen.

"Elsa?" Rachel's voice was thin and gritty. She was still blinking repeatedly, her eyes adjusting to the bright light overhead. "Oh no. Did he get you too?"

"No, sweetie. We're here to rescue you."

"Oh thank God," Rachel sobbed, leaning against Elsa. "How are you going to get me loose?"

The chains rattled as she moved, even with the little amount of slack in them. Her bloodied manacles were pulled tight against the wall, threaded through the first of several grommets that trailed up to the ceiling. Dante followed the lengths of chain to where more grommets suspended the taut metal above them before the chains trailed back down to a winch firmly anchored on the floor.

He stepped forward, determined to free Rachel. "Do not be afraid. I will have you free presently."

Rachel turned her haunted eyes toward him. "Dante?"

"Did you not recognize me with my new look?" He was trying to distract her, to give her some respite from her terrifying circumstance.

He kept his tone light, belying the turmoil within him at what had been done to her.

The skin of her wrists would be scarred. Every time she saw those scars, she would remember this event. The horror of it. After escaping her bonds, she would still have to free herself from the cage of fear Michael had created for her.

But Rachel was surrounded by friends. She would not be alone in this.

Dante managed to work the winch, slowly letting out all of the slack in Rachel's chains. Once that was done, he began to use the tool to try to pry the anchor of the chains free from the floor. It was much safer than trying to break the manacles.

Rachel let out a low moan. "That will take forever. Dante, you have to get Elsa out of here."

Elsa smoothed Rachel's hair away from her face, making shushing noises and holding her close. "It's okay, Rachel. I'm not leaving without you."

"You don't understand. He wants you too."

"Well, he can't have me," Elsa said. "And he can't have you, either."

Rachel clung to Elsa, sobbing against her as Dante kept trying to get the chains free. Rachel would be able to move about now, but she was still trapped in the garage. If only they could find the key to her manacles.

"Dante…" Elsa said.

"I know," he said. "I am hurrying."

A chill swept over Dante's neck, and he turned back toward the door. He saw a flicker of movement through the shelves.

"Elsa, run!"

He turned back to her, but his words were drowned out by a loud bang. The sound of shattering glass accompanied it, along with a searing pain that ripped across the side of his face.

His vision clouded with red. Dante fell to his knees. He lifted his hand to his cheek, but his fingers flinched away faster than he could command them to—pricked by sharp objects embedded in his flesh. Elsa screamed, possibly his name, but it was hard to hear over the rushing sound of blood in his ears.

She appeared at his side, but he waved her away, back between the workbenches. She had to stay out of the aisle he was kneeling in, out of Michael's sight.

She looked stricken, but nodded. She grabbed the tool from where it had landed nearby, then disappeared around the side of the workbench.

That was not what he had intended. He wanted to keep her safe. Instead, knowing her, she was planning to sneak up on Michael to attack him.

The best that Dante could do was provide a distraction. He managed to rise to his feet, using the workbench to steady himself, though the movement sent threads of agony worming through his brain.

The pain clouded his thoughts. Blood was flowing freely down his neck, coating his chest beneath his T-shirt and making it stick to his skin. His only thought was that he had to help Elsa, to protect her and Rachel.

"Whatever it takes," he whispered.

Chapter Thirty

"This is more than I hoped for." Michael emerged in the space between the shelves. He kept his gun pointed at Dante. "I get Elsa hand-delivered, and the freak thrown in for free." He laughed, then said, "I think I've made an improvement on your face."

Elsa had never hated anyone more in her life. She ducked back out of sight, praying that Rachel was staying hidden now that she could at least move within a few rows of the workbenches.

Elsa clutched the tire iron in her hand tightly as she crept up behind Michael. His attention was on Dante. If she could sneak up behind Michael, she could clock him. It was the best plan she could come up with.

"I can't believe that Jazz wanted me to share the opening with you," Michael said. "I'm a true artist. Not like you, with your boring little landscapes. How much are you willing to sacrifice for your art?"

"Art is about creation, not sacrifice," Dante said.

"There is no creation without sacrifice. I'm willing to give up what I love most. Over and over again. I imbue the canvas with their essence. It's how I immortalize them."

Elsa could see the backs of Michael's legs. He had stepped closer to Dante, giving her more room to work. She slowly stood, brandishing her weapon, though her hands shook.

"And how many women have you immortalized?" Dante asked.

"How many paintings have I done?"

She thought of all those canvases in Michael's exhibit, each one representing a lost life. All of her hesitation vanished.

She brought the tire iron down on the back of Michael's head as hard as she could, hearing a sickening crunch. He crumpled to the ground, and his gun skittered underneath the workbenches, toward the far wall.

Dante's knees gave out just then. Elsa tried to run to him, but Michael's hand snaked out, grabbing her ankle.

She fell to the floor hard, hitting her chin with enough force that she saw stars. Dante was dragging himself toward her, but Michael pulled her back, out of Dante's reach. Michael's hands locked around her throat, cutting off her air.

"You think you can make a fool out of me?" he shouted. "You're mine! You belong on my canvas. All of you!"

She struck at Michael's arms, but his grip never loosened. When she clawed at his face, he put even more of his weight on her throat. He straightened his arms to get away from her nails.

The lights seemed to be dimming when another loud bang echoed through the garage.

Michael's grip went slack. He looked down at the rich crimson circle spreading out from the center of his chest, then past her, before falling forward like a puppet whose strings had been cut. His eyes remained open and staring.

Elsa hacked and retched, rolling onto her side as she gasped for air. When she recovered enough to look back toward Dante, she saw Rachel standing behind him, holding Michael's gun. Rachel was still pointing it at Michael's body, as if she expected him to move again.

Elsa wasn't sure he wouldn't. Though his eyes stared sightlessly at her, she wondered if at any moment he might lunge at her again.

Apparently, Rachel wasn't willing to risk it. As Elsa scooted away from Michael, Rachel walked toward him, her chains clattering with each step. She fired round after round into his body and kept pulling the trigger even when the gun merely clicked.

Michael wouldn't be getting up again.

Elsa struggled to her feet and cautiously made her way to Rachel. When Elsa was close enough, she put her arms around Rachel and reached down to take the gun. Rachel's gaze remained fixed on Michael's body.

Desperate to check on Dante, Elsa led Rachel to where he had fallen. Elsa set the gun on the workbench closest to him, then knelt at his side.

There was so much blood. She didn't even know how she could apply pressure to stop the bleeding.

Bits of glass and other shrapnel stuck out from his right cheek and temple. She couldn't keep herself from crying as she looked at him, carefully smoothing back his hair.

"You've never cried when you looked at my face before." He actually chuckled.

Elsa lowered her forehead to his for a moment, then pressed a kiss against his left temple where the skin was still intact. "I'm so sorry this happened to you," she whispered.

"Is Rachel safe?"

"She's okay. She'll be okay. We all will," Elsa said, though there was a part of her that was wondering, doubting. She pushed that part away.

Dante would be fine. He had to be.

Footsteps sounded behind them. She glanced over her shoulder, relieved beyond belief to see Jazz and Garrett standing in the doorway. Elsa heard the sound of sirens approaching.

"Oh my God, Elsa," Jazz said. "Are you okay?"

"No." Elsa's voice broke on a sob. "Dante's hurt."

Jazz went to Rachel and Garrett ran to Elsa's side, his eyes briefly darkening as he took in the bruises that must already be forming on Elsa's throat. She shook her head, then looked at Dante. Garrett's focus needed to be there.

Garrett's expression was grim as he examined Dante, asking questions. At least Dante was able to answer them all. That must be a good sign.

The police and paramedics arrived at the same time. Jazz quickly took charge of answering the officers' questions while the paramedics worked with Garrett on Dante.

After Rachel was freed from her manacles, she and Dante were loaded onto gurneys. It took all of Elsa's strength to move away from him. She didn't want to let go of his hand.

As they were wheeling Dante from the room, he grabbed Garrett's arm, pulling him close. Whatever Dante said, Garrett nodded.

Jazz came to stand beside Elsa. "I'm sorry I didn't believe you."

"But you trusted me enough to help anyway. That's all that matters."

Jazz wiped away an errant tear and nodded. "Dante will need this." She handed Elsa a plain leather wallet.

"What is it?" She opened the wallet, shocked to see a driver's license with Dante's picture, along with a library card, credit card—everything he'd need to answer any questions that came up at the hospital. "How did you—"

"Don't ask." Jazz smiled and shook her head. "Come on. We can ride along in the ambulances."

Elsa saved her questions for later. She held on to her faith that everything would be okay. For the moment, she was grateful for the chance to be back at Dante's side. It was where she belonged.

Chapter Thirty-One

Summer Park, Florida—2016

The sun was shining brightly as Elsa sat at one of the tables in the hospital's outdoor eating area. Dante had refused to let her be in the room while he met with his doctors for his final post-op discussion.

He had spent most of the last few months with his face in bandages, needing several surgeries to recover. Apparently, he wanted a chance to deal with the aftermath on his own before letting her see the final results.

She respected his decision to not have her present when the bandages were removed, even though she hated not being at his side. At the first meeting Elsa had been present for, his reconstructive surgeon told them there might be further permanent damage, maybe even partial paralysis.

She had been preparing herself for the worst ever since, imagining what his face might look like in vivid detail so that she wouldn't wince or flinch in the slightest when she saw him. Already, his face had changed in her mind's eye—new scars added upon the old, his expressions muted from a loss of muscle control.

It killed her to think of him having to endure that. The least she could do was make sure he knew it didn't affect how she felt about him in the least.

All that mattered was that Dante was out of danger. Whatever resulted from the surgeries, they would handle it together. She was so grateful he was still with her.

To keep her mind off her nerves, she reviewed the latest copy of their manuscript. She and Dante had finished the first draft while he was recovering, and they were planning to celebrate as soon as this was behind them.

She imagined all the various ways they might go about that, smiling as her face probably flushed more from her wayward thoughts than the sun.

"Hello."

Elsa glanced at the stranger who stood next to her table. She'd been so engrossed in her thoughts she didn't notice him approach.

"Good afternoon." She turned back to the manuscript in the hopes that he'd get the hint and leave.

"May I?" Without waiting for an answer, he sat in the chair next to her.

Elsa sighed and said, "I'm not sure what this is about, but you should know, I'm not available."

When he didn't leave, she finally gave him her full attention. A slow smile spread across the man's face.

She had to admit it was a nice smile. A nice smile in a very nice face. A strangely familiar face.

The man's brown hair was highlighted from time in the sun and framed his face in gentle waves. He was handsome enough that he probably wasn't used to women rebuffing him.

Elsa stared at the man openly, a nagging doubt in the back of her mind. His eyes were bright turquoise against the pale blue sky, his jaw was strong, and his nose straight. There was a playfulness in his gaze that drew her in and made her like him.

"Have we met?" she asked.

His smile turned into something of a wicked grin, his full lips parting over straight, white teeth. Elsa knew that smile.

"I should certainly think so," he said, his rumbling voice oh so familiar.

"Dante?" Elsa gasped.

His smile broadened, the skin around his eyes crinkling from it. The skin around *both* eyes.

Elsa reached out and cradled his face in her hands, gingerly running her fingertips over his right temple and down along his cheek. She couldn't see any new damage at all, and more than that, his older scars were all but gone. The skin was a bit pinker than the rest of his face, a few white lines crossing the surface.

They'd addressed his scars while performing the reconstructive surgery.

"Before you say anything," Dante said, "I know you were opposed to the idea of me undergoing what you considered unnecessary surgery. However, I had already consulted with Garrett shortly after the dance, and since surgery had become somewhat more necessary in the intervening time, we decided to take care of the matters all at once."

She didn't know what to say. She could tell that her mouth was hanging open, but she didn't have it in her to do anything about it. She just stared. This was Dante?

He scooted a little closer in his chair. "I know it is quite a change, and you would have preferred that we discuss the matter before I made such an important decision, but it was my last decision to make as a single man. So, as Jazz would say…" His grin became downright mischievous. "Deal with it."

Elsa couldn't find any words. She just stared at him. She was so used to how he looked before, it was almost unsettling to see him like this.

"What are you thinking?" Dante asked. His voice was a bit thin, as if he was worried about her reaction.

"I think you've been talking to Jazz too much."

Elsa leapt on him, kissing him probably more passionately than was advisable. But it had been so long since she'd been able to kiss him without worrying about sutures and bandages.

And he seemed *fine*. He didn't show any signs of pain as he smiled or narrowed his eyes, and from what she could see he hadn't lost any of his expressiveness.

She sat on his lap, finally coming up for air.

"I trust that means you like it," Dante said.

"I like that you're well and I can finally kiss you again. I can kiss you again, can't I?"

"I certainly hope so. Otherwise, I'm very confused about what we were just doing."

"You know what I mean. Did your doctor say everything's okay?"

"I am in perfect health, and the procedures went better than expected. We have no need to worry about lingering side effects, aside from the need to adjust to my new appearance."

"I think I'll live. As long as I can keep doing this."

And then she kissed him again, deeply and thoroughly. She didn't stop until something he said earlier rose up in her mind.

"Wait a minute. What do you mean, 'your last decision as a single man'?"

Dante rested his hands on her hips, guiding her first to stand and then sit in the chair opposite him. He knelt on one knee and produced a small black velvet box from his pocket. Elsa could feel her heart beat in her throat.

"Elsa Sinclair, you have given me a new world and a new life. I cannot imagine spending that life without you." The sunlight gleamed off the box's contents as he opened it. "Would you do me the incomparable honor of becoming my wife?"

"A lifetime with you? Absolutely. Yes!"

He paused, feigning a puzzled expression. "It occurs to me, perhaps I should have asked for more than one lifetime, given that you are a time traveler."

"I will gladly spend every lifetime with you."

With a gentle smile, he lifted her left hand in his and slid the ring in place. It was only then that she calmed enough to actually look at it.

"The ring... Your mother's ring. I thought you sold it."

"As did I. Jazz was to broker the exchange, but told me that she held it as collateral instead. She has been able to recoup the money she lent to me and more from selling my paintings and returned the ring when I told her I planned to propose."

"I can't believe you're all still making secret plans around me, and this time I didn't even notice."

"I should warn you that Rachel insists on designing the dress, and

Jazz is already making plans for the event. I know you prefer to be in control of such things, but—"

"Are you kidding?" Elsa laughed. "I get to spend every day with you. I don't care about anything else."

"Don't forget the nights," he said, his smile softening.

"For the rest of our lives."

Dante leaned in to kiss her again. They had found the ending to their book, and Elsa knew in her heart that their story was only beginning.

Epilogue

Garrett leaned against a counter in the doctor's lounge, chugging another cup of coffee to stay on his feet. He didn't trust himself not to fall asleep if he dared to sit down. A dull ache filled his chest.

The bruises on Elsa's throat were mostly superficial. Damn, she had done a good job fighting off that psychopath. She was resting, sedated, so Garrett would need to wait to tell her Dante was out of surgery and doing well.

He wished he had more good news to share.

Last he saw, Jazz was sitting next to Elsa's bed, watching her like a hawk, dark eyes following anybody who dared come into the room. The nurses said it was sweet, but he knew better. Jazz was guarding Elsa, not just watching over her. If anyone dared to make a mistake in Elsa's treatment, Jazz would crush them, any way she could.

And she would come for him soon, full of questions. She would want to see Rachel, and Garrett would have to explain why that wasn't possible.

Rachel was on the fifth floor. The psych ward.

His hands were still shaking. The memory of Rachel being held down, strapped to a bed as she thrashed and screamed, begging Garrett for help, to make *the voices* stop... His stomach churned, the coffee rising into the back of his mouth with an acid finish.

After what Rachel had been through, he'd expected something, but not a full-blown psychotic break. It was killing him that he couldn't help her. And he had a feeling there was more going on with her than she was telling anyone.

As if being abducted and tortured, and then killing a man wasn't enough.

He turned around and punched the cabinet, hard. He'd feel it for days and he didn't care. The pain was a balm, took his mind off the terror of it all for a few seconds. Long enough to remember that Finn had left a voicemail hours ago, when Garrett's world was still bright and his friends all safe and whole. Garrett hadn't been able to listen to it yet.

He pulled out his phone, then hit *play* as he lifted it to his ear.

"Hey, man. I know you told me to stop digging into Dante Lucerne, but you're going to be glad I didn't. He isn't conning Elsa. That *Dante Lucerne* I told you about from the 1800s? It's the same guy! I don't know how she did it, but Elsa brought him here straight from that theatre fire that supposedly killed him. This is so fucking unbelievable!"

There was a pause where the only sound was Finn's quick footsteps. What the hell was Finn talking about? When he spoke again, his voice was quieter, but still thrummed with excitement.

"She didn't call the cops after the break-in because she's terrified of anyone finding out. After how cool you were when I showed you what I can do, I know you'll help her and not freak. And you need to know. I picked up another trail. Someone else is following her."

Garrett's stomach roiled again. Had the voicemail come in time for him to do something, to prevent what happened to his friends? Why hadn't he checked it sooner?

"I have a really bad feeling, Garrett. And you know what it means when I say that. Keep Elsa close, but be careful, man. I'm going to see what else I can dig up."

Garrett kept the phone to his ear, too stunned to move. If Finn said Dante was from the 1800s, Garrett believed it. Finn's word was beyond doubt. And as Garrett thought about it, pieces clicked together in his mind. It made sense.

How insane had his world become that time travel was the most rational explanation for a host of mysteries?

How insane…

His thoughts went back to Rachel on the fifth floor. Sweet, smart, sensitive Rachel, who had saved her friends but not herself.

Garrett wouldn't let her slip away, he wouldn't let this break her. If Elsa could travel through time to save Dante, Garrett sure as hell could help Rachel put the pieces of her life back together.

He would find a way.

———

Read on as Rachel and Garrett face down their demons in *Whispering Hearts*.

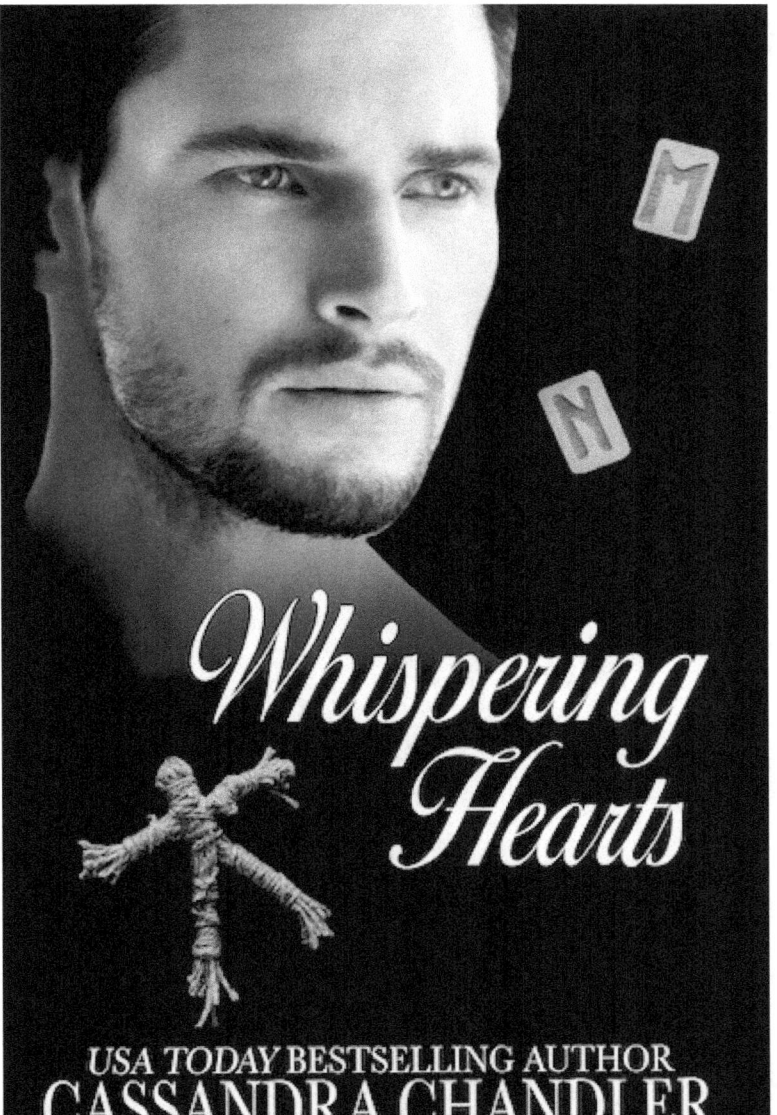

Whispering Hearts

USA TODAY BESTSELLING AUTHOR
CASSANDRA CHANDLER

Whispering Hearts

The Summer Park Psychics
Book Two

Cassandra Chandler

Dedication

For those who listen with their hearts.

Prologue

Rachel hung from the chains that held her to the wall, her arms splayed like a dismal butterfly. Her wrists were searing points of agony, her knees throbbing from the cold cement beneath her. Holding still helped keep the pain at bay.

Nothing could help with the voices.

"The exhibit is opening tonight."

The peculiar echo that accompanied the voices of the dead sent a chill down Rachel's spine that had little to do with her circumstance. This one she recognized as Veronica. Her voice was higher than the others'. Gentler.

"They won't know. All those people looking at our portraits, and they won't even know what they're seeing."

"He'll kill her afterwards."

Pragmatic, forceful. That would be Anna. Rachel wondered if any others were present. From the conversations she had overheard, half a dozen spirits haunted Michael's garage.

"I can't watch him kill another one." Veronica's voice rose in volume, the echo growing with her distress. She let out a long, high wail.

Keening was the worst sound Rachel had ever heard. She couldn't stop the shuddering sob that wracked her body. She only hoped the ghosts didn't figure out it was more from their conversation than anything else. They couldn't figure out that Rachel heard them. She hadn't given up hope yet. If she made it out of this alive, she didn't want the dead to know that she was clairsentient.

Nicole joined the conversation, her deep voice distinct from the other two. *"At least she won't suffer as long as we did."*

"We should be here to help her in case she doesn't cross over,"

Anna said.

"There's nothing we can do to help her."

No one had a rejoinder for Nicole's statement. Finally, a moment of blessed silence.

Except for the thoughts churning through Rachel's mind. Garrett was always at the forefront—with his easy smile and gorgeous blue eyes. Garrett who always showed up whenever and wherever she needed him. This time, she was afraid he'd be too late.

She might never see him again. The idea tore at her heart, but at the same time, she wondered if he would be better off. No more need to rescue Rachel from her poor decisions or step in as her emergency date. No more mixed messages.

She did wish that she had kissed him. But she knew it wouldn't have ended there. If she had ever opened that door, he would've walked right through to meet her and been doomed to a lifetime of this—living with the dead. Knowing they were everywhere. Wondering every time her attention strayed if they were truly alone.

Keeping Garrett at arm's length had been a good choice. She only wished her judgment had been as sound with Michael.

There had been so many things she had explained away. The way he kept scaring Elsa by showing up at her house uninvited. The way he had talked about her friend, Dante.

Rachel had finally ended their relationship. Michael had seemed to take it well. When he'd asked her to sit for a portrait, she'd been too flattered to resist. That vanity might cost her everything.

She had ignored the voices, tuned out the whispers when she walked into Michael's house—even though she could tell there were so many of them. How could she have been so stupid?

Oh, right. Years of practice.

"I'm going to the gallery."

Rachel jerked her arms, startled by Nicole's voice close by. Her wrists sent lightning strikes of pain along her arms, punishing her for her loss of control. She feared the consequences of her lapse would be greater than that momentary increase in suffering.

Several moments of tense silence followed.

"Did you see that?" Veronica's voice. Right next to Rachel's ear. *"You don't think she can hear us, do you?"*

Rachel closed her eyes and focused on the pain. It was an easy distraction, with her nerves clamoring for attention. If the ghosts decided to test her, to shout at her or try to startle her, she could ignore them. When their attempts failed to get a response, they would decide she couldn't hear them.

Please let them decide she couldn't hear.

Light struck her retinas, burning through her eyelids. That was new. Rachel flinched away. She couldn't help herself. It was so bright.

"Rachel? Rachel, it's Elsa."

The voice was solid—no unearthly echo. And it was accompanied by touch. Soft, but firm.

Rachel opened her eyes. The bright lights made them burn, and she blinked several times, trying to bring the room into focus. The shelves and workbenches crowded into the garage filled her view. She turned her head and saw a small blonde woman next to her.

"Elsa?"

Elsa was kneeling on the floor at Rachel's side. How was that possible? Only one theory presented itself.

"Oh no. Did he get you too?" Michael had talked about Elsa after chaining Rachel to the wall. He had told her Elsa was his next "model".

"No, sweetie. We're here to rescue you."

"Oh thank God." Rachel trembled as another sob escaped. She leaned against Elsa and looked around the room, her eyes finally adjusting. No one else was in view. "How are you going to get me loose?"

Dante's face appeared above the workbenches. The fluorescent lights washed out the red scars covering his right cheek and arcing across his forehead. "Do not be afraid. I will have you free presently."

"Dante?"

"Did you not recognize me with my new look?" His tone was playful, but Rachel could see the strain around his eyes, the tightness to his smile. He was wearing one of the new outfits that Rachel had bought for him. Dante's exhibit was opening tonight as well.

Rachel's heart seemed to freeze in her chest. Dante and Elsa were supposed to be starting a new life together—a life Rachel had helped him create. She had walked blithely into this nightmare, and now her friends were being dragged into it as well.

Metal clanked and rattled as Dante worked the winch that controlled her chains. Elsa helped support Rachel's arms as enough slack was let out for them to drop to her sides.

The winch was lined up so that Rachel could see Dante work. He was using the crowbar arm of a tire iron to try to pry loose the moorings that attached her chains to the floor. Michael always had a sick smile on his face when he let out slack or pulled them tighter, delighting in watching her suffer.

There was no way Dante could get her loose with that tool. Michael wore the key on his necklace. Rachel had asked about it when they'd just started dating. He'd said it was the key to his success. She shivered at the memory.

A pins-and-needles sensation in her arms let her know her circulation was returning. The burning would be nothing next to her wrists when more feeling returned there.

Rachel didn't care.

How many times was she going to let other people save her? How much longer could she play the fool before someone she loved was hurt trying to help?

She didn't know how they had found her, but Rachel couldn't let Elsa and Dante continue to endanger themselves. They needed to leave and call the police.

Rachel moaned. "That will take forever. Dante, you have to get Elsa out of here."

Elsa pulled Rachel closer, stroking her hair. "It's okay, Rachel. I'm not leaving without you."

"You don't understand. He wants you too."

"Well, he can't have me. And he can't have you, either."

Rachel had said such awful things to Elsa the last time they spoke. Yet here Elsa was, risking her life for Rachel. She gripped Elsa's arms, more sobs shaking her, listening to the rattle of the chains as Dante worked to get her free.

Elsa hugged Rachel tighter. "Dante…"

"I know. I am hurrying."

The voices began to whisper something, the echoes distorting their words, but not their urgency.

"Run."

"Run."

"Run!"

There was a brief pause, then Dante shouted, "Elsa, run!"

A sharp pop and the sound of breaking glass joined the sudden keening of the ghosts. Blood sprayed the shelves as Dante jerked back, then fell to his knees behind the workbenches, out of Rachel's sight. Elsa scrambled toward Dante as Michael stepped into view.

Rachel saw his gun first, then that horrible smile. Michael had them caught. He knew it. And he was enjoying every moment of their pain.

A hand appeared on top of one of the workbenches. Dante pulled himself up to stand, leaning on the heavy table. Rachel couldn't see his face. She knew that was a mercy. She could see the trail of blood still running down his neck, staining his shirt red.

Michael leveled the gun at Dante, stepping further into the garage. "This is more than I hoped for. I get Elsa hand-delivered, and the freak thrown in for free."

When he laughed, Rachel heard a faint echo from the ghosts—a grieving moan.

"I think I've made an improvement on your face," Michael said. "I can't believe that Jazz wanted me to share the opening with you. I'm a true artist. Not like you, with your boring little landscapes. How much are you willing to sacrifice for your art?"

Dante's voice was strained. "Art is about creation, not sacrifice."

"There is no creation without sacrifice. I'm willing to give up what I love most. Over and over again. I imbue the canvas with their essence. It's how I immortalize them."

"No, no, no…" A loud screech pierced Rachel's ears. She shook her head, but couldn't block out the sounds, no matter how hard she tried. Echoes, moans, sobs, prayers.

"And how many women have you immortalized?" Dante asked.

"How many paintings have I done?"

"Don't kill him!" the voices shrieked.

Rachel heard a thud, then something skittered toward her beneath the workbenches. The light glinted off of Michael's gun. Another thud brought her attention back to where Michael had been.

Without thinking, Rachel picked up the gun as she stood. She walked between the benches, ignoring the pain searing through her wrists as the chains rattled along behind her.

Dante was on the ground again, pulling himself toward Elsa. Michael was on top of her, his hands around her throat.

"No, please no. Don't kill him!" The voices were so distorted that Rachel couldn't tell who was speaking.

"She's going to free him!"

Michael was strangling Elsa, screaming at her as he did. "You think you can make a fool out of me? You're mine! You belong on my canvas. All of you!"

Elsa was fighting, but Michael was too strong.

"Don't kill him!"

"She'll set him free!"

Michael straightened his arms to avoid Elsa's fingernails as she clawed at his face, giving Rachel the opening she needed. She lifted the gun and pulled the trigger.

Red bloomed on his chest, spreading in a circle from the bullet hole. He looked down at the spot, then up to Rachel. His eyes were wide, full of surprise. Then he fell to the floor.

Rachel kept the gun trained on Michael's body. She wasn't sure if he was dead. Even with his eyes staring blankly at the room, it didn't feel as if he was dead.

"Run! Run! Run!"

The voices blurred together, growing fainter. Michael's presence remained strong.

Elsa was coughing, but that meant she could breathe. She rolled away from Michael's body as Rachel approached.

He needed to die. Why wouldn't he die? Rachel pulled the trigger again. And again and again. She kept pulling it even when all the rounds were spent.

She still felt him in the room.

Elsa stood and staggered toward Rachel. That wasn't right. Dante should be Elsa's main concern. But Elsa hugged Rachel instead, one hand sliding down her arm to the gun.

She let Elsa take it. Rachel didn't care. There was nothing more it could do to help them.

She wondered if it had really helped them at all.

Chapter One

Two months later

Garrett was about as happy to walk into the Montgomery household as he'd be going in for a colonoscopy. He'd encountered Rachel's mom a time or two at social events and always felt the need to shower afterwards. But Rachel was inside and no one had heard from her in a week.

He sat in his car for another moment psyching himself up, then murmured, "Into the lion's den."

Lioness, really.

The cool air from inside the car rolled past him as he opened the door, leaving him to poach in the steamy summer. Heat from the asphalt hit his legs like he was stepping into a blast furnace. The muggy humidity made his shirt cling to his skin. Sunlight reflected off the white sidewalk, blinding him even through his sunglasses.

Ah, Florida.

Wearing slacks and a long-sleeved shirt wasn't his idea of comfortable, but shorts and a T-shirt wouldn't fly for a visit to Chez Montgomery. It was bad enough that he had opted for his light brown boat shoes. He wasn't even wearing socks.

Scandalous.

The house in front of him was immense, set back from the road on a jewel-green lawn that must cost a fortune to maintain. A few palm trees framed the white two-story mansion, accenting the view of neighboring dwellings just as large.

Garrett was happy with his country home. Summer Park wasn't as heavily populated as much of the state, but it still had tons of people running around. He preferred the quiet outside of town.

Living half an hour or more away also helped him avoid the demands of making too many social calls like this one. If he really wanted out of something, he could always say that gators had crawled up to sun themselves on the one road that led to his neighborhood, blocking his way to the city.

Not that he would ever do such a thing. He let out a tense laugh as he made his way along the front walkway.

At the door, he bent his knees a bit to see his reflection in the narrow window that gave people inside a view of who was calling. He ran a hand through his hair, brushing it back past his collar. It was longer than he would ever have let it grow when he worked the ER. Back then, it had been uniformly brown. The sun had added highlights everywhere. Being a man of leisure had left its mark.

Quitting his job had definitely changed him. After two years, he wasn't sure if it was for the better. He had enjoyed having time to read and think about things at first. But self-reflection was tipping over into brooding and that had to stop.

He'd been spending too much time lately thinking about the reason he left the crazy hours and the constant stress. She was somewhere on the other side of the door.

Damn, he should have shaved. He wiped his hand over the darker stubble that covered his jaw, then shrugged. At least it was in fashion. Hopefully Rachel's mom wouldn't be too offended at his scruffiness and send him packing.

As he stood straight again, he rang the bell and forced himself to smile. Time to turn on the Southern Charm and make his mama proud.

"Yes?" The woman who answered was wearing a maid's uniform. Her eyes widened as she stared at Garrett's chest. She tilted her head back farther and farther to look up at him.

This was the best part of being six-seven. The expressions were always priceless by the time they reached his face.

He upped the voltage on his smile and took off his glasses, letting his southern drawl thicken when he spoke.

"Good afternoon. I'm Garrett Wolfstrom. I'm here to call on Miss

Montgomery."

The woman blinked a few times, then smiled back. "Oh! Doctor Wolfstrom. Please come in."

The staff knew he was a doctor? That meant the Montgomerys must have mentioned him before, even though this was his first visit to the house. Maybe Rachel had spoken of him.

"If you would wait here for a few moments..." The woman nodded to him, then walked briskly from the foyer toward the back of the house.

A mix of emotions churned within him. Worry and hope battling in his chest. He couldn't wait to see Rachel—to know she was all right.

Well, physically, at least. Mentally and emotionally, she had to still be reeling from what had happened to her, no matter what her psychiatrists said.

When she was discharged from the hospital, she had seemed fine. Too fine. People didn't swing from a psychotic break to *everything is roses* after a few weeks of therapy—no matter how intensive it was.

But she had her doctors convinced the medicines were working. Garrett wasn't sure she was taking them.

He had noticed her working on the doctors at the hospital. Doctors with heavy caseloads and light experience when it came to one Miss Montgomery. She had pulled out all the stops. Nobody could turn a head like Rachel. With her vibrant personality and warm smile, her natural charm beat his best efforts by a million miles. To make things worse, she was insanely gorgeous, eyes the pale blue of a morning sky and hair as gold as the sun.

Yeah, he had it for her pretty bad. At least he owned it.

"Mrs. Montgomery will see you in the tearoom."

"I was hoping to talk to Rachel."

The woman was already walking back through the house. Garrett followed.

"Miss Montgomery is resting currently. But her mother would love to speak with you."

Garrett felt a trickle of sweat run down his back that had nothing to do with the heat wave making this summer even worse than usual. How did anyone stand living in the city?

He ducked to avoid smashing his head on the door's lintel as he took the single step down into the tearoom.

Mrs. Montgomery was sitting at a small round table covered by a pristine white cloth. She was holding a tiny teacup and matching saucer, which she set on the table with practiced ease.

Everything about her was fake—from the long, perfect nails on the ends of her fingers to her sculpted and dyed hair. Blonde, of course. Her eyes weren't altered, though. They were the same pale blue as Rachel's. Seeing that bit of Rachel in Mrs. Montgomery fortified him for the encounter.

"Dr. Wolfstrom!" She extended a hand to him, the faintest hint of a Southern accent lacing her voice. "It's so good of you to call on us."

"Ma'am." He took her hand and bowed over her, kissing the air near her cheek. "I apologize for not letting you know I was coming."

"Don't you worry about that. We're always happy to see you here."

Garrett didn't doubt it. Rachel's jokes about her mother wanting a doctor for a son-in-law had been reinforced every time he met Mrs. Montgomery. Too bad Rachel wasn't interested. Whether it was an act of rebellion or just a personal choice in Garrett's case was a mystery. A mystery too painful to try to unravel.

He sat at the table feeling like a full-grown gator in a ten-gallon fish tank. Mrs. Montgomery was built like a porcelain doll, tiny and delicate. It just made him feel worse.

Rachel was taller than both her parents. And she worked out. She had muscle to her and an athletic frame, though she usually dressed to hide it. Usually.

When they had been working together fixing up his house, she'd mostly worn shorts and tank tops. He hadn't been able to ignore the tempting curves and lines of sinew on her body. Or the way her smile hit him all the way down to his toes.

He cleared his throat and pushed the memories from his mind. Now was not the time.

"I was hoping I might have a word with Rachel."

"I'm sure you can have several, but not until I'm done with you." She gave him a flirty smile. He hoped the one he forced in response was convincing.

"It is rather important. None of her friends have heard from her in a while."

Mrs. Montgomery's smile faltered enough to give Garrett a glimpse of the real woman. The cold, reaching woman beneath the surface of civility she projected to the world. He wanted to leave, but couldn't until he knew Rachel was all right.

"She's been resting quite a bit," Mrs. Montgomery said.

"That's good. But she shouldn't be isolating herself. It isn't healthy."

"I don't think she's isolating herself." Mrs. Montgomery lifted her cup and saucer again, slowly and deliberately. "Rather, she's moving on."

"What do you mean?"

She took a sip of her tea, only glancing at Garrett from the corner of her eyes. He hated the social dance she was playing at, but knew she wouldn't give him answers if he didn't match her moves.

"I hope you're not planning on leaving Summer Park," he said. "The Montgomerys are an important part of the city."

It was a bald-faced lie, but stroking her ego might help to loosen her tongue and get him to Rachel faster. Mr. Montgomery was a defense attorney. If Mrs. Montgomery had her way, he would eventually be President.

"Don't you worry, my dear." She set down her teacup again. "Our plans keep us in Summer Park for a little while longer. I have to say, I would very much like to see Rachel settled down before we move on." She gave Garrett a pointed smile.

He wanted to shrug and say, "I'd be game if she'd stop shutting me down," but didn't think that would end well for Rachel.

Adding to her stress in any way wasn't a good idea. Pressuring her about marriage right after what had happened with her latest boyfriend would be downright despicable. How could Mrs. Montgomery even allude to such a thing?

She tilted her head to the side as she raised her shoulder to meet it —a dismissive shrug Rachel had picked up and used too often. "Unfortunately I don't see that happening if she keeps associating with those friends of hers. Present company excluded of course."

Garrett was stunned. "Rachel needs her friends, Mrs. Montgomery. Now more than ever. They can help her get over what happened with —"

Mrs. Montgomery waved her hand in the air and shook her head. "We mustn't speak of that unpleasant matter."

"Unpleasant?"

Rachel's boyfriend had kidnapped her. Tortured her. He had planned to kill her—and she wouldn't have been his first victim. Not by a long shot. But Rachel had survived. She had survived and gunned the bastard down while he was trying to kill two of their other friends.

"She needs to talk about what happened," Garrett said. "Especially with the people who went through it with her."

"They did, didn't they? Doesn't that seem a bit odd to you? That so many of her little group was involved?"

Garrett took a deep breath and held it to keep from yelling. When he trusted himself to speak, his voice was tight and clipped.

"Mrs. Montgomery, I don't know what you have been told, but Dante and Elsa were present because they were trying to rescue Rachel."

Mrs. Montgomery's perfectly shaped eyebrows rose on her forehead. "And how did they know she needed to be rescued?"

Explaining that would give away secrets that Garrett had sworn to keep. He doubted she would believe the truth anyway.

When he didn't respond, she looked back to her tea and said, "Weren't they all associated with that gallery owner Rachel fell in with? That Asian woman with the ridiculous name and reputation for *creative* marketing tactics?"

Garrett clenched his hands into fists on his lap. It wasn't only what

Mrs. Montgomery was saying but how she was saying it. He had never had the urge to shake someone before.

"Mrs. Montgomery. Elsa was strangled and Dante was shot trying to help your daughter."

"Only one person suffered gunshot wounds." She shifted in her chair, the first sign of unease since Garrett entered the room. "I read the police report quite thoroughly. Mr. Lucerne's injuries weren't sustained from a gunshot."

"You read the report?"

"Of course." A bit of an edge crept into her voice. "Since our family was involved, we thought it best to be well informed on the matter. My husband is a lawyer, you'll recall. Which brings me back to Mr. Lucerne."

She took another sip of her tea, then set it on the table.

"I believe he's just launching his career as a painter." She leaned forward slightly and narrowed her eyes. "Doesn't it seem a bit coincidental to you that he was injured only on the side of his face where he was already disfigured?"

Garrett could barely speak. Was Mrs. Montgomery talking to Rachel like this?

"This wasn't some publicity stunt."

"But it was publicity. The worst kind. We can't afford to be involved in such a scandalous event with Edward's political campaign starting so soon."

She was about to get another scandalous event. Garrett was going to lift up her tiny table and chuck it through the window. He stood so quickly, when the backs of his knees hit his chair it went flying across the room.

"Garrett?" Rachel's voice swept through his adrenaline-charged system. His skin felt electrified.

Glaring at Mrs. Montgomery, he let her see his outrage. He couldn't speak his mind at the moment, but he wanted her to know that what she was saying was not okay.

Her eyes widened and her mouth fell open. She leaned back in her chair, one hand clasped to her chest.

He took a few deep breaths to calm himself down. He didn't want Rachel to see him so angry. He made his voice cheery and plastered on his best smile as he turned around.

"Rachel, it's good to see—" He froze, a lump forming in his throat too big for his words to squeeze past.

Rachel stood in the door to the tearoom, eyes unfocused like she was looking through him. Her hair was dull and clung to her scalp in lifeless strands. Her skin was pale, her lips bloodless and chapped. For some inexplicable reason, she was wearing a tennis outfit—complete with wristbands. The white fabric caught and reflected the light in the room. Her skirt was wrinkled as if she'd slept in it for days, and her feet were bare.

Mrs. Montgomery made a tsking sound behind him. "Rachel, how can you let a gentleman caller see you in such a state? Go to your room and clean up."

Rachel hovered in the doorway. "Sorry."

She tended to fade next to her mother, like a flower folding in darkness, but this took it to a whole new level. He was used to her being vibrant, lighting up a room with her conversation and charm.

"It's all those dreadful medicines they have you on. Hurry up and change, dear. And do something with your hair."

"Yes, mother."

Garrett's chest felt tight—too full from everything he was having to process, all the things he could imagine that woman saying to Rachel when no one else was around to hear.

"Don't trouble yourself," he said. Rachel had trouble enough.

She opened her mouth as if she was about to say something, but her mother spoke over her.

"Are you leaving so soon then?" Mrs. Montgomery's tone was smug. She thought she had won some victory. Garrett was through playing her games.

"Yeah. And Rachel's coming with me."

Rachel's gaze came into sharp focus as she started to back away. "I won't go back to the hospital."

"You don't have to. But you can't stay in this toxic environment."

"Excuse me!" Mrs. Montgomery must have been taking another sip of that damned tea, because he heard the cup and saucer clink on the table.

Garrett rounded on her. "There is no excusing the things you just said to me. And if that's how you talk to company, I can't imagine what you've been saying to Rachel since she came home."

He turned back to Rachel, approaching her slowly to be sure he didn't scare her. He didn't want to bring up memories of the nightmare she had endured just two months ago.

The urge to protect her was overpowering. When he was close enough he rested his hands on her arms.

She looked up at him, eyes shimmering with unshed tears. "Where would I go?"

"We'll figure that out." He kept his voice as soft as he could manage, barely above a whisper. "But you don't have to stay here. Please let me help you."

She pressed her lips together tightly. He knew that look. She wanted to argue. But she nodded instead. She must be worse off than he thought.

He let out a breath of relief, only then realizing he was dusting his thumbs back and forth over the soft skin of her arms. He stopped and said, "Go and pack a bag. Holler from the front door when you're ready."

Mrs. Montgomery rose from her chair. "I will not be disrespected in my own home!"

She started toward Rachel, but Garrett turned and crossed his arms, shifting so that he entirely blocked the door to the small room. Sometimes being a giant was very useful. He let himself be intimidating.

"If you think I'm going to let you near Rachel again, you are very much mistaken. Sit down and finish your tea."

Mrs. Montgomery raised her voice enough for Rachel to hear. "If you leave now, don't bother coming back."

The stunning lack of compassion left him speechless. He looked over his shoulder at Rachel to see how she would take the callous remark.

Rachel paused at the base of a staircase, one hand on the bannister. Without turning to even glance at them she said, "I won't."

Then she vanished up the stairs.

"How dare you come into my house and cause such a disturbance!"

Garrett turned back to the livid woman before him. "How dare you treat your daughter like this?"

Mrs. Montgomery snorted—a sound he never expected to hear from her. Then she narrowed her eyes and smiled.

"She'll come crawling back, eventually."

Garrett laughed and shook his head. "You have no idea, do you? Those friends that you seem to have such a low opinion of? We all *love* her. Every single one of us. We would die for her. Two of us damn near did. She has homes with us all, places where the people will care for her and treat her right. Speak to her with the respect and compassion that she deserves." He tried to stop himself, but he was too angry and kept going. "But you? You deserve to live a long, lonely life. Because that's what you're making for yourself. That's your choice."

She gave him a strange smile, like she knew something he didn't. Then she shook her head and walked to the table, a casual stride instead of her usual elegant glide. It unnerved him.

By the time she sat down, her mask of fine manners had swept back over her face. She took a sip of her tea, once more the proper lady.

"You want to take her off my hands? Fine." Her voice was low and somehow menacing. "But you will find, Dr. Wolfstrom, that my little girl is never alone. And you might not appreciate the company she keeps quite as much as you think."

Chapter Two

Socks, underwear, jeans... Rachel gathered the things she would need, stuffing each into her backpack as she checked them off her mental list. A few button-up shirts followed, then a pair of sneakers on top.

Shoes. Right, shoes.

She shoved her feet into some sandals before she forgot she was barefoot. The pavement would be hot and she didn't want anything to delay her in getting the hell out of here.

Was she really doing this? Leaving her sanctuary?

She had wanted to leave. Of course she had. But her room was safe. The one spot in the world where she knew she could actually be alone.

She glanced around at the powder-blue walls, the white slatted closet doors and canopy bed that had barely changed since she was a child. The stuffed animals and boy-band posters were gone in a vain attempt to make her room look more like an apartment.

Instead it was stark. Barren. Like a prison cell.

This was no way to live.

She told herself she was staying with her parents to help with their political aspirations. Photo-ops were much more effective with the entire family embracing and smiling at the cameras. The pictures were just another kind of lie.

In truth she was terrified—afraid to make the simplest changes in case it somehow opened a crack in her defenses. Even when studying Interior Design in college, she hadn't changed the color of the paint, added different furniture, or even put in area rugs. She kept everything the same.

She couldn't stay here anymore, listening to her mother's daily barrage of deprecating statements and watching the help avoid her or make the sign of the cross when they thought she wasn't looking. A lifetime of that scared her more. She could make other places safe.

She walked to the window and put her fingers behind the plain white poppet hanging there—a tiny doll with no distinguishing features aside from its hominid form. A medley of herbs were inside along with the cotton stuffing that gave it its shape. The few times people caught her making them, she said it was her take on potpourri sachets.

It wasn't.

"Salt." She spoke as if the little doll could hear her. "I'm going to need salt." She let it go and watched it swing back and forth in the window for a moment.

No more time for dallying. She ran to her bathroom and opened her medicine cabinet. The door was plain wood—she had removed the mirror decades ago. She grabbed the large cylinder of salt that was inside, along with her hairbrush. No way she was leaving stray hairs around. The brush and salt went into the top of her backpack, which was lying open on her bed.

There was a medium-sized suitcase in her closet that already held most of what she needed. Books, notes, a few necessary supplies. Hidden away where the staff—and her mother—wouldn't get at them.

She pulled it out, then wheeled it to her bed and opened the zipper so she could shove in a few extra things like toiletries and...more books. She dropped to her knees and pulled her best book on psychic self-defense from under her bedside table.

The tattered thing was wrapped in cloth to prevent further damage to the binding. Rachel had slept with it under her pillow every night for as long as she could remember. Each morning, she hid it in the thin space between the bedside table and floor. She placed it in her suitcase with reverent care.

From the drawer in the small table she grabbed scissors, thread, needles, and white fabric—the basic materials to make new poppets— then shoved them in her backpack. Wherever she was going, she hoped they had a well-stocked kitchen. She would need fresh herbs.

"You about ready?"

When she heard Garrett's voice, she let out a little yell and fell backwards onto her bottom. He ran to her and knelt at her side.

"I'm sorry. I didn't mean to startle you."

He put his hand on her shoulder. Large, strong, warm. The hair on her arms stood on end as a shiver of pleasure swept through her body.

His eyes were dark blue. Deep and rich, like the ocean. But warmer than the waters she had known.

He was ridiculously gorgeous. His face had the perfect symmetry of a model, his jaw and bone structure as strong as a superhero's. And he was *built*. Broad shouldered and barrel chested, but not too bulky.

When he hugged her, he enveloped her. It made her feel safe.

The ideas that sprang into her mind when he touched her were the hardest to handle. Her imagination tortured her with a future she had no right to think about. At least when it came to him.

"How are you here?" she asked.

Garrett was always there when she needed someone. Even when she didn't ask. He always knew.

"Well, it took some poking around, since none of the staff was of a mind to help me. But if I stayed in that room with your mom another minute…" He let out a sigh through his nose, his lips tight. "Let's just say I might have turned ungentlemanly."

She couldn't imagine Garrett being anything but gentle. Case in point, he cupped her elbows and helped her to her feet. Her hands wound up resting on his chest. She couldn't stop staring into his eyes.

He grinned, the lopsided smirk making her heart feel like dandelion seeds. The two of them could float away on a trail of gossamer white to a place where they could put down roots, enjoy the warm sun, press themselves closer together…

"You keep looking at a guy like that, you might give him the wrong idea." His smile vanished as pain and worry shoved it aside. "I'm sorry. I shouldn't have said that. I forgot for a minute…"

"Forgot?"

Oh right. Her ex-boyfriend, Michael. The ex-person, thanks to her.

Her hands curled into fists and she dropped her gaze to Garrett's feet. She started to pull away, but he gently tightened his grip on her elbows. Just enough to get her attention and make her pause.

"Have you been taking your medicine?"

"It's right there."

She pointed at the bedside table, to the army of bottles containing the exact amount of pills she should have left based on the instructions her doctors had given her. She disposed of several every day in case someone counted.

"That doesn't answer my question."

She managed to look at him, then. "The longer we stay the more likely something will happen to keep me here. Please, Garrett. Can we just go? I want to go."

He nodded and let his hands drop from her arms. "Yeah. But I'm going to want to talk later."

"That's fine."

She ran to the table and threw the bottles in her backpack to reassure him. They took up precious space, but getting away quickly was most important. If they took too long, the yard would be crowded with spirits by the time they made it outside. Everyone wanting something from her. She wasn't sure she could handle that.

In a moment, she'd have nowhere left to run to.

"Can you get the glass ball that's hanging in the window?"

He did as she asked, detaching her witch's ball from the swag hook in the ceiling. He stared for a moment at the chords of blue-green glass that had been created inside the sphere. The strands were meant to catch and confuse spirits trying to enter the room.

Taking down her witch's ball would weaken her boundaries. She wasn't sure how much. But she would need it wherever she ended up.

Her heart pounded as they removed the strongest part of her defense. Leaving the others in place would buy her enough time to leave in peace—she hoped.

"It's pretty handy, being tall. You want this thing too?" He reached for the poppet.

"No!"

She took a few steps toward him, but stopped when he jerked his hand back from the doll. His puzzled look turned to concern. She would deal with that later too.

"Rachel?" Her mother's voice carried down the hallway.

"Rachel..." The echo came from her closet.

Rachel's heart leapt to her throat. That was fast. Too fast.

She grabbed the glass ball from Garrett and stuffed it in her backpack with her clothes, cushioning it as best she could. Her hands were shaking as she zipped everything shut. She grabbed her purse and a spray bottle full of saltwater from her desk.

"Can you get the suitcase?" She slung her backpack over her shoulder.

"Sure." Garrett lifted her suitcase by the handle rather than wheeling it around. He nodded toward the spray bottle and said, "What's that for?"

"I'll explain later. We have to go. Now."

The door to the bathroom slammed shut and they both started at the sound. It reminded her of the popping noise Michael's gun had made.

"Is there a window open in there?" Garrett asked.

"No." There were no windows in the bathroom at all.

Too fast and too powerful.

Rachel grabbed Garrett's hand and pulled him toward the hallway. They needed to leave immediately. For that level of manifestation to take place so quickly...

They must have been waiting for her. Waiting for her to let down her guard even a little. Like they had warned her they would.

Her mother was already in the hallway, her small frame somehow taking up the entire space.

"It is highly improper to have a gentleman in your bedroom."

Rachel froze. Her mother was a master manipulator. All she had to do to destroy Rachel was tell Garrett that the voices Rachel had heard in the hospital—the ones that made everyone think she was crazy—hadn't gone away. Rachel doubted it would help if Garrett knew they had always been there.

Voices of the dead.

Garrett was a doctor. He would think in terms of pathologies and cures. He would take her back to the hospital, where the rooms and halls were filled with wandering spirits. She wasn't sure her sanity would survive another stay.

"Don't let it trouble you." Garrett squeezed Rachel's hand, pulling her along. "We're leaving."

He shouldn't be the one facing off against her mother, but Rachel didn't know if she was strong enough to do it herself. She knew what her mother was capable of and was terrified of the woman.

In that moment though, she hated herself. Hated her weakness.

The past few weeks were a gray blur of pain and despair. Her mother's words only seemed like an anchor pulling Rachel deeper into the abyss. An abyss that was calling out to her.

"Rachel..." she heard again.

"And where are you taking her?" Rachel's mother asked.

"You don't deserve to know," Garrett said. Rachel had never heard him sound so angry. His hand was trembling, his grip tight. "I can't believe you're more concerned about bad publicity than your own daughter."

"Don't leave us." The voice was louder, closer. Then another spoke. *"You're supposed to be with us."* And another. *"You were never supposed to leave."*

The voices were right next to her. Her skin erupted in gooseflesh as she felt a breath of icy cold air on the back of her neck. She quickened her pace, but her mother followed along as Garrett led Rachel down the stairs into the foyer.

"My daughter has already been abducted once," her mother said. "I think that's quite enough."

"Mother!" Rachel didn't recognize the shriek that came from her mouth as she wheeled around. Her entire body was shaking. "Don't you dare compare this with what happened to me," she said. "Garrett is trying to help, which is more than you've done since I came home."

Wherever Garrett was taking her had to be better than this—as long as it wasn't back to the hospital. She was fine with whatever he had in mind. She trusted him.

She didn't trust anyone else in the house with the knowledge of where she would be. Why did her mother even care?

Wait—she *didn't* care. She was a merciless, vengeful woman. Rachel's cheeks tingled as she understood her mother's plan.

Either get Garrett to say where he was taking Rachel, letting the spirits in the house overhear and seek her out to torment, or even better, watch Rachel slip up and mention the voices in front of him.

It didn't matter that her mother knew they were real from first-hand experience. Rachel had inherited her ability from her mother—not that the woman would ever let anyone know she was psychic. Without the moonstone earrings she always wore that somehow blocked the voices, her mother would hear the ghosts too.

No, she didn't want to know where Rachel would be. Her mother wanted to punish Rachel for leaving—like she'd punished Rachel for befriending spirits as a child.

Rachel's rage became a living thing inside her demanding release. Thoughts and feelings she had stifled for days, weeks, her entire life pressed against her lips. For one brief moment she wanted to know what it felt like to be free.

She stepped in front of Garrett, walking right up to her mother. She had never noticed how small the woman was.

"That's the first time you even admitted that I was abducted," Rachel said.

She dropped her purse and the bottle of saltwater so she could pull the sweatbands off of her wrists.

"I'm done. I'm done being a marketing prop. You want a picture?" She threw down the wristbands and held up her arms, revealing the shining red and white scars Michael had left behind. "Take one now!"

Her mother's mouth dropped open, but nothing came out. Rachel would remember that sight for the rest of her life. She felt a thrill of victory. Lillian Montgomery, speechless.

"That's why…" Garrett's voice was almost a whisper, so soft

Rachel thought at first it might be one of *them*.

"That's why she had you wearing the tennis outfit," he said. "To match the wristbands. So no one would see and ask questions—no one would know what happened to you."

"It doesn't matter." Rachel bent down to pick up her things. "We're leaving."

"It does matter!" Garrett stepped toward Rachel's mom, glaring balefully. "What the hell is wrong with you?"

She knew Garrett had seen through Lillian's act the first time the two spoke. It was one of the things Rachel loved about him. Her mother had never been able to fool him.

Rachel had been watching him all night at the fundraiser, unable to pull her eyes away. She'd caught the look of revulsion on his face as he walked away from his exchange with her mother. Their gazes had locked across the room.

He'd looked nervous, but Rachel smiled and rolled her eyes at him, then shrugged. His smile had been hesitant—the first one he'd directed at her. Butterflies had swarmed up from her stomach, words sticking in her throat.

She had left early to avoid talking to him.

Rachel put her free hand against his chest. Her voice was shaking. "Garrett, please."

"Where are you going, Rachel?" a voice said. Another whispered, *"Where are you going?"*

Rachel's heart lurched at the sound—at the low, even tone of the women's voices—vaguely familiar. Three people in the hallway. Five voices.

Garrett looked stricken as he gazed down at her. Rachel struggled to appear at least a little bit calm.

"She's your mother," he said.

Rachel cast one last glance over her shoulder at the woman who had given her life and then proceeded to make it a living hell.

"Not anymore."

Lillian stiffened her spine, getting ready to light into them again. "I will not be spoken to in such a disrespectful manner in my house!"

Garrett opened the door and tugged Rachel's hand. "How about in your yard? Because we're heading outside and if you want to follow us and keep being a royal bitch, you'll have to come along."

Rachel wished she could laugh at the scandalized expression on Lillian's face. But all she could think about was getting away.

"Where are you going, Rachel?" The voice was in front of her.

She ducked behind Garrett and quickened her pace, almost stepping on his heels as he led her down the front walkway.

She was reminded of the tale of Orpheus and Eurydice. Garrett was braving the underworld to bring Rachel back to the world of the living. She had a feeling Hades was kinder than Lillian.

Rachel kept her gaze on her feet and softly chanted, "Don't look back. Don't look back."

She matched Garrett's pace until she felt the heat-soaked asphalt nearly scald her legs, burning her feet around her sandals. She walked a little faster.

He led her to the far side of his car, into the green grass along the verge of the road. How long since she'd breathed fresh air?

He set down her suitcase, then dug in his pocket for his keys. The car beeped as he hit the button to unlock it. He opened the back door and set her suitcase on the seat.

"Let me help you." He lifted her backpack from her shoulder.

"Be careful."

"I will."

He stared into her eyes and she knew they weren't talking about her bag anymore. He set it in the car and closed the door without looking away.

Her heart had been thumping like a jackrabbit since he asked her to come with him. The thumping turned to thunder as she realized he was still holding on to her hand. His grip was tight, as if he was afraid she would slip away.

She had tried. Tried to stay out of his life—to leave him alone so he could find a nice normal woman to settle down with. But every time she thought he was moving on, something happened that brought them back together. Like now.

Looking back at the house, she saw her mother standing in one of the front windows, arms crossed and condescending smile firmly in place. Hopefully that smile would fade when she realized that Rachel wasn't coming back. One way or another, she was never coming back.

Rachel stood a little straighter, determined to leave with her head held high. She tried to compose herself while staring at her mother— Lillian—before turning back to Garrett.

The sun glared off the top of his silver car, blinding her for a moment. The car's window reflected back the palm trees behind them, the open sky and white clouds above...and the two dead women standing over her shoulders.

Blonde hair, blue eyes. Michael had a type.

"Where are you going?"

For a moment, Rachel could only stare in shock. Both women were gaunt, their skin absolutely white, which made the dark circles under their eyes stand out like livid bruises.

The spirits lifted their arms for her to see. Their wrists were mangled, bloodied and torn in the same places Rachel's had been.

Michael's victims. Two of the spirits who had begged Rachel not to kill him.

"I'm sorry." Rachel closed her eyes tight, tears spilling down her cheeks. Hearing the women Michael had killed was bad enough. Seeing them was unbearable.

"Hey," Garrett's voice was so gentle it hurt. She felt him dust his knuckles over her cheeks, wiping away the tears—even though more quickly followed. "There's no reason for you to be sorry."

"You have every reason to be sorry!" One of the ghosts shouted right next to Rachel, a blast of cold hitting the side of her neck.

Her eyes snapped open as she pulled away from Garrett, lifting her spray bottle. He held up both hands and backed away as if she was holding a gun.

She wanted to laugh, but knew she would sound hysterical.

"Didn't we suffer enough, Rachel?" one of them asked. *"You barely suffered at all!"*

The other said, *"We told you what he did to us. We warned you not to kill him."*

Rachel tried to ignore the voices. She knew she must look crazed to Garrett. Taking action would only make things worse.

"You killed him anyway. You let him reach us," the first one said.

Rachel shook her head and tried to cover her ears without setting down her spray bottle.

"Rachel, what's going on?" Garrett asked. "Talk to me."

A voice hissed into her ear. *"But now we can reach you!"*

Icy cold pressed against her wrists and around her neck. The spirits hadn't figured out how to cause real damage yet. But they were trying.

"Don't touch me!"

Rachel started spraying in the direction of the voices, saturating the already salty air with concentrated saltwater. Any spirits in her immediate vicinity would be disrupted for a few moments at least— time she needed to use to her best advantage.

She threw open the door and jumped into the back seat, spraying everything. The windows, the seats, the floor, the ceiling. She reached into the front and did the same thing.

Garrett stood outside the car, eyes wide, mouth hanging open. How was she ever going to explain this?

That was a problem for later.

"Get in!" she yelled. "Get in and drive! Please!"

As she slammed her door shut, he ran around to the driver's seat. He slid behind the wheel and started the car, then peeled away from the curb. Maybe he was trying to get her to the hospital as quickly as possible.

She would jump out of the car if it came to that. She wouldn't go back to a place packed with spirits, with environments she couldn't control. The vengeful spirits from her mother's house would probably check the hospital first anyway.

Rachel didn't want to jump out of the car. She wiped the tears from her cheeks and sniffed.

"Please don't take me back to the hospital. They don't know how to help me."

"I don't know how to help you, either."

His tone was flat. Hopeless. He was trying to help her and it was hurting him. Like always.

She'd need a hand and he would appear and make everything better. In the process, the attraction between them would flare like a star, and she would bolt right before anything happened—before a real connection could be made.

If she had explained why, he would have moved on, seeing her for the freak she was. He could be married by now. With kids. She knew that was what he wanted. She wanted it too, but how could she pull someone she loved into the chaos that surrounded her? How could she ever start a family when her life was full of death?

Her tears kept falling, but she ignored them. She shifted in the seat to see him without looking in the rear-view mirror.

"Dante and Elsa are staying in the city. Maybe I can stay at their place in the country with Winston?"

That would be perfect. The lower the population density, the fewer ghosts would be hanging around. Then she could focus on dealing with the ones that were after her specifically.

"Winston's with them in the city."

"Even better. I need to be away from everything. Far from people."

"I'm not letting you be alone."

"There are too many people here, Garrett. Too much history. I can't deal with it."

He nodded, then accelerated again. "Okay."

Maybe he thought she was talking about Michael or her ordeal at the hospital. She didn't care, as long as they kept heading out of town.

She threw herself back against the seat, closing her eyes and taking deep breaths, so grateful he had come for her—was helping her. She would keep herself in check this time. No lingering stares or light touches. No raising his hopes.

Garrett would take care of her. She knew it. She just had to make sure it didn't cost him too much.

Chapter Three

This was the stupidest thing Garrett had ever done. Instead of the hospital, he was taking Rachel to his home.

It made a sort of sense that she didn't want to go back to the hospital. She associated that place with her abduction and mental breakdown. The only memories she had of his home should be positive —painting rooms, cooking, looking at the stars with the telescope she'd picked out for him.

At least, he hoped his house would be filled with happy memories. He wasn't completely sure, with the way she had dropped out of his life.

She had renovated his house—living with him for months—helped him host a few dinner parties after she moved out, and then abruptly stopped visiting. No warning, no explanation.

They had never been more than friends, but he had still been so messed up about it that his friend Jazz had tried to set him up with her best friend Elsa. Jazz said the pairing was destiny, since the two of them even lived right next door to each other. It was a nice sentiment, but not meant to be.

At least Elsa had let Garrett be part of her life after dating didn't pan out. Rachel and Garrett's paths only seemed to cross anymore when she needed help. Sometimes she'd call. More often he'd just stumble into things.

He glanced in his rearview mirror, which he had adjusted so it was mainly focused on the back seat rather than the road. Rachel was sitting with her head against the window, her eyes vacant as the lush scenery sped past. She didn't perk up until Elsa's driveway came into view.

"You're taking me to Elsa's after all?"

"No." Garrett's drive was just past Elsa's. He didn't dare look to see

Rachel's expression. He would read too much into it, no matter what it was.

"Don't go into the garage," Rachel said. Her voice was tight.

Damn. He should have thought of that. It was the first reaction she'd had that made sense.

Michael had kept her chained up in his garage. That was where he had tortured her.

Garrett stopped the car in front of his house. He waited for a moment before killing the engine.

What was he doing?

He heard Rachel open the door and kicked himself into gear. Movement shook his thoughts loose.

He was helping his friend. That was what he was doing. He would sort the rest out later.

By the time he was out of the car, Rachel had already slung her purse and backpack over one shoulder. The spray bottle she had nearly drowned him with was tucked into the strap of her purse. She was just starting to drag her suitcase out of the back seat when he reached her.

"Let me get that."

"Thanks."

She turned and stared at his house—modest compared to her family's or even Elsa's. Garrett didn't need much and didn't want to have to keep up with a big place. It was just him most of the time.

When he'd bought it, he had still been working in the ER with hours so crazy he barely slept at home. Rachel had been delighted to find all the walls blank, the place sparsely furnished, and a budget that let her imagination run wild.

Even with that freedom, she'd kept Garrett's comfort in mind with every choice she made. She had contractors turn all his square doorframes into arches so he didn't feel like he was about to whack his head any time he left a room. The only thing on the windows were blinds, which kept them nice and open and made every room seem more spacious.

He would never have thought to do half the things she had done that made his house feel like home. The memory of her living with him during the renovation was a big part of that, though.

"It's been a while since you've been here." He didn't mean it as a dig, but she winced. Great job making her feel welcome.

He pulled out his house key as they walked to the front door. Once inside he said, "Come on. I'll make us some lunch while you get settled."

"I'd rather cook." There was an urgency to her tone that didn't make any sense. She must have picked up on it because she tried to laugh it off. "It's the least I can do with you taking me in."

"This isn't going to work if you aren't honest with me."

"What do you mean?"

"I know you. I know when you laugh for real and I know you use the fake ones to throw people off your trail. I want to help you, Rachel. I really do. But I can't do that if you aren't honest with me about what you need—what you're going through."

She let out a snort of a laugh. Unladylike and real. It didn't carry any mirth, but it was better than the fake twittering of a trained socialite.

She cleared her throat, then said, "I think I need to work up to that."

"Fair enough. But in the meantime, we need to call your doctor. He can come here to talk, maybe have sessions over the phone."

"I don't need a doctor."

Garrett let out a sigh that he felt all the way to the soles of his feet. "From what I've seen today, you do."

"Can't you be my doctor?" Her voice hitched and grew small. She sounded scared.

He wanted to tell her he could make everything better, but he couldn't. "That isn't a good idea."

"You treat Elsa and Winston. And you consulted with Dante's case. Even Jazz calls you when she's sick."

"That's different."

"Why?"

"You know why." He stared at her. Harsher than he should,

probably. But he was carrying a lot of pain. Pain he knew she was aware of.

He never had figured out why Rachel played dumb with everyone else, but he had seen the woman behind the pretense. The brilliant, funny, caring woman he'd lived with for three months. He was crazy about her and she knew it.

Her lips parted. Some of the color had returned to them already. They were still cracked and dry. He might not be able to treat her as a doctor, but he could treat her like a friend.

The first thing she needed was to settle in. He wanted to comfort her, give her a place of solace.

"Let's get your things put away." He hefted her suitcase again and headed for her room.

Technically, it was a guest room, but he always thought of it as hers. It had been empty when she started redecorating his house. White walls and beige carpet.

Now, it had light brown hardwood floors made of bamboo, walls of warm gold, and a queen bed with matching dresser, table, desk, and a comfortable chair for reading near the window. The lamps were art pieces—ceramic sculptures that caught the light and matched the colorful paintings on the walls.

She had stayed here during the months she was renovating his house. Months when Garrett had found himself questioning his career for the first time in his life.

Back then he couldn't wait to get home and didn't want to leave for work. She'd said she wanted to immerse herself in the environment and oversee everything personally. To really get a feel for how he lived.

What she'd done instead was show him what he was missing. He would come home to gorgeous dinners, usually in the fridge since he worked such long hours, but sometimes Rachel would wait up to eat with him.

She helped him with his schedule, building him a workout room when it became obvious he never had time to get to a gym. She talked to him, really listened, and used that knowledge to transform his home.

Every day he was comforted by things she had done for him. Every day he was reminded of how much he missed her.

During the renovation, Garrett had started to come up with more things he wanted to fix to keep her around longer. When she left, he wanted to ask her to stay, but she'd already made it clear that they were just friends.

That was all she wanted. He would be that for her now.

"I really appreciate you letting me stay here." Rachel set her backpack and purse on the chair, then set her spray bottle on the dresser nearby.

"I'm glad to help." He set her suitcase on the floor next to her bed. "Feels like this thing is full of rocks. What do you have in here?"

"Books. I'll put them away later."

"Whatever you need. I suggest you start with a hot shower and a change of clothes."

He couldn't believe her mother had her wearing that ridiculous outfit to cover up what had happened to her. But it shouldn't surprise him. Her family had covered up the whole thing. He was amazed at how little media coverage there had been. Rachel's name was never mentioned. Lillian Montgomery probably didn't want anyone to see that her daughter's life was anything but perfect.

He felt sick. His eyes burned and he wanted more than anything to put his hand through a wall. Any wall. He turned around quickly to hide his anger. She'd seen enough of that with Michael.

She shouldn't have to be going through any of this. He didn't want to make things worse, so he walked to the window and looked outside at the palm trees that lined the small canal behind his house.

"It's okay." Her voice was close. She must have come up behind him, quiet as a mouse.

He turned around and shook his head. "No it isn't. None of this is okay." He brushed a lock of her hair behind her ear without thinking. She didn't seem to mind. "At least it's over."

Her lips parted on a brief breath and her eyes filled with tears.

If it was over, why did she look so scared?

Maybe she was remembering something. He couldn't change what had happened to her, but at least he could help her process it. He desperately wanted to help her feel safe.

He pulled her against his chest, wrapping his arms around her and burying his face in her hair. She wound her arms around him, grabbing the back of his shirt, pressing herself closer. Her body trembled, and he felt the front of his shirt grow damp.

How could this have happened? Rachel was the brightest, most carefree person he had ever met. Always happy, always smiling. She was the last person he would ever think would get caught up in a nightmare like this.

And yet she was at the center of it—the storm blowing around her. He wouldn't let it pull her away.

He didn't know how long they stood that way and he didn't care. Eventually he felt her grip loosen, her hands flatten against his back.

"Tell me what you need. Anything, and I'll do it. I'll make it happen. You need to cry or scream. You need somebody to wail on…"

She leaned back and laughed, wiping her nose on her arm. Her mother would be mortified. Garrett smiled.

"I need a shower."

"That one's easy. The bathroom's right where you left it."

"Could you…"

She clamped her mouth shut and looked away.

"Could I what?"

With a sigh, she said, "Could you stay outside the door for me? I'm…scared."

"Sure. Sure I can." Hell, he'd sit inside the room if she needed it. Eyes shut, of course. He was pretty sure he could manage that.

"Thanks." She smiled at him, then pressed a hand against his cheek. "Thank you. For everything."

He gripped her hand in his, squeezed it, didn't trust his voice to speak. He would give her everything. Everything he had, everything he was. He would give anything for this to have not happened to her. But that was outside his power.

Instead, he nodded and let her hand slip away as she headed to the bathroom. She paused by the chair and unzipped her backpack, then pulled out the pretty blue-green glass ball Garrett had taken down from the window in her bedroom.

"I don't suppose you could hang this up for me while I'm in there?"

"I think I can manage that. There's a hook in the ceiling and everything."

"Thanks." She gave him one last smile before picking up her backpack and heading into the bathroom. She left the door open a crack behind her.

Garrett waited till he heard the water start before hanging up the globe. Strands of molten glass formed crisscrossing patterns inside, connecting the sides of the ball like pathways.

The light caught and reflected from its surface and the little tunnels within. It was pretty and interesting. He'd never seen anything quite like it. The tiny doll in her window was new to him too. He'd ask about it later and why she had flipped out when he touched it.

That reminded him of the other weird thing she'd brought along. The spray bottle.

He walked to the dresser and picked it up, inspecting the cloudy water inside. It probably wasn't toxic, with how she had liberally sprayed it in his car and all over him.

He sprayed some into his hand and smelled it. Nothing.

Rubbing his fingers together, he detected a bit of grit.

He touched a fingertip to his tongue. Salt overwhelmed his taste buds. He wiped his mouth on his sleeve. Yeah, they were a bastion of manners, he and Rachel.

Putting back the bottle, he tried to come up with a rational reason that she would spray his car with saltwater. She treated the thing like it was some kind of weapon—like it was vital for her survival.

The list of questions he wanted to ask her grew, as did his concern. He should call her doctors, but knew what they would say. They would want her to come in for another assessment.

She would never go for that. He didn't want to find out what she would do to avoid it.

He moved her purse to the dresser, then sat in the chair. His head ached and he rubbed his temples to try to ease some of the tension.

At least Rachel was here with him. She was safe and he could take care of her. Scratch that. He could make sure she took care of herself. Help her while she got back on her feet and sorted things through with her actual doctors.

There were too many blurry lines. Too much gray space between them. They were friends, but could have been more. She needed a doctor, but Garrett couldn't help her in that way—not in good conscience. And she knew it.

But when she was at the hospital, she had still asked for his help—even cried out for him. She had begged him not to leave her side.

And she had come with him today without hesitating. She trusted him. He couldn't betray that trust by carting her off to the hospital right away. Not until they had talked and he could ease her into the idea.

The delay might cost her, though. Like when Garrett waited to listen to Finn's voicemail the day after she was abducted.

Finn was Garrett's best friend and a private investigator. He had been working on a case for Garrett—a case involving Elsa and Dante, not Rachel. And Garrett had called Finn off, asked him to stop digging.

He had done it for Elsa. She had been terrified when Garrett told her that he had hired Finn. But instead of barging in and taking charge of things as usual, she asked Garrett to take care of it. She had never trusted him to do something like that before, and he didn't want to let her down.

Now he knew that she'd been afraid that Finn would discover that she had a psychic power. And she was right to be afraid. Finn had ferreted out her secret—and Dante's.

Garrett should have known Finn wouldn't be able to walk away from that case. Still, when Garrett had noticed the voicemail, he'd thought it was nothing—an invitation to a jazz club, Finn calling to give Garrett a hard time about something. He never thought it could be so important.

His stomach cramped at the memory. He had gone over the details hundreds of times, thought of the different ways he could have spared Rachel from even a moment in Michael's garage or kept Elsa and Dante from being hurt. Garrett had done the math, figured out when the call came in and when Rachel was taken, when Elsa and Dante showed up to help her.

Garrett had been consulting with another doctor when Finn called, but could have listened to the voicemail right after. Instead Garrett had gone home to get ready for the new exhibits opening in the gallery. His stomach had been upset all that day and he'd felt weirdly out of it, but he had wanted to see Rachel again—even if she was on another man's arm.

Jazz had happened to drive past him while he'd been walking from his car to her gallery. She'd slammed on her brakes and nearly ran into another SUV, cutting him off on the sidewalk, then she screamed for him to jump in. When she'd told him what was happening, he'd never been so scared in his life. Not since...

He shook aside a memory that was even darker.

He *would not* lose Rachel. He wouldn't let her slip away.

Chapter Four

Steam surrounded her, clinging to her soapy skin. Rachel stood in the tub and let the hot water pound on her back.

She hadn't been able to shower for a week. She couldn't bring herself to be naked in her parents' house. She felt vulnerable enough as it was. Sloughing off all that grime and oil felt as decadent as a full body massage.

Knowing that Garrett was right outside, she felt safe for the first time in months. Safe and awful.

She was taking advantage of him. She knew it. He cared about her. More than cared.

No matter what was going on in her life, he was always there for her. And every time she walked away, she saw how much it hurt him. Every time, it was harder for her to leave.

She couldn't pull him into the chaos and darkness of her life. Helping her out from time to time was easier to handle than living with what she could do, with what she knew.

She had to get on her feet—and out of his house—as quickly as she could. To spare him from getting his hopes up. To spare them both from their connection starting to build, only to be severed again. But where could she go?

Jazz's apartment was in one of the most densely populated parts of the city. It would be thick with ghosts. The same went for Elsa and Dante's loft.

Their house was a different matter. And it was next door.

Rachel could run over, cleanse the place, put up poppets, and hide until she was strong enough to tune out any voices that didn't belong to the living. If she waited long enough, maybe word about her among the spirits would quiet down.

Right. Like that was going to happen. The only reason they had left her alone for this long was because her friend Hiram had been around to convince the other ghosts that Rachel's powers were fading as she grew up. Hiram was gone. He had crossed over decades ago.

Elsa and Dante's house was still her best bet. If she could convince Garrett to give her the key, she could leave him in peace. She might need to borrow a laptop till she could get one of her own. Then she'd be able to order everything she needed without leaving the property.

But she would be isolated. As much as she wanted to avoid the dead, she knew she needed the living. Being alone reminded her of the time she had spent chained up in pitch darkness while Michael had her in his power. The memory made her shiver.

Garrett wouldn't go for it anyway. He was set on her not being alone. Knowing him, he wanted to keep an eye on her, to watch for signs that she was a danger to herself or others. He would want to keep her close, to help her heal. To protect her.

She didn't deserve it. She was lying to him—to everyone. People she loved had risked their lives to save her without really knowing who she was. All they saw was the socialite's daughter, the role her mother had raised her to play.

If they knew what she could do, would they still care about her? If they knew she was a coward?

She had hidden herself away from ghosts for as long as she could. Then she had run. And she hadn't even managed that on her own. Garrett had come to her rescue again.

At least she had finally stood up to her mother.

Lillian. Saying terrible things about Rachel was one thing, but Garrett... Apparently Rachel reserved causing him grief for herself.

The only thing that made staying with him bearable was that she loved him too. She turned around, eyes stinging as her tears mingled with the hot water.

The numbness that had enveloped her over the last few days fell away, leaving her heart flayed and bleeding. Not from shock or horror over what had happened to her, but from the loss of what could have been between her and Garrett. If she had been born normal.

But Rachel wasn't normal. She never would be. And Garrett deserved better. It was bad enough he was saddled with her as a friend.

She shouldn't keep him waiting. She finished cleaning herself quickly, then turned off the water.

After wiping the excess moisture from her skin, she looked for a towel. Several were stacked on a shelf built into the wall just beyond the sink. Which presented a problem—she hadn't thought to cover the mirror when she entered. She had ducked her head and raced for the shower.

The mirror was fogged with steam. And Garrett's house was far enough from the city that she hoped there were no haunted places nearby. Unless *she* was haunted now, and that was a very distinct possibility.

Michael's other victims had not been happy with Rachel when she killed him. They were very clear on that point, even before they were certain she could hear them. They were afraid of what would happen when Michael's spirit was no longer trapped in his body.

She didn't want Michael to be able to hurt anyone, living or dead. But she hadn't known what else to do. She'd had to stop him, to save Elsa and Dante. In that moment, she had made her choice.

As soon as she had been discharged, she'd started working on helping the spirits of Michael's victims. Luckily, her parents had gathered all the information they could on *the incident*—including what had been done with Michael's body.

No family had come forward to claim it, so it had been cremated. Rachel felt a sigh of relief flow through her every time she thought about that.

With no earthly remains to link him to the physical plane, his spirit would be forced to move on to whatever came next. She had that on excellent authority, and her research corroborated what she'd been told.

Michael couldn't be the reason the ghosts at her mother's house were angry. Not directly, anyway. She didn't understand why they were so upset that she had escaped and they hadn't, why they hadn't moved on when Michael died. What was keeping them here?

They could want Rachel's help, like many spirits did. Tying up loose ends that had been left unraveled when they died.

She wasn't a stranger to ghosts trying to scare or bully her into helping them. That was the norm rather than the exception. It was a big part of why she did her best to ignore them all. Even the ghosts who were comparatively nice were just too numerous. It was overwhelming.

She shuddered as she remembered her mother's harsh lessons about toying with the spirit realm.

"You want to play with ghosts? Fine. Here are some new playmates."

Yeah, her mother was going to Hell. Except Rachel didn't believe in Hell. Or Heaven. She knew there was something *after*, but didn't think she could conceive of what it was like.

People made their own Heavens and Hells right here on Earth. Both the living and the dead. Whatever the reason, it wasn't right that Michael's victims were still suffering. She had to do something to help them.

She would check her books. She would find a way. But first she had to give herself a safe sanctuary, a place where spirits couldn't enter without her permission. To do that, she had to leave the bathroom.

She looked toward the mirror again, but couldn't bring herself to move. The AC was running and the water left on her skin began to evaporate, chilling her.

If she called to Garrett and asked him to cover the mirror, it would be one more mark against her, one step closer to him giving up on her and taking her to the hospital. She was shocked he hadn't done so already. She sank down in the tub and curled into a ball to stay warm while she thought of a plan.

She could crawl out of the bathroom. No, too weird.

Close her eyes as she passed? Her reflection would still appear in the mirror, making it that much more likely a ghost would find her.

She could just deal with it. Walk out and say, "Hi," to anyone who might be in the room with her. Not brave enough.

Just the thought of talking openly to a ghost made her tremble. Too many memories poured through her mind.

Whispers in the night, shadows flashing across any reflective surface, wicked smiles as they reached for her, let her know that they were touching her, even if she couldn't feel them—and worse, the ones she *could* feel.

Closing her eyes, she shook her head. She wasn't that terrified child anymore. Was she?

"Rachel?"

She shook her head harder, pressing her hands over her ears.

"Rachel?"

"Stop," she said. "Stop talking to me."

She felt a hand on her shoulder and jumped sideways, her shoulder slamming into the tile of the shower.

"Rachel! Are you okay?"

Garrett was kneeling next to her, leaning over the tub. He wrapped his arms around her and pulled her up against his chest.

"I'm getting you all wet," she said.

"I don't care. Come on." He helped her stand, then tried to ease her out of the tub.

"Wait."

He stopped, staring into her eyes. The pain she could see there would be etched on her soul forever. How could she do this to him?

She should tell him. Just explain everything.

But that would buy her a one-way ticket back to the hospital.

His gaze briefly wavered, a deep red blush coming to his cheeks. He looked away, but kept his hands on her arms.

"What do you need?" he asked.

"A towel."

He nodded and released her. The room was small and he was huge. He only had to take a step to reach the towels. He turned back to her with one in hand and offered it to her, averting his gaze from her body.

"Thanks." She wrapped it around herself, then pointed at the mirror. "Could you cover that, please?"

"The mirror?"

"Yes. I—" Inspiration hit and she said, "I don't like looking at myself since…it happened."

Her heart was pounding painfully against her ribs, as if it wanted to punish her for the half-truth. She had *never* liked looking in mirrors and only used a compact so she could control what she saw.

He stared at her for a few moments, the lines on either side of his mouth deepening. It was obvious he wasn't buying her story. But he picked up another towel and draped it over the mirror anyway.

"Thanks." Tears pricked her eyes again.

He helped her from the tub. His hands didn't linger this time and he pointedly avoided looking at her. Since he had just seen her naked, that kind of made sense. He was also keeping his body as far from hers as he could.

She was used to them gravitating toward each other, especially in close-quarters like these. Her heart squeezed painfully at the absence of that contact. It was the least she deserved for putting him through this.

"Are you going to be okay if I step outside while you get dressed?"

"Yes. I'm fine, really."

He looked at her then, pinning her with his gaze. "No you're not. And you don't have to be. Not with me. But you will be okay. You're going to get through this."

He lifted his hand as if he was going to touch her, but stopped himself and let his arm drop back to his side. He stepped out of the room again, pausing in the doorway.

"I'll be right outside."

A lump formed in her throat and she could only nod. After he pulled the door mostly shut, she stood still for a few moments while she composed herself. If she could pull herself together, maybe she could keep Garrett from being hurt again. More than he was already hurting.

She grabbed another towel to blot her hair. She dried herself, then threw the towels in the hamper.

She'd do the laundry while she was staying with him. And the dishes. And cook. Cooking would give her inconspicuous access to the spice cabinet, which she would need to make a new poppet for the window in her room.

Her bag was already open on the floor. She pulled out a pair of pale jeans, a deep blue button-up shirt, and her brush. Within minutes she was dressed and presentable. She put on her best smile as she opened the door and stepped into the guest room.

"Thanks so much. I feel worlds better after that."

Garrett was sitting in the reading chair, glowering so intently Rachel could almost imagine storm clouds over his head. His hands gripped the arms of the chair and his lips were pulled into a deep frown. Creases at the edges of his eyes cut grooves where she was used to only seeing laughter.

The quips she was hoping would lighten the mood dropped from her mind. She wanted to tell him not to worry about her, that she didn't need it or deserve it. She wanted to throw herself into his arms and kiss him until they both forgot all their troubles.

Instead, she walked to the bed and sat near him. She folded her hands in her lap and stared at the floor.

"You are not okay," he said. "You are not taking your medicine. And there is more going on here than you're telling me. More than you're telling anyone."

Even her psychiatrists were convinced that Rachel was on the mend and doing well. Garrett could see right through her. He always knew when she put on her fake smiles and hollow laughter.

He knew because she had been weak and let him in—let him see through the masks she wore for her parents and friends. She'd felt safe with him and let him get too close. He'd been paying for her mistake ever since.

"I am not okay," she said. "I am not taking my medicine. I'm grinding it up with a mortar and pestle and mixing it with coffee grounds and throwing it away. I didn't want them to get into the water supply."

He snorted, then leaned his elbow on his chair, rubbing his eyes with one hand.

"Well, at least you considered that." He let out a deep sigh before looking at her again. "Did you consider how not taking your medicines would affect you?"

His question wasn't patronizing or condescending. He didn't even sound angry or concerned. He asked it as one doctor might ask another during a differential, trying to get to the root of the problem—her.

"I did."

No one had all of the facts except Rachel. Her doctors gave her drugs to stop her hallucinations, but she knew that what she heard was real. She had never met a doctor she thought might believe ghosts existed, let alone that people could perceive them. Even if she opened up to someone, the more she shared, the crazier she sounded.

Garrett leaned forward, hands steepled between his knees as his long arms rested on his thighs.

"I know you wouldn't make this choice without a reason. A damn good reason. I would really like to know what that is."

She wanted to tell him. It would explain everything. Why she was often distracted in public, why she wanted everyone to think she was a flake, why she carried those stupid spray bottles with her. Even the perfume bottle in her purse was just saltwater, for moments when she needed to disrupt a ghost without raising suspicions.

But more than anything, she wanted him to understand why she had turned him down every time he asked her out. Why she turned away every time he looked like he was about to kiss her.

Her vision blurred as tears filled her eyes again. She didn't let them fall.

"I am not your doctor," he said. "I'm your friend. I've always been crystal clear about that. But even still, I'm legally and morally bound to make sure you are safe, that you are healing properly—that you aren't a danger to yourself or others."

She nodded, sniffing as her nose started to run. "You need to protect yourself. I get that."

"I don't give a damn about that. I care about you. I have to be sure you're getting the help you need."

He let out another sigh, then leaned back in his chair and rubbed his eyes again. She hadn't noticed the deep circles underneath them or the layers of extra stubble on his jaw.

How much sleep had he managed in the last two months? Every time she'd woken up at the hospital, he had been at her bedside. And he always had news about Elsa and Dante, or Jazz. Rachel didn't know how he did it.

She leaned forward and grabbed the hand that was still resting on his knee. "You don't have to take care of us all. We're stronger than you think."

He looked more than a little bewildered when he lowered his hand from his face. "We?"

"Elsa and Dante. Jazz and me."

"You sure that's what you meant?"

"I don't understand."

He stared at her for a few moments in silence, then said, "When you met with your psychiatrists, did anybody mention DID?"

"Of course not." She laughed and shook her head. "The only acronym they threw around was PTSD."

"Did they talk about schizophrenia?"

"I know what's real and what's not, Garrett. And I only have one personality. Why are you even asking me this?"

"Because I've been wondering about you for a long time. When we were working on my house, you were like a completely different person. A person I've caught glimpses of from time to time, but seems buried under this—"

"Ditzy socialite?"

He snorted again, and his lips quirked up in a tiny smile. "You said it. Not me."

She let go of his hand as she debated how much to share with him. He couldn't truly understand her choices unless he knew what she was dealing with. But she couldn't bring herself to tell him. Not yet, anyway.

The only way to convince a skeptic was with proof. For that she needed a spirit who would talk to her and who knew things that would convince Garrett she was really speaking to a ghost.

As far as she could tell, he didn't have any spirits haunting him. And Rachel didn't have connections on the other side anymore. Not since she'd started to pretend her powers had vanished and that she was so hapless no spirit would turn to her for help. Not since she started hanging poppets in her windows and spraying everything with saltwater.

"The truth is I don't really know who I am."

The words slipped out before she could think them through. But they were honest words—ones she had longed to share with someone. With him.

"My parents didn't shelter me. They *sculpted* me. To be the perfect daughter. The perfect accessory to my father's political career and my mother's social aspirations."

She had never really let herself think about it before, let alone talk about it. Garrett didn't prompt her to go on, but let her take her time to formulate her thoughts.

"I tried to live up to what they wanted. Live down to it, really. My mother always told me not to sound too smart. She didn't want me offending people or scaring away suitors. 'A proper lady is neither smart nor...'" Rachel stopped herself from finishing her mother's standard statement—*nor psychic.*

Garrett took in a quick breath as if he was about to say something, but stopped, then let it out slowly. Rachel shook her head, laughing to try to cover her near mistake.

"Anyway, you know how boring those social events can be. I was always relieved when you were there. At least I would have someone to talk to without...pretending."

"You never have to pretend with me," he said.

If only... She took a deep breath as she figured out the best way to share her thoughts without giving away too much.

"I've always been different. Strange, even. I have what I like to call idiosyncrasies. Hanging poppets in the windows and using my spray bottle everywhere to sort of mark my space... The behavior isn't a warning sign that I'm heading for a psychotic break because of what happened to me. It started way before *this*."

She leaned back and straightened her arms a bit, which pulled her sleeves up far enough to reveal her scars. There were still pressure marks over the bands of pink and silver flesh from the stupid tennis outfit.

Garrett's gaze went to her wrists and seemed to get caught there. His jaws clenched, muscles standing out along his cheeks.

She pulled down her sleeves, breaking the spell her scars had cast over him. His gaze shifted back to hers.

Sitting next to him, staring intently at his face, it was impossible to ignore how beautiful he was, the warmth that spread through her body from his closeness, the way her heart seemed to become as infinite as the sky when he looked at her.

"Right now, I am okay," she said. "Being here with you, I'm okay."

His eyes glistened. The sight nearly broke her, but she forced herself to be strong.

They were together. They were safe.

In that moment, nothing else mattered.

Chapter Five

"How many more of these do you intend to make?"

Garrett mentally counted the windows in his house. "Ten more. That'll make an even sixteen. One for every window."

They were sitting on barstools that lined the counter dividing his kitchen from his living room. Behind them, his couch, recliner, coffee table, and a big-screen TV filled the room. When he cooked for gatherings, his friends would hang out in the living room and they could all still talk. Well, if he ducked down lower than the cabinets that hung above the counter.

"You don't have to hang them in all the rooms. Mine would be enough."

"They make you feel better. We're putting them up everywhere."

He made another stitch in the tiny doll, pulling the thread tight, but not too tight. He tied it off, then started carefully turning the doll inside-out with the seams tucked away inside like she had taught him.

Rachel set to work cutting out more figures from some plain white cloth she'd brought along.

"Only in the windows," she said.

Poppets. He didn't know why the featureless things made her feel better. She called it an idiosyncrasy. He would call it a neurosis. There was more to it—he was sure. Until she was ready to tell him everything, he would play along.

Helping her make the dolls was an excuse to stay near her. He could observe her to make sure she wasn't having the relapse he feared. And he had to admit he just plain enjoyed being with her. She was tense, but he kept seeing glimmers of the way she had been when their relationship was just starting.

"Whatever you need." He lifted his latest poppet and wiggled it like it was dancing. "These things are kind of cute." Halfway between cute and creepy.

"Yours look better than mine ever did."

He grinned and said, "Never thought I'd use my medical school training like this."

She laughed—an honest-to-God laugh—and his stomach did a somersault.

"I'm sure the poppets are honored to have such a skilled physician working on them."

He snorted as he added the finished doll to the pile, then picked up another set of cloth and started to sew. For a while, they worked in silence, settling into an easy companionship.

"Why did you quit, anyway?"

Her question came out of the blue, and he almost answered it honestly.

"Because I wanted more of this—more time with you—and working crazy hours at the ER wasn't going to get me there."

Instead, he said, "Too stressful."

"Sure." She arched an eyebrow and cast him a wry grin. "It seems a waste to retire so early. Can't you start up a private practice or something?"

"I'd have to do another residency. I'm not up for that. Anyway, I keep myself busy."

"*We* keep you busy."

"I don't mind. It's nice having someone to take care of."

She looked up at him, her face curiously unreadable. "Who takes care of you?"

"I'm a big boy. I can take care of myself."

"Size is not commensurate with competence. Look at Elsa. She's tiny, but when she's around, she's in charge of us all."

"I can't argue with that."

After a moment, he laughed and shook his head.

"What's so funny?"

"You. 'Size is not commensurate...' Throwing around three-dollar words like that, you'll never get anyone to think you're a ditz again."

She smiled and said, "I never felt like I had to be a ditz around you. Not when we were alone."

"I noticed." He set the latest finished doll on the stack, then started another. "Why is that?"

"Because when it was just you and me, I felt safe."

The floor seemed to drop out from under him. He wished he was sitting on something more substantial than a barstool.

He made her feel safe. Warmth spread through his chest.

He wanted her to feel safe with him. He wanted her to always feel safe.

"I kept trying to get them to let me sign papers that would enable you to make medical decisions for me, but they said you couldn't because you had privileges at the hospital. How does that make any sense?"

He remembered her doctors asking him about it—and the nature of their relationship.

"Friends," he'd kept saying. "We're just friends."

But he still wouldn't consult on her case.

"It's a good rule. It protects everybody from doctors working cases..." He stopped himself from saying *they're too close to.* Instead he finished with, "...they shouldn't."

She gave him a half-shrug, lifting one shoulder. It wasn't the flirty gesture he'd seen dozens of times before. More like she was tuning him out.

"It made sense to me. I mean, you're a doctor."

The warm feeling in his chest chilled.

He shouldn't push it. He knew he shouldn't. But he was afraid she was reeling him in again. Telling him she felt safe with him, sharing that, then turning around and focusing on his medical knowledge...

It reminded him of when she had lived there before. One minute she'd say things that seemed to bare her soul, the next she'd laugh coquettishly and joke that she could never get involved with a doctor because it would make her mother too happy. She'd shut down or flit away.

The worst was when they'd be sharing a moment, and she'd abruptly start telling him about the type of woman he should find and settle down with. He already knew the exact woman he wanted to settle down with. He was looking at her.

"Is that it, then? It was just because of the credentials?"

"Of course not."

She glanced up at him, but whatever she saw on his face must have been too much for her. She quickly turned back to her poppets, lips pressed tightly together.

"I'm sorry. I shouldn't have—"

She cut him off. "No. You have every right to…feel that way. I get it. I'm flaky and confusing." Almost under-her-breath she added, "Especially for you."

She lifted one of the dolls and started to gently fill it with cotton balls she had found in his bathroom and fluffed up to act as stuffing.

"A lot of things are going to need to change," she said. "I realize that now. I don't think I can play the ditz anymore. It's outlived its usefulness."

"You ever going to tell me what the *use* was in the first place?"

She set down the doll and gave him a calm, level look. "I hope not."

"Why?"

"For a start, you wouldn't believe me." She picked up another poppet and stuffed it like the first.

Garrett smiled. He couldn't help it. He wouldn't believe her? That was rich. He shook his head and laughed.

"What?" she asked.

He tried to stop laughing. It was hard.

"I think I might surprise you there." He grinned. For once it seemed that he had confused her. "I'm very open-minded about all sorts of stuff."

"Really?" She arched an eyebrow. "How about Bigfoot?"

"Never met the fellow. Can't say one way or the other."

She snorted and rolled her eyes, turning back to her work. "See? I knew you wouldn't believe me."

"I didn't say I didn't believe. I just said I never met the guy. There could be a whole troop of Bigfoots running around in the Everglades for all I know."

"Don't make fun of me."

She glared at him for a moment, genuine hurt playing across her features.

Well, damn. She'd given him his first clue about what the hell was going on. And it was…Bigfoot?

"I'm not making fun," he said. He was sure to keep his tone serious. "As soon as you're both up for it, we're having Elsa over. Once you've had a chance to catch up, you tell me what I won't believe."

"Elsa? Come on. If there's one person in our group more grounded in reality than you, it's her." Rachel kept filling the little dolls, stacking them up like cordwood.

"My definition of reality expanded a while back. I get that there are things going on that we don't understand yet. That science can't explain."

"I'm not talking about things like the placebo effect."

"Neither am I."

Garrett's best friend had shifted his world view years ago. Finn's demonstration had knocked Garrett on his ass, as did the follow-up experiments Finn let Garrett run. It had taken a few weeks for the world to feel real again. Garrett was absolutely convinced that the world was full of mysteries well beyond what science could handle at the moment.

He was grateful Finn had shared his abilities with Garrett for many reasons, not the least of which being that Garrett hadn't flipped out when Elsa explained her own powers.

Time travel.

Once his mind wrapped around that whopper, everything else seemed tame in comparison.

Maybe Rachel had something going on too. Garrett couldn't guess what, except that it might deal with the voices she kept screaming about during her psychotic break—if that was actually what it was.

He looked at the poppets she had finished, a chill sweeping over his skin. They reminded him of bodies in the morgue. White sheets and...

Ghosts.

That was it. Had to be. He almost stabbed himself in the thumb as things started to fall into place.

Rachel had been fine in the ambulance, coherent and taking everything remarkably well. Once she was settled in her hospital room, she went out of her mind with fear.

She didn't mention what had happened to her, didn't ask about her friends. She just kept screaming about voices, covering her ears and thrashing her head. She begged Garrett to make the voices stop, to sedate her. Eventually, her doctors had to knock her out just to treat her injuries.

At the time, he'd thought the trauma of what happened to her had fractured her psyche. He'd never considered that the voices she was talking about were real.

Relief flooded through him, washing away the worry he'd been carrying since that night. Garrett didn't know how it worked, but he was sure he was right.

People died in hospitals every day. If spirits tended to linger, there had to be an abundance of them walking those halls. And if Rachel could hear them, that would have to be its own kind of hell.

He reached for her hand, brushing his thumb over the backs of her fingers. "You can tell me anything. You know that, don't you?"

"I know." She smiled at him faintly, then pulled her hand away.

Maybe she wasn't ready to talk about it. He didn't want to push, so he went back to his little pile of poppets, taking the matter quite a bit more seriously.

When they were finished, she had a stack of sixteen little dolls with loops of thick white string attached to their heads for hanging them in the windows. They still had openings in their sides where Rachel had added the cotton stuffing.

"Is it time to close them up?"

Rachel shook her head and said, "They aren't ready yet."

They looked exactly like the one that had been hanging in her bedroom window. Garrett set down his needle and thread.

"Okay. What's next?"

"Do you still do a lot of cooking?"

"Yeah." He'd picked up the hobby after he retired, imagining family dinners and special gatherings with friends—like the dinner parties she had helped him host.

She let out a little breath and smiled. "Great."

She slipped from her barstool and walked around the counter where they were working. She opened some cabinets and started pulling down spices.

"If you're hungry, I can make us something."

"I want to get this done first." She took out a bowl, then started sprinkling spices into it.

"Anything I can do to help?"

She paused, her gaze sliding to the nearly empty spray bottle she insisted on carrying around with her. He hadn't seen her use it since the car.

If she understood that he was open to helping her, she might decide to tell him about what she could do. And he wanted her to tell him. He didn't want to trick it out of her or confront her with it. He wanted her to want him to know—to trust him enough to share it with him.

Garrett slid from his stool and walked around the counter. He reached into the open spice cabinet and pulled out a big cylinder of iodized salt, then picked up the spray bottle.

"What's the ratio?"

She blinked a few times, like her brain was slipping gears trying to process his words. "What?"

"The ratio. Salt to water." He held her gaze, noted how her lips thinned, her throat worked to swallow. He had her thinking, and that was perfect.

"About an inch of salt at the bottom, then fill it with cold water and shake it."

"Anything else go into the mix?" He had never seen such intensity in her eyes.

She stared at him for a long time before saying, "No."

"Should I dump it and rinse it first?"

"Yes, please." She turned back to her concoction, getting out a fork and stirring everything together.

After he rinsed out the bottle and added salt and water, Garrett showed it to her before shaking it. If this thing was as important as she acted, he wanted to get it right.

"This good?"

"Yes. Thanks."

He sealed it and shook it up, then walked back to his seat. He set the bottled saltwater on the counter within arm's reach.

Wasn't there some TV show where the people were always using salt against ghosts? But they used the actual crystals, not saltwater. There had to be some connection, though.

When she was finished, she put everything away except her bowl of spices, then joined him. She looked pensive.

"You're not going to ask?"

Garrett shook his head. "You'll tell me when you're ready. I can wait."

Her lips pulled into a frown and she fixed her gaze on the poppets. She picked up a pinch of the spice mix and put it inside the doll.

"You can seal it now. Just don't let anything spill out."

"We doctors generally don't like letting things spill out when we're closing up a patient." He was trying to lighten the mood, but all she gave him was a tiny smile.

He turned his attention to finishing the poppet, pinching the cloth together so the seams were inside. He kept his stiches as tiny and unnoticeable as possible while sealing it up.

Rachel handed him doll after doll until her stack was empty and his was full. She gathered them all up, then held them close to her chest, closing her eyes and whispering something. It was almost like she was praying over them.

She probably was.

"They're ready."

"Is that it? We just hang them up?"

That intense stare was boring through him again. "No. We have to do it in a special order. We'll start on one side of the house and work our way to the other. And there's a little more to it than hanging them in the windows."

"Lead on."

He smiled at her, but the lines of tension around her eyes only intensified. Her stare turned into a glare.

He cleared his throat and gestured toward the dolls. "I can hang them up for you."

She handed them over, then bent down to dig around in her backpack. When she stood, a small bronze cup suspended on three small chains dangled from her hand. Openings in decorative patterns covered the lid and sides.

"I've seen one of those before," he said.

"Priests sometimes use them during ceremonies. It's called a censer." She set it on the counter, then opened the lid.

She bent to her backpack again and this time came up with a box of matches and some cones of incense. She put the incense in the censer, then lit it. She extinguished the match and set it in the bowl that had held the poppets' spice mix.

Smoke from the incense pricked at Garrett's nose, the scent strong and not entirely pleasant. He was a fresh-air kind of guy. But if this would help Rachel, he didn't care how it smelled. She grabbed the spray bottle, then handed him a box of thumbtacks.

"We're going to have to put a hole above each window. I hope you don't mind."

Her voice was thin and low. She wasn't looking at him at all anymore.

He wanted to make a joke about her being the one who would have to fix it the next time he asked for help repainting, but thought better of it.

All he said was, "Not a problem."

They started in her room at the far end of the house. Rachel had him hang the poppet in the window, then she sprayed the window with saltwater.

She swung the censer through the whole room, in every corner— even in the closet. Especially in the closet. Then she sprayed the doors with saltwater as well.

"This one is done." Her voice was tight and she was still frowning.

Garrett kept his mouth shut and nodded. Better cut his losses and not dig himself in deeper. They treated the whole house in the same way, moving from one end to the other as if they were herding something, pushing it away. His confidence in his theory grew.

After reaching the far end of the house, they doubled back to the front door, which Rachel sprayed down liberally. She turned to the last space in his house and paused. This time, it only took Garrett a second to remember why.

The garage.

"You don't have to," he said. "I've seen enough. I can do it."

"No." She shook her head. "It has to be me."

Chapter Six

Rachel saturated the door that led to the garage with saltwater before opening it. Her heart was pounding in her chest. For a few moments, she stood in the doorway looking inside. The space was empty except for a washer and dryer with a counter built into the wall next to them.

When she'd worked on Garrett's house, he'd told her that he loved natural light and wanted it everywhere. She never thought it would be such a boon when she changed out his garage door for one that had windows in it.

This was the antithesis of Michael's garage. His had been packed with workbenches and shelves lined with mason jars full of bizarre and disturbing things—the space a labyrinth of the macabre.

In Michael's garage, her shackles had been mounted on the wall opposite the door. Even in the dim light filtering in from the windows in Garrett's garage door, she could see the beautifully blank wall right in front of her. She let out a sigh and stepped down into the room.

"Do we need to hang a poppet over the garage door?"

Rachel started at Garrett's voice, not quite as at-ease as she thought. She tried to laugh it off, one hand to her chest, a forced smile on her face.

"Sorry. I'm a little jumpy."

"You never need to apologize to me. And you don't need to do that either." He briefly bobbed his head up in a gesture he usually saved for greetings.

"Do what?"

"Pretend you're okay when you're not."

She stammered out, "I...I know. It's just habit."

"It's okay. I'll keep reminding you as often as you need me to."

He eyed the windows set in the garage door, then past her shoulder to the door that led to the side yard. It also had a window. The glass in all of them was lightly frosted, obscuring the view from both sides.

"Only one left." Garrett held up the last poppet. "Where do we put this guy?"

"I'm not sure what to do with this space."

"Why don't you explain to me what we're doing? Maybe I can help."

Sure. If she tried to explain, he'd *help* her by taking her straight back to the hospital. No matter what he said about being open-minded or believing things that might surprise her, she doubted he would accept that ghosts were real and she could communicate with them.

Still, she wanted to give him something. He deserved that much.

"They're sort of good luck charms. I hang them in the windows to keep bad luck away."

"There are four windows in the garage door. Five counting the door to the yard. Should we make more poppets?"

"I don't think so. This space is challenging."

"Does the garage door really count as a window? The front door has glass in it, but you just sprayed it down. No poppet."

"That's a good point."

A really good point. Could he be grasping more of what was going on than she thought? She stared at him for a few moments trying to assess his expression, his body language, anything that might give her a clue. All she saw was a man desperate to help her.

She should have been more distant when they were working on his house together—refused the job outright. But she couldn't stay away. Like now. She wanted to be with him—no, *near* him. She could never be *with* him.

He deserved a normal partner, someone he didn't have to rescue constantly. Someone who didn't have trouble tracking a conversation with the living because of whispers from the dead.

She played into Garrett's weaknesses—his compulsion to help people. She knew it. And she still couldn't stop herself from calling.

Because it meant another few hours—even minutes—in his company.

"The bottle's running low. Should we go make some more?"

"I need to stay here with the incense."

The hair on her arms lifted at the thought of being alone in the garage. She pushed aside the terror that was leaping up from the pit of her stomach trying to find purchase on her thundering heart.

Of course he picked up on it.

"Can't I do that? Stay in your place?"

If only. But this was her ritual and she had to be the one to finish it. Backtracking into the house would weaken the work she had already done. She smiled at him and shook her head, then handed him the spray bottle.

"Just be quick, okay?"

"Can I at least turn on the light?"

"I prefer the sunlight."

He nodded, his mouth a tight line underscoring the tension in his face. She would make this up to him. She would find a way.

He handed her the last poppet, then ran from the room. Full-on ran. He would be back as fast as humanly possible.

Human speed couldn't match inhuman.

Seconds after he left, the light in the room dimmed. The afternoon's thunderstorm was rolling in early.

She wanted to walk to the garage windows and look at the clouds, but she couldn't will herself to move. She felt rooted in place, fear spreading through her muscles in an icy grip that paralyzed her.

Darker. Darker. The light in the garage faded, shadows deepening, lengthening, reaching for her.

She clutched the poppet in her hand, focused on the scent of the incense. The house was already cleansed and warded. All she had to do was make it across the threshold from the garage to the hallway and she would be safe.

She was already safe. She hadn't heard so much as a whisper.

"Rachel."

Closing her eyes, her entire body began to shake. Had they found her already? Even out here?

"Rachel?" A warm hand gripped her shoulder. She screamed.

"Rachel! It's me!"

There was no mistaking Garrett's silhouette against the light from the hallway. Why hadn't she let him turn on the light?

Because the artificial light reminded her of Michael's garage. His had no windows, no sunlight, only the cold, controlled buzzing of the fluorescents overhead. And that was when he decided he would spare her from utter darkness.

She shook her head, forcing the fear away. The adrenaline flooding her system was making her shake.

"Sorry, I guess I'm just..." *Hearing things.*

She should be able to say it without the risk of landing in a psych ward. But she couldn't. Because she wouldn't tell him the truth.

"I wish you'd stop apologizing to me. To anyone."

"Old habits."

"Yeah, well it's high time to make some new ones. Like instead of carrying around one spray bottle, let's make it two."

She laughed—a sound that bubbled up like the last breath when being held underwater. Her chest was too tight. The room was spinning.

"Come on." He handed her the full bottle. "Let's finish this and get out of here."

She nodded, focusing all her attention on that task.

Half the bottle was empty by the time she finished with the doors in the garage. She set the poppet on the counter next to the washer and dryer, positioned as if it was watching over the space, and set an intention to match.

It would have to do.

When they were back inside, Garrett shut the door behind them and locked it. His front door was a few feet away, connected to the same foyer. He checked that it was locked as well.

"I'm not worried about burglars or anything like that," Rachel said.

"Yeah, well you make yourself feel better in your way and I'll do it in mine." He grinned.

Garrett was being too supportive. Even for him. He wasn't asking questions about her odd behavior. The way he was acting, it was almost as if he understood what was going on.

Either that or he was humoring her for long enough to call in reinforcements. One way or another, she had to know.

"We need to talk," Rachel said.

"We need to eat."

He led her back to the kitchen. She set down her spray bottle on the counter and took out a trivet to place under the censer. The thick scent of the incense surrounded them.

Her body had gone numb while standing in the dark garage, but she knew she must be hungry. She wasn't sure she could keep anything down though.

"I'd just like some water."

Thunder clapped nearby and they both jumped. The sound of rain pelting the roof quickly followed.

"That was weird timing," he said. "Have any other wishes you want granted?"

She spoke before she could think better of it. "I want this all to have been a bad dream. I want to be normal."

"I'm with you on the first one a hundred percent. But I can't back the second."

"Why?"

"I want you just as you are."

Her mouth fell open at his honesty. She could read it a couple of ways, but she knew how he meant it. He accepted her, cared for her, as she was.

But he didn't know everything.

Maybe telling him would help. Maybe it would push him away.

He headed for the refrigerator. "I hope turkey sandwiches are okay. As I recall, you really like them."

"Garrett." She waited to speak till he was crouched in front of the fridge, the door blocking her view of him. Somehow, that made it easier.

"Yeah?"

"I'm clairsentient."

"Clair-what-now?"

"Clairsentient. It means I can perceive things using Extra Sensory Perception. ESP."

He kept rattling around in the fridge. "What kind of things?"

"Ghosts. Voices of the dead."

He stood up, mustard and mayo tucked under one arm and bags of turkey and cheese in his hand. "I think I saw that movie." His face was deadpan, but he had to be joking.

"I'm serious."

"So am I. I'm trying to get a common frame of reference. I want to understand what you're telling me."

She hadn't expected that. He was being rational about it. Hearing her out. Part of her was excited at the opportunity to explain herself. Maybe, just maybe, he would believe her.

But a bigger part was terrified. She wasn't sure which she dreaded more—him thinking she was crazy or...believing her. This was supposed to push him away, not open possibilities.

"I only hear them. I don't see them. Well, except in reflections."

"That's why you had me cover the mirror in your bathroom."

"Yes."

He nodded. "Okay. After lunch, we cover the rest of them. There aren't many, so it won't take long. And let's cut up a sheet or two instead of using towels. They'll stay put better."

"Are you listening to me? Ghosts are real. They're around us constantly. And I can hear them."

"Yeah. I get it." He set down the food on the counter, then closed the door to the fridge. He kept working on lunch as he talked. "And that's why you aren't taking your meds. There's no point in taking anti-hallucinogens when you aren't hallucinating."

It couldn't be this easy. He must be trying to keep her calm. As soon as he had a moment to himself, he would call someone to come get her or figure out a way to take her to the hospital himself. In the meantime, he was casually making them sandwiches.

"I'm not going back."

She bit out each word. She would run into the swamp before going back to the hospital. At least there all she'd have to face were alligators. And snakes. And bugs.

Okay, maybe she wouldn't run into the swamp, but she sure as hell wasn't—

"I know."

He spoke so softly her furious thoughts almost drowned him out. His voice was tired, gentle, resigned. If he had said it any other way, she probably wouldn't have registered him speaking. But there was a power to his quiet.

"How can you know? How can you believe me?"

He handed her the sandwich. "First we eat. Then we talk."

She had seen that look before. He wasn't going to budge.

She took a tentative bite. Her stomach didn't balk at food as she had feared, and she was hungrier than she thought. She still glared at him the whole time she ate. He just smiled.

When she finished inhaling her sandwich, he handed her his own, then made another for himself and brought her some iced tea. How could he be so nonchalant about this?

When they were done she said, "You really believe me?"

He aimed a dazzling smile at her. "Being able to hear ghosts isn't the most outlandish thing I've heard *this month*. Your ability is kind of mainstream in comparison."

Garrett knew other psychics? She had trouble believing it, then realized the hypocrisy of her thought. Adrenaline fired through her system, this time tinged with excitement instead of fear.

He shook his head and said, "I'm starting to think you can't throw a rock in this town without hitting a psychic."

"Only the ones without precognition."

He laughed. It wasn't much of one, but it made her heart skip in her chest—which was a bit hard to notice, since it was already flipping out from the joy of knowing she wasn't the only one.

Well, aside from Lillian. And Lillian didn't count.

"Let's move to the couch," he said. "This might take a while."

He picked up the spray bottle, then pointed at the censer. "Do we need to bring that?"

"No, it just needs to burn itself out."

She followed him into the living room, then sat on the couch and curled her legs up under her. Instead of sitting in his recliner, Garrett joined her. He pulled out his phone and set it on the coffee table.

"How many do you know?"

She wanted names, phone numbers, ability descriptions. But if they were anything like her they would want their privacy. Maybe she would have Garrett give them her contact information and pray they were as curious about her as she was about them.

"With you, it's an even four."

"Seriously?" She leaned forward, rising up on her knees.

He laughed again. "Don't get too excited. There's only one that I know for sure wants to talk to you about it. The others... Well, their secrets aren't mine to share."

"Wait, why would they want to talk to me?" Unless they already knew about her. "Do they have precognition?"

"Not exactly." He picked up his phone, then pulled up a contact. "You need to talk to Elsa."

Icy dread threaded through Rachel. Her veins crackled with it. She hadn't spoken to Elsa or Dante since they'd been hurt.

"Elsa is busy taking care of Dante. And I don't want to wake them if they're sleeping."

"It's the middle of the day. They'll be awake. Plus, Dante is doing great. She'll be glad to hear from you, trust me."

Rachel shook her head, shrinking back on the couch. Her vision blurred with tears. "No. No, she won't."

"Why not?"

"Because I'm the reason that she and Dante were hurt. They were trying to save me. I'm the one who was stupid enough to get involved with Michael."

"Stop. Stop right there. I won't let anyone speak against my friends like that. Even if it's them doing the talking. And if Elsa was here, you know she'd say the same."

He took Rachel's hand in his, letting his strength and warmth seep into her. "It isn't your fault that this happened. Michael fooled everyone. Even Jazz was clueless, and you know how good she is at reading people."

"He didn't fool Elsa. She knew something was wrong. She tried to warn me, but I wouldn't listen." A flash of insight hit Rachel. "It's not... It can't be Elsa, can it? Can she see the future?"

Garrett sighed, holding the phone out to Rachel. "You need to talk to her. I'll stay or go. Whatever you need."

"Stay. Please. I don't want to be alone."

"All right."

For this call, she wanted all the support she could get. As if he sensed her need, he draped his arm over her shoulder. She nestled against him before taking the phone.

Elsa's number was already displayed. Rachel took a deep breath and made the call.

Chapter Seven

This was a level of Hell. Pain and pleasure tore at Garrett's heart as Rachel snuggled next to him on the couch.

He'd dreamt of holding her like this. The circumstances were vastly different in his imagination.

Rachel put the phone on speaker and held it in front of them so he could share in the call. He felt a tremor run through her and pulled her closer.

"Garrett! How are you?" Elsa's voice was lighter than ever. He'd never seen or heard her as happy since she and Dante became a couple.

Rachel must have heard it too. She seemed stunned, staring at the phone with her mouth slightly open.

"Doing good. I'm here with Rachel."

"Rachel? Hi! How are you?"

"I'm...good, thanks. Thanks for asking." Rachel wiped her eyes and sniffed, then beamed at the phone. "I'm glad you guys are okay."

A peal of giggles drowned out the end of Rachel's sentence. She looked at Garrett, her eyes wide. She must feel like she'd slipped into *The Twilight Zone.* He was right there with her.

Normally, Elsa was the reserved one and Rachel was ebullient. Things changed.

"Stop that!" Elsa said. "You're supposed to be resting."

"Dante's with you?" Garrett asked.

"Yes. I'll put the phone on speaker."

"Only if Winston isn't around. This conversation is going to be a little bit sensitive."

There was a slight pause, as if Elsa was picking up on the tension on the other side of the line. Her voice was more subdued when she spoke again. "He's in his room listening to audiobooks with the door closed. You're on speaker now."

Elsa and Dante were staying in their loft in the city to be close to Dante's doctors. Garrett missed having them next door, but agreed with their logic.

It did make having private conversations like this one a bit more problematic, since Elsa's butler, Winston, was staying with them in the much smaller space. They had even moved their cat, Leonardo.

"Hey, Dante," Garrett said. "How are you feeling?"

"Marvelous. Modern medicine's modalities are mesmerizing," Dante said.

"He's been doing this for the last half-hour. Alliteration was not listed in the side effects of his medicines. Do you have anything to make him stop?"

There was laughter in Elsa's tone and Garrett chuckled.

"I think this conversation will put a stop to it," Garrett said.

Dante laughed. "Quell it quickly to quash any quarreling."

"Quiet," Elsa said.

Garrett waited for them to stop laughing before asking his question. "Dante, when were you born?"

"Quite a question."

"Dante!"

Dante's tone became a bit more serious. "The second of April."

"The year," Garrett said. "Rachel needs to know."

There was a long pause. When Dante spoke again, his voice was low and the playfulness was gone.

"Eighteen hundred and forty-five."

Rachel turned to Garrett, her eyebrows knitted. He nodded in what he hoped was a reassuring manner, then said, "And how did you get here?"

Elsa jumped in. "I brought him."

"How?" Rachel's voice was weak.

"According to Jazz, I used astral projection to travel back in time and brought him forward 'through sheer stubborn willpower'. I haven't had a chance to research it myself, but it's Jazz, so she's probably right."

Rachel was shaking her head, as if she couldn't believe what they were saying. "Wait, you didn't know what you were doing when it was happening?"

"I knew what I was doing, just not what it was called. I've always thought of it as 'traveling'. It's something I've been able to do since I was a child. I never researched it because I was afraid to be seen with books about paranormal phenomenon."

When Garrett had been helping Dante get settled in the loft a few weeks back, Elsa had explained her powers and that she had saved Dante's life by pulling him through time to the present.

Jazz had been there and had already been clued in. She seemed to know more about Elsa's powers than anybody. It had confused Garrett initially, but made more sense now that he knew Elsa hadn't researched her own abilities—which still struck him as odd. He hadn't said anything at the time because he had been too busy pretending to be surprised.

Finn had already been looking into Dante at Garrett's request, and straight-out told Garrett that Dante was from the 1800s and Elsa had teleported him to the present. That plus the pre-surgery blood work that showed Dante had never received any inoculations...

Yeah, Garrett had come to terms with the idea of time travel before Elsa had said a word.

Being friends with Finn had given Garrett plenty of practice wrapping his mind around serious weirdness. He wondered how Rachel would hold up to learning about what Elsa could do. At least she had personal experience with the paranormal to draw on. Garrett hoped it would help.

"Garrett, you know I trust you," Elsa said, "but some context would be nice."

Her trusting him—or anyone, really—was another amazing change. She hadn't hesitated to answer his questions. She had been the biggest control freak he'd ever met until she became involved with Dante. She took charge of every situation, never trusting anyone else to do anything for her.

Garrett still wasn't sure how Dante had helped Elsa let go and start enjoying her life. Garrett sure as hell appreciated it though. They all did.

Rachel had the opposite problem. She seemed to be enjoying life, flitting through it blithely, but deep down she had been suffering the whole time. She used her poppets to control her environment, but she was trapped in the space she created.

Garrett didn't know what to do about that. Yet. But he could help her now—take the pressure off so she wouldn't have to share her own ability until she was ready.

"It was time," he said. "That's all."

"Is that..." Rachel's voice crackled. It was low and raw. She cleared her throat and said, "Is that how you knew? About Michael?"

"Yes, my powers helped me find you."

"No, I mean... Is that how you knew he was dangerous? You tried to warn me."

Rachel covered her mouth, her eyes clinched shut as tears streamed down her face. She was trying not to let Elsa and Dante hear the pain—shielding them from it.

Garrett wasn't so lucky. The cracks along his heart where it had broken time and again with Rachel started to bleed as she shuddered and silently cried in his arms. He pressed a kiss against the top of her head and helped hold the phone still. From the way her hand was shaking, she looked ready to drop it.

"No." Elsa's voice became cold. "My parents hurt each other. Sometimes they hurt me too. I can recognize the potential for violence."

Rachel's hand moved to her chest as her breathing became rapid. "What?" She choked back a sob. "I'm so sorry. I didn't know."

It was news to Garrett too. His grip on the phone tightened.

"Nobody did. And it almost cost me Dante. It almost cost you your life."

"I don't understand," Rachel said.

"If I had explained how I knew about him, maybe you would have listened. I'm so sorry, Rachel." Elsa sniffed.

This was not what Garrett had planned. He wanted Rachel to understand that he believed her, not to have both her and Elsa upset and crying.

Garrett pulled Rachel closer, gently running his hand up and down her arm. He hoped Dante was comforting Elsa too.

"Please don't be sorry," Rachel said. "It's my fault, not yours. You were only hurt because you were trying to help me."

Dante spoke up, sounding much more focused and coherent. "The only involved party who bears responsibility is Michael."

Next time Garrett saw Dante, a manly hug was in order. Everybody was blaming themselves for what happened. Even Garrett, every time he thought of that damned voicemail from Finn. It needed to stop.

"I think we can all agree on that," Garrett said. "Can we also agree that we're done with the apologizing?"

"Absolutely," Elsa said.

Rachel nodded. "Yes. Of course."

"I can't believe you've been blaming yourself this whole time," Elsa said. "I hope we never go through anything like this again, but no matter what you're dealing with, if something's bothering you and we can fix it just by talking, please don't wait to call me."

Garrett suppressed a little laugh. That was the Elsa they all knew and loved. Telling people what to do. Order was restored to his universe.

"I won't. In fact that's why we called." Rachel looked at Garrett and smiled, eyes bright with tears.

His heart seemed to lurch toward her. He wanted to pull her closer and kiss away her tears. She turned back to the phone before he could do anything so stupid.

"I have a gift too," Rachel said.

"A gift?" Elsa asked.

"A psychic ability."

"You're kidding!"

Rachel laughed. "I told Garrett about it, and when he believed me right away I thought he was humoring me."

"Yeah, he does that." An edge of playfulness had returned to Elsa's tone. "Can you travel too?"

"No, mine's more...mainstream."

She grinned at Garrett. He smiled back, trying to pretend that everything was okay, that his heart wasn't constricting in his chest, suffocating from having her so close and knowing he couldn't do a damn thing about it.

"I hear ghosts," Rachel said.

"Ghosts are real?"

"Yeah."

"And they talk to you?"

"It's more like they talk near me. I've been trying not to let them know I can hear them, but I think the cat's out of the bag. It tends to make them clingy when they find out. The whole thing is not as fun as it sounds."

"I can imagine. Can you turn it off?"

"Not really. But there are things I can do to keep them away."

"That sounds awful." There was a short pause, then Elsa asked, "It isn't Michael, is it? You're not hearing him?"

Garrett's heart dropped through his stomach. He pulled Rachel closer against his chest, looking all around.

How the hell had he not thought of that immediately when Rachel told him about what she could do? His relief that she was confiding in him—that he finally had an explanation for her behavior—had clouded his mind.

"No, it's not Michael. His body was cremated—I checked. There have to be earthly remains for a spirit to linger."

Garrett lowered his head to Rachel's shoulder for a moment, willing his heart to slow down. She briefly leaned her head against his.

"That is still a very scary thought," Elsa said. "Being surrounded by people you can't see."

She wasn't kidding. Garrett would make a dozen more of those poppet things. Hell, he'd make Rachel a dress out of them.

"What can we do to help?" Elsa asked.

Garrett listened with keen interest.

Rachel wiped her face dry with the back of her hand and seemed to melt into Garrett's chest, her tension flowing out of her. He hoped she couldn't feel his heart beating, fast and urgent.

"Just knowing you believe me—knowing I'm not the only one with a gift—really helps. Thank you."

"Of course. I still wish there was more we could do."

"Don't worry about me."

"I do not wish to add to an already tense subject," Dante said, "but I must inquire... Is Elsa safe when she travels? If there are spirits about that she might encounter while outside her physical form, some of whom may be dangerous, I would rather we know and address the situation."

"I've never heard of people running into ghosts during astral journeys," Rachel said. "Maybe they're on a different wavelength or something. The bigger issue is protecting your body while you're journeying."

"I always make sure I'm in a locked room when I travel and I'm the only one with a key."

Rachel's brow knit together and she cast a glance at Garrett that was not reassuring. "I meant protect your body from possession. Florida is filled with spirits. An unoccupied body is easy pickings for any coherent ghost. They just step right in. If a spirit's personality is strong enough, they can even possess occupied bodies."

Garrett felt a chill shoot down his spine. How many times had Elsa left her body unattended, flirting with disaster without even realizing it?

"That is a most alarming bit of information," Dante said. "What can we do to protect her?"

"First you stay calm," Garrett said. "Stress won't help with your recovery."

"She just needs to refrain from traveling," Rachel said. "Until I can make a talisman to protect her."

"You know how to do that?" Elsa asked.

"I have a pretty good idea. I'll research it more to be sure. I'll need materials, but I'll take care of it. Don't worry. You just focus on taking care of Dante."

"Thank you," Dante said.

"Yes, thanks. And thank you for telling us, Rachel. I know how hard it can be to open up about these things. But secrets between friends aren't a good idea. Not like these."

Rachel nodded. "I'm starting to see that. You guys take care, okay?"

"You too."

Rachel disconnected the call and immediately dialed another number. She didn't put the phone on speaker, but lifted it to her ear instead.

"Hey, Jazz. Yeah. Yeah, I know. Yes, I should have called sooner. I've been distracted."

Rachel rose to her knees, which took her out of Garrett's arms. He tried to hide his disappointment. She was focused enough on her call that she didn't seem to notice.

"I need your help. I'm going to text you a list of things I need from Bookwyrm. Yes, the hippie bookstore you like. Yes, I've been there. Well, I never mentioned it because... Look, I'll explain when you bring me the things on the list." She rolled her eyes at Garrett and shook her head. "Can you bring it to Garrett's house this afternoon? I'm staying with him for a while. Yes, I left my mother's house."

Garrett could hear Jazz's enthusiastic response from two feet away. Rachel moved the phone from her ear. She sighed when she started listening to Jazz again.

"I know, I should have done it sooner. I'll explain everything when you get here. Okay. Thanks! Bye."

She disconnected the call, then set the phone on the coffee table. Her lips were pulled into a broad smile.

"Thank you for doing that for me," she said. "For believing me, for letting me stay here, for...everything!"

She threw herself forward, wrapping her arms around his neck.

Garrett rested his hands on her back and closed his eyes, letting the feel of her soak in—warmth and joy and the brightest essence he'd ever felt. He took a deep breath, filling his lungs with her scent.

Something shifted in her embrace. For a moment, she softened against him. Her cheek grazed his, her breath tickled the fine hairs on his neck.

Warmth turned to heat and the thought of cradling her face in his hands and kissing her senseless became almost overwhelming. But then she stiffened and pulled away. Again.

It didn't surprise him anymore, but it still hurt like hell.

"I need to get my books," she said. "To research the talisman for Elsa."

Garrett nodded. "I'll help. Any way I can."

She wouldn't meet his eyes and her cheeks were flushed. There was attraction between them. He knew she felt it too. But there was something else standing between them—something he couldn't see, couldn't touch, couldn't tear apart.

Damned if he knew what it was.

Chapter Eight

The coffee table was covered in open books when the doorbell rang. Rachel didn't jump at the sound. She let out a little sigh, realizing she was more relaxed than she'd been in months.

She felt safe. Safe enough to convince Garrett to take a shower and leave her on her own for a little while.

"Coming!"

She ran to the counter to grab the censer before heading for the door. She had already refilled it and lit fresh incense, knowing Jazz would arrive soon. Now Rachel had the fun of explaining why she needed to smudge Jazz when she came inside.

The windows along the side of the front door let Rachel see Jazz standing on the stoop, holding a bright green bag decorated with a picture of a dragon lying on its back and reading a book. Its tail wound around a crystal ball.

Rachel smiled as she opened the door. "Hi!"

Jazz hesitated before saying, "Hi."

Her dark eyes glittered strangely in the late-afternoon light and her long black hair hung around her shoulders as if she hadn't done more than brush it. She still wore her signature black leather pants, but instead of her usual white V-neck T-shirt, she had on a dark, oversized sweater that practically engulfed her slight frame.

Rachel panicked. Where was the cocky smile and knowing gaze? Aside from a few times when Jazz lost her temper, Rachel had never known Jazz to be genuinely upset.

"What's wrong? Did something happen?"

"Are you kidding me?" Jazz's voice was shrill instead of her normal rich tenor. "Yes, something happened. I haven't seen you since you left the hospital, and you've barely texted or called!"

She stepped over the threshold and swung the door shut, then grabbed Rachel in a crushing hug. Rachel wanted to make a joke to try to lighten the moment, but she couldn't. Jazz's affection was usually lots of light touches and quick hugs. She had never hugged Rachel like this before.

A tight ball of emotion filled Rachel's chest, making it hard to breathe, to think, to do anything but not cry. Careful of the censer, she hugged Jazz back.

"Are you okay?" Jazz asked. "You look better."

"I am better. Getting there, anyway."

"Why does it smell like a temple in here?"

Rachel laughed, finally pulling back from the hug. "That would be from this." She lifted the censer, streamers of smoke following its movements.

Jazz arched an eyebrow and waited patiently for an explanation. Much more normal for her.

"If you don't mind, I need to smudge you."

"You want to cleanse my aura?"

"That's the idea."

Jazz stepped away from Rachel and lifted both arms. Rachel moved the censer around Jazz's body, wafting the smoke closer with one hand. Knowing about auras—the energy field around people's bodies—was one thing. But understanding smudging? Compared to discussing her ability with Garrett, talking to Jazz would be a breeze.

"If you need me to open the bag to cleanse the stuff inside, let me know," she said.

Rachel finished her circuit, holding the censer under the bag for a few moments.

"That should be good enough." She let out a small laugh. "I know we've never discussed paranormal stuff before, but I have to say I'm very grateful you're into it and already know so much."

"I didn't know you were into it at all."

"It's kind of been a necessity for me. Let's sit down and talk." Rachel took the bag from Jazz, then led her into the living room. "Can I get you a drink or anything?"

"I'm good." Jazz walked around the coffee table to sit on the couch, looking over the books Rachel had been using for research. "I'm guessing this isn't a passing interest."

"No."

Jazz looked around the room and noticed the poppet hanging above the stationary side of the sliding glass doors that led to Garrett's back patio. "I see you're already redecorating."

A little surge of jealousy ran through Rachel. How often was Jazz a visitor that she noticed such a small change to Garrett's house so quickly?

Rachel shook it off. Jazz was super-observant. And Garrett could have over whomever he wanted. If he and Jazz hooked up, great. Great for both of them. Rachel wanted them to be happy, even though her heart sort of stuttered at the thought of Garrett with someone else. Anyone else.

"It's a poppet. They keep away spirits." Rachel cleared a small space on the coffee table, then sat on the floor in front of it.

She opened the bag from Bookwyrm and pulled out the supplies she had asked for. Some silver jewelry wire and a wire cutter, a silver chain in a velvet pouch, and a small clear plastic bag that held a few stones.

"Snowflake obsidian, fluorite, and opal, as requested," Jazz said. "I picked out three that looked like you could make them work in a necklace."

"These are perfect, thanks."

Rachel emptied the bag of stones onto her palm, then placed them on the table in front of her. The first, black with speckles of gray that looked like snow, the second a translucent mix of rich purple and blue, and the last a milky white with iridescent colors only visible when viewed from the right angles.

Jazz had managed to pick specimens that would work well together aesthetically. That was good, since Rachel hoped Elsa would wear it constantly as soon as it was hers.

Rachel set to work.

"I spoke with Elsa on the phone today," Rachel said. "She told me what she can do."

"Elsa can do a lot of things."

"So can I."

Rachel paused in her work. She looked up at Jazz, wanting to see the expression on her face when she heard about Rachel's abilities.

"I can hear spirits. Sometimes I see them in reflections. Especially mirrors."

Jazz was silent, her lips slightly pursed and one eyebrow arched on her forehead. She stared at Rachel for what felt like a long time.

"Aren't you going to say something?"

"I'm being inscrutable. It's an Asian thing."

Rachel laughed and Jazz finally smiled.

"Okay," Jazz said. "I need more information."

"You know how I sometimes get distracted? That's usually when I'm hearing spirits having a conversation. Florida is filled with ghosts. That's why I'm making this for Elsa."

"I don't see the connection."

"Elsa travels astrally. She leaves her body behind, ready to be occupied."

Rachel was still a little nervous talking openly about what she could do, but at least Jazz would understand the logistics of it. She had always been openly fascinated by the paranormal.

"Occupied?"

"It's easy for a spirit to enter an empty body."

"You're talking about possession."

Rachel nodded. "Some ghosts can even take over bodies that have souls in them. If they have a strong enough personality, they can overcome the existing consciousness. All they need is an opening or conduit. It would be easy for a spirit to take over Elsa's body while she's traveling."

Jazz's lips thinned. She gestured at the necklace that Rachel was wiring together.

"Are you sure this will protect her?"

"It should. She's been lucky."

"What about a salt circle? Would that help?"

"If she can control when she travels, yes, that would keep spirits away. I'm not sure how the circle would affect her, though. It might trap her inside or keep her from being able to get back. We can run some experiments and see."

"She's not going to want to try anything until Dante is better. Since she can control her ability by not being around any art, it shouldn't be a problem."

"Art?"

"That's what triggers her ability. I guess it's like you only seeing spirits in reflections."

Rachel nodded. "That will buy us some time."

"What about you? Are these poppets enough to keep spirits from bothering you?"

"That plus spraying saltwater on all the doors and windows. Florida is so humid and there's already salt everywhere from the ocean being close. It doesn't take much extra to ward entryways."

"I'll keep that in mind. What do you do when you leave the house?"

Rachel was quiet for a moment. She wasn't sure how to respond. Elsa's warning about secrets resurfaced in Rachel's mind. The truth, then.

"I don't."

Jazz's eyebrows hiked up her forehead. "You can't stay here forever."

"I'll figure something out. If Dante and Elsa are staying in the city for a while, maybe I can stay at their place."

"That isn't what I meant. You can't let ghosts keep you imprisoned for the rest of your life. They can't hurt you, can they?"

"It's difficult for them to hurt people physically through direct contact. They're more likely to try to startle me so I jump out in front of a car or maybe impel an animal to bite me or something."

"That's not reassuring."

"It's hard for spirits to control animals. They'd have to be extremely willful and focused. Death tends to distract people and scatter their thoughts. It takes them a while to regroup and be able to think rationally."

Unless they had a single-minded focus in life. Like tormenting people. She wished that Michael was her only experience with that type of personality—on both sides of corporeal existence. She had done her best to convince spirits she couldn't hear them anymore with very good reason.

"What about—"

"Michael is dead and gone. His body was cremated. Without any remains, his spirit can't linger." Hopefully, that would be the last time she had to talk about the matter.

Jazz let out a huge breath and nodded. "Okay. What about these other yahoos? How do we get them to stop bugging you?"

"I'm still working on my long-term plan."

She could ward her mirrors—very carefully—and make herself a set of earrings like her mother wore to deafen herself to the voices. If Rachel had spent less time and energy on ignoring her abilities, she would have thought to do so years ago.

"There's more you're not telling me," Jazz said. "I want to help."

"The best thing you can do is get this to Elsa."

Rachel held up the necklace for them both to see. It had actually turned out pretty well. The stones were balanced, and Rachel had positioned them to enhance the color and beauty of each component. The silver chain matched the jewelry wire she had used and would look gorgeous against Elsa's perpetual tan.

Jazz shook her head. "You are a miracle worker. I keep telling you I could sell your work in the gallery easily."

"I have a trust fund, remember?"

"Is that why you fought me so hard on getting a paycheck?" One corner of Jazz's mouth twitched in the barest hint of a smirk.

"The knowledge you've shared with me is worth more than any paycheck. You've given me a chance to do something meaningful that I love."

"How's that working out for you?" There was a bitter edge to Jazz's voice.

"Are you kidding? I've learned more from you than anyone."

Rachel looked up to Jazz for how she handled herself and others. Jazz didn't put up with crap from anyone. She didn't even put up with the crap Rachel piled on herself.

She had pushed Rachel to try new things and take on responsibility for projects that had intimidated her. Jazz refused to accept the limits Rachel had set on herself, and because of that, Rachel had become a stronger person. Strong enough to stand up to her mother. Strong enough to finally leave.

"If knowledge is all you wanted, you could have gone back to school," Jazz said.

"There are no schools that could give me the experience I've gained working with you."

Jazz opened her mouth, but shut it abruptly. It was unnerving to see her censoring herself. Not as unnerving as the way her eyes started to glisten again. She cleared her throat, but her voice was still gravelly when she spoke and even lower than usual.

"Is there anything special I need to do when I give the necklace to Elsa?"

"No, but I need to charge it with an intention first. If you give me a moment, I can do that now."

Jazz nodded, then leaned back against the couch. Setting the intention in front of someone was going to be a little weird. After cleansing the entire house with Garrett, Rachel was starting to get used to performing rituals around people, though.

Holding the necklace cupped between her hands—like it was a butterfly that might try to fly away—Rachel closed her eyes and cleared her mind. She shut out all her doubts and fears and focused on what she wanted.

Elsa safe and sound, authentically herself, no outside influences present or affecting her in a harmful manner. Rachel held the thought for a few moments, then imagined the thought as energy and pushed it into the necklace.

She chose two runes to go along with it. For protection, Algiz—which looked like a vertical line with a capital "Y" superimposed over it. And Uruz—an upside-down, angular "U"—for strength. She focused on each symbol, merging them with the energy she visualized infusing the necklace.

When she was done, she opened her eyes. She set the necklace on the coffee table, then flicked her hands to release any residual energy.

"Seriously? That's it?"

"The simplest solutions are usually the most powerful."

"I might have taught you about running a gallery, but I'm guessing you had other mentors."

"I had two teachers," Rachel said. "One on each side."

"Each side of what?"

"One was a spirit. The other was a medium."

"I suppose that makes sense. Actually, a lot of things I wondered about you are making sense now. Like why you try to get people to think you're scatterbrained when you're actually brilliant."

Rachel felt her eyebrows leap up her forehead. She faked a laugh, trying to recover, but she was off her game.

"I don't know about that. But I appreciate the compliment."

"It wasn't a compliment. It was a statement of fact. And you're doing it right now." Jazz let out a long sigh. "I wish you would stop."

"I don't know what to say."

"Forget it. I'm just glad you're away from your mother. I've been trying to get you out of that pit since we met. Garrett's going to get a deep discount on his next piece for accomplishing that."

"A pit? I've been living in a mansion."

"That's putting lipstick on a pig. Your mom could suck the joy out of a sold-out opening show. I've seen her do it. Belittle your accomplishments and demean you in front of a room full of people."

It wasn't the worst thing her mother had ever done. Rachel forced a laugh again, but it was an uneasy sound, even to her ears.

"You're the one who makes the sales."

"Stop. Now you're doing it to yourself."

"You sound like Garrett."

"Good. If we all remind you to disregard the crap she's told you over the years, it might help you to stop telling yourself the same lies she taught you."

Rachel felt herself tear up. She always tried not to think about the things her mother said, pulling a comfortable numbness over her heart during the worst of it. That shield was cracking, along with all of Rachel's boundaries.

She shoved thoughts of her mother into a tiny box in the back of her mind. There were other things she needed to address. Friends to protect and spirits to help.

"Thanks," Rachel said.

Jazz nodded. "Will it disrupt the energy if I touch the necklace?"

"It's best if others handle it as little as possible." Rachel slid the necklace into the velvet bag that had held the silver chain, then handed the pouch to Jazz.

"I'll see that she gets it tonight," Jazz said. "But what about you? How do we get all these ghosts to leave you alone?"

"I can take care of myself."

Jazz reached across the table and grabbed Rachel's hand. She squeezed it hard.

"We take care of each other. Now more than ever."

Rachel couldn't speak. A few choking sounds came out of her throat, her eyes burning as she held back tears—tears she saw mirrored in Jazz's eyes.

Jazz dropped to her knees next to Rachel and hugged her again. Rachel buried her face in Jazz's hair and squeezed her just as hard.

When Jazz pulled back, her eyes were red. She actually sniffed. Rachel's stomach felt weightless, like she was on a rollercoaster just before a drop-off.

"You need me—you need *anything*—you call. Understand?"

Rachel nodded.

"Okay." Jazz put her hands on Rachel's cheeks and kissed her forehead as she rose. "Give Garrett my regards. And be sure to lock the door after me."

Rachel nodded again. She couldn't do anything else in that moment, couldn't even will herself to move.

She was stunned. She stayed where she was on the floor as she watched Jazz leave.

Chapter Nine

Living in the subtropics, steaming up a bathroom wasn't hard. Water condensed on the cooler glass of the windows that lined the top of Garrett's open shower area. The whole room looked like it was part of a fog bank.

Garrett let the hot water pound on his shoulders for a while, trying to get rid of some of his tension. When he'd worked the ER, he was used to long stints of light sleep and heavy activity. Too much time had passed since he left—he was out of practice. The last few weeks had drained him.

Heck, the last few *hours* had drained him. He couldn't believe so much had happened in such a short amount of time. He'd thought he was already emotionally exhausted, but facing off against Mrs. Montgomery, that talk with Elsa, Rachel's ghost issue, and having her living with him again... It was a lot.

At least he knew Rachel wasn't as bad off as he thought. What she was dealing with sounded pretty terrible, but she was being open about it. Garrett would make sure that she had the help and support she needed.

Dante and Elsa were doing well and Michael was gone. Garrett let out a sigh. Things were finally looking up.

Then he heard the scream.

He bolted out of the shower space, barely aware of opening the bathroom door before running through his bedroom and down the short hall that led to the kitchen.

Rachel had her back to him as she grabbed a glass from the cabinet. She was holding a spatula in her other hand.

"What the hell happened?" All the fine hairs on his body were standing on end, the cold air on his wet skin mixing with an adrenaline rush strong enough to make him lightheaded.

Rachel laughed, but it turned into a choking sound when she turned toward him. It took him a moment to realize why.

Her eyes widened and her cheeks flushed scarlet. That plus her gaze locking on to his privates helped to clue him in. He grabbed the hand towel from the handle on the oven door and used it to cover as much of himself as he could.

"Why'd you scream?"

"Um," she cleared her throat, her gaze stuck to the towel. "There's a scorpion in the dishwasher. It startled me."

"A what?"

"A scorpion."

"Did it sting you?" He barely recognized his own voice, high and tight. His heart pounded.

The few scorpion species in Florida weren't considered that dangerous, but they all had venom. Everyone reacted to venom differently.

"Relax. It's just a common striped scorpion."

He would hyperventilate if he wasn't careful. He took a deep breath and let it out slow. His voice lowered to a register he was more used to.

"Did it sting you?"

"No. I was going to catch it in this glass and use the spatula to keep it trapped, then take it out back and let it go."

He felt bile rise up in the back of his throat. No way was he letting her near it.

"Give me the glass."

She laughed, tossing her head so that her hair fell past her shoulder. Such a casual gesture. She really wasn't afraid at all.

He was scared enough for both of them.

"I can catch the little guy and take him outside. I'm not afraid of scorpions."

Her words sent a chill down his spine. Garrett had heard a similar sentiment plenty of times when he was a kid. Dylan had always been overconfident when it came to wildlife. Reckless.

"Relax, little bro. I've got this."

Garrett held out his hand, forcing it not to shake. "Give me the glass."

"It's going to take two hands to get him and you're a little…busy." She let her gaze return to his towel, then looked back to him and laughed. "I can handle it, really."

No. Way.

He tossed the towel onto the counter and held out his empty hands. "Hand them over."

Rachel's gaze shot back to his privates, her eyes seeming ready to pop out of her head. She extended her arms slowly.

As a doctor, he was used to viewing the human body with clinical detachment. He wasn't used to being the one under inspection. And she was examining him thoroughly. He didn't know if he was more flattered or chagrined.

She snapped her gaze back to his at last and did one of her fake laughs. "I guess now we're even after what happened earlier."

Earlier? Right. When he'd helped her out of the tub.

That was just a day in the office, though. She needed help, he gave it. He had done his best not to look.

This was different. The way she stared with that unfocused look, as if she wasn't just seeing him but was thinking about things she'd like to do with what she saw—that was different.

She was ogling him. No doubt about it. And if he kept thinking about that, there was going to be more to see.

Garrett took the glass and spatula from her, then knelt on one knee next to the dishwasher. The scorpion was near the drain. How had it managed to squeeze through the drain cover?

Its tail was curled over its back and its pincers extended. An aggressive stance.

"Did you poke it?"

"Poke…"

Sweet Lord, have mercy. He cocked his head to the side and gave her a look that said, *really?*

Apparently it was enough to get her mind back on task. There was a potentially dangerous animal right next to them. Now wasn't the time for flirting or games.

She cleared her throat and said, "Of course not."

He reached into the dishwasher—grateful for his long arms—and quickly dropped the glass over the scorpion. It immediately lashed out, its tail and pinchers bouncing off the glass with a *tink-tink-tink*.

"Are these things always this cranky?" he asked.

"It could have come across some soap or something that set it off."

He lifted the glass just enough to slide the spatula beneath it. Rachel had picked one out that didn't have any slats. There was no chance for it to escape. When the scorpion was secured, he flipped the glass over, keeping the spatula flush with the top.

"Nice form," she said. "I mean, with the trap. Not that the rest isn't nice as well." She gestured to him, then looked away, her cheeks reddening further. "I'm going to stop talking now."

He tried to give her a smile, but what he managed felt more like a grimace. He stood, and this time she kept her face pointing at the ceiling.

"I'm going to take it outside." He headed through the living room to the sliding glass door that led to his backyard and she followed.

"I'll get the door for you."

He slipped into the shoes he kept by the back door, feeling absolutely ridiculous. Six-foot seven, dripping wet, and carting around a pissed off scorpion while wearing nothing but a pair of sandals.

Rachel slid open the door and Garrett stepped into the brutal late-afternoon heat. The air was humid enough that the water on his skin didn't even feel like it was going to evaporate.

He crossed his backyard, glad for the privacy provided by living away from the city. The canal was a good thirty yards from his back door, but he didn't want to chance the scorpion finding its way back into the house.

There was a sheer drop-off to the water on both sides of the canal and it wasn't more than six or seven feet across. The occasional gator passed by, so even though they didn't have a slope to get onto Garrett's lawn, he carefully scanned the area for any visitors.

He paused by the edge of the water, then removed the spatula and swung the glass so that the scorpion flew across the canal and landed in the grass on the other side. There was his good deed for the day.

Garrett shivered, even though the heat had killed the last of the chill from the AC on his wet skin. Buttonbush and saw palmettos grew thick among the yellow pines and palms on the other side of the water. There were probably hundreds of scorpions out there. Snakes, spiders, all kinds of things that could hurt Rachel.

If he thought about it too much, he'd never sleep again. And those were just the threats he could see. Living in the country gave him privacy from the living, but who knew what wandering ghosts might happen by.

He headed back to the house at a brisk pace, eager to put on some clothes. Rachel was staring at him through the kitchen window.

He slowed, unnerved by the intensity of her stare. He glanced over his shoulder, wondering if she was seeing something he couldn't. She didn't look scared though. Maybe she was checking him for tan lines.

When he reached the house, he scraped the bottoms of his sandals against one of the landscaping rocks next to the patio to knock loose the few sandspurs he'd picked up. Cold air hit him as Rachel slid the door open again. He stepped inside and kicked off his shoes.

She was waiting for him with two big towels from her bathroom. She handed one to him as soon as he set the glass and spatula on the counter that ran between the kitchen and living room.

"Thanks," she said.

"What for?"

"For not killing it. The poor thing was probably lost and confused."

She handed him the second towel once he had secured the first around his waist. Garrett wiped his chest and arms dry, then started on his hair. He didn't miss the way she kept staring at his chest and arms while he worked—lips slightly open, eyes heavy-lidded.

He was grateful for the towel, but he needed more to keep himself from getting into an even more embarrassing predicament. Diverting her attention would help.

"Only you would call a scorpion *poor thing*. That was a slick containment system you came up with on the fly."

"I just used what was available."

He shook his head and laughed. "Well, it worked pretty well. Remind me to call the lawn service later. That grass is too long."

Rachel peered out the window, then looked back at him, one eyebrow arched. "Your yard has a buzz cut. I can see patches of sand everywhere."

"I'm more concerned with the things you can't see. Cutting the grass shorter might not help much with scorpions, but it'll give us a better chance at spotting snakes."

"We could go out with a black light at night some time to see how many scorpions are out there."

"What, they'll all come out for a rave?"

She laughed, her broad smile soothing his frayed nerves. "Scorpions phosphoresce in black light. They should light up with a pretty blue glow."

Pretty wasn't a word he would use to describe a bunch of scorpions. He was certain there'd be plenty if they checked—that was a downside of being out from the city.

"How do you know this stuff?" he asked.

"I read a lot."

"I'd rather not know how many are out there. I like to spend time on the patio and I don't want to be worrying about how many scorpions are in my yard. Unless those citronella candles and box fans you started me using will take care of them too?"

"Sadly, that's only for repelling mosquitoes. How are they working for you anyway?"

"Haven't been bit for a while, thanks."

"Do you still take out the telescope?"

"Sometimes." Every chance he had.

He would crack open a beer and spend hours looking at the stars and planets, thinking about Rachel and her astronomy lessons.

"We should take it out tonight. I can test you on your constellations and see if you remember what I taught you. It'll be just like old times."

"That sounds like a great idea."

Primarily because she wouldn't be able to see how he was blushing if they were hanging around in the dark. He wasn't sure he'd ever stop with how she kept looking at him.

He'd imagined her seeing him naked many times. His daydreams were a far cry from the reality. For one, they were usually both naked in his fantasies. And he had never dreamed she'd have such a...hungry look to her. It was hard to ignore and even harder not to do something about.

He cleared his throat, then asked, "Do we need to do anything to keep ghosts away while we're out back?"

She shook her head. "It would be a huge undertaking and I doubt it's necessary. I've never detected a ghost out here. That's one of the reasons I loved staying with you during the renovations. It was peaceful."

His heart sank. Those months with her had been the best of his life. The way she'd opened up to him—the person she had revealed herself to be—had made him feel special.

But what if all her talk of feeling safe with him had more to do with an absence of ghosts rather than his presence? Thinking about it was too depressing.

"Well, I better get dressed. Be careful around that dishwasher and make sure it's shut tight. We don't want any more unexpected guests showing up."

"Right."

He felt her gaze on him as he retreated to lick his wounds.

Chapter Ten

Dinner had been quiet. After gawking at Garrett, Rachel could barely work up the courage to try to make eye contact. When she managed to glance at him, he was always looking away. Now he had her off prepping the telescope while he did the dishes.

He'd blushed all through the meal—unless his tan had managed to turn to a burn in the few minutes he was out back. Her face was probably red too. Her cheeks—among other parts of her anatomy—hadn't stopped tingling since he appeared in his kitchen absolutely naked. She tried not to think about it. And failed.

She had known he was built from the way his clothes hugged his frame. She'd used her imagination countless times to fill in what was hidden underneath. Imagining was very different from seeing with her own eyes.

He wasn't totally ripped with hard angles and rock-hard planes, though he obviously had plenty of muscle. The lines of his body were smooth, inviting her to explore them. That touch of softness amid his masculine lines did way more for her than abs that looked like rows of rumble strips.

Six-foot-seven and he was proportional. Everywhere.

The tingling in her cheeks intensified till they almost stung. Her bra started to chafe.

The things she could do to that body of his.

She shook her head, and whispered, "Not now." Not ever, in fact.

Everyone came with baggage. Hers extended to include the unresolved business of any ghost around that knew she was psychic. She wasn't dumping that on Garrett.

The telescope was in the hall closet, a six-foot long refractor she had picked out for him. The shorter optical tube of a reflector would have been much more practical for Garrett's use, but he had insisted on a refractor when she said that was her preference.

She liked the old-fashioned look of refractors—and that they used lenses instead of mirrors for magnification. If a spirit happened by the aperture of a reflector telescope while she was viewing the sky with such a powerful mirror... She had no idea what would happen.

The thought gave her a chill. His refractor might be more cumbersome, but she was grateful for his choice.

As she pulled the telescope from the closet off the foyer, she noticed there wasn't a speck of dust on the case. The huge tripod was also easily accessible—a good sign he was using it often. She was glad the scope wasn't languishing. It took several trips to cart everything outside and set up in the center of the patio.

Garrett joined her. He lit a couple of citronella candles and set up box fans for the mosquitoes. It didn't take much of a breeze to keep them at bay. The candles might not be as effective, but their dim light wouldn't interfere too much with stargazing and would help keep them from stubbing their toes.

He turned off the outside lights when everything was ready. The lights inside the house were already off. He walked to the patio table and set down an open bottle of beer—presumably for her since he held another in his hand.

Her heart gave a little tug as she remembered the first time he'd given her one and the many they had shared on this very patio while looking at the stars. It would be so easy to pretend that nothing had happened—nothing had changed—and fall back into that comfort zone. But it wasn't really comfortable. For either of them.

While waiting for their eyes to adjust, Rachel said, "I can't believe you wanted to cover your patio." She tilted her head back, following the thick cluster of stars that made up the Milky Way. "You have the most amazing view of the sky. Can we start with Lyra?"

He leaned against the back of one of his wrought-iron chairs, his empty hand in the front pocket of his jeans. At least, she presumed it was empty.

"Whatever you want."

Whatever she wanted? She imagined walking up behind him and sliding her hands into his pockets, seeing what all she could reach. Or she could approach him head-on, unzip his pants, and let her fingers follow the dark path that led to his manhood.

She bent over the telescope, working to bring Lyra into view. If she could draw him into a conversation, maybe that would distract her from her thoughts.

"I can barely see Lyra's Alpha star in the city, let alone the rest of the constellation. The light pollution in Summer Park becomes worse every year." He didn't say anything, so she tried harder. "Do you remember the name of the star I'm looking for?"

"It's probably rattling around in here somewhere." He pointed to his head with the hand holding the bottle.

"What about what I taught you about Alpha and Beta stars in constellations and asterisms?"

He took a deep breath and said, "If you don't mind, could we maybe skip the astronomy lesson this time?"

"Absolutely." She tried to sound upbeat and hoped the dim light hid her disappointment.

No astronomy lessons. Okay.

She started to wonder if he'd actually enjoyed her teaching him about the sky when she was staying with him or if he was just being polite. The possibility was crushing. He had always seemed eager to learn. It had reminded her of how excited she was to receive astronomy lessons from Hiram when she was a child.

Rachel lined up the scope with Vega, pushing away the doubtful thoughts. She let her mind fill with the wonder of seeing something that was so far away, imagining the vast distance between her and the star— the dark space between them.

The light she saw from Vega was actually cast by the star twenty-five years ago. She had always thought of stargazing as the closest she could come to time travel. Now she knew that wasn't the case. She had met Dante, held his hand, even hugged him. She never imagined she might meet someone from another time. It was incredible.

Starlight from twenty-five years in the past paled next to a human traveling over a hundred years through time. What must that have been like? She couldn't wait to talk to Elsa and Dante and learn more.

Except Rachel *would* wait. She would force herself to be patient. They had other priorities—and so did she. As soon as she found her footing, she would figure out a way to help the ghosts of Michael's victims.

But not tonight.

Stepping back from the scope, she said, "I have Vega lined up for you. Take a look."

Garrett nodded, then set his bottle on the table. He wiped his hands on his jeans as he approached her, walking slowly as if he was nervous. He bent to the scope, candlelight catching in his hair. Rachel wanted to reach out and run her fingers through the pale brown strands.

His hair was as soft as silk. She knew, because once she had lost control and let herself do the very thing that tempted her. The memory came back, sharp and full of pain and longing.

They had been laughing about something while working on his house. Reaching for him had been instinct, the pull she felt toward him irresistible. He'd responded immediately, leaning in to kiss her.

It had been the most abrupt dodge she had ever done. She'd felt his breath ruffling her hair as she stepped away. The awkwardness of the following moments had been brutal—she still hated herself for letting it happen and putting him through that.

"Lyra is filled with double stars." She started to talk just to hear something other than her own thoughts. "It's really a fascinating constellation. If I'm remembering correctly, Vega is the third brightest star visible from the Northern Hemisphere."

He stood up straight, but didn't move away from the telescope. And he still didn't say anything back.

"But you didn't want an astronomy lesson. Right." She fished around for anything to say instead. "Have you ever heard of Tanabata?"

"Can't say I have."

"It's a celebration in Japan that involves Lyra. There are a bunch of myths about the stars Vega and Altair being lovers separated by the Milky Way. My favorite version portrays Vega as a Celestial Maiden who fell in love with a human. When her father found out, he forbade them from being together and put the Milky Way between them to keep them apart."

Even in the near-darkness, she could feel the tension build in him. A warning sounded in the back of her mind, but her momentum carried her forward. It was a beautiful, sad story.

"On the seventh day of the seventh lunar month, the Sky Gods take pity on them and create a bridge of magpies so that they can be together. I guess technically that would make it take place in August, but if you go by the Gregorian calendar and wanted to celebrate it here, Tanabata would have been yesterday."

"It sounds like a sad thing to be celebrating."

"They're focusing on the time the lovers can be together. You can look at the bitter or look at the sweet."

"Take what you can get, huh?" He snorted and shook his head, then walked back to the table. He picked up his beer and held it for a while before taking a drink.

The idea of a star-party for two had been impulsive, like almost everything Rachel did. Instead of making Garrett feel better and easing any embarrassment or tension between them, she had only made it worse.

"I'm guessing you aren't interested in lessons on Japanese culture and religious festivals either," she said.

"I was actually thinking we could just enjoy the view."

"Sure."

Like she had enjoyed the view earlier—especially watching him walk to the canal. She doubted she would find any dust on his exercise equipment, either. Judging by his backside, he must do a few dozen squats every day.

The assessment of her plan to ease the awkwardness between them with some stargazing shifted from failure to dismal failure. It wasn't even keeping her mind off his body. And the more she thought about his body, the harder it was to resist him.

The last thing Garrett needed was to get involved with her. It would condemn him to a life filled with the dead. He deserved better.

Rachel was skirting the issue, trying to avoid or deny what had happened and hope it would go away on its own. It was how she dealt with everything in her life—her powers, her family issues, even her feelings for him. For once, she wanted to face something head on and just deal with it.

"Listen," she said. "We should probably talk about what happened earlier."

"It's been a full day. You'll have to be a bit more specific."

"The thing with the scorpion. How I behaved." She wasn't surprised when he stayed silent. "I'm sorry I kept staring. I didn't mean to. It's been a really long time since I've seen a naked man and well, you're just…"

She lifted her hands toward him and waved them up and down like she was showcasing his physique. "It was difficult to look away. But I should have. And I'm sorry."

She forced herself to pause so that he could respond. Silent moments dragged on, time seeming to dilate as she shifted from one foot to another. Finally, she couldn't take it.

"Aren't you going to say something?"

"That's a lot to process. How could you have not seen a guy naked when—" He shook his head. "I'm sorry. I shouldn't go there."

"When what?"

"Well, you were pretty serious with…"

The hair on her arms stood on end. Her stomach cramped, the pasta from dinner feeling like a lead weight.

"Michael."

She didn't blame Garrett for not wanting to say the name. She didn't want to say it, either. But she refused to let Michael have power over her anymore.

Garrett let out a huge breath of air and ran his fingers through his hair, holding it back from his face. "I don't want to bring up bad memories."

"No, it's all right. Talking about it is supposed to be healing."

He shrugged and let his hand drop to his side. "But you don't have to push yourself. You can take your time. As long as you need."

"I don't *want* to take my time. I don't want to still be talking about this a year or even a month from now. I want to move on with my life."

He nodded and simply said, "Okay."

Rachel walked over to him and sat in one of the patio chairs. He sat next to her. She picked up her beer and took a long drink before she began.

"Michael told me he wanted to take things slow. That was fine with me. I didn't want... Well, I haven't done more than kiss a guy for a couple of years now."

Garrett sat back, his eyes wide and glittering in the light from the candle on the table. He let out another huge breath that he must have been holding, and shook his head.

"I'm glad you didn't..." He shook his head. "I'm glad you don't have that to work through on top of everything else."

"Me too."

Her chest felt tight, but the dread in the pit of her stomach was lessening. Talking to Garrett was lightening the burden she carried. And it seemed to be doing the same for him.

"I know I've been dating a lot, but none of those relationships were serious at all. I was trying to distract myself more than anything."

"From the ghosts?"

She felt her eyebrows rise, the warm citronella-laced air tickled her tongue as her mouth dropped open. The candlelight couldn't be covering her reaction. He had to see it too.

"Among other things."

He had asked for her honesty, but telling him how she felt about him would ruin their friendship. Worse, it would make him even more impossible to resist because he would want to take action based on that knowledge.

Then he'd be stuck with a weirdo who could see spirits and constantly spouted awkward factoids. When she wasn't pretending to be a socialite at the beck and call of her somewhat—totally—evil mother.

"I'm dealing with a lot," she said. "I understand that. But it isn't as much as you think. I had already broken up with him."

"What?"

She shivered at the memory. Michael had been calm when she told him. He said he understood and wished her the best. He only had one request—that she sit for him so he could make a portrait to remember her by.

At the time, she'd thought of the paintings in his gallery room. His opening show consisted of a dozen portraits of women in painterly style. The portraits evoked despair, with the women having distorted bodies and either hiding their faces or keeping themselves turned away from the viewer.

As grim as they appeared, the dark red and gray paint he used hid a more disturbing secret—he had mixed the paint with the blood of his victims, the subjects of each painting.

He had started Rachel's portrait before she was rescued.

She'd ignored her own misgivings when he asked her to sit for him, like she ignored the voices of the dead around her. She was too practiced at ignoring things. She had agreed and gone with him to his house.

"It might have accelerated things," she said. "After I told him."

Garrett looked like he was going to snap his beer bottle in half. She reached over and took it from him, then set it on the table.

"I'm sorry," he said. "I'm having trouble with my poker face. I don't want to make this harder. I want you to be able to talk to me."

"You don't have to put on a face for me. I guess that's what makes our friendship so special. We can both let our guards down."

"I suppose. I still appreciate you sharing this with me."

"I want you to know that I'm doing better than you think."

"Yeah. I kind of noticed when you lit into your mom." He smiled, one side of his mouth curving up and a deep dimple appearing in his cheek.

Oh she had missed that dimple. She wondered if she could bring out the other one. But that would be a bad idea. His smile was devastating. It made her want to crawl into his lap and kiss him.

"That kind of surprised me too," she said.

"It was a long time coming."

"Jazz says she's going to give you a big discount on the next piece you buy for getting me out of my mother's house."

"That was all you. I only gave you a lift."

"And a place to stay and the motivation to finally do something." She couldn't believe how much her life had changed just since that morning.

"Yeah, but you're still the one who did the work. It took courage to walk out of that house—way more than I understood at the time."

"I feel like I had help. Watching Jazz over the years and how she doesn't take crap from anybody has been very educational. It was like I was channeling her or something."

"Not literally, right?"

She knew he was joking by the way his smile deepened. *Dimples...* Keeping her focus on the conversation was difficult, but she managed.

"No. That would require training to be a medium. I'm just psychic." A thrill went down her spine and she shivered. "It's strange to say it out loud. But it feels good."

"I'm glad." He leaned closer and asked, "What's it like? If it's uncomfortable to talk about, you don't have to answer."

"I don't think you could ever make me feel uncomfortable." Her voice had a bit of breathiness to it she hadn't intended. Consciously, anyway. She laughed and looked away.

"Give him a kiss."

Rachel was so caught up in the moment, the quiet voice caught her off-guard.

"It's obvious you want to. Him too, from the looks of it."

Rachel leapt to her feet.

"What is it? What's wrong?" Garrett rose right after her.

"Someone is here."

"Who?"

"I didn't mean to ruin your moment." The voice was male. He sounded older, genial.

She didn't care if he sounded like a super-friendly grandpa. Rachel shook her head, then ran to the house. She kept her eyes shut tight as she approached the glass doors. Whoever it was, she didn't want to see him in the reflection from the candlelight.

Seeing always made it worse.

Scrabbling for the handle, she managed to slide the door open and jump inside. She still couldn't bring herself to open her eyes and bounced off something—probably Garrett's recliner. As upset as she was, she couldn't remember the room's layout.

She dropped to her knees and wrapped her arms around her middle, waiting for Garrett to come to her rescue—again.

Chapter Eleven

Garrett ran after Rachel and shut the door behind them. When he turned back around, she was huddled in a ball on the floor.

"It isn't Michael, is it?" he asked.

She had said Michael was gone, but with the way she reacted, Garrett had to wonder. His hands kept flexing into fists. If it was...

If it was, he couldn't do a damned thing about it. His insides boiled at the thought.

"The water bottle," she said. "Spray down the door."

He grabbed it and did as she asked, then knelt at her side. "It's done."

She was trembling, shaking her head. She started to rock back and forth, like she had at the hospital. He did not want to go down that road again.

"I'm going to touch your back," he said. He gently placed his hand on her back and let out a little breath when she didn't scream or jerk away. "Do you still hear the voice?"

"No. I don't." She shook her head again and her rocking slowed.

Garrett rubbed her back, trying to soothe her.

"All right, then. Rachel-1, ghost-0."

She stopped rocking, but the trembling increased. At first he worried he had made things worse, but then he realized she was laughing. She leaned toward him. As soon as her shoulder touched his chest, she reached up to wrap her arms around his neck. Her eyes were still pinched shut.

He sat and pulled her into his lap.

"What can I do?"

"I'm just trying to build up my nerve to open my eyes again."

Garrett glanced around the room. "I don't see any reflections."

She pressed herself closer to his chest and opened first one eye, then the other, looking around carefully. She let out a huge breath and leaned her head on his shoulder.

"Thank you."

"No problem."

But it was a problem. Rachel curled up in his lap with her arms around him, her face nestled close enough that her warm breath fanned his neck... Biology took over. He had never held her so close, felt her press herself against him this way.

He shifted beneath her, trying to get more comfortable and keep her from noticing his predicament. The citrus scent of her shampoo was driving him crazy. He could tilt his head a few inches and kiss her if he wanted to. And he did want to.

Trouble was—he wanted a whole lot more than kisses from Rachel.

Desperate to distract himself, he asked, "Do you know who it was?"

"No. I didn't recognize the voice."

That was a relief.

She shook her head. "I don't understand how he found me so fast."

"I still don't know how it works. Do ghosts have to...walk to where you are? How do they even get around?"

"They sort of will themselves to go places—if they aren't tied to a person or place. If the ghost is haunting a location, they're usually stuck in one spot. But if they're haunting a person, they can follow them around. If the person dies or somehow severs their connection, the ghost is free to roam."

The thought of people being haunted... And the voice was male. Garrett's stomach tightened. Maybe the ghost wasn't tied to Rachel at all. Maybe it was him.

"Were there any other distinguishing characteristics?"

She shook her head. "He sounded older. With a bit of an accent."

Garrett felt some of the tension ease from between his shoulders. If the ghost sounded older, it wasn't Dylan. The thought of his brother's spirit lingering for so many years was more than Garrett could deal with on a good day. It had been a long time since Garrett had experienced a good day.

"What did he say?"

"Nothing scary." Her face reddened and she looked away. "He didn't even ask me for anything, which is kind of strange. Ghosts usually are pretty fixated on getting what they want. He actually reminded me of Hiram."

"Hiram?"

"He was the only ghost I ever became friends with. He watched over me. In life, he had been an astronomer. He's the one who taught me the constellations." She smiled, her eyes getting a faraway look. "We would sit out back and look at the stars and talk for hours sometimes."

No wonder she loved the scope so much. Garrett doubted her mom had been more loving when Rachel was younger. At least Hiram had been there.

How messed up was it that the most supportive adult in her childhood had been a ghost?

"Could it be him?" Garrett asked.

She shook her head. "No. Hiram crossed over decades ago."

"You sure about that?"

Her eyes filled with tears that immediately spilled over.

Dammit. He wished he would stop stumbling into topics that obviously caused her so much grief.

"I was there," she said. "He did it to protect me. He was always protecting me. He's the one who told me to act like I couldn't hear spirits anymore and helped to convince the others to leave me alone."

"Why do I have a feeling there's a lot more to that story and I'm not going to like it?"

She laughed and leaned against his chest again. "Because you know me better than anyone."

Sometimes he felt that way. Sometimes he felt he didn't know her at all.

"Could Hiram have come back?"

"I don't think so."

Garrett let out a sigh. "I have a lot to learn."

"You can borrow some of my books if you want. I've managed to collect a few good resources over the years."

"Thanks."

"I'll go get you some. Could you bring in the telescope? I can help put it away after we spray the door again."

"Don't worry about any of that," Garrett said. "I'll take care of it."

"You're really good at taking care of people." She lifted her hand to his face, resting it along his jaw.

He tried to stop himself from sucking in a fast breath—and failed. Her smile faltered and she shifted away.

She braced herself on his shoulders as she rose. It was all he could do not to reach for her and pull her back. She didn't say anything else as she walked away.

Garrett sat on the floor for a few minutes, trying to find a sense of equilibrium. A frantic night at the ER was nothing compared to the emotional toll of being this close to Rachel.

He needed to get up and move around. Shake it off.

Bringing in the scope would help. And maybe he'd have a word with whoever was out there. Bolstered at the thought, he jumped up and headed for the patio.

Outside, insects were droning loud. Garrett glanced up at Lyra, remembering Rachel's story of the star-crossed lovers.

He blew out a breath and shook his head. Best not to go there.

He carried in the scope and packed everything up, then went back for the tripod and fans. When he was done inside, he grabbed the spray bottle and stepped back into the muggy summer night. The candles were still flickering, putting off a sharp scent. It was eerie—knowing there was a ghost hanging around—a stranger he couldn't see.

Garrett wondered why Rachel didn't use mirrors more often. If he could, he'd be checking his surroundings constantly to be sure he was alone.

Then again, maybe it was better not to know.

Rachel said Florida was filled with spirits. He imagined what it must be like walking past a mirror in a busy store and not knowing if the people he saw were dead or alive. He wondered if the ghosts showed signs of how they had died...

Garrett was more grateful than ever that he lived out in the country. Only one ghost to deal with—at least, for the time being. But how the hell did you start a conversation with a dead person?

He glanced at the spray bottle in his hand. It felt like a weapon. That wasn't him. He set it on the table, then ran his fingers through his hair.

Best to focus on the *person* part. Garrett decided to talk to him as such.

"I don't know who you are or what you need, but Rachel's been through a lot. Give her some time. Please."

He blew out the candles and grabbed the spray bottle before heading back inside. He closed the door, then sprayed it down twice.

"You're starting to be paranoid, like me."

Garrett jumped at Rachel's voice. The creepy atmosphere outside must have hit him harder than he thought.

"Sorry," she said. She was holding a small stack of books, hugging them to her chest.

Garrett shook his head. "No need to apologize. Guess I'm just feeling a little high-strung after today."

"I feel like I should apologize for that too. You wouldn't have had such a stressful day if you hadn't come to my rescue."

He couldn't have slept another night without knowing she was okay. Not that he'd been sleeping much lately anyway.

"Friends help each other out."

"Yeah."

Her voice was small, like the fake smile pasted on her face. It couldn't break through the tension around her eyes. All he saw there was sorrow.

She walked to the kitchen counter and set the books down. "Here are the books you wanted to borrow."

"Thanks."

"Could I have the spray bottle?"

He nodded and handed it over. "Rachel—"

"It's late. We should try to get some sleep."

"Yeah. I guess we should."

"Well…good night."

"Night."

She turned and walked away without another word. Something was obviously upsetting her. Beyond what she'd been through and knowing that there was a ghost close by. For once, she didn't seem to want to talk.

Garrett didn't know how to help her. Yet.

He picked up the books and headed to his room. Once there, he closed his blinds before stripping and pulling on his pajama pants. The thought of someone lurking outside—watching them, listening… It was freaking him out. And Rachel lived with that every single day.

He couldn't imagine how awful that must be. Surely there was a way to keep the ghosts away. He was even interested in the solution for himself. It was creepy as hell to think about walking around not knowing how many ghosts he might be brushing elbows with.

He made sure the bedside lamp was on before turning off the overhead lights. At this rate, he would probably sleep that way. He slid into bed with Rachel's books, but didn't open them immediately. His thoughts were spinning too much to concentrate.

She'd dropped several information bombs on him. Of all the ones to fixate on, he kept thinking about her saying that she hadn't been with a man in years. She had dated at least a dozen guys in that time span. Garrett hated every single one of them.

They disrespected her, talked over her, didn't seem to pay attention or listen when she spoke.

He wanted to think that he would have been happy for her if she settled down with a decent person, but couldn't be sure. It didn't matter, because she had seemed to seek out the worst example of a human being to date. If Rachel brought any of them home, her mother must have been mortified. But then, that might have been part of the allure.

Garrett wondered again if her mother had something to do with why Rachel kept shutting him out. It was obvious she felt the chemistry between them. She seemed to enjoy his company. But damned if her mother wasn't practically trying to arrange a marriage between the two.

His own mom had repeatedly mentioned that she was surprised to receive so many invitations to events hosted by the Montgomerys. Rachel's mother had even openly talked to his mom about what an attractive pair they would make.

His mom would never push the matter. She just wanted Garrett to be happy and could tell there was something not quite right with the dynamic. When he said Rachel wasn't interested, his mom dropped it.

Then Jazz had decided to try to match him up with Elsa. It hadn't worked out, but at least he and Elsa had managed to build a strong friendship. She came to him when she needed help, big or small, and he appreciated that probably more than she knew. He was well aware of how much he needed to feel...needed.

Now that he thought about it, Rachel hadn't actually asked him for help at all. Sure, she took him up on his offer of a place to stay, but she had other options. She could stay at Elsa's house.

If she did, he knew he'd lie awake wondering if she was okay the whole night. Sharing a roof helped him as much as her. He needed to know she was safe, even if he had no clue how to protect her himself.

He had the books to read—a way to learn more about how he *could* help her. He needed to get to it. If things did blow up eventually, he wanted be useful.

He cracked the first book open. It landed on an etching of a man holding his hands over his head as a seriously creepy ghost flew at him.

Garrett heard a soft rapping sound. The hair on his arms stood on end. The sound came again—from his bedroom door. His heart was hammering in his chest. It had to be Rachel... Didn't it?

"Come in," he said.

She opened the door slowly and stepped inside. Garrett's pulse jumped for a different reason, scenarios playing through his head about why she might be coming to see him in the middle of the night.

Because we're both awake, jackass.

"I forgot to bring—"

Her eyes grew wider as she looked at him, her gaze slowly trailing down his chest and over the sheet that covered his hips and legs.

He forced a smile, trying to get her to laugh off some of the tension between them. "Don't worry. I'm not naked under here."

She gave a quick laugh—a bit too high to be real. He'd take it.

"What do you need?" he asked.

"I...forgot to bring pajamas. None of my clothes are comfortable for sleeping, and being naked in the dark is not high on my list of things I'd like to do right now."

Her mouth dropped open for a second, but then she clacked it shut, cheeks glowing scarlet—betraying her thoughts. He was thinking the same thing.

Being naked in the dark with Rachel was about at the top of Garrett's list of things he'd like to do any time, any day. Increasing the awkwardness between them by letting her see just how much that idea appealed to him was close to the bottom.

He tried to look casual as he strategically placed his book over his lap, then nodded toward his closet. "Help yourself."

"Thanks."

She didn't waste any time, quickly walking to the closet and pulling out a couple of T-shirts. She was tall, but his shirts would still be huge on her.

The thought of his shirt dusting across her long, slender legs, her breasts brushing the fabric...didn't help his predicament. He shook his head and picked up another book, burying his nose in it as if it held all of his attention.

He couldn't let himself look up at her. No way could he hide how much he wanted her. He wouldn't burden her with that knowledge.

Clearing his throat, he said, "If you need anything else, don't hesitate to come get me. Okay?"

"Yeah. Thanks again."

He didn't set down the book till after she had gone and shut the door behind her. He closed his eyes and leaned his head against the headboard.

This was torture.

If she wanted him, she could have had him at any time in the past couple of years. Garrett made no secret of that. Hell, she could have him right now.

No matter her reasons, she *didn't* want him. Not really. He had to keep reminding himself of that. And maybe that emotional pain would help him keep his physical reactions to her under control.

He wouldn't hold his breath.

Chapter Twelve

There was a ghost right outside the house. A stranger.

If the voice had been one of Michael's victims, menacing as they were, Rachel would have understood their presence. With that understanding, there would have been some twisted form of comfort. But this ghost was a complete unknown.

She sat on the edge of her bed, staring at the window. The blinds were closed, but even still there were little cracks around the edges that would allow glimpses into the room from outside. Why hadn't she put in curtains?

Because Garrett loved natural light—and she didn't want to deny him even a particle of it.

Every room in his house only had blinds to cover the windows. Well, except for her bathroom, which had no windows at all. She considered sleeping in the bathtub, but that wasn't an option. As much as the windows bothered her, the mirror in that room—even covered—scared her more. The living room had the sliding glass door, so that nixed the couch.

There was always Garrett's room, with only one clear-glass window that would have a limited view from the backyard. A narrow row of frosted windows lined the wall that faced the front of his house, high up and running parallel to the ceiling. His bed was huge and looked very comfortable—especially with him in it.

Her mind immediately pulled up an image of him walking back to the house after the scorpion incident. That memory was burned into every synapse. His confident stride, the determined set to his features, his strong chest, his muscled legs, a certain other part of his anatomy...

The things she wanted to do to that man.

She knew he was thinking about it too—acting on their mutual attraction. But he was most concerned with protecting her. He wouldn't even let her get close to a tiny scorpion. It was sweet, but unnecessary.

She went through her list of all the reasons that she shouldn't be with him in the first place. At the top was how being involved with her would affect his peace of mind.

Learning about her powers—and that ghosts were real—had already impacted him negatively. When she went to borrow a shirt to sleep in, she noticed the blinds in his room were closed. He had always kept them open before. Always. He must be freaking out, trying to protect her yet again by shielding her from how much his new awareness disturbed him.

At least Rachel was used to dealing with this kind of thing. Now that Garrett knew ghosts were real and how prevalent they were, he might never be able to truly relax again.

She didn't want that for him. For any of her friends. Having Rachel around was a constant reminder of death. It robbed them of even the small comfort of thinking that death held finality.

Jazz wanted to help. So did Elsa. But Rachel wanted to preserve their peace of mind—just like she wanted to preserve Garrett's. She needed to figure this out on her own, to keep them out of it as much as she could.

The more they tried to help, the more they would internalize that none of them were ever really alone. It didn't make for a happy life.

She leapt up from the bed and started pacing. The soft fabric of Garrett's T-shirt brushed against her legs as she walked, distracting her from her anxious thoughts. It carried a hint of his scent. She paused and took a deep breath to saturate her senses with him.

She wrapped her arms around herself and closed her eyes, imagining that Garrett was holding her. He'd been doing a lot of that lately. It was taking a toll on both of them.

She was having trouble resisting the pull she felt toward him. The desire to be with him was stronger than ever. The more time they spent together, the worse it became.

But she was weird. He deserved normal. A happy, loving family to join with his, a partner who didn't get distracted by—

Something tapped on her window. Rachel's eyes snapped open. She backed toward the bed.

It happened again—a fluttering thump.

She took a deep breath, then slowly approached the window. At least it was shut. She was certain of that. Still, the persistent flutter-thump was making her heart beat in her throat. When she was close enough, she pulled on the cord that raised the pleated blinds.

Outside the window, all she saw was inky darkness. The light cast by the bedside lamp was strong enough that she could see the reflection of the room around her in the glass.

And of the pale, blonde ghost staring back at her—*from inside the room*.

Rachel's heart beat even faster. There couldn't be a ghost in the house. She had cleansed and warded the whole thing.

She took a deep breath and let it out. So did the woman in the window.

Her heart seemed to stop. It wasn't a ghost at all. It was her own reflection.

Rachel avoided any mirror bigger than a compact. She couldn't remember the last time she'd actually seen so much of herself at once. Her eyes were wide and there were dark circles beneath them. Her hair was a tousled mess.

No wonder everyone was worried. Especially with the obvious fear on her face, the lines of stress etched around her eyes. In the dark glass of the window, her reflection was translucent. It was as if she was the ghost, haunting her own life—a living shadow.

Rachel leaned closer to the window just as something huge and bright yellow whacked into the glass. She yelped and jumped back. She was still holding onto the cord for the blinds and it tangled around her arm. As she tried to free herself, her movements caused the blinds to bang against the window with an awful racket. She quickly grabbed at them, pushing them against the glass to stop the noise.

Still holding the blinds, she looked at the windowsill. Two lubber grasshoppers stared back at her. Each was at least three inches long, with bright yellow and orange carapaces. Lubbers were everywhere in Florida, but she'd never noticed them being active at night. One crawled a few inches toward her while she watched.

"Rachel?"

She jumped again, jostling the blinds and getting her wrist tangled in the cord even more. Garrett ran forward before she could extricate herself. He was just wearing pajama bottoms.

She was staring again, but she couldn't bring herself to care. His chest was covered in fine dark hair that flowed together and cascaded down his stomach, all the way to—

"I didn't mean to startle you," he said.

"It's okay." She laughed and shook her head, trying to force the image of Garrett naked out of her mind with limited success. She tried to lighten the mood, wiggling the cord as he helped free her hand. "I guess I'm a little high-strung too."

Apparently, he wasn't in a laughing mood. He didn't say anything until he had lowered the blinds.

"Was that ghost bothering you again? I thought the poppets were supposed to keep them away."

"It's not always ghosts." She wanted to help him normalize what he'd learned. Maybe he wouldn't fixate on the idea of ghosts if she gave him another explanation. "There were some grasshoppers flying against the window. They must have been drawn to the light coming out from around the edges of the blinds."

"Grasshoppers at night?"

She shrugged. "I didn't mean to disturb you."

Again.

"I was already up."

"You can't sleep either?"

He shook his head. His gaze kept flicking to her wrists, his eyes getting an angry, haunted look.

She was tired of it. She was tired of people—especially Garrett—asking her if she was okay and looking at her like she might shatter at any moment. He had done enough for her. Maybe she could do something for him.

"Do you need me to tell you about it?" she asked.

"What, the bugs? I was born here too. I know all about the pesky things."

"About what happened with Michael."

He looked away and shook his head. "You don't have to tell me."

"I think I do. I need to tell someone what really happened."

"I thought you talked it all through with your doctors and the police."

A lump was forming in her throat. She shook her head.

"Only part of it. What they could believe."

His mouth opened and shut. His chest stilled as he held his breath, waiting for her. Always waiting. She walked to the bed and sat, then patted the spot next to her.

"Sit with me?"

Garrett hesitated for a moment, but then joined her.

How to begin?

Not with the feeling of dread when she entered Michael's house—yet another warning sign she had ignored. Not with the chloroform or waking up in darkness chained to a wall.

As bad as that was, she wasn't haunted by what Michael did to her. She was haunted by the voices of the other women. The ones he had killed.

The voices had started before she woke. She was dropped into the middle of a conversation between half a dozen ghosts sharing the room with her. Sharing their darkness.

They spoke in whispers, even knowing Michael couldn't hear them. They were that afraid.

How could Rachel help Garrett understand? Hearing those spirits, she could almost feel their pain—pain strong enough to keep them chained to this world even after death.

"What you're imagining is… It's not what happened," she said. "It's not what anyone thinks."

He was quiet for a moment, then said, "I'm listening."

She took a deep breath and blew it out to steady her nerves before she began.

"I had been avoiding Michael all week. I would tell him I was busy setting up Dante's loft after work at the gallery—which was true. But I went out of my way to make sure I didn't have any spare time. When opening night for Michael's show was close, I realized I couldn't avoid him any longer. We met for lunch and I told him we were done."

"I can't imagine that went over well."

"That's the thing—it did. He said he was proud of me for figuring out what I wanted and saying something about it. That it was high time I took a stand for myself." Her stomach churned at the memory. "I ate it all up. Every word. When he asked me for one last favor, it seemed such a small thing. He seemed reasonable."

"What did he want?"

"He wanted me to sit for him. To pose for a final portrait so that he could *keep a piece of me near him forever*." She let out a tinny laugh. "Little did I know."

She shivered. Garrett scooted closer to her, but she didn't let herself lean into him for comfort. The whole point was to let him know that she was stronger than he thought—that this hadn't broken her.

"Rachel, you don't have to tell me this if it's too hard."

"What's hard is the way you've been looking at me. How worried you are about what Michael did."

"How could I not worry?" he asked.

"I won't lie. It was terrible and sickening and for a while I didn't know if I would make it through with my sanity intact. But there were other things going on. Things that made what he did to me more bearable—less awful in comparison with what he had done to others. Because I escaped. Do you understand, Garrett? *I escaped*."

Garrett looked perplexed. His brow furrowed and he shook his head. "I don't understand."

She didn't want to come out and say it. Saying it made it more real. But she had to. She had to help him understand.

"The others didn't."

Her eyes burned with tears, but she held them back. Understanding flowed over his features as he sucked in a breath.

"There were ghosts with you? People he had…"

"Killed. Yes. Half a dozen that I could distinguish. I heard whispers as soon as I arrived at his house. They were so quiet, I could barely hear them. But I didn't even try. I tuned them out, like usual. If I had only tried to listen to them, maybe I could have escaped. Prevented what happened to Elsa and Dante."

Garrett shook his head. "No. You can't let yourself go down that road again. Remember what Dante had to say on that. None of this is your fault. You can't keep beating yourself up over what Michael did."

She closed her eyes and the tears she had been fighting spilled over. The lump in her throat grew. She forced out the words anyway, her voice raw with guilt and fear.

"I can't keep hiding my head in the sand, either."

She had to start helping people—the living and the dead. She was sick of always being the one who needed to be rescued.

"After I woke up, the women kept talking about what happened to them. About what was going to happen to me, in graphic detail. They said I was lucky because…"

"Rachel—"

He started to put his arm around her, but she needed space to get through telling him. She shook her head and put her hand on his chest, which was…probably the best possible thing she could have done.

The sadness and fear dispersed as she took in the feel of him. The soft texture of the hair on his chest. The heat of his skin and the strength of the muscle beneath.

Warmth flooded her—not the fiery chemistry she was used to fighting with him, but soft waves of well-being and safety. She felt his desire to comfort her and drew on that strength to go on, her voice much stronger than before.

"They said the women he had killed more recently were lucky because he had more practice. He was better at taking blood and knocking us out when needed—even at using the blood for his paintings. He had it down. They said I was lucky because it would be over quicker."

She could feel each deep breath he took, her hand rising and falling with the movements of his chest. Focusing on the rhythmic motion helped her go on.

"Thanks to Dante and Elsa, I was only there for one day. The other women were held for days or even weeks. And the ones that couldn't move on after... The ones haunting him were with him for *years*."

"God, Rachel. That's awful."

"Do you see now? Those women—they were alone when this happened to them. They couldn't hear the voices of the others hovering near them."

She shook her head. "What happened was terrible. But I didn't go through it alone. They were with me. Knowing what they went through forced me to make peace with whatever was going to happen to me. To accept my fate. If I didn't, I knew my spirit would linger."

She wiped the tears from her cheeks. She never wanted to lead the existence of the ghosts she heard. Whatever was on the other side, she wanted to be willing and able to cast herself into it instead of clinging to a shadow of her life.

"And it's terrible and yes I have nightmares about it still, but I can handle all that. What I can't handle is knowing that those women are *still* out there. Still suffering. And I don't know how to help them."

"Why didn't they move on when he died?"

Rachel's heart gave a little sideways-leap, like it was trying to escape her chest. She was about to chisel away another bit of his peace of mind.

"I'm sure some did. But not all of them. Some were too hurt, too angry."

"How can you be sure?"

"Because they're directing that rage at me. That's why I freaked out when we left my mother's house. I saw them in the reflection in your car window."

"That doesn't make any sense. You didn't have anything to do with what happened to them."

"Toward the end, some of them figured out that I could hear them. They begged me not to kill Michael. They were afraid he'd be able to hurt them on the other side—to pick up where he left off."

Garrett hissed in a breath. "But they were wrong. You said Michael is gone."

"He is now. Now that his body has been cremated. For those few days after his death and before that, I…I don't know for sure what happened."

Garrett's voice lowered to a growl. "Did you ever hear him?"

"No. Usually it takes a while for a spirit to collect itself enough to figure out what they are and remember who they were. He might have been able to manifest more quickly."

The guilt from her choice was still crushing her. She didn't want Michael to inflict even a moment's more suffering on those women. But she also couldn't let him hurt anyone else. He had to be stopped.

"For whatever reason, some of his victims are still lingering. They need help to move on and I don't know what to do for them."

"We'll figure it out," he said.

"No. *I* will. You've done enough already."

He shook his head and let out a deep sigh. She could sense his disappointment, sharp and bitter through her chest.

"I don't understand what happened," he said. "What made you stop letting me help you?"

"You help me all the time."

"No, I rescue you when you've gotten yourself in so deep you can't see a way out. You call me in as a last resort."

"I wouldn't say that."

She would just think it.

She started to pull away, but he covered her hand with his, pressing it firmly against his chest.

"Listen to me. I know you're dealing with a lot. And I know you're trying to handle it on your own. You said those ghosts helped you through your ordeal. That it was easier for you because you weren't alone. You aren't alone now. You haven't been for a while."

She knew her friends would help. But she didn't deserve it, didn't want her own drama to impact people she loved so dearly.

"Garrett—"

"You're not an echo of your mom," he said. "You're not set-dressing for her life—something to be seen and not heard. You don't have to figure out all your problems on your own."

It came out of left field, but it was exactly what she needed to hear. How did he always know just what to say? She felt enveloped in his warmth and compassion. Accepted. And he wasn't done.

"You're a vibrant, brilliant, kind-hearted person, and you deserve to be surrounded by people who appreciate you and are happy to help you. Like I am."

She let out a little laugh and said, "Are you trying to make me cry again?"

"Never." He put his hand on the back of her neck and drew her forward, placing a gentle kiss on her forehead.

God, she wanted so much more than that. She wanted to plant her hands on his shoulders and push him back on the bed. She wanted to put all this talk about ghosts and death far behind her and just sink into him.

She wanted so much—too much from him. She was already tilting her head up, staring at his lips. Their faces were close enough that her nose grazed his cheek. His stubble tickled her skin.

He smelled like the ocean. Salt-tang and open spaces.

Flutter-thump.

They both jumped. Garrett muttered something under his breath that sounded like, "Damn grasshoppers."

But it was a good thing. A strong reminder of what it meant for someone like Garrett to be with her. Someone who didn't know what he was signing up for.

Lubbers weren't active at night. She was sure of it. Which meant something was influencing them to fly against her window. Something or someone.

She remembered the ghosts at her mother's house. The anger in their eyes as they lifted their arms to show Rachel the bloody wounds they had once all shared.

The accusation.

If Michael's victims had found out where Rachel was staying, going outside might become outright dangerous—for her and the people around her. The people who dared to help her.

Even the genial ghost who had talked to her on Garrett's patio was at risk. If they thought he was standing in their way... She almost felt bad for him.

She felt bad for everyone at the moment.

"They seem to like this window. I think I'll sleep on the couch tonight," Rachel said.

"You can have my bed. I'll take the couch."

"I wouldn't hear of it."

He shook his head. "If you think I can't be as stubborn as you, you're wrong. I'm taking the couch. Come on."

She didn't have it in her to fight him on it or resist as he stood and pulled her up after him.

Chapter Thirteen

Garrett's couch was not meant for someone his size. He sat against the cushions, another of Rachel's books open in his lap.

The things he was reading about made his skin crawl. Bad enough to know that ghosts could be walking around him all the time, but learning that they could actually affect the physical world? He shuddered at the thought.

The chapter on poltergeists had been a particularly rough read. He'd seen enough movies to know about them throwing around stuff. He didn't know about the scratches, scrapes, bruises, and *bite marks* that sometimes came along with it.

How did Rachel do it? How did she walk around with a smile and pretend that everything was normal when she knew about all this—when she heard them all the time?

His appreciation for her grew. Along with his desire to help her. To support her any way he could.

The book also explained how salt helped to neutralize ghosts. It was all about energy. Salt could disrupt them. What he was still struggling with was how intention factored in. He was having trouble wrapping his mind around...the mind being able to influence the spiritual world.

According to the books, some clairsentients—people like Rachel who could perceive ghosts—weren't just receivers but could transmit energy into the ghostly realm as well. He wondered if there were any spectral objects on the other side that could be thrown around by psychics. Give the poltergeists a taste of their own medicine.

He snorted and turned the page. The next chapter was all about possession. Great.

He skimmed the introduction, but stopped cold at the first section header. In bold print, it read, "Spectral Influence on Animals."

Attention caught, he read each word with care.

No. Freaking. Way. Ghosts could control animals?

The text used words like *impel* and *motivate*, but it boiled down to the same thing. Some ghosts could get animals to do what they wanted. If the ghost was powerful enough, they could even control several animals at a time.

Shit.

Garrett thought back to the scorpion in the dishwasher. To the lubbers bouncing off the windows. The possibilities were chilling.

What if the ghosts who were ticked at Rachel were *impelling* animals to try to get into the house? To get to Rachel. What if they were pissing the animals off in the process?

Grasshoppers were no big deal, but that scorpion could have been a problem. Florida had any number of dangerous and mobile species running around. An angry ghost could find a sick bat and get it to fly at Rachel, or send wasps her way, pathogen-carrying mosquitoes, snakes...

His mind reared back from that concept like a startled horse. He set aside the book and leapt up from the couch, then paced back and forth in his living room.

If there was more than one ghost after her, and they figured out how to send more than one animal at a time... Things could get hairy fast. How could he possibly keep Rachel safe at this rate? The poppets and saltwater kept the ghosts outside, but they hadn't been effective against that scorpion.

He had to deal with this. To address the issue at the source—the ghosts. Maybe there was some way he and Rachel could help them to move on. Resolve their issues, like the books talked about.

That seemed the best solution. The permanent solution.

But once they had dealt with these ghosts, what about the next batch? Rachel hadn't hedged around the fact that Florida was filled with lingering spirits. If they all came for her, wanting closure or resolution or whatever, how could she handle that?

He wouldn't let her do it on her own. That was for damned sure.

If she wouldn't let Garrett help her, he'd recruit Elsa and Jazz. Rachel couldn't stand against that pair. And if they all worked together, they could find a way to make sure that Rachel could lead whatever kind of life she wanted. He was certain of it.

Too bad that life didn't include him.

She had been opening up with him about so many things. He hoped she would explain her mixed messages at some point. The way she kept touching him, nestling close, then pulling away...it was driving him crazy.

When she'd patted the bed next to her, part of him had wondered if it was a different kind of invitation. Then she had put her hand on his chest and left it there for what felt like forever. His heart had pounded the whole time—from what she was saying and her touch.

Nuzzling his neck, his cheek... Her breath warming his skin.

He had nearly lost it before that lubber went and broke the moment. Damn bugs. He couldn't help but wonder what would've happened if they hadn't been interrupted. Scenarios danced in front of his mind, an array of possibilities he had longed for.

There was no time to feel sorry for himself. He had too much to do. Too much to learn.

He picked up the book again and opened it, then flopped down on the couch. The topic he happened across was psychometry—the psychic ability to read the history of objects through touch. Finally, something he knew about. He shook his head and started to read, just in case the book had more to teach him.

Chapter Fourteen

Sleep had eluded Rachel until light was just starting to peer around the edges of the blinds in Garrett's room. His sheets, his pillow, everything smelled like him. That alone would have been enough to keep Rachel awake in his huge bed.

His huge empty bed.

Everything else going on—the spirits outside, Garrett on the couch, her with no ideas about where to go or what was going to happen next —that didn't help either. It also didn't help that her resolve to stay away from him was breaking apart after only one day.

Instead of thinking about why they shouldn't be together, her mind kept conjuring up possibilities that just might work. What if she could shield him from the spirits in her life?

Her parents seemed happy together, though Rachel doubted her father was in on the secret Rachel and her mother shared. If Rachel could block the voices, she might be able to lead a normal life with Garrett.

A fake normal life.

No. She was tired of pretending. She wanted to be real, to feel real.

She was different. It was time to admit it. Embrace it. *Do something with it.* Like help the women that Michael had killed.

Rachel checked the clock when she woke up after a fitful few hours of rest. Ten in the morning. She had slept late.

She slid from the bed quietly and made her way to the kitchen. The living room came into view as she approached the counter that separated the rooms. Garrett was sprawled on his couch on his stomach, one arm under his chest and the other above his head.

He didn't even have a pillow, poor guy. He must be exhausted.

His chest rose and fell with his breath and his hair was splayed over his cheek. Rachel was tempted to dust his bangs away from his face, but she didn't want to risk waking him. Making breakfast was out, since the noise would certainly disturb his sleep.

She decided to start in on her plan to help Michael's victims. And she was going to listen—in part—to Garrett's advice.

She would ask for help, but from the ghosts themselves. They were the ones who knew what they needed. She just had to find a way to get through to them, to get them to understand that she wanted to help.

The first thing she needed was more information. She didn't know why they were lingering when Michael was gone. Did they want Rachel to tell their families what had happened to them? Was there something the police had missed? What could help them let go and move on? She headed for the sliding glass door.

Opening it slowly and quietly, she glanced back over her shoulder at Garrett. Still asleep. She slipped outside into the muggy morning air, then slid the door shut behind her.

Initiating a conversation with a ghost wasn't something she had done before. Even with Hiram, he had been the one to introduce himself.

Sweat was beading on her chest before she finally said, "Hello?"

"Good morning, my pet." The voice was male—the older ghost from last night. *"Did you sleep well?"*

"Well enough, thank you."

Her heart was beating fast and she had the urge to run back into the house. But that would wake up Garrett and then he'd insist on helping her—rescuing her again. She watched for possible threats to keep herself safe. Flying insects, birds, even fire ants.

"You don't need to be concerned, my dear. It's just the two of us."

The thought was mildly comforting. She glanced around at the palms swaying in the breeze and took a deep breath, trying to calm herself.

After all the hours of social etiquette classes her mother had sent her to and all her practice, she was having trouble making small talk. The ghost bailed her out.

"Where is your gentleman friend?"

"He's still asleep. Just inside." She corrected herself quickly. No sense in letting the ghost think she didn't have backup, even if she didn't want to call on Garrett.

"Goodness. Well... I remember those days." The ghost gave a chuckle that made her blush.

"He's not... We didn't..."

"My dear, I didn't mean to embarrass you. It's nature, regardless. I thought your generation was less stogy about such things."

"We are. I just don't want you to get the wrong idea about Garrett and me."

There was a pause, as if the ghost was considering her words. *"How on earth could that idea be wrong? A beautiful woman, a handsome man. You're obviously attracted to each other."*

"That doesn't mean we should do something about it."

The ghost chuckled again. *"My dear, when you cross over to this side, do you think you'll regret a night with that handsome man or all the nights you spent alone because you never dared to reach for him."*

His words struck her soul like a tuning fork, chills flowing over her skin. He was right. He was absolutely right. Rachel would go to her own grave regretting never having the chance to be with Garrett. But she had reasons. Good reasons.

The irony that a ghost was giving her tips on how to live... Her irritation was tempered by how much he reminded her of Hiram.

"Who are you?"

"My name is Misha. I think you knew a late colleague of mine."

"You knew Hiram?" Her voice rose to a squeak. She coughed to clear her throat.

"Yes, pet. We weren't much more than acquaintances in life, but grew a bit closer afterwards. He was always so fond of you. He asked me to keep an eye on you after he moved on. I've done my best, but you didn't make it easy."

"I didn't know."

Hiram hadn't mentioned anything to her. But it did seem like something he would do. He was always looking out for her. Protecting her.

"Well, I'm glad to finally get a chance to talk. I've been watching you with the good doctor and I haven't been able to figure out for the afterlife of me why you aren't together. It's obvious you care deeply for each other."

"Garrett deserves a better life than I can give him."

"Has he said that? He strikes me as a man who would rather have a choice."

"He can't make an informed decision. What I'm offering is too... alien."

Misha scoffed. *"So you string along other men who don't really have a chance with you? How is that fair to anyone?"*

Advice was one thing. Criticism was another. She didn't like his tone or what he was saying, even if there was truth to what he said.

She hadn't thought about her dating distractions in those terms at the time. She hadn't thought at all. Thinking made things harder.

Most of the men she'd dated seemed self-absorbed. She joked with Jazz that they didn't even notice when Rachel broke up with them. Maybe Misha had seen things she hadn't.

"I didn't mean to hurt anyone," she said.

Misha was quiet for a long time. Long enough that Rachel wondered if he had left.

"Misha? Are you still there?"

"Yes, pet."

His voice was a bit thinner. Sharper. The hairs along her arms stood on end.

"You sound angry."

"I apologize, my dear." His tone was genial again. *"I'm a bit distracted keeping the others from speaking with you."*

"Others? What others?"

"Those bothersome women who have been troubling you."

Her stomach lurched. Michael's victims *were* there.

"How are you keeping them from talking to me?"

"*I can be persuasive.*" He laughed shortly.

"I need to talk to them."

"*That's not a good idea. They're quite angry with you.*"

"I want to help them. Can you tell them that for me?"

"*Help them how?*"

"If they tell me what they need to be able to move on, I might be able to do something for them."

"*Oh, pet,*" he said. "*I don't think you'll like their answer. The afterlife has not been kind to these women. They're focusing all that rage on you.*"

"But I want to help."

"*It's kind of you, but they've made their choice.*"

"No. I'm not going to let them keep suffering. I'm not going to give up. Let them talk to me."

He was quiet for a moment, then said, "*I'm afraid they've gone away for a bit. As I said, I was keeping them from you. But now that I know your wishes, I won't do that again.*"

"Can you tell them I want to help? Try to get through to them?"

"*I shall do my very best. But in the meantime, perhaps I can help you.*"

"I don't need any help."

"*Oh but you do. My sweet pet, you are wasting your life by focusing on the dead. You fear us so much that you haven't really even started living.*"

She didn't like hearing it from him, but couldn't argue his point. "What do you suggest?"

"*I think you should walk right into that house and kiss the good doctor.*"

"You seem keen on us getting together."

"*What can I say? I'm a romantic. I'm also keen on seeing you happy. And I think you two can make each other happy—unlike your other misadventures in romance.*"

"I know he would make me happy, but all I would bring him is... strangeness and anxiety. He was happier before he knew that ghosts were real and everywhere. Having me around is a constant reminder."

"I hardly think his mind is occupied with thoughts of death when you're standing close." He paused for a moment while she digested his words. *"Have you talked to him about it? Asked him what he thinks? What he wants?"*

"No…"

"Maybe you should. You of all people know how terrible it feels when others make decisions for you."

Another good point. "I guess you've sat in on some family dinners."

"A few. Your mother is a most intriguing woman."

"That's one word for it."

He chuckled again. *"Pet, I know that you are lonely. It's difficult to watch you prolong your suffering—and that of the good doctor."*

"I don't mind suffering if it gives him a chance at a normal life."

"He doesn't want normal. He wants you."

Rachel snorted and shook her head. "You have a weird way of giving pep-talks."

"Forgive me. My manners are a bit skewed from dealing with the dead for so long. But please believe me that my sole purpose is to make you happy."

Strangely, she did believe him. She wasn't sure she trusted him yet, but he seemed sincere in this at least. He had been watching her—and Garrett. And whatever Misha had seen convinced him that they were right for each other.

If she could admit it to herself, she already knew they *felt* right together. Being with Garrett felt like home—like…forever.

She didn't want to have regret at the end of her life. She wanted memories. Wonderful memories. She didn't want to deny either of them that potential.

Rachel smiled at the thought, excitement bubbling up through her. Maybe it was time that she started focusing on living her life instead of avoiding the dead.

Chapter Fifteen

Too many nights of not enough rest were taking their toll on Garrett. He woke up to the groggy state of half-sleep, disoriented and stiff. His left arm was numb from being pinned under his torso and he had drooled on his couch.

Light was filtering into the room from the blinds that covered the sliding glass door. They had shifted a bit, enough to let the morning sun stretch across the bamboo floor.

Something was wrong. Why were the blinds open at all?

He jumped up, nearly cracking his shins on his coffee table, then ran to the door. Rachel was sitting on one of the chairs outside. She was still wearing his T-shirt. She hugged her knees to her chest and had her feet resting on the chair. And she was laughing.

Garrett paused, trying to triage the situation. She looked relaxed. Comfortable. She wasn't scared. But she was talking to someone. Her voice was too low for him to make out what she was saying through the glass.

Had she already made contact with one of the ghosts they had talked about helping? It seemed quick work to win them over so fast, even for someone as charming as Rachel. If anyone could do it though, she could.

The thought of her outside alone with a ghost was unsettling. Especially now that he knew there was more danger involved than she had let on.

He opened the door, the heat from the stone of his patio blasting him. Rachel turned at the sound, her smile stopping him in his tracks.

How long had it been since he had seen that smile? He felt an odd sense of loss that someone else had brought it out of her. He had been trying so hard to be supportive. Whatever ghost she was talking to had done a better job lifting the weights from her spirit.

"Hi Garrett. I was just talking to Misha."

"Misha? Who's that?"

"He was a friend of Hiram's. It turns out he's been hanging around me for a long time." She paused as if listening to something, then laughed again.

Garrett bristled. He wasn't sure why.

Whoever this Misha was, he was helping Rachel feel better. Shouldn't that make Garrett happy too? Instead, his stomach coiled up like a rattler. He wanted to get her back inside the house, safe behind the wards.

"Have you had breakfast yet?"

"No, I was waiting for you to wake up. Do you think I should take down some wards so he can join us?"

Chh-chh-chh-chh. The hair on his arms stood on end. Who the hell was this guy that Rachel was talking about letting her guard down? Letting him into Garrett's house?

"I don't think that's a good idea. Misha isn't the only one hanging around."

"Right." She shook her head. "Sorry, I guess I wasn't thinking. Misha, I hope you don't mind. Would you excuse me?"

She was quiet again, her head cocked to the side, then she laughed. She stretched out her legs and put her feet on the ground, then yelped and pulled them right back up. They must have been talking for a long time, since she hadn't realized the stones had heated up.

"Hold on." Garrett slipped on his sandals, then stepped into the sun. At least Rachel had been sitting in the shade of the umbrella attached to his patio table.

"Garrett, you don't have to—"

He picked her up before she could finish her sentence. She smiled at him and wrapped her arms around his neck, but he couldn't bring himself to smile back. Even feeling the soft skin of her bare thighs resting on his arm couldn't quell his misgivings.

When he stepped inside, his top priority was to grab the spray bottle and make sure the door was secure. Rachel leaned into him, breaking his concentration.

Holding her close against his chest felt too good. His mind was already coming up with excuses to keep holding her. He pushed the thoughts away.

When he started to set her down, she left her arms around his neck and slid down his torso. He could feel the T-shirt she was wearing bunch up against him, moving up past her hips as he lowered her. Her legs had to be completely bare—at the very least. Her T-shirt felt like it was bunched above her waist.

She was probably wearing panties. No, she was definitely wearing panties. He had to believe that. If he envisioned anything else, things would get embarrassing fast. Even that brief thought was enough to set things stirring down below.

He cleared his throat and locked his gaze on the spray bottle, stepping away from her. "I'll take care of the door."

He slid it shut as he stepped to the counter. Then he sprayed the whole thing down and pulled the blinds shut. Rachel was heading for the kitchen when he dared to look at her again.

Those long legs stretching out past the hem of the T-shirt she was wearing caught his attention. The way she swished her hips wasn't helping, the fabric rippling against her backside. She paused by the barstools, resting one hand on the counter as she looked back at him over her shoulder and smiled.

It wasn't exactly a fake smile, but it wasn't a real one, either. It was flirty. Coquettish.

He'd seen her use that walk—that smile—before. He always felt sorry for the poor saps blasted by it. And now, he was in the line of fire.

Holy shit.

"What would you like for breakfast?" she asked.

He took a step toward her, felt his hands flex like they wanted to reach for her. But he stopped himself.

She caught every nuance. Her smile turned to a smirk, her gaze softening as it flowed over his body then back to his face. She knew she was pushing his buttons, and she was doing it on purpose. Garrett just couldn't figure out why. Why now, of all times?

She'd had years to make a move. Why do it during the storm of chaos surrounding them?

Unless that was exactly why she was doing it. Because she needed to feel in control of something when her life seemed to be in a tailspin. And she knew she could control Garrett, if she really wanted to.

God help him, it looked like she did.

"I could make French toast," she said. "Or pancakes and eggs."

She turned toward him, giving him a new view. He let out a little grunt, but wasn't sure she heard it. He stifled it as best he could. His chest felt constricted.

The soft fabric of his T-shirt clung to her full breasts, faint outlines showing him where her nipples had stiffened beneath. She leaned forward on the nearest barstool, both hands planted firmly on its surface so that her arms pushed her breasts together and exaggerated the effect.

Dammit, that was not okay. He could feel himself starting to get hard.

If she needed to feel in control of something, this was not the way to do it. He pulled on the anger rising up in him to help calm his body down as he kicked off his sandals.

"Cereal is fine."

"Are you sure? You've done so much for me. I'd like to do something nice for you in return."

He could think of a slew of nice things they could do together. None of them involved food. Wait, no there was a can of whipped cream in the fridge.

He needed to rein this in.

"I'll take care of breakfast. Maybe you should go get dressed."

She looked confused, the seductress façade slipping. The tightness in his chest eased up enough that he could breathe again.

"You seem upset," she said.

He could hardly deny it. But voicing his immediate concerns didn't seem like a good idea. He chose some from earlier instead.

"What were you doing out there by yourself?"

"Talking to Misha."

"But you didn't know it would be Misha," he said. "It could have been one of Michael's victims. The ghosts that are pissed off at you."

"They can't hurt me."

"Not directly. But those grasshoppers weren't having a mosh party against your window last night for no reason. And don't think I haven't figured out that's why the scorpion was in the dishwasher."

His anger spiked as he remembered the jolt of fear brought on from that knowledge. The ghosts were already sending insects after Rachel —even venomous ones. What if they started sending something worse?

No way he was letting her go outside alone again, especially barely dressed as she was. Too much unprotected skin waiting to be bitten or stung. His stomach clenched at the thought.

"I was being careful. Besides, Misha told me the ghosts who are mad at me aren't here right now. He scared them away."

"Did he?" Garrett didn't buy it. Something about this Misha character was off.

"I told him my plan—that I'm going to try to help them. He thinks it's worth a shot and is going to let them know the next time he sees them. If they even come back." She shrugged as if it was no big deal.

"You seemed pretty determined to help them last night."

"I was. *I am.*" She sighed, then walked back to him, stopping so close he could almost feel her body heat. "Do we have to talk about this now?"

Leaning forward even an inch would bring their bodies together. He clenched his hands into fists to keep from touching her.

"I'm worried," he said. "You wanted to let this guy into the house. That doesn't seem safe."

"That was a mistake—I admit it. But lucky for me, I have you looking out for me."

The playful teasing was coming back to her voice again. Garrett wouldn't mind it a bit if the circumstances were different. But they weren't.

Of all the messed up twists of fate, having Rachel come on to him now... He steeled his resolve, doing his best to ignore the way she stared at his lips, the way she radiated desire.

It wasn't happening. Not like this.

Chapter Sixteen

"Rachel, this is serious. You wanted to let a ghost into the house."

The conversation was not going the way Rachel had expected. The fact that they were still talking at all baffled her. She'd expected them to be naked by now.

She let out a sigh and said, "Misha isn't just a ghost. He's a friend."

"Really? You just met the guy last night. And you couldn't get away from him fast enough then."

"I was wrong. Last night I was afraid of every ghost. But I'm seeing things differently now. You even said you wanted to help me with them."

"That's exactly my point. You should have waited for me to come with you."

"You were sleeping."

"You could have woken me up." He shook his head. "I know you're...spontaneous, but there's too much at stake for you to not be more careful."

"*I'm* the one in danger."

"And do you think the rest of us wouldn't be hurt if something happened to you?"

His words felt like a slap. She amended his sentence in her head. If something *else* happened to her.

Everyone in their circle of friends had been hurt. Some physically. Horribly. And it was her fault—no matter what they said.

What had she been thinking, trying to start something with Garrett? Even if he could handle her ghost issue, which he clearly couldn't, Rachel still had too much baggage.

Her eyes filled with tears and she crossed her arms. "Right. Because I'm such a terrible judge of character. That's how we all landed in this mess in the first place."

"Rachel…" He reached toward her, but she threw her hands up and backed away.

"I'm sorry I'm not perfect like Elsa or Jazz. I don't always know what to do next. I screw up."

And that was probably what Garrett saw in Rachel in the first place. He was a classic rescuer. An ex-ER doctor, for crying out loud.

Rachel's string of mistakes and failures gave him something to focus on. No wonder things hadn't worked out between him and Elsa. Elsa was always on top of everything.

"That isn't what I meant at all. And everybody makes mistakes," he said.

She snorted and shook her head. "Not like this."

She sniffed to keep her nose from running and wiped the back of her hand across her eyes. "Listen, I said I was going to handle this myself. And I will. I'll get on your computer and find a place and be out right away."

"No. Hell no."

Garrett let out a huge sigh and ran his hands through his hair. Instead of leaving them there and staring at her like he usually did, he dropped his arms to his sides. He walked over to his recliner and sat, then rested his elbows on his knees.

"This is exactly why doctors aren't allowed to work on people they're involved with." He glanced at her quickly and said, "I mean care about."

He shook his head and laughed, then ran his hand over his face. With another sigh, he leaned back in his chair. He looked exhausted.

"I'm messing this all up," he said. "Nothing I say is coming out right. Please let me try again. Can I start over?"

Her anger fizzled. Garrett asking for a second chance… How could she say no to that? Even if they didn't have the huge mass of things he had done for her—second, third, fifth, eleventy-ith chances he'd given her—she would have melted at the request.

He was hurting. It was probably the clearest thing they'd

communicated to each other yet, etched in the lines around his eyes, the furrows between his brows.

She sat on the edge of his coffee table in front of him. "I'm listening."

He leaned forward in the chair again, which brought him close. Really close.

His jaw was coated in dark stubble that accentuated his strong cheekbones. She wanted to run her fingertips across the coarse surface, but shook herself internally and brought herself back to task. He deserved her full attention.

"I'm just going to lay it all out there," he said. "You've always been the first to admit that you're impulsive."

She opened her mouth to argue with him, but realized that was true. It stung, but she kept her silence and heard him out.

"I don't know if that's your nature or how you've been dealing with these voices your whole life or a little of both. But it's who you are and I—"

He lowered his head for a moment and took a deep breath, then let it out slow. When he looked up at her again, his expression was shielded.

"I care about you. I don't want you to have to change because of this. Because of what Michael did to you or being born psychic or anything."

"I appreciate that."

He nodded. "What I do want is for you to be safe. I've seen your other side—the reflective, detail-oriented person who pauses and thinks things through before acting."

"In other words, you want me to be more like Elsa." It felt like he was using her heart as a punching bag.

"Not at all. If you'll recall, I met you first. If anyone's the baseline, it's you."

Rachel had forgotten that she had worked on Garrett's house before he and Elsa met. It helped. A little.

"I want you to be more like *you*. I think if you let yourself stop playing the socialite and take some time to figure out who you really want to be, you'll be a lot happier. And I want you to be happy. You can stay here as long as you need while you sort it out."

"I don't want to impose."

"It's not an imposition. I love...hanging out with you."

He winced as he obviously changed the direction of his sentence. She didn't dare let herself think of what he might have been about to say.

"I know I had a great time during those months when you stayed here before," he said. "I thought you did too."

Her throat felt thick again. "It was wonderful."

"I'm glad." He smiled at her, so sad it broke her heart. "I think I'm the one messing things up now and I promise I'll work on that. I just have a lot of anger when I think of what happened to you. It's hard for me to hide it and it's making everything become exaggerated. I'm sorry."

"You don't have to be sorry."

She lifted her hands to his face, cradling his cheeks. The prickling of his hair against her palms made her shiver. He closed his eyes and lifted his hands to her arms, taking more slow, deep breaths.

When he opened his eyes again, Rachel couldn't look away. They stared at each other, gazed into each other's eyes. It was incredibly intimate. She felt exposed, vulnerable, but he was right there with her. As always.

He was so beautiful.

She wanted to kiss him, but if she did, their friendship would be over. She couldn't fool herself into thinking that they could go back to the status quo after that.

And if they did become involved, she'd have to stay in constant crisis to keep him interested, to keep giving the rescuer part of him that hit. That wasn't any better than the way she'd been living up to this point.

She wanted to be partners with him. She wanted to take turns shopping and paying the bills and doing laundry. She wanted to live as they had when she'd been working on his house.

Wait... That was when their relationship started—when she had been basically living with him over those months.

At first he'd been at work most of the time, but it hadn't been long before he was coming home earlier and taking more vacation days. They had spent tons of time together, talking, laughing, taking care of themselves and each other.

They had been partners then, and she had never felt more at ease in her own skin. She hadn't needed any rescuing. Her life had been calm. And he had been interested in her. Obviously, deeply interested.

Rachel had run away because she thought he couldn't handle her ability to see ghosts. Now she knew that wasn't a valid fear. He could handle it. In spades.

He could even handle her mom—who already loved him and had been pushing Rachel to try to seduce him into a marriage. Which had only inspired Rachel to run away more.

Reacting. Always reacting.

That was the impulsiveness that Garrett was talking about. It had grown the more she pinballed her way through life, bouncing off of whatever obstacles rose before her. Calling Garrett for help because she couldn't stay away from him.

She sat up straighter as another thought rocketed through her mind. Garrett might be a bit of a rescuer, but she was the one who kept initiating the problems by making ridiculously bad choices. Every time she dug herself in too deep, she had an excuse to call him. And every time, he came to help her out.

He wasn't a rescuer. She was a rescue-ee.

She had a list. Didn't she have a list? Reasons she shouldn't pursue a relationship with Garrett.

She played into his weaknesses as a rescuer. No, she was artificially creating crises to give herself an excuse to call him.

She could hear ghosts, and that would be too weird for him to handle. Well, that was impacting him, but he didn't seem too put off by it. He just wanted her to be safe and use caution when dealing with them. That was fair enough.

Her mother was...her mother. Garrett had already stood up to Mrs. Montgomery when he helped Rachel leave her house. He could handle that matter.

Didn't she have a longer list than that? She couldn't remember anything else.

Like a lightning strike, she realized there were no actual reasons for them to not be together. Nothing but the shadows she had conjured up from her own mind.

She looked at him again, sitting patiently right in front of her. Waiting.

He had been waiting long enough.

Chapter Seventeen

Something shifted in Rachel's expression. Garrett couldn't miss it. He watched closely as she thought over what he said. Thought long and hard, from the looks of things.

She started off looking troubled, then shifted through perplexed and concerned before...relieved? Hopeful?

He didn't know how it was going to land.

Would she be mad? Hurt? Would she get up and walk out like she always did, leaving him to patch up his heart as best he could?

All he could do was wait. He held her arms lightly, let her stare into his soul, her hands gentle on his face.

She leaned in and kissed him.

He felt the shock of it in every cell of his body. Her lips—velvet soft—played across his mouth. A few tentative preludes before she became more aggressive. Her tongue found his, their breath mingling, her grip tightening to hold him right where she wanted him.

Was this still playing out from before? Was it about control or something else? Something deeper?

After everything he'd laid down on her, this wasn't at all what he expected. But he couldn't bring himself to stop her.

She pushed him farther onto his recliner and molded her body against his in a graceful lunge. The force of her movement made the chair kick back and flatten. She brought her knees up on either side of him, pressing their hips together.

He groaned as he felt her heat through her panties and his thin pajama bottoms. When had he grown rock-hard?

Damn, she knew how to kiss. He had imagined this so many times, but it was never this intense. There was always a slow build. He should have known better with Rachel.

414

She raked her teeth along his jaw. He felt it echo in every nerve ending in his body. She started rubbing against his erection as she lightly bit down on his neck.

Garrett sucked in a breath, trying to form a coherent thought. All he could do was groan and rock against her.

So many years full of *want*. And now he had her. Finally.

He let his hands glide down her back, past her waist, and cupped the fullness of her backside. She let out a little grunt, then moved her kisses up along his neck so she could suck and nip his earlobe. His fingers clenched against her flesh as electric pleasure crackled through him.

This was happening too fast. He needed a moment to catch his breath, to make sure they were on the same page.

If she was just doing this to say thanks or to give herself comfort... Well, he could comfort her in other ways. But not like this. This was too important.

She ran her nails over his chest, letting her fingertips burrow through his chest hair as she explored his torso.

"Rachel..."

She lifted herself from him a bit. He thought maybe she was going to stop so they could talk, but instead she pressed her hand against his abdomen, sliding it all the way down, right past the waist of his pajamas so she could grip his erection tight.

His head hit the back of his—thankfully—cushioned chair as his back arched. She didn't waste any time before starting to work him, pumping her hand up and down.

Her skin was soft as silk. His body must be glowing white-hot from how his nerves were firing off. They wouldn't be the only thing firing off any second now if she kept that up.

"Rachel—"

He grabbed her hand to stop its movement, but she didn't let go. Apparently she wasn't nearly done with him yet.

She nuzzled his cheek as she brought her lips back to his. The kiss was slow and deep. It gave him time to enjoy the taste of her, the warmth of her skin.

He had a chance to kiss her back. Really kiss her. Maybe it wasn't all about control after all.

He indulged himself, holding the kiss for long enough to saturate his senses with her before moving his mouth across hers, pulling first one lip then the other between his.

Her hair fell across his face and neck, feather-light. He let go of her arm to tuck it back behind her ear, then slowly slid his tongue into her mouth.

This was more the give-and-take he had imagined.

She didn't start up her hand again, and he couldn't say that he minded. He was way too close to the edge. Even holding still, her hand wrapped around him was sending lightning arcs of stimuli through him.

He needed to get her to let go—to give him a chance to cool down. There were still things he needed to talk to her about before this went any further.

As if she sensed his need, she finally let him go. She kept her hand down the front of his pants, though—playing with the sensitive skin above his hip and along his lower abdomen.

She shifted above him, kissing his cheek and jaw, then down along his neck. His eyes rolled shut as her gentle touches relaxed him.

Still, he managed to say, "We need to talk."

She nuzzled his earlobe, and whispered, "There are much better things I can do with my mouth."

He didn't doubt that one bit after what they'd just done. He groaned at the thought of doing more, but it wasn't the time. There were things they needed to work through.

She started to slide down toward the edge of the chair. Garrett kept his eyes closed for a minute and took a deep breath to help himself focus.

He needed to calm his body down, but he was wound up too tight. And she still had her hand down his pants. It was planted on his thigh for some reason. Probably so she could sit up.

The cool air of the AC hit his erection. That was the only warning he had before she wrapped her lips around him and sucked him deep into her mouth.

He let out a guttural cry as his body rocketed back up, his nerves singing in ecstasy. Her tongue flicked along his length, swirled around in circles that stoked him even higher. And all the while, she kept pumping him, lips wrapped around him tight.

He wanted to grab her and move her away. Part of him really did. But a stronger part, a more primal part, couldn't resist this pleasure. He looked down at her, watched as her golden hair slid across his stomach, and he came.

It was harder and faster than any climax he had ever experienced. His fingers dug into the arms of the chair, he couldn't catch his breath or stop the low grunts that escaped him.

And she never once stopped. She never slowed down. Even when his hips bucked up against her, she just rode him until he was spent, taking everything he was giving her, till the edges of his vision seemed to darken as the sensory overload threatened to make him pass out.

When she finally had mercy on him and let him slide from her mouth, she gently released the waistband of his pajama bottoms, then glanced up at him and gave him a wicked smile. She had just taken him down to the most primal level a man could reach, and she knew it.

And he wasn't sure why.

She slid back up his body, kissing a path to his mouth. He was still thrumming from what they had shared—physically more relaxed, but more on edge in every other way.

He tried to form his thoughts while she kissed him, but they all blurred together. When she was done, she leapt up from the chair.

"Why don't we skip breakfast altogether," she said. "It's late enough that we can just have lunch."

What. The. Hell.

Chapter Eighteen

Rachel had never felt more energized. She and Garrett were together. *Finally!* She couldn't wait for things to get back to how they had been when she lived with him before. Only this time it would be even better.

There were no more secrets between them. No more reasons to stay apart.

They were already living together again. It was amazing. The house was cleared and warded, and as soon as they solved the problems of the ghosts that were unhappy with her, they could focus on each other fully.

She was absolutely going to start taking care of him now. That little episode in the recliner was just the appetizer. They would need their strength for the next things she had in mind.

As he rose from the recliner, she said, "Is there still lunchmeat in the fridge? I can make us more sandwiches."

Garrett was staring at her with his mouth slightly open. Oh yeah. He had enjoyed himself. She felt her smile broaden.

"Rachel, what the hell was that?" he asked.

She wanted to say *foreplay* but something in the way he was looking at her made her stop. He ran his hands through his hair, resting them on top of his head and holding his bangs away from his face. The supermodel pose accentuated his broad chest and narrow hips.

He was unbelievably beautiful. With his hair out of the way, she had a clear view of his strong cheekbones and jaw—those rich blue eyes.

She wanted to push him right back down on the recliner. Except his eyes were pinched around the edges. And he was frowning—not what she expected after what they had shared.

"I don't understand," she said.

"*You* don't understand?" He let his arms drop to his sides. Even under all that stubble she could see a muscle in his cheek twitching.

He shook his head and said, "I can't keep up. One minute you're happy to be here, the next you're out the door any second. You ask for my help, but you don't listen to what I say, then you do a one-eighty and are going to do everything on your own. You're terrified of ghosts, then you're inviting one to breakfast."

"If this is about Misha—"

"This isn't about Misha! It's about *us*. It's always been about us. How you look at me like...something's there, then laugh it off and flit away." He pointed at the recliner and said, "And then you do *that* and immediately jump to lunch like nothing happened?"

"I—"

"You can't blow me just to let off steam! It has to mean something."

"Of course it means something." Her heart felt like it had stopped beating, like it was curled up in her chest.

"What? 'Thanks for letting me crash here'?"

"How can you say that? I would never—"

Anger and disappointment clawed at her throat, cutting off her words. She would never be so casual about what she'd just done. Especially with him. How could he think that of her?

He put his hands over his face for a moment, then slid them along his cheeks till they were held in front of his lips as if he was praying. He dropped his arms to his sides again, letting out a deep breath. Somehow, it seemed to diminish him, like more than air was escaping. He looked crushed.

"I'm sorry. I said I would get a handle on myself, and I...messed it up again." He bowed his head and murmured, "Shit. There's no going back now anyway."

When he looked up at her, his eyes were blazing. It wasn't anger or frustration. It warmed her—made heat pool deep in her belly—even in the midst of this awful conversation.

"I love you, Rachel. I have since the night we met."

The room started to spin around her. No matter how confident she was about his feelings for her, there was always room for doubt. Until this moment. Hearing the words was so much better than making assumptions about how he felt. And he had more to say.

"When you were staying here working on the house… I've never been happier in my life. It felt like how forever should be. I thought we had both found *the one*. Then it was gone—you were gone—and I didn't know why. Still don't."

He shook his head and went on. "But I still want it. What we had, whatever it was. I want it so much it eats me up inside. I've tried to get over it. To get over you. But every time I started to give up on the dream of us being together, you'd throw me a crumb and I'd think maybe we still had a shot."

Rachel's heart was pounding so much she was lightheaded. She knew she had hurt him in the past and wanted to make up for that. She thought that was what she had been doing. That she was starting something beautiful with him. But she had only managed to make things worse—to hurt him more.

"I can't keep doing this. I can't—" His voice broke. It actually broke. Rachel's heart cracked along with it.

He cleared his throat. When he spoke again, his voice was low and quiet—so gentle it made her ache.

"You can stay here as long as you need. I will help you any way I can, except…" He angled his head slightly toward the recliner. "Except that. But I need to know where I stand with you. Once and for all."

Rachel couldn't speak. Her chest was so tight, she could barely breathe. She felt the tears on her cheeks but didn't move to wipe them away.

All she could do was nod.

"Take some time," his voice was still painfully gentle. "I'm going to go cool off."

She closed her eyes so she wouldn't have to watch him walk away, but she felt him passing. She wanted to reach for him, to tell him he had it all wrong. But that would be reacting again. She couldn't risk hurting him any more than she already had.

She still didn't understand what had happened. She replayed that last few minutes in her mind, picking everything apart for clues.

They were talking... He wanted her to be more authentically herself. She thought that was what she was doing. Showing him how she really felt, letting herself be free to express who she was, passionate and adventurous and energetic.

And he couldn't keep up.

She was mercurial. She couldn't change that. She didn't want to have to change to be with someone. With Garrett, she never felt that she had to. Until now.

He kept going on about how she could be practical and focused. It was true. When she was working on a project, she did feel different. Confident... In charge. She didn't need to jump from one topic or activity to another just to keep her mind occupied.

Which was the real her?

Both. She couldn't deny it. And because of that, for the first time she truly wasn't sure if she and Garrett should be together. Not for any of the paranormal reasons or issues with her dysfunctional family. But because of who she was.

The hopelessness of that thought weighed her down. She felt like she would sink through the floor at any moment.

She wasn't right for him after all. He wouldn't be happy with her.

Something thumped against the sliding glass doors. And again and again. More freaking lubbers.

Dammit! She had enough problems in her *own* life. She didn't need to be distracted by other peoples' afterlives.

She wasn't going to feel guilty that she was the only person to escape from Michael. Those other women needed to know that she was going to help them, but on *her* terms.

Going outside wasn't safe. She couldn't control the environment well enough. Plan B, then.

Rachel went to the kitchen and grabbed the container of salt, then stalked to her room. She trailed a thick line of the crystals across the entire threshold of her doorway, but left the door open. The barrier she'd made could be disturbed too easily. Besides, she wanted to be able to leap over it if she needed to. No ghosts would be able to cross that line.

They'd definitely need to get more salt soon. Rather, Garrett would. There was no *they* involved.

Wiping the back of her hand across her eyes and nose, she stood, then went to the bathroom. She grabbed a washcloth and wet it.

For a moment, she thought about tearing the sheet away from the mirror so she could face the women when she confronted them. Remembering their expressions, their wounds... Not a good idea.

She went back to her room and opened her blinds all the way. She wiped down the window, getting all the saltwater off the glass, then pulled her reading chair closer to it.

With a deep breath, she climbed up on it and took down her witch's ball and the poppet.

Nothing happened at first. That wasn't too much of a surprise. She climbed back down and tucked the poppet and glass ball under the sheet on her bed.

Turning the chair to face the window, she sat and waited.

Moments ticked by. She was getting restless. Her thoughts went back to Garrett and her stomach clenched.

"You look unhappy."

The voice whispering close to her ear made her jerk away. It was male, but didn't sound like Misha. A chill swept over her skin.

"I didn't mean to startle you, pet." The genial tone returned. *"Is everything all right with your doctor friend?"*

"I don't want to talk about that. Were you able to find the women I'm looking for?"

"Goodness but you sound serious. No, I'm afraid I didn't have much luck there."

"I know they're close. They keep sending grasshoppers to bounce off the windows and they impelled a scorpion to crawl through the drain in the dishwasher."

"That sounds unlikely. Impelling animals takes skill and a certain mindset. I doubt those women have enough self-control to do so."

Rachel bristled on their behalf. "Excuse me?"

"Because they're upset, of course. They would need to focus their emotions to channel them properly to get an animal to do what they want."

What he said made sense, even though she didn't like how he said it. What didn't make sense was the grasshoppers' behavior. One isolated incident wasn't suspicious. Three? That couldn't be a coincidence.

"Something is making them act strangely," she said.

"Does the doctor have a lawn service? Perhaps a chemical sprayed in the yard recently upset them."

"I suppose it's possible..."

"What's truly troubling you, pet?"

"I'm not a pet. Stop calling me that."

"Of course. My apologies."

She shouldn't have snapped at him, but the level of despair she felt was reminding her of her time in Michael's garage. Her hopes had risen higher than ever in her life, and then been dashed. Even the dream of being with Garrett was gone.

If she thought about it more she would start crying again. And she was sick of crying.

She stood and started pacing the room. "There has to be something else going on. Those women I saw at my mother's house must be around here somewhere."

Rachel remembered how angry they had been, how terrified. Both at her mother's and in Michael's garage. They weren't walking away from this—from her.

"My dear, if you would tell me what is wrong, perhaps I could help you."

"Find me those ghosts. That's how you can help."

"Patience is required in this case."

Rachel snorted. Misha wanted her to slow down too. More waiting. If she hadn't delayed so long with Garrett, things might have worked out differently. But could they have lasted as a couple, knowing the issues he was having now?

"I'm beginning to grow worried. Is Dr. Wolfstrom all right? I would check myself, but you've warded the house quite effectively."

"This isn't my first rodeo. I doubt it will be my last."

Her voice had a growl to it that even surprised her. Misha was quiet for a while. Good. Let him know—let them all know—she was done being messed with. She was done having people tell her who to be or how to act.

She was psychic. She was smart. She was weird. And most of all, she was tired of hiding it all. Hiding who she was and how she felt.

And how she felt…

She loved Garrett.

"Does he know you took the wards down?" Misha asked.

"Of course not," she said. "He would never have let me."

"He has good reason for his concern."

"I get it! He only sees me at my worst! When he's picking up the pieces after I make bad decisions. But this is the last time. After this, he won't be seeing me at all. He's done with me."

The words—the thought of it—tore at her heart. No more Garrett. He was out of her life forever. She had ruined everything.

"I highly doubt that."

She sat heavily on her bed, shoulders slumping. "He'll be better off. He as much as said so."

"There is no way he said such a thing."

"He can't keep up. That's what he said."

Misha chuckled. *"No one can keep up with you, my dear! I don't have a body to exhaust, and I still get tired following you around. That doesn't mean he doesn't want to be with you. Accept who you are and believe that he does the same and you'll both be happier."*

"No. I've put him through enough."

There was a long pause, then Misha said. *"If you walk away now, you'll destroy him."*

Misha's voice was somber and low. The hair on Rachel's arms stood on end. Ghosts only spoke like that if they had an ace up their sleeve.

"How can you be so certain?"

"Because I understand why he's so overprotective. Why the tiny scorpion brought out such a huge reaction."

She had thought it was weird at the time, but was distracted by Garrett naked in his kitchen. Even now, the memory of seeing him in all his glory—and nothing else—made her body tingle.

"He has a brother," Misha said.

"No he doesn't."

Garrett had never mentioned a sibling of any sort. Rachel knew his parents, had seen them at tons of social events. Garrett was the only person they ever brought along or talked about.

"Forgive me, I misspoke. He had *a brother."*

Had... Her heart sank at the thought, weighed down by countless tragic scenarios that played through her head.

It must have happened years ago—decades, even. She had never heard anyone, living or dead, speak of Garrett's brother.

"Garrett was with him when it happened," Misha said.

Rachel jumped up and shook her head. "No. You can't tell me this. If Garrett wants me to know, he'll tell me himself."

Why hadn't he told her? It must have been terrible for him. She wanted to know more, wanted to run to Garrett and hold him and for once be the one to comfort him.

"He won't have a chance if you run away after this. I know you, Rachel. It's what you do."

Misha's voice took on that strange cast again toward the end of his sentence. He sounded angry. She wasn't having it.

"Why does it matter to you? You already had your shot at life. This is mine. I can mess it up if I want to."

"Forgive me. It's just painful to watch someone I care about throwing away their best chance at happiness."

"Maybe I don't get to be happy."

The words escaped before she had a chance to think about them. Saying them hollowed her out, made her feel empty.

She had always considered happiness a choice. It was about

choosing the way she thought about events, even when life rose up again and again to knock her down. Now, she wasn't so sure.

"What about Garrett? Does he deserve to suffer too?" The ghost let out a derisive snort. *"You two are perfect for each other. Punishing yourselves for imagined errors and perceived imperfections. I truly hope you work this out if only so you won't inflict yourself on other unfortunates who are blinded by your charms."*

"Excuse me?" Rachel practically shouted the words.

What the hell was this guy's deal? He said he wanted to help her, then insulted her? His voice had changed again too. He sounded younger.

Why was he so angry? It was her life that she was messing up. Well, Garrett's too, according to Misha. She didn't understand why he cared.

Unless...

Unless he wasn't who he said he was. A chill shot down her spine as she thought of Michael. But no—it couldn't be him. Who did that leave? Who might be lingering around one or both of them, mad about choices they were making?

Whoever this was, he seemed to really want them to be together and to believe that was best for them both. Especially for Garrett.

She thought back over what Misha had said, about Garrett having a brother. Garrett's brother had to have been gone for a long time for Rachel not to have heard of him. Young children didn't linger, but if his brother had been older than Garrett by several years...

His spirit might have stayed. He might have watched as Rachel flirted and flitted away, over and over again. He might have seen Garrett fall in deeper, loving Rachel, wanting to be with her. He might have seen how happy she made Garrett once upon a time.

He might be pissed as hell that she was planning to run away again.

"Misha, I don't think Garrett and I will work out in the long term." She kept her voice as gentle as she could manage. "He deserves a woman who won't put him through so much."

"He wants you."

"That doesn't mean he should be with me. You've probably noticed how upset he's been since I came here. I want him to have a peaceful life. A chance at a normal family."

Misha let out another snort. He sounded much younger now, even the cadence to his speech changing. *"There are no normal families."*

"There are always challenges, but if he can't love me as I am, I can't be with him."

"You think you're so special that you're unlovable?"

Rachel was taken aback. She didn't know what Misha had been like when he was alive, but he sure was a jerk in the afterlife. And he wasn't done with her yet.

"All you have to do is say the word and Garrett would be yours. You're the one keeping the two of you apart. Don't lay this on him."

"He can't keep up with me."

"Then slow down!"

"It's not that simple."

"Excuses. It's always excuses with you."

Brother or not, Rachel was reaching her limit with this guy. "You don't know me."

"Do you? Does anyone?"

Rachel opened her mouth to argue, but couldn't think of a response. Of everyone on the planet, Garrett understood her best. If she couldn't make it work with him, she knew in her heart she would be alone for the rest of her life. Except for the ghosts.

A life filled with spirits seemed easy compared to a life without Garrett.

Misha had regained some of his composure when he spoke again. He still sounded different, but the anger was contained.

"All you have to do is tell him how you feel. That's all he needs. Please, at least try."

Chapter Nineteen

Garrett didn't look up when Rachel walked into his bedroom. He sat at the foot of his bed, elbows on his knees and hands clasped together. His eyes were burning. She could probably see how damp they were. He was past caring.

"Hi." She hovered just inside the doorway.

He parroted back, "Hi."

"Can we talk?"

"You sure I'm the one you want to talk to?"

"I don't understand."

"I heard you," he whispered.

"Heard me what?"

He cleared his throat. "I came out to talk things through, but you weren't in the living room. I heard you talking to someone in your room. I'm guessing it was Misha."

After a short pause she said, "Yes."

He nodded, her confirmation hollowing him out.

"I made a salt barrier at the door," she said. "He can't come in further than the guest room and bathroom."

"Great."

Like that made it okay.

Yet again, she had turned to someone else—let someone else in—while she kept Garrett at arm's length. She was moving away from him already. He wanted to follow after her, but he didn't think he had it in him anymore. At least he knew she'd be back next time something blew up.

Was that all he had to look forward to?

He felt the bed move as she knelt next to him. He could see from the corner of his eye.

Please, Lord, don't let her try to start anything again.

He wouldn't be able to handle it if something happened between them before he had the answers he needed. If she so much as touched him, he would probably leap across the room like he was snakebit.

His stomach churned as he remembered Dylan again.

"I'm in a difficult situation here," she said. "And you are too. Because of me."

"I knew what I was signing up for."

Partly, anyway.

He knew she was going through a lot—it just turned out to be a different kind of hurting, from a source he would never have guessed. Being surrounded by ghosts... What she was dealing with was awful. He didn't mean to be putting more on her.

"But you didn't," she said. "Not really. You thought you were helping out a friend who had been through a traumatic event. You didn't know you were getting all of this. I did."

Her voice crackled for a moment, but she cleared her throat and went on in a strong tone.

"I knew how you felt. I knew you loved me. And I let you help me even though I knew it was hurting you. And I am so, so sorry for that. But I didn't do it to use you or lead you on. I did it because I couldn't stay away. I knew I was all wrong for you, but I just...wanted you so much. I hope you can forgive me. I know I never will."

"Rachel—" He glanced up.

Looking at her was a mistake. When their gazes met, it was like being struck by lightning. His heart seemed to want to break out of his chest to get to her.

Whenever they were close he felt it—electric energy, pulsing just beneath his skin. Never this strong before, though. His entire body was charged and ready to do whatever she needed, wanting just a little more time with her any way he could get it.

The pull toward her was like gravity—or a black hole.

Her lips parted and she leaned toward him. She felt it too. He was sure of it. What he wasn't sure of was whether it was love or lust on her part. And the ever-present question with her remained—when would she run away again?

"You asked me to think," she said. "But that's part of my problem. I think too much about some things, but not enough about others. I can be focused and calm or full of frenetic energy. I'm a person of extremes."

She shook her head and leaned back on her heels. "I'm passionate. I feel everything deeply and I process things so fast. It can come out... intense. I know it can be off-putting. Even *I* want to run away from me sometimes. Maybe that's what I've been doing. Running away from everything."

Garrett had never thought that Rachel might be exhausted by her own contradictions. "That doesn't seem like a good way to live."

"It isn't. I don't want to live that way anymore. I don't want to run away from you, Garrett."

His heartbeat instantly picked up. He could feel the blood rushing in his ears.

He tried to stay calm. She didn't want to run away. Okay. But what *did* she want? A casual fling? Or something more?

"I've never seen you yell or get as worked up with anyone else as you do with me," she said. "I don't know that it's a good thing I bring that out of you."

"I have a temper. That's not your doing."

"I know. I'm trying to explain why I act this way with you." She let out a breath and said, "Do you remember the night we met?"

"Of course. It was one of your mom's fundraisers."

"I'm not talking about seeing each other across a room. I mean the first time we talked."

He had seen her half a dozen times before they ever spoke. They had exchanged glances across rooms, even sometimes grinned and raised their eyebrows or nodded their heads, sharing a joke that no one else seemed to get.

But the first time they talked... That was something he would never forget. It had put his life on a different trajectory.

He cleared his throat and said, "Jazz had that Halloween party at the Orange Grove Inn."

"And we both stepped outside to get some fresh air because there were too many people. You said you had already used up your quota for crowds with an event we both attended earlier that week. I told you I'd had my fill of crowds too. But it wasn't the kind you were thinking of. I couldn't tell you then, but I was freaking out from seeing so many people in costumes."

It only took him a second to figure out the issue this time. Everybody had shown up as monsters. The room was full of people dressed as the dead. That night must have been an ordeal for her.

"Why did you go?"

"The idea was hers, but Jazz had me do all the planning. It was the first big event she let me handle on my own. I couldn't not show up. When you and I were talking, I kept thinking she might fire me for being gone so long, but I didn't want to go back inside. Not because I wanted to avoid the costumes but because I wanted more time with you. There was something about you. Even then, I could feel it."

"It was probably the beer."

She laughed, and the sound tugged at his chest.

He wanted to make her feel better. If jokes would work, great. But the more they talked—with her kneeling next to him on his bed—the more he wondered if it would be so bad to have a one-night stand. If that was what she needed...

"That was the first beer I ever drank from a bottle," she said. "You had nabbed it from behind the bar and shared it with me. You've always shared whatever you had with me."

It didn't feel like sharing. After that night, everything he had—everything he was—was hers.

"You talked to me and I felt calm," she said. "Centered. I felt like I could finally let go of my socialite veneer, at least for a little while. I felt like I could be myself. We were out there for hours."

She had a soft smile on her face. She laughed again as she went on. "When you first ran into me on the balcony, you offered to leave. You said I was there first and you didn't want to trouble me."

Garrett nodded. "I remember."

"And I asked you to stay. I'm always asking you to stay. I can't say I'll always be right at your side. That isn't who I am. I'm flighty and full of energy and movement and I need you to be okay with that. But I ask you to stay because I want to be with you."

Yeah. He got that. She wanted to be with him on her terms. When, where, and how she wanted. He needed more.

"There are lots of ways to be with someone," he said. "Different relationship dynamics. This is all really...nostalgic, but it doesn't let me know where I stand. I don't get why you can't just come out and say—"

"I love you."

He blinked. He felt his eyelids close and open like shutters.

Love? His mouth went dry and his heart seemed to stop.

"Love means different things to different people..." he said.

She sighed and inched closer.

"I love how gentle you are and how passionate you can be. I love your intelligence and generosity. I love how you take care of everyone. I love how you can charm people without letting them past your guard. I love that you give me glimpses of who you really are and share sides of yourself with me that no one else gets to see."

Was she talking about how she felt about him or the other way around? He had thought these same things about her more times than he could count.

She paused for a moment, then said, "I love that you let me get away with just enough that I feel free to take risks and be myself, but not so much that you don't let me know when I've crossed a line, like I did earlier."

"Rachel—"

"I'm not finished."

She inched closer, resting her hand on his thigh for balance. He remembered the softness of her skin and felt himself start to get hard again. This time, it didn't bother him.

"Your house is the only place that ever really felt like a home to me. I thought at first it was because it's out in the country and so it's more peaceful for a clairsentient. But it was because of you."

She squeezed his thigh, sending a jolt of pleasure through him. He wanted to grab her and kiss her, to wrap his arms around her and never let her go. But even more, he wanted to hear what she had to say. He wanted to understand her—who she was and what she was offering him.

"I loved going to bed in your house every night and waking up knowing that you were going to be the first person I would see. I loved cooking for you and laughing with you. And I wanted to stay so much that it terrified me. Because then, I didn't think I could do that to you. It felt like it would be a punishment, and you deserved better."

"How could living with you ever be a punishment?"

"Because I'm weird and I see ghosts and I go off on tangents constantly and my mother is actually kind of evil and I say things without thinking them through, like that part about my mom."

He laughed and shook his head. "You don't see me arguing the point."

She smiled, shifting closer. He could lean forward and kiss her if he wanted, and he really wanted to. But damn, if he wasn't shaking inside. She was dangling everything he wanted right in front of him. If he reached for it, she might jerk it away.

Yeah, that killed the moment. He looked down, but she lifted her hands to his face and turned his head back toward her.

"You said you laid it all out for me before. Let me do the same now. What I want? I want you. Not just your truly exquisite body, but all of you. I want to see you every day. I want to go to sleep in this huge bed with you and wake up in your arms. I want—"

She locked her gaze with his, more serious than he'd ever seen her. Warmth flooded him from her hands on his face, her knees pressing against his thigh.

"I want the white-picket fence," she said. "To be your wife—your partner. With three kids and a dog and two cats. I want to go to family cookouts with you and make jokes that only we get. I want you to bring me breakfast in bed on mother's day and to send the kids to a friend's house on father's day so I can give you better memories in that ugly recliner that I know you'll never let me get rid of."

That one memory in his favorite chair was being painted in a whole new light with every word she said. She was still holding on to his face, as if she was the one afraid he was going to bolt for a change.

"What I want," she whispered, leaning in so close that her breath warmed his lips. "Is you. Forever."

Chapter Twenty

If she didn't kiss Garrett immediately, she was going to spontaneously combust. His lips were slightly parted as if waiting for her—welcoming her.

She hoped she was reading him right this time. She couldn't bear to bring him more pain. She also couldn't bear to not touch more of him.

His stubble prickled against her hands, strong muscles tensed beneath. She didn't dare let go. She would never let him go again. He had to understand that she was done running. This was it.

Gently, she pressed her lips against his. He wanted slow. She could do slow.

She let the feel of him soak in—his breath light on her face, the warmth of his lips and softness of his mouth. And for once, she waited for him. Waited for him to make some sign that this was okay. That it was what he wanted.

She didn't have to wait long.

He lifted his hands to her back, running them up along her spine and over her shoulder blades, then pulled her closer. His lips started to move in a slow, sensual caress that made heat pool between her legs. When he slid his tongue into her mouth, it felt like the most natural thing in the world.

No wonder the episode in the recliner had gone so wrong. She gave him a flash-fire when he was after a slow burn. The heat of his kiss spread through her body, resonating, echoing deep within her. She had never felt anything like it.

Primal energy uncoiling in waves that rolled through her instead of crashing around. His lips gripped hers, sucked and nipped. The sensation spread along her nerve endings as if they were each getting a massage.

Her muscles relaxed into him, tension dropping away even while a throbbing ache built in her core. He held her against his chest with one arm while he reached down with his other hand and pulled her thigh across his lap so she was straddling him on the edge of the bed.

A sharp spike of nerves rippled through her. Perched on the edge of the bed, she could easily fall off. But he was holding her up, keeping her safe—as always.

She pressed her hips down to feel his erection. She wanted more.

He thrust up against her, tantalizing her through the thin cotton of her panties. She was so wet. She could feel it. Aching and hollow and longing for him to fill her.

She wrapped her arms around his shoulders as he moved his kisses down her neck and over her collarbone, making a steady trail to her breasts. He nuzzled her through the soft fabric of her T-shirt till her nipples were so tight they almost hurt.

She was very glad she hadn't worn a bra.

He ran his nose over the point jutting toward him, then clasped his mouth around her, laving it with his tongue. She groaned low, not recognizing the sounds she was making. Her T-shirt was damp and clinging to her skin when he moved to her other breast.

No one had ever done anything like this to her before. Sex was always over quickly and then she was on to the next thing. She could tell with Garrett this *was* the next thing. And the next, and the next. She wasn't sure they would ever leave his bed again.

He ran his teeth over the inner side of her breast, then trailed his nose up along her cleavage.

"Stand up." His voice was rough—lower than usual.

At this point, she would do anything he said. She slid to her feet, standing between his knees.

His shaft was sticking out from the top of his pajama pants. Even after what they had done in the recliner, she felt like she was seeing him for the first time. Thick and glistening and ready for her.

She wanted to drop to her knees and take him again, but resisted the urge. Things would be over too fast. She wanted to keep savoring him, keep basking in this incredibly erotic experience.

"Look at me."

Her gaze flicked to his. The intensity of his stare sent another wave of electric sparks through her. Not in little trails or isolated parts of her anatomy. Everywhere.

There was really something to be said for taking their time. Every touch was magnified, the connection more intimate. She was saturated with him. From the way his blue eyes burned, he was only getting started.

He ran his hands up her sides underneath her shirt, cupping her breasts and kneading them. She gasped as he flicked his thumbs across her nipples, the jolt of pleasure echoing in her core.

She put her hands on his broad shoulders, wanting to knock him back onto his bed, but resisting. She could have him inside her in seconds. This was torture. The most exquisite, erotic, pleasurable torture she had ever endured.

"Look at me," he said again.

She didn't know when her eyes had rolled shut or her head had listed against her shoulder, but she snapped herself back to attention. She didn't want to miss a single nuance of what he was doing to her.

She shifted her weight and let out a moan. Even that small movement sent shivers up from between her legs to her breasts, intensifying the effect of his touch. With his right hand, he dusted the backs of his knuckles along her stomach. His left lovingly traced the curves of her backside before he rested his forearm firmly against it.

She wasn't sure what he had in mind until he slid his right hand past the waistband of her panties, his wrist stretching the elastic down to give him access. His fingers raked through her curls, finding her core and sliding in effortlessly.

She had known she was ready for him, but not how ready. She could only imagine what it would feel like for him to bury himself deep inside of her, to feel her body expand to welcome his shaft.

She groaned as her body clenched around him instinctively, her grip on his shoulders tightening as well. His hands were so large he was able to press the heel of his hand against her most sensitive spot, rubbing it in slow circles while his fingers stayed buried deep.

Her knees weakened as the pleasure he had been building in her burst into a bright flame. He was already helping to hold her up, pulling her closer as he scooted to the very edge of the bed.

Her body was on fire, sparking, more alive than she had ever felt. Her nerve endings sang his praises with every languid thrust and pull of his fingers.

He brought his mouth to her breasts again, his kisses more aggressive, demanding. She lifted one knee to rest on the bed, bringing herself closer to him. She wanted him buried inside of her—as deep as he could go. She had never wanted anything or anyone with such intensity.

"Garrett, please," she moaned. "I need you. I want you."

"Look at me." His voice had devolved practically to a growl.

She blinked her eyes, staring down at him as if becoming aware she was dreaming while it was still going on. His fingers kept moving, palm pressed firmly against her.

Watching his face while he was pleasuring her made it even more intimate. Her quim was already starting to pulse around him, the sensations building to a tipping point.

"Come for me."

"I…thought we would do that together."

"Please, Rachel. I need this."

He increased the speed of his fingers, arcing his hand away from her so he could press his thumb against her sweet spot, gently circling it. He stared into her eyes the whole time.

She held his gaze as long as she could, letting him see how his touch affected her, hoping that sharing this intimate moment would help him believe.

She was done running. This was the life she wanted. In his arms, in his bed, in his life. She rocked her body against him, letting the sensations flow through her, push the pressure building between her legs and deep in her abdomen higher than ever before.

On a gentle breath he said, "I love you."

Her body seemed to collapse in on itself and then explode with infinite energy. She threw her head back and screamed as the release tore through her body, a shockwave of ecstasy that left her panting and writhing in his hands.

He finally stopped thrusting, but left his fingers buried within her, his chest heaving in time with her own. She felt her body continue to clench around him, sending aftershocks rippling through her.

He pulled her closer and she draped herself across his chest. She nuzzled his ear, then ran her tongue along its edge and nibbled his earlobe. As amazing as that orgasm had been, she still wanted more. Wanted to be closer, to feel him inside her. She wanted to share the deepest intimacy with him that she could.

When she thought she could speak again, she whispered, "I love you too."

Chapter Twenty-One

The relief Garrett felt made his heart pound. That and watching Rachel's uninhibited, absolutely open responses to his touch. There was no faking what she had felt, what *he* felt from her body through his hands.

The look in her eyes… He had almost lost control so many times, wanting to slide his shaft into her.

There was no need to rein himself in anymore.

He slid his fingers from her and pulled down her panties in one stroke. Most of her weight was already on his chest, and his arms were long enough that he only had to bend sideways a little to get the thin cotton fabric out of the way.

He stood, bringing her with him. The soft cotton of his waistband held his erection tight against his stomach. When her feet were firmly planted on the floor, he lifted her shirt over her head and tossed it aside.

He went to pull off his pants, but she was already there. She tore them off about as eagerly as he had stripped her, barely waiting for him to step out of them before leaping up and wrapping her arms around his shoulders.

Pulling him down a bit, she crashed her lips against his, tongue hungrily seeking his out. He met every thrust, savoring the velvet feel of her mouth.

He loved that she was tall. He still had over half a foot on her, but he didn't loom over her like he did most women. She had to be pushing six-feet. He cupped her backside, squeezing and kneading the firmness of it.

She pressed herself against him, rubbing her stomach against his shaft. Her skin was so soft. She worked one arm between them to grip him, wrapping her fingers around his erection and starting to work her magic. Then she stopped abruptly and pulled away.

This was not happening. No way after everything they had just done was she stopping this. He couldn't believe it.

"I'm not going too fast am I? Do you want me to go slower?"

He let out a laugh that took the tense energy with it. That had scared the crap out of him.

"I want you to do whatever the hell you want."

Her lips pulled into a smile that was pure sex. His breath rushed out as if he'd been kicked in the chest. She let go of his shaft, then put her hands on his shoulders and pushed him down so he was sitting close to the edge of the bed.

As much as he wanted to feel her lips on him again, nothing could compare to being inside of her. And he wanted that so bad he was bursting at the seams.

She must have felt the same, because she put her knees on either side of him, using her grip on his shoulders to keep her balance. He grabbed her backside to help.

"You should know I was always smart with the few guys I slept with," she said. "We used protection and I get tested regularly."

"Okay." Of all the times to bring that up. Yeah, he supposed this was a pretty good one. "Well, my experience is the same."

"I just want you to know because I was serious with that talk about kids. I want them. Tons of them. I don't want to wait."

He swallowed hard. What she was suggesting...

It was fast and sudden, like everything with Rachel. He started to do the math, calculating their ages and thinking about genetic risk factors, how many years they had left and how long they should wait between each child. Then there was the danger the ghosts presented.

No. He wouldn't let fear make up his mind. He thought about what he wanted instead. The decision was obvious.

A house *full* of children, a life full of love. With Rachel.

They would always face challenges—ghostly and otherwise. But they would figure them out together.

He couldn't force words around the lump in his throat so he nodded.

Without any more of a prelude, she lined herself up on him and slowly inched down. Bliss cascaded through him, a buzz of pleasure cantering along every nerve fiber.

Her flesh parted around him, unbelievably soft and slick. And the heat... It soaked into him, flooding his body as she pushed him deeper, taking all of him in.

For a moment, she stayed still, her hands gripping the back of his neck, gazes locked. His heart was pounding, his blood rushing through his body. His hands were trembling.

She loved him. This was what the rest of his life looked like.

He let his gaze slide down her body, lingering on the fullness of her breasts before grazing her flat stomach and finally resting on where they were joined. He took a deep breath to keep himself from getting too worked up. He wanted it to last—this first time of complete intimacy.

She started to move again, slower than he'd expected after the way she mounted him. She lifted herself up onto her knees, sliding along his length as far as she could, then lowered herself back down. He brushed his thumbs along her hips and squeezed her backside as he watched.

So. Fucking. Erotic.

She clenched her sheath around him, as if asking for his attention elsewhere. He was more than happy to oblige.

He let his gaze climb again, lingering only for a moment on her breasts as they swayed with her movement. He swallowed hard and kept going.

Her cheeks were flushed, her lips bright pink and full. Her eyes were open wide, like she was as moved by the experience as he was and didn't want to miss a thing.

She leaned forward to kiss him. Slow and deep, same as her hips. She was savoring him—giving him the chance to savor her. This was night and day from the recliner. Not that there wasn't a time and place for quickies.

His imagination went crazy with possible scenarios. The kitchen counter, the shower, the couch... Any horizontal surface was fair game.

Hell, the vertical ones, too. He wanted her anywhere he could have her. He knew she could satisfy him, but he'd never get enough. He wanted her—forever. Just like she'd said.

He broke off the kiss and said, "There's a Justice of the Peace I know. He could hitch us this afternoon."

She laughed, the vibration traveling through her body and into his. His fingers tightened on her backside reflexively and he took another deep breath to calm himself.

"I want a big wedding, *Doctor* Wolfstrom."

"That is the first time I've ever liked being called that."

She bent down and nibbled along the length of his ear. Goose bumps scattered over his skin, heightening the sensations everywhere they touched. Especially where they were joined.

She whispered into his ear, "I promise I'm not going anywhere."

Rising back on her knees, she wrapped her arms around his neck again and quickened her pace. "Lean back on your arms. I won't fall."

"Yes ma'am," he drawled.

She grinned—her nose crinkling up the way he liked. When he placed his palms on the mattress, she gripped his shoulders for balance and upped her pace again.

The view was unbelievable. With the better leverage, he thrust up into her, meeting her hips with his own. It deepened each stroke, amped up the friction. His skin was thrumming with sensation, nerves lighting up everywhere.

The pleasure coaxed him to move faster, land harder. She matched him perfectly, taking everything he had to give her. He bent his head forward far enough to kiss her breast and she gasped, arcing her back so he could reach her nipple.

He ran his tongue around the tight circle, then sucked it deep into his mouth till she groaned. He had no idea she was so flexible. He was definitely going to have to work on his core strength after this.

He released her breast as she increased her pace again, focusing on matching every movement. She held on tight, eyes clenched shut as she pumped him even faster.

His hips rose to meet her, crashing into her as more sparks ran through his body, pressure building until he felt her spasm around him. She threw her head back and screamed his name.

The pressure within him exploded and he rammed his shaft into her as fast and hard as he could, spilling himself deep inside of her. Her muscles pulsed around him, coaxing everything out of him, everything he had to give.

It was hers. He would always give her everything he could.

She let out a moan and her breath hitched. She was still writhing on him. He kept on thrusting, even as he felt himself growing soft.

She dug her nails into his shoulders, eyes shut tight, head back. Another climax?

She let out a huge breath and finally sagged against him. He could still feel her pulsing around him.

Good Lord. And he thought he had trouble keeping up with her before…

Chapter Twenty-Two

After the incredible afternoon she had spent in bed with Garrett, Rachel didn't expect to wake up from a nightmare. She shot up in bed, glancing around the room frantically. For a few moments, she was disoriented, trying to figure out where she was and what was going on.

Garrett sat up and wrapped his arms around her. "What's wrong?"

"Nothing." She shook her head. "Just another nightmare."

"Do you want to talk about it?"

"I don't know. It felt so real."

He shrugged. "It might help."

What a novel concept. Talking openly about something she had been keeping secret for decades. The chill of the dream receded at the thought of sharing this with Garrett—something she hadn't told anyone about.

"It isn't just from recent events. I've had nightmares for about as long as I can remember. Not every night, but more often than I'd like."

"That sounds awful."

"It used to be standard ghost stuff. I had actually acclimated to it. But since what happened with Michael, they've changed. Now there are two men reaching for me. One of them feels cold and…twisted. Like Michael. But the other one is warm and loving."

"Maybe that one's me." Garrett nuzzled her neck and she leaned into him.

"No. There's definitely a different feel to this one. More…familial." She shook her head. "It's strange, even for me. It felt like the warm energy was trying to find me, but couldn't because of Michael. Like Michael was keeping the other one away."

"Is it possible your powers are trying to tell you something?"

"I hope not."

445

Garrett leaned far enough to the side that she could see his quizzical expression.

"There's an urgency to the dreams that has been building. And this last one…" She shivered at the memory. "Whoever was trying to find me, the warm energy, it was grabbed by Michael's energy and… absorbed or something. It was awful."

She leaned into Garrett's chest to calm herself down. The fear from her nightmares usually faded quickly. This one left her with a lingering sense of anxiety.

"I hate to keep asking this, but—"

"Michael is gone. He has to be. Spirits need a corporeal connection. I have it from people in-the-know."

"Don't ghosts ever lie?"

"Of course they do." She thought of Misha and her suspicions. This didn't seem the best time to bring up the topic. "Hiram isn't the only one I talked to about it."

"Another ghost?"

"I keep telling you, it isn't always about ghosts."

"Who then?"

"The woman who owns Bookwyrm is a medium named Chloe. She does readings in the store sometimes. She's into the showmanship of the whole divination thing and really dresses for the part." Rachel laughed and said, "You should have seen my mother's face when Chloe showed up at the house the first time."

"Sounds like you should have sold tickets."

"Yeah. Chloe's the one who taught me about poppets and how to use a witch's ball. She still sometimes sends me books, but we have to be careful."

"Why?"

"For one, my mother threatened to sue her. I didn't take that threat lightly. Lillian would have found a way to ruin Chloe. And Chloe and I were trying to keep the ghosts from figuring out I could hear them so they would stop bothering me. Hanging out with her would raise their suspicions."

"She doesn't have your problem with ghosts?"

"Chloe isn't clairsentient. Not like me, anyway. She has to do all sorts of ritual preparations to contact the other side."

Chloe had always told Rachel what a gift her powers were. Now that things had changed, maybe Rachel could go to Chloe and learn more. For the first time since Rachel was a child, she was actually excited about what she could do.

"Can she help us with Michael's victims?" Garrett asked.

"I was just thinking something along those lines. I think she can. She'll be very happy I'm away from my mom."

"We're all happy about that. Especially me." He kissed the side of her neck—a small nip, but then he nuzzled her ear and moved to her lips.

This was much better than talk of nightmares and dysfunctional families. Rachel wrapped her arms around Garrett's neck and kissed him back. She was about to push him flat on the bed when her stomach growled loudly.

Garrett broke off the kiss.

"Sorry," she said. "I think we forgot to eat."

"We should take care of that."

He slid to the edge of the bed, holding on to her hand as she followed. He didn't let go while they walked to the kitchen. She stood on her tiptoes to kiss him, and finally dropped his hand so she could open the fridge.

"Sandwiches?"

He laughed and retrieved some plates from the cabinets. "What is it with you and turkey sandwiches?"

"They're nature's perfect food."

Rachel rooted around in the fridge for what she needed, then set everything on the counter. They worked in silence, exchanging a few sidelong glances and smiles. Garrett filled a pair of glasses with a sports drink and his grin turned wicked.

"We need to keep ourselves hydrated after that afternoon," Garrett said.

"And for tonight."

Rachel ran her hand down his chest, trailing her fingers almost all the way down the dark river of hair that bisected his torso. If she went too far, it would be a while before they ate.

"Maybe we should have put some clothes on…"

She hadn't even thought about the fact that they were standing naked in his kitchen. She was that comfortable with him. And he must be that comfortable with her. The thought delighted her and she giggled.

"When a man's body starts to get ready to please his woman, he's not looking for giggles."

Her gaze dropped past his waist and a different kind of hunger altogether stirred in her.

"Stop. Stop looking at me like that." He turned her around and playfully swatted her backside as she walked toward the living room. Then he slid the plates and glasses across the counter.

"Hand me a couple of towels, will you?"

He didn't ask why she wanted them—just opened a drawer and grabbed a pair, then handed them to her. She draped them over the barstools.

"They look cold," she said.

"Good thinking."

He joined her on the other side of the counter and they started eating, sitting so their knees touched.

When they were about done, Garrett said, "I have to ask. Did you ever tell your parents about what you can do?"

Rachel snorted. "My dad—no. And I didn't have to tell my mom. She already knew."

"How?"

"Because she can do the same thing."

Garrett choked on his last bite of sandwich. Rachel reached out and patted him on the back. He took a long sip from his glass when he'd cleared his throat.

"Lillian Montgomery is psychic?" he asked.

Rachel laughed again. "Please do not ever tell her that you know."

"I wouldn't dare. She'd probably have me killed."

Fear clawed at Rachel's heart suddenly. Her mother was capable of much more than hearing ghosts. Terrible things.

"Garrett, you really need to be careful with my mother. She's much more dangerous than you think."

He laughed. "I think I can take her."

"No," Rachel shook her head. "You don't know what she's capable of."

"You mean aside from hearing ghosts?"

"Listen to me. I told you that Hiram crossed over to protect me. Something happened... Something terrible."

"This is that story you mentioned earlier. The one I won't like."

She didn't want to have to tell him this, but it was a vital part of her past. He needed to know, both to understand the regular nightmares when they returned and so he knew the true horror that was Mrs. Lillian Montgomery.

"I talked about Hiram all the time when I was a kid. Even in front of strangers," Rachel said. "When I was younger, my mother could explain it away as an imaginary friend. But when I grew older, people started giving me strange looks. Then they started giving *her* strange looks."

Lillian Montgomery had found that unacceptable. Rachel felt her cheeks tingle with rage over what her mother had done to control her disobedient daughter.

"What did she do?" Garrett's voice was a low rumble. This wasn't going to go over well.

"My mother took me to a town a few hours away. She never paid much attention to me before that day. She had nannies for that. I was so excited." Rachel shook her head. She refused to cry over this. Not anymore.

"We walked into this abandoned building on the outskirts of the town. It had burned down years before. I was scared, but she was with me and I thought she would keep me safe, because that's what mothers are supposed to do. We walked to this huge empty room and she said, 'Playing with ghosts isn't all fun and games.' Then she stood there and smiled while they came for me."

Rachel was shaking. *Dammit!* She shouldn't be shaking. She dared to look at Garrett. His jaw was working again, his lips so tight they were bloodless.

"It had been a maximum security prison before a riot that killed dozens of prisoners in addition to several of the guards. I was eight."

"Jesus!" Garrett grabbed her hands and squeezed them.

She didn't let him pull her close. Didn't dare rest against his chest and cry. This was an old pain. She wanted him to know she could deal with it.

"After that, word spread about what I could do among ghosts that were not as kind as Hiram. That's why he brought Chloe to me. He contacted her during one of her rituals. He's the one who came up with the plan to pretend that I lost the ability after..."

Rachel shook her head, trying to turn her mind away from those horrible memories.

"Chloe taught me about poppets and helped me learn, and Hiram..." Rachel couldn't stop a few tears from rolling down her cheek at the thought of losing him. "Hiram crossed over as part of a ritual Chloe designed. He was able to grab a couple of the ghosts who had been especially...unpleasant...and take them with him."

Garrett didn't need to know just how bad those spirits had been. Judging from his reaction so far, Rachel had better not tell him about the ones who were able to affect the physical plane. About the scratches and shoving and the light touches to her hair she could almost convince herself she imagined.

Chloe had assured Rachel that Hiram wouldn't be dragged to the same place as those spirits. Rachel wouldn't have let them try the ritual otherwise. She was sure those ghosts were headed for suffering.

"How could your mother just stand by and listen to that?" Garrett asked. "How could she subject you to it?"

"She wanted me to stop talking about ghosts. Her plan worked. And she didn't know exactly what they said. Have you ever noticed that she wears two sets of earrings?"

"That's kind of a non sequitur. You're going to have to build me a bridge."

He would get it in a moment. "One set is always the same. Understated little moonstone studs. They block the voices. Apparently, they were passed down from generation to generation in my family. Hiram asked around and told me. All the women are clairsentient."

"That is…a lot to process. I mean, I would never guess in a million years that your mom knew a thing about any of this, let alone that she could do something so awful to her own daughter."

"She always told me, 'Watch what you say—a proper lady is neither smart nor psychic.'"

Rachel felt her grimace as she said her mother's favorite bit of advice. How many thousands of times had Mrs. Montgomery whispered those words in Rachel's ear to keep her daughter in check?

The set line to Garrett's jaw made Rachel uncomfortable. He was planning something and she doubted she would like it.

"I'm getting you those earrings. One way or another."

"You don't have to—"

"No, I *shouldn't* have to. She should have given them to you already."

Rachel let out another scoff. Her mother doing something supportive like that was such an alien thought.

Chloe had said that families with powers like Rachel's usually gave the children whatever tools were available to help them until they could control their powers. Lillian must have skipped that lesson from the grandmother Rachel had never met.

"It's okay."

"No, it's not okay! She's waltzing around like the Queen Bee while you're trapped in here behind poppets. She's your mother. She should have taken care of you, not…" He snapped his mouth shut, fuming.

Lillian had never taken care of Rachel. That was what the nannies were for.

Rachel kept the comment to herself. Garrett seemed ready to explode already.

"I'm okay," Rachel said. "I'll figure something out."

"What about our kids?"

Rachel's breath caught in her chest. Even though she had mentioned kids and he seemed on board, they hadn't actually talked about it. She had always wanted a big family, but didn't think it could happen for her because of her ability. With Garrett as her partner, anything seemed possible.

"Our kids?" she squeaked.

"What if we have three girls?"

She could see the wheels moving in his head. He wanted to take care of Rachel, and he was already worrying about kids they didn't have yet.

Yet... Yet!

The reality of her future was just hitting her. Rachel jumped up and threw her arms around his neck, kissing him long and deep.

As she trailed her kisses along his neck, he said, "I don't see how this is helping us find a solution."

"We'll figure it out," she whispered in his ear, then gave it a nip. "Someone made those earrings for her. I can make my own and sets for our girls."

Their girls!

Rachel leaned back and gave him a fake-serious look. "We get to have boys too, right?"

He lifted her up and she wrapped her legs around his waist. The smile on his face matched hers. He seemed as enthralled at the notion as she was.

"We can have as many kids as you want."

"Then what are we waiting for?"

They were going to do this right. Their children would be loved. So loved. Rachel's chest felt over-full, warmth and love washing away the pall of remembering such awful events.

"Okay," he said. "But afterwards, we're going to talk jewelry.

Including rings."

Garrett grinned and carried her back to the bedroom.

Chapter Twenty-Three

"We're going to need a bigger house." Garrett couldn't believe they were already talking about kids. Lots of kids. His heart beat faster just thinking about it.

Rachel was sprawled across his chest after yet another round of lovemaking. She made a soft cooing sound and shifted her legs closer to his.

"You should design it for us," he said. "With plenty of bedrooms for the kids. Maybe one of those climbers like you see at playgrounds in the back."

She laughed and tightened her grip around his waist. "How about a pool?"

"We can plan to put one in later, but not right away. Not until they all know how to swim." The thought of a pool plus kids made his stomach sour. There were too many chances for them to get hurt. "Maybe not out in the country, either."

She pushed herself up on her elbows to look at him, her brow furrowing. "I thought you loved living out in the country."

"Too many wild animals." More variables he couldn't control.

"Cities have too many people," she said. "More people equals more ghosts."

"Right, I forgot for a moment."

He didn't want Rachel to be plagued by spirits. Or their girls, for that matter. His chest tightened at the thought of a flock of girls running around in the backyard in dresses, squealing in delight as they played.

"I like the look on your face right now," Rachel said.

He glanced back at her and smiled. "I'm not surprised. I suppose we can live in the country."

At least in the country the dangers were tangible. Rachel wouldn't be the only one who had to stand guard. He hated the thought that some ghost could be talking to his kids and he wouldn't know what they were saying or that they were even there.

"It went away," Rachel said.

"What?"

"The look on your face." She ran the backs of her fingers along his jaw. "It makes me wonder what I need to do to bring it back."

That mischievous expression gave him some pretty good ideas about what she had in mind. He could think about their future later. Like she said, they would figure it out. For the moment, he wanted to focus on her.

She was already sliding down his stomach when the room darkened quickly enough for them both to notice. Rachel rose to her knees, staring at the window.

"The storm's late today," she said.

"It rained a little earlier while you were sleeping. This must be another one."

Florida's humidity didn't just come from the ocean. The afternoon summer rainstorms did their part. It didn't rain long, and usually at the peak of the afternoon heat. Garrett glanced at the clock. It was already past five.

Thunder boomed in the distance and rain started to pound on the roof. Rachel stared at the ceiling.

"That's really loud. Did you ever pull your car into the garage?"

"No."

The noise above was rising, interspersed with pings and thuds that were unmistakably hail. Garrett jumped up and pulled on his pajama bottoms.

"I can bring it in for you," she said.

He leaned over the bed and kissed her for longer than he'd intended. When he finally was able to pull himself away, he said, "Darlin', there's no way I'm letting you go out in this."

She raised an eyebrow and smirked at him. "*Letting* me?"

"How about, 'I'd really prefer if you stayed inside.'"

"Fine. But I'm coming along to watch and help if I can."

She grabbed the T-shirt she had borrowed from him earlier and pulled it on. Garrett was mesmerized by the thin fabric floating down over her body, imagining the feel of it against her skin.

Rachel clapped her hands. "Let's go!"

Smiling, he trotted out of the room. His keys were on a table in the foyer. He picked them up as he opened the door to the garage and stepped through it. Rachel was right behind him.

"You don't have to come in with me."

"I'm okay," she said. Her smile was a bit strained. "I'm going to have to go into garages again eventually."

"But not now if you don't want to. You're already doing enough. You don't have to go so fast."

She crossed into the garage and stepped in close to him as she ran her hands up along his arms. "I like to go fast sometimes."

Damn. He was starting to tent his pajamas. He leaned down to kiss her again, deep and wet. Maybe he could give her some better memories to drown out the others.

There was a table next to the washing machine at just the right height to set her on. She could wrap her thighs around his waist while he rocked into her.

He was already reaching down to lift her from the ground when a thunderclap brought him back to earth. They both jumped. It probably wasn't the safest time to be doing anything too adventurous.

She smiled at him as she pulled away. "We should get the car in the garage before it's covered in dings."

"I suppose so."

She hit the button to open the garage door and the sound of the rain instantly intensified. Her smile faltered along with his.

Water ran into the garage from what could only be described as a torrential downpour. They walked as close to the door as they dared. Mist floated in and stuck to his chest. He couldn't even see the car.

"You need to go inside," he said.

"It's not that bad."

He shook his head. "I'm going to have trouble seeing. I don't want you here when I pull the car in."

"I guess that makes sense. I'll be waiting just inside the door, though."

"Okay."

She grabbed his hand and pulled him down for a quick kiss.

"For luck," she said.

He smiled and watched her walk away, waiting to turn around till she was safely out of the garage. Unlocking the door with his key fob, he took a deep breath, then plunged into the water.

It was always colder than he expected. In the middle of the summer, when the air was oppressively hot, the rain should match. But it didn't. And this storm was colder than most. It took his breath away.

Hail bounced off his shoulders and stung his scalp. Running flat out for the twenty or so feet to his car, he was still soaked when he slid into the driver's seat. They were going to have to dry off the upholstery. At least the driveway kept him from getting sandspurs lodged in his feet.

The rain was even louder inside the car. Hailstones almost as big as golf balls pelted it. They seemed to be getting bigger. Nearby, a dark looming shape shook itself frantically back and forth—one of the palm trees in his front yard. The thing was practically bent in half.

"Jesus," he murmured under his breath.

He started the car, eager to get back inside—back to Rachel. The wiper blades did almost nothing to improve his visibility. Luckily, he knew his drive well enough that he made it into the garage without scraping anything. His car was definitely going to have some dings.

As soon as he was in, he killed the engine and stepped out, then closed the driver's side door. Rachel was standing in the doorway to the house, holding some towels.

"I wanted you to know I stayed safely inside the whole time."

"I appreciate that." He smiled at her as he slicked his hair back from his face, water trailing down his back.

She hit the button to close the garage door, then walked over to him and handed him a towel. He wiped his chest and arms, then went to work on his hair.

"I'm sorry you're so wet." She walked around behind him and started to work on his shoulders. "But I am really going to enjoy drying you off."

His teeth were chattering. "I think I'll enjoy it a lot more when I'm warmer. We should take a shower later."

She dabbed the water from his back with her towel. "What are you doing in five minutes?"

"You, I imagine."

She laughed, and he turned around and grabbed her, pulling her against his chest and lifting her feet from the ground. Her laugh deepened—the sweetest sound he'd ever heard.

So what if his car was all wet. He had a gorgeous, brilliant, incredibly imaginative woman to bed. He turned back toward the house with her already nibbling on his neck.

After one step, he froze. His heart was pounding, and the chill on his skin shot right through to his bones.

"What's wrong?" She tightened her grip on his neck and looked around.

Garrett couldn't breathe. On the floor between them and the door to the house was a snake—a snake with black, red and yellow bands.

A coral snake.

His stomach churned and his muscles felt both electrified and paralyzed. He had to move. He had to get her to safety.

"Oh, look at that," Rachel said. She sounded delighted. "It must have come in when the garage door was open to get out of the rain. Poor little guy."

"Get on the car."

"*On* the car or *in* the car?"

"Do it!"

She pushed away from him and he set her down. The car doors were unlocked. Maybe once she was safe, he'd be able to move again and could deal with this intruder. But instead of heading for the car, she took a step forward, between him and the snake.

"Rachel!"

"Stop shouting at me!"

The sharpness of her tone was enough to make him glance at her. The look she gave him then made him wonder what was the deadliest force in the garage.

She took a deep breath and let it out. "That is a scarlet snake. They're completely harmless."

"You don't know that."

"I do. I recognize the band pattern."

"Since when are you an expert?"

"I grew up here too. Knowing there's dangerous wildlife, I researched them. I can tell the difference between a scarlet snake and a coral."

His skin started to buzz when she said the word. His ears were ringing.

Shit—he had let it out of his sight. He looked back at it, infinitesimally relieved that it was in the same spot.

If she knew about coral snakes, she knew how deadly they were. She knew you did not fuck around with snakes in Florida. Any snakes —even if you thought you knew for sure they were harmless.

"We can throw one of the towels over it and help it outside."

"No! We are not going near that thing."

He kept watching the snake, making sure it wasn't moving. It was coiled and seemed placid. But that could change in an instant. Especially with some asshole ghost prodding it.

Her voice was gentle when she spoke again. "Okay. You are obviously phobic about snakes. I didn't know. But don't worry. I've got this."

The blood rushed from his head and the room spun a little.

"That's the same thing…"

"What 'same thing'?"

"The same thing Dylan said. Right before he got bit."

"Dylan?"

"My brother."

"Your... Oh God, Garrett. I'm so sorry. I didn't—"

"He was sure it was a scarlet too." Garrett could barely force out the words. "He was wrong."

She gently touched his arm. "Listen to me. We need to get the snake out of the house. One way or the other. We can try to call a service, but the snake might move and find a hiding spot in the house before someone gets here."

What a nightmare. A snake hiding somewhere in his house?

If it made it inside... He'd have to burn the place down. They could stay at a hotel. They should move to Alaska before they had kids.

No, Alaska had bears.

Dammit!

"Can you trust me?" Rachel asked. "Trust me that I know what I'm doing here and can keep myself safe."

She didn't know what she was asking. Or maybe she did. He risked a glance at her and the earnest look on her face—the caring, the love—it melted some of the icy fear.

"I won't go near it," she said. "I'll treat it as if it's...dangerous. I promise. Please, Garrett. This is my chance to help you."

She had said she wanted to be his partner. He wanted to be hers too. That meant taking care of each other.

God help him. He nodded.

She took him by the arm and pushed him back a few feet closer to the car. He was tall enough that he could still see the thing, but if it went for his car, it could easily slither out of sight. Then again, if it went for his car, he could run the damn thing over.

Instead of going for a towel, Rachel walked toward the side door that led to the yard. As she opened it she said, "We don't have the means to capture it and relocate it. Is it okay if I get it out into the yard?"

"I just want it out of the house."

"Okay."

The rain had stopped, thankfully. The patchy grass beyond glistened in the dim light. More rain might be on the way, but the snake didn't have to know that. Maybe it would go out on its own.

Rachel wasn't waiting around. She picked up the broom that was tucked behind the washing machine, then walked slowly toward the snake, giving it as wide a berth as she could.

It angled its head toward her. Garrett felt that tiny motion in his heart, a lurching tug of fear.

She was totally focused on the snake. Sliding the broom between the snake and the door to the house, she moved closer, but kept herself at least six feet back, her arms outstretched and her body arched away from it. What was the strike radius on that thing?

He would surely have a heart attack any moment. His chest was too tight to breathe.

The snake uncoiled and started toward him, but Rachel was right there, placing the broom sideways between them and herding it so it made a bee-line for the door.

Or the space underneath the washer and dryer.

Please please please... He willed the thing to keep going straight, to head outside.

It did.

He let out a huge breath as he watched it disappear into the grass. Finally, he could move. He jumped forward and slammed the door shut. He knew it was ridiculous, but he locked it, too, for good measure.

His whole body was shaking, only partly because he was freezing and still dripping wet. Rachel dropped the broom, then set her hands on his shoulders and turned him around. He leaned down, wrapping his arms around her and holding her tight. She stroked his hair and whispered in his ear—soothing words that only half-registered, he was so wired with adrenaline.

It could have bitten her. Scarlet snake or...not.

He wanted to keep her safe. But he hadn't been any help. When he had finally been able to do something, the threat was over. Again.

He couldn't live with himself if anything happened to her. Especially if it was because of him. Because of a lack of action. Because he was too late.

He thought about Finn's voicemail—the warning that might have come sooner if Garrett had kept pushing the investigation instead of telling Finn to back off at Elsa's request. The hours that Rachel might have spent free of Michael if only Garrett had listened right when the message arrived.

"Come inside." She took his hands in hers and walked backwards, leading him into the house.

Chapter Twenty-Four

As soon as they crossed the threshold, Garrett latched on to her again. Rachel needed to get him dry and warm.

His skin was freezing—still coated with rainwater. The blast from the AC couldn't be doing him any good.

"It's okay," she said. "We're okay."

Except Garrett wasn't. He was shaking, but she wasn't sure if it was from the cold. His reaction had seemed extreme at first, but the more she thought about it, the more sense it made. She kept her arms wrapped around his neck, giving him the time he needed to sort himself out as her mind filled in all the details for him.

His brother had been killed by a coral snake. And Garrett had been there when it happened.

Garrett had grown up in the country. He mentioned playing in the swamp a few times, but never gave many details. Coral snake bites were pretty rare and didn't manifest as many would suspect. They didn't hurt like a rattlesnake's. The neurotoxin caused respiratory failure.

Antivenom wasn't always on hand.

She couldn't imagine how terrified Garrett must have been to see that snake in his home, not knowing what it was or how dangerous. Scarlets were mistaken for coral snakes all the time. But she was sure the one in the garage had been a scarlet.

Still, she hadn't taken any chances. It was only about a foot long. Even if it had been a coral snake, she never came close to entering its strike radius. Better safe than sorry, and Garrett was right—she wasn't a herpetologist.

"I'm sorry," he said. She was so deep in her thoughts it took her a minute to realize he had spoken.

"For what?"

"Not helping."

"I'm glad I had the chance to help you for once."

"You help me all the time," he whispered. "Just by being with me."

"Garrett—"

She was going to try to laugh it off, to lighten the mood, but when she leaned back to look into his eyes, the tears streaming down his face made her stop. Her own eyes filled immediately, her heart lurching toward him, trying to give him comfort.

"You're the only one," he said. "The only one I've ever really felt I can be myself with. It's always been on me to take care of people. To be the responsible one. Even before it happened. But you... You're the only one who ever took care of me."

She couldn't take it. Seeing him bared down to his soul right in front of her, the wounds he kept hidden, the pain. It was almost like seeing a ghost—seeing his soul through the shield of his body.

She lightly gripped his face and pulled him into a kiss. A slow kiss. Deep and long and healing. She let him sink into her through that simple connection, imagined her own soul wrapping around his and soothing him.

When she pulled back, he had a stunned expression. His eyes were wide as he stared at her. She wasn't sure what had happened, but she felt different. Strong. Empowered. She felt like...a healer.

"Tell me," she said.

He started to lean away, but she took his hands in hers again and looked into his eyes.

"Please."

Garrett cleared his throat before he began.

"He said it was a scarlet snake. That the bite didn't even hurt once he got the thing off him. We were out in the country. Too far to get help."

His eyes were unfocused as he watched his memories play out in his mind. The more he spoke, the thicker his accent became.

"Dylan was older than me. He was in his teens and I wasn't even ten." Garrett let out a short breath, not a laugh, but a release of energy. "I hadn't had my first real growth spurt yet, but he had. He always seemed so grown-up to me. Reckless, though."

Another wave of emotion hit him. Rachel felt it even as she saw him wince, his jaw tightening and his eyes narrowed in pain.

"He saw I was upset. Wanted to reassure me that he was fine. So he said…" Garrett's voice broke over his words. "He said, 'Race you back home.' Then he took off. Just flew over the sand. God, he could run. It only made the poison circulate faster through his system."

He cleared his throat, then said, "I lost sight of him right away, but tore ass for home as fast as I could." He sniffed once and shook his head. "I found him in a fennel grove. Laying on the ground—so still. I turned him over and…"

Garrett pulled his hands from hers. He covered his face and tilted his head back. She gave him space to do it, but moved her hands to his chest. Her instincts told her she had to keep touching him. When Garrett looked at her again, he didn't bother trying to hide his tears or his pain.

"I had to get him home. He was so much bigger than me, but I got him over my shoulder somehow and carried him as far as I could. I had to drag him the last couple hundred yards."

Wave after wave of grief and guilt rolled through her. She tried to take the emotions in—to let them pass through her, channeling them away from Garrett and letting them sink harmlessly down through the floor. He had been carrying this for too long.

"My mom came out and saw that. Saw me dragging his body. But it was the best I could do. I was screaming so loud. But the noise my mom made… I never knew what keening meant till I heard that sound. She fell to her knees, grabbed him up from me and held him and just rocked making that terrible sound."

He shuddered and another wave of energy flooded her. She opened herself to it, letting her heart feel his anguish, pulling it away from him.

"My dad came running out and grabbed Dylan—he had to fight my mom off to get to him. Dad was shaking all over, barely holding it together. He told me to call 911, but he already knew. He took one look at Dylan, and he knew it was too late."

Garrett looked back down at Rachel, dazed. His gaze slowly came back into focus. He covered his eyes for a moment, then wiped his face.

"Since then, I've always felt it was on me to protect everyone. I became a doctor so I would know what to do, how to help. But I don't always know. I can't always protect the people I care about, and that terrifies me."

She kept her voice as gentle as possible. "It's not your job to protect us, Garrett. We help each other out when we can, but we're all stumbling through this life together. All we can do is our best."

"It doesn't feel like enough. Not when people are still getting hurt. Elsa and Dante. You..."

"Don't. Dante was right. The only person responsible for what happened to us is Michael. And I took care of him."

Garrett shook his head. "I guess you did. And that snake too. And the scorpion. I knew everybody else was underestimating you. Didn't know I was too."

"I think I've been underestimating myself. Or not estimating myself at all."

She was beginning to feel like she'd been sleepwalking through her whole life. But the jolt of what had happened to her, the trauma, had awakened parts of her she didn't even know were there.

Hearing ghosts? Yeah, she was used to that. Full-on empathic bonding? That was new.

The tether she felt leading from her to Garrett vibrated like the strings of a harp and she knew he was going to say something before he even took in the breath to speak.

"I've never told anyone else. We never talk about him. I've tried, but my folks just won't."

Rachel felt a hollowness inside of her. The loss of a sibling, so complete and utter that it was like he never even existed... It resonated within her somehow. Deep and echoing.

His parents should have talked to him about Dylan. They should be keeping Dylan alive by remembering the joy and love they all shared.

She thought about Misha again and tamped down the worry that bubbled up within her—just in case the connection with Garrett went both ways. Now was not the time to bring that up. Garrett was too vulnerable, too wounded.

But soon. She would have to tell him her suspicions soon.

She wrapped her arms around his shoulders and held him as tight as she could. He buried his face in the nape of her neck, his arms around her waist, holding her close.

"Thank you," she whispered. "Thank you for telling me."

When she leaned back enough that she could look into his face, he looked lighter. The lines around his eyes had softened and his brow wasn't as furrowed. She needed to build on that, to help them both get distance from the pain she hoped he was starting to leave behind.

"You can talk to me," she said. "About this—about anything. Always."

"I know. That's part of why I love you."

She smiled up at him. "It's nice to hear you say that when we aren't in bed. And when you're not mad at me."

"I'm sorry about that. I was really confused and hurting."

"And now?"

"Now..." He considered her words for a few moments, as if he was assessing himself. "I feel good. Lighter, I guess."

"Let me see if I can make you feel even better. Starting by warming you up."

She led him to the master bath just off his bedroom. She started up a hot shower, then turned back to him and pulled her shirt over her head and threw it in the hamper. He smiled and slipped from his pajama pants, tossing them after her shirt. They held hands as they stepped into the water.

When she designed the open shower, she never thought she would have a chance to share it with Garrett. It took up a third of the room, filling one corner, with windows that let in the fading sunlight set high in the wall.

She nudged him under the water first, wanting him to get warmed up as quickly as possible. Jets sprayed their bodies from three sides. He put his hands on her hips, shifting them so she was enveloped in water and steam as well.

The hot spray first hit her shoulders, coursing down her spine and giving her goose bumps. She leaned into the water to wet her hair, then slicked it back. When she looked at him, he was staring at her.

"You are so beautiful," he said.

Those words had never meant so much to her. When she'd heard them before, it was always a sign that whoever was talking thought they'd already figured her out. The politician's pretty daughter. Nothing else to see but the surface.

Garrett looked deeper.

She ran her fingertips over his face, lingering on his lips. "So are you."

He grasped her hand and pressed a kiss into her palm, then pulled her closer, bending to kiss her. His hands followed the water's path down her back. He cupped her backside, as his tongue slid between her lips. Warm and wet everywhere.

She slid her hands over his chest, exploring the muscles, relishing his strength. The water coursed over their bodies, washing away their tension and all the residual negative energy.

Breaking off the kiss, he said, "Turn around."

As she did, he shifted so that she was facing the main jets. He moved behind her, pressing his chest against her back and pinning his shaft between them. Her hips squirmed and she rose on her toes without really thinking about it. All she knew was that she wanted him inside her again.

He kissed the side of her neck, lingering enough to leave a mark, then made his way up to her ear. As he nipped at her earlobe, her nerves lit up again.

He wrapped his arms around her, one hand lifting and kneading her breast and the other delving between her legs as he rocked his hips against her, rubbing his shaft on her backside.

The jets were lined up to hit all sorts of interesting parts of her anatomy. He shifted her again so they alternated between massaging her breasts and bouncing off the hand that shielded her most sensitive spot. When he moved his hand away, the intense stimulation almost set her off immediately.

"Garrett…"

"I know."

He bent down and grabbed the shower stool just outside the sprays of water, sliding it close. He ran his hand down the back of her thigh, then lifted her leg to rest her foot on the stool, opening her further to the jets. She gasped as the pleasure increased.

He reached for her again, kneading one breast while he lined himself up at her core with his other hand. Slowly, he inched himself inside, moving his hands to her hips as he slid all the way home.

Feeling her core tighten around him, his hips flush against her backside and his hands gripping her as the water pounded against her… Her head snapped back as her body started pulsing around him, so many sources of stimuli, she couldn't keep up with where the pleasure was coming from.

He held her up as she reached out to the cool tile, resting her hands against it to support her. She was still throbbing when he started to move.

The water was merciless, massaging her breasts and where they were joined as Garrett thrust into her over and over again. He would pull out almost all the way, moving slowly, then ram himself back in. He ran one hand over her raised leg, shifting her to reach deeper, to move faster without making her lose her balance.

Heat built in her, a diffuse inferno that ran beneath her skin like lava. He thrust faster, harder, his hands finding both breasts and holding them, using them to pull her tight against his chest, her back plastered to him.

She shifted her arms so that she only needed one to keep her propped up against the wall, wrapping the other around his neck and twisting so she could kiss him. He groaned against her mouth as her tongue slid into his. His pace increased, his shaft pulsing within her.

Her climax tore through her body, heat running over her skin. She had to be radiating light, so much energy coursed through her body. Even her eyes were tingling by the time he slid from her body and moved her from the jets.

He turned her around so that the water hit her back, his strong hands rubbing her shoulders as she leaned against his chest. She had never felt more relaxed or at peace. She had never felt as safe.

"Thank you," she whispered, her body yearning for his big bed and some sleep.

He held her tight. "Any time."

Chapter Twenty-Five

Waking up next to Rachel the next day was one of the happiest experiences of Garrett's life. He couldn't keep himself from smiling.

Her legs were tangled with his, one arm sprawled over his chest and the other folded against his side. She was as close to him as she could get and he loved it. Of course, his own arms were wrapped around her, holding her tight even as he slept.

He was never going to let her go again. He wouldn't have to.

His arms flexed around her and he kissed the top of her head. She let out a contented sigh.

"Morning," she mumbled.

"Good morning."

She yawned and nuzzled his chest. "I'm starving. Want some eggs?"

"Sounds like you need more sleep. Why don't I go make us breakfast?"

"Because then you won't be with me." She rose on her elbows to kiss him, erasing his thoughts of breakfast. But then she slid to the edge of the bed and stood. With a smile, she said, "Come on. Let's go."

Rachel standing naked in front of him—yeah, he'd go wherever she wanted. As he rose, she went to his closet and pulled out two T-shirts. She tossed one to him and put on the other.

"If we're going to be cooking, we probably shouldn't be naked."

"Good point."

He pulled the shirt over his head, then grabbed a pair of pajama pants from his dresser and put them on. Rachel waited for him—she didn't take off to get started on breakfast.

She took his hand when he reached the door, but he pulled her close instead of walking to the kitchen. He bent down and brushed his lips across hers, satin-soft and sweeter than honey.

After a good long while, he leaned back to see her eyes half-shut and her breathing quickened. He would have walked them right back into the bedroom, but her stomach growled. They both laughed at the sound.

"Sorry. My stomach is very opinionated."

"I'm the one stalling breakfast. Let's go."

They worked side-by-side in his kitchen, bumping into each other or at least brushing elbows often. No words were necessary. She made the eggs, he made toast and coffee.

As they ate at the counter, they kept smiling at each other. He felt ridiculous—like he was a kid again, free-falling into that first love. Rachel wasn't his first, though. She was his last.

"I was thinking about the house," he said.

"The one we're going to fill with all those children?" The way she smiled as she spoke made his heart fill with warmth.

"That's the one. I was thinking we could build on a solarium, sort of like what Elsa has, only more detached. If ghosts are going to keep pestering you, we might as well make a sort of waiting room so we can deal with them on our terms."

"'Our' terms?"

"Partners in everything. I'm sure as hell not going to leave you to deal with this alone."

"I'm not sure how much you can do."

"Just because I'm not psychic doesn't mean I can't help." He would damned sure find a way. "I can make poppets, spray saltwater…look menacing."

She laughed at that, and he felt his smile deepen. His cheeks hurt, he'd been smiling so much.

"And I have resources," he said. "My friend Finn is a private investigator. You need to dig up facts on anybody who comes to you for help, he's your guy."

"Are you sure he'd be okay helping out a psychic?"

Garrett laughed and shook his head. Finn's secrets weren't Garrett's to tell, but the irony of her question was too much.

"He'll be fine with it. And he'll be more help than you can imagine. Finn's the best."

"A PI would be extremely helpful in many cases, I imagine. Tracking down descendents or lost items. Those are the main requests I get hit with. The ghosts want me to tell someone something or get something to a particular person."

"Why was Hiram hanging around?"

"'Scientific curiosity'. That's what he always said." Her smile softened as she spoke about him. "He wasn't done learning about this life when he passed on. He was the exception rather than the rule, though."

"I'm glad you had somebody to help you with all this."

"Me too."

"Speaking of helpful spirits, what about Misha?"

"What about him?"

"Do you think he might be helpful? Kind of act as an intermediary for you?"

That gorgeous smile of hers vanished, her eyes crinkling at the edges and the slightest line appearing between her eyebrows. She took a breath and held it, mouth open like she was on the brink of saying something. Something he was not going to like.

"What?"

"I...don't think Misha will be much help. I think he *needs* help. Closure of some kind. I haven't figured out what, though."

"I thought Hiram sent him to watch over you."

"That's what Misha said. But ghosts sometimes lie. And they talk to each other. He could have asked around, found someone who knew about my friendship with Hiram when I was a child."

Garrett's stomach soured. The idea of an entire network of ghosts using their knowledge to manipulate people... No wonder she had stopped listening to spirits.

"We're putting mirrors in the solarium. Lots of them." At least if she could see them, she would have a better idea of who she was talking to.

"That's...a really good idea."

Her gaze shifted from him, her demeanor intensifying. Her mind was carrying her away on that tangent. She was probably designing the room already.

"Do you have any idea what Misha wants then?" Garrett asked, bringing her back to the more immediate issue.

"I'm not sure." The pain and hesitance crept back into her expression. "But I don't think he's who he says he is. For one thing, he's younger than I thought."

Garrett's skin felt electrified. "He isn't... It can't be Michael, can it?"

"No, Michael was cremated."

She didn't seem as convinced as she had been. If it was Michael and he had somehow found a way to harass Rachel from beyond the grave, Garrett would find a way to make him pay.

"He mentioned Dylan," she said. "Before you did. He said you had a brother who died."

How would a ghost know anything about Dylan? He'd been gone for thirty years. Misha might have asked around about Garrett, but why would he? Unless...

Garrett's heart started to pound.

"Wait, you don't think—"

She didn't have to say anything to give him his answer. The way her brow pulled together above her nose, how she leaned toward him as if ready to put her arms around him, to hold him together...

Yeah. She thought it might be Dylan.

Garrett's eggs threatened to come back up.

Imagining dead people hanging around was unnerving enough— serial killers or not. But Dylan couldn't be among them. He couldn't.

Garrett dropped his fork and pushed away his plate, then covered his face with his hands, leaning his elbows on the counter. His skin prickled, a sensation of warmth surrounding him like Rachel's arms.

But she wasn't touching him.

Her arms wrapped around him, giving the feeling a source. After-the-fact.

He dropped his hands so he could look at her. "What was that?"

"What was what?"

"I felt you touch me before it happened."

She started to pull away, but he caught her arms and kept them on his shoulders.

"Please don't," he said. "Don't pull away. Not now."

He needed her. Especially now that he knew Dylan might still be around—might have been lingering since his death decades ago. If so, Garrett had to help his brother find peace.

She took a deep breath, then let it out. Warmth washed over Garrett again, taking the edge off his pain and worry. She grasped one of his hands and pressed it against her chest just above her heart, then placed her free hand in the same place on him.

What he felt was indescribable. His mind still tried to put it into words.

Peace, happiness, contentment, hope, excitement—a kaleidoscope of emotions poured through him. He could feel his own emotions connecting to her and traveling through her as well, like they had closed a circuit by opening their hearts to each other.

He covered the hand she rested above his heart with his other hand. "What is this?"

"I'm not sure. It's kind of new to me. But if I had to guess, I'd say it's some sort of empathy."

"Is it part of your power?"

"I don't know. It's never happened before."

"When did you first notice it?" Damn, he sounded like he was starting an exam.

"It started after the snake in the garage."

Dread crashed through him, but even that ebbed quickly. "It's not because of..." He swallowed hard. "Dylan, is it?"

"Not directly. I think it was triggered by how upset you were and how much I wanted to help you feel better."

"So this is another thing you can do."

"Apparently."

It would probably come in handy when helping out ghosts. Starting with his brother.

The pain and guilt of it tore through him again. Rachel was right there, carrying it with him, easing his burden.

"Don't," Garrett said. "You don't have to do that for me."

"I know. But I want to. This is what you've done for me since we met. Helping me to feel less alone, more at peace with myself. This connection has always been there, I think. We're only just now exploring it."

He couldn't deny that. Since the first time their gazes met, he had felt it deep in his gut, in his soul. She was the one for him.

"What are we going to do about it?" he asked.

"I guess see where it takes us."

He wanted to see where it could take Dylan, how it could help him. With it being an unknown, a new power, Garrett wasn't sure how safe it would be for Rachel, though. He didn't like the idea of her using any kind of empathic ability to connect with an unknown ghost.

"It's okay," she said. "You'll be right there with me."

"What, can you read my mind now? Because then we might be in trouble."

She gave a light laugh and said, "No, I could feel you worrying. And I can feel you wanting to act. We can see if I can help Misha, whoever he is. We can try to find out if he's Dylan."

Her voice trailed off at the end. She must have been waiting for another spike of dread or fear or guilt. But they were all overpowered by the one prevailing emotion he felt in that moment. Gratitude.

This gorgeous, generous woman was willing to walk into a situation that a few days ago would have terrified her, just on the chance that it was Garrett's brother. She wasn't running away from him. She was walking at his side, as a partner.

He didn't feel like he was out on a limb with her anymore. It was more like they were standing on a bridge that they were building together, one that would lead wherever they wanted it to go.

"That is…heady," she said.

"It's what I've always felt for you."

"I'm sorry I made you wait so long."

He shook his head. "It was worth it."

"If we aren't heading back to the bedroom now, we might want to try to tone this down."

The bedroom sounded really good. But if Misha was Dylan, Garrett couldn't let that go for another moment.

"What do we do?"

Rachel took a deep breath and closed her eyes. The warmth he felt from her lessened, but was still there. She moved their hands away from each other's chests, letting out a long, steady exhale. The feeling of connection faded till it was just a tingling along his skin, a calmness in his heart.

"Did that work?" she asked.

"You're the psychic. You tell me."

"I think that's as good as we can do with toning down the connection for now. Come on. Let's go talk to Misha."

Garrett was still nervous as hell, but he nodded and stood. She grasped his hand again and led him to the guest room.

Chapter Twenty-Six

It was hard to believe she was doing this. Willingly opening herself up to a ghost to help them. After everything she'd been through, the sacrifices she'd made to get them to leave her alone...

None of that mattered. Word was out about her abilities anyway. If Misha really was Dylan, she had to help him for Garrett's sake. But that wasn't her only reason.

She *wanted* to help Misha. Whoever he was. She wanted to help all the spirits that needed her and were aware enough to come to her for aid. First Misha, then the spirits of Michael's victims that were haranguing her.

If her mother had raised her in her family's traditions, this wouldn't have even been an issue. She would have been protected as a child and trained in how to use her powers. She would have been helping spirits for years by now.

Looking back wouldn't help anyone. She needed to be looking forward. To a future with Garrett. Embracing her abilities and exploring them more, honing her skills. She had the book knowledge. It was time to start putting it into a deeper practice.

"When we go into the room, be careful not to disturb the line of salt that's over the threshold." She pointed at the barrier she had made earlier.

"I thought spraying the door with saltwater was enough."

"Since there's already so much salt around in Florida, it generally is, but I wanted to be sure no one could get into the rest of the house. I left the door open and took the wards down from the window. With the window and the mirror, there are too many access points in there."

"The mirror is an access point?"

"Reflections are a link between this plane and the next. Mirrors are powerful enough that they can be used as doorways from the other side. They magnify and focus spiritual energy."

She hadn't talked to anyone about it since she was a little girl. When all of this was over, she was going to have a long conversation with Chloe and rekindle that relationship. In the meantime, she had to try to explain this better to Garrett.

"Ghosts can move around like people through doorways. That's the easiest way for them to get around. I think it's because that's what's most familiar to them from when they were alive. But they can also sort of teleport to different places by willing themselves to go there, especially the ones who are focused or have been around a long time and have lots of practice. They still need something to connect to. Either a person or a place they're familiar with. Hence hauntings."

"Okay, that makes sense."

"Good." She took a deep breath and went on. "Ghosts tend to think of themselves in terms of their human existence. Doorways and windows are obvious ways to get into someone's house. Warding them keeps ghosts from being able to enter and usually stops them from even seeing or hearing anything that goes on inside."

"What if a ghost doesn't see themselves as human?"

She shivered as she remembered her conversations about the topic with Hiram. Garrett was dealing with so much. She didn't want to burden him with yet more knowledge that most people never had to deal with.

"You don't want to tell me. I can feel it."

"I would rather protect you from knowing this."

"I think I've proven by now that you can tell me anything. I can handle it."

She nodded, then said, "If a ghost stops thinking of themselves in human terms, their soul devolves. Over time, they become what most people think of as demons. Different rules apply. They are much more dangerous than ghosts. Thankfully, it's very, very rare for a ghost to become a demon."

"Okay. That's a pretty scary thought."

"Sorry."

"Don't be. I'd rather know—be prepared for it if something comes up."

"Well, hopefully we'll never need to worry about that. Anyway, Hiram told me that everything is kind of foggy on the other side. Trying to look through doors and windows is a little bit like looking through frosted glass. Unless it's warded, and then it's all opaque. But mirrors make everything crystal clear. And they glow on the other side."

"Do you like beards?"

She blinked at the sudden shift in topic. Her penchant for non sequiturs might be rubbing off on him.

"I guess they're okay."

"Good. Because I doubt I'll be shaving again anytime soon."

He gave her a small smile and she laughed, grateful for him easing the tension of the moment.

"So that's why you can see ghosts in reflections. Because those are the *real* windows from the other side?"

"Exactly. That's also why I have to be so careful around reflective surfaces. Mirrors especially can act like a sort of amplifier. Ghosts can use a mirror to get to a place or person they don't already know. I cover them so that I don't see anything disturbing and so they can't see me in a warded environment. If I tried to ward one and did it wrong…"

Her skin crawled at the thought. She knew some psychics used mirrors extensively in their work. With her already amplified abilities, putting any sort of energy on a mirror seemed like a colossally bad idea. Not until she had learned more. Had more practice.

Garrett squeezed her hand. She could feel him willing reassuring energy into her and welcomed it gladly.

"Then we keep the mirror covered and we don't mess up the line of salt. Got it."

"Are you sure you're ready for this?"

"Doesn't matter. One way or another, we're getting this done now."

She nodded, then turned back to the door.

Strangely, when Misha had been an unknown, she was less nervous around him. Not as much was at stake when she thought she was just talking to an easygoing ghost who was hanging around like Hiram had been.

But Misha wasn't like Hiram. She was certain of it.

Which meant one of two things. Either the ghost in the guest room was Garrett's brother Dylan and they were about to have an emotional reunion—or the ghost was a stranger pretending to be a friend.

As much as she hated the thought of Dylan lingering, the second was infinitely more frightening. One way or another, they needed to know.

With a deep breath, she stepped over the threshold. Garrett followed right behind her.

"Misha? Are you here?"

No one answered.

She walked deeper into the room, holding tight to Garrett's hand. "Misha, we'd like to talk to you."

After another few moments of silence, Garrett spoke up. "Dylan? Is that you?"

Still nothing.

"He might not be here," Rachel said. "I asked him to find the spirits of the women who are haunting me and tell them I want to talk. Maybe he decided to help with that after all."

"I'd like a few words with them myself. They need to stop stirring up bugs and snakes. Immediately."

When Garrett had offered to look intimidating, Rachel had laughed it off. Seeing the look on his face at that moment was anything but amusing. His jaw was set, brow drawn together and lips in a tight line. She could practically see lightning sparking from his eyes.

He might be able to scare ghosts after all.

"We should hear them out first. Try to talk. If they ever show up, that is."

She glanced around the room. No reflective surfaces to try to catch a glimpse of ghosts. No voices. Nothing.

"I don't want to have to do a summoning," Rachel said. "Those always ruffle the ghost's feathers, so to speak."

"I read a little about those in the books you loaned me. It sounded like an involved process."

"It can be. Or it can be a simple one, depending on how you go about it. I don't go in for show. My rituals are always simple and practical. Like the poppets and saltwater."

"I didn't know that qualified."

"If you do it in the right mindset, anything can be a ritual."

They could just wait for Misha to return, but who knew how long that would take. Rachel was already feeling antsy.

"Maybe I could use a rune…"

"Like a Norse rune?"

Rachel had always felt a pull to runes and collected volumes dedicated solely to their use. But they weren't mentioned in any of the books about ghosts she had loaned Garrett.

"How do you know about runes?"

He snorted, then gestured down the length of his body. "Witness my heritage."

She laughed, leaning into his broad chest. "Just because your ancestors were Nordic doesn't mean you've read up on them. And runes are a pretty obscure subject."

"With a last name like Wolfstrom, I was curious. I've read a bunch of myths. Runes came up from time to time. The stories made them seem powerful and dangerous."

"Anything powerful can be dangerous. The trick with runes is to use them with the correct intention."

"I stand enlightened."

She laughed again, until a sudden icy feeling shot through her. Looking around the room, she sought out the threat.

"What is it?" Garrett asked.

"Misha?"

"*I found them!*" Misha's voice sounded even younger, a sure sign that he was in distress, even without the urgency in his tone. If this wasn't Dylan, it was someone who had been carrying a lot of emotional baggage when he died.

"Hello, Misha." Rachel tried to keep her voice calm. She wanted Garrett to be part of the conversation as much as possible, even though she also wanted to shield him from what might be said. "Thank you for finding the ghosts for me. I still want to talk to them, but I'd like to speak with you first."

"There's no time to talk. They're getting ready to act."

The near-panic in his voice confused her. He sounded as if she and Garrett were in imminent danger. What could the spirits possibly do to hurt them? Glancing around the room, she didn't see any animals or bugs. Unless the ghosts had found a herd of rhinoceroses to stampede into the house, they seemed fairly safe.

"The house is warded," Rachel began.

"They aren't just after you. They're mad at Elsa for escaping too."

"What?"

Garrett pulled Rachel closer. "What is it? What's he saying?"

"Misha, what are the ghosts planning to do to Elsa? How are they going to harm her?"

"Christ," Garrett hissed.

"By going after Dante. He's in surgery and they're controlling insects that they've hidden in the room. They're going to startle the doctors while they're cutting him."

"Oh God…" Rachel shook her head. This was too awful.

Dante had already had one emergency surgery after Michael had shot at him. Even though the bullet missed, it hit nearby mason jars full of debris. The shrapnel had hit Dante in the face.

The only reason he needed surgery in the first place was because he tried to save Rachel. She didn't know he was going back under so soon. It had only been two months.

Her cell phone was on the bedside table. Rachel dove for it and dialed Elsa's number. Nothing happened. She looked at the screen and saw that there wasn't a signal.

"Garrett, we have to warn Elsa."

"Hold up a minute. What is he saying? Warn Elsa about what?"

"The ghosts of those women aren't just mad at me. They want payback against Elsa too."

"What! Why?"

"Michael wanted both of us. And we lived."

Garrett's forehead crinkled and she heard his teeth grind together.

"Tell me what to do."

"I don't know! I can't get a signal to warn her. Where's your phone?"

"In my bedroom." He had already turned and was headed for the door. In his haste, he scuffed the salt line in the threshold. "Dammit!"

"I'll fix it later. We don't have time to waste."

They ran to his room and he picked up his phone. As he looked at the screen, his shoulders slumped.

"No signal."

"Have you ever had that happen before?"

"No. Maybe one of the towers got hit in last night's storm?"

Rachel shook her head. Her stomach was doing somersaults. "It's possible that the ghosts are messing with the signal. But that's a good thing. If they're here messing with our signals, they can't be at the hospital."

"Hospital?"

The urgency in his voice had spiked. She hadn't filled him in on the vengeful spirits' plan yet.

"Misha said that Dante's in surgery right now. The ghosts are planning to hurt him by distracting his doctors at the worst moment. They've already herded insects into the room. But if they can block cell signals, they're more powerful than we imagined. Working together, they could do all sorts of things."

A single ghost that was this angry, this focused on revenge wouldn't need to make a bug fly into a surgeon's face. It'd be able to bump their hand, maybe even throw scalpels across the room. It could kill the lights, bite or claw at someone, give them a chill at just the wrong moment.

And more than one was after her. After Elsa.

All of the research Rachel had done on hauntings by angry spirits surged up from the back of her mind. All of her memories of her own experiences. She had shoved them away so that she wouldn't be too terrified to ever leave her house.

Garrett pulled her against his chest, wrapping his arms around her. "Take a breath and calm down."

He was feeding steady emotions into her. Calmer than her own, but tinged with fear. They still helped, and she let them in, using them like an anchor to keep from being pulled into the memories that clawed at her mind.

"They might be able to move things." Her voice was muffled by the fabric of his shirt.

"What?"

She stepped away and took that deep breath he suggested. As she let it out, she made herself focus. Solutions. That was what they needed.

"It's possible that one or more of them has become a poltergeist. If so, they'll be able to move things. Nothing too heavy, but in a room full of surgical equipment..." She shook her head, her imagination taking her to places too dark to think about. "How fast can you get us to the hospital?"

"Twenty minutes. But Dante shouldn't be back in surgery for another couple of weeks. He has to heal before they can do anything else."

"Something must have already gone wrong, then. Misha says he's being operated on now."

"Shit." Garrett started to pace.

"We have to get to the hospital to warn them. We can ward the room to keep Dante safe while they work."

"No, *I* will ward the room. If these ghosts can throw around scalpels, they might have tricked Misha to lure you into a trap. Plus the hospital staff won't let you into the OR. They're not going to like me spreading salt in the doorways, either."

Garrett ran his hands through his hair, leaving them on top of his head so his bangs were pulled back from his face. "I don't know how to help him."

"If you can at least be there, maybe you can run interference. You'll know that something might go wrong."

He dropped his arms to his sides. "I won't leave you alone in the city. You'll be swamped by ghosts."

"Then I'll stay here. I can re-cleanse the house and put the wards back up. Elsa and Dante will need a safe place to stay anyway. And Winston and Leo. When Dante is able to be moved, you can bring them all home with you. I'll keep trying to call so I can warn them. Maybe talk them through setting up some wards of their own."

She could sense how torn he was—wanting to help his friends and facing the overpowering urge to protect her. Pulling him into a hug, she said, "I'll be okay. Misha is here and seems to genuinely want to help. He can warn me if they start to focus on something more than blocking the cell signal."

Honestly, she'd be the safest one of them all. She hated the idea of staying behind, but at the same time, she didn't know what would happen if she went back to the city now.

All of her mental energy would be spent just sifting through the voices that would undoubtedly be piled on top of each other vying for her attention. And she doubted the ghosts of Michael's victims were the only ones savvy enough to make physical contact.

She remembered all the pinching and shoving, invisible hands grabbing at her wherever she went. She had to stop thinking about this. If Garrett sensed her fear, he'd never go.

Instead, she willed her determination into him. They were going to help their friends. She would make a haven for them when they returned. Garrett would make a temporary safe spot for Dante in the hospital. They could do this.

"I get it," he said. "Enough with the psychic pep talk. I'll go."

She followed him to the foyer. He quickly pressed his lips to hers in an urgent kiss. Then he grabbed his wallet and keys from the table and headed for the car.

Chapter Twenty-Seven

At barely lunch time, the sky was so dark it looked to be dusk. Clouds hung above—thick and heavy, and low enough he felt he could reach up and touch them. Garrett's grip on the wheel was turning his knuckles white. Twenty minutes to the hospital meant he was driving fast enough that there was no room for error.

The sky opened up as soon as he had the thought.

"Shit!"

Water hit the windshield like a tidal wave. His instincts told him to slam on the brakes, but he refused to listen. His arms tried to spasm from the jolt of adrenaline in his already saturated system. Years of training and experience helped him control his response.

Surprises happened in the ER all the time. Twitching could cost someone their life. In this case, it would be his.

He eased up on the gas pedal and let gravity and the weight of the car slow him down steady and safe. Florida might be full of bugs and snakes, but at least it was flat. Hills and ditches could have meant disaster.

Even though the road had to be slick, it traveled through the countryside in a straight line toward the city. All he had to do was keep himself calm and let physics do the work for him.

When the speedometer was in a more reasonable range, he turned on his wipers and checked his bearing. He was driving down the center of the road, but at least he wasn't close to running off either side. Rain that thick would turn the ground to quicksand as far as his car was concerned.

The wipers swung furiously back and forth over the glass. The deluge instantly replaced the water they flung away. Lightning crackled right next to his car, bright enough to blind him briefly. Thunder pounded his eardrums right after.

"Fuck!"

This time, his nerves got the better of him and the wheel twitched to the side. The roads were as slick as he thought. The back end of the car swung around so that he was facing the wrong direction.

His momentum kept him going, coasting backward down the straight road. He used the passenger's seat headrest for leverage as he twisted around to look out the back window and keep himself on the asphalt.

He said a silent prayer of thanks that he lived far enough out of town that the roads to and from his home were deserted on weekdays. Gently hitting the brakes, he slowed the car to a crawl. He was planning to stop it, but was too stunned when bright sunshine dazzled his eyes.

Turning back to face the front of the car, he finally stepped on the brake fully, his inertia making the seatbelt pull across his chest. Steam was already rising from the hood as the summer sun heated the water running down its surface.

Rain while the sun was shining wasn't new to him. But this... This was something else. Garrett put the car in park and stepped out so he could see the sky.

In front of him, a wall of dark gray clouds rose up through the atmosphere—a smooth wall that curved away from him. It was like the storm was centered right over his house. A house where Rachel was trapped. Alone.

Well, not exactly alone. She was with Dylan.

Or Misha...

A sick feeling filled Garrett's stomach, spreading out through his body. Something was very wrong. Beyond the bugs, the snakes, the storm, the pissed off ghosts behind it all. They were missing something.

Dante's doctors were at the top of their fields. Garrett had hooked Dante up personally, calling in every possible favor to ensure he received the best care. If Garrett could keep himself from wrecking during that freakish storm, Dante's surgeons could handle a moth in the face or a poke in the ribs. They were trained to deal with distractions, power outages, emergencies.

If Rachel had taught Garrett anything over the past few days, it was that he didn't have to be the one to run in and fix things. He pulled out his phone and saw a full-strength signal.

Letting out a huge breath of relief, he called Elsa.

"Hi, Garrett."

She giggled. Not the sound someone makes sitting in a waiting room while the love of her life was undergoing emergency surgery.

"Is Dante with you?"

"Where else would he be? Stop it!"

"Elsa!" Garrett didn't mean to yell, but he needed her full attention.

Dante came on the call, his voice low and filled with a quiet challenge.

"Good morning, Garrett. I trust you have good reason for speaking to Elsa in such a harsh tone that I could hear it even sitting next to her."

Dante sounded as pissed as he ever had, and Garrett was near giddy with relief. Hearing Dante on the phone meant that he was okay. It also meant he wasn't in surgery.

The ghosts that were after Rachel might have tricked Dylan—no, Misha—into leading them astray.

Or Misha had lied.

When Garrett didn't respond, Dante went on. "I will ask you to nonetheless forgo using such a stern tone in the future, as she is quite sensitive to it."

"I'm sorry." Garrett ran his hand through his hair. He had forgotten about Elsa's parents. Not that he had the full details on that. They could catch up later.

"Listen, we're kind of in a shitstorm here."

"I beg your pardon?"

Right. Dante was from the 1800s. *Shitstorm* probably wasn't used back then.

"A mess. Problems. Danger."

"What do you need?"

"First, I need to know that you're okay."

"We are both fine."

There was a pause, then Garrett heard Elsa say, "You're on speaker." Her voice was a bit colder than usual, but at least she seemed focused. "What's going on?"

Damned if he knew.

"Dante, are you due for surgery anytime soon?" Garrett asked.

"Not for at least several weeks. While the preliminary reviews have been promising, the doctors wish to see how well I have healed from the initial surgery before following up with additional procedures."

That was the first thing that made sense all day.

"Okay. Good. Listen, I don't know for sure what's going on here, but there are some ghosts that are threatening Rachel. They've even brought you both into it, trying to trick us and..."

And get Rachel alone.

The churning in Garrett's stomach intensified and a chill swept over his skin making his hair stand on end. When it came to the ghosts threatening Rachel, Garrett wasn't sure who he was talking about— Michael's victims or Misha.

Michael.

It had to be.

Michael had been enough of a narcissistic prick to call himself "Michael Angelo" as a painter. Going by Misha as he fooled Rachel into thinking he was a friend of Hiram's would be just the thing to play to his ego. She had said ghosts sometimes shared information. Michael could have learned about Hiram and...

Fuck!

Garrett jumped back into his car and pulled on his seatbelt. Who knew what was in store for him once he drove back into that storm. He had to be alive to help Rachel. He had to get to her.

He also had to warn Elsa. She was in even more danger than they thought.

"What can we do?" Elsa asked.

"I don't have time to explain, but Michael is back. I'm sure of it."

How the hell was he supposed to protect everybody? Rachel was miles away in the center of what was building up to a landlocked hurricane from the looks of it, Elsa and Dante were miles in the other direction, ignorant of the issue and how to protect themselves. Even Winston and Jazz might be on Michael's list.

"You know that little bookstore on Sunny Lane with the dragon reading a book on the sign?" he asked.

"Bookwyrm. Yes, I did a signing there last year."

"Good. Then you know the owner."

"Chloe."

He relaxed the tiniest bit. "Call her. She's a medium and can help you. Tell her there's at least one poltergeist coming after you and everyone you care about. If you can't reach her—"

This was going to sound crazy, but he barreled on. "Make up some saltwater in spray bottles. Spray it on the windows, doors, any entry to the loft."

"Our windows are two stories high," Elsa said.

Shit! He'd forgotten about that. "Then make lines of salt across all your windowsills and the door to your place. And cover your mirrors. Make sure Winston and Leo stay inside too. And call Jazz and tell her what's up."

"How great is the danger?" Dante asked.

Lightning streaked from the sky and hit the ground less than a mile in front of Garrett. The thunder rolled in after like a warning. Or a challenge.

Garrett's jaws tightened, the muscles nearly cramping. He bit out each word. "Ward your place. I'll take care of the rest."

He ended the call, then dropped his phone in the drink tray and knocked the car into drive, flooring the gas. Once he was home, he was going to figure out a way to end this once and for all.

He felt the car hit the water like it was a solid thing, but then it gave and he was back in the downpour. He just had to keep the car going straight. And not miss his driveway.

The rain started to lessen. It made him more anxious. What else did Michael have up his sleeve? What was distracting him from trying to drown Garrett?

By the time Garrett neared his home, the rain had all but stopped. He started to turn into his driveway when something huge lurched up from the brush lining his property. Swerving to miss it, his car went off the drive and into the sand.

"Shit!"

He looked out his window to see an eight-foot alligator walking toward his car. He hit the gas again, but all his wheels did was spin, throwing up patches of grass and digging in deeper.

The gator opened its jaws and hissed. Rows of sharp teeth surrounded the pale flesh of its mouth. Its eyes should have been black, but they glowed bright blue.

At this point, it was just one more weird thing. He pushed it from his mind and focused on what to do next.

His drive was long. Maybe fifty yards. Gators were faster on land than most people knew, but if he had a head start, Garrett could outrun it.

He slid his chair back and climbed into the passenger's seat. As he opened the door to jump out, something slammed against it. The door hit him in the head with enough force to send him sprawling back, seeing stars.

The tip of another gator's nose came into view through the passenger's window.

His heart was pounding. He took a few breaths to calm himself. Looking at his hands, he saw they were okay. If they'd been in the door when it shut—hell, if he'd made it out of the car...

Best not to think of that.

He was a little dizzy and his forehead itched. He looked in the rearview mirror and saw blood flowing down along his temple.

The wound was superficial. Head wounds always bled more. He could fix it later.

At the moment, what he needed to do was think of a way out of his car. Crawling out the windows or using the doors wouldn't work. A gator could jump up and grab him easily. And if he hit the ground too close to one, the same thing would happen. They could strike like a snake.

His heart sank.

Please don't let there be snakes waiting out there too.

Surely gators were enough. Right?

One way or another, he was getting to his house. He would get to Rachel.

He looked around the car for a way to escape. There was no sun roof. Damn, he should have bought a convertible. He could pop the top off, climb on the hood, jump clear of the gators, and run like hell for the house.

Wait...

He turned around to face the trunk of his car. He pushed his chair flat and crawled into the back. The releases for the back seat were a little hard to track down, but once he did, he lowered it so he could reach into his trunk and dig out his tire iron.

He pushed the seat up again and took a deep breath, staring out the glass of his rear windshield as he tested the weight of the metal in his hand. He really wished he was wearing thicker clothes.

Covering his eyes with his elbow, he pulled back his other arm and struck the window as hard as he could.

Chapter Twenty-Eight

As soon as Garrett left, Rachel went to work. She lit incense in her censer and refilled the saltwater bottle, then headed to Garrett's room. Walking through the house, she tried to keep her focus. Her mind kept wandering to her friends.

Were they okay? Was Garrett putting himself in even greater danger by trying to help them?

There was nothing she could do about that. All she could do was make the house safe for them whenever they managed to arrive.

She also wanted it to be safe for Dylan. Or Misha. Whoever he was. She even still wanted to help the women who were haunting her, though at this point that probably meant helping them to cross over rather than resolving their issues. She couldn't believe how far they were going—how angry they felt just that she had survived.

Rachel's own issues were fighting against her as well. She made a line of salt in front of the garage door rather than cleansing it. Garrett would be returning through the garage and she'd have to cleanse the space again anyway after he pulled in, especially the way it was raining. She had never heard such a storm. Better to just block off the garage from the rest of the house for now.

When she reached the guest room, she paused again. Misha or Dylan—whoever he was—had seemed comfortable talking to her in this room. And she preferred the comparatively controlled environment to talking outside. There were too many variables in the yard, too many ways things could sneak up on her.

Plus, she liked the idea of letting Dylan stay inside with them. As Garrett's brother, she wanted this to be his home too.

She made a new line of salt across the threshold, then took the censer back to the kitchen and set it on a trivet on the counter. After hesitating for a moment, she set the spray bottle next to it. Walking into the room carrying the equivalent of a shotgun wasn't the reception she wanted for the troubled spirit—Misha or Dylan.

It was time to figure out who this guy was and what he needed. Rachel headed back to the room. She stepped over the barrier carefully.

"Misha? Are you here? I'd like to talk to you."

She listened intently for his response, but heard nothing but the rain pounding against the window. A shrill sound broke in, rattling around in her head. She jumped, heart pounding.

It was her phone. She had brought it back to her room before cleansing the house so that she wouldn't lose track of it.

Strange that it suddenly had a signal again. Maybe a tower had been struck by lightning like Garrett thought and repairs were just finished.

She ran to the bedside table and picked it up. The caller ID read *Jazz*.

"Hello?"

Without preamble Jazz said, "Are you absolutely sure that Michael is gone?"

Rachel felt a chill that shot straight through to her bones. Why did people keep asking her that?

"He was cremated." She sounded unsure, even to herself.

Jazz's voice kept cutting out as she spoke, like the signal wasn't stable.

"I know…if…found…connection…could…possess…someone?"

"Possession?" Rachel's stomach clenched again and the icy feeling in her bones intensified.

No way. He would still need an anchor, some physical remains. He couldn't—

Jazz said, "Oh God—" just before the call died.

The door slammed shut.

All the hair on Rachel's arms stood on end as the room dropped in temperature. She felt a cold breath on the back of her neck.

"Hello, Rachel."

She dropped her phone on the bed, then ran to the door and tried the handle. It turned, but the door wouldn't budge. She pulled as hard as she could, then threw herself against it, but nothing happened. Slowly, she turned around and took a few hesitant steps back into the room.

"Dramatic as always, I see."

She pinched her lips shut and closed her eyes, tears spilling down her cheeks.

Michael...

"You look lovely, my dear." Lines of cold traced down her arms like fingertips, lingering over the scars on her wrists. Michael let out a contented, *"Mmm..."*

"What do you want?" Her voice crackled as she forced the words out.

"You, of course. I have a little harem on this side, and you will be my crown jewel." He chuckled. *"I thought Elsa was the strongest one, but you... You surprised me, Rachel. When you* killed *me."*

The paintings on the walls rattled as the room shook. How was he so powerful? How was he even here? None of it made sense.

"It was self-defense," she whispered.

"It was selfish. Short-sighted. Like everything you do." The cold traced over her cheek, freezing the tears on her face. *"Don't worry. I forgive you."*

She turned her face away from his touch, just like she had done in his garage when he held her prisoner. It had been so long since she had felt a spirit's hands on her. Her flesh was crawling.

"My ladies can't wait for you to join us. They told me they warned you about what would happen if you killed me. But you didn't listen." He laughed again. *"Another of your strongest suits—only paying attention to yourself."*

Her heart broke at his words. She had been selfish for so long, focused on not hearing ghosts to the point that she didn't listen to her friends.

Elsa had warned Rachel about Michael, and she hadn't listened. Rachel had known Garrett loved her, but she'd ignored it instead of telling him straight out that they couldn't be involved or explaining the situation and discovering that they could.

She had wasted so much time. And she wasn't sure how much she had left.

"I'm grateful, actually. Death is much more fun than being alive. If I had known, I would have arranged this years ago. There are so many things I have to teach you, but I want to wait till you're here with me. I want you to feel everything I do to you—and you will *feel it."*

His hands were on her shoulders. She had nowhere to run.

"I've been practicing on the others," he said. *"Warming myself up for you."*

Bile rose in the back of her throat. Those poor women. She had to help them somehow.

"I've been experimenting on someone else too. Someone close to you, though you've never met."

What was he talking about? Hiram maybe? But Hiram had crossed over. She prayed it wasn't Dylan.

"He's been teaching me all kinds of interesting tricks—how to slip into bodies like a fine suit. When I'm done with him, I'm sure I'll have no problem finding another meat-puppet to play with. And another and another."

His cold breath brushed her ear. *"I will kill so many women, Rachel. In so many ways. Ways I haven't even imagined yet. And the men I use to do it…"*

He chuckled. *"They won't be able to stop me. I'll twist them around inside until they won't know where they stop and I begin. I will remake them in my image. And you'll be right at my side to watch. Forever."*

No. No no no. This was not going to happen. She would find whatever part of his body was left and destroy it. She would find a way to end his twisted soul permanently.

"I can see what you're thinking," he half-sang. *"I studied you, remember? I'm in your head as much as his. He just doesn't realize it yet. But he will. The moment I use his hands to crush Ms. Zhou's throat. When he hears me laugh while she dies and tries again to sort out his thoughts from mine."*

"Stay the *hell* away from my friends!"

Rachel dove for the reading chair and hefted it over her head, then threw it at the window. Glass shattered, some of it falling into the room as a blast of rain-drenched wind hit her.

The chair lodged in the window. Rachel shoved it as hard as she could. It crashed to the ground on the other side. She hopped up onto the windowsill, ignoring the warning from her primal brain about the sharp glass that was scraping her arms, ignoring...

A low rumble sounded from the ground below. Instinct kicked in and she lurched back just as an alligator struck, its jaws clacking shut inches from her face.

She stumbled backward through the broken glass, not stopping when the backs of her knees hit the bed. Even though the alligator couldn't climb into her room, she kept moving away, crab-walking over the mattress. She was breathing so fast her vision was tunneling.

Calm. She needed to be calm. She couldn't help anyone if she was unconscious. And goddammit, she was going to protect her friends.

She took a few deep breaths, her body quaking with adrenaline. The sheets were sticking to her arms and legs where she'd been cut. Pain began to register.

She checked her wounds and found that most of them weren't too deep. Some still had small bits of glass in them. She steeled her nerves and picked them out, throwing them toward the window.

"Keep cutting." Michael's voice was right at her ear, but she didn't flinch. *"That's a nice piece there. Use it on yourself. Maybe I'm haunting you, and it will stop me. Or you can have a go at me from this side."*

He nuzzled her ear, the cold almost burning. *"I would love to see you try."*

Rachel was adept at ignoring spirits. She used that skill, picking up the edge of her sheet and wiping away some of the blood on her arms. A flash of blue-green glass caught her eye and she quickly covered it back up.

The witch's ball. She had forgotten about it after taking it down and putting it under the sheet.

Her mind began to race. With Michael in the room already, using it would be the equivalent of a flash-bang grenade. He would probably be confused and startled at the least.

But he could retreat to the person he was possessing. Having a living body as a shelter in addition to whatever piece of him was anchoring him to the physical plane... That explained a lot about his strength and abilities.

He had been strong-willed and extremely charismatic when he was alive—his psychopathic focus was no doubt serving him on the other side. She had seen his type before in the prisoners her mother exposed her to. But Michael... He was even more dangerous.

From what he said and the powers he was already demonstrating, he was well on his way to becoming a demon—if Rachel didn't stop him.

Hiram and Chloe weren't here to help this time. She was on her own. All she had was the ball, and while it would distract Michael, she doubted it would affect the alligator outside her window.

Slowly, she rose to her feet, keeping the witch's ball hidden in the sheets she brought with her. She pretended she was using them to staunch the blood on her arms.

Pain from the cuts on her feet lanced up her legs. She didn't let that stop her from approaching the window, carefully avoiding more glass. Water was still coming in through the hole she'd made, wetting the floor. Her blood stained it red.

Peering out, she saw the alligator sitting on the wet ground. Its eyes glowed blue, the same shade as Michael's only lit with a preternatural light. She jerked back a few steps as it opened its mouth and hissed.

Michael laughed. *"Do you like my little pets? They certainly liked your friend Garrett."*

She turned her head toward the sound of his voice. Garrett should be at the hospital by now.

"What do you mean?"

"I mean he made them a substantial meal."

"No, Garrett left, he—"

"Do you really think after you strung him along for years, then finally let him rut in your body that he would be able to go? He turned around to come back. Of course, with this little storm I prepared for him, he didn't get far. I made sure my friends gave him an exuberant welcome."

Michael clacked his spectral teeth together.

She was shaking again, but this time it was rage. Garrett couldn't be… Especially not that way.

Michael must have read her expression.

"The good doctor is dead. He is dead because he loved you. And love is the most dangerous thing of all. Women are not to be trusted. They will trap you and torment you. He learned this at the end. My gift to him."

The storm had stopped. She noticed it with numb detachment. The storm that Michael had used to kill Garrett… Only a gentle drizzle remained.

"It was my gift to you too, Rachel. I can do more than make you suffer. I wanted you to see I can make you happy as well. Give you what you want. Pleasure is an excellent appetizer for pain."

A chill breeze hit her ear again, creeping down her neck and along her back and arms. Michael was standing right behind her, running his hands along her body.

He was still playing God, only this time with her heart instead of her life. He had pushed her toward Garrett, made sure she had a taste of happiness greater than any she had ever experienced. And then he had taken it away.

"I am the only one who truly understands you," he said. *"Who you are, what you can do. We don't need to worry about anyone getting between us anymore. Garrett has already crossed over. He didn't even think to wait, to help you. But I waited. I'm here. For you. All you have to do is join me."*

He wanted to break her, to control her. But instead of despair, all she felt was rage.

If she thought she had a chance of taking Michael out from the other side, she just might try. But with how well he could manipulate the physical world, she didn't want to think about what he could do to other spirits. He had always been a master manipulator.

Rachel was finished being his puppet.

She felt his hands on her shoulders as if he was urging her forward. His voice was gentle. *"Take your pick—my pet or the glass. I recommend the window. It'll be cleaner."*

"I recommend you go fuck yourself."

She dropped the sheet and held up the witch's ball, directing all of her rage and grief through it. The ball acted as an amplifier for her already enormous pain. She wanted Michael to hurt, like she was hurting. Worse.

The emotion blasted through the room. She could feel it. And even without that, the way Michael screamed let her know it was working. The remaining glass in the window exploded out into the yard.

That was unexpected...

Still holding the ball in front of her, she walked toward the empty space. Water and glass slid out of her way as she approached, pushed by the force of whatever the hell she was doing.

Outside, the alligator was already leaving, heading for the canal at the back of the property. She could sense that Michael had left—for the moment. Her heart was racing, but even that sensation was muted at the stark reality she was left to face.

Garrett was gone.

"Rachel!"

Rachel looked around the room. That was Garrett's voice. But he had crossed over... Hadn't he?

"Rachel!"

Someone was pounding on the front door.

Garrett!

She flung the door to the room open and ran through the house, chucking the witch's ball onto the couch as she passed it. Garrett was still pounding on the front door. It sounded like he was trying to break it down.

"Garrett! I'm here!" she shouted as she unlocked the door and threw it open.

Time seemed to pause. Garrett was standing on the stoop, his hair plastered to his face, rivulets of red streaking across his forehead and down his cheek. His clothes were pasted to his body and his chest was heaving as his gaze roved over her as well.

"Jesus…" he gasped.

He crossed the threshold and picked her up in one movement, crushing her to his chest as she wrapped her legs around his waist to hold on to him. He kicked the door shut and turned so that her back was against it, then he kissed her.

His lips crashed down against hers, his fingers firm against her backside as he held her tight. She wrapped her arms around his neck, returning his kiss, wanting to feel him, all of him, to know he was truly all right.

With their chests pressed together, their hearts were so close—only a few inches of flesh and bone between them. She could feel their energy mingling, merging.

She needed more.

Chapter Twenty-Nine

This didn't seem like the time to start something. Both of them were bleeding, though it all looked superficial. Who knew what kind of danger they were in. But Garrett could feel how much Rachel needed him, needed this. He sure as hell needed it too.

Her legs were wrapped tight around his waist, her tongue delving into his mouth and fingers burrowing through his hair. He pressed her against the door, grinding against her till she groaned.

How could this be happening? Gators outside, ghosts everywhere...

And Rachel opening herself up to him completely—heart, body, and soul. He could feel her fear, her relief, her grief. And a hell of a lot of lust and love thrown into the mix.

Just about the same as him.

But he was only getting the tip of the iceberg of what she was feeling. He sensed the weight of it lurking under her skin.

She arched her neck as he trailed his mouth along her trachea and down to her collarbone. Her hips were already moving on him. She was aching and hurting and needed an outlet for too many emotions. Quickly.

"Garrett..."

"I know," he murmured against her skin.

She hadn't bothered with underwear when they threw on clothes to make breakfast. Stretching his arm around her thigh, he pulled down his waistband and lined himself up. He plunged in deep, holding on to her thighs. Their gazes locked.

Her body relaxed against him as she let out a shuddering breath. And then another.

"Kiss me," she said.

"Any time."

A faint smile crossed her lips before he claimed them. He thrust his hips, her body warming him, sending frissons of pleasure all along his nerves. With the adrenaline already coursing through his system, he knew he wouldn't last long. Lucky for him, he could feel she was in the same boat.

Using her arms on his shoulders for leverage, she moved in synch with him, arching her hips away then back with each of his thrusts to get every drop of stimulation possible from their union. She sped up and he matched her, until the sensations were blurring together in a cascade effect.

All the adrenaline that had coiled in his body focused around where they were joined—on the primal energy of this act of love and longing. It gathered deep in his gut, pressure building until it burst through his body.

He felt himself shifting, like part of him was moving into her as they came and part of her merging with him. Something beyond the physical, something new and bright and full of possibilities. It left his skin tingling and his legs weak.

He leaned against her, pinning her to the door, while he pulled himself back together. She was still pulsing around him, holding him tight everywhere she could. When he slid from her at last, he lowered her feet to the ground, then reached down to pull his pants back up.

Her face was burrowed into the side of his neck, the vibration of her voice traveling through him when she spoke.

"I thought I'd lost you. He said…" Her voice broke. "He said you were dead."

"Look at me."

He waited for her to straighten up so they could look in each other's eyes again. Tears streaked her cheeks, tugging at his heart.

"Never gonna happen." He kissed her again, then rested his forehead against hers. "While you're here, this is where I belong."

She nodded and sniffed. He gathered her up in his arms and carried her to the couch in the living room.

After setting her down, he pulled his T-shirt over his head. He should really get the First-Aid kit, but he couldn't leave her. At least the wounds were as superficial as he first thought. They must sting like crazy, though.

He knelt in front of her and dabbed at her legs with his shirt. "What happened?"

"It's Michael. He's back. He never really left."

Garrett nodded. "Yeah, I figured that out when he tried to drown me in that storm and sent some gators after me."

"How did you escape?"

"Broke a window and climbed on top of my car, then jumped off and ran like hell. They chased me farther than I thought they would, but when I reached the house, they sort of lost interest. Good thing too, because I left my keys behind in my hurry."

He chuckled and glanced up at her, hoping he could ease her worry even a little bit. Nope. There was a crease wedged between her brows and she was getting ready to cry again.

"I'm so sorry," she said.

"Michael's the one that needs to be sorry. And we're going to see to that next."

There had to be something in one of her books that would help them. Otherwise, they were trapped in his house with no way of calling for help. He didn't like the idea of that at all.

"How did he hurt you?" He could hear the change in his voice as he asked the question. The low tones almost hitting a growl.

"He didn't. I broke a window too."

"With your arms?"

They seemed to have taken the worst of the damage, but all the scratches were shallow. She had a few scrapes on her knees and the outsides of her legs, and needed to stay off her feet for a few days. Those were the cuts that worried him the most. None were deep enough to need stitches, at least.

"I used the reading chair in the guest room."

"I didn't know you had it in you."

"He said he was going to kill Jazz. The door to the guest room wouldn't open and I couldn't think of another way to get to her. God, Garrett, the things he said..."

Garrett held her face so she had to look at him. "We're going to stop him. Do you hear me? He's not going to hurt anybody else."

"But he already *is* hurting people. The women he killed—they were right. He's able to get to them again. He's torturing their spirits in the afterlife. And Jazz..."

Garrett's stomach curled in knots. "What about Jazz?"

Rachel gripped his hands and pulled them into her lap. "She called me right after you left. The signal wasn't very clear, but she was trying to ask me about possession. And then Michael told me that he's already taken someone. He's going to force the person he's possessed to kill Jazz if we don't stop him. That poor man... What he must be going through right now."

Garrett's thoughts were spinning. All his friends were in danger—again. And even though he knew it was happening, he had no way to get to them. No way to help.

"He'll go after Elsa next. He's going to kill everyone I care about to punish me. I know it." Rachel leaned forward as if she was getting ready to jump up.

"You need to stay off your feet."

"I need to get to my friends!"

Garrett let out a deep breath, knowing how upset she was going to be when he told her the truth about their situation. Knowing he had failed her again.

"The car's stuck in the sand. There's no getting it out. And I'm not sure how far away those gators went."

And his phone was in the car along with his keys. Shit. He didn't bother bringing up that cheery point. They would check her phone for a signal as soon as they could.

"For the time being, we're stuck here," he said. "And that means you stay off those feet."

"No. There's more we can do."

"Rachel, you're going to start bleeding again if you walk around."

"Good. I can use that."

His heart sank as he saw the determination in her gaze, felt it echo in his soul. There was no talking her out of whatever she was thinking, even if it meant more danger, more harm to herself. All he could do was make a stand with her.

"Tell me what to do."

Chapter Thirty

Blood magic was powerful. One of the most powerful magics.

Michael might have been a ghost long enough to figure out tricks and gimmicks, but Rachel had been studying the paranormal her entire life. She had just never opened herself up to her powers before. Powers she had grossly underestimated.

She remembered the water—red with her blood—moving away from her and taking the broken glass with it as she walked to the window. Psychokinesis.

Yes. She could use her blood. But she would need more if she was going to put a stop to Michael.

Runes. Definitely something with runes.

She wasn't naïve enough to think that she could get Garrett's car out of the sand. But she could make the wards incredibly stronger if she reinforced them with her blood. That helped her and Garrett, but no one else. Michael was still free to go wherever he wanted at the speed of thought.

She surveyed the room, taking stock of her resources. Censer with incense, salt, saltwater spray bottle. Those were small-scale compared to what she was facing.

If Chloe were there, she might be able to channel Michael's spirit into her own body and banish him. Rachel had heard of séances for that purpose. But she had never been part of one. Never been taught how to do it.

Sometimes, other people were used as receptacles for the spirit while the medium remained outside and could focus fully on banishing the ghost. Rachel looked at Garrett kneeling in front of her.

She knew he would have faith in her ability to keep him safe. He would jump at the chance to help, even putting himself through that hell. He was probably the most powerful resource she had, but she couldn't—wouldn't—use him like that. It wasn't safe. It wasn't right.

There had to be some other way.

She glanced down at the couch, her gaze caught by the witch's ball. Caught...

The tunnels of glass within the orb were meant to trap malicious spirits. What if she could lure Michael back and somehow trap him in the ball?

She picked it up, wiping her hand over its surface. How could she possibly get him into it? If she hung it back in a window, he'd simply stay outside or find another way into the house. He could wait them out, like a siege.

She couldn't stop staring at the witch's ball. It was the key. She knew it. But if she couldn't use it in a window...

"A mirror!"

Garrett started and fell over backward. His eyes were wide, but he must have been encouraged by the smile she felt pulling on her face.

"Warn a guy next time," he said.

Her grin turned wicked. "Oh, there will be no warning. What I have planned will be a total surprise."

From the guest room, a tinny sound called out to them. Her phone again.

"Like that?" Garrett asked. He jumped up and started toward the room.

"Wait! I'm coming with you."

She ran to the counter, ignoring the pain in her feet and the way she slid on the bamboo floor as they started to bleed again. She grabbed up the container of salt and the spray bottle, pinning them to her body with the arm that held her witch's ball. She didn't dare drop it with what she had planned.

"Dammit, I told you to stay off your feet."

"I'll heal. Now let's go before we miss the call."

She pushed past him, running down the hallway to the guest room. Garrett was right behind her. She made sure they crossed the threshold together. Being trapped in the room alone with Michael once had been quite enough for her.

Her phone was still ringing, buried in the sheets that she had dropped near the window. Garrett threw them aside and picked it up, then hit the speaker button while Rachel set down what she carried on the bed.

He held the phone up between them and said, "Hello?"

"Garrett?" Jazz's voice. She sounded wrecked. "Where's Rachel? Is she okay?"

Rachel's stomach started doing flip-flops again. She had never heard Jazz sound so upset. Nowhere close.

"I'm here. I'm fine."

Garrett glared at her, but Rachel stared him down. Now wasn't the time to go into details. They could lose the connection at any moment.

"Thank God."

At the same time, Rachel and Jazz both said, "Listen to me," then paused.

"Me first," Jazz said. "He'll find me any second."

"Who will?"

"Finn. I mean Michael. I don't even know anymore! I'm losing him. He's losing himself. Michael is possessing him."

Garrett let out a breath like he'd been punched in the stomach. As if that and the feeling of loss and dread pummeling through Rachel from Garrett wasn't bad enough, Jazz sniffed loudly, her voice hoarse as she continued.

"He's coming for you and Elsa. You have to warn her. He's going to kill you and… You don't want to know what he has planned then. If I can't save Finn—"

"Stop," Rachel said. "We're saving everybody. And we're taking Michael out in the process. Permanently."

As in *eternity*. Michael was done hurting people Rachel cared about. He was done hurting anyone.

Even without their bond, she could see that Garrett was barely holding it together. With it, she could sense how much he cared. He loved Finn like a brother. She wouldn't let him lose another one. And whatever Finn was to Jazz...

"Where are you?" Rachel asked.

"I don't know exactly. I was knocked out. But I'm in a swamp. Probably somewhere near Clearview."

"Why Clearview?"

"Finn and I were trying to find out more about Michael's other victims. It's Michael's home town. We found the house where he grew up."

"Listen to me carefully. I am certain that Michael's body was cremated but there must be something of him left behind. Something acting as an anchor in the physical realm. With how powerful he is, it can't just be a lock of hair. It has to be something with more substance."

For a brief moment, she was actually sorry she and Michael hadn't been intimate. She hadn't had a chance to check him for surgery scars or find out if he'd ever had something removed. All those jars of *keepsakes* in his garage... Maybe one of them held an organ. Even his tonsils or appendix would be enough.

If Jazz couldn't find an anchor in Clearview, they at least had a lead on where to try next. In the meantime, Rachel had a plan to keep him contained.

"I think I know where it is," Jazz said. "What do I do with it?"

"Burn it. Can you do that?"

"Yes. But what about Finn?"

"Once you destroy the anchor, I'll be able to take care of Michael and Finn will be free. We'll be working from here to try to weaken Michael, but we need you to help Finn keep fighting."

If Finn was half as worked up about Jazz as she was about him, they stood a good chance.

"Jazz, you have to reach him," Garrett said. "Any way you can. He won't be able to live with himself if he hurts anybody."

"I know."

Garrett was frowning deeply, his brow lowered over his eyes.

"Watch out for wildlife too. Michael can control snakes and gators and the swamp's full of them."

"It's good if he's spreading himself thin," Rachel said. "The more fronts we can hit him from, the better. Work on your connection to Finn. Try to reach him and help him to hold on."

Jazz's voice dropped to a whisper. "Hurry."

The call ended.

"Tell me your plan is going to work," Garrett said.

"It's going to work. But you're not going to like it."

"What do you need me to do?"

She wasn't entirely sure. She was cobbling things together from all the different books she'd read, everything Hiram and Chloe had taught her. Mostly, she was going on instinct.

"I don't know. I'm not sure how this will play out. I just know I need you with me."

So much was at stake. She had never been more frightened in her life. If she failed, everyone she loved would die. And that was just the beginning. What Michael had planned, the lives he would take, the people he would destroy—

No. Just...no. She was going to stop him. Right now.

Garrett nodded. "What is it you're going to do?"

"Ask you to trust me."

She pulled him down for a kiss, lingering more than she probably should. A small part of her warned that it might be their last one. She pushed the thought away.

The witch's ball sat on the bed with her other supplies. She handed the container of salt and the spray bottle to Garrett, then picked up the glass sphere and headed to the bathroom with him right behind her.

This is where it had to happen. The mirror and the witch's ball were her best weapons. Plus her blood and her knowledge.

She made a line of salt across the door's threshold and another along the back of the sink's counter underneath the mirror, then handed the container of salt to Garrett. It was starting to feel disturbingly light.

"Mix up more saltwater, please," she said.

As he did that, she pulled some towels from the shelf and wrapped the witch's ball, then set it on the floor in a corner where it would be safe. When Garrett was done using the sink, she put in the stopper and filled it with warm water, then added more salt. Having the saltwater easily accessible would help with her work.

"Close the drain in the tub and then spray it down. Put a towel over the toilet tight enough that nothing can crawl out of it. See if you can find something to put on top of the toilet seat too. Just in case." She thought about that, then added, "Maybe make a salt line around the whole thing as well."

Garrett raised an eyebrow, but did as she said. He put a sturdy metal trash can on top of the seat when he was finished spraying and salting everything. Hopefully anything that might try to come up from the toilet wouldn't be strong enough to lift it.

"What next?" he asked.

"Spray me down."

He hesitated. "With those cuts, it's going to hurt like hell."

"I'll deal. And you're next, by the way."

She didn't let herself wince, even though the salt stung each and every wound. Turning in a circle and spreading her arms, she made sure he was able to get her covered in a fine coat of saltwater. Then she did the same for him.

It didn't feel like enough.

Using her blood to protect him was out of the question. Not only would he not stand for it most likely, but with what she had planned, it would make him a target. Their connection already opened him up to Michael more than she liked.

If he had her blood on him, it would act like a beacon—like the one she was about to set up. But a saltwater symbol on his chest would hopefully be lost among the others she was about to draw. She had just the rune for the job.

She dipped her fingertips in the saltwater in the sink, then lifted them to his chest and traced the shape of Eihwaz—like a backwards letter "Z"—a powerful rune of protection. She visualized him being surrounded by a bright golden light, strengthening his aura and keeping him safe.

She wished she could do the same for herself, but the saltwater spray would have to be enough. She didn't want to scare Michael off.

"Help me get the sheet down."

"Won't Michael be able to see what we're doing or use it as a door if we do?"

"The salt line should act as a barrier."

The way he scowled let her know that he didn't like the idea of taking down the sheet as clearly as the waves of apprehension flowing from him. Still, he moved to one side and carefully lifted the sheet off the corners of the mirror, making sure he didn't disturb the line of salt. He dropped the sheet on the floor behind them.

Rachel bent and picked up the witch's ball, then set it on the counter within reach but not too close to the edge.

"I'm going to need a few minutes of silence," Rachel said.

Garrett nodded and she went to work.

First Thurisaz—a straight standing line with a triangle jutting out from its middle pointing to the right. Thorn. She traced it in the top left-hand corner with the saltwater from the sink.

Upright, it was another rune of protection. As she drew it, she thought about herself and Garrett—all her loved ones, even the people she didn't know who stood to lose their lives if Michael was free.

Then she drew it in the corner opposite, with the arrow pointing to the left—a mirror image of the first rune. Reversed it meant ill-fortune, things not turning out as one hoped. She focused her thoughts on Michael.

The next rune was Sowelu, the sun. A symbol of victory. It had always looked like a lightning bolt to her. She thought of Michael's narcissism and played into that. Let him think this energy was for him —let it lure him in, make him feel secure.

But it wasn't for him. Or even for her. It was for Fate.

The next rune finished her thought. Jera—two arrow-heads facing away from each other, touching so they defined a sealed space between them. It also looked a bit like a "Z", but with an open rectangular space in the diagonal line. The harvest time for karma.

"Reap what you sow," she murmured as she traced the symbol.

She continued to tell their story through the runes. Kenaz reversed, a single arrow-head. Darkness. Loss. Symbolizing both what she had felt during her time chained up in his garage and what Michael was about to experience at her hands.

Each rune flowed from her fingertips onto the mirror, her skin buzzing with energy, her arms crawling with it. Uruz, a little like an upside-down "U". The wild ox. Untamed. She wanted Michael to know he hadn't broken her.

In the mirror, she noticed her grim smile as she traced Tyr—justice. A single arrow pointing up.

She was placing the runes in a spiral pattern, visualizing a vortex, a spinning whirlpool of energy that would trap him.

And finally, in the center of the mirror, a single vertical line—Isa, the ice that held the whirlpool in check. The stick that held up the cage. The snare beneath the leaves.

It was ready. All she had to do was place the bait.

Her.

Chapter Thirty-One

The air grew heavier by the second, charged with energy like the moment before lighting struck. Goose bumps ran over Garrett's skin. With each design Rachel traced on the mirror, he felt it thicken.

And she was smiling.

That unnerved him most of all. The way she smiled into the mirror, like she was daring Michael to come. Daring him to do his worst.

Taunting him didn't seem wise. Almost everyone Garrett cared about was on the line.

What Finn must be going through, having that sick fuck playing around in his head. And Jazz trying to help Finn through it, sounding like her heart was being dragged across razorwire in the process.

Elsa and Dante were somewhere hiding behind a line of salt with Winston and Leo. Damn, even their cat wasn't safe. And it wouldn't end with his circle of friends. For Rachel, it might not end at all.

He could sense she was keeping things from him. Trying to protect him. But that just left him with his wild imaginings.

What if they failed and Michael managed to take them all out? Could he grab her spirit and keep it from moving on? She had mentioned Michael's other victims, that he was already tormenting them on the other side. There was no way Michael would let Rachel go if he had any say in it.

Garrett thought he might be sick, his nerves were so bad. He fought the bile in his throat back down. There was no way he would lift that toilet seat after what Rachel had implied. He imagined a rattler springing out and hitting him in the face, or dozens of scorpions crawling from under the lid.

The thought made him shiver. What Rachel did next made it worse.

Reaching out to the counter beneath the mirror, she drew her finger through the line of salt, breaking it.

Garrett shifted so that he stood behind her, ready to help however he could. Their reflections caught his attention. He outlined her perfectly, framed her smaller form, but didn't dwarf it. The result was harmonious. Balanced. It calmed him to think of how perfectly they fit together.

He had seen pictures of auras in her books. The image was almost the same as what he was seeing. It gave him faith.

He was going to protect her. They were going to get through this. All of them.

He rested his hands on her shoulders and sucked in a breath as their bond blew through him, electrified him. She was radiating power.

Garrett's eyes were tingling and he blinked a few times. The mirror was illuminated—all the symbols she had traced glowing with a faint silver light. He had no idea what they meant, but felt a tug, like he was looking into a pit instead of sideways into a mirror.

But not a mirror. Not anymore.

Their reflections and the room around them blurred and vanished. Instead, the glass was filled with gray fog and dark shadows.

Holy shit…

His disorientation grew worse as a silhouette emerged. The features were fuzzy, but gradually came into focus. Tousled blond hair, three days' stubble around a broad smile, straight nose, large eyes… Finn. But not Finn.

Those eyes were supposed to be gray. The same blue-gray as Rachel's, in fact. Instead, they glowed bright blue. Blue like the gators'. Blue like Michael's.

Garrett sensed Rachel's confusion. He shared it himself. If Michael had appeared, that would have made a sort of sense. Reflecting his soul and all that. But even possessing Finn, why would he appear that way?

Unless Michael was using more than Finn's body.

Shit! Why hadn't Garrett thought of that before? Finn was psychic too. And from what Garrett knew, Finn's powers made him a prime target for a ghost looking to jack someone's body.

If having some sort of special anchor already gave Michael a boost, what would riding around in Finn do?

Make it easier to get in people's heads. Or animals. Make it easier for him to charm people, to connect. Especially through his hands, one of which was lifted as he reached out toward Rachel, that disarmingly charming smile on his face.

Rachel lifted her arm in return. Garrett could feel some sort of feedback loop, energy rippling out from the mirror and from Rachel as well. There was some sort of connection there, a pull that neither of them understood. But Garrett did understand that she should absolutely not touch the mirror. He grabbed her arm to hold her back.

Finn's gentle smile twisted and another face lurched toward them. Garrett could still see Finn standing in the mirror, his expression pained and his hands reaching for the translucent *thing* coming out of him. Superimposed over Finn in a sick parody of Garrett and Rachel's reflections earlier, Michael's features took shape.

In life, Michael had been handsome by any measure. Death had wiped that out. His cheeks were sunken, dark circles surrounding eyes blazing with that unholy blue light. Straw-like strands of hair floated around his face, and his teeth were serrated like a shark's. His skin was waxy and bloodless.

"Hello, Rachel," Michael said.

He lunged at them, his face and shoulders coming out of the mirror. On this side, they looked solid. How was that possible? He reached out and locked his grip on Rachel's arms—and pulled.

She screamed, and Garrett tightened his hold on her, keeping her tight against his chest. His feet started to slide on the tile floor.

"What do I do?" Garrett yelled.

"The ball! The witch's ball!"

The…? Right. That glass ball she'd hung in her room. It was close enough for him to reach. He wrapped his arm around her chest, keeping her pinned to him, and picked it up with his free hand.

Michael let go of one of Rachel's arms. The pull toward the mirror lessened and Garrett gained some ground, bringing Rachel with him.

But it gave Michael the opening he needed.

Laughing, he swatted the ball away. It hit the floor and shattered.

"Trinkets and baubles," he said. "Oh Rachel, I have so much to teach you once you're on the other side with me. Stop fighting it, love. We're all waiting for you."

Then Garrett saw them—dark forms lurking behind Michael in the mirror. The ghosts of his victims.

Their spirits looked like the portraits Michael had made using their blood. Distorted bodies, faces hidden or turned away. The pain and despair Michael captured on his canvases blew out from the mirror like a cold wind, freezing Garrett down to his soul.

Police had identified a dozen different victims from DNA testing of Michael's portraits. There were more than a dozen spirits in the mirror. So many more.

Rachel began to cry. Her right arm was turning blue where Michael's spectral hand held her.

"Rachel..." Garrett's teeth were chattering. "Rachel, sweetie, I need you to focus. I know you're scared. I am too. But everyone is counting on us. Including those women. We need to help them, remember? That was always the plan."

"The plan..." She sniffed loudly, then nodded.

Reaching up with her free hand, she dug her nails into one of the deeper cuts on her right arm. Blood welled to the surface.

Shit! He did not know this part of the plan. His stomach churned. He stopped himself from trying to staunch the blood that ran down her arm and dripped onto the floor.

Michael smiled. "Perhaps I don't have as much to teach you as I thought. But save some fun for me."

She let Michael pull her closer to the mirror. Garrett's instinct screamed at him to keep her away, to run, but he had to trust her—that she knew what she was doing.

When she was within reach, she slammed her hand onto the mirror, pushing most of Michael back into the glass. His features became translucent again, superimposed over Finn's.

Garrett could see that Finn's eyes were closed, his eyebrows scrunched together. He was fighting Michael's control.

"Using blood..." Michael said. "You surprise me, my love. We're an even better match than I thought."

Rachel was gulping air. The mirror glowed where her hand touched it.

"Come to me," Michael said. He still had his grip tight on her arm. "Come to me and I may spare you one of your friends. You may choose. Any but the good doctor. He must die, of course, for tasting your forbidden fruit. But Elsa perhaps? That dear lovable butler of hers? The cat? Your—"

Whatever he was about to say, they didn't hear it. His face contorted in agony, mouth a wide "o" with all those teeth showing. Finally, he let go of Rachel's arm, his image retreating fully into the mirror.

Finn cried out, then his reflection vanished.

Garrett's breath rushed out of him in a sob. What had happened to Finn? Was he okay? Was he...

Rachel made a straight line down the center of the mirror—a streak of red that bisected it—then stepped back, pushing against Garrett hard enough that he staggered. He struggled to keep his hold on her.

She didn't lose her balance. Feet planted, she glared at Michael in the mirror.

Michael glanced around as if he was searching for something—like maybe a way out. From how Rachel was laughing, Garrett didn't think he'd find any.

Garrett kept his hands on her shoulders as she approached the mirror again, matching his stride with hers. When Rachel spoke, her voice was eerily calm and filled with confidence.

"Ladies, find your peace," she said. "You are free."

Rachel ran her finger through the blood on her arm and then traced what looked like a large "M" on one side of the mirror's surface and a blocky "R" on the other.

The gray fog in the mirror began to move, forming a whirlpool. Garrett felt it pull at something deep in his gut, like his energy was trying to move toward the mirror. He felt it bump into Rachel, then settle back into him.

What the fuck...

But the dark forms in the mirror didn't have anything to block them. Some seemed to fight the current, while others swam with it. They all flowed into the center of that spiraling vortex, wherever it went.

Michael started to turn, but Rachel snapped, "Not you."

She smeared the "M" and "R" with the heel of her palm. The swirling stopped. Only Michael and the gray fog remained before them.

The mirror changed again, the room around them coming back into focus as the fog dissipated. Garrett still couldn't see their reflection, though. Only Michael's, as if his spectral form stood in the room instead of them.

Rachel ran her fingertip through the blood on her arm again. Her face angled enough so that Garrett could see that she was smiling. It was not a kind smile.

She traced over the line bisecting the mirror. Michael's pallor intensified and he started to shimmer as if shivering. Mist rose from him, like breath on a freezing day.

"You won't be hurting anyone ever again," Rachel whispered.

Chapter Thirty-Two

"Garrett, please hand me the trash can."

She pointed toward the toilet without looking. Her eyes were locked on Michael's in the mirror. If she looked away, she wasn't sure what would happen. She was scared to even blink now that she finally had Michael where she wanted him.

In her periphery, she saw Garrett pick up the heavy metal bin and set it on the counter. He didn't let go of it.

"Is he trapped in the mirror?"

"For now." For about the next thirty seconds—the last of his existence on any plane.

"Are Finn and Jazz okay?"

"I don't know."

"Shouldn't we find out before we do anything else?"

She had to blink—she couldn't stop herself. Michael stayed in the mirror. She let out a breath of relief. At least she didn't have that to worry about. But she could feel him trying to slip out of the mirror, trying to get away.

"I don't know how long I can hold him. We can't risk him getting away."

Garrett's voice was quiet when he said, "What are you going to do?"

She didn't want to say. But she had to.

"I'm going to end him. Eternally."

"You freed the spirits of his victims. Can't you just—"

"I don't know where those other spirits went. I don't know what's on the other side. What if it's a revolving door and spirits are instantly reincarnated? What if he retains his memories, his personality?"

Michael smirked. "So many *what ifs* deciding my fate. I only have one question. What gives you the right to decide whether I cease to exist?"

That question could plague her for the rest of her days. But it wouldn't.

"When you chained me in your garage, you kept saying that you were God. That you decided when and how I would die."

"And now, you do the same to me." He made a clucking noise. "Love, we are so much more alike than I ever guessed. I truly found my match in you."

"*Met* your match. Not found. I am the one who will end you."

"You would really utterly destroy me? All I wanted was to immortalize those women."

"You wanted to control them."

"So now you control me. Does it feel good to hold my fate in your hands?"

"No." She shook her head. "It isn't in my hands."

For the first time, Michael looked uncertain.

"When I opened the gateway, it pulled in the other spirits," she said. "I felt it. Felt Garrett being affected too. But not you."

Michael's frown turned to a grimace, his lips pulling up from his teeth.

"I thought so." Rachel nodded. "You didn't have any trouble staying right where you were. I thought it was the rune at first. Isa—ice—holding you in place. But what I felt was warmth."

She smiled as she remembered it. Comforting energy. Restfulness and home. She hoped kindness was waiting for the spirits she had sent to the other side—a place that they could heal and rest. Maybe Hiram would be there to greet them—to help them on their journey, like he had helped Rachel.

"I felt it," she said. Something had guided her, something beyond her intuition.

"Not your hand but the hand of Fate? Is that how you'll absolve yourself of guilt?"

"This is my choice. Whatever that force was, I choose to help it."

She was finished sitting on the sidelines. She reached for the trash can and rested her hand on its lip. Garrett was right behind her. He hadn't said anything, but she felt the turmoil in him.

Softly she said, "You don't have to stay."

"No, he doesn't." Michael sneered. "But he will. He'll stay with you through the long years, thinking of how the woman sharing his bed and bearing his children was capable of destroying *a soul*. The most precious part of our existence. That you felt you had the right to decide not just between my life or death but my very existence."

Rachel's heart picked up. She knew it was a risk. Garrett was a doctor. Sworn to help people. What she was about to do... Even with what she had sensed from the vortex, the calm encouragement that this was the right thing, she knew she would wonder what Garrett thought of her after it was done.

"The doubt on his face is beautiful," Michael said. "The anger and the pain. And you are the one putting it there, Rachel. It's your masterpiece."

She gripped the trash can, but Garrett wouldn't let go.

"Garrett, please trust me. I know what I'm doing."

"I know," he whispered.

Michael spat out, "That won't change anything. He'll never truly trust you after this, after seeing what you're capable of. You aren't the one who gets to decide when I'm done!"

"No," Garrett said. "I am."

He pulled her tight against his chest as he lifted the trash can out of her grasp, then smashed it into the mirror.

Rachel saw the look of disbelief and fear on Michael's features just before it hit.

Lightning fast, cracks spread over the mirror's entire surface. They seemed suspended in place for a brief second—as Michael's ghostly form exploded into mist, dissipating almost instantly.

Then the pieces of the mirror fell. Her ears rang from the sound of them striking the counter. Garrett tightened his grip on her. She could feel his heart beating against her back.

They stared at the fragments for a few moments before Garrett asked, "Is it over?"

She nodded. "Yes. He's gone."

Chapter Thirty-Three

Garrett's heart was beating so hard it was painful. He had never been more scared. Life and death decisions he was used to. Immortal souls? Shit, that was outside of his depth.

All he had been sure of the entire time was one guiding truth—he trusted Rachel. And he could feel how certain she was, even with the pain of what they had to do.

He dropped the trash can and spun her around, pulling her into a crushing hug. He buried his face in her hair and kissed her neck.

"It's okay," she said. "We're okay."

Not entirely. Her arm was bleeding where she'd dug into her cut. His stomach churned at the memory.

He pulled her with him as he took a few short steps to the shelf and grabbed the First-Aid kit. His hands were shaking so bad she had to open it for him.

A cursory glance at the wound told him it still probably didn't need stitches. It might leave a scar, though. Another one from that bastard.

She set the kit on the back of the toilet and took out an alcohol wipe. Without pausing, she opened it and started on her arm.

"I can do that," Garrett said.

"I thought you weren't allowed to treat me." She grinned up at him.

How could she already be smiling? She wasn't even wincing while she cleaned up her wound.

She threw the bloody wipe into the bathtub and said, "I could use some help with the bandage, though."

Garrett cleared his throat. "I can do that."

Now that her cut was cleaned up, it wasn't as bad as he had feared. He let go of her long enough to open the bandage and put it in place.

She put her hand above his heart. "I really am okay. Are you?"

"Yeah."

"You didn't have to do that," she said. "I would have taken care of it."

"I wanted you to know that I understood. That I believed you. From what you told me about demons, I wouldn't be surprised if he was heading down the road to becoming one. And that guy with even more power... It's something the Universe doesn't need."

"I can't believe how much faith you have in me."

"I can. And I also..." He took a deep breath and blew it out. "Elsa told me she felt that she was being guided to save Dante. She knew she could pull him from his time and bring him here. What you said reminded me of that. The way you trusted your power and listened to your intuition." He shook his head. "If something's out there, some force that wants to help good people and stop bad... Well, I'm in."

"I hope you're right. It would be nice to know we aren't alone in this."

"I've been trying to tell you—you're not alone. None of us are. Not while we have each other."

Rachel's phone started to ring in the other room.

"We should get that," she said.

"What about..." Garrett looked at the shards of glass coating the bathroom counter.

"We'll take care of that later. It's only broken glass now. But I'm thinking we should bury it in a salt-lined hole. Just in case."

"Maybe add some cement."

"You're thinking too corporeally," she said. "Come on."

She led him to the guest room, carefully stepping over the remains of her witch's ball. Sunlight was streaming in through the broken window, catching and reflecting on the broken glass along the wall below. Picking up her phone from the bed, Rachel hit the speaker button.

Before they could say any kind of greeting, Jazz screamed, "Are you guys okay?"

Garrett's heart picked up again. Finn had been the closest thing to a brother Garrett had since Dylan. He couldn't stand the thought of losing him. Not to Michael.

"We're fine," Rachel said, squeezing Garrett's hand tight. "What about you two?"

"We're okay."

Garrett blew out a huge breath. His eyes burned and he felt tears on his cheeks—and he did not give a damn. His body was shaking with relief. Rachel wrapped one arm around his waist, holding the phone closer.

"Finn, you SOB," Garrett said, wiping his eyes with the back of his hand and sniffing. "What the hell did you get my friend Jazz mixed up in?"

"Are you *crying*?" Finn's mocking voice came over the line—the best sound Garrett had heard all day.

"Shut up," Garrett said.

"Oh, I am never going to shut up about this."

Garrett laughed. He hoped so. He wanted Finn to give him a hard time about it for decades—for the rest of their lives, laughing and joking and poking fun at each other as usual.

"Ugh, bromance," Jazz said.

"I think it's adorable." Rachel laughed and squeezed Garrett's waist.

There was a silence on the line that made Garrett uncomfortable. "Finn, you okay?"

"Yeah, man. Yeah." But his voice was a little more serious than Garrett was used to. Gravely.

"Wait a minute," Garrett said. "Now are *you* crying?"

"You'll never prove anything."

Jazz laughed. "Don't worry, Garrett. I'll get some pictures."

The next sound to come out of the phone sounded suspiciously like kissing. Which seemed like a really good idea to Garrett. He kissed the top of Rachel's head. There would be time for more later.

"Look, we've got a mess to clean up here," Jazz said.

Garrett laughed. "Funny, I was about to say the same thing."

"Ours is going to take a while. We need to call the Clearview police

—"

Finn broke in. "Already texted them. They're on the way."

"When did you text them?"

Jazz sounded supremely annoyed for some reason, and Finn instantly went on the defensive.

"As soon as you called Rachel!"

Garrett loved hearing Finn exasperated. It meant Garrett was right about the pair. Double-dates were in their future. He was sure of it.

"I didn't want them to check our phone records and see that we called our friends before them when—"

"Enough!" Jazz cut him off. Garrett could imagine her waving one hand in the air dismissively. "We can explain all that later. Bottom line is, you two need to call Elsa and Dante and give them the all-clear. We are all clear, right?"

"Yes," Rachel said. "Michael is gone—for good this time."

"Thank you." Finn's voice had that somber cast again. Unnerving.

Garrett was used to his friend being worked up about cases or laughing about… Anything, really. This was a new side, brought out by whatever he'd gone through. Another scar for his friends, courtesy of Michael.

Yeah, Garrett wouldn't be losing sleep over ending Michael any time soon.

"We couldn't have done it without you," Rachel said. "We make a good team."

She looked confused for a moment, staring intently at the phone as if she was trying to see something. But then she shrugged and laughed.

"I'll text you after I call Elsa to let you know they're okay," Rachel said. "But I'm sure they are. We let them know what they needed to do to protect themselves and it sounds like we were all keeping Michael pretty busy."

A loud whirring noise sounded in the background.

"Okay," Jazz said. "The cops are pulling up."

"Is that an airboat?" Garrett asked. How deep in the swamp were they?

"Yeah. We better go. But we're headed your way as soon as we're done. And I'm bringing guests, so clean up."

"Guests?" Rachel emphasized the *s* at the end.

"Deal with... I know you can handle it," she said, then ended the call.

Garrett looked down at Rachel. One eyebrow was arced on her forehead. She shrugged.

"I'll call Elsa," Rachel said.

"One thing I need to do first." Garrett pulled her against his chest and kissed her. He meant it to be quick, but once he had her taste, he was lost.

Her mouth was so warm, her arms strong around his neck, pulling herself up to kiss him back. She lifted her thigh, sliding it along his leg.

Breaking off the kiss, he said, "Make the call fast and send that text."

"We still have a bunch of cleanup to do."

"Can it wait a few minutes?"

Rachel cast him a wicked grin. "I think we can make the time."

She dialed Elsa's number and hit the speaker button. Elsa seemed to answer before the ringing even stopped.

"Is everyone okay?" Elsa asked.

Rachel leaned into Garrett's chest and he squeezed her tight.

"Yeah," she said. "Everybody's fine."

Epilogue

A solarium wasn't quite right for Rachel's needs. She preferred the greenhouse they had built onto the back of their new two-story house. She sat at a round table nestled against the outer windows, watching Garrett run after the twins while Hiram, their eldest, wrestled with Dante and Elsa's daughter, Alexis.

Deirdre took a tumble and started to cry, but Garrett swooped her up into his arms, checking her knees for scrapes, then giving her kisses and tickling her till she laughed. Dylan clung to his leg, giggling madly.

Life was good.

Rachel turned her attention back to her notebook on the table. Elsa and Dante were planning a signing at the Bookwyrm to celebrate their latest collaborative effort—a children's book they had written together and Dante had illustrated.

Rachel was designing an exhibit for the paintings Dante had made for the book. They would hang in Jazz's gallery and tie in with the signing. All the proceeds were going to fund a new wing for the local hospital that would specialize in pediatric medicine.

A high squeal outside made her smile. Such a good cause.

The wind chimes hanging above her head sounded, a cold breeze stirring the pages of her notebook. Rachel planted her hand on the paper and let out a sigh.

"Rachel..." The voice was right at her ear.

In a calm voice Rachel said, "Yes?"

She took a sip of her tea.

There was a pause. Most spirits were confused when their introductions were met with nonchalance. The windows rattled in their panes. Great. One of *these* again.

Rachel frowned. "There's no need for theatrics. We're having a cookout this afternoon. Please don't make a mess."

"I will do what I want!"

The rattling kicked up and one of the plants scooted closer to the edge of its shelf.

"I can make your life hell. Make you wish you were—"

"Let me stop you right there." Rachel smiled as the ghost paused in its spectral posturing.

Rachel pulled on the cord that hung down next to her seat. It flowed through grommets set into the greenhouse's frame and ended on the far side of the space. The cord was attached to a gauzy cloth that covered a large mirror suspended high in the opposite corner. The lever that let her adjust the angle of the mirror was also right at hand. She took another sip of her tea, adjusting the mirror so that she could scan the room.

"Ah, there we are."

The ghost was standing next to her. They usually did. Rachel barely ever had to move the mirror at all.

This one was a woman. She might have been in her early twenties when she died.

"I'm sorry for your loss," Rachel said. "But that doesn't excuse such poor manners."

"I... You can't talk to me that way!"

"Oh sweetie..." Rachel smiled. "Let me tell you how this works."

She set down her tea and dipped her finger into the warm liquid, slowly swirling it around in a circle. As she did, the runes she traced in saltwater on the mirror every morning started to glow.

The ghost turned to face the mirror, eyes widening in her pale face as she saw her reflection. Gray clouds swirled around her, pulling her into the glass and trapping her there.

Rachel set aside her cup and flicked the tea from her finger. Her mother might not have taught Rachel how to handle her powers, but Lillian Montgomery *had* taught Rachel how to dominate social interactions. Rachel only cast an occasional glance toward the mirror, letting the ghost know that she was not worried in the least by the presence of a spirit.

"I hope the accommodations will be comfortable for you while we work to resolve your issues. Please understand that I can't have ghosts who are willing to throw their weight around running freely near my home. There are children to consider. The safety of my family and our guests."

"How did you..."

"It's neat, isn't it? One of my friends used to be a set designer for a theater. He's a brilliant engineer, though he mostly paints nowadays. Set the whole thing up for me."

Dante had used cords and pulleys rather than electronic motors. The manual system was much more difficult for ghosts to interfere with and had a cool steampunk look.

"I understand that you might have lost touch with certain aspects of your civility," Rachel said. "But I must ask you to try to remember to treat me and mine with respect. I will do my best to reciprocate."

She paused to let that sink in with the ghost. Mutual respect or mutual antagonism. Those were the choices. Rachel wanted to be sure the ghost understood just what it would mean if she chose to make Rachel her enemy.

"You will remain in the mirror until I am certain that you pose no danger to anyone, living or dead. If you threaten me, my family, or anyone else..." Rachel stared at the ghost. "Ready or not, you *will* move on to the next plane, and whatever is waiting there for you."

The ghost shrank back from Rachel, becoming a bit more transparent. Good.

"But if you are willing to be courteous and explain your situation calmly, I'm willing to hear you out."

Rachel smiled.

"Now. Let's see what we can do for you."

———

Think you know everything? Think again! You can see what Jazz and Finn were doing during the events of *Whispering Hearts* as they face a new threat in *Lingering Touch*—and it's not just from beyond the grave. Secrets will be revealed that shock the group of friends to their core and show them that they're even closer than they thought.

Lingering Touch

CASSANDRA CHANDLER

Lingering Touch

The Summer Park Psychics
Book Three

Cassandra Chandler

Dedication

For those who dare to try again.

Prologue

Summer Park—May 2015

Time travel was impossible. There was no such thing.

Finn had worked plenty of weird cases as a private investigator. This one might break into his top ten.

He picked the lock on the theatre's back door, then slipped into the building. The most recent production had wrapped almost three weeks ago. That meant only construction crews would be around. They'd be focused on the stage. Finn was interested in the theatre's seating.

All he needed was a few minutes in the box reserved for Elsa Sinclair—famous novelist and professional recluse. His best friend, Garrett, had hired Finn to figure out if Elsa was being conned by the guy she was living with—Dante Lucerne.

It seemed likely. For starters, Dante Lucerne had been dead over a hundred years. Finn turned up that little gem of information within an hour of working the case. The original Dante had been killed in a fire in London in 1881. Finn couldn't find any other men matching the name and description Garrett had provided. And it was a very unusual description.

Six foot tall, short dark hair, thin build, blue-green eyes, and scarring over a quarter of his face centered on his right temple. Oh, and he dressed like a guy from the 1800s...who chose to wear a *Phantom of the Opera* mask.

Yeah, this case had definitely cracked his top ten.

Garrett had turned around and told Finn to drop the case right away, but it was too late. Finn's curiosity had been piqued. The more Finn learned, the more curious he became. He had even already brought out his secret weapon—psychometry. He'd used his psychic ability to read what had happened in the limo Elsa rented the night Dante appeared in her life.

Finn snorted and shook his head as he remembered Elsa telling Dante that she had basically teleported him from 1800s London to modern-day Florida.

Time travel. Yeah, right.

Finn could buy into a lot of things—psychometry and telepathy, for instance. His very personal experience proved those were real. But going back in time and bringing someone to the future? No way.

Dante had been really convincing, though. Not only had he been wearing the old-timey clothes Garrett had mentioned, but Dante had been covered in soot and sweat. He had the accent down, speech cadences sounding like something from a period piece.

Only one explanation seemed plausible—Elsa was researching a new book. She was going all out and had hired an actor to help her get into the spirit of things. For all Finn knew, this was how she researched all of her stories. It would explain why everyone talked about how real they felt. Hell, even Finn's dad was a fan.

Finn might have to read her next book. The horror novels he usually read right before sleep were finally getting to him. It had been decades since he'd woken up screaming from a nightmare. He was a grown man, for crying out loud. He couldn't quite remember what had happened in his dreams the night before, but he felt in his gut that it was somehow related to this case.

He'd never had an investigation get under his skin like this. He'd been on edge all day, jumping at the smallest things and feeling... honestly, kind of terrified. He didn't understand where it was coming from. He did understand that it needed to stop.

If sifting through the memories of the dozen or more people who had been in the limo since Elsa and Dante would help him figure out the mystery, it was worth it. Even the ones that were a graphic and unwelcome reminder of his last encounter with Jazz. They had broken up after a disastrous date in a limo.

That was Fate's punchline. Elsa wasn't just tight with Garrett—who was as close to a brother as Finn was going to get this lifetime—she was best friends with Finn's ex, Zhou Jazz.

Who was he kidding? Jazz wasn't just an ex-girlfriend—she was *the* ex-girlfriend. The only woman Finn had ever wanted to spend the rest of his life with. Their relationship had escalated so quickly, even though they'd only been together for a couple of months. He'd been certain she was the one he was meant for. Part of him still thought so.

Normally, he used his work to avoid thinking about her, letting himself get lost in the puzzles his investigations presented. With this case, everything reminded him of her.

He had even seen her a few times, talked to contacts that he introduced her to. For some reason, she was putting together a fake ID for Dante. If Dante was conning Elsa, he was conning Jazz too. Finn took a deep breath and willed his body to relax, his hands to uncurl.

If Dante was conning Jazz, if he tried to hurt her in any way… It would not end well for him.

Finn made his way to the box that Elsa had reserved for every single showing of the play. It was unlocked. Two chairs sat facing away from him. The curtains were already closed. Apparently, she insisted they were kept that way—yet another of her eccentricities. No one had bothered to open them yet.

It worked in his favor. He could check things out without being seen. Her memories should be all over the place.

Finn closed the door behind him and set to work. He held out his hands and shifted his awareness, letting the feel of the place soak in. A few deep breaths would open him to…

Holy shit.

The tiny room was bursting with energy. Finn felt like he was on a roller coaster, his stomach lurching and doing flip-flops. He staggered forward and grabbed one of the seats in front of him to stay upright. A jolt of energy lit him up like the Fourth of July. His eyes were electrified, his body tingling from head to toe. He blinked a few times, waiting for his perspective to shift as his powers kicked in.

Normally, he felt like he was floating above the place he was viewing—his awareness on the shoulder of whoever had touched what he was touching. This time, he was booted out of his body like someone rammed him in the gut. The vision was different too—the colors more vivid. Too vivid to be real.

He looked down from the ceiling to see Elsa standing in the same spot that Finn's body must be occupying. She was staring at...nothing. Between the no-blinking and standing completely still, she looked like a mannequin.

It would have been creepy if not for the ribbons of golden light whipping around, centered on her. They cast off little fireworks of energy that filled the space. Finn felt like he was inside a glitter-filled snow-globe that was being swirled around.

The light started to gather in front of her, taking on the shape of a man. Elsa's arms shifted so that she was embracing him, clinging to him. The light was painfully bright. In a final flash that made Finn wish he had eyelids to shut, Dante appeared in her arms.

What the fuck! What the flaming flying fuck!

Dante collapsed. It looked like he was convulsing.

"Dante? Dante, are you all right?" She grabbed a dark cloak from the back of the other chair. "I'm so sorry. I didn't think it would be this bad."

She draped the cloak over him, then dropped to the ground. She snuggled up against his back, spooning him and rubbing his arms and chest. He was shivering and breathing heavy.

"Stay with me. Please stay with me," she said.

Finn watched, dumbfounded. After a few moments, Dante's tremors subsided. He gripped Elsa's wrist and said, "I assure you, I have no plans to go elsewhere."

They sat up slowly. She knelt next to him, hovering like a hummingbird, her face pinched with worry. The pair finally faced each other, and damn, Finn could sense the chemistry even without his body. A much dimmer version of the golden lights was hovering around their bodies, linking them together like she was still holding on to him.

"How do you feel?" Elsa asked.

"I scarcely know where to begin."

"Are you hurt?"

"I do not believe so. For the most part, I am confused."

That made two of them.

"That's understandable. I'll explain everything as soon as I can. But right now, we have to go."

Elsa rose to her feet and offered her hand to help Dante up. Of course, he took it. The two stood close, staring into each other's eyes like...

Like Finn wished he and Jazz would have. He groaned at himself, then forced thoughts of Jazz out of his mind.

"Where is it we are going?" Dante asked.

Elsa smiled. Finn realized he had never seen her look happy before. Not that they'd spent much—or any—time together. Jazz wasn't keen on incorporating Finn into her life.

"Home," Elsa said.

She stepped toward the door. The vision faded as she and Dante moved away. Finn blinked a few times as his awareness returned to his body. He was sitting on the floor where Elsa and Dante had been talking. When had Finn fallen?

The conversation Finn had viewed in Elsa's limo took on a whole new depth of meaning. She really *had* brought Dante forward over a century, had saved him from the fire that supposedly killed him.

Finn stood, careful not to touch anything. Once was enough for being pulled into the current of such a powerful memory. He staggered out into the hall, closing the door behind him. His thoughts whirled as he leaned against the dark wood, still clutching the doorknob.

Finn's hearing cut out suddenly, his perspective shifting so he was looking down at the door. Another vision? What the *fuck* was up with his powers today?

A blond guy was standing in front of Elsa's theatre box, stroking the door. Yeah, that wasn't suspicious at all.

Finn recognized him as one of the people he had sifted through when finding Elsa's memories in the limo she rented. He remembered the guy because he had just sat there, completely still, for a long time the day after Elsa and Dante rented it. That was too much of a coincidence.

Finn made a note of the guy's height and weight, his build, his clothes, anything that might help ID him later. The vision ended gradually, letting Finn sink back into the awareness of his own body again.

He had a call to make. Garrett needed to know that Dante wasn't the one Elsa should be concerned about. And after that, Finn would start looking for the blond guy.

Chapter One

Garrett's car was in his driveway. Jazz parked her SUV behind it, clutching her wheel with a white-knuckled grip. The day was already oppressively hot. His car was going to be an oven. Why wasn't it in the garage?

The garage. Right.

She had never really thought about garages before. Now she hated them. She couldn't imagine how they made Rachel feel after what had happened to her.

No, Jazz could. She just didn't want to.

"Get off your ass," she said. Rachel was waiting for her.

Jazz grabbed the green bag sitting in the passenger's seat. Apparently, Rachel was in the mood for some metaphysical arts-and-crafts. If it helped her feel better, Jazz was all for it. She opened the door and slid to the ground.

Heat reflected up from the white concrete of Garrett's driveway. Her leather pants held on to the cool from the AC, deflecting some of it. The big black sweater she had decided to wear—not so much. She stood for a moment as the humidity penetrated the fabric, baking her.

Today's wardrobe choice brought to you by yet another lapse in judgment.

"Fuck. This."

She slammed the door shut. It was even more satisfying than swearing—a habit she had picked up from Finn.

Don't think about Finn.

She repeated the mantra a few times as she marched up to the house and rang the doorbell.

"Coming!"

Rachel's voice. She sounded...happy. How could that be possible after everything she'd been through?

Rachel opened the door. She had a broad smile on her face. It was almost like nothing had happened. No, not quite. The lines of tension around her eyes had deepened.

She always had a haunted quality about her that made Jazz want to kick her parents' asses. It had never been this bad before. She ran through a quick, assessing check.

Rachel's hair was brushed but otherwise left alone. Simple blue shirt, jeans, sneakers. No jewelry, no makeup... Yeah, Rachel was still healing. The dark circles under her eyes weren't the only sign. She kept one hand behind her back, as if she was hiding something.

"Hi!"

Jazz knew Rachel's enthusiasm must be at least partially forced. Probably to benefit Jazz. Her eyes were burning. She was grateful that Rachel was okay. Would be, anyway. They would all make sure of it. Especially now that Rachel was at Garrett's.

"Hi."

Rachel's brow knitted and her smile vanished. "What's wrong? Did something happen?"

Did something...

"Are you kidding me? Yes, something happened. I haven't seen you since you left the hospital, and you've barely texted or called!"

Jazz walked into the house and shut the door, then grabbed Rachel and hugged her. Rachel stiffened as the awkwardness of the moment sank in. Dammit, Jazz needed to start hugging people more often. The idea that she could have missed the chance to make up for it...

It was too much. Her eyes were still burning. No way in hell would she cry. If she did, Rachel would try to comfort Jazz, and that was not okay. Rachel was the one who needed comforting.

"Are you okay?" Jazz asked. "You look better."

"I am better. Getting there, anyway."

Jazz sniffed to keep her nose from running. The air was thick with incense. Not freshen-the-air incense, either. It was the same scent that Chloe used at her metaphysical bookstore, Bookwyrm.

"Why does it smell like a temple in here?" Jazz asked.

Rachel laughed and stepped back. "That would be from this."

She held up a small brass incense holder with holes punched in patterns along the sides and lid. Three tiny chains attached to it led to a small hook at the top that Rachel had looped over one finger. The thing —a censer, Jazz remembered—was used in rituals and religious observations. Smoke trailed out of it, slowly wending its way up Rachel's arm.

"If you don't mind, I need to smudge you," Rachel said.

How did Rachel know what smudging was? Jazz was the only member of her group who was into metaphysics. Well, aside from Elsa. But Elsa wasn't so much interested in the topic as forced into it from first-hand experience. Maybe Rachel didn't know what she was talking about.

"You want to cleanse my aura?" Jazz asked.

"That's the idea."

Okay, she does *know.*

Jazz stepped back toward the door and lifted her arms to give Rachel space to work. Like a pro, Rachel wafted the smoke around Jazz's body, clearing and cleansing her energy field.

Auras were kind of mainstream. Lots of people knew what they were and Jazz wouldn't have been too surprised for that topic to come up in conversation. But smudging was a level deeper.

The question of "how Rachel knew" wasn't as disturbing as "why was she doing this?" Jazz actually cleansed and combed her aura on a regular basis. She smudged herself and her apartment every month during the dark moon, banishing thoughts and attachments she wanted to clear out.

Finn's smiling face popped into Jazz's mind—his cocky grin surrounded by dark brown stubble and those pale blue eyes that she could dive into. She had never been able to bring herself to try to clear Finn's energy from her life, even though she constantly told herself to stop thinking about him.

He and Rachel had the same exact eye color. It had unsettled Jazz at first. Now she found it weirdly comforting. Nostalgic even.

Bullshit.

It just gave Jazz an excuse to think about him—let her blame it on an external stimulus instead of the soul-deep longing that kept her up at night and made her that much more dedicated to her work.

Dammit, stop thinking about Finn.

Her mantra wasn't working. Then again, it seldom did with him.

One month, three weeks, six days, and twenty-two hours. That was how long they had been together before he left. Even after all this time, she still thought of him every day.

She needed to be thinking about Rachel.

"If you need me to open the bag to cleanse the stuff inside, let me know," Jazz said.

Rachel paused briefly with the censer under the bag. She let the smoke float up around the green plastic.

"That should be good enough." She laughed abruptly. "I know we've never discussed paranormal stuff before, but I have to say I'm very grateful you're into it and already know so much."

"I didn't know you were into it at all."

"It's kind of been a necessity for me. Let's sit down and talk." Rachel took the bag and led Jazz into the living room.

Necessity. Like Elsa.

Jazz wondered if Rachel might be psychic too. It was pretty common in Summer Park. Something about the place seemed to call to people with gifts, drawing in whole families sometimes.

Like Finn and his dad, Tommy.

Her stomach tightened as she remembered sitting around their kitchen table and laughing till her sides hurt. Finn hadn't just given her his heart—he'd given her a family. She had messed up and lost them both.

She modified her standard mantra, trying to get a better handle on her emotions.

Do not think about Tommy.

"Can I get you a drink or anything?" Rachel asked.

"I'm good."

Garrett's coffee table was covered in an impressive library of metaphysical texts. Jazz recognized several of the same books she had in her collection. Chloe was doing good business.

Jazz sat on the couch and said, "I'm guessing this isn't a passing interest."

"No."

Where was Garrett? Jazz broadened her attention and heard water running at the other side of the house. He must be in the shower. While she was scanning the room, she noticed a poppet hanging above the sliding glass doors that led to the patio.

A poppet?

It was made of plain white cloth and shaped like a person, but didn't have any other defining characteristics. Jazz checked the kitchen window with her limited view from the couch. Sure enough, a poppet was hanging there as well. Rachel was warding away spirits. Not just a specific spirit—otherwise, there would have been more detail to the things. She was keeping away all of them.

That explained the smudging.

"I see you're already redecorating," Jazz said.

Rachel's smile faltered and the tension around her eyes increased. She'd said she wanted to talk metaphysics, but maybe she was like Elsa and new to the whole thing.

"It's a poppet," Rachel said. "They keep away spirits."

Maybe not-so-new.

Rachel made herself a workspace on the coffee table, then sat on the floor and opened the bag. She placed what Jazz had picked up at Bookwyrm on the table. Silver jewelry wire, a wire cutter, a silver chain, and three stones.

"Snowflake obsidian, fluorite, and opal, as requested," Jazz said. "I picked out three that looked like you could make them work in a necklace."

"These are perfect, thanks."

They were in a small sealed plastic bag. Rachel opened it, then let the stones tumble gently onto her hand. She set them on the table reverently.

The snowflake obsidian was black with little gray speckles that looked like snow. Obsidian was used in metaphysical work with the subconscious. Snowflake obsidian specifically could be used in meditation and rituals designed to help a person manifest their most authentic self.

Fluorite, on the other hand, was about boundaries and concentration. Jazz used it when she really needed to focus on a project and didn't want to be distracted by outside influences.

The one she'd picked out had lots of blue and purple flowing through the translucent body of the stone, which would bring out the iridescent qualities of the otherwise milky-white opal. Opal was used for journeying and balance.

Journeying... Was the necklace meant for Elsa?

Rachel was linking the stones together, wrapping the jewelry wire around each one to hold it in place. While she worked, she said, "I spoke with Elsa on the phone today. She told me what she can do."

Yup. It was for Elsa.

The choice of stones suddenly made sense. No, not just sense—they were genius. Opal to aid journeying, fluorite to aid focus. Using those stones together, Elsa's psychic ability of astral projection would be heightened. They would give her more control. Jazz wasn't sure how the snowflake obsidian factored in, though.

She also wasn't completely certain that she and Rachel were on the same page. Until she was, Jazz wouldn't spill Elsa's secret, even though Elsa said she was planning to tell Rachel eventually.

"Elsa can do a lot of things," Jazz said.

"So can I."

Rachel let her hands drop to her lap and stared at Jazz intently. She had never seen Rachel look so serious.

"I can hear spirits," Rachel said. "Sometimes I see them in

reflections. Especially mirrors."

Damn. Was Jazz a psychic magnet or something? She knew she didn't have any abilities herself. She would have discovered it over her years of practicing, researching, trying to reach the other side.

Plus, Chloe had tested her.

One of the reasons Jazz settled in Summer Park was to be closer to Chloe and work with her. She had been the most promising lead in Jazz's ultimately futile quest.

Aside from "having a heightened sense of people's character", Jazz was within the normal levels of sensory perception. And even that ability hadn't helped to avoid—

Do not think about Michael.

Her mantra didn't keep her stomach from knotting. She hated that Michael could affect her so viscerally. She took a slow, deep breath through her nose and let it out through slightly pursed lips, hoping that Rachel wouldn't notice.

"Aren't you going to say something?" Rachel asked.

"I'm being inscrutable," Jazz said. "It's an Asian thing."

As she hoped, Rachel laughed. Jazz felt her own face pull into a stiff smile.

"Okay. I need more information."

Rachel nodded. "You know how I sometimes get distracted? That's usually when I'm hearing spirits having a conversation. Florida is filled with ghosts. That's why I'm making this for Elsa."

How did ghosts intersect with astral projection?

"I don't see the connection."

"Elsa travels astrally. She leaves her body behind, ready to be occupied."

The knots in Jazz's stomach tightened.

"Occupied?"

"It's easy for a spirit to enter an empty body."

"You're talking about possession."

Rachel nodded. "Some ghosts can even take over bodies that have souls in them. If they have a strong enough personality, they can overcome the existing consciousness. All they need is an opening or conduit. It would be easy for a spirit to take over Elsa's body while she's traveling."

Shit. Jazz should have thought of that as soon as Elsa had told Jazz what she could do. Jazz had been too dazzled and happy and proud of Elsa's ability.

Elsa didn't just use her power to let her soul travel through space—she traveled back in time *on a regular basis*. No wonder her novels were so rich in historical detail.

As if that wasn't enough, she had discovered Dante, basically fallen in love with him while observing him, and saved his life by pulling him forward through time *physically*. Jazz had never heard of anything happening on that level. She was still kind of in awe of the whole thing. Even so, she should have realized the danger inherent in Elsa leaving her body empty.

Jazz knew that mediums could channel spirits through their bodies during séances and that sometimes the spirits didn't want to leave. She had studied the phenomenon of walk-ins, even a bit about possession. Finding out more about how spirits and the living could interact had been a near-obsession of hers for years after her father's unexpected death.

Never think about Father.

Her mind shied away from the topic instantly, like the thought was made of shards of broken glass. She pulled her focus back to Rachel again.

The snowflake obsidian finally made sense. The necklace wasn't meant to boost Elsa's powers. It was meant to keep her safe.

Jazz pointed at it. "Are you sure this will protect her?"

"It should," Rachel said. "She's been lucky."

"What about a salt circle? Would that help?"

"If she can control when she travels, yes, that would keep spirits away. I'm not sure how the circle would affect her, though. It might trap her inside or keep her from being able to get back. We can run some experiments and see."

Chloe needed to be there when that happened. Her experience would be invaluable. But Jazz was getting ahead of herself.

"She's not going to want to try anything until Dante is better. Since she can control her ability by not being around any art, it shouldn't be a problem."

"Art?"

"That's what triggers her ability. I guess it's like you only seeing spirits in reflections."

Rachel nodded. "That will buy us some time."

The knots in Jazz's stomach lessened a tiny bit. Elsa was safe for the moment. Dante was doing well. Garrett was apparently at-ease enough to take a shower, which was a relief, since he'd been so busy taking care of everybody else he'd been neglecting himself for the last two months. That left Rachel.

"What about you?" Jazz said. "Are these poppets enough to keep spirits from bothering you?"

"That plus spraying salt water on all the doors and windows. Florida is so humid and there's already salt everywhere from the ocean being close. It doesn't take much extra to ward entryways."

Jazz had never bothered warding anything. She'd fix that as soon as she went home.

"I'll keep that in mind. What do you do when you leave the house?"

Rachel paused for a moment before saying, "I don't."

What?

"You can't stay here forever."

"I'll figure something out. If Dante and Elsa are staying in the city for a while, maybe I can stay at their place."

"That isn't what I meant. You can't let ghosts keep you imprisoned for the rest of your life. They can't hurt you, can they?"

"It's difficult for them to hurt people physically through direct contact. They're more likely to try to startle me so I jump out in front of a car or maybe impel an animal to bite me or something."

"That's not reassuring."

"It's hard for spirits to control animals. They'd have to be extremely willful and focused. Death tends to distract people and scatter their thoughts. It takes them a while to regroup and be able to think rationally."

The most recent ghost that Jazz could think of was also the worst. Michael.

You will think about Michael if it helps Rachel be safe.

Michael Angelo, the brilliant artist whose works inspired such a visceral response in viewers because his paintings were made from the blood of women he *killed*. Jazz felt her stomach heave, but clenched her muscles, willing herself not to be sick. His works had been set to exhibit in Jazz's gallery—*her own fucking gallery*.

He had targeted Rachel and Elsa, kidnapping Rachel first. Elsa's ability had been triggered when she went into Michael's exhibit room. She'd traveled to where Rachel was being held in Michael's garage.

On one level, Jazz was grateful. If Elsa hadn't seen the paintings, she and Dante wouldn't have been able to run to the rescue, having Jazz call in reinforcements in the form of EMTs and the police. But if Jazz hadn't brought Michael's pieces into the gallery, her friends might not have been hurt at all.

Heightened ability to read people's character. Right.

Michael had shot at Dante and injured him, had strangled Elsa, and had...tortured...Rachel. And then Rachel had shot him. A lot. If Michael's spirit wanted revenge, she would be his first target. The first of many.

"What about—"

"Michael is dead and gone. His body was cremated. Without any remains, his spirit can't linger." Rachel recited the information as rote. She and Garrett must have already covered this ground.

Jazz let out a huge breath and nodded. "Okay. What about these other yahoos? How do we get them to stop bugging you?"

"I'm still working on my long-term plan."

"There's more you're not telling me. I want to help."

"The best thing you can do is get this to Elsa."

Rachel held up the finished necklace. It was gorgeous. The stones were secure, but still showcased. She had even added little flourishes with the silver wire, making spiral patterns on the stones.

"You are a miracle worker," Jazz said. "I keep telling you I could sell your work in the gallery easily."

"I have a trust fund, remember?"

A trust fund from parents that didn't give a damn about Rachel. Her dad was absent except for photo shoots, and her mom was a grasping, conniving, undercutting woman. Jazz wasn't into hating people. It took too much energy. Rachel's mom had earned it, though, after too many gallery openings where she attended seemingly just to humiliate Rachel.

Even with a trust fund, Rachel had wanted a job. Wanted to contribute. How the hell had such a beautiful person come from that pair?

"Is that why you fought me so hard on getting a paycheck?"

Jazz almost managed a smile at the memory. Rachel worked hard at the gallery. Jazz had to shove a check in Rachel's purse and threaten to fire her if she didn't cash it.

"The knowledge you've shared with me is worth more than any paycheck. You've given me a chance to do something meaningful that I love."

Something that had almost gotten her killed.

"How's that working out for you?"

"Are you kidding? I've learned more from you than anyone."

"If knowledge is all you wanted, you could have gone back to school," Jazz said.

"There are no schools that could give me the experience I've gained working with you."

Experiences like being chained to a wall and exsanguinated for a painting. Jazz bit back the acerbic comment. When Rachel was ready to talk about what happened to her, Jazz would be there. But she wasn't going to bring it up herself.

Dammit, she was tearing up again. Rachel didn't need to see that. Jazz coughed to clear her throat, but it was still tight when she spoke.

"Is there anything special I need to do when I give the necklace to Elsa?"

"No, but I need to charge it with an intention first. If you give me a moment, I can do that now."

Jazz nodded, then leaned back. Rachel held the necklace in her closed hands, presumably to block out any of the ambient energy floating around the room. She shut her eyes and murmured something so quiet Jazz couldn't make it out.

After a few moments, Rachel opened her eyes and set the necklace on the coffee table. She flicked her hands to shed any residual energy. Yeah, she knew what she was doing in the energy-manipulation department. That still seemed like a very small-scale ritual.

"Seriously?" Jazz asked. "That's it?"

"The simplest solutions are usually the most powerful."

That sounded like something Chloe would say.

"I might have taught you about running a gallery, but I'm guessing you had other mentors."

"I had two teachers," Rachel said. "One on each side."

"Each side of what?"

"One was a spirit. The other was a medium."

"I suppose that makes sense. Actually, a lot of things I wondered about you are making sense now. Like why you try to get people to think you're scatterbrained when you're actually brilliant."

Rachel's eyebrows hiked up her forehead and her mouth dropped open. She let out a fake laugh, trying to throw Jazz off her scent. It was way too late for that.

"I don't know about that," Rachel said. "But I appreciate the compliment."

"It wasn't a compliment. It was a statement of fact. And you're doing it right now." Jazz sighed. "I wish you would stop."

"I don't know what to say."

"Forget it. I'm just glad you're away from your mother. I've been trying to get you out of that pit since we met. Garrett's going to get a deep discount on his next piece for accomplishing that."

"A pit? I've been living in a mansion."

"That's putting lipstick on a pig. Your mom could suck the joy out of a sold-out opening show. I've seen her do it. Belittle your accomplishments and demean you in front of a room full of people."

Rachel's laugh was tinny and hollow. Jazz could only imagine the things echoing in Rachel's mind. Ghosts were probably easier to deal with than memories of her mother's passive-aggressive abuse.

"You're the one who makes the sales," Rachel said.

"Stop. Now you're doing it to yourself."

"You sound like Garrett."

"Good. If we all remind you to disregard the crap she's told you over the years, it might help you to stop telling yourself the same lies she taught you."

Rachel's eyes filled with tears and she muttered, "Thanks."

This topic was too sensitive. Jazz needed to distract Rachel. Immediately.

Jazz nodded and asked, "Will it disrupt the energy if I touch the necklace?"

"It's best if others handle it as little as possible."

The silver chain had come in a velvet bag. Rachel slid the finished necklace into the little pouch and handed it to Jazz.

"I'll see that she gets it tonight," Jazz said. "But what about you? How do we get all these ghosts to leave you alone?"

"I can take care of myself."

Jazz grabbed Rachel's hand and held on tight. "We take care of each other. Now more than ever."

Rachel was trying to say something, but only little coughing sounds came out. If her throat was as tight as Jazz's, it was no wonder.

No more talking. No more thinking. Just this offer of comfort.

She knelt next to Rachel and pulled her into a hug. Rachel buried her face in Jazz's hair and hugged her back, hard.

Jazz pulled away and sniffed. "You need me—you need anything—you call. Understand?"

Rachel nodded.

"Okay." Jazz put her hands on Rachel's cheeks and kissed her forehead as she stood. They both needed time and space to collect themselves, to give the emotions and memories they had stirred up a chance to settle. "Give Garrett my regards. And be sure to lock the door after me."

Rachel nodded. She didn't walk Jazz to the door. It was probably for the best.

Chapter Two

Finn splashed cold water on his face, hoping it would chase off the aftereffects of his latest nightmare. It didn't.

He dried off, then chucked the towel on a pile of dirty clothes. He needed to do laundry, but hadn't been able to motivate himself to do much of anything lately. Dad was stuck doing all the dishes and Daphne was cooking for them both. Finn needed to get this under control.

Letting out a snort, he shook his head. Nothing was under control.

He ran his fingers through the tangled mess of his hair and it stayed standing on end. He needed a shower. Dammit, he was *going* to shower. And get dressed. And leave the apartment. Today.

"Finn! Get in here."

After he found out what Dad needed.

"Coming."

In his thirties, and his dad still shouted for him like he was a kid. Finn shook his head as he headed for the kitchen.

Dad was sitting at the table, a grim expression deepening the lines on his face where time had left its mark. His hair was almost entirely gray, though it had once been dark brown. He was chewing on his lower lip. The upper was hidden beneath a full mustache.

"What's up?"

Finn was already in the room when he noticed Daphne leaning against the counter. Her dark curls hung loose around her shoulders and she stared at him with warm brown eyes. She was already dressed for working the bar downstairs—jeans and a plaid flannel shirt with the sleeves rolled up.

Finn was in his boxer-briefs.

"Dad, warn me next time."

"It's nothing she hasn't seen before. Sit down."

Finn paused, already halfway back out of the room. He looked at their faces again. Very unhappy. Nervous.

"What is this, an intervention?" Finn laughed.

Neither of them smiled.

"Something like that," Dad said. "Sit down. Please."

If he hadn't added that "please" at the end, Finn might have balked. But the strain on their faces was too much for him to walk away from. He sat across from his dad.

"What's going on?"

"That's what we'd like to know," Dad said.

"What do you mean?"

Dad tapped his finger on the table. "You aren't taking cases. You're not looking after yourself."

Finn shook his head and started to rise. He did not have it in him to deal with this right now. Dad reached for his hand, but Finn jerked it away. It was too dangerous for them to touch at the moment. The last thing Dad needed was to see the messed-up thoughts in Finn's head. Since they shared the same psychic abilities, Dad would be able to read Finn in a heartbeat.

"Son, I know you're still having nightmares."

"Yeah, so you know it's not a good idea to touch me right now."

"Tommy." Daphne's quiet voice cut into the conversation, reminding them that they had an audience and shouldn't just let each other have it.

Dad leaned back and took a deep breath. "I'm not trying to read you. Yet. But I'm getting close."

He didn't need to see the nightmares that were plaguing Finn or feel the hopelessness that grew every day. He wasn't sure his dad's heart could take it. If they touched, Finn wouldn't be able to hide the darkness he was struggling with. He wouldn't burden his dad with that knowledge. Not when they'd almost lost him a few months ago.

Anyway, whatever this was, it would pass. It had to.

He thought about the nightmares—of the woman chained to the

wall and being tortured. The woman whose awareness Finn shared during his dreams. He felt every shuddering breath, every stab of the needle. He could feel death surrounding him. Every night, he saw her killer's face.

It was too late for Finn to go after the guy. The serial killer known as Michael Angelo had not only been caught but killed. That case was solved, but not closed. Not for Finn. He had no idea why this one victim's memories were so firmly implanted in his mind. He didn't even know who she was.

On good days, when he felt like he might be able to accomplish something, he tried to find out more. He was amazed at how little media coverage there had been after Michael's murders were discovered. Usually, serial killers were all over the papers, reporters swarming the story and splashing it on every TV screen they could reach. Not even the local media had run with the story. It had been buried.

Finn had learned more from Garrett, who had been at the scene when the cops arrived. Elsa and Rachel, two of Garrett's other friends, had both been targeted by the killer. Bad move on his part. The pair had teamed up and taken him down—permanently.

Good for them.

They both had considerable resources. Elsa could probably buy and sell Dad's bar a dozen times over. Rachel was both rich and the daughter of a powerful lawyer. The papers weren't shy about her dad's upcoming political campaign. In a town as small as Summer Park, the local papers couldn't afford to piss him off by plastering pictures of his daughter next to a serial killer.

Garrett was torn up over the whole thing and sketchy on the details. Finn knew that Dante, the guy Garrett had originally thought was a threat to Elsa, had been hurt pretty bad. Finn had cleared Dante as a suspect when Garrett first became aware that someone was after Elsa.

Finn's investigation had revealed that he and his dad weren't the only people in Summer Park with special gifts. Summer Park was a happening place for psychics.

Garrett was supporting Elsa as best he could, and now that Dante was in his good graces, Garrett would do everything in his power to help. From the sound of things, his friend Rachel needed him too. So Finn would get by on his own.

He wouldn't call, even to check in. Garrett knew Finn too well and would be able to tell that something was wrong. It would have been great to have Garrett to talk to, though. Finn missed him.

Garrett had a tight circle of friends who all supported each other. Finn was more like a satellite on the periphery. He would have loved the chance to join their club, but since he and Jazz split, that wasn't an option anymore. It never really had been.

He couldn't believe how much it still hurt that she didn't want to include him in her life anywhere outside the bedroom or Dad's bar. Finn had been in the same room as Elsa, but never been introduced. He'd never laid eyes on Rachel. Garrett didn't know Finn and Jazz had been a couple. She had insisted on secrecy.

Finn had offered her everything he had, everything he was. She hadn't wanted to be seen in public with him. Not as a couple, anyway.

In private, though... He could feel the warmth she kept locked away. Her smiles would make him forget whatever had been bothering him. Her touch had ruined him for other women, and not just because she was the only person he'd ever met that he couldn't read.

"Finn?"

Dad's voice snapped him out of his thoughts. Dammit, it was so hard to focus.

"I didn't say anything when you buried yourself in your work or when you dropped most of your friends except Garrett. But you're not even hanging out with him now. You don't talk to Daphne. Or to me."

"Dad—"

"You're isolating yourself. It's not healthy. You wake up screaming every night and drag around here all day. You haven't been right for years. You've been living like a monk ever since—"

"Not everything is about Jazz, okay!"

Finn picked up the salt shaker on the table and chucked it at the wall across the room. It embedded itself in the cheap plaster. Daphne gasped and stepped away from the counter, as if she was concerned Finn wasn't done with his tantrum.

Shit.

Finn took a deep breath and let it out slowly. He covered his eyes with one hand as he tried to get control of himself.

Nothing was in control.

Dropping his hand, he said, "I'm sorry. Look, I'll fix it later. Today." He was going to get a handle on this, dammit.

"I'll take care of it," Daphne said.

"You don't have to."

"I know," she said. "But I will."

"If you don't want to talk to us, fine," Dad said. "But you need to talk to someone. Call Garrett."

Finn was glad *that* was the name Dad had chosen. Usually when Finn was in a funk, Dad bugged him to call Jazz and see if he could patch things up. Beg her to come back to him. If only Dad knew—Finn was the one who had broken things off. Still, he doubted she'd be coming back any time soon. Or ever.

For some reason, Dad never urged Finn to move on. It was like he knew that wasn't an option.

Three years. Three years and Finn thought about her every damned day. When he wasn't thinking about the woman from his nightmares.

Finn had seen a news story about Michael Angelo the day after he'd been killed. The details were sketchy, but Michael's picture was in a little box on the screen as the reporter spoke.

"A serial killer who went by the name of Michael Angelo was caught and killed yesterday evening. Police are investigating several missing persons cases that may be related..."

Finn was shocked to recognize the killer from his nightmares. It didn't take long for him to realize he was the creepy blond guy that had been stalking Elsa. Maybe it was the readings he did trying to track Michael down, but something about the guy had made it under Finn's skin.

Even Finn's powers had gone crazy. When Finn tried to read objects, he saw the memories attached to them as if he was the person involved—not as a detached observer. It was visceral, like he was there in that moment.

Touching someone to read their thoughts was even worse. The only way he'd made it out of their heads was when they jerked away, looking at him like he was nuts.

He had to get his powers back under control. Otherwise, he really would have to become a monk. Being around people was too dangerous.

Finn stood and started toward his room. Daphne stepped in front of him.

"Where are you going?" she asked.

"Out."

He had a sudden urge to do something, to get out of the house, to leave. It was overwhelming.

The nightmares were tied to one of Michael Angelo's victims. Finn was sure of it. He had to figure out why she was haunting his dreams. To do that, he needed to find out more about who she was and what had happened. He looked back at Dad.

"I do have a case," Finn said.

And it started with Michael Angelo. That was Finn's only lead.

Chapter Three

The gallery had been her life for almost a decade. Now, Jazz could barely stand the thought of stepping inside. It had been rough after breaking up with Finn, with so many memories of the two of them together when no one else was around. That was nothing compared to this.

To hell with it. This was *her* gallery.

She unlocked the door and stalked inside, heading for the alcove that hid the alarm panel. She keyed in the code to shut it off—Finn's birthday. She should really change it, but that would mean letting go of one more part of him. At least she could keep this little piece in her life.

Ugh. Maudlin thoughts.

"Enough!" She actually waved her arm in the air to cut herself off.

Great. Now she was talking to herself.

She flipped on the lights for the foyer, then pulled her sweater over her head and walked to the front door to lock it. The white T-shirt she wore reflected from the glass.

She was trying to put on a show of having her shit together. Same black leather pants as always, matching boots up to her knees, the V-neck shirt, minimal make-up, and the same attitude. She wanted her friends to know they could count on her.

They didn't really seem to need much help anymore. That left her alone with her thoughts, which would not shut the hell up.

Peering out at the dark street gave her the creeps, especially after her conversation with Rachel. Jazz already believed ghosts walked among the living. Hearing Rachel's firsthand account of encountering them—knowing they were *everywhere*—that was a bit much.

Not the ghost I was looking for, though.

But that was a good thing. Her father had crossed over. Chloe told

Jazz during their first séance. It had taken a while for Jazz to accept it, but after all these years, she was glad. She believed he was in a happier place.

Her eyes filled with tears again. She was sick of it. People were counting on her, people she had already let down. She had to find a way to make it up to them.

Rachel was staying with Garrett. That was a huge blessing. Elsa had the necklace that would protect her during her travels. Dante was in good spirits, considering...

Jazz clenched her eyes shut and turned back toward the gallery. She didn't want to remember seeing him with his face covered in bandages. She really didn't want to remember what he had looked like when the EMTs had taken him away.

She had been so proud of Dante. So happy for him and Elsa and the life they were about to start together. A life Jazz had helped them create.

A wave of anxiety rippled through her. She had wanted Elsa happy. Wanted her to find love. That was part of what had blinded Jazz to Michael in the first place. Setting him up on a date with Elsa had been the first mistake—the one that let him into their inner circle.

How much had she talked Elsa up to Michael? What had Jazz said to Dante? She couldn't remember. But if she had been too ebullient in her praise, too obviously affectionate in her own feelings toward her best friend...

This could all be her fucking curse again.

Every fortune-teller Jazz had ever been to had given her the same reading. No matter what divination method they used, the message was always, "You are an implement of Fate." They said Jazz would play a vital role in facilitating the fates of the people in her life, helping them on the paths to their destinies.

She wished they had warned her about how dark those destinies could be.

Jazz had thought the readings were weird and amusing the first few times she visited psychics, until Fate struck her down over and over again—any time she bragged too much about someone she loved. And the stronger her emotion was, the worse the consequences would be.

It would have been easier to handle if Jazz was the one who bore the brunt of it, but the curse targeted the object of her affection. Whenever she was too happy and let anyone know, whoever she loved most paid the price.

At least this time no one had died. Well, no one who didn't deserve it.

Her friends didn't deserve what had happened to them, though. They were good people. They shouldn't be suffering.

Even doped up on medicines, Dante seemed to sense Jazz's distress and tried to ease her conscience, making jokes and pleasant conversation. It only made her feel worse.

She was used to his mask. The Phantom one was her favorite. The first time she saw his scars, she hadn't reacted well. He'd caught her off-guard, and she had already been worried about Elsa at the time.

What would he look like when the bandages came off?

"Goddammit, Jazz," she said. "Get it together."

He would still be gorgeous. He would still be Dante.

Watching Elsa dote on him earlier that afternoon should have been hilarious—like Winston's running commentary while he made everyone dinner. How could they laugh so soon? Jazz was still raw, especially after visiting them. She practically vibrated with the need to *do* something.

God, she missed Finn. If they had still been a couple, going back to his place would have been the first order of business. Or heading to the office in the gallery. She needed an outlet for her frustrations. Finn had always been so great about that, sensing when she'd had enough with talking and thinking and needed to just feel—even if he obviously had more he wanted to say.

And you wonder why he bailed.

She would be grateful to have him as a friend at this point. He was the only person she ever felt she could talk to. She gave Rachel orders, teased Elsa, chatted with Garrett, but only really talked to Finn. He knew her plans for the gallery, everything she hoped to accomplish with it.

She wanted to build up her business so that she could become an integral part of the community, could change Summer Park for the better. Hell, she had even shared her dreams for retirement—filling her twilight years with travel and new experiences.

If they were still hanging out, she could ask him for another self-defense lesson just to have someone to wail on. He'd encouraged her to let herself go as much as she wanted. He told her he could take whatever she dished out.

Apparently not. It didn't take long for him to decide he didn't want her in his life at all.

She was supposed to be over him by now. Dammit, she *was* over him. She had moved on.

She threw her sweater down on the bench seat near the door, then headed for Dante's exhibit room. Looking at his paintings would help clear her head and calm her. It might help her feel less alone.

She turned on the lights for his room and took a deep breath as the soothing artwork entered her peripheral vision.

A portrait of Elsa at her writing desk hung on the wall opposite the entrance to the exhibit. In the painting, Elsa's blonde hair glowed with gold tones that warmed her brown eyes. She was dressed in a pale pink tank top and pajamas that picked up splashes of color in the sky visible through the windows of her solarium.

Jazz loved the piece. If she thought Dante would sell it, she would buy it in a second. He had beautifully captured Elsa's balance of vulnerability and strength. The cautious hope on her features left Jazz breathless. The brushstrokes were bold and gentle at the same time. How did he do it?

She stood in the center of the room, turning to look at Dante's landscapes. She felt herself smile, her cheeks stiff and bewildered. It had been a while. His paintings lifted her spirits. If she had Elsa's ability, that lifting would be literal—Jazz would be able to go back in time to when Dante had made the pieces.

She still wouldn't be able to warn them.

This wasn't helping. Not her, not anyone. She needed a plan, a focus. Some sort of direction.

One of Dante's landscapes caught her eye. It was Elsa's backyard, which seemed as big as a freaking football field. Jazz didn't want to know how much her friend paid to make the grass green and thick in such a large space. Normally, Jazz thought of it as wasteful. But it had helped Dante create this masterpiece.

There was a wistfulness in it. He had captured the gentle swaying of the palms and pines along her property line. The painting almost seemed to move. Garrett's house was right on the other side of those trees, a much smaller dwelling on a bit less land.

For a moment, Jazz actually felt homesick.

Maybe she should throw in the towel and move back to Kansas. Join her mom on a swing on the front porch and watch her little sister raise those three adorable nieces. The idea was good on paper, but the reality would be anything but peaceful. Her sister would light into her immediately, like she always did.

"When are you going to have kids? You should really settle down with someone. You're not getting any younger you know. My kids need more playmates."

Their mom would just sit and stare at them, letting them work it out between themselves and not taking sides. Jazz knew what that side would be, though. Her mom had married and had kids, after all. Jazz just wasn't interested.

Her sister wouldn't take no for an answer. Even when Jazz had confided that she'd already gone through with a tubal ligation and had no interest in government-sanctioned ceremonies to legally bind her to another person, Mei had just said, *"You can adopt. Hire a nanny with all that art-money."*

Mei could really be a pain in the ass.

"Dammit!"

This is not helping.

Jazz needed to get out of her head. Or at least switch what she was focusing on.

There was a mountain of paperwork waiting for her in the office. Bills, schedules, emails—all the gallery work that she'd been putting off while focusing on getting her friends back on an even keel. Everyone else seemed to be doing better, but Jazz felt like she was drifting around in a fog. She was sick of it.

She headed for her office, stopping long enough in the alcove to turn off the main lights before scaling the stairs two at a time.

Chapter Four

Finn couldn't believe he was doing this. Breaking into Jazz's gallery in the middle of the night.

All his leads had come up empty. He was sure the Montgomerys were the ones burying the story. Everyone Finn talked to had been nervous. Enough so that he was considering looking into that family when he was done with this case. Bribery only went so far. The people he spoke with acted more like they were being threatened.

He didn't dare try to read their minds with his powers out of control. He had to solve this case first and get back to normal. The gallery was the only option he had left. He hoped he wasn't getting in over his head.

Luckily, he'd helped Jazz design and install her security system. He knew where the cameras pointed, where the blind spots were, and the interior layout. He even had a key to the back door, though he was sure she'd changed the lock.

He walked up to the edge of the back camera's field of view, which was a few feet away from the door. Black gloves protected him from picking up random memories and leaving prints anywhere. If anyone reviewed the footage, the long raincoat and his dad's fedora would disguise his features once he was visible. Of course, if he could get in and out like he hoped, no one would think they needed to look...

His thoughts trailed off as he looked at the doorknob. Same shade of gray, same model, same scratch on the handle where Jazz had lost her grip on an unwieldy metal sculpture and dropped it—a secret he was sworn to take to his grave, even though it hadn't been damaged.

She'd felt so bad about it, she'd purchased it from the artist and then donated it to the local hospital. And sworn to him that she'd hire people to help her move heavier pieces in the future. It was a big concession for her. She was a hands-on kind of person. In many, many ways.

He shook off the slew of memories that floated right at the back of his mind. The gallery was full of them, like when she'd given him the key on their one-month anniversary. At the time, he'd thought it was a great sign—that they were on the same page and headed toward a lifelong partnership. Turns out, she trusted him with her business. Not her heart.

It still didn't make sense that she hadn't changed out the lock. She'd had years to do it. Maybe she'd only replaced the tumbler and kept the rest of the hardware. Maybe she'd expected him to come crawling back after he left. If so, he doubted these were the circumstances she had in mind.

He pulled out his key ring. The gallery key was still on it. Ducking his head, he quickly walked to the door, then slid the key in the lock and turned it.

Click.

There was no time to reflect on what that meant—which was probably nothing. He slipped into the dark gallery and shut the door behind him, then turned to look at the motion sensors.

Green light. Bad news.

That meant someone was already in the gallery. Unless the alarm had been left off. He doubted that was the case. Jazz loved her gallery. She wouldn't leave it unprotected. At this time of night, she was probably the one hanging around. He hoped so…and he hoped not. Seeing her would be too much to deal with right now.

He needed to be quick.

The streetlamps outside the big front windows gave him just enough light to see vague shapes and doorways. Finding Michael Angelo's exhibit room was easy. It was the one roped off with police tape. He couldn't believe Jazz hadn't dealt with that yet. The doorway leading to Michael's room wasn't visible from the front foyer at least.

It wasn't like her to let anything interfere with her business. Two months was a long time to keep the gallery closed.

He pushed aside his unwelcome concern as he ducked under the yellow ribbon of plastic crisscrossing the doorway and turned on his flashlight. The small beam cut a weak line of light through the darkness.

The room was cold. Colder than the rest of the gallery. Colder than it should be. The hairs on his arms were standing on end, even under his coat. He half expected his breath to come out as fog.

What the hell?

It was probably his imagination. He was already dreading what he had to do. Terrified, actually. He was going to try to read the walls.

The chance of him getting anything was slim. He wasn't reading an object—he was reading a wall that had touched an object. And the paintings had been removed months before. The more time passed, the more the energy dissipated.

But this was a special case. The paintings that had hung on these walls were covered in blood. Blood put in place while Michael's victims were dying. They watched it flow from their bodies and be spread on the canvas.

Sick fucking bastard.

Finn was glad Rachel had killed Michael. After reliving the memories of one of Michael's victims every night for two months, Finn wanted to kill the guy himself.

What he didn't want was to read these walls. He almost hoped he would come up empty. Except then, he'd be stuck like this indefinitely. At least reading the walls would be safer than reading the paintings. Finn was counting on that.

The paintings had to be filled with terrible energy. Too much energy —memories that were so dark, Finn was afraid of becoming trapped in them, of taking on more and losing himself entirely in the memories of Michael's victims. The residue left from the paintings would be easier for him to pull back from.

Please, let me be able to pull back from this.

Best to get it over with quickly. He put away his flashlight, then pulled the glove off his left hand and stuck it in the pocket of his jeans.

He did not want to do this. He so did not want to do this. But he touched the wall anyway, his fingers splayed over the smooth surface.

Voices began to echo in Finn's mind, their words distorted as he strained to listen. Yelling. Jazz's voice mixed in. Elsa's name. A man's voice as well. Accented. Crisp. *Dante.*

Finn pushed back farther. Sweat broke out on his forehead. He was keeping as tight a hold of his powers as he could, holding on to the tenuous threads of the past while trying to not lose control in the present.

A man and a woman speaking quietly. Her voice—her energy—was so familiar, but he couldn't place her. Dante again. They were talking about Michael's paintings.

Finn pushed more.

Jazz barking orders. Just her—in her element.

His breath hitched and he felt himself leaning forward, wanting to be closer to her, even now. He stopped himself, the strain increasing as he tried to control his body and his powers at the same time.

This used to be so easy.

He paused at that moment, listening to her voice. The measured cadence of her speech was comforting. It was the last comfort he was going to have for a while. He pushed again, rewinding the memories imprinted on the wall.

The room became colder. His skin prickled and he felt a pull, like gravity was shifting and the wall wanted to suck him in. His stomach lurched and his knees weakened. He had felt similar things working some of his early cases—before he had learned how to spot trouble and brace himself for it. Domestic investigations that had gone south. Way, way south.

He sensed death. Violence. Fear.

His stomach kept churning. He didn't want to hear anyone die. And if he became lost in the memory... He sure as hell didn't want to experience it with them.

At least in his nightmares, he always woke up before the victim died.

He couldn't feel his body anymore.

The wall was sending out ripples of energy, like it wanted to cleanse itself of the paintings it had touched. Then the ripples became a spiral, pulling him in, thick as tar.

He heard someone yell. He thought it was a memory beginning, but it was male. All of Michael's victims had been women, hadn't they?

The whirlpool that ensnared him vanished. Finn was on all fours on the floor, his right knee sending sharp spikes of pain to his brain. Before he could register what was going on, a strong, slender hand clasped his right wrist and pulled that arm out from under him, then twisted it around behind his back. His assailant jammed their knee into his back, further throwing him off balance so that he fell forward onto his face.

"Struggle and I will dislocate your shoulder."

Jazz.

Christ, her voice was sexy even when she was pulling his arm out of its socket. Trying to, anyway. She twisted his arm a bit further, just like he had taught her, making pain arc through him intense enough to beat out the throbbing in his knee for a moment.

"Ow."

The pressure lessened a miniscule amount. "Finn?"

Dammit. Why was he flattered that she knew it was him from one word? His idiotic heart was doing flips in his chest, as if it didn't remember her stepping on it. Repeatedly.

"Hi, sweetie," he said. "Thought I'd drop by and check out the gallery for old time's sake."

"In the middle of the night."

"I was trying to avoid an awkward encounter."

"How's that working for you?"

Man, he'd missed the snarky sarcasm. Truly, he had. He chuckled, face against the hard wood, waiting for her to be ready to let him up. Her weight disappeared from his back. She kept her grip on his wrist, though, and used it to help him turn over.

She was standing above him, long legs silhouetted against light that filtered in from the doorway. If she dropped to her knees, they could pick up right where they left off. More meaningless sex. More dashed hopes.

Not this time.

"Do you mind?" There was a bite to his tone that seemed just about right for how he was feeling.

Instead of stepping away, she bent down, sending his heart and other body parts into overdrive. Maybe meaningless sex wasn't such a bad thing. But then she gripped both his hands to help him up, and his lust instantly flipped to panic.

They were touching skin-to-skin. Their *hands* were touching skin-to-skin. At least, one of them. It might be enough for him to be pulled into her thoughts, to lose himself there.

Jazz was the only person in his life he had never been able to read. But that was before his powers went off the rails. He didn't want to read her thoughts now. He didn't want to see that she really didn't give a damn.

"Let go!"

She jerked back her hands as if he was made of lava. "Fine. Keep your ass on the floor."

"Come on, Jazz. Could you just give me a minute to try to get my bearings?"

"Once you do, find the door and get the hell out of my gallery." She walked to the wall near the door and flipped on the lights, blinding him.

He held up his arm to shield his eyes. "Right. Go for the weak spots to disable your opponent."

"That's what you taught me to do." She let out a sigh. "What are you doing here, Finn?"

Something in her voice was off. She sounded tired in a way that went beyond the physical. He'd never known her to be anything but charged with enough energy to power the state. Lifting himself on his elbows, he finally laid eyes on her again.

Damn...

Her skin was flawless, shining over her smooth cheekbones and highlighting the graceful curve of her jaw. Her black hair fell over her shoulders in thick locks. It was longer than he remembered. She looked thinner too. She didn't have the weight to spare, and his worry grew.

Her eyes were the same, though. Two spheres of onyx sparkling with intelligence and passion. Her lips were full and lush. He couldn't stop staring at them.

Memories flooded his mind, but at least this time, they were his own. He remembered those lips pressed against his body, how her long legs felt wrapped around his waist, how she would smile at him and make him feel as if he was the only man on Earth.

Finn's breath caught in his chest. Gorgeous wasn't a strong enough word to describe Jazz. Her presence filled the room, commanded him to focus on her and her alone.

"Stop looking at me like that."

Finn didn't have to ask what she meant. He scowled and lay back flat on the floor, covering his face with his hands. Jazz was forged from iron. Unyielding. No wonder he could never read her.

"Are you okay?"

"No, I'm not," he said.

That tentative edge was in her voice again. She almost sounded vulnerable. Shit, what the hell had happened? Where was her unshakeable confidence? Finn rolled onto his side, then rose on all fours.

"Let me help you."

He probably still couldn't read her. If she only touched him through his coat, he'd be fine either way.

"Thanks."

She held on to his arm as he tested putting weight on the leg she had kicked out from under him. Even when he was steady, she didn't let go.

He wanted to bury his hands in her hair and kiss her and never stop. Hell, maybe melting into her wouldn't be such a bad thing. Except the unshakeable woman of iron he had dated was holding him with a trembling hand, and for the first time since he'd known her, there was uncertainty in her eyes.

Which only made him want to kiss her more. To hold her close and tell her he would make it right. Whatever was wrong, he would fix it.

One case at a time...

There was someone else he needed to help first. As much as he could at this point. The woman from his nightmares. He had to know what happened to her, why she was haunting his dreams. Hopefully then his powers would come back under control and the nightmares would stop.

"I'm working a case that involves one of Michael Angelo's victims."

"One of..." Jazz's gaze became unfocused for a moment. She shook her head brusquely. Her lips tightened and her eyebrows pinched together. Her eyes started to blaze.

Uh-oh.

"What do you need?" she said.

"I was just going to read the walls and see what I picked up."

Jazz was one of four people who knew about Finn's ability. The others were Garrett, Daphne, and Dad—who shared the gift. Apparently, it was hereditary and passed through sons. His line would end with Finn, which was okay by him. He had family up north to carry it on.

"You think you can get something from the wall even though the paintings are gone?" she asked.

"I'm hoping so. Especially since you've kept the place roped off." He gestured toward the yellow ribbon. "You thinking of making this a permanent display?"

"I'm thinking of burning it to the ground."

Shit. That was...extreme.

She crossed her arms and nodded. "Hurry up and get it over with. I don't like being here."

Finn felt his hatred of Michael ratchet up another notch. The bastard had driven Jazz out of her own gallery. There was no way she would have let this room stay as it was if she'd been around. It shook him to realize how deeply Michael had affected her. Finn didn't want to keep her there any more than necessary.

"I don't suppose I could get a little privacy?"

"I'm staying. Deal with it."

His jaw clenched at his most hated catchphrase. The only thing about their breakup he had been whole-heartedly grateful for was that he would never hear those words from her again.

And now she was about to see him use his wonked-out powers. This night was getting better and better.

He would have to stay in control. He *could* stay in control. Repeating that thought, he turned back to the wall and pressed his hand to its cool surface.

Chapter Five

Jazz had returned to the gallery to try to set at least one corner of her world right. Instead, everything had been turned upside-down by finding Finn in the Cursed Display Room. That was what Jazz was going to call it forevermore. At least in her head.

Finn Connelly, the great love of her life. Who had kicked her to the curb before they had a chance to experience how great they could be together.

He looked like hell. Well, in an *I'm-too-sexy-to-do-laundry-or-shave* kind of way. The white tank top he wore under that ridiculous raincoat was rumpled and she wouldn't be surprised if he'd been wearing those same jeans for a week. His level of stubble was dangerously close to becoming a beard, and... She wanted to kiss him. Her skin burned from it, her heart pounded, and even her stomach seemed to be trying to reach out and touch him.

Just touch him...

Every part of her body was in agreement. But not her mind.

This was the guy who had broken her heart. He was the one who walked away. And she would *not* go crawling back to him. She wouldn't beg him to take her back, no matter how much she wanted to.

Even obviously exhausted, Finn was the most gorgeous man Jazz had laid eyes on. And hands... And mouth... And...

Something was wrong. His breath was coming out in little grunts. He raised his right hand slowly, as if someone or some*thing* was trying to hold it down and he was fighting against them.

He punched the wall. Hard. Hard enough to hurt. She was surprised the drywall held. The impact propelled him backward, away from the wall. He ended in a crouching, fighting stance, eyes wild, glancing around the room as if he expected to be attacked.

Jazz knew better than to approach anyone standing like that, even before Finn's lessons. She waited for his breathing to calm, his body to straighten and relax.

"Are you okay?" she asked.

He didn't reply. He seemed to be looking right through her.

"Finn?"

"Yeah?" He spoke as if he hadn't heard her.

"I asked if you're okay."

She watched his throat work as he swallowed. He put both hands on his face and shook his head, then dropped his arms to his sides and let out a huge breath.

"I'm fine," he said.

"Seriously? That is the biggest load of bull."

He glared at her, but she didn't care. He had scared her. She was sick of being scared for people she cared about, and dammit she still cared about him.

"What the hell was that?" she asked.

"That was me using my powers."

"I've seen you use your powers before. It never looked like that."

"This is a special case."

No kidding. What had he seen that affected him so profoundly? She couldn't believe that even an echo from the paintings would do that to him. Then again, she'd seen with her own eyes what Michael had done to Rachel. The mangled flesh on her wrists, the waxy cast to her skin from so much blood loss—blood *theft*.

Jazz didn't let herself think about what had happened in that garage before she and the police showed up. She couldn't bear it. She wasn't sure she could stand watching Finn try to read the wall again, either.

You can and you will, if it helps him.

"Did you find what you're looking for?" she asked.

"No."

Her stomach sank. "Finn…"

"You don't have to stay."

But she did. She absolutely did. Dante still had multiple surgeries ahead of him. The bruises on Elsa's neck had only faded a few weeks before, and Rachel was trapped in Garrett's house until they could figure out a way to keep ghosts from haunting her. Michael might not be among the ghosts bothering her, but even the residue of what he had done was still hurting people.

There was no *fucking* way she would let Michael hurt Finn from beyond the grave. Not if she had anything to say about it.

"I'm staying. Tell me how to help."

His mouth opened, then snapped shut. There was something she could do, but he didn't want to tell her.

Typical. They had never really been partners.

She might not want a marriage contract, but she still wanted a companion. Part of that was having someone to lean on and part was wanting to be the one giving help. It had never been easy for either of them to ask.

"I'll get it out of you," she said. "You know I will."

"Yeah." He sighed. "If I seem to get…stuck, snap me out of it. Just go for the left knee this time. The right one's already taken a beating."

He gave her his best cocky grin. She saw right through it. Still, that flash of teeth, all the memories that gorgeous fake smile brought out of her made her stomach flood with butterflies. Her heart was pounding again and heat started to build deep within her.

And she'd thought she was over him. What a joke.

Finn must have grown tired of her meaningful stare. He headed to another spot where a painting had been. The track lighting was still set up for the exhibit, making it obvious where the pictures were supposed to hang.

Jazz had considered Michael's work dark, brilliant, and compelling. Her stomach cramped at the thought.

Each space represented a lost life. Each one had left a family grieving that would never find closure. Michael had carried the names of his victims to the grave. She hadn't thought of that, either. She'd been too busy taking care of her friends. Still in shock over what had happened.

All those people... If Finn could help even one family find closure, Jazz wanted to help him. Finally, she could *do* something. Something to try to make things better. To set the scales right. It was a start, at least.

Finn shook his left hand, like he was trying to remove any residue from the first spot he'd checked, then he placed it on the wall. He was wearing a glove on his right hand. She'd never seen him wear gloves before. That and the coat were weird wardrobe choices for Florida. *Says she of the leather pants.*

Working on such a disturbing case, it made sense that he'd want to protect himself from seeing things when he wasn't ready. Maybe the gloves were supposed to help with that.

When he'd told her about his powers, he said they worked primarily through his hands. He could read memories off objects and actually read peoples' minds if he maintained contact. Luckily, he couldn't read her for some reason. The idea of having sex with someone who could read her thoughts during skin contact was not a turn-on.

Jazz wasn't sure how he was getting anything from a wall that touched a painting. The energy imbedded in the paintings must have been intense. She thought of Elsa and her ability to travel through art by using the emotional energy infused into creating or even observing it.

Finn's powers didn't seem to be based on any kind of heightened emotion, though. He could read anything that happened around an object. He said the further back he went, the blurrier the memories became. The paintings had been gone for almost two months. He had to be pushing his limits.

He started to lean toward the wall he was reading. That didn't seem good. He pressed his forehead against the surface, bringing his right hand up to help support himself. He shifted his weight to his left leg. She had kicked his right knee pretty hard when she'd thought he was a burglar.

"Finn? You okay?"

He didn't respond at first. When he did, his voice sounded strange. Lighter, more breathy.

"You are so beautiful."

He turned his right hand and ran the backs of his knuckles over the wall's surface. That was weird.

"Look at me," he said. "Look at me!"

Jazz jumped at his sudden shout. The change in his demeanor was so fast and unexpected.

"What the hell, Finn."

But he didn't turn. He didn't even register that she was there. Did that mean he was stuck or was he just immersed in a memory? She didn't like that he was acting things out. Besides being creepy as hell, he was reading the memories of *a murderer*.

Finn pinched his index finger and thumb together, like he was offering the wall a treat. She had seen that gesture before. Michael used to tip Rachel's face toward him by putting his hand under her chin that way.

"There, now. Isn't that better," Finn said. "You shouldn't have spilled the blood, Nicole. I can't finish your portrait without more."

"Shit!" Jazz's stomach seemed to drop through the floor.

"Don't worry. I'll get you something to eat and drink. We'll spend a bit more time together than I planned. That's all right, though. I forgive you. This is my first masterwork. Delays are to be expected."

Was this what Finn meant by getting stuck? She thought he meant he could get stuck viewing a memory, not that he'd actually become part of it. She never would have let him read the wall if she'd known.

She grabbed his shoulders and pulled, but he didn't budge. She yanked on just his right arm, but that didn't work either. He was half a foot taller and at least a hundred pounds heavier than she was. She'd always loved how his body was all muscle, admired how he sculpted himself. Now she just wished he was smaller.

He shifted closer to the wall, as if he was going to lie against it. She had no idea what that would do to him. There was still a narrow space, and she slipped into it, putting herself between Finn and the wall.

His body pressed against hers, bringing back her own memories. They hadn't been able to get enough of each other. Any closet, any private space was fair game. They'd had sex in her office in the gallery more times than she could count.

This time, her skin crawled at the close contact. This time, it wasn't Finn.

Finn was thick with muscle—carefully controlled muscle. He had always seemed to envelop her, melding himself to her body as if they were made for each other. It made her feel delicate and strong at the same time. Finn owned himself, his body and his movement. The body pressing against hers was tense, hesitant.

"Finn, look at me."

She put her hands on his cheeks, forcing him to face her. The pale blue-gray of his irises had hints of a brighter, darker blue bleeding in around their edges.

What the hell?

"Dammit, Finn!"

Pain had snapped him out of it before. Maybe it could again. She slapped him, hard. He didn't even blink. The blue kept seeping into his eyes as he murmured disturbing things to a woman long since dead.

"Finn, please…"

She slapped him again, even harder. This time, he blinked and shook his head. Jazz used the opportunity, bracing herself against the wall and shoving his chest as hard as she could. They stumbled away from the wall together.

He shook his head, then turned toward the ceiling. He covered his face with his hands as he took deep breaths. On the last burst of an exhalation, he lowered his head and hands, then opened his eyes.

Pale blue again. He was himself.

Chapter Six

"What the hell was that?"

Finn had never heard Jazz yell so loud. His head already hurt, and the noise was like a jackhammer on his skull.

"Could you keep it down a little bit?"

"No, I can't keep it down! You need to tell me what just happened."

Finn ran his hands over his face. His cheek stung like crazy. "Why does my face hurt?"

"Because I slapped you. Twice."

He let out a snort, then walked to the low viewing bench that ran along the middle of the room and sat down.

"I hope you didn't enjoy it too much."

Her rage kicked up higher, rolling from her in palpable waves that he didn't need his powers to detect. The volume of her voice lessened, but that just made her more intimidating.

"Fuck you."

Damn. Yeah, that was past the line.

"Sorry."

"Your eyes changed color," she said. "The things you were saying, it was like you were *turning into Michael*. You just scared the shit out of me."

His eyes had changed? That was scary for him too. He knew he was having trouble pulling himself from other people's memories, but he didn't think it was manifesting externally. He didn't think his powers *could* manifest that way. It brought up too many terrifying possibilities.

"I'm sorry. I didn't know that would happen." He leaned forward with his elbows on his knees and put his head in his hands. "I don't know what I'm doing, Jazz. I'm trying to fix things, but I just can't put them right."

"What are you trying to fix?" The fire had left her voice.

"Me. My powers."

In his periphery, he saw her stoop to pick up Dad's hat. He hadn't even realized it had fallen along with him earlier. She set it next to him, then joined him on the bench.

"Start at the beginning."

Feeling her body so close to his, he didn't trust himself to look at her while he spoke. The need to touch her was almost overwhelming. He stared at the floor, clasping his hands in front of him. He wished he could hold her. Hell, he wished she would hold him, but it was way too late for that.

"Two months back, I woke up from this screaming nightmare. Dad came running into the room, asking what was going on. I didn't know. I tried to shake it off. Told him it was nothing."

"But it wasn't."

"Yeah." Finn nodded. "It was something. Big time."

"Did Tommy believe you?"

Her tone warmed just mentioning Dad. It was so obvious how much they loved each other. Finn never understood why she was fine with becoming part of his family, but wouldn't tell her own or even any of their friends they were dating. Old indignities tried to rise up in him, but he was too tired for them to take hold.

"At first. But the nightmares didn't stop. Every night, I'm either sleeping so hard no one can wake me, or I wake everybody up screaming. It's been wearing on them."

"Them?"

Right. Daphne had moved in after Jazz was out of Finn's life. He didn't know why the thought of telling Jazz made him uncomfortable. There had never been the tiniest spark between him and Daphne. She was much more interested in Dad. If he'd stop being blinded by the difference in their ages, he'd see it.

"The new bartender has been living in our guest room."

He glanced over at her in time to see her smile, the tension easing in her features. He caught a glimpse of the face she had shared with him and his dad and no one else—not that he'd ever seen, anyway. No cockiness, no bravado. Just Jazz. It only lasted a moment, but it was enough to send him reeling.

"Finally." She let out a brief laugh. "I told you guys you needed more help."

"Yeah, you were right, as always. Daphne's been a big help in and out of the bar."

Jazz went completely still. From what he could see, she wasn't even breathing.

Crap.

"We're not...together. Never have been."

Goddammit, why was he compelled to explain himself? He could practically hear ice crackling around her, a thick coat of cold blocking her off. That was another thing he hadn't missed—her freezing him out.

"Not my business," she said.

Yeah. That was a familiar sentiment.

She launched herself from the bench and headed for the wall. He expected her to lean against it, cross her arms, and glare at him. Her arms were already lifting when she balked, then turned away and started to pace. She didn't so much cross her arms as hug herself as she walked.

That was new. She probably didn't want to touch the walls after what she had seen and heard from Finn. He wished he could un-see it himself.

Nicole had been a thin blonde woman with blue eyes. Similar to the one in Finn's dreams, but not the same. Nicole was much smaller, for one thing.

In his dreams, Michael used a needle, tubing, and jars to siphon blood from his victim's body. Nicole...

Her body had been covered in cuts. Michael was using a knife.

Finn ran his hands over his face again. If he thought this case was about bringing Michael down, he would be all over it. He'd be charging in and reading everything he could to bring the bastard to justice.

But Michael was already dead. Finn seriously didn't know what he was accomplishing with any of this, aside from figuring out the identities of the victims. Like Nicole.

Did she have a family somewhere? Were they still hoping, waiting for her to come home? How would they react if Finn walked in and told them she was gone? He hoped they never found out what had been done to her.

"Tell me about the nightmares." Jazz's clipped voice was commanding. Somehow, that reassured him—made him feel that he wasn't in this alone. At least for the moment.

"I'm inside someone else's body, sharing their experience. I'm chained to a wall in darkness. My wrists are burning, my arms sore where they aren't numb. There's cold cement under my knees and my lungs are full of stale air."

Jazz stopped pacing and stared at him. He knew that look. It would be a while before she spoke. She wanted more information. He could provide it.

"I've only been able to see and hear things in dreams before. These are different. I have all my senses. I can feel everything, and I... Whoever it was, she was so scared. They always end the same way. Light floods the room, and this guy comes in."

"Michael Angelo." Jazz said the name like a dirge. Appropriate.

"I recognized him from the news. I can see his face clearly in the nightmares. I know he was the one hurting me. Hurting her."

"Do you know who she was?"

He looked over at Jazz and let out a short chuff of breath. "I wish. Maybe then I'd have a clue what the hell is going on. I mean, why am I having these dreams? I didn't touch anything or anyone related to this case. I would have known if I did. Nothing like this has ever happened before."

"What did Tommy say about it?"

"I haven't told him."

"Why not?"

Finn let out a sigh that felt like it emptied him out. "Dad had a heart attack not too long ago. We almost lost him." Finn's voice cracked a bit, but he didn't let it slow him down. "It scared the crap out of me. He's worried enough already. If he finds out my powers are…"

He paused when he looked up at her. All the blood had drained from her face and her mouth was hanging open.

"You okay?"

"I…um…" She shook her head and swayed on her feet.

Finn leapt up and grabbed her, pulling her against his chest. She gripped his arms tight, taking slow, steady breaths. She murmured something too quiet for him to hear.

"What was that?"

"You should have called me!"

She shoved him hard. Pushing him away. Always fucking pushing him away. She staggered to the bench and sat down with her head between her knees.

After a few moments, she said, "Is he going to be okay?"

Affection and jealousy were fighting it out inside of Finn. She loved his dad so much. Why the hell couldn't she love Finn that much? Like he loved her—passionately, completely.

"The doctors say he needs to be careful. Dad did their rehab and is seeing a specialist." And the bills were still rolling in. Bills Finn was doing his best to intercept so Dad didn't worry more. "He's exercising more and we're watching what we eat. And he isn't working so many late hours."

"Okay." She let out a shaky breath. "That's good."

She was worse off than he thought. It made sense, though. She had almost lost Elsa and Rachel. Hearing about Dad when Jazz was already off her game… Yeah, he understood why it was hitting her hard. He was glad to know at least she still cared about his dad.

"Has Tommy ever been haunted?" she asked.

Her voice was a little muffled since her face was pointed at the floor. Finn couldn't have heard her right.

"What?"

"Haunted." Jazz sat back up, looking more stable. "Has he ever run into any ghosts?"

Finn laughed and shook his head. Jazz didn't join him.

"Oh, you're serious."

Her stare turned into a glare and he cleared his throat.

"He's never mentioned it. And he would have told me when he taught me about our powers."

Jazz nodded. "We need to talk to Tommy. I get that you don't want to worry him. We'll figure out a way—"

"Hold up." Strolling down his own memory lane had been... awkward and uncomfortable. But he was done. Jazz was a distraction. Being around her was too damned painful. "There is no *we. I* will figure out a way."

"Not this time. I'm in, whether you like it or not."

"All I need is more time with this room. I already have a name now. Nicole. I can check with missing persons files and see if I can find more leads."

"I'm. In. And there is no way in hell I'm letting you read more of these walls. Not after almost losing you like that."

"Look, your concern is touching, but—"

"You try, and I'll have you arrested for trespassing."

He stared at her, stunned for a moment. "You wouldn't."

She cocked an eyebrow at him, then stood and pulled out her phone. Yeah. She would. He shook his head and smiled.

"Same old Jazz."

If he could manage half of her self-control and determination, he doubted his powers would be acting up at all. Maybe having her along would help. She could keep him from losing himself in the memories he read. He just needed to be sure he didn't lose his heart again.

Right. As if it wasn't already hers.

He rose to his feet without realizing how close she was standing. A few inches of space separated their bodies. It might as well have been an entire universe.

Chapter Seven

Jazz wished that Finn was farther away. Or closer. She wasn't sure which she would prefer. He was too close for her to ignore the effect he always had on her, but not close enough for her to really enjoy it.

Now that he wasn't trying to crush her against the wall, she was back to appreciating his size. He wasn't nearly as tall as Garrett—then again, who was?—but Finn was packed with muscle. She could see the outlines of his pecs through his tank top, traces of his chest hair peeking out.

Do not think about Finn's chest.

She needed to focus on the issue at hand. He was trying to shut her out again, and she wouldn't stand for it.

"I'm not going to let this go," she said.

"I kind of figured."

She felt herself relax an infinitesimal amount. At least their history helped him know when she wasn't about to back down.

"I'm not saying you shouldn't try to figure this out. I'm just saying you can be smarter about it. If these walls are pulling you into Michael's memories so strongly that you can't find your way out on your own, maybe you should try less visceral spots."

The paintings were physically linked to the women Michael had killed. Strongly linked. It would be as bad as reading the chains in his garage. Jazz stifled a shiver at the memory of red-crusted metal— Rachel's blood on the manacles attached to those chains.

There would be other places in Michael's house that Finn could read, though. Places that might not be as strongly connected to Michael but could still give them useful information. She doubted Finn would have come to the gallery if he knew where Michael lived. They could go there and try to find another lead. Very carefully.

"You sound like you have something in mind," Finn said.

"I do, but I'm not telling you until we've talked to Tommy."

Tommy. She couldn't believe she'd get to talk to him. She had missed him too. Her head started to swirl again as she thought about his heart attack. She could have lost him without having a chance to say goodbye. Just like she'd lost her own father.

Never *think about Father.*

Tommy. Think about Tommy.

She wanted to see him with her own eyes—to know he was okay. There was no way Finn could move on without her this time. He was stuck with her.

"I'll drive," she said.

"Aren't you afraid people will see us together?"

They were *not* going to have this argument again. Not after all these years. Not now.

"I have tinted windows."

He glared at her, but then let out a sigh and shook his head. "Fine."

She had expected more of a fight. Finn giving in so easily only made her more worried.

"Come on, then."

Her SUV was parked right in front of the gallery. In this part of town, shops closed up and people went home early. At least, on a boring Wednesday night. She could actually find parking on the street.

"That is a big-ass SUV," Finn said. "I thought you didn't want to own a car."

Jazz shrugged. The car beeped as she hit the button to unlock the doors. "I need it for transporting art."

She had removed all but the seats right after buying it and laid out a tarp for extra padding. She wasn't even sure where the seats were anymore. Maybe somewhere in the gallery or the storage unit for her apartment. At the moment, the back space of the vehicle was empty and roomy. Big enough for two.

Dammit. Stop thinking about Finn. Especially that way.

They climbed in and buckled up. Finn was sitting next to her. It was like a dream. If only the circumstances were different.

The bar was halfway across town. He broke the silence after a few minutes.

"Dad's been reading tons of Westerns since the doctors told him to take it easy." Finn fiddled with the brim of Tommy's hat. "When the library ran out of new ones, he started reading romances set in the west. Now he's hooked and reads anything he can get his hands on, no matter where or when it's set. He especially likes the historicals, though."

"I can absolutely picture your dad reading a romance novel."

Jazz laughed, and Finn joined her. She couldn't believe how good it felt to hear. Her heart skipped from the sound. What kind of a fool was she?

"Yeah, he's not shy about liking them. He's been chatting up the regulars, going on and on about the stories."

She imagined Tommy leaning across the bar, holding a dog-eared paperback with the cover bent backward as he pointed out a particular passage. Tommy had a way with people. He was always kind, an incredible listener, and gave good advice when asked. Everybody loved him.

It warmed her heart to think of Finn and his dad still living together and taking care of each other. Talking to Finn like this... It was bringing back memories of the first few weeks when they were dating, before things had become complicated.

"You're still above the bar?"

"We like it above the bar," he snapped.

And the moment passed. "I know you do. I didn't mean anything by it. I just thought you might have moved into your own place at some point."

"Dad needs me."

"I get that. I was thinking about before his..." She couldn't even bring herself to say it. She shook her head. "It's been years, Finn. Things happen. *Change* happens."

Finn let out a huge sigh and ran his fingers through his hair. It was down-soft. She knew.

"I'm sorry. It's been hard to keep a lid on my temper with all of this crap going on."

"It's understandable." Rather than wade into the nebulous waters of their emotions, she pulled on her pragmatic façade. "When did your powers start acting up?"

"The day Michael Angelo was killed. I ran it down with the little bit of information I could find. I never would have guessed such a big story could be squelched like this was."

"It was a good thing. The people involved have been through enough."

Jazz felt her fingers tighten on the wheel. She wished she could break it in two. It might make her feel better since there wasn't a damned thing she could do to change what had happened to her friends.

"I know Elsa was involved." He spoke gently, but Jazz felt as if she'd been slapped. She stared at him, wondering how he had found out.

Elsa had ridden in the SUV a couple of times since that night, but Finn's hands were carefully folded in his lap. His gloves were on. While she stared, he suddenly reached for the wheel, jerking it toward him.

"Watch the road!"

Adrenaline flooded her system. Jazz looked back through the windshield at the parked car she had almost side-swiped.

When her heart stopped pounding in her throat, she asked, "How did you know?"

"That we were about to crash? I looked out the window."

"You know that isn't what I meant."

She heard him sigh.

"I didn't read your car, if that's what you're worried about. I know how you feel about that." He was quiet for a few moments, then said, "Garrett told me."

She let out an exasperated burst of air. The more word spread about Elsa and Rachel's involvement, the more chances there were for people to start bothering them about what had happened. Jazz was going to have to remind Garrett of that fact the next time she saw him.

"I know you're blaming Garrett, but I would have figured it out anyway. I can see how upset you are about the whole thing and know the only person you care about that much is Elsa."

Jazz let out a snort and shook her head. "I care about a lot of people."

Including the dumbass sitting next to her. She bit her tongue before saying more. Fate was always listening.

"Yeah."

That edge of tension she hated so much was coming to his voice again. It had always preceded their fights.

Instead of a snarky retort or escalation, he asked, "Is she doing okay? I haven't heard from Garrett in a while."

"She'll be fine. Her boyfriend got the worst of it."

"How's Dante doing?"

"He'll be fine." She refused to believe otherwise.

Finn seemed to sense that he shouldn't push that line of inquiry. He let out a little scoff. "I still can't believe Elsa's shacking up with someone."

"She's an amazing woman. Why is it so hard to believe?"

"I don't know. I guess I just imagined you two becoming spinsters together."

"You think *spinster* is part of my life's plans?"

She glanced over at him. He was glaring at her. Then he looked away.

Yeah. There it was.

She had always guessed that Finn wanted the whole package. Marriage, kids, picket fence. Jazz wasn't interested. She didn't need rings or ceremonies to bind herself to Finn. He shouldn't either. And even though Jazz loved her nieces and kids in general, motherhood was not for her.

She'd tried to bring up the subject once while they were dating. He'd scared her off from the topic before she could ask if it was a deal-breaker.

"Kids? Kids are great. I have all of these cousins with bunches of them. I wish I had nieces and nephews to enjoy, but...you know. Curses of an only child."

The whole conversation had been so awkward and his reference to curses had freaked her out. They'd only been dating for a few weeks at the time. His position seemed pretty clear, though. She had hoped maybe after they'd been together longer if she brought it up again it wouldn't be an obstacle. He'd left her before she had a chance.

She'd known she was fooling herself anyway.

"Yeah, well, I guess it's just going to be me knitting on the porch in a rocking chair."

He let out a sharp laugh.

"What is it now?"

He ignored her cutting tone.

"That is the funniest mental image. No matter how I try to picture it, I always see you standing up and throwing aside the needles, and saying, 'Seriously?' before storming off the porch."

At least he understood that domesticity wasn't for her.

They didn't have a chance to say more. Jazz pulled up to the curb in front of his place. A few cars still dotted the street. The bar had probably just closed. Her heart beat in her throat as they walked toward the front door.

Tommy had named the place Connelly's and their name was painted on a tasteful and understated sign that stuck out above the street. Jazz had tried to get Tommy to let her upgrade the storefront, but he wouldn't budge. He had teased her that she'd have to wait till Finn ran the place, since she had more sway over him.

The windows were coated with opaque dark green paint to give the people inside privacy. Finn popped his dad's hat onto his head and opened the door, then held it in place with his foot. Even wearing gloves, he seemed not to want to touch anything for too long. That handle was probably layered with memories, some of them recent, most of them clouded from drink.

She slipped past him quickly so he could get away from the door.

Connelly's... She had missed this place too. The smells had changed. At closing, the scent of cleaner was front and center. But instead of the air being thick with grease, it was lighter. The sharpness of smoked meat was the main note she detected instead of the fryer.

"When did you guys start doing BBQ?" she asked.

"Daphne talked dad into setting up a smoker. She's a really good cook."

Daphne again. Jazz's replacement.

"I know how you feel about BBQ outside of KC," Finn said, "but you really should give it a try."

There was laughter in his tone, and for a moment, Jazz could almost believe things were back to the way they had been before. They used to meet at the bar most weeknights. The three of them would eat dinner together and talk, then Tommy would go to bed. Finn and Jazz would sit up and talk before finding their way to his room.

Jazz couldn't care less about Daphne's BBQ. She *could* care a hell of a lot less about Daphne cozying up to the Connellys.

The woman of the hour stepped out from the kitchen—at least, Jazz assumed it was Daphne. She held a plastic tub that reeked of bleach in one hand and a rag in the other.

Why couldn't she be ugly?

No such luck. Her black hair was lustrous and hung down to her shoulder blades in soft curls. She had a pale complexion and eyes that were a rich mahogany brown. Her bone structure was delicate, like the rest of her.

Great. The pair of them were Snow White and Prince Charming. Finn said they weren't a couple, but it was only a matter of time.

Not my business. Not anymore.

"Hi Finn." Daphne had a soft, gentle voice. "Who's your friend?"

Finn hesitated. Yeah, they weren't a couple.

"This is Jazz."

Daphne's big cartoon eyes widened and her jaw dropped.

Enough! Jazz pulled her uncharitable thoughts to task.

Daphne was helping Finn and his dad with the bar. That was more than Jazz had been able to do the last couple of years. If Finn and his dad were happy and Daphne was part of that, Jazz should be hugging the woman, not letting catty thoughts run through her mind. Jazz wouldn't heap her own issues on someone else. She would deal with it.

Daphne set her cleaning supplies on the bar. "You're Jazz?"

Daphne knew who Jazz was? Why would Finn and Tommy still be talking about her after all this time?

Daphne stammered and smiled. A genuine smile. Jazz didn't want to trust it. She felt herself warming up to Daphne anyway.

"It's nice to meet you," Daphne said. "I've heard so much—"

Daphne looked over Jazz's shoulder and shook her head as if parroting someone else's movement. Changing tack, she said, "I mean...I've heard nothing. Nothing at all about you."

Jazz couldn't stop herself from laughing. "Wow, you are a terrible liar."

Daphne gave Jazz another of those heart-melting smiles. "I've never put much effort into it. The truth is usually good enough for me."

"That makes two of us."

"Daphne, when you're done wiping down the bar—" Tommy stepped through the door that led to the kitchen.

Jazz felt like she'd been punched in the stomach. Tommy had acted like a father to her—had *felt* like a father. He had helped fill that gaping hole in her heart. She had thought she and Finn were headed toward a lifelong commitment. She had let herself get attached. Too attached. And she'd been paying for it for years.

She should have known better—that she and Finn wouldn't work out. There were too many obstacles.

You don't name your bar "Connelly's" without expecting a long line of heirs to run the place.

Tommy smiled at her. "Well, I'll be. Jazz Zhou. Sorry, I mean Zhou Jazz. I never could quite get the hang of that."

Dammit, she was tearing up. She forced herself to smile back. Not that smiling at Tommy took much effort.

"Hey, Tommy." Her voice was high and tight.

Tommy made her feel like a teenager. Ever since the moment he'd walked in on her in Finn's bed—naked after they'd slept together for the first time. Tommy had blushed furiously while trying to make conversation until Finn walked in and introduced her.

Tommy had quickly retreated saying, "You kids have fun."

Her father had never walked in on Jazz with a boy. Jazz hadn't started dating till college and her family couldn't afford visits back then. They had planned to come out to celebrate Jazz's graduation.

They hadn't made it.

And now Tommy was staring at her with that quirky smile half hidden under his ridiculous mustache. He looked older. More frail, but still strong. Like time was slowly wearing him away.

Tommy walked over to her and stared at her for a moment. Then he said, "Come here," and pulled her into a hug.

Keep it together. Keep it together.

How was she supposed to do that when everything she ever wanted was right next to her and completely out of reach? Finn was a few steps away, she was surrounded by the place that felt more like home than anywhere she had ever lived, and she had let it all slip through her fingers. She had messed up.

"It's good to see you." She forced out the words.

Finn put his hand on her shoulder. Clenching her eyes shut, she fought the tears away. They didn't need to see how much she…needed them.

Deal with it, Jazz. You made your choices. Now live with them.

Chapter Eight

"We need to talk," Finn said.

He might have underestimated how much Jazz cared about his dad. She was clinging to him like her life depended on it. Finn shoved down the jealousy that was trying to rise up in him for the millionth time.

"In a minute, son. I'm not quite ready to let go."

Neither was Jazz, from the look of it.

Finn used to try to comfort himself by thinking that Jazz wasn't affectionate with anyone in public. He wanted to believe that was why she only ever scowled at him when other people were in the room. He had seen her give Elsa and Garrett quick hugs, though. And she was never shy about hugging his dad in front of people.

When it was just the three of them in the bar, she seemed to smile all the time. She'd pat their shoulders and give them hugs. Hell, she would even sit in Finn's lap with a beer when they were having their late-night discussions. She'd acted like they were a family.

And when it was just the two of them...they'd been so much more. He could never read her, and yet always felt more connected to her than anyone he had ever known. He didn't think he'd ever understand how she could seem so open one moment, then build a wall of ice the next.

He'd ask to take her out on the town, and she'd respond with stony silence. He would yet again beg her to tell Garrett or anyone that they were dating, and she'd shake her head and tell him no. Any time he tried to talk to her about it, she shut down. It drove him crazy.

Finn had to stop thinking about the past. She needed him right now. He would be there for her. He had never seen her so shaken. He knew she loved his dad, but still...

He kept his hand on her shoulder, hoping to lend her support and for a moment feel that connection they had all shared. Jazz finally stepped back. She actually ran a fingertip under her eye and leaned against Finn's side.

He wanted to wrap his arms around her and nuzzle her hair. If Daphne hadn't been in the room, he might have, but Jazz had conditioned him too well. No affection in front of anyone but Tommy.

Anyway, it only took her a second to realize what she was doing. She stiffened and moved away.

"It's damned good to see you, Jazz." Dad cast a glance at Finn that was all too clear. *"Don't screw this up again."*

"I can finish in the kitchen," Daphne said. "Why don't you three go upstairs?"

Dad shook his head. "No. We're all family here. Come on and pull up a chair."

"It needs to be upstairs, Dad." Finn started for the front door, but Jazz ducked in front of him.

"I'll do it." She locked the door, keeping Finn from having to touch it again.

"Thanks."

Dad was staring. Better to get this over with and keep him from building false hopes.

"Is that my hat?"

"Yeah." Finn took it off and handed it over.

Dad ran his fingertips over the brim. He was reading it, trying to figure out what was going on.

Finn sighed. "Can we go upstairs? There's way too much...ambient energy down here."

"All right."

Dad looked worried. The last thing he needed was more stress. Finn followed the group up the stairs, letting Jazz and the others go first. Once they reached the kitchen, Daphne took up her favorite spot leaning against the counter in front of the sink. Dad hung his hat on its hook on the wall, then sat at the table with Finn. Jazz sort of hovered nearby.

How to begin? Finn rubbed the bridge of his nose briefly, feeling a headache starting to build. He needed to just come out with it.

"You guys know something's wrong. I didn't want to worry you, but I haven't been able to fix things myself."

Tommy nodded. "What's going on?"

"My powers aren't working right. I'm getting stuck in memories. I don't always remember...myself when I'm in a vision. And when I touch people, I read their thoughts almost instantly. Same deal. It's like I'm them instead of me. I'm getting lost." He raised his hands and wiggled his fingers. "That's why I'm wearing gloves."

Dad narrowed his eyes and looked at Finn's hands intently. "Then why did you go with leather?"

Shit. Finn realized his mistake as Dad started explaining for Daphne and Jazz. This was rookie stuff Dad had taught Finn when he was a kid.

"Leather transmits. These gloves might muffle readings a little, but you want silk to block energy."

"I've read that before," Jazz said. "You're supposed to keep tarot cards and other metaphysical tools wrapped in silk to protect them from stray energy and cleanse them after use."

Finn let out an exasperated sigh. He took off the nearly useless gloves and tossed them on the table.

Yeah, he should have come to his dad sooner. Even talking to Jazz about it more would have helped. She'd never taken him to her favorite bookstore, but talked about Bookwyrm often. She had studied all kinds of paranormal phenomena.

"I forgot about that," Finn said. "Thanks. My head hasn't been right for a while now."

"We noticed." Dad laughed.

He was trying to ease the tension, help Finn feel more comfortable. Man, Finn was a lucky bastard to have such great people in his life. Topping it off, Jazz stepped up behind him and put her hand on his shoulder, prompting a sigh that was anything but exasperated.

She gave his shoulder a squeeze and said, "Finn's powers are somehow being disrupted by a connection to the serial killer from a couple months back."

That was way too blunt. Finn was trying to figure out how to tell Dad without giving away any details. He just…hadn't worked out how to do that yet.

"Dammit, Jazz! I can tell them myself."

She jumped, as if his outburst surprised her. Funny, they never had before. Sure, they'd prompted plenty of freeze-outs, but she had barely registered them in the past. A brief look of hurt crossed her face. That was new too.

"I'm sorry."

It was too late, though. She crossed her arms and walked to the other side of the room, glaring at him.

"I'm sorry. I'm just raw."

"We get that, son, but lashing out isn't going to help anyone."

Dad was probably more concerned about Finn chasing away Jazz than anything else.

No, that wasn't fair. Dad was worried about Finn.

"I wish you'd come to us sooner. You shouldn't have let it eat you up inside like this."

"Yeah, well hindsight's twenty-twenty."

"There's nothing wrong with asking for help now and again," Dad said.

Not this again.

"And if your powers aren't working right, this is serious."

"I know. I get it." Finn could hear his voice rising. He closed his eyes and took a deep breath, then let it out.

Dad turned to Daphne. "Can you run to Finn's closet and bring back that dark blue silk shirt of his?"

"Sure."

As soon as she had left, Jazz said, "You kept it?"

"Yeah, I kept it." Finn would never let go of that shirt.

Jazz had given it to him early on. It reminded him of their best times together, when they had just switched from a professional relationship to a personal one. They had met when Jazz hired him to investigate an artist she thought might be a fraud. The case had been…

complicated.

She'd learned about his powers before it was over, they'd worked together, and after the case was closed, they'd pretty much jumped each other. He still wasn't sure who had started it.

Finn stood and took off his coat, then draped it over the back of his chair. He was wearing a cotton long-sleeved shirt over his tank top. He took the shirt off too and set it on top of his coat.

The silk shirt had short sleeves, but would still do a better job protecting him from random readings. Daphne returned and handed it over.

"Thanks." He slid it on, aware of the many stares on him as he did. They were waiting for him. No more stalling. "The connection isn't to the killer. It's one of his victims. I'm having nightmares about what happened to her."

As soon as Finn sat back down, Dad started his interrogation. "Was she someone you'd met before?"

"I don't know. I guess she does seem familiar somehow, but that could be because I'm dreaming about her every night."

Dad leaned on the table. "What happens in the dreams?"

"I basically experience what she did when she was being held by Michael Angelo. I'm chained to a wall and he's... Well, the dreams are unpleasant and I can say wholeheartedly that I'm glad the sick bastard is dead."

Daphne shifted her weight and said, "Could you have touched something the victim came into contact with? Maybe in the bar?"

"I thought about that. I don't know how that could have happened. For these memories to be available, it would have to be something that she touched while she was being held captive. Only one person escaped, and I doubt she kept any mementos."

"Two escaped," Jazz said. "If you count Elsa."

"You know one of his victims?" Daphne asked.

"I don't know any *victims*," Jazz said. "I do know both of the women who took him down."

"Are they okay?"

Jazz nodded at Daphne. "They're going to be fine. I'm more worried about Finn right now."

What an admission. And after only knowing Daphne for a few minutes.

"Rachel's the one who shot him," Finn said.

"That's Garrett's friend," Dad said. "I've heard him mention her."

"Yeah, and if you would watch the news or read anything other than your books, you'd know Rachel's dad is running for office soon. The whole thing has been swept under the rug. The lid they're keeping on this is insane. They have to have something they're using as leverage on a whole lot of people."

Dad shook his head. "I can't fault a man for trying to protect his daughter."

Jazz let out a snort and everyone turned to her. She shrugged. "Rachel's parents don't give a crap about her. She's a prop they use to appear like a perfect family. They're covering their own asses, not hers."

"That's a cheery thought," Daphne said.

"It's the truth."

"Where's the connection, though?" Dad tapped his finger on the table. "Break it down for me."

Finn's dad was even more of a hidden weapon for his investigations than Finn's powers. Finn could always count on him to give new insight into cases. Dad was the one who told him to start tracking Elsa when Finn's investigation into Dante hit a wall. And really, that was when this had all started.

"Okay. So, Garrett calls me to look into Elsa's new roommate."

"He did *what*?" Jazz broke in.

Finn sighed. "It was after the break-in, when she refused to call the cops."

Jazz looked like she was about to light into him again, but then cast a wary glance at Daphne.

"I already know about Dante being from the 1800s and Elsa's ability to time travel," Daphne said. "Finn was kind of flipping out when he figured things out, and the walls are really thin up here."

"Great." Jazz glared at Finn. That was going to cost him.

"Could we maybe stay focused?" Dad said. "You worked Garrett's case and found the creepy guy, but never told me what came of it. You just said he was out of the picture."

"Yeah," Finn said. "Permanently. That was Michael Angelo."

Jazz took a step toward him. Her hands were balled into fists at her sides.

"You knew that Michael was stalking Elsa?"

"I knew *someone* was stalking Elsa," Finn said. "You all did. And I let Garrett know what I'd found out as soon as I could. Turns out it was a little too late."

"Come on now." Dad tapped the table harder. "Let's focus here. That was the first time you felt the guy's energy. When did the dreams start?"

"The night he was killed."

Dad leaned back, crossing his arms and staring at the ceiling. "So, you've got the killer's energy signature on you. He dies."

Jazz cut in. "It can't be his ghost."

Everyone turned to stare at her.

"I'm just saying, it can't be his ghost. His body was cremated. What?"

Finn finally turned back to Dad. They hadn't really talked about ghosts before. But if psychometry and time travel were possible, why not ghosts?

"I can't be haunted, can I?" Finn asked.

Dad turned back to stare at Finn.

"Michael killed a lot of women," Jazz said. "Maybe one of them is trying to communicate with Finn. To get closure or something."

"Why Finn?" Daphne asked.

"She could be sensing his power," Jazz said. "Using it as a conduit."

"No," Dad said. "There would have to be a stronger connection than that. Something or someone that links them."

"I really *really* hate to ask this," Jazz said, "but has anyone in your family ever gone missing?"

Finn turned back to look at her. He had talked about his family a lot when they dated—not that there were many running around locally. Only Finn and his dad were in Florida. The rest were from Boston.

Of course, Jazz never bothered to share more than that she was from Kansas City. He didn't even know which side of the state line.

Focus, Finn. Focus.

"Do the police know if Michael worked anywhere else?" Finn asked. "Any other states?"

"Not that they've mentioned," she said. "The last I knew, the only clue they had is that Elsa and Rachel are both blonde. The police said maybe he had a type. They're compiling a list of missing persons—" Jazz glanced over at Dad. "Tommy, wait!"

Finn turned to his dad, only to see him lurching across the table. He grabbed Finn's hand and pulled him forward, holding it against his chest.

"Dad, let go! You don't want to see—"

Shit, he hated it when Dad read him like this. It hadn't happened since he was a kid. He felt the pull, the feedback from both of their powers colliding, then the click as they synched up.

Then Dad drew out the vision.

The rattle of chains. The weight of the manacles digging into her flesh, tearing it as she struggled to get free. The prick of needle after needle in her arms. Darkness. Fear. Knowing that death surrounded her —feeling it close. Michael Angelo's smiling face. And blood. So much blood.

Finn could feel Dad's hands trembling even through the vision. Then something strong yanked him back from it, pulling him free. He landed on the floor, sitting between Jazz's legs. She had her arms wrapped around him and was crushing him to her chest.

He might have enjoyed her warmth, her closeness, except his dad and Daphne were on the floor right in front of him—and Dad was clinging to Daphne's arms, sobbing.

"Dad. Dad!"

Finn scrambled to his dad's side and wrapped his arms around the pair. Dad was shaking so bad. Finn had never seen him cry. Ever. And this? This was a complete breakdown.

The vision was terrible, but Finn didn't understand his dad's reaction. Had he seen something Finn couldn't? Was that even possible? They had always shared the same visions when he read Finn before, the same memories or experiences, like Finn did when reading objects.

"Dad, come on. You have to calm down."

Jazz put her hand on Finn's back. He closed his eyes to let her calm sink into him. Except her hand was shaking too. He looked at her over his shoulder.

The blood had all drained from her face again. Her lips were set in a grim line. Instead of looking like she was about to pass out, she looked like she wanted to kill somebody.

She reached between them all and pressed her fingers against Dad's neck. Checking his pulse. Finn's heartbeat skyrocketed. He should have thought to check that first thing.

Jazz's face seemed to relax a bit and she nodded. Finn closed his eyes and took a deep breath, letting it out slowly. When he opened them again, he mouthed, "Thank you."

She actually gave him a tiny smile. She dropped to her knees and pulled Finn's head against her neck. They were touching skin-to-skin, and all he felt was comfort. No memories, no thoughts. He still couldn't read her. He swore he felt her press a kiss to the top of his head, though. Then she wrapped her arms around the group.

They sat in a heap on the floor for what felt like eternity while Dad cried it out. Finally, exhausted, he leaned into Finn.

"I thought it was for the best," Dad said. "I thought she'd take care of her. Give her a good life. Protect her."

"Who, Dad?"

"Your sister."

What the ...

Shit, had Dad picked up some part of the memory and lost track of who he was? Finn had been able to shake off other people's thoughts and memories as soon as he stopped touching them or whatever object he was reading. At least, so far. Surely Dad could do the same.

"I don't have a sister."

"You do. You did. Oh God, how could your mom have let this happen? I thought I was doing what was right."

"Dad, you're not making any sense."

Finn's heart was in his throat. Dad had never mentioned Finn's mom before. Whenever Finn tried to bring up the topic… It didn't go well. It didn't go anywhere. He'd stopped asking when he hit his teens.

"I recognized her," Dad said. "The connection. I felt it." Dad's blue eyes were bloodshot and lined with red. Tears were still streaming down his face. "I know my own daughter. That was Siobhan. Your sister, Finn. Your twin."

The blood rushed from Finn's head fast enough to make him dizzy. Luckily, Jazz was right there, keeping him steady.

"Your mom wanted more than I could ever give her," Dad said. "I thought maybe when we had you two, she'd settle down. Be happy. But it made her miserable. We were living in Boston with my family. She took up with some lawyer and told me she was divorcing me and taking Siobhan with her. She said I could keep you as long as I didn't try to find them, but if I did… She said they'd take you too. And I knew her new husband could do it."

"Christ, Dad. Why didn't you ever tell me?"

"I didn't want you to know that she didn't want you. Didn't want *us*. When Pat and I got the chance to open the bar down here, I moved us away so we could start over."

Finn's uncle Pat had passed away a decade ago, leaving his half of the bar to his brother.

"You never looked for her?"

"How could I, when I let your mom take her? When I…" Dad swallowed hard. "When I kept you for myself rather than making her take you too. They could have given you so much. Anything you ever wanted. But I couldn't let you both go. I was afraid if you found out about the kind of life I had kept you from you wouldn't forgive me."

Finn thought of all the years barely scraping by. Hell, he thought about the stress he'd been under the past few months, trying to make sure they had what they needed and could pay for Dad's medical bills, let alone be ready if something else should happen.

He thought about all the fights they'd had, when Finn wanted to use their powers to make some money and finally be able to stop struggling. How Dad had stayed strong and never once wavered or seemed to be tempted.

Then he thought about the woman who had given birth to him. Who he finally had learned something about.

She didn't want him. Worse than that, she was willing to use Finn— her son—to blackmail Dad into abandoning his daughter.

No matter how bad it was, Dad was always crystal clear in how much he loved Finn. How much he wanted to be part of Finn's life. Not many adults could stand to live with their parent when they were grown. Finn loved spending time with his dad. They relied on each other, took care of each other.

What had Siobhan grown up with?

Finn was reeling. Too many emotions were running through him. He was too shocked to process them all. Anger passed by his awareness and he latched on to it.

He couldn't let himself be angry with Dad. Not after almost losing him. So he directed it at the woman who had torn their family apart—a family Finn didn't even know he had.

"Are you kidding? If she didn't want us, that's her loss. I'd rather have been raised by someone who wanted me."

Dad wrapped his arms around Finn's neck and held on. Finn hugged him back hard.

He couldn't imagine what it must have been like to hold on to this for all these years. He wished his dad had told him, had come to him with the truth before it came out in such an awful way.

"We have to find out what happened to her, son. If she's haunting you, we have to help her find peace."

Chapter Nine

Tommy had been so exhausted he had passed out as soon as Finn and Jazz tucked him in bed. Jazz didn't want to leave. Even more, she wanted to have answers for Tommy when he woke up.

Finn stepped into the hallway with her and quietly closed the door to Dad's room. Daphne was downstairs finishing up closing the bar. As soon as they were settled, Jazz would...do something. Figure out a way to help, whether Finn wanted her to or not.

He paused with his hand resting on Dad's door. She couldn't imagine what he must be thinking. Seeing his dad go through that, finding out about his twin—knowing he'd lost her and that he was feeling her death over and over again. Jazz was amazed at how well he was holding it together.

She kept her voice as low as she could. "What do you need?"

He looked wrung out. She wanted to take care of him too. Food, water, sleep. Those were at the top of her mind.

He turned around and grabbed her, molding her against him and covering her lips with his.

Right. This.

Her body responded instantly. It always had. She buried her fingers in his hair, pressing herself against him. His tongue slid into her mouth, picking up the old dance as if it had been only yesterday.

Jazz moaned as he pushed her back against the wall, his hands sliding down past her hips to grab her thighs and lift her from the ground. She locked her ankles behind his waist. He was already hard, grinding against her, turning the heat building between her legs into a firestorm.

In the back of her mind, she recognized the pattern. Extreme emotion of any sort always led to sex. Whether it was an argument or...

Okay, usually it was an argument.

She knew she needed to hold on to some semblance of self-control, but at the moment, she couldn't even think. All she could do was feel. And she wanted more.

"Psst! Guys!" Daphne's voice cut through the euphoria of Finn's kiss.

Jazz was panting when he pulled away. He kept staring into her eyes for a long time. Daphne stalked up to them and started pointing toward the kitchen.

Finn turned to her and hissed, "Do you mind?"

Daphne pointed at the wall next to Tommy's door. "Paper thin, remember? You want to have sex with your girlfriend, fine. Just do it in your room and be quiet about it."

"I'm not his girlfriend," Jazz said.

At the same moment, Finn said, "She's not my girlfriend."

She tried not to scowl at him when he looked back at her. Good to have that clear.

"I don't *care*," Daphne said. "Just move."

The last of Jazz's jealousy vanished. Daphne had taken on the role of mother-hen for the Connellys—and now Jazz too, from the look of it. Jazz hadn't been replaced after all.

Finn let Jazz's legs slide to the floor. He kept his hand on her back as they walked into the kitchen area of the apartment. It annoyed her. She still didn't want him to stop.

"Downstairs." Daphne pointed and Finn and Jazz obeyed.

Once they were back in the bar, they could speak in normal tones. Jazz had been there enough to know that the ceiling at least was sound-proofed well.

Daphne was glaring at them. Jazz almost wanted to laugh. Yet again, she'd been caught in a compromising position. A tiny glimmer of hope stirred deep in her soul. The last time she'd felt this way was when she and Finn first made the leap from working together to being lovers.

That was a long time ago. He was probably just reacting because of the stress. It was part of his nature. He was impulsive, passionate. She was still tingling from that kiss—and everything that went along with it.

The timing was horrible to rekindle anything, even if Finn was interested. She shouldn't be thinking about it at all right now. Or ever. Finn had trampled her heart. He would probably end up leaving her again. He had been just as quick to correct Daphne when she called Jazz his girlfriend.

Ardor effectively dampened.

Daphne didn't light into them. Instead she said, "I'll stay with him while you work the case."

"I can't go," Finn said. "Not until I know he's okay."

"I took care of my mom for years before she passed. I know how to look after people."

Daphne walked over to Finn and rested her hand on his arm. No, she left it hovering an inch away, not touching his skin. She really did know how to take care of people.

"What he needs are answers," she said. "And what you need is to run this down. It's what your sister needs too. If she's hanging around and so upset that her presence is messing up your powers, you need to find a way to help her."

Damn. Daphne knew them well.

"I know where to start," Jazz said.

Finn turned to look at her. "Where?"

"Michael's house. Remember, I was there right after everything went to hell. I know where Michael lived. I also know that the police have pretty much finished with the place."

Finn nodded, his gaze becoming unfocused as he thought things through. "So no one will be there right now."

"Go." Daphne stepped back. "I'll take care of things here. You just take care of each other, okay?"

Finn glanced at Jazz, but quickly looked away. He nodded again. "Thanks, Daphne."

Daphne smiled and almost slipped and patted his shoulder. She looked puzzled about what to do for a moment, then patted the air above it. Finn let out a tiny chuckle. It was such a sweet gesture and had helped ease his pain, even a little.

"I know the shirt is supposed to help, but I don't want to take any chances," Daphne said.

Jazz felt a lump forming in her throat. She coughed to clear it.

"Let's go." She headed to the door and unlocked it, then held it for Finn. "Lock up after us."

"Of course." Daphne was already headed for the door.

Jazz waited for her to be close before murmuring, "Thanks for taking such good care of them."

Daphne smiled and Jazz felt a little tug on her heart. Yeah. Jazz was pretty sure she loved Daphne now. She tried to figure out how that would work as she unlocked the SUV and climbed into the driver's seat.

She would have to keep Daphne separate from her other friends. If she introduced her to Elsa and Rachel, there was no way Jazz could keep her relationship with Finn a secret. Daphne was too open. Then there would be endless questions and all the angst and drama of explaining why Jazz hadn't told anyone and why things hadn't worked out.

Jazz didn't have the stomach for it.

"Why didn't I tell you? Because he was mine. I didn't want to share him."

And the deeper truth.

"Because I loved him so much, I was afraid if I let anyone know, Fate would take him away from me."

It wouldn't have been the first time. Not by a long shot.

She had lost Finn anyway. But now he was back in her life and he needed her. He was letting her actually help him with something. No matter what came of it, she couldn't let the opportunity pass.

Being with Finn and Tommy had felt like Fate's reward for all the crap Jazz had gone through. Like being repaid for every loss she'd suffered. Their home was her oasis—the one place she could show Finn how she felt, even if she still didn't dare to say anything out loud.

Maybe this was her chance to even out the scales a bit and pay him back for everything he'd shared with her, everything he'd offered and she'd been too afraid to accept.

She pulled away from the curb, heading toward Michael's house. Finn didn't say a word.

"You okay over there?" she asked.

Finn was staring out the window. He glanced over at her and shook his head.

"Just trying to sort things out. I can't believe I had a sister. All this time and Dad never told me."

"I'm sure he had his reasons."

Finn snorted. "No wonder you two got on so well. You love your secrets."

Her grip on the wheel tightened.

He sighed. "I'm sorry. That was a shitty thing to say."

Whoa. Another apology. He sure was doing that a lot. She couldn't remember him doing it much before.

"When did you become so self-aware?" That sounded better in her mind. "I didn't mean that to be catty."

He laughed a little. Just a tiny fast exhale. But it made her smile, warmed her up inside. She wanted to help him feel better.

"You know, I think we've talked more in the last few hours than the last few weeks of us dating." He looked over at her and grinned.

God, that smile. The streetlights caught and reflected in his pale eyes, gleamed on his straight teeth.

"As I recall, we were busy doing other things toward the end," she said.

His smile faded and he turned back to the window. How had that killed the mood? It was true, anyway. At the end, all they did was argue and have angry make-up sex.

Amazing angry make-up sex.

Her skin tingled as she remembered some of the more spectacular encounters. The argument was always the same by that point. He wanted to come out about their relationship. She didn't.

Going out meant being seen. Summer Park wasn't a big enough town to avoid the grapevine. Their friends would find out. Then the playful banter would start.

"When are you going to get married? How many kids do you want? What breed of dog? What's your retirement plan?"

Hell, even strangers felt they had the right to weigh in on her personal life. Just the other day, the sandwich shop owner where Jazz often picked up lunch asked her when she was going to meet a nice man and settle down.

Right, I need to find a new lunch place.

Her sister Mei complained that after the first kid, people would ask when she would have her second. And after her second, they asked about her third. It never ended.

Okay, after three kids, Mei had stopped mentioning it. Then again, she'd pretty much stopped talking to Jazz. The girls kept her busy.

Jazz missed her family, but Kansas City held too many memories of her father. She hadn't been back since the funeral. Mei and her family had come to Florida every other year for a while, along with their mom. They had visited various state attractions and Jazz had driven up for a day or two to visit.

It had been a long time since they'd made the trip. Not since just before her break-up with Finn.

She hadn't told him they were visiting. Her family was in the same state, and she didn't even tell him, let alone introduce him. Meanwhile, he had opened his home, his family, his heart to her.

Yeah. She had messed things up with Finn big-time. Trying to keep him compartmentalized. Trying to keep herself from bragging about her amazing boyfriend and letting anyone know how happy she was. The crashes always came when she was at her happiest.

The first one was literal. When she was a kid, her puppy had been hit by a car and killed while she had been walking it to a friend's house to show off. She shuddered at the memory.

She had bragged about a scholarship to a prestigious performance academy. The teacher she was supposed to study with had fallen ill right after Jazz told everyone at school about it. She could think of half a dozen times she'd been over the moon about something and told everyone about it, only to have it snatched away.

It took her too long to learn her lesson. Right before graduation, she had talked to her father about her fear—had even shared her suspicion that it was a curse. She told him she was afraid to be happy that things were going so well. Agents had already contacted her, wanting to represent her. She hadn't told anyone, because she was afraid something would happen to them.

He had laughed and told her not to be afraid. He encouraged her to enjoy this part of her life and said that whatever Fate had in store for anyone, she couldn't change it, especially just by being happy. He told her the universe wasn't cruel and to lay down her fear.

She had bragged to her friends after that. Not about the offers, but about him. What a wonderful father he was. How supportive. How he believed in her ability to make it as a singer.

The entire month before graduation, she wouldn't shut up about him. She told all her friends how much they were going to love him and how great he was and didn't they wish they had a father like hers.

She hadn't sung a note since her final performance in college. Not at birthdays, not lullabies to her nieces, not even alone in the shower.

She had thought her family was in the audience. They hadn't even made it to the state.

Jazz had never admitted that she loved anyone out loud again. She was cautious every time she was with the people she cared about, trying to hide how she felt. Trying to stifle her feelings.

It was suffocating.

Now she was wondering if other people were falling to her curse. She hadn't said anything about how happy she was for Elsa and Dante when they found each other, but she'd thrown that party. In her heart, she'd known it was to celebrate them getting together.

She'd worked with Dante behind Elsa's back to help him set up a life for himself, knowing her best friend wouldn't be able to relax and really enjoy being with him until she knew Dante was self-sufficient.

Then Michael happened.

What if it had somehow been Jazz's fault? She'd had way more than her share of bad luck in her life, and was convinced there were powers working behind the scenes—scales that insisted on being balanced, energies that influenced the course of human events. Beyond the obvious, mundane precipitator—Jazz was the one who had fucking introduced Michael to everyone.

Goddammit, Jazz. Get your head out of your ass and back in the game.

She could feel sorry for herself later. Finn needed her now.

Michael had lived outside of town in a small house built near the edge of swampland. Jazz hadn't been back since Rachel's rescue. Thinking about that night was just what Jazz needed to renew her focus.

Michael's house was haunted with her own memories. She would keep Finn away from the garage—that was certain. Even still, how could they sort through Michael's memories safely? She didn't want to see Finn get lost in a vision again, especially now that they knew Michael had killed Finn's sister.

Jazz was tempted to call Rachel and ask for help. If Siobhan was hanging around and somehow messing with Finn's powers, Rachel would be able to help them figure out what they needed to do. Siobhan could just tell her.

But Rachel was dealing with her own issues. Jazz had to try to sort this out herself first. She didn't want to drag Rachel into it. Not unless it became absolutely necessary. They would try Michael's house first and see what they could find.

Jazz turned onto the gravel driveway, her lights flashing across the windows of Michael's brown and tan single-story house.

"We're here."

Chapter Ten

The house looked ordinary. Finn could hardly believe so many terrible things had happened inside. At the same time, he could feel a chilling energy creeping out from it, even from inside the SUV. Jazz had her door open already, letting in the muggy night air.

"You ready for this?" Jazz asked.

"Yeah. I think so." He reached for her hand on instinct. Having her near him... Well, he wasn't sure how well he'd be coping without her.

She pulled away. It was standard procedure for her, but every time it felt like she kicked him in the chest.

"Cut me some slack," he said. "I wasn't trying to start something."

Not this time, anyway.

That moment in the hallway had been intense. He hadn't been able to stop himself from reaching for her. And yeah, it was instinct again that made him want to hold her hand, to touch her. It wouldn't have escalated, though. Probably.

"That isn't why..." She sighed and slid from her seat, her boots crunching as she hit the gravel. She slammed the door shut.

That was not-so-standard.

He followed her out, closing his door a bit more gently. He was walking on her heels. When she stopped abruptly, he almost ran into her.

"I was trying to protect you, you ass," she said. "I didn't want you to be flooded with my thoughts."

"Oh."

Damn. That was the first time he could remember her unloading on him like that. Now that he knew why she pulled back, it was well deserved.

He'd always felt alone in their fights, like he was talking to a wall.

She never yelled back. She always stayed so calm. It made him wonder if she cared about him at all. Eventually, he'd start shouting, trying to be heard. They always ended up in bed, his last resort to establish some form of connection.

"It's okay if you touch me," he said. "I still can't read you, even with my powers messing up."

"Oh."

He shook his head and smiled. "Didn't you notice before when we made out in the hallway?"

"I wasn't *thinking* then." She was quiet for a moment, then said, "Wipe that grin off your face."

"How do you know I'm grinning? It's pitch black out here."

"I don't need to see you to know you're smiling."

"I guess you just have that effect on me."

Her breath hitched and she turned away, walking toward the house fast enough that he had to trot to catch up. What had he stepped in this time? Talking to her had often been challenging, but this was like walking through a minefield. She hadn't been volatile before.

She had actually once told him, "I suck at talking. Can't we just have sex instead?"

It had sounded great at the time. With how anxious he was, it sounded great at the moment too. It had always comforted him, made him feel grounded.

Remembering their time in bed wasn't a good way to keep his focus, especially with the recent reminder of how well they fit together. Talk about losing control. But in that moment, when she asked what he needed, all he could think about was being closer to her, holding her.

She had always been the one person that he could touch without worrying about reading her thoughts. Now she was the only person he knew he wouldn't lose himself in.

At least, not his mind. His heart was another matter.

She pulled out her phone and turned on the flashlight as they walked to the side of the house. Windows lined a door tucked behind some bougainvilleas. One of the panes had been broken out and was taped over.

"I don't suppose you brought along your gloves?" Jazz asked.

"They're back home on the kitchen table."

"Forget it," she said. "I've got this."

She hit the tape with her elbow a couple of times until it gave way, then snaked her arm through the gap and opened the door. Holding her phone up, she led the way into the house. The door opened into a narrow laundry room.

"Is the AC on?"

The house felt at least twenty degrees cooler than outside. The night air was stagnant and oppressively hot, even in the pre-dawn hours they were approaching. The house was an ice box in comparison.

"I don't know. I think they shut off the utilities, so probably not." She ran her light over the washer and dryer. "It is cold in here."

Cold and creepy as hell. Finn's skin was crawling and he hadn't even touched anything.

"Tell me again how this is less visceral than reading the walls of the gallery?"

"I'm not going to have you read the garage or anything."

"The garage?"

Jazz was silent for a moment. "That's where he kept them."

"Oh." Finn had never been able to see past the workbenches in his dreams. Shelves and tables blocked his view.

He shivered, walking a little closer as they made their way into the kitchen. A small square table was tucked against a wall. Two chairs. Michael must not have entertained often. The counters were mostly bare.

"Maybe we should start in here." Jazz moved the light over the cabinets and counters. "I don't know where he kept his empty jars. Let's avoid the cabinets."

Jars? Oh right. To hold the blood. Finn would avoid the cabinets unless absolutely necessary.

"How about the table?" he asked.

She turned around and flashed the light across its surface. It seemed innocuous enough. Then again, the whole house did. On the surface, anyway. The longer he was in the dwelling, the more he sensed the malice lurking there, as if it had soaked into the walls, the ceiling, the floors.

"That's a good idea. Rachel said Michael brought her here after a date to capture her. He might have sat with his other victims before..." Jazz shook her head and stepped closer to him. "Maybe start with the chairs?"

"Okay." Finn scooted one of the chairs away from the table with his foot. Jazz grabbed his arm before he could sit down.

"Don't sit. I'll need to be able to break your contact if something goes wrong. It'll be easier if you're standing."

He hesitated, wanting to keep feeling her hand on his arm, the softness of her touch. He loved having her with him, knowing she was thinking about him, that she cared what happened.

That was as far as they'd ever gone conversationally. She admitted she cared about him.

Now is not the time, Finn.

He tried to keep things light. He laughed and said, "Easier for you, maybe. My knee still hurts from the gallery."

Her voice softened. "I didn't know it was you."

"It's okay. I'm glad you didn't forget everything I taught you. That was a pretty good takedown."

She hadn't wanted to learn self-defense at all. She said words were her best weapon and that she always had her phone handy for calling the police. He had kept after her about it. She worked such late hours at the gallery—usually alone, on the nights he wasn't with her.

When she'd asked him to hang around more, acting as her bodyguard, she could tell it set him off. They never talked about it, but he thought maybe she had agreed to the lessons to sort of make it up to him.

Acting as her bodyguard was another form of working for her. He didn't mind playing the part on occasion, but he wasn't interested in her being his boss. That was another reason he didn't want her helping him.

She'd take over, ordering him around, running everything.

Yeah, he was proud and didn't like asking for help. He knew that. But he especially didn't like asking for help from someone he saw as a partner but who treated him like a minion.

And on that cheery note...

He turned back to the chair.

The wood was old and the paint worn and peeling. Finn would have thought someone who called themselves a painter would be more particular about that. Then again, when Finn thought about what Michael used for paint... Definitely a good thing the chairs hadn't been redone.

Get it over with.

He grabbed the back of the chair with one hand, keeping his weight a little off-balance. If Jazz needed to push him loose, it would help her out.

The room lightened as if the sun was rising in fast-forward. Illuminated, it looked less creepy and more normal. Homey, even. The eerie atmosphere was gone.

Finn didn't feel like he was floating. Instead, he was sitting at the table across from Michael.

Finn felt his hands curl into fists. He wanted to punch Michael in the face. Wanted to make him hurt for all the pain he had heaped on others.

This is the bastard who killed my sister. I'll never get a chance to know her because of him.

Michael was smiling as he leaned back in his chair and spoke. "This next piece will be spectacular. Not one, but *two* subjects. I don't know why I didn't think to try this sooner."

He was staring at the ceiling, a dreamy look on his face. He interlaced his fingers and put his hands behind his head, stretching out his legs. He looked relaxed. As if he hadn't a care in the world.

"The canvas is prepared. I just need to gather the materials. They're already selected. Both subjects are friends of the gallery owner. I'm hoping to be able to display the piece in an exhibit there. Can you imagine?"

Michael laughed. He actually laughed.

Sick psychopathic bastard...

"She keeps me on my toes, that one. Always trying to see through me. It's too bad she's not a match for my needs. Perhaps someday I'll expand my subject matter and the little gallery owner can grace her own wall."

Michael's gaze became unfocused as he stared at the ceiling again, casually contemplating *killing Jazz.*

Finn wanted to leap across the table and—

"Stop looking at me like that."

He felt a chill sweep through him. Holy shit. Michael couldn't see Finn, right? Now that he knew time travel was possible, he wasn't as sure.

"Pig! Stop looking at me."

Finn's gaze dropped, as if he had lowered his head to look at the floor. Except he wasn't looking at the floor. He was looking at somebody's lap.

"Did you take care of it?" Michael asked.

Finn's view bobbed up and down, as if he was seeing through someone else's perspective and they were nodding. At least he was holding on to his sense of self. Whoever this was, Finn was just along for the ride.

Michael nodded. "Good. The alligators near Auntie's house are getting fat helping us clean up after my work. I hope they're hungry for what's next."

Alligators...

Finn felt sick. He wanted to leave the memory, but couldn't. Michael stood and walked to the sink. Whoever Finn was seeing through watched out of the corner of his eye. When Michael turned back, the person quickly looked back at their lap.

While Finn was stuck there, he might as well do some good. He looked for details that might help him ID the person he was occupying.

The man's hands were bony, calloused and leathery—and curled into tight fists. His arms were emaciated. Judging by the length of his legs, he was pushing six-feet in height. His pants ballooned around his body. He couldn't weigh more than one-hundred-thirty, one-hundred-forty pounds. Tan skin. Mud stains on worn boots. A bit of sphagnum moss stuck to the side.

Michael walked back to the table.

"Poor piggy. Are you hungry too?"

Finn felt the man's chest catch, saw his fists tighten further. He looked up, but before he could say anything, Michael's lips pulled back in a snarl and he flat-out punched the guy. The blow sent him reeling, the room spinning in Finn's view until his face hit the floor.

"Finn!"

Finn sucked in a huge breath. He felt like he was drowning. The cold linoleum pressed against his cheek. Warmer hands were on his shoulders.

Jazz helped him sit up, pulling him against her chest and wrapping her arms around him. Finn's body was shaking violently. But it was *his* body. He'd made it back.

"That was so not-okay." His teeth were chattering and he felt... weird. Oddly disconnected. He focused on the soft feel of Jazz's body behind his, closing his eyes and trying to take deep breaths. Something thick and wet was interfering.

"You're bleeding."

"What?"

He lifted his hand to his nose. When he pulled it away, he could see red on his fingertips from the dim light of her phone, which was sitting on the floor next to them.

"I must have hit my head when I fell."

"You didn't. I caught you. Well, I tried to anyway. You're heavy."

Finn let out a chuckle. It sounded a little hysterical to him. Nothing felt real.

Auntie's house...

"What do you know about Michael's family?" he asked.

"Nothing. We didn't talk about anything but art and the gallery."

"But you knew his body was cremated."

"Rachel told me."

If Michael had any family, they probably weren't too eager to come forward and claim his remains. The state would have taken care of the matter. But just because no family came forward, that didn't mean they didn't exist.

He pulled a handkerchief from his back pocket and wiped his nose, then picked up her phone and stood. He ran the light over the floor, table, and chair to make sure he hadn't bled anywhere. They needed to leave behind as little evidence of their visit as possible.

Jazz rose and crossed her arms, glaring at him. "What did you see?"

No way was he filling her in on all the details. He still felt half-sick from what he had learned, what he knew in his gut to be true. He stuck with the basics. What she needed to know.

And that knowledge was chilling.

"Michael has a cousin who helped him. He wasn't working alone."

Chapter Eleven

Jazz couldn't believe that Michael had an accomplice. Someone who had taken part in his crimes was walking around free. That part of this awful situation was supposed to be over. Justice had been served. Right?

"The police would have caught that," she said.

"The police might have talked to the guy and not realized his role in it. From what I saw, he was cleanup."

"Cleanup?"

The light from her phone was enough for her to see how Finn grimaced. He didn't want to tell her what he knew.

"I need to know. I'll deal with it."

Finn let out a tired laugh. "I've never heard you use that phrase on yourself. I thought you only used it on other people."

"Finn…"

He sighed. "Michael's cousin helped him get rid of the bodies. I only got a nickname, but I could tell enough about what the guy looks like to give me a good lead. Once I track down Michael's hometown, I should be able to find him."

"Don't you mean *we*?"

Finn shook his head. "I was only okay with you coming along when I thought the killer was dead and you'd be safe. If this other guy was working with Michael, we have no idea what he's capable of."

She bristled. Finn was *not* benching her. He was not leaving her behind again.

"Well, you know what *I'm* capable of. Or does your knee need a reminder?"

"Jazz…"

"And we know what you're *in*capable of. You can't control your powers. You need me." At least for this.

"I can't risk you being hurt."

She let out a laugh. That was just too rich. No one had ever hurt her like Finn had. Her heart had never healed, never moved past him. She still felt butterflies in her stomach when they were close, still wished things could have been different—that he hadn't chosen to walk away.

"You're forgetting that I drove," she said. "Unless you're walking back to town to pick up your car, you're stuck with me. Deal with it."

His jaw was tight and he was frowning so hard deep grooves were shadowed on his face.

"Don't ever say that to me again." He bit out each word, clipped and tense.

"What? Walk back to Summer Park?"

"*Deal with it.* Do you even know what you're really saying? What that means? 'I don't give a shit about what you feel. Sort it out yourself.' I don't *ever* want to hear that phrase again."

She felt like the floor had dropped out from under her. That was her catchphrase. She used it all the time with everybody. No one had ever complained. She had never thought it could be taken that way. But…he had a point.

If he hated that expression, she must have upset him dozens of times while they were together. He never mentioned it.

Talking was something they had never excelled at.

"Finn, I'm—"

"Just forget it. We have a job to do."

What the hell? She had been about to apologize—something she *never* did. Her skin prickled as rage surged up. He shouldn't rock someone's foundation and then walk away.

But that was what he did with her. Turned her world upside-down, then walked away.

Not this time.

She grabbed her phone from his hand, then turned around and headed for the laundry room. He fell in step just behind her.

"Where are you going?"

"Back to the SUV. Unless you think you can safely read something else in here to find out where this cousin lives, we're probably better off searching for him on the Internet."

She opened the door and held it, staring at Finn expectantly. He only hesitated a moment before walking back into the steamy night air.

After the chill of Michael's house, it felt good. The moisture carried the heat right into her bones. She couldn't wait for the sun to come up and chase away…everything from this night.

Not everything.

She had reconnected with Tommy. She was even happy to be with Finn, even though he was driving her crazy. She was so scared he was going to leave. Watching him walk out of her life again was something she couldn't bear to think about. But she was more afraid he'd try to do this alone and get hurt.

Once they were back in the SUV, she said, "Wherever Michael is from, there are bound to be other people around. It won't be too dangerous. And you need me to back you up, whether you'll admit it or not."

He sighed, but then pulled out his phone and started searching the Internet. That was a good sign. She thought over what she knew while she waited for him to find something. She needed to be as useful as possible so Finn would admit that he needed her.

Things were starting to make more sense.

Someone was out there who played a part in the deaths of those women. Someone who needed to pay. Finn's sister was using the only connection she had to help get herself—and hopefully the other victims—some peace about what happened to them. Jazz would do everything in her power to make that happen.

"Clearview. Michael was from Clearview." Finn put his phone in the cup holder and pulled on his seat belt. "It's a small town a few hours to the northwest."

Jazz picked up his phone and looked at the map he had brought up. She memorized the highways and turns.

One of the best parts of living where they did was that not many roads passed through. The cities were small oases in the middle of sand and swamp. It was a fairly straight shot to Clearview. They could be there shortly after dawn.

She handed him his phone and buckled up, then started the engine. Finn put his hand over hers as she gripped the gearshift to kick it into reverse. They stared at each other for a few long moments. She resisted the urge to flip her hand over and lace their fingers together.

"Are you sure about this?" he asked. "We can head back to town so I can pick up my car. You don't have to come."

She did. She would never find peace with herself if she didn't help Finn's sister find her own.

"I'm coming with you. Deal—"

She sucked in a breath, stopping mid-sentence. Turning to look through the back windshield, she put the car in reverse, then pulled her hand out from under his and hit the gas. "You're not getting rid of me this time."

They were well away from Michael's when Finn spoke again.

"I never wanted to get rid of you."

She let out a laugh. Was he really going to go there? Fine. She'd play along.

"That's funny. As I remember it, you're the one who jumped out of the limo. I'm surprised you waited for it to stop, you were so eager to get away from me."

He shook his head. "There was so much wrong with that moment."

She shrugged. "You wanted out."

"No, Jazz. I wanted *in*. That's all I ever wanted with you. But you always kept me at arm's length. Hell, not even arm's length. It was more like a ten-foot pole. Like you kept yourself in a fucking castle surrounded by a moat filled with…" He shook his head and looked out the window.

Was he kidding? She had never let anyone get closer to her than Finn. She told him about her dreams for the gallery, funny stories about her clients. She shared every moment of her life with him.

Unless they involved Elsa. Or her family.

That had always been her boundary. Her line in the sand. But Jazz didn't talk to *anyone* about her loved ones. It wasn't safe. The only reason she talked about Elsa with Garrett and Rachel was that they all knew each other. Even then, Jazz was careful to keep it low-key and not give away how much she loved them all.

Finn had barely grazed the outskirts of her social circle, which was what Jazz wanted. There was no way she could hide how much she loved Finn if they were all hanging out. No way she could avoid talking about it.

He was Garrett's best friend, but he'd only met Elsa in passing and Jazz didn't think he'd even been in the same room as Rachel. Yeah, she didn't tell Finn stories about her friends, but he still knew how much she cared about them all. Her friends knew *nothing* about Jazz and Finn. Their relationship was sacred.

If she had told the others, they would have insisted on meeting him. Rachel would have started pressuring Jazz about a wedding, wanting to plan it and design a dress. Elsa wouldn't say anything, but she was a romance novelist. Who knew what sort of daydreams she'd create. And Garrett...

Garrett would be over the moon about it. He'd insist on double dates, even though he wasn't dating anyone—hadn't dated anyone since Jazz tried to hook him up with Elsa. And it would be awkward all around. Awkward and dangerous.

The more people who knew about Jazz and Finn, the worse it would be when something finally happened to him, especially with how much she loved him. That was how the curse worked. She loved him too much to risk it.

Curse aside, she didn't want to deal with the inevitable pressure her friends would heap on her with their well-meaning comments, building up dreams for how they wanted her life to be. Settle down. Get married. Have kids. People loved pairs and spawning.

Even Jazz had fallen into that mindset. She kept trying to set up her friends. Then again, she *knew* they wanted families and partners. They'd told her as much during uncomfortable conversations where

Jazz had to work to keep the focus off of herself.

She sucked at matchmaking anyway. Rachel and Garrett had seemed a natural fit, but something had kept them from ever connecting, even when it seemed like Fate kept bringing them together over and over again. He and Elsa hadn't worked out either. But they became great friends after Jazz introduced them. They all had.

Jazz had known they would get along. She didn't know what she had been thinking when she sent Elsa on a blind date with Michael.

I wanted her to have a chance to find the happiness I had lost.

Okay. Maybe she did know.

Chloe had once told Jazz that she was a "nexus". It was just another way of calling her Fate's tool. Supposedly, Jazz had an energy that brought the right people together at the right time. But she was the one who had brought Michael into everyone's lives. How the hell could anything be right about that?

At least Elsa had Dante now. Jazz was so happy for her—for them both. She was so grateful they had...survived. Dante would heal. Rachel was already doing much better. And Finn...

His forehead rested against the window and his eyes were closed. Either he was asleep or trying to avoid conversation. Jazz let him be. She wouldn't know what to say even if she tried. She *hoped* he was sleeping and did her best to keep the ride smooth for him.

The miles rolled by, dark scenery turning to slate gray as dawn approached. The sky brightened to a cloudless blue. They were nearing the coast. It would be a hot and humid day.

Finn lurched forward in his chair shouting, "No!"

Jazz jerked on the wheel. The SUV shimmied as she tried to regain control. She barely kept it from rolling.

"What the hell, Finn?" Her heart was pounding and her mouth had gone completely dry. She glanced over at him.

He was clutching the dashboard, his chest heaving and eyes wide. He swallowed a few times and pressed his head back against the headrest.

"Are you okay?"

"Yeah... Yeah."

She was not buying it. It must have been one of the nightmares he talked about. His eyes were haunted.

"How bad was it?" she asked.

"What? It wasn't..." He shook his head, then ran his hands over his face. "I don't want to talk about it."

"Fine."

She could hear his heavy breaths, and they weren't slowing down. Glancing over, his eyes were still wide.

"You doing okay?"

"Yeah."

"Bullshit."

"Jazz, please just leave it." He closed his eyes and shook his head.

"Okay." Whatever he had seen in the dream must have been horrible. She let him be for a while, trying to figure out what to say. "You had quite a night."

Lame.

He laughed. "That's an understatement. Not all of it was bad though."

"Really?" What could he have enjoyed?

He shrugged and grinned at her. "That part in the hallway was kinda fun."

She snorted. "Only kind of? I must be losing my touch."

"I wouldn't say that."

"That was always our strongest suit. Touching."

"Yeah. Too bad we sucked at the rest of it."

"We had some good times out of the bedroom. Didn't we?"

She hated how small her voice sounded. Hesitant. But she wasn't sure if she wanted to know the answer. Had he really wanted her to be part of his family? Had he enjoyed those times together?

"In the bar. Upstairs."

The bitter edge to his tone cut deep. He'd wanted to tell Garrett and everybody about their relationship. Jazz kept saying she wanted her privacy. It was nobody's business if they were dating.

When they were at the bar, just the two of them or with Tommy around, Jazz could let herself be happy. Somehow, she felt like it was the one place Fate wouldn't peek, the one concession to Jazz's calling as a *nexus*. If they had ever gone out, she would have constantly been on guard, trying to make sure no one realized how much she cared for Finn. The few times Garrett had seen them together, Jazz had scowled so much that Finn later told her Garrett thought she hated him.

Why couldn't Finn have been as happy as she was to carve out a corner of the world where they could be together? A place they could retreat to and be safe. She hadn't been able to risk losing him and because of it he had left.

Maybe Fate found out anyway.

For their last date, Jazz thought she had come up with the perfect compromise. Rent a limo for the night and drive around town. She had arranged for take-out from an upscale restaurant to celebrate their two-month anniversary, which was no small feat in itself. The chef had been offended when she first approached him with the idea, but she turned it around.

The back of the limo was spacious enough for them to have a nice dinner and even a good time, if he'd been up for it. She had dressed to the nines, spent hours preparing for the evening, trying to make it perfect—trying to make him happy and keep him safe.

Finn had been uncomfortable from the beginning. When she explained the evening she had planned, he pounded on the glass partition hard enough she was afraid it would break. The driver opened it to see what he needed, and Finn demanded they pull over.

He hit the curb the moment the limo came to a stop.

She tried to talk to him afterward, and he told her he was done. She remembered the moment with crystalline clarity.

"I want to really be with you. To start a life with you. Not this sneaking-around crap. I used to work divorce cases. This isn't a relationship—it's an affair. I won't be 'the other man'. That isn't what I want for us. If you're not all-in, I'm out."

But she *couldn't* be all-in. Not with anyone. Beyond the

supernatural obstacles, it wasn't what she wanted, what she was meant for. It just wasn't who she was. She didn't want to treat their relationship like an affair, but the alternative...

If he had asked again to tell their friends, she might have considered it. If he wanted to go out that badly, she would have managed. But what he was asking... It was something she couldn't give.

Would it have been so bad to marry him?

She felt like she had asked herself that question a thousand times since he left. Along with wishing they had talked about the entire situation more. She thought they would have more time—like she always did right before Fate took someone from her.

If he really needed the traditional lifestyle, they could have adopted some kids, picked up a dog somewhere, bought a house in the suburbs...and lived a lie. Had children she loved but would never connect to the way a mother should.

She didn't want to be a mother or a wife. She just wanted to be *Jazz*.

Apparently, that wasn't enough for him.

Chapter Twelve

"This is the turn."

Finn pointed at the exit. A rusted sign with a few bullet holes read *Clearview*.

Jazz didn't say anything. Just turned the SUV and headed to the town. She hadn't said anything since he'd brought up how their relationship ended.

Great idea there. Really good form.

He knew he was still raw over it. He didn't expect her to be after so many years.

Isn't it right that she's suffering as I am?

Wait... What?

No. Absolutely not. Finn didn't want her to suffer. He didn't want either of them to. He would honestly have been glad to find that she'd moved on and was happily having a purely physical relationship with someone else.

Okay, maybe not *glad*. But it would have helped him move on to see that he was right all along about what she was looking for from him. Knowing she was still upset about the breakup made him question things.

Including his decision to end their relationship in the first place.

If he was being honest with himself, they hadn't only clicked in the bedroom. She had been part of his family. She and his dad got on so well, sometimes Finn wondered if Dad liked her better than him. Finn used to tease them both about it all the time.

Finn and Jazz would have been great together—if she'd let them actually make a life together instead of hiding their relationship. He knew Jazz hadn't been involved with anyone else, but it still drove him crazy that she acted like Finn was *the other man*.

After the initial phase of pretty much constant sex, he'd spent all his energy trying to get them out of the damned house. When they should have been talking about what they wanted out of their relationship and where they were headed, he was busy trying to understand why she wouldn't let their friends know they were involved.

It seemed a necessary first step before getting into the heavier conversations, like kids and marriage—and why Finn wasn't interested in either. That didn't mean he didn't want a long-term commitment from her. It didn't mean he didn't love her.

She had kept herself so guarded. Never once—not a single time—had she ever told Finn she loved him. Even after he said it. She just sat up in the bed and walked away. Said she wasn't comfortable talking about feelings.

He might have jumped the gun, telling her how he felt after only a month, but he'd thought they were on the same page. He hadn't brought it up again. He hadn't had a chance to.

Now she was back in his life and it was messing with his head. He was losing his focus. Not that he'd had much of that lately, either. At least she'd be there to pull him out if he became trapped in a memory again.

"Where are we heading?" Her question snapped him out of his spiraling thoughts, thankfully.

"Let's take a pass through town. See what's off the main strip."

"We're going to be conspicuous. All I'm seeing are old trucks and rusted-out compacts." She smiled at him briefly. "Maybe we *should* have gone back to Summer Park to pick up your car."

He bristled. "I junked it."

"No way."

"It might have fit in here, but I was sticking out like a sore thumb in Summer Park. I had to upgrade for stakeouts."

Of course, he had bought his new car—topping out his budget—just a few months before Dad's hospital stay. Dad insisted he keep it, and Finn couldn't argue. It really was helping with stakeouts. He and his dad were doing okay so far with their savings and what the bar brought in, but Finn needed to get this squared away so he could get back to work.

"I liked that car," Jazz said.

"Seriously?"

She shrugged and glanced over at him. "It had character."

"That's one word for it."

Maybe the car was a happy reminder that she was above me.

What the fuck? Where were these thoughts coming from? He shifted in his seat, staring out the window at the few buildings they passed.

The thought was an unwelcome reminder of one of the main doubts that plagued him through their relationship. He had wondered the whole time they were together what Jazz saw in him. She was self-made, well off, and *owned* herself. Finn tended to fly off the handle. Jazz was always in control. What could she want with a private eye living above a bar with his dad?

Then he'd look in the mirror and remember.

Finn never had trouble getting a date before her and he doubted he'd find it challenging if he decided to put himself out there again. Jazz had made no secret of enjoying his body. She even made jokes that she could display him in the gallery if she didn't want to keep him all to herself.

If she was only into him physically, how could he keep her interest over time? He wanted to grow old with her. He didn't want to constantly be checking his physique, wondering if she was getting bored or looking to trade up. No matter what she said, her secretiveness kept reminding him of too many cases he'd worked.

Switching to investigating insurance fraud had helped him move away from seedy hotels and some truly disturbing moments gathering evidence that he wished he could forget. He was gaining a reputation with his new cases as someone who could crack seemingly impossible mysteries.

People had already started asking him what his secret was. He had to be careful.

If anybody figured out that he was using his powers to read objects —and people—involved in the cases... He'd lose all his business in a heartbeat. No one would believe what he did was real. He'd become a joke.

Dad disapproved of what he did. They weren't supposed to use their powers to make money. Their gifts were meant to help people. That was what his granddad passed on when teaching Dad about his powers. But Finn *did* help others with what he could do. He just also helped himself and his family.

"You're walking a gray line, Finn." Dad always let Finn know when he was about to take on a case that would cross the line, no matter how big the payout. Finn was grateful. He'd been tempted a time or two, but his dad always kept him on track.

Now he had Jazz to help him.

They passed the last building, the scenery reverting to thick foliage crowding between palm trees and pines. Damn, Clearview was tiny. Most of the buildings had busted-out windows and peeling paint.

"That was one shitty town," Jazz said.

He couldn't disagree. People were struggling here. He could feel it.

"I saw a bar that wasn't boarded up," he said. "That's our best bet."

"Let's hope Michael's cousin is a drinker then."

From what Finn had seen, he wouldn't doubt it. Not much of an eater, though. That nickname Michael kept using was just cruel. Finn almost felt sorry for the guy.

Almost.

She turned the SUV around using a side street, then headed back the way they had come. The parking lot for the bar had tons of potholes filled with sand and gravel. The SUV bounced as if they were driving off-road.

"Pull around so you're facing the street." He scanned the area, looking for the best place to park. "There. Park there. If we need to, we'll be able to get out fast and it'd take several trucks to block us in."

She raised her eyebrows and glanced at him, but did as he said. "You get to think about fun stuff in your line of work."

He shrugged. "Things happen. I don't like repeating mistakes."

Like being with you.

What the fuck. He was seriously about to reach into his head and punch his brain. The lack of sleep must be getting to him more than he thought. Or the nightmares.

The most recent one... It was different. He suppressed a shudder.

Dreaming from his sister's perspective made a lot of sense now that he knew their relationship. He'd researched psychic powers enough to know about the twin bond. Even non-psychic twins had heightened connections.

Experiencing what happened to her was horrible, but he understood it. What he didn't understand was the dream on the way to Clearview—the nightmare from *Michael's* point of view.

Finn had seen Siobhan's memories so many times. Maybe his brain had decided to mix things up a bit. It was sure doing its own thing with the extremely unwelcome thoughts that kept popping into his head.

Yeah, he was bitter. But when had he become an asshole?

"Are we going to go in or just sit in the parking lot all day?"

He didn't bother responding. Just scowled at her and opened the door. She fell in step beside him, keys in hand.

"Wait." Finn grabbed her arm before she could lock the doors. God, he missed touching her.

She stared into his face. Didn't ask. Didn't say anything. Just waited for him to make a move.

He cleared his throat. "I don't want them to hear the car arming itself and look out the window. We need to keep a low profile."

She nodded. "I can lock it without it making a sound."

He felt the muscles in her arm shift as she pressed the button to lock the door. He couldn't bring himself to let go of her, even while she put the keys in her pocket.

He wanted to kiss her again. That was a bad idea. Whether she went along with it or not, he was certain the results would gather attention. He finally let go of her and turned back to the bar.

Trees lined the parking lot. There were too many places people could be hiding and watching them. He headed for the bar at a brisk pace. At the door, Jazz ducked ahead of him and opened it so he didn't have to touch the handle.

"Thanks."

She actually smiled at him. "No problem."

The bar was busier than Finn expected. The smell of grease and eggs explained that. It was quite possible that they were in the only restaurant in town, unless there were others tucked away down a side street. A wiry woman stood behind the bar, wiping the counter. She was maybe in her late thirties and looked pissed as hell.

Tread carefully, Finn.

He walked to the bar, making sure Jazz stayed close as he kept track of the patrons. A table of four guys with full plates. They'd be busy for a while. The pitcher at their table was full of beer instead of orange juice, though. That was an early start and a bad sign, especially since their glasses were still half-full from a previous pitcher.

Two other tables had guys sitting at them, but they were solo and focused on their food. Finn wasn't as concerned about them. Numbers gave people false courage. Drinking would make matters worse.

He turned his attention back to the bartender. Flirting was out. He didn't need his powers to detect the "do not fuck with me" mojo she was putting off. He'd need to be direct, but not give too much away.

This will be fun.

Finally, something he and his brain could agree on. Unless he wasn't being sarcastic…while he was thinking to himself.

I'm worse off than I thought.

He brought his mind back to task and smiled as the woman made eye contact. He waited to speak until they were close and he could keep his voice down while being heard.

"Good morning."

She nodded. "Morning."

The rag on her shoulder had what looked like raw egg yolk on it. She was probably also the cook. He kept that in mind while figuring out how to get information from her. Using his powers to read her mind was out. He was pretty sure she'd cut off his hand if he tried to touch her.

At the very least.

Shut up, brain.

He sat on a stool, careful not to touch the counter. "Could we get two plates of eggs and toast with some orange juice?"

"Just some bottled water for me." Jazz was glancing around with a grimace on her face. She looked revolted—like she didn't want to touch anything herself.

The bartender snorted. "I can pour some from the tap into an empty. That work for you?"

Finn was sure Jazz was about to say something impolite in response. He reached over and touched her arm, giving her a pointed look. She seemed to get the message. He turned back to the bartender and smiled.

"Orange juice is fine," Jazz said.

"I'll have it right out."

As soon as the bartender left Finn whispered, "What the hell was that?"

Jazz stood near the bar, but didn't sit. "What do you mean? You're going to get rabies eating the food here."

"Come on."

She leaned closer and pointed to the door that led to the kitchen. A possum was hanging right above it. It didn't move as he stared at it. After a moment, he realized it was stuffed.

Great décor...

"At least it's not going anywhere," she murmured, crossing her arms.

"I don't plan to eat anything." Especially after seeing that. It would be a while before his appetite returned. "I just wanted to buy something so that I can overpay when I ask my questions."

"Oh. So that's how you do it."

"Would you please sit down?"

"No thanks." Jazz eyed the barstool. "I'm having enough trouble thinking of you sitting in my SUV in those pants."

She shifted closer, scanning the room. Her arm brushed his shoulder.

"I could always take them off first."

Dammit, he couldn't keep himself from flirting with her, even now. Especially now, with her standing close, being there for him when he needed her. She had dropped everything to help him. He only just realized that.

She smiled at him and he felt it reflected on his face. He had forgotten that smile. How could he have forgotten it? It made him feel like he was the center of her universe. Her eyes softened, her lips parted, and...

He was already leaning in when she snapped out of it and pulled away. Damn good thing one of them was keeping a level head.

"Sorry," he said.

"Forget it."

She crossed her arms and looked at the bottles lining the shelves in front of them. Most were fairly empty.

The bartender returned and set two plates with wet eggs and burned toast in front of them. There was nothing floating in the orange juice, but Finn didn't actually want to chance it.

He pulled four twenties from his wallet and set them on the counter. "Thanks."

She didn't reach for the cash as he'd expected. Instead, her eyes narrowed. She put her hands on the counter and leaned forward in an aggressive stance.

"What do you want?" she asked.

"My friend and I are just passing through town."

"Good for you. Get on with it."

Finn smiled at her, turning up the charm. Her lips pressed together more tightly. Perfect. She might be resisting him, but that meant he was at least affecting her.

"We're hoping you can settle something for us." He glanced at Jazz, then said, "I was telling my friend that this is the town where that serial killer grew up. You know…" He lowered his voice to a whisper and leaned forward. "Michael Angelo."

"Get the hell out of my bar."

Jazz jumped in. "I told you this isn't the town. If it was, they'd be cashing in on the publicity."

The bartender snorted again. "Right. Cops and reporters hassling your regulars is great for business. They didn't find anything here for them and neither will you."

Her gaze lingered on a seat a few spots to Finn's right.

"I'm not talking regulars," Jazz said. "I meant tourists. Florida is already full of them. If Clearview is where that guy grew up, you could advertise it and draw in more business. Charge an admission fee just to get into the place for special events."

"Events?"

Jazz had the woman hooked. Damn, she was a natural at this. He should have known, with the way she ran her gallery.

"His birthday. Halloween. You could make a whole show of it. Cash in on the creep factor."

The bartender leaned back, considering. Jazz kept on, pressing her advantage.

"Of course, you might catch some flak from his family. Does he have any in the area?"

The woman's gaze flicked back to that seat. Finn was able to track it better this time. Three stools over.

"You leave him alone. Travis is a good man."

Perfect. Now we have a name.

Finn leaned forward, keeping his elbows on his knees so he didn't touch the counter. "She didn't mean anything, Nell."

The woman and Jazz both stared at Finn. He wasn't sure why.

"What?" he asked.

Nell lowered her voice to a very menacing register. "How do you know my name?"

Shit. Did he? He hadn't even touched anything. How could he have picked that up? His mind spun, trying to come up with an explanation.

He needed to keep it together. He needed to get her off their case for long enough to read Travis's spot.

"Okay, you caught us," Finn said. "We had this idea for building a tourist trap in Clearview. My friend here is a marketing genius. We thought maybe we'd scope the place out. See if there's partnership potential."

"There's not," Nell said. "So you keep on moving out of town."

"Okay, okay. We get it." He held up his hands and nodded. He gave her his best smile and said, "Can I at least finish my eggs?"

She snorted, then snatched up his money and stalked away.

Chapter Thirteen

Jazz was ready to leave. She wanted to head back to Summer Park, burn their clothes, bleach the inside of her SUV, and spend three days in the shower. Maybe she could convince Finn to join her.

As soon as the bartender went back into the kitchen, Finn stood up. He didn't head for the exit as Jazz had hoped. Instead, he walked to a different barstool and sat.

"What are you doing?" she asked.

"This is where Travis always sits. I need to read the spot."

"That's a terrible idea."

They were in a public place. He could get lost in the memory. He could get a horrible disease from touching something in the bar. Jazz had looked at the floor once since coming in. Things were...moving.

"We need to know more about him. Who he is, where he lives. Scoot my plate over here, will you? It'll be less conspicuous."

She glanced at the plate. The eggs were half-liquid. It was one thing to have a ratty place, but the bartender—*Nell*—could have at least cooked the eggs properly.

"How did you know the bartender's name?"

"I must have picked it up somehow."

"What, by reading the seat through your ass?"

He busted out laughing, then shook his head. Part of her delighted in hearing him laugh. Most of her was terrified.

"This is serious. Have your powers gone airborne or something?" she asked.

If they did, she would have to get him away from people, away from civilization. It would be the only way to keep him sane.

"No. It must have been something I picked up from reading Michael's memories earlier. Or maybe from Travis."

She wasn't buying it. Something about the whole thing felt wrong —beyond his powers being whacked out.

"Jazz, please. You've been so keen on helping me. I need you now."

Dammit.

She pushed the plate over to him, then set up her dishes at the seat next to it. She still couldn't bring herself to sit down.

"I'll be right here."

"Give me ten minutes tops. If I'm not done, shake me out of it anyway."

"Okay."

She didn't like it. She didn't like anything about this. Her stomach was still in knots from giving that woman ideas for ways to use Michael Angelo as a *marketing tool*. Jazz hadn't known what else to do. If she ever found out this place was acting on those suggestions, she wouldn't forgive herself.

But they had made progress. They had a name for Michael's cousin. And if this worked out, they would know even more.

Finn put his hands on the counter. No more time for self-recrimination. She needed to keep her attention on him.

His eyes became blank. Maybe that was a good sign? At least he wasn't talking to himself. If she needed to snap him out of it, she could kick the barstool out from under him. Comforted by her plan, she crossed her arms and watched him work.

He was handling everything remarkably well. Yeah, he kept making snarky comments and he had yelled a few times, but he had flown off the handle on a regular basis when they were a couple. Either time or this had calmed him down. She hoped it helped him find happiness. With someone else.

Enough with the maudlin self-pity.

She was tired. She hadn't slept in over twenty-four hours and had no idea when she'd sleep again. But she was with Finn, and he kept looking at her with those soulful eyes, holding on to her longer than was necessary.

She wanted to put her hand on his back. Run her fingers through his hair. Okay, she wanted to pull off his tank top and see if he really was in just as good of shape as the last time she'd seen him shirtless.

She wanted to do much more than that. She wanted to hold on to him and never let go.

One touch. One tiny touch…

But she had no idea how that would affect him. She kept her hands to herself.

"Look at that."

The hair on the back of her neck stood on end at the voice that was too close for comfort. She turned around slowly, uncrossing her arms and shifting her weight to put herself between Finn and the four guys blocking the door to the bar.

They reeked of beer, and the smell wasn't just coming from the pitcher in the front man's hand. Each was smaller than Finn, but there were four of them. Jazz wished she had let Finn teach her more about fighting.

"You lost, little lady?"

"I'm fine, thanks."

How much time did Finn need? How much time was left before she was supposed to snap him out of it?

"I heard you talking to Nell about trying to bring in some tourists. I think that's a fine idea."

"Great. Take it up with your local Chamber of Commerce."

They all laughed and the three men behind him said, "Woooo."

"Sounds to me like you've already got it all worked out. We were just saying we can take you around. Show you what Clearview's got to offer."

"*My friend* and I are fine on our own, thanks."

She didn't want to call their attention to Finn, but needed them to know she wasn't alone. And at the same time, she kind of wanted to start screaming for help. She doubted there were any police nearby. To make things worse, the last solitary customer stood and half ran out of the place, as if he was scared.

Shit. What did he know that she didn't?

She focused on the four men in front of her, took in the way they were looking at her, and panicked. She pushed it down.

Where was the bartender?

"Your friend over there seems more messed up than us. When did he start in, anyway?"

The three guys laughed while the ringleader just smiled at her.

"He really likes eggs," she said.

"I'd be paying more attention to you. I bet he spends more time with that shiny SUV outside. That thing's barely got a speck of dirt on it."

She hadn't noticed the guy leave or come back. It unnerved her to imagine him eyeing her car while thinking about her and Finn.

"A man shouldn't spend more time on his ride than his woman. Unless of course—"

She refused to let him finish his lewd comment. "Actually, the SUV is mine."

"Is it now? I do like a woman with fine taste. Why don't you let your friend there finish his eggs and we can all go for a ride in that fancy car of yours. We can show you those sights and maybe talk about those plans you got."

"My only plan is to stay here."

"Come on. I heard your friend say you're a genius. You gotta have a few more ideas for bringing people to the bar in that gorgeous head of yours."

How the hell did this guy have such good hearing?

One of the guys behind him laughed. "I have one. Wet T-shirt contest."

He grabbed the front guy's arm and flung the pitcher of beer at Jazz. Her shirt was doused and she stumbled back into Finn, knocking him off the stool.

"What the fuck?" she shouted.

The men started to laugh. Jazz felt her shirt plastered to her front. She didn't bother crossing her arms to cover herself. They probably wanted her to feel cowed, and she refused to give them the satisfaction.

Also, she was wearing a bikini top under her shirt—she always wore bikinis under her clothes so she could hit the pool the moment she went home at night. They weren't getting the view they were after.

Mostly, she wanted her hands free so she could grab some bottles from behind the counter and smash them over these guys' heads.

She felt strong hands clasp her arms and lifted her foot to stomp on the guy's instep. She realized it was Finn just in time. Before anyone could say anything else, the bartender stormed out of the kitchen. With a shotgun.

"What the hell is going on out here?" she shouted.

"Hey, Nell." The front guy—all of them—acted contrite. He pointed at Jazz and said, "We were just welcoming these two strangers to Clearview."

"And flinging my good beer all over the place for me to clean up."

"If she'd been a little friendlier—"

Nell shook her head. "I don't want to hear it. You're all banned for a week. If I see you in here before then, I'll call the sheriff."

"A week? You can't—"

"I can and I did. Now go home and sleep it off. Unless you'd rather spend the rest of the day in the drunk tank. Again."

As the men filed out, the glares they cast at Jazz made her skin crawl. It took all her strength not to lean back into Finn.

The bartender was Jazz's new hero. Nell walked over to them and threw her rag on the floor in the center of the beer that hadn't soaked into Jazz's clothes.

"Thank you," Jazz said.

"Thank me? You just cost me four of my best customers for a week. Do you even know what that's going to mean for my business?"

She didn't, but from the looks of things, the bar was barely making ends meet.

"I can make up for it," Jazz said. "I have money."

"Keep your goddamned money. Just get the *fuck* out of my bar and don't come back."

Finn gripped Jazz's arm more tightly and led her to the door.

"Finn—"

"I know. Just keep walking."

The men from the bar were clustered around a truck parked in the back corner of the lot. Jazz unlocked her doors quickly, her heart pounding.

When they were in the car, she said, "Is Nell going to be okay?"

"They won't take this out on her. She's their source for a bar. We're a different matter, though. We need to leave. Now."

Jazz started the car and kicked it into gear, trying not to seem too much in a hurry. She wanted to floor it. She wanted to go back to the parking lot and run them over.

"What the hell was wrong with those people? Who throws beer? Seriously! And the whole, 'Hey baby, let's all go for a ride in your SUV.' Give me a fucking break."

"They tried to get you to leave with them?"

Finn's voice was quiet. Disturbingly so.

"It was no big deal."

"You should have snapped me out of it."

"You were busy."

"Jazz, don't dismiss this. Guys like that can do a hell of a lot worse than douse you in beer."

"They didn't make a move. I was ready to scream for help."

"And who would have come to your rescue?" He let out a deep sigh. "Some small towns, even down on their luck, the people pull together and help each other. Others go bad. This one is about the worst I've ever felt. In a town like this, you keep your head down and your mouth shut. You don't look too close at what other people are doing."

"I handled it. Deal—" She stopped herself again, clamping her mouth shut.

Finn shook his head. "This is why I didn't want you coming along. You're too cocky. You're going to get hurt. We should turn around and head back to Summer Park."

"I can take care of myself."

"Against four guys? Come on."

"I had you to back me up."

"Four guys, Jazz. I would have gotten my ass kicked if it wasn't for Nell."

The thought of Finn trying to fight them off—and failing—sent ice shooting through Jazz's veins. Her imagination painted a scene with him on the ground, them surrounding him…

"And they wouldn't have been finished after me. Do you even realize how dangerous that situation was?"

Yes. She did. She just didn't want to think about it. That had honestly been one of the scariest moments of her life. She didn't need to be psychic to see what the ringleader at least had in mind.

She wanted to have the courage to help Finn, to keep moving forward with him. *Nothing* would stop her.

"If something happened to you…" he said.

Her heart was still pounding, but suddenly for a different reason. She wanted him to finish his sentence. Wanted to hear him say he still cared.

"If something happened to me what?"

"Forget it." He shook his head. "I know who we're looking for. I have a good idea of where he lives. Head back to Summer Park. I'll pick up my car and take it from here."

"What about your powers malfunctioning? You need me."

"They worked fine back in the bar. Maybe now that I'm on the case, Siobhan's spirit is taking it easy on me. Hell, maybe she'll even help."

Replaced by a ghost. Harsh.

"What if you're wrong?"

"As you so often say—I'll deal with it."

And that was it. No more chances to fix things between them. Maybe they'd never be a couple again, but she had missed him. His absence in her life left a gaping hole. She wanted them to at least be friends.

She hadn't even realized that hope had bloomed in her until he stamped it out. End of opportunity.

Except she didn't want it to be. She didn't want things to be over.

The thought of Finn lost in a serial killer's memory while an accomplice crept up on him sent a chill through her. She needed time to change his mind.

She needed to change.

"I stink," she said.

Finn turned back to her.

"I stink like cheap beer. I don't want the smell getting stuck in the upholstery. Summer Park is hours away. Let's find a place to clean up first. Okay?"

He sighed, but nodded. "Okay."

Chapter Fourteen

An hour later, Finn was standing in a shower stall in a cheap, relatively clean hotel room that he had paid for in cash under an assumed name. They had wolfed down some power bars and bottles of water he grabbed from the office. The SUV was parked around back to keep it out of sight from people cruising down the highway. He hoped that would be enough.

He had called to check in on his dad, and Daphne had answered. She said Dad was sleeping, but seemed okay when he was awake earlier. Withdrawn and devastated, sure. But physically she didn't think he was in danger. That was enough to help Finn keep going. Daphne would update Dad next time he woke up and Finn would keep his focus on the case.

Jazz had showered first and borrowed his shirt to wear while her T-shirt and pants dried. She had definitely taken the brunt of the pitcher of beer, blocking it with her body as she'd fallen into him.

If she hadn't knocked him off his stool, he might have stayed lost in that memory too long to help her. When he came out of it, she might have been gone.

He was certain those guys were capable of…things he didn't want to think about. He wasn't sure how he knew. Just like he wasn't sure how he knew Nell's name before reading anything.

He didn't want to think about that either.

His focus needed to be on getting Jazz back to Summer Park. Once he knew she was safe, he could track down the guy who helped kill his sister. His twin.

A pang shot through his chest as he thought of Siobhan again. How could he miss her when he'd never even met her? He was having a hard enough time keeping it together as it was.

His thoughts kept running on bizarre tangents that just weren't him. No matter where they were, he felt like he was being watched. The case was getting under his skin. He needed to regroup as much as he needed to get Jazz out of harm's way. Focusing on the warm water pouring over his shoulders helped.

Last he had seen of her, she was sitting on the queen bed, bare legs stretched out and crossed at the ankles. She had one arm bent behind her neck and was leaning back as if staring at the ceiling, but her eyes were closed. He'd taken off the comforter for her and folded it on top of the dresser. The bar had reminded him that she wasn't used to dives.

His shirt looked so damned good on her. She left the top few buttons undone. The sleeves dangled past her elbows. He wondered if she had put her swimsuit back on underneath.

The first time he had seen her had been at her condo's pool. He had stopped by to introduce himself after Garrett had recommended Finn for a case involving one of the exhibits at her gallery. It had been late and she had been alone, standing on the other side of the clear water. While he watched, she'd peeled off her shirt and pants. He hadn't known she wore swimsuits under her clothes.

His brain had sort of stalled out before letting him realize what was happening. By then, it had been too late. His dick was already at full attention. He had planned to introduce himself and try to score her number before he'd found out she was his new client. It had been an awkward moment.

He never mixed business and pleasure, but had still hoped to make a move after the case was finished. They were definitely on the same track there—like two trains heading for each other.

He shouldn't be thinking about this. Even the memory of her sleek body cutting through the water was enough to get him hard. He turned the temperature on the shower down a notch, then braced his arms against the tile and closed his eyes as the cooler water washed over his body.

He felt her hands on his shoulders.

Shit. This isn't happening.

At the same time, it felt inevitable. The two of them trapped together, with their history and all that was unresolved between them... Okay. Yeah, it was happening.

Her fingers glided down his back, playing with the planes and valleys of his muscles. She always said she loved his back. Then again, she'd been a fan of everything about him—physically, at least.

She slid her palms over his hips. One traveled up along his abs while the other went straight for the prize. He groaned as she wrapped her slender fingers around him and squeezed, then started slow, rhythmic strokes.

"Jazz..."

She shifted so she was kneeling in front of him. He could feel her moving around him and clenched his eyes shut tighter. If their gazes locked, she would see the conflict in him and this would be over. And if this was all he had left of them right now, dammit, he would take it.

Her lips slid over his dick, pulling him deep into her mouth. Her tongue joined in the stroking, her hand still working the base of his shaft. Damn, he had missed this. The heat, the energy.

His body relaxed under her touch, his tension and unease vanishing as he fell into the familiar rhythm. His hips rocked against her. He wanted to fuck her so bad, but she didn't seem ready to stop what she was doing. He sure as hell wasn't ready to stop her. Maybe she'd missed this as much as he had.

There's no possible way.

Finally, she slid up his chest, wrapping her arms around his neck, jumping up to lock her legs around his waist. She nipped at his neck and pressed her chest against his.

Somehow, he could still feel the water from the shower running along his skin. That wasn't right.

He opened his eyes.

Jazz wasn't there. No one was. He was standing in the shower alone, hard as he'd ever been, water pouring over his chest—and he could still feel her all over him.

Her thighs were tight against his hips, calves gripping his back. Her arms distributed her slight weight across his shoulders. He felt the softness of her skin, the heat of her body, the slickness of her core as she lined herself up.

But she wasn't there.

He lurched back and she went with him. At least, the sensation of her. He reached for her instinctively to keep her from falling. He felt the warm skin of her back—dry, not wet—felt her tense for a split-second, then the...whatever the hell it was...vanished.

Moments later, Jazz flung the door to the shower open. Cool air from the AC flooded the tiny space.

"What the hell was that?" she shouted.

He tried to cover himself, but basically ended up just holding his dick against his stomach.

"What are you talking about? And do you mind?"

"Yeah, I do! You used your powers on me."

Oh shit.

He fumbled for the knobs to turn off the water, panicking. Stepping from the shower, he grabbed a towel and wrapped it around his waist.

"Jazz—"

"I felt your hands on my back."

"Wait... Just your back?"

"Yeah. What the hell difference does it make?"

Relief rushed through him. He had thought she felt the whole thing —that his imagination was somehow manifesting on her body. He would never touch Jazz—or anyone—like that unless they wanted him to, through his powers or otherwise.

Wait a minute...

"You only felt my hands on your back?" He had to be sure.

She crossed her arms and shifted her weight, raising one eyebrow and glaring at him. "Yeah. So?"

"Because I felt a hell of a lot more than that. For the last five minutes at least. What have you been doing out there?"

Her mouth dropped open. She snapped it shut, then turned on her heel and stalked out of the room.

Yeah, his powers were acting up again, but *she* had prompted it. He could tell from the look on her face, the way her cheeks and the skin of her neck and chest were flushed.

She was thinking about him, imagining or remembering what they had experienced together. And he had felt every moment.

He still wanted her. Of course he did. But now he knew she wanted him too. Damn, did she want him.

He followed her into the bedroom. "We need to talk."

"You're right." Jazz stopped on the far side of the bed, crossing her arms again. "I'm not going back to Summer Park."

"What? That's not what I meant." He would save that argument for later. And it *would* be an argument. "We need to talk about what just happened."

"No we don't. Your powers are malfunctioning. End of story."

"That's not... Do you even listen to yourself? You can't put this all on me."

She let out a snort. "Pardon me for not being more careful with my thoughts around a telepath who told me he can only read people when touching them—and that I was immune to his powers. Anything else I should know?"

"What the fuck, Jazz. Are you kidding me? I didn't try to read you. My powers have never done anything like that before."

"I get it. It's not your fault. I don't get why we have to talk about it."

"Because it shouldn't have happened. On so many levels, it shouldn't have happened."

"Well it did and it's done. You're dripping on the carpet. Go dry off."

Seriously? That was her diversionary tactic?

He'd had enough.

He pulled the towel from his waist and roughly dried his chest and arms, then his legs. He glared at her the whole time. Well, at first, anyway.

The more she stared back, the less angry she looked. He started to forget what they were fighting about. Her lips parted and her arms dropped to her sides.

He ran the towel over his back and scrubbed his hair, then ran his fingers through it. When he was done, he threw the towel over the back of a chair and just stood there. One of them had to make a move, a gesture, anything to break the icy silence between them. He couldn't stand being so close to her without touching her.

And that was always the problem.

"Jazz…"

She didn't give him a chance to finish. She ran across the room and grabbed him. Her arms locked behind his neck, pulling her up so she could crush her lips against his. Her tongue slid into his mouth, not so much demanding as starved.

He pressed her against his body—thrumming as anticipation built. He let his hands slide down to her ass, lifting her off her feet. She wrapped her legs around his waist, deepening the kiss as her weight was taken off her arms.

God, he had missed this.

He walked them to the bed, then laid her down and covered her with his body. She ran her legs along his thighs, the softness of her skin making him want to just plunge into her. He couldn't risk hurting her, though. He had to be sure she was ready.

Sliding a hand between them, he let his fingers follow a familiar path through the soft curls at the apex of her legs. She was already slick. Maybe she wouldn't need as much warming up as he thought. He ran his fingers through her wetness, then drove two in deep.

She gasped against his mouth, back arcing as he started moving within her, steady thrusts, thumb circling her clit. She melted back into the mattress. The more she relaxed, the more worked up he became. His dick was so hard he could probably cut glass with it. It would be so easy to sink into her.

He felt her shift beneath him. He didn't want to break the kiss. He was afraid of what would happen when they made eye contact.

Would she pull away? Freak out? Say something that made his heart reach for her or shrivel up in his chest?

He forced himself to pull back. She didn't even look at him. Just reached for the bedside table—and her wallet. She pulled out a condom, then flung the wallet back on the table.

Practical, as always.

He tried not to care—tried not to let it get under his skin—but who was he kidding? She lived under his skin. Had since the beginning.

He sat on his knees, waiting for her to do her thing. She'd probably want to be on top and run the show. He never really minded. Hell, it was great to be with someone who told him what she wanted instead of making him figure things out on his own.

Other guys probably thought Finn was lucky to be able to read people's thoughts through touch. He always knew what his partner enjoyed or didn't enjoy. But the running commentary wasn't what it was cracked up to be.

It didn't usually take him long to realize that most of his lovers were so smitten with his looks that they didn't care at all about who he was as a person. Others compared him with previous lovers, which was almost worse. The result was that his experience outside of Jazz was actually pretty limited. Sex was too complicated when he could read people's thoughts.

Jazz opened the wrapper and slid the thin plastic over him without missing a beat. Her skill set didn't seem rusty at all. A surge of jealousy hit him in the chest. Dammit, now was not the time to be thinking about that—or anything. This could very well be his last chance to be with her like this. He wanted to enjoy it.

She kissed him again, slow and deep. Then she knelt next to him and unbuttoned the shirt she was wearing. She let it slide down her arms before tossing it away. Instead of pushing him down on the bed, she wrapped her arms around his neck, gently pulling him toward her as she lay back.

That was new.

He'd take it. He'd take her any way he could get her. He nestled himself between her thighs, perched right at her entrance, trying to hold on to the moment, to remember every touch, every look.

And the way she was looking at him…

It was unguarded. She actually looked vulnerable.

"Jazz—"

She shook her head and wrapped her legs around the backs of his thighs. "No words. Just this."

Then she pulled him home.

Chapter Fifteen

Jazz felt Finn enter her as a cascade of bliss flowing along all her senses. He slid his hands beneath her back, embracing her as he slowly thrust in and pulled out, over and over again.

Wrapping her arms around him, she held him as close as she could, nuzzling his neck and pressing kisses along his warm skin. She let her legs glide up along the backs of his thighs, then locked her ankles so he could land deeper.

He made a little grunting noise and his fingers tightened against her back. He was trying to hold on to the moment, to make this union last. She couldn't blame him.

She didn't know what would happen when it was over.

He buried his face in her hair, his stubble tickling her ear. "I missed you."

"I missed you too."

He pushed himself up on his elbows and stared down at her, his hips still making languid thrusts into her body. She didn't want to talk, didn't want to think. She only wanted to feel.

She lifted her lips to his. He kissed her, pressing her back against the pillows. She nipped at him, urging him on. She met his tongue as it slid into her mouth. He was still drawing his shaft out slowly, letting them savor the friction, the building heat. But then he'd drive himself back in quickly, as if he couldn't stand being apart from her.

The pace of his thrusts increased, his kiss deepened. She distracted herself from the pressure building within her by tracing the muscles of his back as he moved above her, exploring the valley of his spine just above his waist. She dropped her legs to the side so she could spread her fingers over his ass and feel them flex.

They should have done this more often. She had taken the lead most times when they had sex. It might not be safe to tell him how she felt, but she had always thought she could at least show him. She could give him as much as he gave her.

At the moment, she needed to feel as much of him as possible. She wrapped her legs around his, pulling against his thighs as he buried himself in her over and over again. The rough hair of his legs prickled against her skin.

He shifted his mouth to her neck, sucking and nipping. His weight pressed her into the mattress, his heat surrounding her, filling her. Every time he buried himself in her, he ground against her most sensitive spot. He was moving faster, each pump increasing the pressure she felt deep in her belly, sending tendrils of pleasure out through her body.

He pushed himself up on his arms, letting the cold air from the AC flow over her. His pace quickened, the pull against her skin, the grinding of his thrusts, setting off an avalanche along her senses. The tension he had built shattered as waves of pleasure pulsed through her body from where they were joined.

She wanted to pull him in even deeper, but he wasn't done. Gasping as she caught her breath, she looked up at him. His eyes were shut tightly, his lips parted as he started pumping into her even faster. She wrapped her legs around his waist again, running her fingernails lightly along his back as he landed hard and deep.

Finally, he threw his head back and groaned, burying himself as deep as he could, pinning her to the bed. She felt him pulsing within her, spending himself. With a last shuddering breath, he lowered himself so their chests were pressed together again. He wrapped his arms around her back, embracing her without crushing her.

"That was...amazing," he said.

There was a lump in her throat blocking her words. She ran her hands gently down his back instead of trying to talk.

Panic started to set in.

He was going to pull out soon. She felt him softening. Then they would go back to being...what? Friends? Ex-lovers? Friends with benefits? She had no idea.

They couldn't pick up where they left off. She didn't want to be the couple who always fought. How long could they really be together anyway? She couldn't give him a family, didn't want to settle down. She didn't even want to live with anyone. She wanted her own place to retreat to. She needed her space.

But she wanted Finn. She wanted to be with him.

She felt him slide from her body. He rolled over, taking her with him, then reached to the nightstand and grabbed a handful of tissues. He managed to take off the condom and bundle it up with one hand before tossing the whole thing in the trash.

She wrapped her arms around his chest and willed her body to relax. He wouldn't need his powers to detect her tension at this rate. The longer she could put off talking, the longer she could stay in this moment, this fantasy of them being together.

Everyone always thought of her as brave. Her friends had outright said it on many occasions. But labeling her as brave was dismissive. She was human. She felt fear. They only thought Jazz was brave because she never let them see it. She was terrified of losing all of them, just like she'd lost Finn.

Now he was back in her life and she wanted to keep him there. If she was honest with herself about it, she was desperate to.

She knew that he would never have had sex with her if he was involved or even interested in someone else. Adultery was one of his triggers. She had witnessed that enough times when he flipped out about her keeping their relationship secret.

Back then, she had felt like she was protecting them—*keeping* them together. If they told people, Jazz had been sure something would happen to tear them apart. Instead, their relationship had deteriorated.

What if this was a second chance? What if Fate was cutting her some slack at last, *giving* her someone instead of taking him away? What if her curse was finally breaking?

They both seemed to have changed. Jazz wasn't sure if she'd changed enough. But she could try. She *would* try. If Fate was giving them the opportunity to see if they could work out, Jazz wouldn't waste it.

And if Fate was messing with her...Jazz wouldn't tolerate it. She'd done everything she could to help people along their paths, to be Fate's implement. It was her turn to guide her own life. And she wanted a life with Finn. She would *make* that her destiny.

The trouble was, she had no idea how to go about it.

No, she had one. She needed to talk to him. She needed to tell him how she felt. Even though the thought of it scared the crap out of her. She would find a way to keep him safe, even if she had to go up against Fate to do so.

His breath had evened out and his eyes were closed. She felt her own exhaustion catching up with her. Eventually, his steady heartbeat lulled her to sleep.

Chapter Sixteen

Finn was walking through a swamp. He felt the weight of...
something in his right hand. He looked down to see that he was holding
a machete.

Why was it in his right hand? He was left-handed. Wasn't he?

He stared at the ground. Some kind of animal trap had been sprung
by a squirrel. The poor thing had been snapped in half. Finn poked at it
with the end of the blade. He tried to stop himself, but couldn't.

"Leave it, Mikey!"

Finn turned as a gangly teen ran up to him. The boy's clothes were
worn and dated. He had short-cropped brown hair and bright blue
eyes. He was taller than Finn, which didn't seem right. The kid was
maybe five-six, but Finn was looking up at him.

Finn turned back to the squirrel, noticing that the hand holding the
machete—his hand—was smaller than it should be. His feet were bare
and crusted with sand. It looked like he was about the same age as the
other kid. Maybe a little younger.

"You're going about it all wrong, Travis." The words came out of
Finn's mouth, but he didn't recognize his voice. "If you want the pelts,
you have to use live traps. Oh, right. I forgot. You're too much of a
coward to kill anything yourself."

Travis... The gangly kid was Travis? Finn tried to commit the boy's
face to memory, updating it with time. Finn was surprised at how
healthy he looked. He was thin, but not gaunt.

"They don't all get hit like this one." Travis knelt down and dug a
length of chain out from the sand. He pulled it, and the trap and
squirrel came with it. He stood and said, "If the pelts won't work for
practice, the meat's still fine for dinner."

Finn felt his mouth open again, his voice young and strange. "Is food all you ever think about? Ma isn't that good of a cook."

Travis grabbed the collar of Finn's shirt and jerked him forward.
"She's not your mom."

Finn laughed. "It doesn't matter. She still likes me best."
Travis looked like he was about to punch Finn. Finn wouldn't blame
him. Instead, Travis shoved Finn in the chest. He stumbled back, the
machete slipping from his hand.

"Mikey!"

Travis dropped the trap and grabbed Finn's arm, his face horror-
stricken. Finn looked at the ground, at the crimson spreading from his
foot, at the digit lying in the sand next to the blade.

He started to laugh.

Finn jolted awake. He sat up, frantically searching the room for…
He didn't know what. He was alone.

"Jazz?" he called.

"Just a minute." Her muffled voice came from the bathroom. He
could hear water running.

He was cold. How low was the AC set? Finn threw his legs over the
side of the bed and stood. The room spun around him. Had he always
been this tall? He felt kind of drunk.

His clothes were draped over a nearby chair. He stumbled to it and
pulled on his jeans and tank top. Jazz must still have his shirt. He slid
his feet into his shoes, then ran his hands over his face, trying to shake
off the dream's effects while remembering what had happened.

Travis. Finn had dreamt about Travis. But when they were both
younger. No, not him. Michael. In the dream, Finn had seen everything
from Michael's point of view again. It was visceral. He had actually
been *in* Michael's body.

Why did he keep dreaming he was Michael?

Pushing that…admittedly terrifying thought away. What did you
learn?

They were in a swamp. Their house was close. Finn wasn't sure how he knew, but there it was. Travis was trapping animals for practice. He wanted the pelts.

Finn remembered the stuffed possum at the bar and Nell's instant defense of Travis. Taxidermy. As if this wasn't all creepy enough as it was.

Finn scoffed. *He actually thought those ugly little pets of his were art.*

Wait... Where had that thought come from? That laugh? Finn shook his head again. The room was still spinning.

"These are ruined."

Finn jumped at the sound of Jazz's voice behind him. He could feel his heartbeat in his throat, making it difficult to swallow. She was holding her leather pants and staring at him.

"You okay?" she asked.

"Yeah, I'm fine."

He and "fine" weren't on the same continent.

She tossed her pants on a chair. She was wearing her bikini with his shirt, which was completely unbuttoned. The swimsuit was wine-red and more string than fabric. The dark blue silk of his shirt flowed around her body as she walked.

Finn had always thought she moved like she'd been trained for the stage. He asked her about it once, but it brought on their first big freeze-out. Watching her now, though... The room seemed to warm as he looked at her.

Her T-shirt was wadded up in her hand. She sniffed it, then curled her nose and tossed it on the chair after her pants.

"Do you mind if I keep wearing your shirt for a while? I'm not up to trying to shimmy into that leather, and the whole outfit reeks."

"You can walk around in a bikini and one of my shirts for the rest of my life, as far as I'm concerned."

She smiled at him. Honest-to-God smiled. He felt himself calm down, the last chill from the dream receding. Good thing she didn't throw her smelly clothes on the bed. He had other plans for it. But no condoms.

Dammit.

He hadn't needed any in so long, he didn't bother carrying them anymore. He hadn't been with anyone since Jazz and he knew he couldn't get her pregnant. Depending on how active her social life had been, maybe they could go without. The idea of sliding into her heat, feeling her skin-to-skin in the most intimate way possible...

He wanted her again. And again and again. The room was paid up through the next morning. They could rest, recover, and reconnect. But first he needed to find out if she was on board.

She'd brought up the subject of kids once. Finn had panicked, his mouth running off about how much he loved them—which was true. Up to a point.

He was worried if she found out he'd already made the decision not to have kids and taken steps to make sure it didn't happen that she would freak out or something. He'd never been with anyone long enough for the topic to come up and didn't really know how to handle it. He wasn't sure how she'd react now.

"We should talk."

Her smile faltered. "Okay."

She walked to the empty chair and sat, pulling her slender legs up and hugging her knees. The curve of her hips against the lines of her legs... It was not conducive to a coherent conversation. Finn would make it work somehow, though. He was enjoying the view too much to ask her to move.

"What do you want to talk about?"

She looked like she was bracing herself for something, her lips pulled in a frown and her gaze laser-focused. Preemptive freeze-out.

Great. Even the room seemed to drop in temperature.

"Cut me some slack, Jazz. This isn't an interrogation."

"I know. I'm just..." She shook her head. "You said you wanted to talk."

Finn felt his fatigue hit him again. He was suddenly bone-weary. He sat on the edge of the bed and leaned forward on his elbows.

Go ahead and offer her your heart again. Watch her laugh as she crushes it beneath her feet.

Man, he was being hard on himself today. He was too tired to even fight back.

"Do you ever wonder if things would have worked out differently if we talked things through instead of always jumping into bed when one of us was angry?"

"I'm not the one who got angry. And you're the one who left."

"Thanks for the constant reminders."

What else did you expect?

"I'm sorry," Jazz said.

Whoa. Had he heard her right? She had never apologized for anything before. Not to him, not to anyone as far as he knew. For a moment, he wondered if he was hearing things.

"I'm not good at this," she said. "I don't talk about feelings with anyone. When you would get upset, I didn't know how to respond. Not with words anyway. Sex seemed a reasonable solution."

A reasonable solution? She's talking as if you're an equation.

"Is that what this was?" He gestured toward the bed. "A *reasonable solution* for dealing with me when I'm upset?"

"That's not what I meant. I was talking about when we were together before. Not now."

A convenient excuse. She sees you as something to be managed, like she managed you after your shower. She pulled you right back in. She only ever wanted you in bed.

Dammit. Was she really only interested in his body?

"So what about now? What was that after the shower, just a farewell fuck?"

Her mouth dropped open and her eyes filled with tears. Actual tears.

"Go to hell," she snapped. She jumped up and stalked to her boots, then shook them out before pulling them on.

Finn buried his face in his hands. He was prone to losing his temper. He knew that. But he never hurt people. Ever. Not with his body, not with his words. Why was he turning into such an asshole?

It's the effect she has on me.

No. Goddammit, no. He was not putting the blame on her. This was his problem. He needed to sort it out. He had *hurt* her. Hurt Jazz. He had to get her away from this. Away from him. Until he could get himself back under control or at least figured out what was happening to him.

"Are you okay?" she asked.

Why the hell was she asking him that? She shouldn't care anymore. She had tried to talk—finally, really and truly tried. And he had fucked it up so royally, he would probably never get another chance.

Give up.

"Finn?"

He felt her kneel in front of him. She gently touched his arms, her grip feather light. She pulled his hands away from his face and gasped. She grabbed his cheeks, hard. He was glad. The room was spinning and it helped him feel more connected to his body.

He must have it for her worse than he thought.

"Finn!"

"What?" Nothing felt real. The detachment increased. He felt vaguely nauseated.

"Your eyes are turning blue."

"My eyes have always been blue."

"Not this color."

He closed his eyes tight and shook his head. Not the best move. Her hands shifted to his shoulders as she helped him stay upright.

"Finn? Finn!"

She grabbed his face again and kissed him. Full-on, no build. Her lips were all over his, tongue demanding attention. His body knew her so well, his hands went to the warm skin of her sides like they were magnetized. He pulled her against him, grabbing her legs and pulling them up on either side of him on the bed. He rocked against her, heat building within him.

His jeans chafed his dick as it stiffened. He didn't care—was grateful, even. Because it was grounding him. Her touch, their bodies locked together, it brought him back to himself.

What the fuck is going on?

He was about to start tugging on the strings that held her bikini in place when she pulled back from the kiss—hands on his cheeks, eyes searching his. She let out a sigh and relaxed in his lap.

"It's okay. They're normal now." She smiled at him.

Then the fireball crashed through the window.

Chapter Seventeen

Heat hit her back as the room exploded into fire behind her. Jazz heard the window shatter. The next thing she knew, Finn had pulled her against his chest and was rolling them across the bed to the floor.

"What the hell?" she yelled.

"Molotov cocktail. We need to go out the back."

The curtains were on fire, flames dropping onto the carpet. Some smoldered out. Others caught.

"Shouldn't we try to stop it?"

As she said the words, another projectile flew into the room, landing on the bed. The sheets caught instantly as the accelerant poured over the mattress.

"Shit!"

Finn leapt forward, blocking her body with his, pushing her toward the bathroom.

"Wait."

Jazz ducked under his arm so she could grab her wallet, phone, and keys from the nightstand. He took her hand and pulled her toward the bathroom, both crouching low to stay beneath the smoke. Finn slammed the door shut as soon as they were in the smaller room, then rolled up a towel and tucked it along the crack at the floor.

There was a small window above the sink. She could fit through easily. She wasn't sure about him.

"Finn…"

"It'll be fine."

He jumped up onto the sink, then opened the window and punched out the screen. He scanned the area outside. "I don't think they're back here. They might have taken off to avoid the cops, but we can't assume anything."

"Is it those guys from the bar?"

"Probably," Finn said. "Come on." He helped her up onto the counter. "Be sure to check the SUV before you get into it."

As if he wouldn't be with her.

"You go first," she said.

"Jazz—"

"I will balk. I swear to fucking God, I will kick and scream and fight you on this. I'm not going through that window until I'm sure you can fit through it. You go first."

He stared at her for a moment.

"We're wasting time," she said.

He sighed, then turned and pulled himself up into the window. Shifting his shoulders, he managed to get himself halfway through. She shoved on his legs, helping him the rest of the way. There was a loud *thump* as he hit the ground on the other side. She hoped it was mostly sand.

There were noises coming from the other room that she didn't understand. Crackling, popping. Smoke was seeping in around the edges of the door. She turned and practically dove through the window. Finn was on the other side to catch her, which was good, because she was still holding on to her things with one hand. It wasn't like her bikini had pockets. Thank God she had put on her boots.

He grabbed her empty hand and ran with her through the brush that edged up to the back of their room. He pulled her to a stop just before they hit the parking lot.

Jazz didn't see anyone around. Finn waited a few moments longer, then said, "Okay."

They ran across the lot. Jazz hit the button to unlock the doors as they neared the SUV.

"Get in on the passenger's side," he said.

It was the closest. She pulled the door open and jumped up. Finn put his hand on her ass, pushing her across the space. She climbed into the driver's seat as he sat next to her.

Her hands were shaking so hard, she had to use them both to get the key in the ignition and start the SUV. She peeled out of the space Finn had told her to back into. At the time, she wondered why it would matter. Now she understood.

Two loud pops sounded and Finn yelled, "Get down!"

She ducked low. Finn put his arm around her, trying to shield her with his body and yet not interfere with her ability to drive. She floored the accelerator, tearing out of the lot and onto the highway.

Her heart was pounding so hard she thought it might burst. Finn pulled back from her, wrapping his arm around her headrest as he stared out the back window.

He turned to look out the windshield, and said, "Take the next turn. Slow down. You're going to miss it."

"That isn't a road, it's a dirt track."

"I know. They won't think we'll turn here. Trust me."

She turned, praying the SUV wouldn't get bogged down. A few minutes later, he had her turn again. Then again and again, until she wasn't sure she would be able to find her way back to the highway. He seemed to know where he was going, though.

"Pull off here."

Sphagnum moss brushed the roof of the SUV as she took the last turn onto a graveled stretch that was so overgrown she doubted anyone had used it for years. She stopped the car in the shade of a huge gnarled oak tree, knuckles white on the wheel.

Finn reached over and turned the key, killing the engine.

"Where are we?" she asked.

"About a ten-minute walk from Travis's house."

Jazz turned to look at him. "How do you know that?"

He swallowed hard. She saw his throat work at it.

"I don't know."

"What is going on, Finn?" She was scared. So was he. She could see it in his eyes.

He shook his head and said, "I wish I knew."

She reached across the small space between them and put her arms around his neck, pulling him into an awkward hug. He hugged her back as best he could.

She kissed the side of his head and said, "We're going to figure this out. Okay? I promise you."

He nodded as he pulled back.

Her wallet and phone had fallen to the floor when they jumped into the SUV. She tossed her wallet into the drink tray, but held on to her phone. She handed Finn the keys, then opened her door and slid to the ground.

Her knees felt weak. She left her door open, holding the grab handle and closing her eyes as she regained her equilibrium. She heard Finn's door open and shut and waited for him to walk around the SUV and join her.

She opened her eyes when she heard him stop a few feet away. His face was pale and drawn. He was staring at the bottom of her door.

"What is it?"

She followed his gaze, her stomach clenching with icy dread when she saw what he had noticed. There were two small holes near the bottom of the driver's side door.

That was why Finn wanted them to go in through the passenger's door—the side that was away from the street. He wanted the SUV to provide them with cover from gunfire.

Jazz felt dizzy. She was angry and scared and for once in her life she had no idea what to do. The look on Finn's face made her think he wouldn't be much help. He just kept staring at those holes.

"If they had been a foot higher—"

She didn't let him finish that thought. Either of them could have been hurt. Killed. She wouldn't let him say it—think it. She grabbed his arm and turned him to face her.

"They weren't. Deal—" She cut herself off again. Closing her eyes, she took a deep breath, then let it out slowly. "We're okay."

She opened her eyes to look at him again. He was swaying on his feet. She grabbed his face in her hands and forced him to look at her. "We are okay."

He nodded.

Now that he was reassured, she needed to get a handle on herself. A foot higher and one or both of them would be dead. Fate could have taken him away so easily—but hadn't. Jazz dared to let a little more hope into her heart.

She finally remembered that the shirt she was wearing had a pocket on the chest and dropped her phone in it. The shirt was unbuttoned, so she fixed that immediately. She really wished she had pants. Or bug spray. Wildlife was the least of her worries, though.

The group from the bar had seemed dangerous. She still had trouble believing they were capable of this. Burning down a hotel? Shooting at them? Jazz hoped no one else was hurt.

The hotel was a single-story building laid out like a strip mall, with each room opening out to the parking lot. Finn had mentioned that he had asked for a room away from other guests. Maybe he'd thought something like this might happen.

No. If he had, he would have insisted that they go back to Summer Park immediately. He probably always asked to be secluded. His job made him cautious about everything.

She couldn't believe this was his life. He'd even parked his car strategically. The self-defense lessons he had given her were just the tip of the iceberg. She wanted to learn more, to be able to help him assess situations. She had his back already—when he would let her. She wanted to be sure it counted.

"We can't head back to town," he said.

Her hope picked up. He wasn't trying to bench her, to push her out of his life.

"It's too dangerous. They're probably cruising the highway, and we don't know which direction is safe. They might be using more than one vehicle, based on the attack at the hotel."

Okay. Necessity was keeping her with him. She would take it.

"We should call the police," Jazz said.

"And tell them what? Did you see who threw the bottles? All we have is conjecture."

"But we could tell them what happened at the bar."

"Which would lead to more questions. Clearview is still the closest town. It's obviously strapped for resources. All the emergency personnel will be tied up with the hotel. Besides, I don't want to answer their questions yet. Not until I've had a look at Travis's house."

"That's too dangerous. You can't keep reading things. It's affecting you—"

"She was my sister, Jazz. Do you have any idea what that's like?"

She bristled, felt the familiar walls come up.

No. Not this time.

She was so keen on him not pushing her away, but he'd been right before. She had kept him at arm's length for their entire relationship. He said he wanted in. She wanted to let him. And if Fate decided to try to take him away because of that, he, she, it—whatever that force was —would have to go through Jazz. She was sick of her curse. Sick of stifling herself and living half a life. It ended now.

"Yeah, I do, actually. I have a younger sister back in Kansas. If anything happened to her…"

Shit. Yeah, if anything happened to her, Jazz would let *nothing* stand in the way of getting justice.

Finn stared at her blankly. She wondered if he was having another episode. At least his eyes were still pale blue.

"What?"

"You have a sister?" he asked.

"Yeah. Her name's Mei."

Jazz forced herself to stand still, even though she wanted to pace— as if putting physical distance between them would make it easier to let him closer emotionally. She couldn't stop herself from crossing her arms tight across her chest. It reassured her. A little.

"That's the first time you've told me anything about your family," he said.

She was aware. She tried to shrug it off, to maybe fool herself into thinking it wasn't as big of a deal as it was.

"What do you want to know?"

His eyes were wide and he smiled. He genuinely smiled. She felt her lips tug up at the corners. She hadn't seen him look so happy in a long time.

"Everything." He shook his head. "I want to know everything."

Her stomach felt like she was on a roller coaster. She hadn't even talked to Elsa about her family. Neither of them discussed their pasts, so they never pushed each other for details or information they'd be uncomfortable sharing. That was one of the reasons they were best friends.

Now that Jazz thought about it, she and Elsa never sharing their histories was also what had made Jazz accidentally give Dante some advice for handling an argument with Elsa that had nearly destroyed their relationship. Maybe she and Elsa needed to start talking more too.

Finn had wanted to share Jazz's life. It was obvious he still did. And she wanted to share it with him.

She took a deep breath. She could do this. She could tell him about her family. Especially if she stuck with the facts and didn't wax poetic about how much she loved them all.

"Her husband's a professional football player. They have three daughters. They live with my mom in a huge house. My brother-in-law dotes on them all. My mom still insists on doing all the cooking, but I think they at least have a maid service."

"I didn't mean right now." Finn laughed. "Although I should probably make the most of it while you're in a talking mood."

"I'm not in a talking mood. I'm *never* in a talking mood." Even without the curse, she just wasn't that kind of person.

"Then why are you telling me this?"

"Because you asked. It's important to you to know."

His mouth was actually hanging open.

"You don't have to look so shocked."

He closed it and laughed again.

This was the Finn she remembered. Always laughing. He had seemed so carefree. It was probably part of what drew her to him. They were opposites in that regard. They both had laser focus when it came to their careers, but he knew how to shut it off. Jazz was always thinking. He knew how to let go and just have fun.

"What about your dad?" he asked.

Shit.

Her insides turned to ice and her mouth went dry. This was one of the reasons she hated talking to people about personal things. It was never enough—always led to more questions, whether she was ready to answer them or not.

She swallowed a few times, then shook her head and murmured, "Not yet. Okay?"

His smile faded, his expression turning gentle. His voice was equally so as he said, "Yeah. Sure."

She tried to shake it off, focusing on the task at hand.

"If we're not going to call the police and we're stuck here for now, should we try to find Travis's house? You said he lives nearby. We could hang out in the bushes and watch for him."

The idea made her skin crawl. There would be bugs and lizards and snakes. Who knew what else this far into the swamp. Alligators, probably.

She pushed down her fear. She would help Finn however he needed it.

"He's probably out checking traps right now. He does it every morning and evening."

"Checking traps?"

"He's a taxidermist."

"Oh." Jazz felt a shiver. She had never understood the allure of stuffing an animal and displaying it. "Family reunions must have been creepy as hell."

Finn laughed again, and shook his head. "I don't doubt it. Look, it's not safe for you to stay with the SUV."

"Not safe for you, anyway." She glared at him. "If you try to leave me here, I will kick your ass."

"I don't doubt it."

"Good. Besides, you can't touch anything. The way your eyes keep changing... It's scaring me. I don't want you to get lost in these memories. You need to stop reading things."

"I'm not sure if I can promise not to. If it means helping Siobhan."

Dammit. She was so keen on helping Finn. She needed to remember that he was just as adamant about helping his sister. She couldn't really blame him for taking the risk. She'd do the same and more to help her loved ones.

He took her hand in his. "I need you with me. Are you up for this?"

She nodded. "Yeah. Let's go."

Chapter Eighteen

Wild fennel brushed against Finn's face and arms as they headed toward Travis's house. Finn didn't know how he was finding the way, but was sure they were going in the right direction. A saw palmetto grazed his jeans, reminding him that Jazz's legs were unprotected. He glanced back to see how she was doing.

Damn, she looked sexy. Okay, the boots were a little silly, but she was pulling it off. He loved seeing her legs stretch out from beneath his shirt. The view of her chest when she bent forward to duck under something was riveting. He felt guilty enjoying the sight of her, knowing that she was assuredly not having a good time herself.

"Eyes on the road." She smirked at him.

He turned back to look where he was going just in time to be smacked in the face by a low-hanging branch. He heard her let out a stifled laugh.

Okay, maybe she was having a little fun.

He was glad there weren't paths cleared to the little stretch of side-road where they were parked. It was a good sign that Travis didn't get out that way and wouldn't discover them. They were lucky to have a base of operations to investigate his house. Still, it would have been nice not to be swimming through foliage to get there.

My kingdom for a machete.

You got that right.

He sighed. Now he was talking to himself. At least it was just in his head. He stopped abruptly. Jazz appeared at his side.

"What is it?" She peered around at the wall of green surrounding them.

"This is it."

He pushed back one of the fennel plants as if it was a curtain. On the other side, the brush had been cleared for a few dozen feet leading up to a run-down house. The paint was light brown and peeling and the roof was covered in moss.

He checked the windows and layout. From what he could tell, it probably had two bedrooms, one bath, a kitchen, and maybe a small family room. All of the rooms had to be tiny. The screen door facing them was barely hanging on its hinges.

Behind the house was swampland. True swamp. A small aluminum fishing boat was tied to a dock that stretched a few feet out over the water. The dock and boat were in much better condition than the house.

Finn remembered what Michael had said about well-fed alligators. He imagined Travis on the dock feeding them…leftovers.

He snorted.

What the fuck?

"Is something funny?"

"No." Nothing about that was funny. Why the hell had he laughed? "Come on."

He started for the yard, but Jazz held him back.

"How do we know he's not home?"

Finn pointed to the gravel drive that led up to the side of the house. "His truck isn't here."

He headed forward again, feeling an almost magnetic pull toward the house. When he reached the front door, he didn't hesitate to open it.

"Finn, let me do that! You shouldn't be touching anything."

"There's a trick to it."

He lifted the door slightly in its frame to keep it from falling off the hinges. Jazz stared at him.

"What?" he asked.

"How did you know to do that?"

How indeed.

"Just…let's go inside."

She kept staring at him as she slipped past into the house. Dim light filtered through the curtains. The inner door was open. Finn shut the screen door behind him and looked around.

It was even more depressing inside than out. Aside from the worn furniture, faded wallpaper, and truly disgusting carpet, there were pelts and stuffed animals everywhere.

"They look so real," Jazz said. She leaned a bit closer to a raccoon, then backed away.

"Travis did develop quite a knack for it over the years."

She turned and stared at him again. "What did you say?"

Finn shrugged. His head was starting to hurt. "They look real. Like you said. He's pretty good at this."

"That's not what you said."

"What does it matter?"

"Finn, you don't sound right."

Troublesome woman.

Finn shook his head. The room shifted as he did. "I'm fine. Let's look around."

"Just don't touch anything."

She's always telling me what to do.

She reached for his hand, but he pulled it away. Why did he do that? He loved it when she touched him. And to have her reaching for him... It was a nice change.

He didn't miss the hurt look that crossed her face.

"I just...need some space."

No he didn't. Why had he said that?

"Are you okay?"

He wasn't sure. He glanced around the room, at the ratty green couch with an old blanket over the back. He was sure Travis was sleeping there at night—on the nights when he slept at all.

Travis had always been plagued by insomnia. His nervous energy was everywhere. Finn could practically see Travis pacing the room. Always pacing. *Taking up too much space.*

A wave of nausea flooded his body. Finn felt dizzy. He had to get out of that room.

"Let's go to the kitchen." He walked past Jazz, being careful not to touch her, and headed to the archway that led to the small tiled room.

Finally, he could breathe again. Travis's energy was much lighter here. He must not spend much time in the kitchen. Finn didn't doubt it, with how emaciated Travis appeared. He walked to the fridge and opened the door.

"Don't touch anything, remember?" Jazz grabbed the door from his hand. They both looked at its contents.

Mustard. A jar of dill pickles. Half a loaf of bread that looked like it was starting to go green. That was it. Aside from being kind of pathetic, it wasn't scary at all. No severed heads or body parts. Finn chuckled.

What. The. Fuck.

"Why do you keep laughing?" she asked. "What's so funny?"

Nothing. If there had been something frightening in Travis's fridge, like trophies from Michael's victims, they might have come from Finn's *sister*.

What the fuck was wrong with him?

"I need... I need to go outside," Finn said.

He staggered to the side door that led to the yard. Jazz was right behind him. This door was closed, but not locked. He jerked it open and practically ran out into the fading sun. He bent over, hands on his knees, and took deep breaths.

Someone put their hands on his back. He yelled and whirled away, swinging his arms to fend them off.

"It's just me," Jazz yelled. She was holding her hands up in the air and had backed away.

Thank God she was so fast. He might have hit her while he was flailing. His heart was pounding and he couldn't seem to catch his breath. He needed to get control of himself again. She took a step toward him and he jerked back.

"Don't touch me!"

Her mouth dropped open. She stared at him for a moment, then shut it.

Where had that come from? He still couldn't breathe. His chest felt tight, like something was crushing him. The light was starting to dim, his vision tunneling. He fell to his hands and knees, retching.

"Finn!"

Jazz wrapped her arms around him. The tightness in his chest vanished.

"Finn, hold on to me. We have to get out of here." She helped him kneel, cradling his face with one hand. "I hear an engine. We have to go. Please, Finn. Come on. Get up."

She was trying to pull him to his feet. She was making better progress than he would have guessed, given how much smaller than him she was. He draped an arm over her shoulders and lurched up. They staggered through the yard together.

"Come on," she said. "Keep moving. You can do this."

They made it through the brush and collapsed, panting. Jazz turned back to the house, crawling on her stomach to get closer so she could see without being seen. Finn flopped forward to join her, dragging himself along. The fennel was thick enough that they should be hidden from the other side.

He won't see.

Finn remembered lying not far from where they were, watching the house, laughing as Travis and Auntie had another of their fights.

Wait, no. That wasn't Finn's memory. Another of Michael's rising to the surface.

He closed his eyes and took a few deep breaths, centering himself, reminding himself that this was *his* body. His mind. He was Finn.

Jazz was right about not touching anything. It was too dangerous. They would have to find another way.

A dark gray truck pulled up to the house. Travis leapt from the driver's seat. He looked shaken. He practically ran to the house's side door. The kitchen door.

The one they had left open.

Shit.

Travis slowed as he approached it. He stopped a few feet from the house and turned, scanning the yard and the brush. Finn felt Jazz stiffen. He put his hand on the small of her back, hoping to comfort her, to silently tell her to stay still.

Normally, Finn would absolutely be able to take Travis down. But not now. Not when Finn could barely stand without Jazz's help.

Travis seemed to stare at them for a moment. He took a step forward. A squirrel ran out from the fennel nearby, charging him. Travis screamed, stumbling backward. The tiny squirrel was terrifying him.

Finn started to laugh. Jazz clamped her hand over his mouth. Lucky for them, poor Travis was still screaming. Because of a squirrel.

Poor Travis. The voice in his head was mocking.

What the fuck was happening to him? How were memories surfacing, causing outbursts, when he wasn't even touching anything? And why *the fuck* was he thinking things—thoughts that obviously weren't his—that weren't even memories?

"We have to go," Jazz whispered. "Now."

Finn nodded. They backed away from the edge of the fennel. She pulled his arm over her shoulders again and helped him to his feet. They had to get away. Away from Travis and the house where Michael had grown up. Away from his childhood stomping ground.

Even as they ran, Finn felt an oppressive energy, like it was riding on his back, weighing him down. He stumbled more times than he could count, but Jazz was always right there, pulling him up, alternating between whispering encouragement and threats.

Distance wasn't helping. They finally reached the SUV. She popped open the back hatch and helped him sit. When that was too much for him, he lay down on the tarp that covered the big space.

"Finn, what the hell is going on with you?"

"I don't know." He covered his eyes with his hands.

"No you don't," she said. "Cut that out."

He felt her crawl up next to him.

"Let me see your eyes. Finn, come on."

She grabbed his arm and started tugging on it. When she couldn't get enough leverage to budge him, she straddled his stomach, gripping his hands tightly and pulling. He let her win, but kept his eyes closed. He didn't want to know what she'd see. He was too afraid.

"Please Finn. Let me see your eyes." She put her hands on his cheeks, her touch gentle. "Please."

Begging. I like it.

Shut up shut up shut up! Finn's stomach started churning again. The thoughts popping into his head weren't memories. They were new.

A horrifying theory presented itself.

He had been focused on avoiding getting lost in memories while he was reading things. As long as he made it out, he figured he was fine. But what if he was wrong? What if he was picking up Michael's energy with each reading and it was somehow staying? What if Finn couldn't get rid of it?

He felt like Michael's memories had become ingrained in Finn's mind. Worse—like part of Michael's *personality* was stuck in him.

Finn felt a darkness within him laugh. Whatever it was, it wasn't even bothering with trying to hide. Not anymore.

Shiiiit.

"Finn, please. I'm scared. You're scaring me."

He was scared too. He couldn't move. The darkness was creeping along his limbs, paralyzing him. He was trapped in his own body.

"Please, I can't lose you again," she said. "Do you understand? Can you even hear me?"

Jazz's hands were trembling. Her grip tightened. Then she kissed him.

The darkness evaporated. Finn felt it retreat. He wasn't sure what it was or where it had gone, but for the moment, he was just himself again. It was only him and Jazz.

She pulled back from the kiss. He opened his eyes.

She smiled, her gaze searching his face. Then she laughed and lowered her head to his chest.

"Oh thank God."

She slid her arms around his neck and held him, thighs tight against his sides, chest pressed to his. He wrapped his arms around her and held her to him. He didn't ever want to let go. She was his anchor. Somehow, she had pulled him back from that darkness.

At least for now.

Chapter Nineteen

His eyes were normal. Pale blue. Finn's eyes. Jazz had half expected them to be bright blue. The same blue as Michael's.

The things he said back at the house and the way he was acting... It wasn't him. Finn was confident, but not arrogant. And he knew way too much about Travis's home. Finding it was one thing. Being aware of the trick with opening the door? That was another.

He had only mentioned being concerned that he would get lost in a memory while using his powers. Why was he acting weird when he wasn't touching anything? At least when she touched him it seemed to snap him out of it.

She didn't know what was happening. Didn't know how to protect him. She couldn't stand the thought of losing him again. Not to Michael's memories. So she did the only thing she could. She held on.

Finn nuzzled her neck. She shifted so that she could kiss him again.

He brought his hands to her face, brushing her hair out of the way. His tongue slid into her mouth, coaxing her to relax into him. He brought his hands to her hips, holding her tight to his body as he rocked against her. His erection prodded her through his jeans.

They needed this—needed to connect on a deep level. Words had never been their strong suit. Touch was their best form of expression.

She leaned back, slowly unbuttoning her shirt. He massaged her hips as he watched. She left it on, hoping it would add to his pleasure, keeping him focused on what they were doing. The fabric whispered against their skin as she moved.

She lifted his shirt so she could explore the chiseled rows of his abs with her fingertips. There was no padding to soften his muscles. Only lines and curves, dips and valleys defining every inch of him. He was exquisite.

She tugged on his shirt to let him know she wanted it off. He sat up and lifted his arms so she could pull it over his head and cast it aside. Dark hair graced his pecs, fanning over his chest and running down his stomach like a waterfall.

Running her fingertips over the softness of it, she took her time, watching his gaze intensify with each stroke. She pushed him back onto the floor of the SUV, then started to undo his jeans. As she opened his fly, he gripped her hands to stop her.

"Jazz…"

"What's wrong?"

"I don't have any condoms."

Condoms. Right. And they'd used the only one she had. One that had been sitting in her wallet since they dated, now that she thought about it. But why didn't he have any?

"Please tell me you've been practicing safe sex," she said.

He let out a short laugh and sat up next to her. "I haven't been practicing much of anything. Not with a partner, anyway."

She stared at him. They had talked about their histories when they were dating. She had been surprised that his was as brief as her own. When he explained about being able to read people and the logistic issues with not being able to touch someone during sex without reading their mind, it made more sense. Still…

"Finn, it's been years since we were together. Surely you've slept with someone. I mean, everybody has urges."

"I don't need anybody else to deal with my *urges*." He laughed and shook his head. His tone was more serious when he went on. "I haven't been with anyone since we broke up. I tried a date or two, but just… wasn't interested."

"Oh."

She hadn't been interested in even trying to date anyone. She had thrown herself into her work. The only romantic indulgences she allowed herself were her attempted hook-ups for her friends. Knowing that he hadn't been with anyone either, hadn't even really felt like trying… It gave her hope. He still cared. She wasn't the only one who hadn't been able to move on.

"This is the part where you say something," he said.

"Okay."

"Okay...what?"

"Okay, we don't need to use a condom." They never really did, in her mind. "Neither of us engaged in risky behavior before we started dating or since."

He winced, then looked away. "Great. Good to know."

"I didn't mean..." She let out a sigh. "I haven't been with anyone else either. Since you."

"Oh." His face actually lit up.

Apparently he was feeling relieved about their mutual lack of activity too. She had to admit the thought of him with other women was upsetting. She really had wanted to keep him all to herself, not even sharing him with her friends. She would fix that mistake too, if he gave her a chance.

He grinned and said, "I suppose I ruined you for other men."

She laughed. She couldn't say that he had ruined her for other men. There had really only ever been him. No one else had made their way into her heart.

"Don't be so cocky," she said.

He feigned a confused expression. "But I thought we were going to —"

She covered his lips with her fingertips briefly. "How could I have forgotten what a comedian you are?"

"There are many things I'm eager to remind you of." He lifted his hands to her back, running them along the sides of her spine.

"There's something else you should know," she said.

His smile dimmed. She knew she must sound serious. Then again, she was broaching a serious topic. Possibly a deal-breaking one.

He leaned back and said, "I'm listening."

Her heart was beating in her throat. She forced herself to swallow as her moment of truth approached.

"You don't have to worry about me getting pregnant either," she said.

"Okay."

He was too flippant. He didn't understand, probably thought she meant she had an IUD or something.

"I can't get pregnant," she said. "Ever."

"Oh."

She waited for him to say something else. Ask questions. Offer comfort or something. He just stared at her.

"That's it? *Oh?*"

He shrugged. "Lots of people can't have kids."

"It's not a condition. For me, it was a choice."

His mouth dropped open. Here it came.

Why would you do that? What if you change your mind? But you're so young.

Instead, he laughed.

"What's so funny?"

He kept laughing for a moment, shaking his head. "We could have saved so much money on condoms."

"That's very practical of you." She wasn't sure which was worse, him grilling her about her choice or joking about it.

"We were really going hardcore on birth control."

Yeah, this was worse. She bristled and shifted away from him, but he reached out and picked up her hand.

"Jazz, I'm laughing so hard because I did the same thing. I made the same choice."

"What?"

He shook his head and laughed. "It took me five years to find a doctor who would finally give me a vasectomy. They all kept saying, 'You're too young to make a permanent decision like this. Wait for a while. If you find the right person…' And on and on. Such bullshit. As if I don't know my own mind."

Jazz had heard the same lines. It had taken her *seven* years to get her doctor to perform a tubal ligation.

"But you love kids."

"I do. For about an hour. Then I'm ready to move on." He smiled at her, then brushed a lock of hair from her face and tucked it behind her ear. "Come on. I'm sure you love those adorable nieces of yours. But that doesn't mean you want your own. I get that. I'd sure as hell rather figure it out before having kids than after."

She couldn't argue with that. But this was so unexpected. It felt surreal.

"I thought... I thought you wanted a family."

"What? Why?"

"Your dad named the bar Connelly's. You kept talking about your family up north."

"Because I miss them sometimes. And I was trying to draw you out to talk about yours. My dad named the bar that because he opened it with his brother originally." He grinned at her. "Man, talk about jumping to conclusions. I am never going to let you hear the end of this."

Jazz couldn't believe it. She had built up such a fantasy around Finn —a story of why they couldn't be together. Maybe she had just been trying to feel better about keeping him at a distance.

He shook his head, still laughing. "We *really* should have talked more."

"Do you want to get married?" she asked.

His smile vanished and he paled. "Wow. Okay, that is sudden. Look, we have a lot of things to work out. And marriage..." He shook his head.

"Wait, I'm not asking you to marry me. I'm asking if marriage is something that you're interested in."

"Oh." He visibly relaxed, shoulders lowering as he let out a deep breath. "That's reassuring."

"Well?"

"Damn. I know I wanted us to talk more about meaningful things, but this is venturing into 'be careful what you wish for' territory."

"Finn."

He smiled, but it was subdued, then he shook his head. "No. I'm not interested in marriage. I've seen too many people break vows and ignore the spirit of the arrangement. Paperwork doesn't make a union. Partnership does."

She couldn't speak. How could this be so...perfect? For the first time she could remember, she felt as if Fate was smiling on her.

"Besides, it always struck me as a lot of trouble for what? A tax break on buying a house together? No thanks."

"You like it above the bar. If someone tried to get you to move, they wouldn't be right for you."

He smiled at her. "You never asked me to move."

Jazz smiled back. Her stomach was doing somersaults. She had always felt that she and Finn were a match. She just didn't know how much of one. Talking definitely had its advantages.

Then again, so did other activities.

"I'm going to ask you to move now."

His smile faltered.

She put her hand on his chest and said, "Lay back."

He grinned as he did as she asked, shifting so that he was in the middle of the empty space. She had never been gladder to have a roomy vehicle. And the padded tarp made it downright comfy.

Kneeling at his side, she picked up where she'd left off. She pulled off his shoes and socks, then unfastened his jeans and slid them down his muscular legs. He was already tenting his boxer-briefs. She gave herself a moment to enjoy him through the thin fabric. She ran her fingers along the length of his shaft.

He closed his eyes and folded his arms behind his head, using them as a pillow. She wanted him relaxed. She also wanted better access. He lifted his hips as she pulled off his boxer-briefs, leaving him naked before her.

Finn naked. She hadn't taken the time to look at him before in the hotel. There had been too much need, too much fear. She had thought if she said or did the wrong thing, he would bolt again.

Things changed. Quickly, sometimes. She smiled as she ran her hand over the strong muscles of his stomach, gently skimming his shaft before tracing her nails along his thighs. His breathing relaxed.

Never in a million years had she thought she would be back in this situation—back with Finn. She wouldn't waste a moment.

She kicked off her boots and slid her shirt from her shoulders, then untied her bikini top. After slipping out of the bottoms, she looked back at Finn. His eyes were open as he watched her, smiling.

"You know you're the most gorgeous woman I've ever seen, right?"

She smirked. "Yeah, I get that a lot."

He laughed, but then a shadow crossed his face. He murmured, "I bet you do."

"I don't think I'll be hearing it nearly as often now, though."

"Why's that?"

"Because you'll be with me."

His expression remained guarded. "I guess I'm pretty good at playing the heavy when we're out in public."

"I was thinking of a different role."

"Which is?"

What word could she use? *Boyfriend* seemed too trite for what she wanted them to be. She was so relieved to know he had no interest in the title of *husband. Mate* just made her feel ridiculous. But she wanted him to know she was all-in, just like he'd once told her.

She settled on the phrase that made the most sense to her.

"Partner."

He practically beamed at her. "That sounds good to me."

Chapter Twenty

The day had definitely taken a turn for the better. Finn's life might have been flipped upside-down, but Jazz had tumbled back into it. Naked. Ready to finally talk—to *commit* even. It was a little overwhelming. Still, he said a silent prayer of thanks to any benevolent force that might be listening.

Then he sat up and kissed her. He slid his hand to the back of her neck, tracing her skin with his fingertips. His tongue delved into her mouth. She leaned into him, their chests brushing. She pushed him back, her fingers trailing over his chest as he lay down.

She had let him lead last time, but apparently this time she wanted to take the reins. He was fine with that. More than fine.

Her hair lightly brushed his skin as she moved her kisses along his neck, then further down. Focusing on the feel of her, he was more at ease than he had been in months. It was like her touch was grounding him in his body.

Her hand found his dick first, slender fingers wrapping around him and squeezing. Then her lips pressed against him. His breath hitched as her mouth took him in, waves of pleasure rippling through his body. He ran his fingers through her hair, brushing it away from her face so he could watch her.

Her tongue swirled, her hand kept moving, her lips pulled on his flesh. He was getting too close.

"Jazz…"

She let up at last, shifting to lie next to him. He cupped her cheek, kissing her again and rolling her onto her back. He skimmed his hand over one breast, gently squeezing it, brushing his thumb across her nipple.

Her breath picked up. She arced her back, pressing herself into his touch. He dusted the backs of his fingers against her stomach, not stopping as they trailed through her soft curls. Two fingers slid into her with ease. She groaned against his mouth. He circled her clit with his thumb.

She was so hot and wet. And he was going to be able to feel that, burying himself in her without a condom, with nothing between them. He was sure she was ready. He hoped she was ready. He didn't want to wait anymore.

He moved his hand away so he could grip her thigh and use it to pull her over on top of him as he rolled to his back. He wanted her to enjoy this every bit as much as he did. If being on top helped, he was good with that.

She kissed him deep, rubbing her wet center along his dick. Damn, she felt so good. He thought about sports, traffic, food, anything to try to keep the beautiful contact from sending him over the edge. She lined him up, then slid down over him slowly. He sank into velvet fire.

He felt every pulse of her body as she stretched to fit him. She sat back on his hips and brought her knees to his sides, then rose, bracing herself on his chest. Without asking, he knew what she needed. He brought his hands to hers, interlacing their fingers and supporting her so she had better leverage to move.

She rose up on her knees, leaning against his grip, then sank back along the length of him. Over and over again. He rose up to meet her, hips thrusting against hers. He wanted to go off so bad, but even more he wanted to hold on to the connection they shared. No powers, no walls. Just them.

Her muscles contracted around him, clenching as she upped her pace. He let himself go a bit more, still fighting the ecstasy that beckoned from deep in his gut. She groaned, her eyes shut tight and head tilting back as he felt her pulse around him. Finally, he stopped trying to hold back.

He pumped himself into her, fast and hard. Her grip tightened on his, holding on as she matched his pace. His skin felt like it was lighting up as the pressure built in him, finally exploding through his body. He felt himself fill her, mixing with her heat, her wetness. He landed as deep as he could and held himself there, back arcing off the floor, breath held tight in his chest.

It was a while before he came back down.

Jazz collapsed on his chest, breathing hard. He brought his hands to her back, wrapping his arms around her.

"That was incredible." He panted between each word.

"Yeah."

He didn't want to leave her body, but felt himself softening. There would be time for more later. He just needed to rest a bit.

And this is what it would be like *every time* now. At least, he hoped so.

She nuzzled his neck, then lifted herself from him. He felt a brief surge of panic, wondering if she was pulling away. Instead, she nestled against his body and let out a contented sigh. He kept his arms around her, holding her tight.

It seemed Finn only blinked, but when he opened his eyes again, the sun had already set. He felt better than he had in weeks, even after only a few hours of sleep.

Uninterrupted sleep. No nightmares, no dreams.

Jazz must have the light on the ceiling of the SUV set so that it had to be turned on manually. Either that or the battery had gone dead. It was completely dark. She was fidgeting next to him, then sat up suddenly.

"Shit, we left the back door open," she said.

She lunged for it, but he grabbed her and held her in place. The door was open, she had just woken up, and it was pitch black in the SUV. He didn't want her to fall out.

"Relax."

"You relax. We're going to be eaten alive by mosquitoes—if it hasn't happened already. Bugs and snakes..."

"How exactly would a snake get into the SUV?"

"I don't know. They could crawl up the tires or something. Climb the tree and drop down."

He laughed. He knew Florida had a reputation for bugs and other wildlife, but had never been bothered by them before. Honestly, he didn't know what the fuss was about.

"What about bats? They can fly in. And there are tons of flying insects, even in the city." She shifted closer, leaning against his chest. "And lizards. They can climb."

"Nothing is going to bother us."

She snorted. "Right."

"Has anything bitten you yet?"

After a brief pause she said, "No."

"So don't worry about it. We're more likely to suffocate from the heat if we close the door."

"This is weird. Why hasn't anything bitten us? We're totally naked and without bug spray. I can hear them chattering away right outside."

He shrugged. "Bugs have never bothered me. They steer clear."

She snorted again, but then he felt her lean a bit away. "Wait, seriously? Is it part of your powers?"

"I don't know. Not that Dad ever said."

She pushed him back and straddled him. Waking up for this was fine by him. He could catch up on sleep later. He put his hands on her hips, then slid them back over her ass. He was already getting hard.

"It kind of seems like a big oversight," she said.

He sat up, bringing their chests together, massaging her back as he drew her closer. It wasn't enough to steer her from the current topic.

"Being able to control animals would be awesome," she said.

Control...

"I don't get how it would relate to psychometry, though. Unless you can somehow extend your energy field. Maybe push your energy into others."

He stopped rubbing her back.

"What?" she asked.

"There's one aspect of my powers I never told you about because I never use it. Dad taught me it's like the ultimate taboo."

"I thought the worst thing you could do is read someone's mind with the intent of using what you learn to hurt them."

He wasn't surprised she remembered that. It still made him smile. She had been amazing when he told her about his powers. She'd been studying the whole field of metaphysics—not just psychometry—for years. Finn had never really ventured much outside of his abilities.

She had taught him about metaphysical principles, especially what boiled down to basic karma. *Don't use your abilities to hurt people.* It tied in with what Dad had said about not using his abilities for profit, along with the other warnings he'd been given.

If he was helping people, he was still okay. If he ever gained from using his powers at other people's expense... Finn wasn't sure what would happen, but his dad had implied there would be a swift and terrible reckoning. That was what he meant when he talked about walking the gray line.

Then there was plain stepping over it.

"You know I can read people's thoughts if I touch them long enough with my hands."

"Present company excluded."

"Yeah." He smiled and laughed, then said another little silent prayer of thanks that she, of all the people in the world, was the one person he could touch in peace. "There's something else I can do once that level of connection is achieved."

When he hesitated, she said, "Which is?"

"I can sort of...get them to do what I want. I've never actually tried it out before, because my dad seriously scared the shit out of me when he told me about that. But I can feel it when I'm listening to people's thoughts. One small step and I'd be in their head running the show."

She went completely still. She seemed to be holding her breath even.

"I would never do it. I mean, risks aside, it's just wrong. I'd have to be morally bankrupt to do anything like that."

"What kind of risks did he talk about?"

"Aside from it majorly pissing off the universe and invoking instant karma? You can get lost, I guess. Some of their memories can get embedded in your mind and you can forget which ones are yours."

"Kind of how your powers are acting up now."

He hadn't thought of it before because he never thought about this aspect of his abilities. He had locked it away in a corner of his mind under a glass dome labeled, *Don't*. What he was experiencing did sound like the consequences Dad had laid out.

"Yeah. But I didn't make anybody do anything. I've never used my powers that way. I never would."

There had to be another explanation—a reason his powers were acting up in this particular way. He wasn't controlling anyone. Hell, if anything, he wished he could use those powers to gain better control over himself. That moment when the darkness had spread across his body... He felt more like his powers were being used against him somehow. But that wasn't possible.

Jazz sat back on his thighs, her arms draped over his shoulders. Powers or no powers, he could practically feel her thoughts filling the space as her mind raced trying to put the pieces together.

"Do you think..." She didn't finish her question.

He prompted her to go on. "Do I think what?"

"What if Siobhan has the same powers? Could she be using them to try to push you into getting her justice, and somehow putting Michael's memories in your mind?"

It was a chilling thought.

"Dad said the ability is passed from father to son."

"Even with twins?"

"Honestly, that never came up." When they went back to Summer Park, Finn was going to have a long list of questions for his dad. If he was up for it, anyway.

Even if Siobhan did have the same powers and had retained them on the other side, using the forbidden aspect of those powers wouldn't make Finn take on another person's memories. She would be the one who had to pay the price.

Right?

"I don't think that's it," Finn said. "Michael had a really strong personality. I can feel it in everything I read that was close to him. His energy was dark and twisted, but powerful."

"So it might be enough to leave a kind of retina-burn in your brain."

He laughed again. "That is an excellent way of putting it." He really, *really* hoped she was right. Her other theory, though... It kept running through his mind.

If Siobhan had the same powers and retained some version of them in death... Who knew how that would affect Finn? With his dad, there was always a kind of feedback loop, like static in the channel. Finn hadn't felt anything like that yet. If anything, his powers were stronger, everything he read clearer.

Maybe instead of feedback, she was amplifying him? That would explain the sort of retina-burn Jazz had mentioned. Michael's memories might not be implanting themselves in Finn's mind, but just be strong enough that it was taking him a while to shake them off.

Finn hadn't felt any kind of weird disorientation or disconnection since they had reached the SUV. More accurately, since he and Jazz had started having sex. Being with her chased away all memories and thoughts beyond each moment, each touch.

Yeah, his life had turned into a shitstorm, but Jazz was back with him. And this time, she was all-in. Whatever the universe dished out next, they would face it together.

"I can't see your face at all," she said. "What are you thinking?"

"That I am a lucky bastard. And very glad you're here. No matter how lost I get, when you touch me it pulls me back from the edge. Reminds me that I'm me."

"If that's a line, it's working."

She kissed him, pushing him back to the floor. He gratefully let all thoughts fade away in the presence of her touch.

Chapter Twenty-One

Jazz never dreamed she would think of a restroom at a gas station as a luxury, but after a night in the swamp something as simple as running water made her ridiculously happy. Finn hadn't been keen on the idea of driving to anywhere near civilization so they could freshen up and get food, but had relented when he saw she wasn't going to let it go.

She was not an outdoorsy person. She usually wore leather pants, for crying out loud. She wanted air conditioning, filtered water, and chlorinated pools.

The compromise they had reached was that she would wait for him to get her the key to the bathroom and not go into the store. She was okay with that. Her outfit—or lack thereof—would attract too much attention.

After the run-in with the guys from the bar and what happened at the hotel...she was scared. Dammit, she hated being scared. As soon as they could, she would call the police and tell them everything she knew about the group. She was sure they were behind the fire. The police needed to know how dangerous those guys were.

Finn had assured her that his powers were back on track, or she would have gone in with him anyway. He said he was feeling better after a night of good sleep. Not that they'd slept through all of it. They were definitely making up for lost time.

Finn had gone back into the gas station to return the key. She chewed on another power bar while she waited for him to come back. He'd been in there for a long time. Too long.

She was starting to open the driver's door when he walked out. He paused, hands in his pockets. He had pushed the door open with his foot, so he was still avoiding touching things. Probably wise. She didn't understand why he wasn't making a beeline for the SUV. In fact, he was kind of meandering around. She started the engine, then drove up next to him, rolling down the passenger's side window.

"Finn?"

He didn't respond. That wasn't good.

"Finn!"

He seemed disoriented when he glanced over at her. Shit, had his powers gone off again? He wasn't touching anything, so how could he be lost in someone's memories?

She hoped she wouldn't have to make out with him in the gas station parking lot. But then he opened the door and climbed in, saving her from bringing unwanted attention to them. It was a start.

"You okay?" she asked.

"Yeah."

"You don't sound too sure about that."

"There were a lot of memories on that key."

Probably some pretty gross ones now that she thought about it.

Do not think about that.

"I thought your powers were behaving."

"They're better. Not perfect."

He sounded tense. After last night, she was kind of surprised. She had felt more relaxed than she had in months when they woke up. As soon as they were alone, she'd try to help him back to that state.

"What do we do now?" she asked.

"Head back to Travis's house. I want another look at it. Maybe this time we won't be interrupted."

"That's not a good idea."

"Why, because you didn't come up with it?"

She was stunned for a moment. She felt her mouth drop open. "Where the hell did that come from?"

He looked confused again, then he shook his head and turned to look out the window. "I don't know. I'm sorry. Could we just get out of here? I need to be away from people."

That part made sense at least. She wondered again if his powers might somehow be working long-distance. They could figure things out once they were back in the wilderness.

She drove onto the highway, heading toward their little grove near Travis's house.

"I don't know if we can do this on our own," she said. "No matter what you said earlier, your powers are still acting up."

"I've got it under control."

She snorted. "That didn't seem the case a minute ago."

"There were too many people back there. Too many memories to sort through."

"And you think it's going to be better at Travis's house? Last time we were there, you looked like you were suffocating."

"I'll be ready this time. Besides, that was before last night."

He put his hand on her leg. Heat immediately flared deep in her belly. He leaned over and kissed the side of her neck, trailing his hand further up her thigh.

"You're trying to distract me."

"Is it working?"

Yes. She wouldn't tell him that, though.

"We should call the police. Someone besides us should know about what we're doing."

He sighed, then sat back in his seat. "I already told Daphne what we've learned. I called while you were in the bathroom."

"Do you think that's a good idea? Tommy shouldn't get too worked up."

"I know. She won't tell him more than he needs to know. Right now, all she's telling him is that we're following some promising leads that took us out of town. I don't want him to worry about us, but they need to know where to look in case..."

She glanced over at him, caught the grim expression on his face, and knew what would come next. He was worrying about her again, wondering if he should be doing this alone.

"Don't even think about it," she said. "I'm not going back to Summer Park."

"I know." His voice was barely over a whisper.

"Seriously? I thought you'd fight me on it."

"We're not just investigating the case anymore. We have some seriously pissed-off locals who are willing to commit major crimes to settle the score. After what they pulled at the hotel, you can bet those thugs are watching the highway. There's a long stretch from here to Summer Park. Before we head back, we need to talk to the police."

Thank God.

"But that will take up time," he said. "Alert more people to our inquiries. Nell and Travis are tight. I think she's a little sweet on him. If she hasn't already told him about us, you can bet it'll happen soon. He'll destroy any evidence that might be left before we can get to him."

Crap. Jazz hadn't thought of that.

"And if he gets really spooked, he can disappear into the swamp."

Camping anywhere had never appealed to her. She was more of a five-star-lodge vacationer. Not that she actually took vacations. She loved the pools, the sky, the palms, and even the heat of the city—as long as she had air conditioning close by to retreat to.

"Ugh, how can anyone stand that? The swamp must be full of bugs and alligators and all kind of dangerous animals." She shivered.

Finn laughed. "Tasty, you mean."

"What?" She glanced over at him. He was staring out the window.

"Travis loves living off of what he can forage for himself. Squirrels and vermin. He used to disappear for weeks into the swamp when he was in a mood."

"Finn?"

He looked over at her, a blank expression on his face. But his eyes were turning bright blue. He wasn't touching anything, and his eyes were changing.

Jazz gunned the engine. The road that led to their hiding spot came up and she slammed on the brakes, taking the turn faster than was probably safe.

Finn reached for the grab handle above his door. "What are you doing?"

She didn't have time to head back to their safe spot. As soon as they were out of sight of the highway, she hit the brakes and put the SUV in park.

"What are you doing?" He bit out each word.

She ignored him—rather, the memories that were trying to assert themselves again, if that was what this was. Whatever was happening, she needed to stop it. She unfastened her seat belt and crawled into his lap.

He raised his hands and tried to back away, but had nowhere to go. She grabbed his face and kissed him. At first, he was tense, but the more she leaned into him, the more he relaxed. His hands drifted to her waist, then around to cup her ass. His tongue slid between her lips and she let out a sigh.

This was Finn.

The new immediate problem was that she didn't want to stop and they weren't exactly out of the way if someone decided to use that road. Like Travis, maybe. She forced herself to pull back.

Finn smiled at her. "What brought that on?"

She felt half-sick. He wasn't even aware of how he had changed. She kept her hands on his cheeks, then leaned in and touched her forehead to his. She wouldn't let him slip away.

"Jazz?"

"Your eyes changed again." Her voice came out hoarse. Her throat was tight with emotion.

"What? No they didn't."

She sat back on his thighs and glared at him. "They did."

"You were driving. You can't be sure—"

"I can and I am. I know what I saw. What I heard. It wasn't you, Finn. It wasn't you."

Chapter Twenty-Two

Finn's stomach was in knots. He couldn't have been lost in a memory. He wasn't touching anything. And yes, sometimes Michael's memories had seemed to try to resurface in his mind, but he had *felt* them. He had always known when it was happening. Like when that darkness crept along his nerves.

What does she know?

Finn shook off the thought. She knew him. Always had. If she said he was losing it, he was losing it.

Christ, the thought was scary, though.

"Keep your hand on my leg," she said.

"What?"

"I need to get us out of sight. Touching keeps you grounded in your body, so I need you to hold on to me till we get parked. Then we can sort this out."

Could they, though?

The memories he had read so far were powerful—especially the ones back at the gallery. They had manifested physically on multiple occasions. The link was already strong enough that reading Michael's kitchen chair made Finn share in Travis's bloody nose after Michael hit him in the memory.

What if it was permanent?

Finn couldn't believe that Siobhan would do this to him. He knew she was a good person. He could feel it through his dreams. She would be trying to help him, not throw him to the wolves.

Jazz slid back into the driver's seat and put the SUV in gear. He left his hand on her thigh, trying to keep himself from gripping it too tight. For the first time, the softness of her skin, her warmth, wasn't a turn on. It was a lifeline.

"Tell me about ghosts," he said.

She glanced over at him quickly, then back to the bumpy side road. "What do you want to know?"

"Everything. How do they stick around? What can they do?"

She turned down another road as he pointed out the way, nearing their destination. "From what I've learned, it's usually the standard story—they feel like they have unfinished business or suffered some sort of trauma that keeps them from letting go."

"Like Siobhan."

"It's hard to say what made her stay. It could have been how she died. Maybe she wants justice or closure or something."

"How do we find out? Can we talk to them like with a séance or something?"

She let out a scoff. "Those aren't as effective as you might think."

There was a bitter edge to her voice. He started piecing together what he knew about this other mystery. She had talked to him about her family at last. A mother and sister. Three nieces. But she couldn't talk about her dad. Not wouldn't, *couldn't*. Adding that to her fascination with the paranormal and her comments and knowledge of ghosts...

"I'm sorry," he said. "About your dad."

Her grip on the wheel increased till her knuckles were white. A muscle he wasn't used to seeing stood out along her jaw. Mystery solved.

"Thanks."

She pulled into their spot and killed the engine, but didn't look at him. Instead, she turned her face to the window and quickly ran her arm under her nose.

He didn't know what to say, so he gave her a minute to pull herself together. She had never liked showing emotion. She was crystal clear about that. He wanted to give her privacy, but he couldn't let her go without risking losing himself again.

After a few moments, she said, "Sudden massive coronary. Completely unexpected."

Shit. His own heart started pounding in his chest. He couldn't believe she was sharing this with him. No wonder she had freaked out when Finn told her about Dad. Jazz loved him about as much as Finn did. He couldn't imagine how scared she would be to hear about his dad when her own had been taken from her that way.

"It happened in an airport." Her voice lowered nearly to a whisper. "They were on their way to see me—to celebrate my graduating from college."

"Jazz..."

She went on quickly, like she was afraid her courage would give out. "I was obsessed with finding him after it happened. I just wanted to talk to him one more time." She sniffed again, still staring out the window. "It's good that I was obsessed. The things I learned are helping people now."

As if that made what she had gone through okay. He understood her attachment to Dad that much more.

"There's something else you should know about me. Something I should have told you a long time ago."

"Okay."

His stomach started to twist. They'd covered a lot of ground already, but she seemed so much more serious about whatever she was about to tell him.

"Being close to me is dangerous."

"Dangerous how?"

She paused for a moment, then said, "I'm cursed."

He would have laughed if it weren't for everything they'd been through. His reality had shifted way too far for him to not take this seriously.

"What kind of curse?"

"Whenever I care about people, things happen to them."

"What kind of things?"

"Bad things. Like what happened to my father. I want to fight it to be with you. But you need to know the risk going in."

Shit. She blamed herself for her dad's death?

"Jazz, you can't take that on."

She shook her head. "You of all people know that there are forces at work that we don't understand. Fate is one of them."

"Yeah, but you don't control people's destinies."

"No. I facilitate them."

"How does that work?"

"I'm a nexus. Supposedly I gather people together at the right time and place. It's one of the reasons I'm so good at running the gallery and finding the next hot thing."

"I can't argue that point, but I don't know about the rest of it."

"I've been to dozens of psychics. They all say the same thing. I'm an instrument of Fate. And for whatever reason, she doesn't want me to be happy."

"No. No way. I'm not buying it."

"Finn—"

"I'm not saying you aren't a nexus or whatever that is. That part actually makes sense. But caring about people can't put them in danger. I mean, what kind of fucked-up universe would it be if that was the case?"

She chuffed out a breath and shook her head again. "The one I live in."

"Not anymore. Bad things happen to people all the time. You can't take responsibility for it. Siobhan was a good person. I can feel it. And she…" His throat tightened up and he had to cough to clear it. "None of us know how much time we have. No one gets to decide that. But we can make choices that make us happy while we're here."

"Being with you makes me happy," she said.

Finn felt like his stomach dropped through the ground.

"And I'm sick of living this way. Always afraid to let myself…" She shook her head, her voice trailing off.

He reached over and picked up her hand, then kissed the back of it. When she looked at him, she was so raw. He could barely stand it.

"Listen to me." He spoke each word crisply, making sure she knew he meant it. "Fate. Isn't. A dick."

Jazz busted out laughing.

"Good things happen," he said, his voice growing softer. "Bad things happen. What we've been through in our lives, and what the people close to us have gone through—it's all brought us here. This is where we're meant to be. Everything happens for a reason. I honestly believe that. And I don't believe that Fate is an asshole."

Her eyes filled with tears. She looked away quickly. It would probably be a while till she was comfortable really letting all her walls down with him. That was okay. He could wait. At least he was starting to feel that there was hope for them on the other side.

"Rachel would be a better source of information," Jazz said. "About ghosts."

He could sense that she needed to move on from the topic. She had just faced down one of her demons. He could play along.

"Your assistant?"

"Yeah. She's clairsentient—she can communicate with them."

"You're kidding. She always sounded so normal when you guys talked about her."

Jazz shrugged. "You seem pretty normal too."

She pulled the key from the ignition and tossed it in the drink tray, then opened her door to let in some air. He did the same to give them a cross-breeze.

Finally, she turned toward him. Her cheeks were dry, but her eyes were red around the edges. Seeing it felt like being punched in the gut. Jazz looked away quickly. She pulled her phone from the pocket of her shirt and stared at it for a moment.

"No signal." She put her phone in the drink holder with her key. "We should try to call her as soon as we can and tell her what's going on. Ask her advice. When we head back to Summer Park, we should head straight to Garrett's house."

"She's staying with Garrett?"

"It's a good thing," Jazz said. "She needed to get out of her mom's house. That woman is evil."

Finn snorted, playing along with the conversation. Jazz wanted to gloss over what she'd shared. He could help do that for her.

"But how do you really feel about her?" he asked.

Jazz smiled and shook her head. "Maybe this time, they won't be idiots and will finally hook up."

He laughed outright. "Wait, she's into him too?"

"Big time. She tries to play it down for some reason, but it's obvious how they feel about each other."

"Well shit. He's been pining for her for years. Why didn't they just…"

"Talk about it?" She arched an eyebrow.

Finn shook his head. "At least you had a really good reason."

"I thought I did. Maybe they do too."

"Okay, I guess I shouldn't be pointing fingers."

"I think I'm going to call those years we didn't talk, *the lapse*."

"The lapse?"

"Yeah. As in, *lapse in judgment*." She became more serious as she said, "I should have fought for you harder."

"I should have insisted we talk things through."

She smiled again. "While I'm willing to work things through verbally when we need to, I really am not used to all this talking about feelings. Now that we've settled all that, can we please crawl into the back and have sex again?"

"Absolutely."

He unfastened his seat belt so he could lean closer, pulling her in for a kiss. He heard the click as she undid her seat belt, and then she was in his lap again, pushing him back into his seat. Her tongue slid along his lips, her fingers burrowed through his hair.

He knew what it was like to seek solace in her touch, could feel that was what she wanted—needed—from him. She was still raw from what she had shared. He grabbed the lever to push the chair back, giving them more room to work.

She didn't waste any time. She reached between them and undid his jeans. With her attentive hands, his dick became rock hard in about six seconds. He was still amazed at how her touch could relax him so deeply while working him up at the same time.

The intrusive thoughts and disconnection that had been plaguing him also vanished. Maybe Siobhan *was* to blame, and seeing her brother go at it made her run away. He'd be the same way.

Not the time to be thinking about ghosts, man.

Jazz moved her kisses along his jaw and down his neck and he stopped thinking period. She grazed his skin with her teeth and nipped at him. Damn, she remembered just what he liked. She pumped her hand up and down, increasing the pressure. He leaned back and closed his eyes letting himself relax into the chair.

She slid down between his legs, pushing his shirt up so she could kiss his stomach and trace the lines of his abs with her lips and tongue. That was something she had always liked—playing with the lines of his muscles.

She never had trouble talking about how much she loved his body. It didn't bother him anymore now that she had given him hope that there might be more to it. She wasn't just in it for the physical part of their relationship. Knowing that let him sink into the sensations, to enjoy them on a level he'd never reached before.

The wind had picked up a bit. It drifted through the open space, lifting her hair across his stomach. She kissed him lower on his abdomen, on the sensitive skin below his navel. She held his dick so she could draw her cheek along the length of it, then wrapped her lips around his crown.

So damn good.

She took him in deeper, swirling her tongue, running her fingertips lightly over the base of his shaft. He trailed his fingers through her hair, resting his palm on the back of her head to feel more of her movements. Up and down, a steady rhythm rippling through his body, reminding him that he was Finn and he was hers. He always had been.

She picked up on the pulsing beat starting to build at the base of his shaft and eased him from her mouth. She kept herself pressed against his side, kissing his stomach as she reached down and slid her bikini bottoms down her legs. Then she crawled back up to straddle him in his chair.

Bracing her arms against his shoulders, she lined herself up. He rested his hands on her hips as she inched down over him, her body stretching to hold him tight.

"We need to keep doing this forever," he said.

She smiled, then leaned forward and kissed him, tongue plunging deep, hips rocking on his body. He thrust himself up into her, meeting every movement. The pull of her flesh against his was bringing him too close. He wanted to be sure she was right with him.

He pulled away from the kiss and said, "Sit back."

She kept her hands on his shoulders as she leaned back, using the leverage to steady herself as she slid up and down along his length. Damn, she felt too good. He was going to go off any moment.

He put one hand between them to find her clit, circling it as she moved. Her breath hitched and her eyes rolled shut. He used his free hand to push her bikini top up over her breasts, then drew one into his mouth as he cupped the other, lightly tracing his thumb over her nipple till it was a tight bud.

"Finn…"

His name came out as a moan. God, he loved it when she said his name like that.

His dick was pulsing, pressure building deep. The pull of her skin against his, wet and hot, the softness of her breasts—it was too much. He let go of her breasts but kept the hand at her clit, circling, flicking, feeling the pre-quake tremors start echoing out through his body.

He pressed his back against the seat, his feet against the floorboards, and started thrusting up into her harder, faster. She flung back her head, eyes clenched tight, fingertips digging into his shoulders as she moaned his name again.

At last he let himself go, ramming up into her as he held on to her hips. Her body tightened around him, drawing out his orgasm as he spilled himself inside of her. He buried himself as deep as he could and held himself there, holding tight, pinning her against him, feeling the pulsing in their bodies answering each other.

She fell forward against his chest, breathing heavily. He felt her heart pounding against his.

When they were together like this, it was like they created their own tiny world. It was just the two of them. He wrapped his arms around her, enjoying the moment of peace while it lasted.

Chapter Twenty-Three

After the truly glorious session in the passenger's seat, they had moved to the back for round two. Jazz had been only too happy to fill their time in each other's arms as they waited for the best moment to go back to Travis's house.

Finn said Travis checked his traps out in the swamp in the mornings. She didn't want to think about how he knew so much from so few readings. There was still something going on they hadn't figured out, and it was scaring her. But they needed to focus on what they were doing. They would sort everything out in time. She had faith in them.

He held her hand tightly as they made their way through the brush surrounding the house. Jazz pulled him back before he could step out into the yard.

"His truck is still here."

Finn pointed to the small dock behind Travis's house. "Yeah, but his boat's gone."

Her heart was beating fast. She didn't like the idea of going into the house for many reasons. At the top of the list was her fear that Finn would get drawn into a memory again. After the incident in the SUV, where he seemed to be falling into Michael's memories without touching anything, she was even more afraid of that happening.

What if the next time she couldn't pull him back?

"We won't be able to hear him," she said. "The boat doesn't make noise like the truck."

"You can stay outside as a lookout."

"Like hell I will. Where you go, I go."

"Then you're going into the house. I have to get some answers, Jazz. I need to know what his role in all of this is. It's the only way to make this stop—to help my sister. I'm sure of it."

She didn't like it. Her instincts were screaming for her to run. "We can try to call Rachel again."

"You just did. No signal, remember?"

He cupped her cheek and kissed her—a gentle kiss, not building to anything. Just a reassurance. It didn't do much for her nerves.

He pulled back and said, "You don't have to go with me."

"I do and I will. I'm all-in, remember?" She let out a deep breath that did nothing to ease her nerves. "Let's just get this over with."

She stepped into Travis's yard, pulling Finn after her. This time, she insisted on opening the front door. She didn't want him to touch anything. She managed to not knock the door off its hinges.

Inside, things had changed. The animals, the pelts, they were all gone.

"Someone's been redecorating," Finn said.

Jazz felt a chill. She stepped closer to Finn.

"How is it that it's somehow even creepier now?" she asked.

"Travis's talent lies in being creepy."

She looked over at Finn. That didn't sound like him. He was looking around the living room, a strange smile on his face.

"Finn?"

"Yes?"

The lighting was dim. She couldn't see his eyes clearly enough to note their color.

"Let's go to the kitchen."

"Okay."

Two steps forward, and he stumbled into her side. She grabbed his chest to try to hold him up.

"Finn!"

"Whoa. Whee…" He laughed.

"This isn't funny."

She draped his arm over her shoulders. Damn, he was heavy. They staggered a few feet closer to the kitchen before he fell to his knees.

"Dammit, Finn, get up! I am not making out with you in this shithole!"

He laughed again. "Honestly, is that all you ever think about?"

He listed to the side. She grabbed his face in her hands and tried to see his eyes. They were closed.

"Show me your eyes. Finn, dammit, show me your eyes!"

The grin on his face was unnerving. It was worse when he finally opened his eyes.

They were glowing. *Glowing* blue. She could see the color creeping over his irises, making his own color look gray in comparison—blotting it out.

"Shit. Finn…"

She kissed him. She hoped—prayed—it was enough.

He shoved her away. She scrambled after him as he bolted for a door that led from the room. He ran into the small bathroom, retching into a sink. Dim light filtered in from the living room. The window in the bathroom had been painted over and an acrid scent of chemicals overpowered her sense of smell.

She didn't care. She brought all her attention to Finn. She wrapped her arms around him, holding him tight. When he was done, he managed to stand up again. He tilted his head back and let out a huge sigh. He didn't push her away.

"Finn?"

"Yeah. It's me. Shit, at least I think so."

Thank God. She buried her face in his chest, gave herself a moment —just a moment—to feel him, to regroup, to try to figure out what to do next.

"This doesn't make sense," she said. "If your sister wants you to help her—sees that you're trying to—why is she making your powers go crazy? She has to know that messing with you is making Michael's memories have a stronger effect."

"I don't know what's going on. I wish I understood." He held her tighter. "I'm scared, Jazz. I feel like I'm losing myself. Like he's taking me over."

"That sounds like possession."

"How can he possess me if he's gone? You said he can't be

haunting me."

"Rachel said he was cremated. Without physical remains, he should have been forced to cross over." Jazz had learned that in her own studies, even before Rachel had told her. "I'm calling Rachel. Something's not right."

She pulled her phone from her pocket. The signal strength was weak, but there. She hoped it would be enough. Finn rested his head on her shoulder as she dialed the number.

Rachel answered after only a few rings.

"Hello?"

Jazz barely gave herself time to register relief that she had reached Rachel. It was too early to be reassured anyway. Who knew how long their signal would hold?

"Are you absolutely sure that Michael is gone?" Jazz asked. A sharp bite of static hit her ear.

Through the noise, Jazz could hear the hesitance in Rachel's voice. "He was cremated."

"I know, but if he found a strong connection, could he possibly possess someone?"

If Finn's twin had the same power, maybe Michael's personality had implanted itself in her. Jazz had seen documentaries about twins and their psychic links. Or even worse, maybe Michael had latched on to Siobhan's psychic energy and was using it to stick around. Michael could be using their connection to get to Finn, to try to influence the corporeal world.

Finn reached behind Jazz and flipped on a light switch. The room went from dark and creepy to bright and...gross. Jazz turned away from the sink. String crossed the room just above her head, filled with photographs hanging from clothespins. Was this a dark room?

She forced herself to finish her thought as she glanced at the pictures. "Maybe someone with psychic abilities?"

"Possession?" Rachel's voice rose to a squeak.

Jazz looked more closely at the pictures. Her heart pounded, her breath catching in her chest as full-on panic set in. The pictures hanging on the string were of Elsa and Rachel. Rachel through the windows of her mom's tea room, taken with a telescopic lens. Elsa standing at the window of her loft, arms around Dante's waist. He had bandages on his face.

These were recent.

"Oh God—"

In a huge burst of static, the call went dead.

"Jazz..." Finn was looking at the pictures, his eyes wide.

"Yeah. I see them."

He reached up and plucked one of the pictures from the line.

"Finn, don't!"

Her warning was too late. She waited for the change, for him to stiffen and pull away, to look at her with that condescending smile. His hand was shaking.

Her chest was so tight, Jazz felt like she was going to pass out. She pulled herself together. Finn needed her, dammit. From the look of things, all of her friends did.

Travis was stalking Elsa and Rachel. Maybe that was the real reason that Siobhan was messing with Finn. She wasn't trying to get help for herself—she was trying to save Elsa and Rachel.

"This... It's her. I know it." Finn's eyes were perfectly, pristinely gray-blue. And full of tears.

"Who?"

"Siobhan. This is my sister."

Jazz looked at the photo. "That's Rachel."

"No. No, this is Siobhan. I'm sure of it."

"It can't be. Finn, that is Rachel."

"This doesn't make any sense."

"Okay, we need to figure this out—back at the SUV. We need to call the police."

He nodded. Jazz let out a tiny breath. There was so much more at stake than she had imagined.

"Put the picture back. We don't want to tip off Travis that we were here."

She kept one arm around Finn's waist as she twisted around to turn on the water in the sink and rinse it clean. She hoped it would dry before Travis came home. Finn kept staring at the picture in his hand.

"Finn, put it back."

Slowly, he lifted his arms and placed it back on the line. He kept staring at the other photos.

She had to get him out of there.

"We're going to figure this out," she said. "If Travis has these, he probably has other trophies around. We let the police know, they search the place with a warrant, and they stop him before…"

She couldn't finish that thought. She had no idea what Travis had planned for Elsa and Rachel. Jazz couldn't convince herself it was nothing. She turned off the water in the sink and flipped the light switch, then pulled Finn back into the living room.

A quick survey of the room showed her they hadn't disturbed anything else. She pulled the door to the bathroom shut, then headed for the front door. She kept her arm tight around Finn's waist. He didn't seem to want to leave.

The sooner they were out of this house the better. They stumbled out the door and through the yard. Fennel brushed against them as they made their way back to the SUV. A lingering scent like licorice floated around them, cleansing her nose from the stifling bathroom.

She opened the back door of the SUV and helped him sit down. He looked like he was in shock.

"How can Rachel be my sister?" he asked.

"She can't. I've met both her parents. Your powers must be acting up again."

"No. Not this time. I'm sure of it." He shook his head. "Is she adopted, maybe?"

"Not that she's ever told me. Then again, her mother is a lying, manipulative—"

Wait… Her mother *was* a liar and a master manipulator.

Jazz remembered what Tommy had said about Finn's mom. The picture he painted was not rosy. It did, however, remind her of Lillian

Montgomery.

"What?"

"Your dad said your mom left for a lawyer."

"Yeah."

"Rachel's dad is a lawyer. Tommy said your mom warned him not to try to find them. What if they moved and changed her name?"

"How could we all wind up in Summer Park?"

"Summer Park is a magnet for psychics. I'm friends with the owner of the local metaphysical bookstore. There's a huge population of them here."

"It still seems like too much of a coincidence."

"Maybe it isn't a coincidence. Maybe it's Fate."

She was starting to wonder.

"I don't know. If Rachel is Siobhan, that means my powers aren't off the rails because of being haunted. I'm back to square one solving that problem."

"I don't think so. When exactly did your powers go out of control?"

"It was the day Michael died. No, the day before."

"The day Rachel was abducted. You started dreaming about what Rachel experienced that night—as it was happening. Twins often have a psychic link. With both of your heightened powers, maybe the trauma of it activated a connection and it sort of went haywire."

"That's a hell of a lot better than being haunted or possessed." Finn shook his head. "Do you really think it could be her?"

Jazz looked at his pale blue eyes, remembering again how similar they were to Rachel's. But it was more than that. They were both tall and had similar athletic builds, like Tommy. Straight noses, strong features… How could she have not seen it before?

She laughed. She couldn't help it. She was so relieved, almost giddy. Finn's sister wasn't dead after all. And she was *Rachel*.

"Yeah," Jazz said. "I think so."

"Damn," he said. Then he laughed too. "I have to tell Dad. I mean, I'll check with him on the details first, but he has to know about this."

He jumped up and pulled his phone from his pocket. He looked at the screen, then he started walking around waving it in the air.

"There has to be a signal around here somewhere."

Jazz couldn't stop smiling. This was the best news she'd heard in a long time. Tommy would be so happy. Even Rachel would be glad to know that she actually had a decent family. It was perfect.

Except something wasn't right. Rachel's trauma might have Finn's powers out of whack, but that didn't explain how Michael's memories were strong enough to take him over. From what Finn said, Michael's memories were potent, but they shouldn't be enough to change his appearance...

Could they?

"Let's drive somewhere that has a signal," he said. "We need to call Dad and let the cops know to—"

He gave a sharp cry. Jazz heard creaking and a loud crack from the other side of the SUV. She bolted around to see Finn hanging upside down, his body slowly rotating in the air.

"Finn!"

She ran to him, grabbing his sides to stop his movement. A rope was caught around his ankle. He had stepped in some kind of snare. It looked like it had been set up to pull him against the tree. He must have hit it hard to make such a loud noise. He was out cold.

"Shit! Finn..."

His chest was still moving. He was breathing. She had to get him down. Maybe there was something in the SUV that could help. She turned back to it, vaguely registering Travis standing right behind her, his arm seeming to fly toward her face. She felt a brief moment of pain. Her vision filled with blinding lights and then went dark.

Chapter Twenty-Four

Wake up. Wake. Up.

Finn's head was pounding. He blinked his eyes and looked around, trying to figure out where the voice was coming from. His shoulders ached. He couldn't move his arms. Pain lanced through his wrists as rough rope bit into his skin. He was tied to a chair.

A moment of panic shot through him. He had dreamt something too close to this over and over again. He had to calm himself down. Assess his situation, his surroundings. Directly across from him, Jazz was tied to a chair too. Her head was bowed forward, her dark hair obscuring her face.

More panic, but longer than a moment. She wasn't moving.

"Jazz!"

Finn tugged against the ropes, tried to hop his chair closer. The floor of the place was sand. He couldn't get enough purchase to move.

"You pathetic fool."

He jerked his head to the side, trying to find the voice. The world spun around him and he felt nauseated. He closed his eyes till the feeling passed.

"I can't believe you let him catch you. I only left you alone for a few minutes."

Finn looked around more slowly. They were in some kind of shed, the dark wood pitted from time and exposure to the elements. The door was open, giving Finn a view of the swamp outside. And it was actual swamp.

The water line was only a few dozen feet from where they sat. If a gator decided it wanted a snack, it could walk right in.

He looked around the room some more. Gators became the least of his worries.

Tables lined the walls of the shed. They were covered in a mix of pelts, hunks of wood in vaguely animal-like shapes, and tools. Sharp, jagged tools. Some of them he recognized as being for woodworking. The rest he could only imagine were for carving...other things. It looked like they were in a torture chamber.

He pulled against the ropes again.

"You disappoint me."

Where the hell was that coming from? The guy's voice sounded like it was right in Finn's ear. Even closer.

He looked around the place again. It must be Travis's taxidermy studio. He and Jazz were the only ones there. Finn craned his neck around to try to look over his shoulder.

Two forms lurked in the shadows.

Shit.

They were small, but in his current state, there was nothing he could do to protect himself or Jazz. If only he was free. He could take them—

"What kind of private investigator were you?" The voice was thick with mockery.

Finn's neck hurt, but he kept looking. The figures didn't move. They were holding too still. Mannequins. They were female mannequins. More specifically, they looked like the frames sitting on the tables. The ones Travis must use for...

Oh shit!

He turned back to Jazz, his breath coming so fast he was almost hyperventilating.

"Yes," the voice practically purred. *"Frames for my little mad elf's workshop. I see you can imagine what he plans to do with them."*

"Who are you?"

"Tsk. It's just the two of us in here. I'd rather keep our conversation private. Besides, you don't want Travis to hear, do you? Once he knows you're awake, he'll come back inside."

Finn looked at the open doorway. Yeah, he didn't want Travis coming back. Not until Finn had figured a way out of this and could kick the sick bastard's ass.

"So violent. You need to learn control. There's so much that you're capable of. You didn't even scratch the surface of your powers."

Finn closed his eyes and took a few deep breaths.

"Who are you?" he thought.

"Better. Much better. But too little, too late."

The light dimmed as Travis stepped into the shed. He was wearing a faded gray and white checkered shirt, jeans, and heavy boots. He glanced at Finn and did a double-take.

"He thought you'd still be sleeping. He didn't know I'd be here to prod you awake."

Finn ignored the voice. "Travis. It's Travis, right?"

Travis's mouth tightened into a line, his lips disappearing almost completely. The guy was a rail. His cheekbones stuck out on his face, his thin arms were corded with muscle and sinew—no fat to soften him anywhere.

He walked behind Jazz and checked her ropes. She stirred. Finn's heart was pounding. He had to get her out of there. Travis headed toward him, stepping behind Finn's chair.

If Finn could reach him—touch his skin—he would push him to let them go. He didn't give a shit about the consequences. He just wanted Jazz safe.

"Do you think it's that simple? That you can turn on that power like a switch, without studying it, practicing it?"

Travis checked the ropes, pulling on them tight enough to make Finn wince. He reached for Travis—tried to anyway. His hands didn't respond.

"That is how it's done. Finesse. Slip in between the cracks so they don't even know you're the one in control. Learn how they think so they can't tell which voice in their mind is their own."

Shit! Travis walked to one of the tables. Finn had to think of another way to reach him.

"What is it that you want?" Finn asked.

"He wants to be like me," the voice whispered.

"Shut up!"

Finn's stomach seemed to drop through his body, carried away with a feeling of déjà vu. This conversation wasn't new. It had been going on since yesterday at least. Intrusive thoughts that Finn believed were his own, even though they weren't like him at all.

He'd thought Michael's memories were affecting him—getting under his skin—until Jazz shared her theory in the darkroom that Michael was the one haunting him. That somehow his spirit was still hanging around. Hanging around *Finn*.

Maybe he had used Finn's bond with Rachel or used the connection Finn made when he read objects. Either way, Michael was back. And he was in Finn's head. Under his skin.

The voice in his head laughed. *"'Under your skin' is going to have a very literal meaning for you soon."*

Travis turned from the table, a long thin blade in his hand. A skinning knife.

Shit!

Finn drew out the word in his mind. He couldn't help it. That panic from earlier was back in full force.

"Come on, man," he said. "You don't have to do this."

"He wants *to do it. Don't you see? He's trying to live up to the standard I set—to prove he's as good as me. It's pathetic, really."*

"Travis, please. This isn't you. I saw the kid you were before Michael started messing with your head. Don't let him turn you into this."

"Oh, please. I've been sculpting his mind for decades. Do you think you can undo my work with platitudes? When I came to live here, he was a plump little thing just approaching manhood. Disillusioned with the world, but still open-minded enough for me to squeeze in. I would pick at him till he attacked me, then set his mother against him as well. They were excellent practice for learning to control others. You, though. You have so much raw power. Power you never bothered to use."

Dammit. Finn almost felt bad for Travis. The guy's hand was shaking. He really didn't want to do this. Michael had fucked with his head so bad.

"I can help you," Finn said.

"No you can't," the voice said. *"You can't help anyone. Not yourself. Not Ms. Zhou."*

Finn was trying to figure a way out of this, but coming up empty. The sand kept him from getting enough purchase to shift his chair. Travis was right there with them, armed and absolutely dangerous. Jazz was unconscious, at his mercy.

"Please," Finn said. "I'm begging you. Let her go."

Travis was staring at the knife in his hands. He was working up his nerve. Finn had to reach him quickly.

"As if he would ever let either of you go. You both know about what he's done. He's too much of a coward to go to prison. He'd rather kill you."

"Of everybody in this room, I think you're *the one he'd most like to kill."*

Wait… That just might work.

"Travis, I know Michael hurt you. Made your life hell. I know you hate him and you want to prove that you're better than him."

Travis finally spoke, his voice rusty as if he seldom used it. "You don't know a damned thing."

"I do. I know because he's here. Michael is here."

Travis finally looked at Finn. His eyes were wide and his mouth dropped open. He glanced around the small space, shifting the knife in his hand so he wielded it like a weapon.

"You've felt him too, haven't you? You know he's still around."

"My traps…" Travis murmured. "They were all set off last night."

How could Michael have managed that? Finn wished that he and Jazz had talked more about what ghosts could do instead of focusing on Finn's problematic powers. In the movies, sometimes ghosts could move things. Setting off a bunch of traps seemed a bit much.

The voice in his head laughed. Mocking him again. *"You really are clueless."*

Finn was missing something. Michael had already taunted Finn about not knowing what he could do with his powers. And Michael had said he was practicing using them. Finn looked at Travis again, the way his eyes glazed over, the terrified look on his face.

"They weren't empty, were they?"

Travis's gaze flicked to Finn's again and he snapped his mouth shut. Finn went over everything he knew about Michael, remembered the dream about Travis.

Traps.

What if Jazz was right and Finn did have the ability to control animals? What if Michael had been practicing on them while working his way up to controlling Finn's own body with his powers, overriding his mental commands?

"It was squirrels," Finn said. "They had run into the traps and set them off."

Travis's eyes nearly bugged out of their sockets. He flashed the knife toward Finn. "How do you know that?"

"Because Michael is in my head. You want your revenge? Take it. He's right here for you. But let Jazz go."

"Pathetic. As if ending your life would end me."

Travis turned back to the table and set down the knife. He kept scanning his tools, shifting them, lining them up in perfect rows.

"He'll never let her go. You only have one chance at making it out of this alive."

Finn knew the devil was about to offer him a deal. He could feel it. And he didn't have any options to counter whatever Michael was about to say.

"Which is?"

"Let me talk to him."

It couldn't be that easy.

"Step aside and let me take over."

"As if."

"I'll convince him to let us out of the chair and remind him of his place."

There was no way Finn was letting this sick bastard take his body for a spin. The things he might do... No. No way.

"Then die here. Both of you."

Shit.

"You know he's going to kill you. You're helpless to stop him. If I can talk to him directly, I can convince him to let you go. After that, all you have to deal with is me."

That last part caught Finn's attention. Michael noticed.

"This is your body. Do you really have so little faith in yourself that you don't think you can reassert control after you're free?"

Finn wasn't sure. It was too risky. He had to think of another way. Fast.

"There is only one way out—if he lets you go. He will never cut you free. But he will free me. It's been fun to mess with you, but if he kills you, I can always find someone else to possess. Either way, the choice is yours."

Chapter Twenty-Five

Holding still while Finn talked to Travis was taking all of Jazz's willpower. She kept her head dangling loose on her neck, letting her hair shield her eyes as she surveyed the small space where they were held captive.

She could see tables out of the corners of her eyes. Their phones were sitting on one of them, along with carving tools, blanks waiting to be used, and some that had already been shaped into frames for more of Travis's work—including two life-sized female forms just behind Finn.

The hair on her arms lifted as she thought about the implications of those two mannequins. They were the same size as Elsa and Rachel.

Her stomach knotted. There was an acrid scent permeating the air as well. Something had been burned nearby recently. The wind carried the smell just inside the shed occasionally as it shifted. Char and chemicals. Lighter fluid.

There was sand beneath her feet. Her legs were tied to her chair at the ankles—around her boots. If they could get Travis to leave, she would be able to get her feet out of her boots. She could walk to the table and get a tool to cut herself and Finn free.

It was a big if.

Finn was trying to convince Travis to free Jazz. He had been, anyway, before he lapsed into an unexpected silence. Travis was standing at his tables, sorting through his tools. She risked a glance at Finn. His head was bowed against his chest. Had he given up?

No, he was a fighter, like her. What was he doing then? All of his focus seemed to be directed internally. Maybe he was trying to sort through Michael's memories to figure out a way to help them.

That didn't seem safe. The more he delved into them, the more of a foothold Michael seemed to get. And in this dark place... They were in his home territory. She could feel it.

She had listened to their conversation. Finn hadn't been able to reach Travis. Maybe she could. She lifted her head cautiously and kept her voice low and neutral.

"Travis."

He stiffened, but didn't look at her.

"Hi. I'm Jazz."

He kept picking up one tool after another and setting it back in place.

"You haven't done anything wrong yet." It wasn't exactly true, but she needed to win him over. "You can still let us go. Put a stop to this. You have the power to do that—to make that choice."

He said something, but his voice was too low for her to hear.

"What?"

"Be quiet."

"Travis, please. You need to listen to me."

"Shut up." He was still picking things up and putting them down. Over and over.

"It isn't too late."

"Shut up. Shut up. Shut up!"

He turned to her, eyes wild, then he leapt at her. He grabbed her by the throat with both hands, squeezing till she couldn't breathe.

"You are *materials*! Materials don't talk!"

The sound of blood rushing through her ears was distorting what she heard. It had to be. Because Finn was laughing.

"Pig!" Finn shouted. "Pig, pig, piggy!"

Travis's grip went lax. Jazz sucked in air, the room spinning around her.

Travis turned around, his voice eerily quiet. "What did you say?"

Finn laughed again, then made a horrible squealing sound. His eyes were closed, and his head listed to the side. A bizarre smile stretched across his face.

"Finn…" Her throat was sore. She couldn't manage more than his name.

"I said shut up!" Travis backhanded her.

Pain blurred her vision and blood started to pool in her mouth. She blinked away the tears so she could see Finn more clearly. His head had rolled forward, his chin resting against his chest.

"Travis, how many times do I have to tell you?" Finn lifted his head, his smile spreading to show all of his teeth. He paused after each word when he spoke. "Don't damage the canvas."

He looked up at her. His eyes were bright, bright blue.

"No..." Jazz whispered.

Travis pulled back his fist, aiming for her face. He froze when Finn yelled, "Pig!" again.

"You will listen to me, you filthy little pig."

Travis took a menacing step toward Finn. "Stop calling me that."

"But it's what you are. My piggy bank." Finn laughed again.

Travis's face went pale. He lifted a hand to touch his chest just above his heart, his breath coming fast. If they were lucky, maybe he would pass out and Jazz could try to figure out a way to fix this, to bring Finn back to himself.

Travis stumbled toward Finn. So much for luck.

"You... You can't say that. You can't say these things. You can't know these things."

"I know everything about you. All your dirty little secrets."

"No. You can't be him. She killed you. That Rachel, she killed you."

Finn grimaced. "She was *paint*. Do you really think she could end me? Do you think *anyone* can end me?"

Travis shook his head. His hands were twitching, forming fists that Jazz doubted he was even aware of.

"This is a trick," Travis said.

"You know it isn't. Otherwise you wouldn't look like you're about to wet yourself."

"Shut up."

"That's it. Hide in the mud, piggy. Hide from the truth, the truths I know. Like that you're a gutless coward." Finn cocked his head to the side and pursed his lips. "Is that why you like to play with dead things? Hollow them out so they're like you? Is that why you stole everything Auntie cooked for *me*. Trying to fill yourself up?"

"Stop it." The calm of Travis's voice worried Jazz more than his shouting. Shit, Michael had done a number on this guy. She couldn't imagine living with a psychopath.

"You never even had the courage to kill any of your playthings without your pathetic little traps. I had to do it for you. You'd have nothing without me. You *are* nothing without me!"

"Stop!" Travis punched Finn in the jaw viciously.

Jazz gasped. Maybe the pain would snap him out of it, let him escape from Michael's memories. Finn spat out a mouthful of blood and smiled again.

"I'm sorry," Travis stuttered. He dropped to his knees next to Finn. "I'm sorry, I just get so mad. You know how I get mad."

"It's all right, Travis." Finn's voice was smooth and cool, like a snake's skin. "I forgive you. I understand. That's always been your problem. Your violence is always a reaction. Never a *decision*. Never a choice. My violence always has purpose."

Travis was nodding, his gaze on the floor and his hands clasped in front of him like some sort of sick disciple. "I know, Mikey. I know."

"Let me show you," Finn said. "Let me give you purpose."

"What do you mean?"

"You have a grand goal. I applaud you on that. But you need to practice. Beyond your little pets."

Finn looked at Jazz for the first time. Hope swelled in her heart, then burst when she saw the coldness of his eyes. Finn wasn't there.

No. Dammit, no. She could still save him. Help him save himself. She wouldn't give up on them again.

"If you let yourself become angry, you'll bruise the skin and ruin the piece," he said.

"You're right. You always think of these things." Travis looked at Jazz too, an assessing gaze, one that didn't see her as a person. She was just materials to him, to them both. Maybe she could use that to her advantage.

"These ropes on my wrists sure as hell are chafing. Might want to do something about that if you're trying to keep my skin all pretty."

Travis took a menacing step forward, but Finn... No, *Michael*, stopped him.

"Ah-ah, Travis."

"She keeps talking to me." Travis bit the words out, his jaw so tense, muscles were twitching on both sides of his face.

"Then stop her. But do it better."

"How?"

Michael-in-Finn's-body leveled a malicious stare at her, grin wide, head lowered like a predator. "Cover her mouth with your hand and pinch her nose shut."

"Oh, that's perfect."

"Wait..." Jazz said, but Travis was already on her, covering her mouth and nose. She tried to bite him, but he was too strong. When she flailed her head, he grabbed her hair with his other hand and kept her still. Her lungs started to burn, her eyes watering.

"Not too much," Michael said. "We're not done with her yet."

Travis let go, and Jazz gulped down air again.

She was getting a good idea of how this would end. The worst of it wasn't even that she was going to die. Finn was going to keep on moving, trapped in his body while he was being controlled by Michael.

She had to do something. Any time she opened her mouth, it set Travis off. But words were her only weapon.

The first thing she needed to do was get Finn free—his body, anyway. If she could reach him, it would only help if they weren't both tied to chairs.

"You think you're in charge, but you're tied up just like me." Jazz swallowed hard, then leaned back. "*Mikey*."

Something dark crossed his features. Jazz really hoped she could reach Finn quickly. She was sure Michael would come up with some creative ways to punish her for pointing that out.

"Let me up." Michael somehow made each clipped word a threat.

Travis was thinking about what Jazz said, but she doubted he would be able to go against Michael's wishes.

"You're going to be mad because I hit you," Travis said.

"Not as mad as I'll be if you don't get these fucking ropes off of me right now!"

Jazz had never known Michael to swear. The fact that he did so now terrified her. He even dropped the condescending way he normally spoke. She might have gone a bit too far.

Travis could sense the change too—the danger. He started working on the ropes on Finn's feet. When they were loose, he moved behind the chair to free Finn's hands.

"I didn't know you were in there. I wouldn't have tied you up if I'd known, Mikey."

"Stop calling me that."

As soon as Michael was free, some of the menace seemed to drain from him. He rubbed his wrists and shook his shoulders. After a deep breath, he smiled at Jazz again, a look she'd seen dozens of times at the gallery.

"Where is it?" Michael asked.

"I kept it safe for you, Mi—"

Travis stopped himself, which was probably a good thing given the menacing look Michael cast at him. Travis reached into his shirt and pulled out a leather pouch on a loop of dark cord. He took it off and handed it to Michael.

Whatever was in there, Michael was delighted to have it back. He cupped the pouch in his hands, closing his eyes and taking a few deep breaths as he smiled. Then he draped it around his neck, pressing it against his chest above his heart—above *Finn's* heart.

Michael opened his eyes and smiled at her. "Now then. Let's get started."

Travis was staring at Jazz too. He was shifting his weight from side to side. "What's first? Should I get my knives?"

"The skin, Travis. You have to think of the skin." Michael started moving around the room, picking over Travis's tools.

"Right."

Travis joined him in the search for something to use to kill her. He paused and stared at her. Jazz's heart was pounding in her chest.

"Oh, I know!" Travis said. "We can drown her in the swamp."

"That is a wonderful idea."

Michael turned around, holding a large blank for carving a frame for one of Travis's creepy companions. Never slowing his momentum, he smashed the block of wood into the side of Travis's head.

Travis crumpled to the ground. Jazz wasn't sure if he was alive after that vicious blow.

Michael tossed the blank aside, then dusted his hands together. "Well, my dear. Now that we're alone..."

Shit.

But they weren't alone. Finn was still in there, somewhere. She had to believe it. She had to reach him. And if he wasn't...

Her vision blurred. She closed her eyes, feeling tears roll down her cheeks.

"Finn, I'm so sorry," she said. "I never thought it would end this way. I didn't think it was going to end at all. I thought Fate had given us a second chance."

She opened her eyes to look at him. Michael was glaring at her, but there was confusion and uncertainty on his face. He grabbed a knife from the table and stalked toward her. She smiled.

"I'm glad we had a chance to work things out. I wish we had more time for me to make things up to you."

"Stop talking to me like I'm him. Finn is gone. Permanently. You know who I am now."

She nodded. "If that's true—if Michael is all that's left—then I'm ready to go. I don't want to be in a world without Finn."

He let out a snort. "You and he are a pair. Both disappointing. Everyone is always so impressed with you. You're supposed to be a fighter. You're supposed to be strong. How can you give up so easily just because one man is gone?"

Jazz shook her head and smiled.

"I love him."

Michael's mouth dropped open.

"I hope you're in there, Finn. I truly do, if nothing else so that you can hear me say this. God, I hope you can hear me. I love you, Finn. I'm sorry it took me so long to tell you."

He clamped his mouth shut, his eyebrows pinched together above his nose. He was breathing hard, she could hear it, see his chest heave. He walked around behind her, put his hand on her forehead and pulled her head back. He put the knife against her throat.

She looked into his eyes, praying that somewhere in there, Finn was still fighting. She was fighting too, in her own way.

His gaze was so intent on her, he didn't seem to notice that the hand holding the knife trembled.

Then he dropped to his knees and cut her free.

Chapter Twenty-Six

Finn's hands were shaking. He could feel Michael's will flowing along his nerves, moving him around like a marionette. Before, Michael had been the one fighting to control Finn's body. Now, Finn was the interloper.

"Thank God," Jazz said. "Finn…"

He threw the knife away. He had to help her, to give her the best possible chance of surviving this. And the best chance she had was to run.

Finn glanced at her and saw the terrified look on her face. He could guess what she saw. His eyes were still wrong. She grabbed his face and leaned in to kiss him. Finn couldn't even feel her. But he could feel Michael.

He started to laugh.

Jazz pulled back, eyes wide, mouth open. It only made Michael laugh harder.

"Surprise," he said.

She punched him in the throat. Michael's hands went to his neck and he fell to the side, coughing and sputtering.

Finn let out a whoop inside Michael's head. He had never been more grateful she let him teach her basics of self-defense. Sure, that was going to hurt like hell later, if he ever fully made it back to his body, but he didn't care. It seemed like she had pulled her punch at the last second. Finn's body would heal.

She scrambled to her feet, grabbed her phone from the table, and ran.

"Yes! Run, Jazz. Run!"

"We're on an island, you idiot." Michael's voice was cold inside his head. *"There's nowhere for her to go."*

Michael pushed himself onto his knees, using the chair Jazz had been tied to for leverage. He hung there, breath rasping. Maybe she had hit him harder than Finn thought. Good.

"Veronica. Veronica!" Michael's voice was hoarse. Finn hoped it hurt him to talk.

Who the hell was Veronica?

Michael had his eyes closed, so Finn couldn't see anything. He couldn't *do* anything. He was trapped in his body, watching as Michael drove it around.

"Tend me."

Michael opened his eyes.

"What the fuck?"

The clearing outside the shed was filled with people. Women, more precisely. They milled about, clustered in groups, stared at Michael with terrified eyes. They looked almost solid, but Finn could see the faint outline of trees and brush behind them—through them. Sometimes they would sort of shiver and wink out, only to reappear somewhere else.

Michael laughed. *"Meet my life's work. It turned out even better than I imagined. I'm glad I had a chance to see them like this."*

One of the ghosts—and Finn was certain that's what he was seeing —approached and knelt in front of Michael. She had blonde hair and blue eyes. Finn looked around through the windows of his body's eyes. All the women had blonde hair. They were too far away to make out their eye color, but they had similar builds.

"I see you have a type."

Michael laughed in Finn's head. *"I get nostalgic. I had a sister too. If I had known about ghosts and earthly remains, I might not have burned our house to the ground with her and mother inside. Then they could have joined us as well."*

"You sick—"

"It was better than they deserved," Michael snapped.

Shit.

"Killing Rachel will be so much more gratifying when I use your

body—your powers—to do it. Only she won't get to cross over."

Aloud, he said, "Rachel will be joining us. Right, ladies?"

The ghosts inched closer to the swamp, turning their faces away. All but the one right in front of them. Maybe this was Veronica?

Michael lashed out and grabbed her throat. He moved so quickly, Finn barely registered the strike. Michael stared at the ghost he was throttling.

"I want you to see." Michael thought the words. It must be a special message just for Finn.

The ghost was whimpering, then she started making choking sounds. How could Michael choke a ghost? Where his hand touched her neck, the translucence of her skin became more opaque. There had been a shining quality to it, but it dulled and turned gray. Dark cracks appeared, centered on his hand.

"Stop it! You're killing her."

Michael laughed. *"Idiot. She's already dead."*

Dead or not, she was in pain. Finn tried to pull his hand away, to make Michael stop. He didn't budge. After a few more moments of Finn screaming in his head, Michael let her go. She collapsed on the ground, flickering in and out of sight.

"That is so much better." Michael moved his head from side to side, testing out his neck. His voice sounded fine.

"What did you do?"

"Used your powers."

"I've never done anything like that." Finn actually wasn't certain what Michael had done, aside from hurt that poor ghost.

"Because you're a coward who lacks imagination."

Michael stood up and glanced around. Had he healed himself? What the hell...

"You have no idea what this body is capable of. You don't deserve it."

He took a deep breath, then let it out and said, "Let's see if we can't track down Ms. Zhou. I'd love to catch up."

He walked into the sun, glancing around. A few yards from the shed, the remains of a huge bonfire smoldered. Finn could see a few shapes in the pile of charred wood at the center of the scorched earth. Animals.

Pops and crackles were still sounding from deep in the mass and cans of lighter fluid were piled nearby. Michael wrinkled his nose as the scent of chemicals drifted toward them. He shook his head and stepped away from it.

"Travis is so sensitive. Running the squirrels into his traps was genius on my part. You should have seen the terrified look on his face. And when he came home, I shifted his pieces around at just the right moments to have him out of his mind with fear. He gathered everything up—all his precious friends—and burned them."

Michael sounded gleeful. Finn felt sick.

Michael walked to the edge of the water and looked out. *"I have my own friends."*

Half a dozen alligators floated nearby. Their eyes were glowing blue.

"Shit! Shit fuck fuck!"

Michael laughed again. *"Such language. Do you kiss your mother with that mouth? Oh wait, you haven't met her yet. She's an amazing woman, actually. I think after I'm done with Rachel, I'll stop by for a little reunion."*

"Leave her alone."

Finn didn't care about the things Jazz or even his dad had said. The woman was his mother. Finn would do his best to protect her.

"You misunderstand me. I think Lillian and I will get along very well, once I can get her attention. She could actually be quite helpful." He turned and walked inland. *"There are things going on in this town. I can feel it. I intend to be a player rather than a pawn. And you'll have a front-row seat."*

A ghost flickered into view before them. Most seemed to be staying out of sight.

"Nicole."

Michael reached up and ran his finger along her chin. She

shimmered. When she spoke, her voice rippled and echoed, an audio accompaniment to the visuals that seriously creeped Finn out.

"She's this way."

"Fuck! No no no. Please, don't lead him to Jazz."

"She can't hear you. And even if she could, she does as I say. Nicole doesn't even fight me anymore. She's learned her place. You will too, given time."

"Thank you, my dear." Michael gestured before them. "After you."

Chapter Twenty-Seven

Bugs were crawling over her legs. Lots of them. Jazz didn't care. She had run like hell from the shed and found a hiding spot, trying to figure out what to do next. So far, she had come up with exactly nothing.

Touching Finn wasn't working. From what she could tell, it was as if Michael had completely taken over Finn's body. She had no idea how to bring Finn back—if he was even in there anymore.

No. He was. He had to be. Dammit, Fate wasn't an asshole. After her talk with Finn, she refused to believe that anymore. It wouldn't bring them back together, really together, in a way they'd never been before, then take him away. Not like this.

She had to reach him. She needed help.

Checking her phone, Jazz choked back a sob of relief. There was finally a signal.

She dialed Rachel's number, praying with each ring. *Please be there. Please be okay.*

"Hello?" Garrett answered. Not Rachel.

Jazz started to panic. "Garrett? Where's Rachel? Is she okay?"

"I'm here. I'm fine." Rachel was safe. Not only that, she sounded strong, focused.

Jazz let out a huge breath. "Thank God."

At the same time, they both said, "Listen to me."

Jazz cut in. "Me first. He'll find me any second."

"Who will?" Rachel asked.

"Finn. I mean Michael. I don't even know anymore! I'm losing him. He's losing himself. Michael is possessing him."

Jazz wiped her nose with the back of her hand. Her vision blurred with tears. Dammit, she didn't have time to break down. She had to warn her friends of the danger they were all in.

"He's coming for you and Elsa. You have to warn her. He's going to kill you and…" She thought back to the female forms in the workshop. "You don't want to know what he has planned then. If I can't save Finn —"

Rachel interrupted her. "Stop. We're saving everybody. And we're taking Michael out in the process. Permanently. Where are you?"

Rachel had never sounded so strong. It bolstered Jazz, reminded her to hold tight to her hope. They were going to get out of this. All of them. They just needed to work together.

"I don't know exactly," Jazz said. "I was knocked out. But I'm in a swamp. Probably somewhere near Clearview."

"Why Clearview?" Rachel asked.

"Finn and I were trying to find out more about Michael's other victims. It's Michael's home town. We found the house where he grew up."

"Listen to me carefully," Rachel said. "I am certain that Michael's body was cremated but there must be something of him left behind. Something acting as an anchor in the physical realm. With how powerful he is, it can't just be a lock of hair. It has to be something with more substance."

Knowing Michael, he would want to keep it close. He'd only recently re-obtained a body—and the first thing he'd done was take that pouch from Travis and hang it around Finn's neck.

"I think I know where it is. What do I do with it?"

"Burn it," Rachel said. "Can you do that?"

There was a bonfire right next to the shed. It looked like it had nearly burned itself out, but Jazz remembered smelling lighter fluid. If she could find some, she could get it going again fast. All she had to do was get the pouch from Michael and make it back.

Yeah, just that.

She would do it. No matter what it took, she would do it to save her friends. And Finn… How could she help him? Was he really beyond Jazz's reach?

Rachel was the expert. Jazz almost didn't want to ask, but she had to know if Finn was still in there. If there was still hope.

"Yes. But what about Finn?"

"Once you destroy the anchor, I'll be able to take care of Michael and Finn will be free. We'll be working from here to try to weaken Michael, but we need you to help Finn keep fighting."

She could do that. She *would* do that. Finn was a fighter. Jazz had given up on him once before, she wouldn't make that mistake again.

Garrett came on the line, his voice raw. They were best friends, he and Finn. Like brothers.

"Jazz, you have to reach him. Any way you can. He won't be able to live with himself if he hurts anybody."

"I know," she said.

"Watch out for wildlife too," Garrett said. "Michael can control snakes and gators and the swamp's full of them."

She remembered Finn talking to Travis about squirrels. Before Michael had taken over.

"It's good if he's spreading himself thin," Rachel said. "The more fronts we can hit him from, the better. Work on your connection to Finn. Try to reach him and help him to hold on."

Jazz heard a twig snap nearby. She lowered her voice as much as she could while still being heard.

"Hurry."

She ended the call.

Holding her breath, she scanned the area in front of her. She was lying under a saw palmetto, flat against the sand. Its sharp leaves poked her legs. They were easier to ignore than the bugs. She was never leaving the city again after this.

Something particularly big crawled onto her thigh and she jerked reflexively, swatting it away.

Shit...

She looked back out at the clear space in front of her. Nothing.

Suddenly, the leaves above her bent away, leaving her exposed. She looked up to see Finn standing over her. His face seemed to blur as he grabbed her and lifted her from the ground.

"Hello, darling."

She kicked at his knees, punched, clawed, even tried to bite him. He was too strong, too big. He held her at arm's length while she flailed, exhausting herself.

"Are you done?"

"Let me go."

He laughed. "Why on earth would I want to do that? Travis is an amateur, but he did hit on an interesting concept. It would be a shame to waste those forms, don't you think?"

He tucked her against his chest, pinning her arms at her sides and keeping her facing away from him. She tried to head-butt him with the back of her head, but he swerved out of the way.

"Ah-ah-ah. None of that."

He headed toward the shed. That was a good thing. The fire was there. She held still, building her energy, coiling it within her so that she could lash out when they were close. If she could grab the pouch as he dropped her...

Who was she kidding? Finn had always been strong and fast. Michael was somehow even faster, stronger. Inhumanly so.

She needed Finn's help. She needed to reach him, to help him fight, like Rachel and Garrett had told her to.

"I would think that you of all people would be happy to sacrifice yourself for art," Michael said. "Then again, I suppose you've always been more of a merchant than anything else. I do appreciate your believing in me, though. For that, I'll make sure you're unconscious before I drown you."

"Thanks."

"Of course."

"I'd rather have a moment with Finn, though."

He laughed. "I don't think so."

"You don't have to give him control. I just want to talk to him—for him to hear me. There's something I didn't get a chance to explain."

They were back at the shed. Jazz could see Travis lying on the floor inside. She hoped he was still alive. At this point, she counted him among Michael's victims. The guy needed help. And Garrett was right —Finn wouldn't be able to live with himself if his body had been used to kill someone. Even if he wasn't in control when it happened.

Michael walked with her to the water's edge. As if the thought of drowning wasn't terrifying enough, six huge alligators were floating nearby. Their eyes were glowing blue.

What the hell...

She looked away. If she thought about the water, she was going to panic. Panic wouldn't help anyone.

"You were one of the most talented painters I've ever met." It was a revolting truth, but one that might help her. He had twisted his talent so horribly.

"Thank you. But I already knew that."

"Branching into a new medium can be difficult."

He laughed. "It won't be new to me. Who do you think introduced Travis to his little hobby?"

She was grasping, trying to find any way to keep him talking, to give her a chance to reach Finn. If Michael killed her quickly, Finn would lose his hold on himself. She was sure of it. Physical touch couldn't help him anymore, but emotionally she still had a chance to reach him.

"I don't get why you're so scared of me, though."

He stiffened. "What makes you think I'm afraid of you?"

"You won't even let me talk to you—to Finn. You're so afraid of what I'll say that you want to just knock me out and drown me."

"I am a little busy right now. I regret to tell you that you don't hold my undivided attention."

"Of course. I don't need it. This is a done deal. We both know it. Can you blame me for wanting a little more time?"

He set her down on her feet. She craned her neck so she could look at him. His eyes were glowing, just like the alligators'.

Shit.

She pushed down her fear.

"I suppose not." He smiled at her and it actually looked semi-genuine. "You know, I always liked you, Jazz. You're remarkably calm. Even in the face of this, it's just another business transaction. That's probably why it didn't work with you and Finn. He's so emotional."

That was it. She'd found her in.

"I am a businessperson first and foremost. So you can understand why I'd rather not go out with a debt that I can resolve."

"What do you mean?"

"I owe Finn information."

He frowned. She pushed forward.

"All I'm asking is for you to stand there and listen to me for two minutes. I gave you a chance at the gallery. Can't you give me one now?"

"I know you're trying to manipulate me."

"Do you think I actually stand a chance of doing so? Come on. I'm good, but not that good."

He grinned. "All right. This should be entertaining at the least. He's practically having conniptions in here at the moment."

Jazz could only imagine. But that was good. Finn was in there. Michael had just admitted it. And Finn was already worked up, already fighting. He just needed more ammo, a line to grab on to. She had a feeling she knew just the one to cast.

Chapter Twenty-Eight

Something was happening to Finn. Something he didn't understand and didn't like at all. If he could still feel his body, it would probably resemble a panic attack. With only a sense of his energy, he felt like he was made up entirely of fireworks that were starting to burn out, one after another.

The ghosts sometimes shimmered and flickered, winking in and out of sight. Finn felt the same, except if he blinked out even for a second, he wasn't sure if he would come back.

Michael was winning. He was pushing Finn out of his body. Finn could sense it. The more he fought, the more disconnected he became. He was getting to the point where all he could do was hold on. He wasn't able to help anyone, not even himself.

He was going to have to watch Michael kill Jazz.

No. *Goddammit, no!* That wasn't happening.

"Finn," she said.

Michael had granted them this audience. As if he was some fucking benevolent being. He was a monster. Finn felt the darkness in Michael growing, a sense of sharing his body with something that wasn't human anymore. Michael had moved beyond being a serial killer. His soul was twisting into something even worse.

"Shut up and listen. This is all you're going to get."

Every time he spoke, Michael's voice was stronger in Finn's mind. Every time, Finn felt smaller, more distant.

"We covered a lot of ground," Jazz said. "I'm glad we had a chance to fix things between us."

Finn was too. That was the only comfort he had to hold on to. Dammit, there had to be a way… He felt a pressure on what used to be his heart, a weight dragging him down that had nothing to do with the physical.

Jazz stepped closer. She put her hands on his chest. Did she know that Finn couldn't feel her? He only knew what she was doing because Michael was watching her every move.

"We didn't get a chance to cover everything, though. I want you to know, I never had a problem being seen with you. I wasn't embarrassed that we were together. That isn't why I never told anyone about us and asked you to keep us a secret."

"This should be good," Michael thought. *"Of course she was embarrassed to be seen with you. She's above you."*

"Shut up."

Jazz slid her hands up to Michael's neck. Finn sensed Michael's amusement.

"Do you think she knows who she's touching? Do you think it's on purpose?"

Michael was mocking him now, baiting him. Finn kept his attention on Jazz. She was up to something, he could tell. He just didn't know what or how he could help her.

"I felt like I was being punished when my father died. Every time I was really happy about someone in my life, every time I talked about it, they were taken from me."

"Oh look," Michael thought. *"It's about to happen again."*

"If I could find your face, I would punch it."

Michael chuckled.

"That's why I never talk about people I care about. Why I was so desperate for no one to know how much I loved you. I knew if people saw us together, I couldn't hide it. I thought if Fate found out, you'd be taken from me. I talked up my father to all my friends at college, and he died right before I had planned to show him off. That wasn't the first time something like that happened. And with you... I was so afraid, I didn't even want anyone to know we were dating."

"Interesting. My gallery exhibit was set to open just before I died."

"Shut up, you sick fuck. This isn't about you."

Michael laughed in his mind.

Finn wanted to hear more of what she had to say. Having these answers, *finally*... It lifted a weight from him, made him stronger. He felt as if he was drifting toward her, like he could almost reach out and touch her.

"The bar felt safe," she said. "Like it was an oasis. Our little corner of the world where we could be together. I thought as long as we kept our relationship there, everything would be okay. It was the only place I believed I could let myself love you."

She ran her thumb over Michael's lips, then back down to either side of his neck. She kept brushing her thumbs along his jaw. Finn's spirit might not be in control, but his body sure as hell remembered her touch. He focused on what Michael must be feeling, willed himself to connect with the sensations.

Finn could feel Michael suppressing a shudder, vague ripples of nausea flowing through him. He dropped his hands from her arms, as if he couldn't stand to touch her. For whatever reason, Michael didn't *want* to feel this.

Finn was granted a little more space in his body. He prayed that Michael was distracted enough that he wouldn't sense Finn slipping back in.

"What does she think she's doing?" Michael thought.

Finn wasn't sure. But he made himself ready.

"I was afraid if I showed you off, I would lose you. But I hid you and lost you anyway. I understand now that I should have fought for you. I should have let everyone know, stood by your side proudly. I should have fought for you."

Finn needed to fight. That was what she needed, what she was warning him about. She was about to do something, and he needed to be ready to help her.

"I'm so glad for everything we've shared through this, Finn. We have a second chance. To do things right. But we have to fight for it."

She grabbed the cord hanging around Michael's neck with both hands and pulled. It snapped free. She dropped under his arms and leapt past him, running toward the shed.

Michael was still reeling from Finn's body reacting to Jazz's touch. Finn felt himself connecting, fighting for control as he pushed his awareness along his body's nerve-endings. It was enough to slow Michael down.

"What are you doing?" Michael asked. "There's nowhere for you to run. Nowhere to hide that I can't find you."

Jazz was standing near the bonfire of Travis's work. She bent down and picked up a can of lighter fluid, then shook it. She smiled as she stood.

"I don't plan to run."

"Foolish—"

Michael's thought cut off as Jazz lifted the pouch she had taken from him. His hand went to his chest. He felt around frantically, as if he couldn't believe what he was seeing, that she had taken it—had gotten the better of him.

"Give that back!" he roared.

She chucked it on the fire as he ran toward her. Tried to run, anyway. Finn managed to trip him.

He felt Michael's surprise, a wave of rage pummeling him, searing him. Finn screamed. He couldn't stop himself. The pain was beyond anything he had ever experienced.

But Michael's attention was on him. It gave Jazz enough time to spray down the pouch with lighter fluid, soaking it. Flames crept up around it and the leather started to burn.

"No!"

Michael scrambled to his feet, heading for the fire. Jazz ran past him, not toward land but toward the water. Toward...

Fuck. There were six full-grown alligators out there.

Finn grabbed at his arms with his awareness, clawing at them, making the muscles of his physical body cramp. Michael curled into a ball, clutching them.

"You have a choice, Finn." Jazz was standing at the water's edge. "Save the pouch, or save me."

Then she turned and walked into the water.

"No way. No fucking way!"

"The pouch!"

Michael turned to the fire, fighting against Finn. More fireworks erupted in his body as they clashed. Finn visualized himself tackling Michael, taking him to the ground. He pushed all of his energy into that thought.

They fell.

"Yes!"

Michael started to crawl. His hands dug into the sand, pulling them closer to the fire.

"Dammit!"

Finn could feel Michael's spirit crowded against his own—his body overfull from both of their presences. And if he could feel Michael, he could touch him. Finn dug his elbow into Michael's back. Michael screamed.

Darkness suddenly engulfed Finn as his external senses cut out. He was standing in a pitch void, staring at a vaguely person-shaped form made of glowing blue energy. He lifted his hands and saw that he was the same—only his energy was gold.

He didn't have time to notice more. Michael flew at him. Literally flew. He hit Finn in the middle, knocking him to the ground. Finn managed to grab Michael's wrists and hold them, keeping him at a distance. Michael writhed and snapped at Finn, trying to bite him. The energy he was putting off became more frantic, more violent.

Less human.

It was also fading.

Michael threw his head back and let out an inhuman screech, then vanished. Finn's regular senses turned back on as if someone had flipped a switch. He felt himself sort of flood back into his body.

He looked up and saw the pouch fully engulfed in flames. The fire started to die down, all the fuel consumed. Whatever had been in the pouch was destroyed.

He lay on the ground for a moment, trying to get his bearings, to remember how his arms and legs worked. Then he heard Jazz scream.

He jumped to his feet and bolted for the shoreline, leaping from the ground, body forming a perfect line as he dove into the water.

Please, please...

He couldn't be too late.

Chapter Twenty-Nine

Jazz hoped Finn was winning against Michael. She really, really hoped so.

Her boots were full of water. At least they kept her from feeling the greenish stuff that she was walking through. Her skin was crawling. The water closed around her thighs, cooler than she expected.

Any time, Finn.

It was a gamble. A huge gamble. Being knocked out and drowned seemed a lot better than having half a dozen alligators rip her to shreds...while she drowned. The water was up to her waist. She didn't hear Finn behind her.

He would fight Michael off. She knew he would. But he had to feel that the danger was real.

Shit, the danger is *real.*

When the water had reached her ribs, she paused and looked around. She didn't see any alligators on the surface. That didn't seem like a good thing.

Her heart was pounding and her breath coming fast. Passing out would also not be good. She tried to get herself to calm down, to keep herself from hyperventilating.

Something brushed her leg.

She screamed. The shrill sound echoed around her. She leapt back, water slowing her progress. She couldn't run to shore. If Finn thought she was safe, he wouldn't have as much incentive to fight Michael, to save her.

Too much time had passed. What if Michael had won? What if he had already pulled the pouch—with whatever piece of him was inside of it—from the fire? They might have already lost.

Something clamped around her chest.

Shit! She was about to be eaten by alligators.

What was she supposed to do? Go for the eyes. They would try to roll with her, to take her underwater and drown her. Except she was still upright. Upright and screaming at the top of her lungs.

Her voice trailed off as she realized she didn't feel any pain. She looked up over her shoulder. Finn was standing behind her, face scrunched up as he winced at her.

"That was really loud," he said.

She spun herself around and grabbed his face, pulling his eyelids open. His irises were blue—pale blue, not bright. And they weren't glowing.

"Finn!"

She wrapped her arms around his neck and kissed him. He only half-heartedly kissed her back. That wasn't normal. She pulled back and looked at him warily.

"That is you, right?"

"Yeah. But could we maybe get on shore before making out?"

She nodded vigorously.

He smiled as he turned and started toward dry land, pulling her along with him.

"I fucking hate the outdoors," she said.

He laughed.

As soon as they were on land, he wrapped his arms around her and held her against his chest. He buried his face in the nape of her neck.

Smoothing down his hair, she held him too. She never wanted to let go. But they needed to.

"Finn, we need to check on Travis."

She felt him suck in a breath, his body going stiff. Her stomach knotted with worry.

Please let him be alive.

Finn slowly released her, then nodded. He held her hand as they walked into the shed.

Travis was lying right where he had fallen. A small puddle of blood surrounded his head. Finn knelt down, his hand shaking as he pressed his fingers against Travis's neck. After a few seconds, Finn let out a huge breath.

"He has a pulse. It's thready, but there. I don't think we should move him. We should try to get a signal and call the EMTs and police." Finn stood and grabbed his phone from the table. He put his hand on her waist and pulled her against him as they walked outside.

Her mind was whirling. Their part of it was done. But what about Rachel? Was she okay? And Elsa? Jazz hadn't spoken to her best friend since...she couldn't remember.

She pulled her phone from her pocket. The water hadn't reached quite that high on her body. Finn was busy messing with his own phone.

"I have a signal," he said.

Jazz looked at her phone and saw one as well. She dialed Rachel's number frantically, pressing the speaker button. The moment the call picked up, she half yelled, "Are you guys okay?"

Rachel's voice came over the line. "We're fine. What about you two?"

"We're okay." Jazz stifled a laugh. She was so relieved.

Garrett's voice was rough and actually cracked over the words as he spoke. "Finn, you SOB. What the hell did you get my friend Jazz mixed up in?"

She felt Finn's grip on her side tighten and nestled against him.

"Are you crying?" Finn teased.

"Shut up."

"Oh, I am never going to shut up about this."

Finn kissed the top of Jazz's head. She rolled her eyes.

"Ugh, bromance."

"I think it's adorable." Rachel laughed.

Finn's grip on Jazz tightened again. She looked over at him and saw his eyes glistening with tears. He was talking to his sister for the first time. Of course he was overwhelmed with emotion.

"Finn, you okay?" Garrett asked.

"Yeah, man. Yeah." Finn's voice was rough.

"Wait a minute. Now are you crying?" Garrett said.

Finn smiled at Jazz. "You'll never prove anything."

Jazz laughed. "Don't worry, Garrett. I'll get some pictures."

That would have to wait. Finn had other immediate plans. He shoved his phone in his pocket and tilted Jazz's face to his, claiming her lips for a deep kiss. The warmth of his mouth, the softness of his skin against hers…she let herself get lost in the feel of him for a moment. But only for a moment.

She kept one arm around his neck when she pulled back, and left their foreheads pressed together.

"Look, we've got a mess to clean up here," Jazz said.

Garrett laughed. "Funny, I was about to say the same thing."

"Ours is going to take a while. We need to call the Clearview police —"

"Already texted them," Finn said. "They're on the way."

Jazz leaned back, one eyebrow arched and a scowl on her face. How the hell had he managed that? She knew she was off her game, but to not even notice…

"When did you text them?" Her voice had more bite than she intended, which riled him up, of course.

"As soon as you called Rachel! I didn't want them to check our phone records and see that we called our friends before them when—"

"Enough!"

Jazz shook her head. They had to work on their dynamic. It would take time. Time that they now had.

"We can explain all that later," she said. "Bottom line is, you two need to call Elsa and Dante and give them the all-clear. We are all clear, right?"

"Yes," Rachel said. "Michael is gone—for good this time."

Jazz felt Finn relax a bit. She was relieved to hear it as well. Jazz would be sure to ask Rachel exactly how she had managed that.

"Thank you," Finn said.

"We couldn't have done it without you," Rachel said. "We make a good team."

Jazz covered her mouth to stop a choking sob from coming out. Finn fairly crushed her against his chest. She couldn't wait to tell Rachel about her new family.

They had to tell Tommy first. He would be so happy. They'd have to break it to him easily, ask questions to be certain. But Jazz was already sure. Psychic powers or no, she could feel it.

Rachel just went on, oblivious to Jazz and Finn's reactions. They must have been doing a good job hiding them.

A dull whirring noise was approaching. Jazz looked out at the swamp. It was coming from the water.

"I'll text you after I call Elsa to let you know they're okay," Rachel said. "But I'm sure they are. We let them know what they needed to do to protect themselves and it sounds like we were all keeping Michael pretty busy."

The whirring increased. It was an airboat. Jazz relaxed another iota as she saw the reassuring symbol for the police on the boat's side.

"Okay," she said. "The cops are pulling up."

"Is that an airboat?" Garrett asked.

"Yeah," Jazz said. "We better go. But we're headed your way as soon as we're done. And I'm bringing guests, so clean up."

"Guests?"

Rachel didn't seem all that keen on company, but she would handle it. Especially the company Jazz was bringing.

"Deal with—"

Shit. No. Jazz was done dismissing people's emotions—including her own. She took a deep breath and said, "I know you can handle it." Then she ended the call.

"What are we going to tell them?" Finn nodded toward the airboat.

"The truth. At least, as much of it as they can believe. We were investigating Michael Angelo's case, trying to ID his other victims. We came across a possible accomplice, found evidence that he was considering a crime, but were abducted before we could tell anybody."

Finn laughed. "Damn, you're good at thinking on your feet."

She shrugged. "We all have our talents. We need to tell them about the thugs at the bar too. In case they were involved at the hotel."

"We're going to be here for a while."

"Fine by me. As long as we're together." She rested her head against his chest.

"I love you," he said.

She smiled. "I love you too."

Chapter Thirty

Finn stretched out in his bed. After one of Daphne's amazing meals, then a hot shower with Jazz and...follow-up activities, he felt like a new man. No, not new. He felt like himself. For the first time in months.

Jazz was curled up against his side. They might have fallen asleep a little, which meant they were running behind for meeting up with Garrett and Rachel for a late dinner at Elsa's house. Garrett had called and asked for the switch in location. Apparently his house had been damaged while dealing with Michael.

Jazz had suggested they reschedule for the next day so that Dad could rest, but once it had been established beyond any doubt that Rachel was Siobhan, there was no stopping him. Finn didn't blame his dad for wanting to make up for lost time. It wasn't like he could sleep knowing his daughter was alive and well and thirty minutes away.

The door to Finn's bedroom opened and Dad practically ran in. He clapped his hands together a couple of times.

"Come on, let's go!"

"Dad! Give us a break, man."

Finn covered his eyes with his elbow. He was excited to meet Rachel too, but also exhausted. It had been a hell of a day.

Jazz pushed herself up on her elbows, staring blearily at Dad. She rolled over and pulled the sheets up higher, then laughed.

"This is where I came in," she said.

Right. The first time she and Dad met, he had barged into the room, thinking Finn was alone. Instead, Jazz had been by herself in Finn's bed.

Having a history with someone filled his chest with warmth. Especially since it had led them to this moment—this family.

"I'll be waiting for you downstairs in the bar. Five minutes," Dad said. He pulled the door shut, then yelled, "Five minutes, or I go without you!"

"Come on!" Finn let out an exasperated breath.

Jazz laughed and leaned against his chest. "We better get ready."

They jumped out of bed and dressed. Daphne had loaned Jazz a set of clothes that fit reasonably well. In four and a half minutes, they were all standing in the bar, ready to go.

Well, he and Jazz were standing. Dad was sitting down, one arm resting on the table next to his hat.

"Dad? You okay?"

Daphne was the first to realize something was wrong. She ran over to Dad and knelt at his side, pressing her fingertips to his neck. Finn and Jazz joined her in seconds.

"Dad!" Finn's heart was pounding.

Please, God, don't let Dad's heart give out. Not now.

It was too cruel. To be so close to reconnecting with his daughter and never get a chance to meet her.

Jazz's hands were shaking violently as she pulled out her phone. "I'll call an ambulance."

Finn took in the look on Daphne's face, the blue tinge to his dad's lips, and knew there wasn't time. Dad's eyes were clenched shut and his breathing was labored. He was fighting. If only Finn could do something to help him.

Something Michael had said popped into Finn's mind. Of all the people to be thinking about right then…

"You didn't even scratch the surface of your powers."

He remembered how Michael had siphoned off that poor ghost's energy and used it to heal himself—heal Finn's body. Finn knew his powers went both ways. He could read people, and he could control them. If he could heal himself, maybe he could heal other people as well. He was too desperate not to try.

Finn rested his left hand on Dad's chest, just above his heart, and willed some of his energy into him. Healing energy. He remembered how it had felt fighting Michael in the swamp—their energies clashing as they tried to end each other. This time, he visualized his energy entering Dad's body and wrapping around his heart, strengthening it.

The damned feedback started up, just like every time Finn and his dad's powers interacted. Finn tried to focus through the static. He could feel the jerky movements of each beat of his dad's heart, the muscle's struggle to get blood to flow. Finn saw the veins opening up, the blood pushing through, getting to where it needed to be.

His breath rushed out of him as he felt the connection synch up. His entire existence became that one organ—Dad's heart. He heard each beat clearly in his ears, the sounds of the room muting around him.

Golden light flowed from his hand into his dad, illuminating his heart, clearing it out. The beats became stronger, the light-imbued blood traveling throughout Dad's body, healing him not just there, but everywhere.

Finn felt his dad's joints become less creaky, his bones more firm, his muscle tissue becoming more elastic. Finn wanted to laugh. It was such a rush, like he was a conduit between Dad and...something else. Something so much bigger than anything Finn had ever connected to before.

He felt someone grip his wrist, pulling his hand away and breaking the connection. It was Dad. His grip was so strong, Finn could hardly believe it.

"Enough, son. Enough."

Jazz was the first to recover. "What the hell was that?"

Finn laughed. He knew his dad was going to be fine. Better than fine. Better than he'd been in years.

No imagination, my ass.

Finn could heal people. He could heal everyone he loved.

As soon as he had enough energy to stand up. That was going to be a minute.

Dad, Daphne, and Jazz helped Finn into a chair. They all stood around, staring at him with wide eyes. Finn felt a laugh bubble up in him. He couldn't stop it.

"Finn," Jazz said. "What *the hell* was that?"

"A taste of Heaven." He grabbed Dad's hand and squeezed it. "How are you feeling, Dad?"

"I think you know," Dad said. "I saw everything through our connection. Everything you did."

"We saw something too," Daphne said.

Both men looked at her. That was a surprise.

"Your hands glowed," Jazz said. "While you healed him. That is what you were doing, right?"

Jazz was scowling at him. How could she be mad? She loved Dad as much as Finn did.

"What?" he said.

"There's always a price, Finn. Scales that need to be balanced."

"Fine," he said. "I'll deal—"

Her glare increased. He stopped himself from using her old catchphrase.

"She's right," Dad said. "You can't take a risk like that again. Not until we understand this new aspect of your power better."

"I'm not going to go running around healing papercuts and headaches," Finn said. "But if someone I love is at death's door, you can bet your ass I'm going to make that bastard step off."

Finn's fatigue was already lessening. He didn't feel that bad. A dull ache lurked between his eyes, and his hands were still tingling. He was more bothered by the stares of everyone around him.

"I keep telling you, I refuse to think that Fate is some neurotic asshole fixated on *balanced scales* and making people miserable. Maybe Fate is looking out for us, and the only reason we went through all that shit was for us to be right here, right now—the best versions of ourselves to handle choices like the one I just made."

Jazz was staring at him. Dad and Daphne just smiled.

"If we hadn't been through all this, I wouldn't have known how to save Dad just now. You and I wouldn't be together. Hell, neither would Garrett and Rachel. And we wouldn't know about her and she'd be stuck with her shitty-assed family." He shook his head. "What happened sucked. Royally. But I can't say I'd change a damned thing."

He pushed himself to his feet, glad when his legs felt strong beneath him. "Speaking of which, I have a twin sister to meet. You guys coming along or what?"

Dad and Daphne exchanged a glance. She nodded slightly, then wrapped her arms around his neck. She hugged them both all the time, but not like this. Dad buried his face in her neck. That was new too. And about freaking time.

Jazz found Finn's hand and interlaced their fingers. He looked down at her to find her beaming. Finn was even gladder he'd been able to save his dad. There was too much the lucky guy had to live for.

Another laugh escaped Finn. "Should we leave you kids alone?"

Dad turned to him. "Shut up."

Jazz laughed. Daphne gave him a shy smile.

Dad ran the back of his fingers along Daphne's cheek, then said, "You sure you can handle the bar on your own?"

"Of course. But are you sure you're all right?"

Dad smiled. "Never better."

Then he kissed her.

Finn felt his eyebrows shoot up his forehead. Jazz leaned into him, her grip on his hand tightening. The kiss went on for longer than Finn expected. He glanced down at Jazz again, and she elbowed him in the ribs.

When they broke off the kiss, Daphne said, "Go and spend some time with your daughter."

She hugged his dad again, then came over and hugged Finn as well. "Take good care of him, okay?"

"Always," Finn said.

Daphne surprised him by hugging Jazz too. Which wasn't half as surprising as Jazz hugging her back. A real, full-on hug—not a polite pat on the back.

It was like they were a family again. An even bigger one, now that Daphne and Dad were together. And it was going to keep growing as soon as they figured out how to tell Rachel the truth.

"See you all soon," Daphne said.

"Yeah." Jazz cleared her throat and glanced at Finn. She scowled at him when he grinned. She was just as moved by the whole thing as he was.

When they were on the sidewalk, Finn said, "So, you and Daphne, huh?"

"Yeah, me and Daphne." Dad glared at him.

Jazz laughed and they both turned to her. She shook her head.

"Sorry. Just, when I met Daphne, I was afraid she and Finn were... Never mind."

Dad snorted. "Like he stood a chance next to me."

Finn led them to his sleek black muscle car. The darkened windows made it perfect for surveillance. The lack of rust spots helped quite a bit as well, given the neighborhoods he often parked in.

"Wow," Jazz said. "Maybe I won't miss the old car as much as I thought."

Finn grinned at her, opening the passenger's door and pushing the seat forward so she could climb in the back.

"Are you sure you're up for driving?"

"Yeah. I feel fine. Great, even."

She gave him a skeptical look. "Prove it."

"How? You want me to do some pushups or something?"

"Kiss me."

He heard Dad chuckle. Finn looked around the street. It wasn't too busy, but there were a few people walking around. And it was broad daylight.

"Now? Here?"

"Yeah. Unless you're not up for it."

"But there are people around."

Things had changed between them, but she'd drilled this into him so much he hesitated. No public displays of affection. Ever.

She stepped up to him and wrapped her arms around his neck. "Kiss me and I'll be able to tell if you're okay."

He'd have to stop smiling first. He wasn't sure he'd be able to.

She pulled him closer, helping him along.

He brushed her lips softly at first, then deepened the kiss. He put his hands on the small of her back, pressing their bodies together. His tongue delved into her mouth, his lips caressing hers. She melted against him.

After a while—Finn wasn't sure how long—Dad cleared his throat. Reluctantly, Finn pulled away.

Jazz's eyes smoldered. Her lips pulled into a grin.

"Yeah. You're fine."

"Sheesh." Dad was holding the door. He gestured impatiently for her to get in. "If you guys are done showing off, let's go."

Chapter Thirty-One

Elsa lived about thirty minutes outside the city. Finn made it in twenty.

Jazz was grateful for the time to collect herself after the scare with Tommy. Being in the back gave her some privacy to deal with it.

Scare wasn't really a strong enough word. *Terror* was better.

Michael had almost taken away everyone she loved. If Fate had taken away Tommy after she'd just reconnected with him... Jazz wasn't sure what she would have done. Not returned to her belief in her curse, though. She was done with that. Especially after Finn's speech earlier.

Finn had explained about Michael using Finn's powers to heal himself. If they hadn't been through their ordeal, Finn wouldn't have learned about his new power. He wouldn't have been able to save Tommy.

"Everything happens for a reason," Finn had said.

And *"Fate isn't a dick."*

Jazz let out a slow breath and smiled.

Finn's hands had glowed with a beautiful golden light. She'd watched it flow into Tommy's body. The color had returned to Tommy's face, his lips had turned pink again, and his breathing eased. He even sat up straighter.

She was a little worried about Finn, but he'd given her yet another amazing gift—hope. Hope that the universe wasn't out to get her. Hope that maybe it wanted her to be happy.

She knew she would experience sadness and hardships in the future, but didn't think she would take it personally anymore. She was still going to call Chloe as soon as possible to get her take on it all. In the meantime, Jazz enjoyed the silence.

Tommy and Finn seemed content to drive without conversation. It was a nice change from answering questions and filling Tommy and Daphne in on everything that had happened. Well, almost everything. They left out some of the scarier details for Tommy's sake. Thank God, after what had happened at the bar.

Jazz wondered how Tommy would hold up to meeting Rachel. His daughter was a handful, even as an adult. Now that Jazz thought about it, Rachel was a lot like Tommy. They both had outgoing, friendly natures.

Jazz had never met someone as energetic, outgoing, and cheerful as Rachel. She was the antithesis of Jazz's best friend, Elsa, who was reserved, shy, and...well, a huge control freak. But Jazz would never say that out loud.

The two women balanced Jazz's life. Now she had Finn and Tommy back—plus Daphne. And Garrett and Rachel were finally together. Jazz's heart felt over-full. She saw Elsa's drive appear and pulled herself together.

Nobody said anything until they were standing at the front door of Elsa's mansion. Tommy turned to them and said, "How do I look?"

He looked pale. Frightened. Excited. A little overwhelmed. He was holding his fedora so tight the brim was bending.

Finn gripped Tommy's shoulder and gave it a squeeze. "You look great, Dad."

The door opened. Elsa stood there, smiling broadly. Jazz had never seen Elsa smile like that.

Emotions Jazz wasn't ready to deal with started rushing to the surface. She stepped forward and grabbed Elsa, pulling her into a crushing hug.

"Dad, this is Elsa Sinclair," Finn said.

"I know."

Tommy sounded a little irritated. He probably thought Finn was afraid Tommy would think Elsa was Rachel or something. Jazz felt Tommy step closer.

"I've read all your books," Tommy said. "It's nice to meet you."

Elsa laughed, wrapping one arm around Jazz and shaking Tommy's hand with the other. "And you."

Jazz finally let go. She sniffed and wiped at her eyes, then murmured, "I'm glad you're okay."

Elsa bit her lower lip for a moment, obviously fighting back tears of her own. Then she said, "I'm glad you are too."

And that was it. End of moment. Jazz was sure they'd be having more in-depth conversations about...a lot of things. Their relationship would change, but she was sure it would be stronger for it. And so would they.

"Please come in." Elsa shifted to the side so they could all enter the foyer. She closed the door and locked it when they were all inside. It would probably be a while before any of them really felt safe.

Jazz took a deep breath. She hadn't realized the big step she was about to take. Introducing Finn to her friends—as her life partner.

"This is Finn," Jazz said.

Elsa smiled at Finn and shook his hand too. "It's nice to meet you."

Finn was beaming. "You too." Under his breath, he added, "You have no idea."

Jazz scowled at him. Then she wrapped her arm around his waist and rested her other hand on his stomach.

Elsa's eyes about popped out of her head. Her jaw dropped and she stammered a few strange sounds. Then an even bigger grin spread over her face. Her brown eyes shimmered as if she as about to cry.

Jazz sighed. "Keep it together, Elsa."

"I'm a romance novelist," Elsa said. "You can't expect me to not have a reaction when my best friend introduces me to her boyfriend for the first time after all our years together."

"Finn's more than a boyfriend," Jazz said.

Elsa actually made a choking sound. Jazz rolled her eyes.

"Oh, come on!"

"It's okay," Elsa said. "I'm okay."

It was definitely time to change the topic. "Where is everybody?"

"On the patio," Elsa said. "Can you show them the way? I'm

helping Winston in the kitchen."

Jazz's stomach sank. "He's not letting you cook, is he?"

After the bombshell Jazz had dropped—introducing Elsa to Finn—Elsa was certain to be even more distracted than usual. She had tried to make food for them both a couple of times when they were roommates in college. The results were revolting.

Elsa had a tendency to grab the wrong item, like putting cayenne pepper in oatmeal instead of cinnamon. The worst was when she thought she was using honey but had grabbed amber-colored dish soap instead. Jazz shuddered at the memory.

"I'm just bringing him what he needs and carrying things." Elsa glared at her.

"Yes, but you didn't give him any of the ingredients, did you?"

Elsa let out a little huff of breath. "It's just *sandwiches*."

"I've had your *sandwiches*." Jazz made sarcastic air quotes.

"He smelled everything to make sure it was right. Now *if you'll excuse me*."

Jazz and Elsa had been friends for so long, they had their own secret language hidden in regular conversation. Elsa had effectively told Jazz to eff-off. It was an added treat that Jazz was the only one Elsa was comfortable enough to let loose with that way.

Jazz grinned. "Sure."

Elsa stalked away.

"What was that all about?" Tommy said.

"I'll explain later. Come on."

Jazz led them to the patio through the solarium that Elsa had converted into her art studio. The windows that made up the walls and ceiling had steamed up, but still let the last of the evening's sunlight into the room. More filtered in from the double doors that opened onto the stone tile sun and walkways surrounded by plants that hugged Elsa's house. Laughter and conversation floated toward them.

Garrett was sitting in a chair next to the patio table, with its big umbrella coming out of the middle. Dante was lying on the sun lounger. Half of his face was covered in bandages and he was wearing pajamas.

He started to sit forward when they walked outside, but Garrett put a hand on Dante's chest to keep him in his chair.

"You know the deal," Garrett said. "You can rest in the sun lounger or go back to your room."

Dante sighed, then leaned back. "I suppose I can forgo formalities for once."

"And no alliteration." Garrett looked at Jazz and her group. "Dante's been driving us nuts with it. It's only funny for the first five minutes."

"I do believe it comes round again." Dante grinned.

Garrett laughed.

"Wow," Tommy said. "You're Dante Lucerne?"

"I am. Have we met?"

"No, I just..." Tommy glanced at Finn. "I've heard a lot about you."

Finn stepped forward and offered his hand. It must be such a relief for him to not be afraid to touch people anymore. He grasped Dante's hand and shook it gently.

"Finn Connelly. This is my dad, Thomas."

Tommy stepped forward and shook Dante's hand as well. "Call me Tommy."

"I am very pleased to meet you," Dante said.

Tommy was beaming. No wonder. He loved reading historical fiction of any kind. Meeting someone who had actually lived in a different era must have him over the moon.

"If you guys can keep an eye on Dante here," Garrett said, "I'm going to go check on my other patient."

"Other patient?" Tommy asked.

Jazz's stomach clenched. She thought everybody was okay. Winston must be fine if he was working in the kitchen. They had seen everyone except Rachel.

"Is Rachel all right?" Jazz said. "She sounded fine when we talked to you guys on the phone."

"She got cut up pretty bad, but she's going to be okay."

Jazz let out a breath. Garrett passed close to them as he walked toward the house. He put his hand on Finn's shoulder.

"Are you kidding me, man?" Finn shook his head. "After everything we just went through?"

Finn grabbed Garrett and pulled him into a hug, clapping his back and then just holding on.

"Garrett, check out my makeshift wheelchair." Rachel's bright voice rang out behind them. "Elsa said I can use this old broom as a paddle."

Finn stepped away from Garrett, turning to face Rachel who was... pushing herself onto the patio using a broom, just like she'd said. She was sitting in a wheeled office chair, holding her feet off the ground. Jazz would have laughed at the spectacle if Rachel's feet weren't wrapped in bandages. There were more on her arms.

Garrett headed over to Rachel and put his hands on the back of her chair. "That's a pretty slick system, but on this rough stone, I think I'll feel better pushing you."

"I didn't mean to interrupt your bromantic moment," she said.

Tommy let out a laugh. Finn was just staring. Jazz realized she was as well. She couldn't help it, seeing the two together for the first time.

They had the same hair, eyes, and smile. Even their builds were similar—both tall and athletic. Well, when Rachel was standing, anyway.

Garrett wheeled Rachel closer. She patted his hand when they paused in front of Finn.

"You must be Finn," she said.

"Uh...yeah."

Rachel reached for his hand and he let her take it. Jazz stepped forward a moment too late.

"I'm so happy to...meet..." She broke off, eyebrows furrowing. "Wait. I know you. You've been looking for me. I felt you trying to reach me."

Shit. Jazz should have kept them from touching. Who knew how their powers would interact?

She and Finn and Tommy had already decided not to tell Rachel about their relationship until things had settled down. They didn't want to give Rachel any more to deal with than she already had.

So much for that idea.

Rachel's eyes widened and her mouth dropped open for a moment. She snapped it shut and shook her head.

"I've been dreaming about you for months. I don't understand."

"I can explain," Finn said. He tried to pull his hand away, but she wouldn't let him.

"You all have been through a lot today." Tommy stepped forward. "Maybe we should have waited till tomorrow."

"To tell me that Finn is my brother?" Rachel said.

Garrett laughed. "Have you been dipping into Dante's pain meds?"

"I'm serious." She grabbed Garrett's hand as well, keeping her hold on Finn's.

Garrett's brow furrowed as his gaze became unfocused, then his face relaxed and a huge smile spread across it. "Well, I'll be."

"What the hell was that?" Finn said.

"Empathic bond," Garrett said. "It lets me feel whatever she's feeling, including the connection between you two."

Damn, that would be useful. Jazz sort of wished she and Finn had something like that going on. It would certainly cut back on their miscommunications.

Then again, that level of intimacy was not something she was comfortable with. She was pretty sure he'd feel the same. They'd have to muddle through their relationship the old-fashioned way, and just start talking more.

"Well, I can feel enough of what you guys have going on to really want my hand back," Finn said. "Dude, she's my sister."

"And that makes you my brother." Garrett grabbed Finn in a huge hug, pinning his arms to his sides and lifting him off the ground. He laughed the whole time.

Finn let out an exasperated grunt. "God, this is embarrassing. Put me down."

Garrett did, but then ruffled Finn's hair.

"Stop it." Finn ran his fingers through his hair and looked over at Jazz.

She just smiled. "I've got nothing for you. I think this whole thing is disgustingly adorable."

Tommy spoke up in a gentle voice. "Are you two married then?"

"No, sir." Garrett returned to Rachel's side, resting his hand on her shoulder. "But at this point, the wedding feels like a formality."

"A really *big* formality," Rachel said. "With a huge venue, and a jazz band, and... Wait a minute, we're getting off track."

Jazz laughed as Elsa and Winston walked out onto the patio carrying trays loaded with food, paper cups, and pitchers of iced tea and lemonade. She didn't want to leave Tommy's side, and was grateful when Finn stepped forward to help carry everything to the table.

"It isn't fancy," Elsa said, "but since I was helping out, we figured we should keep it simple." She pulled up a chair next to Dante and held his hand. "What did I miss?"

"I do not know where to begin," Dante said.

Winston let out a *hmph*. He angled his head toward the others as he sat in a chair close by.

"Let me help you out there." In his thick cockney accent, he said, "Rachel and Garrett are finally engaged and she wants a big wedding. She and the muscled one who likes to strut are siblings somehow, and their psychic mumbo-jumbo makes them able to read each others' minds or something."

Winston leaned back with a sigh. The silence stretched on for a moment, then he added, "Oh, and Garrett and Rachel have an empathic bond. I miss anything?"

"I don't strut," Finn said.

"You totally strut," Jazz said. "But how did you know all that, Winston?"

"I keep telling you all, I've got ears like a bat." Winston pointed over his shoulder. "That's the kitchen window and the one just past is my bedroom. You people think you're being all sneaky and whatnot, but it's really just a pain in the arse keeping all these secrets."

Jazz had heard that being blind could increase other senses—including hearing. This was outright amazing, though.

Elsa and Dante exchanged looks.

"Do you know about us too?" Elsa said.

Winston laughed. "Oh, my love. I know more about you pair than I ever wanted to." He put on a mock shiver, then smiled at them.

Elsa turned scarlet.

"Great," Jazz said, trying to keep Rachel away from her line of inquiry. "Now everyone knows everything about everybody."

It didn't work.

"Not even close," Rachel said. "I still need to know how Finn is my brother."

"I have to admit, I'm curious about that myself," Garrett said. "You never mentioned anything about that before."

"I didn't know before," Finn said. "We discovered it while investigating the case."

"I don't understand," Rachel said. "Did my dad have an affair or something?"

"No." Finn let out a sigh. "It's complicated."

Her eyes snapped to Tommy. "Why did my question upset you?"

"Uh…" he stammered.

"Enough with the empathic readings already," Jazz said. "Rachel, you know how your mom's an evil, lying, manipulative—"

Three voices of protest cut her off. Jazz was surprised that the Connellys jumped to Mrs. Montgomery's defense. She suppressed a smile thinking of them as a family unit already. Damn, they were good people.

"Am I wrong?" Jazz said. When no one argued the point, she went on. "Did you ever notice that you look nothing like Edward Montgomery?"

"Well, yes," Rachel said. "But not all children favor both parents."

Jazz pointed at Tommy. "Have you not noticed yet that you look *just* like Tommy and honestly more like Finn than I'm comfortable thinking about?"

Rachel stared at Tommy and Finn for a moment, her eyes growing wide. "Oh my God. *You're* my father?"

Tommy looked over to Jazz, and she nodded encouragement. He stepped forward, crushing his hat in his hands.

"Well, yeah," he said. "I know this must be a shock for you. I don't expect you to—"

She launched herself out of her chair and hugged him. Tommy wrapped his arms around her and held her above the ground as best he could. She was almost as tall as he was.

"Sweetie, you need to stay off those feet," he said.

Rachel let out a sob, her eyes clenching shut and tears rolling down her cheeks. Jazz didn't need empathy to guess what Rachel was feeling. Her parents had treated her terribly. It was probably the first time a parent had shown her true concern.

Tommy rubbed her back. "It's okay," he said. "It's all going to be okay."

Garrett approached and put his hand on the pair's shoulders. They helped Rachel back into her seat.

"You're so tall." Tommy face was filled with pride as he smiled at her. "You grew up so beautiful."

Rachel held on to his hand, staring into his eyes. Finn picked up a chair and brought it over so Tommy could sit right next to her, then he knelt at their side himself.

"Finn, don't you dare heal her wounds," Jazz said. "We still don't know how doing that affects you."

Garrett's interest perked up. "Heal her?"

Jazz shrugged. "Yeah, it's something new he can do. Turns out, Finn's the most psychic of them all." She looked over at Elsa and Dante. "Well, except maybe for Elsa."

Dante beamed at Elsa. "As someone saved by her psychic sagacity, I certainly—"

"Dante," Elsa said.

His smile became a bit more subdued.

Garrett shook his head. "Yeah, well wait till you hear about how

Rachel got the better of Michael."

"I'd be really interested to hear about that, myself," Tommy said.

"Well, first I shot him seven times."

Tommy let out a half-strangled laugh. He cleared his throat, and said, "Only seven?"

"I ran out of bullets."

Tommy pressed a gentle kiss on the back of her hand, then set it in her lap, but held on. "That's my girl."

"This is a lot," she said.

Jazz picked up a chair and brought it closer for Finn to use. "There's one more thing. Finn's not just your brother—he's your twin."

Rachel smiled up at Finn and squeaked, "Twin? Really?"

"Yeah," Finn said. "We were split up in the divorce right after we were born."

More tears flowed down Rachel's face. She shook her head, and said, "God, our mom *sucks*."

Jazz let out a big laugh. She pulled Finn up from where he was kneeling so he could sit in his chair, then sat in his lap. He wrapped one arm around her waist and let the other rest on her thighs. It felt like the most natural thing in the world. Nobody said a word about the display of affection.

Buoyed by that, Jazz said, "I've already warned Finn about your mom. Just in case he gets curious or nostalgic and wants to meet her someday."

"Good." Rachel turned to Finn and said, "Whatever Jazz told you, it's all true—and worse."

"Believe that," Garrett said.

He was scowling more deeply than Jazz had ever seen. Whatever Mrs. Montgomery had done to get on his bad side, she'd better watch out for him. Jazz somehow doubted Mrs. Montgomery's dreams of her husband launching his political career in Summer Park would come true without the Wolfstroms' endorsement. From the look on Garrett's face, she sure as hell wasn't going to get it.

"Well, I'm curious right now," Rachel said. "I want to know

everything."

Jazz broke in. "We have time to catch up later. Let's just...be together. Okay?"

Rachel hesitated for a moment, but then nodded. "Sure."

Elsa and Garrett started handing everyone paper plates loaded with chips and sandwiches. Jazz couldn't believe a day that had started out filled with chaos and death could end so...peacefully. Her stomach started to churn as the familiar fear eked in. She felt at any moment the other shoe was going to drop.

Rachel glanced over from her conversation with Tommy.

"Don't," she said. "Don't let fear in. This is the moment we have. Hold on to it."

Everyone was silent for a moment.

"Well said." Tommy raised his cup toward her. "And if I might propose a toast... To family. And a brighter future."

"Here here."

"To family."

They lifted their glasses one by one, then took a sip.

Jazz wrapped her arms around Finn's neck and smiled down at him. This was the moment they had. She was going to hold on to it for all she was worth.

—

Summer Park Shorts

Short Stories Surrounding
The Summer Park Psychics

Cassandra Chandler

Winston

Elsa wasn't happy about needing to hire a chef. She had been putting it off ever since she moved to Summer Park at the urging of her best friend, Jazz. But with a new novel in the works, Elsa's single-minded focus on the fictional story was having unfortunate effects on her reality.

The week before, she had thrown up in her kitchen sink after taking a bite from a tuna salad sandwich she discovered in her fridge. Later she remembered that she had never succeeded in making edible tuna salad. She still wasn't a hundred percent certain what she had tried to eat. She'd been subsisting on cereal and energy bars ever since and felt terrible.

Elsa was practiced at appearing to be on top of everything. In truth, she had always been better at taking care of other people than herself. She needed help. Primarily someone to cook, but it would be nice if they could also remind her to eat, maybe help with laundry, and definitely keep the fridge clear of hazardous materials. She could afford to hire a full staff for her house, but that many people running around...

No, she needed to find one person who could help with all her needs. That was why she was sitting in the waiting room of the *Abrams Hiring Agency*, preparing to interview several candidates and find the best match. Mr. Abrams was late, which was not a good way to—

"What the bloody hell is wrong with you?"

Elsa's heart leapt into her throat at the harsh voice bellowing down the corridor that presumably led to Mr. Abrams's office. A man dressed in a dark suit stepped into view. His hair and beard were snow white and his skin weathered. His voice was heavy with a thick Cockney accent.

"You think I can't take care of people? How the hell do you think I take care of *myself?* Do magical fairies come and do my wash, cook and clean, and maybe fetch the old man a pint at the end of a long day?"

He smacked his cane against the wall as he turned toward Elsa. She jumped out of her chair, noting that the receptionist had already picked up the phone. Security would be on the way in moments.

Another man appeared in the hallway—maybe in his thirties, with glossy black hair and a snappy suit. Mr. Abrams, Elsa was certain.

"Mr. Cooper, please calm down. As I said, we clearly state that applicants must be able to fulfill all of the duties required..."

"You're going to talk to me about my duties? I've been doing this since before *your parents* were born!"

"Nonetheless, you were not honest on your resume. When you stated you could do the job blindfolded..."

"I can."

Mr. Abrams cast a glance at Elsa and looked stricken. He shook his head and held up one finger, as if asking her for a moment. Then he rolled his eyes.

The gesture would have been disrespectful enough if done behind Mr. Cooper's back, but the men were still facing. Elsa was shocked Mr. Abrams wasn't getting another verbal barrage for such poor manners until she noticed that Mr. Cooper's cane was white with red at the end. He was blind.

Elsa clenched her purse, willing herself to stay calm as her fear turned to anger. Making faces at a blind person? She would be taking her business elsewhere.

Mr. Abrams turned his attention back to Mr. Cooper. "In any case, your resume should have noted your disability—"

"I'm *differently*-abled. Not *dis*abled, you pillock. And you can consider my resume withdrawn."

Mr. Cooper popped a dark gray Trilby onto his head to punctuate his statement, then turned to the door. Never once did he have to right his course as he left the office.

Elsa was stunned. *Differently-abled*, he had said. She knew what it was like to be different. And she completely understood why Mr. Cooper had left that fact off of his resume.

"Ms. Sinclair, I'm so sorry that you had to witness that." Mr. Abrams extended his hand to her. She ignored it.

"I'm not." Elsa slid her purse strap over her shoulder and gave Mr. Abrams her coldest stare. He pulled back his hand. *Good.*

"There are several excellent candidates—"

"Please extend my regrets to them."

"Ms. Sinclair, you have to understand—"

"As a matter of fact, I don't."

Whatever explanations Mr. Abrams had ready, Elsa wasn't interested. She turned and walked out the door.

Mr. Abrams followed her with his hollow apologies as far as the sidewalk, sending a spike of panic through her. Was he going to try to stop her from leaving?

She quickened her pace, falling in step with the other pedestrians. Glancing back once, she saw that he was shaking his head as he stepped back into his building. She let out a little breath of relief.

Her car was parked close to the building, but she would wait a few minutes before doubling back. She needed to clear her head and regroup.

Summer Park was a gorgeous city, with old trees shading the sidewalks, flowers spilling out of planters everywhere, and the flawless blue Floridian sky overhead. Elsa still hated going into town.

People made her nervous. Especially strangers. Otherwise, she would have subsisted on take-out and delivery, like she had back in Virginia. But she'd lived there for years, and had built pleasant acquaintances with enough restaurants and dry cleaners to keep herself fed and clothed. Plus, most of those relationships had started in college, when she was just a student and not a relatively well-known historical romance author.

Elsa's new house was a manor. She loved it, but it was huge and didn't have a doorman to screen people or include a maid service as part of the rent. Sure, she had more privacy, but she also lacked a support structure.

Jazz could help Elsa find a chef. And a maid, and a driver, and they would all be amazing and spectacular. But that wasn't what Elsa wanted. She wanted someone she knew would mind their own business and leave Elsa to hers.

She had reached a corner and was waiting for the lights to change so she could cross the street. The group next to her laughed loudly, startling her again.

She needed to get back home—to sort through her thoughts. She needed to get away. Maybe it was time to head back to her car. She turned so abruptly that she bumped into someone.

Muttering, "Excuse me," she started to cross the street.

A strong hand grabbed her arm and yanked her back. Seconds later, a sports car whizzed by, right where Elsa had been headed. Her heart started to pound. If she had taken one more step...

"You all right there, love?"

Elsa turned to see Mr. Cooper staring over her shoulder, a faint smile on his lips. His voice was so different when he wasn't shouting. He sounded playful and friendly, with a touch of gruffness tracing the edges of his wonderful accent.

"I... You... How..."

He laughed and pulled her hand into the crook of his elbow, then led her a few steps farther from the street. "'I hear all things in the heavens and in the earth.'"

"Poe? You're reassuring me by paraphrasing *The Tell-Tale Heart*?"

"You a fan then?" He let out a little laugh. "I suppose I could have chosen something better. I'm in a bit of a dark mood at the moment, and that was the first thing that came to mind."

"Well, thank you, Mr. Cooper."

"Bah. Call me Winston."

Her cheeks felt stiff as she smiled. "Winston. I'm Elsa Sinclair."

"Nice to meet you, Ms. Sinclair."

"If I'm calling you Winston, you're calling me Elsa."

He laughed and patted her hand on his arm. "What I'm calling is a taxi."

"Let me buy you lunch," she said.

Where did *that* come from? Sure, once she thought about it, she was starving. And it made sense to get a properly cooked meal with balanced nutrition before returning to her pathetically stocked kitchen.

Winston looked like he wasn't keen on the idea of going to lunch together either. He was staring at her shoulder, his expression fixed as if he was trying to find the right words to politely decline.

"It's the least I can do," she said.

Now she was trying to convince him to come along? The idea of eating with a stranger usually set her stomach on edge. But Winston didn't *feel* like a stranger. Maybe it was because he had just saved her life.

"Being blind doesn't just make my hearing better than most people's. I noticed the same scent of roses in the waiting room of Mr. Arsehole. That plus you knowing my name and it's fairly clear you had to sit through the spectacle back there."

"Actually, I stood."

He laughed, then said, "Well, I'm just fine, so you can look elsewhere for your good deed of the day."

"*My* good deed? You just saved my life."

She struggled to find words—something she hated experiencing. At least at the page she could take her time. But with Winston right in front of her—getting ready to leave—she knew her opportunity was closing.

"I'd like to interview you," she said.

He snorted.

"I'm serious. That's why I was at the agency in the first place. What happened between you and Mr. Abrams... Well, let's just say that I no longer trust his judgment of character."

"Seeing as how he has none himself?"

She laughed and felt a weird lightness shoot through her stomach. When was the last time she had laughed? She couldn't remember, had only experienced it vicariously through her characters in... Months?

Years? No wonder Jazz had been worried enough to insist Elsa move to Summer Park.

"You all right, love?"

The lightness skittered through her chest, oddly making her heart feel tight. Or maybe making her aware of the tension that was already there.

She shook her head and smiled. "I'm fine, just hungry. And you should know I'll probably starve to death if you walk away thinking that this is me trying to be altruistic."

He let out another snort and started to pull away, but Elsa held on.

"I'm serious. The most nutritious thing I've had to eat in the last week was a rancid tuna sandwich."

"Rancid tuna? Not even 'rancid tuna salad'?"

"I wish. I thought it was tuna salad because the meat was all runny."

"Runny meat..."

"But I don't have any mayonnaise or radishes in the house."

"Why would you need radishes to make tuna salad?"

"I usually chop it up and mix it in. Aren't you supposed to put radish in tuna salad?"

"Relish, not—"

Now that her mouth was running, she couldn't seem to stop it. She hadn't spoken to anyone for a while, and Mr. Cooper had a strangely reassuring presence. She knew that if he had a problem with her, he would tell her straight out. That was a wonderful feeling.

"Come to think of it, the last time I *did* try to make tuna salad, I ended up in the ER."

"I'm afraid to ask, but...more runny meat?"

"No, I have a tendency to be easily distracted when working on a new book and lost my focus with the knife."

He stared at her with pale gray eyes, then shook his head. "Oh, my love. You do need my help. Come on. Let's get that lunch and see what we can work out."

Elsa smiled as they started across the street.

Heinrich

London, England—1881

"You should not be here, Heinrich."

Dante approached Heinrich slowly, taking care not to let the catwalks sway overmuch. Though there were ropes one could use to maintain balance, it unnerved Dante to see his mentor with only a thin piece of wood between himself and the floor of the theater far below.

Heinrich's words were accented by his native German when he spoke. "I suppose that is true. But I like to come up here every now and again. It is good to seek some perspective on one's life, is it not?"

"Indeed."

Dante stopped close enough to catch Heinrich should he lose his balance. There was a pallor to the older man's skin that had increased daily for some time. Dante's concern had also grown, but he was uncertain how far he dared press for answers.

"Is something wrong?" Dante asked.

"Many things." Heinrich's eyes appeared glazed, as if he was not truly observing the rehearsal going on below. "Distance is sometimes necessary to achieve true perspective. Do you believe that, Dante?"

"I do."

"I am glad for that." Heinrich took a deep breath and rubbed his left arm as if he was cold.

"Would you like my jacket?"

"No, just your company." He cast a glance at Dante, then quickly turned away.

"Of course," Dante said. He did his best to keep the hurt from his tone.

That even Heinrich was among those who could not stand to look at

794

Dante pained him greatly. When others saw Dante's mask and thought of the disfigurement beneath, he scarcely felt it anymore. He had grown numb to the masses, to their fear. But Heinrich was his mentor—one of the few people who would actually speak to Dante. He wanted Heinrich to not care about the scars beneath Dante's mask.

Heinrich chuckled. "Do you remember the day I found you at the circus? The mastermind who designed incredible mechanisms for their performances."

Dante would not go into detail about how very much he remembered. Heinrich had not yet grown the beard that currently covered his face, but only a shaped mustache. He had been holding his hat in his hands, and smiled as Dante approached.

After clearing his throat, Dante said, "I will always remember the day we met."

"As will I." Heinrich nodded. "But it was not that day."

"I beg your pardon?"

"I met you the day you were born. The very moment. But the last time I had seen you before I found you at the circus... Well, you were too young to remember me. I and your mother...we were very close."

The board seemed to sway beneath Dante's feet. Why had Heinrich not mentioned this before?

A sleeping dream that Dante had fought since that day at the circus woke within him. He had not allowed himself to think of Heinrich as a father-figure. Only as a mentor. But if Heinrich had been present when Dante was born...

"I had been searching for you both," Heinrich said. "For years, while I also worked to start this theater. I needed a means to support—" He let out a wheezing breath, rubbing his chest.

Dante's heart was thundering in his ears, making him light-headed. If Heinrich was experiencing anything similar, it was most certainly unsafe for the pair to remain on the catwalks.

"You are unwell," Dante said, daring to rest his hand on Heinrich's arm. "Let me help you to your room. We can speak more after you have rested."

Heinrich shook his head. "No. It must be said. Now. The theater is lost to us."

"What?"

"The debt-collectors are circling. It is only a matter of time."

"But the house is full for every show. My devices—"

"Your devices are a great part of what has drawn people to our performances, and for that I thank you," Heinrich said. "But no amount of ticket sales will ever be enough for Klaus. We must start over again. I fear your brother has gambled us into bankruptcy."

"My brother…"

When Heinrich looked up again, his eyes glistened with tears. "I am so sorry not to have told you this before. I thought it safer to moderate my affection for you."

Dante's mind reeled, but at least this he understood. Of course it was safer not to be known as the sire of a deformed freak. He held no ill-will toward Heinrich—his father. All he could feel in that moment was joy and hope.

He had a family. It did not matter if he had to keep it a secret to protect them. He had a—

"Father?"

Heinrich doubled over, clutching his chest. The wheeze of his breath became a gasp.

"Heinrich!" Dante yelled.

Dante heard a matching shout from below just as Heinrich fell forward over the rope railing. Leaping after, Dante grabbed Heinrich's arm with one hand and a rope that looped down from the rafters with his other. The force of their weight jerking against his grip almost made him slip, but he held on.

"Heinrich!"

His father hung limply from his hand, head lolling to the side as they slowly spun from the inertia of their fall. Dante's hands were weakening, the rope biting into his skin as he slid lower.

"Please, you must… I can't hold on! Heinrich!"

There was no sound, no wheezing breath, nothing. Just the rustle of fabric as Heinrich's arm slipped from Dante's grasp.

Time seemed to slow as he watched Heinrich fall. Dante thought their gazes locked for a moment, but Heinrich was just staring—staring at nothing...

He landed in the seats beneath them, the sound sickening, his body, his neck, at angles impossible to support life. Shouts from the actors rehearsing below drowned out Dante's own scream.

His father was dead.

For the briefest of moments, Dante considered letting go of the rope. It would be too easy to stop fighting, to stop trying. To let all the fear and hate that surrounded him daily just disappear. But he could not bring himself to relinquish the gift of life that his parents had given him. Dante pulled himself back up onto the catwalk, laying prone upon the board as his tears soaked into the wood.

People were sobbing beneath him, shock and grief thickening the air. He heard Mary's voice, and Edgar's. They would come to Dante if he did not rise, and he did not want either to risk the catwalks while distraught. If he lost Mary too, he would not survive it.

He rose to his knees, holding the rope railing to steady himself, and saw a light...

At first, he thought it was someone coming across the catwalks with a lantern, but the light was too large and diffuse. He blinked away his tears to find himself staring into rich chestnut eyes set in a golden light that was almost too bright to look upon.

Had he fallen as well and did not realize it? Had he died and this was an angel sent to ferry him to Heaven?

Her form was slight and feminine, but he saw no wings at her back. Sadness seemed to emanate from her, and a deep longing welled up within Dante as they stared into each other's eyes.

The angel reached for him, and he lifted his hand in return. Before they touched, Mary ran through the figure as if she couldn't perceive it at all, and the golden light vanished.

"Dante!" Mary dropped to her knees before him and threw her arms around his neck, sobbing.

Edgar stood behind her, one hand on the rope railing and the other clutching her shoulder to keep her safe. Dante wrapped one arm around her and patted her back, meeting Edgar's gaze. Edgar nodded, then quickly looked away. Though he did not mind Mary's affection toward her own mentor, Edgar preferred to avoid Dante's company.

At the moment, Dante *wanted* solitude. His mind was over-full. Heinrich was—had been—his father, and now gone. His brother Klaus had need of Dante's help if they were to save their family's theater. And the golden light, those longing eyes...

Through his grief and confusion, the comfort the angel provided remained. She had come for Heinrich. And with that, Dante was assured that Heinrich was in a better place. He held onto that hope as he rose, helping Mary to her feet.

All Hallow's Eve...
Part One

Summer Park, Florida —Several Years Ago

Jazz had outdone herself. Garrett stepped into the crowded ballroom at the Orange Grove Inn, looking around at the amazing decorations. A couple of witches on broomsticks flew overhead, a cloud of bats following them. Ghosts and ghouls clung to the banisters of the landing that wrapped around the place. All of the sculptures were made out of paper from the look of things, making it both a party and a gallery showing.

Genius.

A huge full moon hung in the center of the ballroom, thin paper catching the light from the chandelier above to make it glow with a soft light.

Damn. There went his costume.

He was dressed in one of his finer suits, a dark charcoal gray that he hoped made him look a little mysterious. If anyone asked what he was supposed to be, he planned to say he was a werewolf. The punch line was that there wasn't a full moon that night.

He looked at the giant paper moon again. Hopefully, no one would ask.

All he had to do was locate Jazz, let her know he'd put in an appearance, and be on his way. He could be home with his feet up, sitting in his favorite recliner and sipping a beer in two hours.

He spotted the bar and headed over, thinking he could at least enjoy a beer during his search. The bartender was busy talking to another hotel staff member. Garrett took the opportunity to snag a bottle while they were distracted. Maybe the night wouldn't be that bad after all.

He turned back toward the crowd. So many people. He'd had his fill of parties already that week. He scanned the sea of bobbing heads, looking for Jazz, but didn't see her. Sticking to the edges of the room, he made his way to a set of stairs that led to the landing above, hoping to get a better view. Even from up there, he didn't have any luck.

The air shifted, warm and lightly scented with gardenia. Fresh air. He headed in that direction, wanting to get away from the chill of the AC. A set of double doors led onto a dark balcony. Perfect.

The door creaked as he opened it. He stepped outside and closed it behind him. A woman was standing at the stone railing, still as a statue.

"Oh, excuse me," he said.

She was tall, her figure hugged by a dark suit that reminded him of his own. Her hair was pulled up on top of her head. She didn't turn around when he stepped outside. Didn't even acknowledge his presence.

"I didn't know anybody else was out here."

She still didn't respond. He started to grow concerned. A second floor balcony wasn't a great place to jump from, but he'd seen people try worse ways of ending themselves. He walked over to her slowly, watching for any sign that he might be setting her off. He relaxed a tiny bit when she let him get within arm's reach, but remained ready to grab her.

"Ma'am? Are you all right?"

She sighed as she turned to him. His heart started to thud in his chest.

Rachel Montgomery. He'd never seen her from this close. He'd wanted to, even tried a few times, but she had a knack for disappearing right when he thought he was about to reach her. They'd only made eye contact from across crowds or worse—clusters of tables where it would be way too awkward for him to get up and walk through the room to introduce himself.

He'd still considered it a time or two.

Now they were alone together on a dark balcony, close enough to touch.

He'd always thought she was gorgeous. He upgraded his assessment to stunning. Honey-blonde hair and pale blue eyes. He'd managed to get close enough to catch that in the past, though under circumstances where they couldn't speak.

A couple of times she'd rolled her eyes at him across the distance—communicating without words a sentiment they seemed to share. Neither of them liked the fundraisers they were socially obligated to attend. He was pretty sure, anyway.

And she was tall. Taller than he'd thought, even. She must be wearing sky-high heels. He'd never been so close to a woman's face while standing toe-to-toe. Close enough to lean forward and kiss.

She cleared her throat, snapping him out of his train of thought.

"Hello," she said.

"Hello, yourself."

He felt himself smile. He had wanted to introduce himself to her so many times before. Now that he had a chance to talk to her, he wasn't sure what to say.

"You're Rachel Montgomery."

Smooth.

"Yes. That's me."

She laughed. Her smile could light him up from across a room. From this close, it was like being struck by lightning.

When he could finally speak, he said, "I'm Garrett Wolfstrom."

"Right. Dr. Wolfstrom. It's good to meet you."

He quickly moved his beer to his left hand when she extended her right. He was *not* going to miss the opportunity to touch her. He'd imagined this moment too many times to let it slip away.

Her skin was cool, her grip surprisingly strong. The hair on the back of his neck stood on end. His stomach was doing flip-flops of the sort he hadn't felt since he'd been a teenager chatting up a girl.

She was staring at his lips—almost like she was thinking about kissing him, too. Her eyes locked on his, and for a moment, he felt as if the rest of the world disappeared, leaving just the two of them.

Then she let out a laugh and pulled her hand away. The world came back into sharp, harsh focus. Love at first sight was a ridiculous notion. They'd never even spoken. And what? He thought they'd fall into each other's arms the first time they were close enough to touch?

He had spent too much time daydreaming about the mysterious woman who always caught his eye—imagined a connection too strong to be real. But *something* was there. This was his chance to explore it.

"I didn't know you would be here," she said.

"Neither did I. There was a last minute shift change at the hospital."

If he had known she would be at the party, he would've put in for a shift change himself. He said a silent thanks to the universe for helping him out.

"I see." Her tone had become distanced and professional. "Are you enjoying the party?"

He shrugged. "Sure."

"That's not very convincing."

"Sorry."

He could feel her trying to put distance between them. He scrambled for a topic they had in common, something to draw her back again.

"I've reached my quota on socializing this week after that fundraising dinner that dragged on for five hours."

Rachel laughed. "They really needed a better planner for that one."

"Yeah. I just stepped out here to get some fresh air."

"Me, too."

Damn. He was intruding. She wanted a moment to herself, and he was too busy trying to ingratiate himself with her to notice.

"Well, you were here first. I don't mean to trouble you."

Before he could head to the door, she reached out and grabbed his arm. He froze, not sure what to do until she spoke again.

"Stay."

His heart started to pound. If she wanted him to stay, he would stay. Ridiculous time-frame or not, he had never felt such a deep connection with anyone before. He wanted to know what it meant—if she felt it, too. The way she was staring at him, holding his gaze, he had to wonder...

She cleared her throat again and let go of his arm. "It's a big balcony. And there aren't many other places you can get away from the crowds and not outright leave the party. Unless you're ready to go."

He didn't miss the wistfulness in her tone. He wasn't sure if she wanted to talk to him or just wanted someone to talk to in general.

"I was planning to stay for a little while. I haven't checked in with Jazz yet, and I want her to see that I showed up."

"She wasn't expecting you."

It was nice of Rachel to give him an out, but Jazz was more savvy than that. She would find out that Garrett had suddenly been given the night off. He didn't know how she'd do it, but he knew it would happen. And if he didn't show up to her party when his other plans had been cancelled, she'd be upset with him. If Jazz was only his art broker, it wouldn't be an issue. But over the years, they'd become friends.

"She has a way of knowing what's going on in town. She'd never let me hear the end of it if I bailed. I'm scared enough that I phoned in my costume."

Rachel looked him up and down. "I hesitate to guess what you're supposed to be."

"A werewolf."

"I had no idea werewolves had such good senses of fashion."

He straightened his tie, beaming under the compliment. "Not all do."

She laughed and shook her head. "Did you spend the whole day shaving for this event? Filing down your fangs and claws?"

"Didn't have to." He grinned, hoping she'd be amused at his joke. "It's not a full moon."

She burst out in laughter. Real, earthy laughter. She almost doubled over from it.

After a bit, she quieted down. That thousand-watt smile beamed at him.

"That's very clever, Dr. *Wolf*strom." She emphasized the first half of his unusual surname.

"That's where I got the idea."

He must be grinning like a fool. He took a sip of his beer to try to tone down his own smile, then leaned against the railing. She mirrored his posture.

"I have to ask, where did you get that beer?" she asked.

"Swiped it from behind the bar while the bartender was restocking. They're really partying hard in there."

She nodded. "I noticed. We've already had to send one reveler home in a cab."

"I'm glad you're taking care of people. We just dealt with a bad car accident in the ER."

Her face fell. A haunted look entered her eyes as she stared through him. Maybe she had known someone who was involved. He might have stepped in it bad.

After a moment, he said, "You okay?"

"What? Yeah." She shook her head and let out a short bark of a laugh. "It's just... Halloween is already creepy enough. I don't like thinking about that kind of thing."

Welcome to my world.

"I'll let you in on a secret." He leaned a little closer. "Neither do I."

Garrett hated nights like those in the ER. Summer Park wasn't a big town, but he worked in the most advanced hospital in a large area. A lot of accidents were funneled to them. He had seen things that...he didn't want to think about.

He took another swig of his beer, then realized that Rachel's hands were empty.

"You don't have a drink. Can I get you something?"

"I'm fine, thanks."

This time, when she laughed it sounded more genuine.

"You don't have to play the Southern Gentleman with me," she said.

That went against a lifetime of conditioning. If she was going to let him off the hook, the least he could do was the same for her.

"Fair enough," he said. "In that case, you don't have to be a Southern Belle."

"Oh thank God."

She slouched against the rail, her perfect posture falling away. Garrett let out a laugh and she smiled at him, then stood straight again. But not too straight.

She regarded him silently for a moment, then said, "Actually, I think I've changed my mind."

Was she sending him away? The thought that she preferred solitude to his company hurt more than it should. He had daydreamed about talking with her, built a whole fantasy around her without even realizing it until now. He thought those stolen moments—even shared across huge rooms—had meant...something.

Maybe it meant he needed to get out more.

She gestured to his beer. "You don't have to get me anything, but do you mind sharing?"

Sharing? Hell yeah.

He was still in the game. He felt himself grin as he handed her the bottle.

"Not a bit."

Maybe he was setting himself up for disappointment. There was no way she could live up to his daydreams. Then again, the chemistry he'd already experienced with her was nothing short of amazing. He had a feeling when it came to Rachel Montgomery the reality would be beyond his imaginings.

He sure as hell couldn't wait to find out.

All Hallow's Eve...
Part Two

Summer Park, Florida —Several Years Ago

Rachel was surrounded by monsters. Everywhere she looked, she saw vampires, zombies, werewolves, and...ghosts. Her face hurt from the forced smile she was keeping firmly in place. Her eyes burned from tears she *would not* shed.

This was her party, after all.

The main ballroom of the Orange Grove Inn was fully decked out for Halloween. She had commissioned paper art in the form of witches on broomsticks, flying bats, and a giant illuminated full moon that hung from the ceiling. The landing that wrapped around the room giving it a second level had similar sculptures attached to the banisters so that it looked like the people dancing below were about to be pounced upon by various creatures.

Not only did it make the place look perfect for a Halloween costume party, she had supported half a dozen local artists, asking them to work together to turn the place into a sort of art gallery of its own. Which was fitting, since the party was being thrown by her boss—the owner of the Jazz Gallery. Rachel was proud of her accomplishment, even if she couldn't relax enough to enjoy it.

A cool breeze caressed the back of her neck, sending goose-bumps down her arms. She knew what would come next—the echoing voices, impossible to tune out even with the music and conversation that surrounded her. Voices only she could hear.

"This one's pretty. Look at that golden hair."

Rachel felt a slight pull on her hair. Her stomach roiled. Someone was touching her. Someone *dead*.

She had almost grown accustomed to hearing them. Thankfully, touches were much less common. Thoughts raced through her brain. What should she do? If she didn't react, that would be strange. If she over-reacted, that would be even worse. What would a normal person do? Someone who couldn't hear *them?*

She decided to pretend that she had experienced it as an itch. As naturally as she could feign, she scratched the spot where her scalp had felt the tug on her hair.

"Her eyes are so blue. She looks like a doll."

"Shall we play with her?"

Play… She wanted to scream and run away. But if she did, she would completely blow her cover. She couldn't risk them realizing that she could perceive them. Once they knew, they would never leave her alone.

She should have worn a costume. She stood out, wearing a navy blue pantsuit. This was the first party that Jazz had given Rachel complete control over. It was her chance to prove herself. She didn't want to blow it. She wanted to look professional, and honestly she couldn't bring herself to dress up as something. She worked so hard to seem normal.

Rachel glanced around the room, looking for an escape. She remembered a set of double-doors on the second level that led to a small balcony. The main focus of the party was in the ballroom. Bored spirits would be attracted to people. They wouldn't look for anyone out there. She just needed a few minutes to collect herself.

She wove among the people, smiling and saying a few words here and there, hoping the ghosts would get distracted and leave her alone. Finally emerging on the other side of the crowd, she walked up the stairs and made her way out onto the balcony. She walked to the railing and pressed her hands against the warm stone. The sun had only set a few hours ago and it still retained some heat from the Floridian afternoon.

Even in autumn, the air was muggy, but it wasn't oppressively hot.

She took a deep breath and let it out, staring up at the stars. She was alone. She was finally alone.

She didn't want to be.

Why did it always have to be ghosts?

The door creaked open behind her. She pretended not to hear it.

If the ghosts had followed her, she was in trouble. Most would prefer the activity of the party rather than trying to entertain themselves by scaring one person. Even worse, if they were powerful enough to open the door, they would be able to do much more than tug on her hair. She should have brought along her perfume bottle that she'd filled with saltwater. Trying to find some salt nearby to disrupt them with would absolutely tip her hand.

"Oh, excuse me."

Rachel didn't turn around. The voice was deep, with a distinct Southern drawl. Plenty of ghosts in Florida had the same accent, but the speaker's voice lacked the echoing quality of a spirit. Still, she was afraid to turn around. If she was wrong, she'd be letting him know she could hear him.

"I didn't know anybody else was out here," he said.

When she didn't respond, he walked up next to her, letting her see him out of the corner of her eye. She could only see ghosts in reflections. He was alive.

"Ma'am? Are you all right?"

She let out a huge breath, then turned to greet him, her smile becoming a tiny bit less fake. Her words caught in her throat when she saw who it was.

Garrett. Dr. Garrett Wolfstrom.

Oh wow…

She had never seen him from this close.

He was a few inches taller than she was, even in her heels. He had to be at least six and a half feet tall. His hair was brown, cut close on the sides with a little more length on top. He had styled it to spike up so it looked like he'd just woken up and rolled out of bed. His features were decidedly masculine, matching his enormous physique. His eyes were a deep, rich blue.

The only light on the balcony came from the double-doors that led back into the hotel, but she didn't need more to know exactly what he looked like. She had studied him too many times at the various fundraisers they'd both attended—always from across the room. She never let him get too close. She hadn't known why until this moment.

Her skin prickled. Her heart pounded. She felt a flush creep over her cheeks. The pull she felt toward him was incredible. She had already taken a step closer before she managed to stop herself.

She cleared her throat and said, "Hello."

He looked confused for a moment, then said, "Hello, yourself."

He smiled. She had never seen him smile like that—a real smile, if somewhat hesitant. Not one of the practiced smiles he used at public events. A faint hint of dimples formed on his cheeks.

"You're Rachel Montgomery," he said.

"Yes. That's me." She laughed, grinning like a kid and feeling like one. Her stomach kept lurching as if she was on a roller-coaster. It wasn't too surprising that he knew her name, but she still found it ridiculously flattering.

"I'm Garrett Wolfstrom."

"Right. Dr. Wolfstrom. It's good to meet you."

She extended her hand. It would be weird not to. They were really just meeting, after all, and it was only polite. It had nothing at all to do with the fact that she wanted to know if his hands were as strong as they looked, if his skin would be smooth or rough, warm or cool.

He had an open bottle of beer in his right hand. He switched it to his left and took her hand in his.

Her body lit up, fresh goosebumps spreading along her arms, across her back, and even down her legs. His hand was smooth and warm, his grip strong but surprisingly gentle. Then again, as a doctor, he would need a deft touch.

His lips parted. She noticed, because she was staring at them. She snapped her gaze to his, trying to focus on anything but the amazing energy arcing between them. That was a mistake. His eyes had softened and he was looking at her as if…

As if he felt it, too.

She forced a laugh, pulling her hand away. Again, he looked confused.

Desperate to focus on something else, she tried to start a conversation. "I didn't know you would be here."

"Neither did I. There was a last minute shift change at the hospital."

"I see. Are you enjoying the party?"

He shrugged and said, "Sure."

"That's not very convincing."

"Sorry. I've reached my quota on socializing this week after that fundraising dinner that dragged on for five hours."

Rachel laughed. "They really needed a better planner for that one."

"Yeah. I just stepped out here to get some fresh air."

"Me, too."

"Well, you were here first. I don't mean to trouble you." He started to turn toward the door, but Rachel reached for his arm to halt him.

"Stay."

Where had that come from? She hadn't been thinking, just… feeling. She wanted him to stay.

His smile slowly faded. Her mouth went dry as they stared into each other's eyes.

She cleared her throat again, pulling her hand away. "It's a big balcony. And there aren't very many other places you can get away from the crowds and not outright leave the party. Unless you're ready to go."

She hoped he wasn't.

"I was planning to stay for a little while. I haven't checked in with Jazz yet, and I want her to see that I showed up."

"She wasn't expecting you."

"She has a way of knowing what's going on in town. She'd never let me hear the end of it if I bailed. I'm scared enough that I phoned in my costume."

Rachel took in his outfit. It was a stylish suit and tie, maybe a step down from the formal attire she usually saw him in, but still very nice.

"I hesitate to guess what you're supposed to be," she said.

"A werewolf."

"I had no idea werewolves had such good senses of fashion."

He straightened his tie and grinned. "Not all do."

She laughed and shook her head. "Did you spend the whole day shaving for this event? Filing down your fangs and claws?"

"Didn't have to." He gave her a cock-eyed smile, one of the dimples deepening on his cheek. "It's not a full moon."

She laughed. Long and hard. She couldn't stop herself.

When she finally recovered, she said, "That's very clever, Dr. *Wolf*strom."

His grin deepened. "That's where I got the idea."

He drank a sip of his beer and leaned against the railing. The bar wasn't supposed to be giving out beer in bottles. Jazz wanted her events to be in keeping with a certain vibe. His beer did not match her requirements. Rachel started to wonder if there might be a problem she needed to address.

"I have to ask, where did you get that beer?"

"Swiped it from behind the bar while the bartender was restocking. They're really partying hard in there."

She relaxed a little bit. She should probably get back to the party, but she couldn't bring herself to. Suddenly it wasn't because she was avoiding the crowd. She just wanted more time with him.

"I noticed," she said. "We've already had to send one reveler home in a cab."

"I'm glad you're taking care of people. We just dealt with a bad car accident in the ER."

She was aware. Rachel had heard a woman's disembodied voice while she was shopping with Jazz that day. The woman didn't seem to realize she was dead yet. She kept asking people why they were ignoring her and saying she had hurried through her errand as fast as she could before coming back to work. It was heartbreaking.

Rachel had accidentally caught a glimpse of the woman in a mirror behind the cashier's counter. It had taken all of her self-control not to react to the horrific sight. When she heard about the accident on the news later, she already knew people had died.

"You okay?" Garrett asked.

"What? Yeah." Rachel shook her head and forced a laugh. "It's just... Halloween is already creepy enough. I guess I don't like thinking about that kind of thing."

"I'll let you in on a secret." He leaned a little closer. "Neither do I."

He didn't laugh. Neither did she. She couldn't imagine the kind of stress and pressure he dealt with at the ER.

He took another drink, then glanced around. Standing up straight, he said, "You don't have a drink. Can I get you something?"

"I'm fine, thanks." Rachel laughed again, but this time it was real. It felt good. "You don't have to play the Southern Gentleman with me."

"Fair enough. In that case, you don't have to be a Southern Belle."

"Oh thank God." She dropped her proper posture and let herself lean against the rail in what she hoped was a comic slouch. Garrett's laugh let her know she hit her mark.

She smiled and stood straighter again. "Actually, I think I've changed my mind."

His smile faltered. She gestured to his beer.

"You don't have to get me anything, but do you mind sharing?"

It only took a moment for his grin to return. He handed her the bottle. "Not a bit."

She took a sip of the earthy brew—her first beer straight from a bottle. Her mother would be mortified. That only made it sweeter. She laughed as she handed it back to him. This was the closest she'd ever come to "meeting a guy under the bleachers". She'd made it all the way through college without a bit of rebelling. It felt good.

Being with him felt...right. And that was even more terrifying than the ghosts back in the ballroom.

The Limo

It had to be a limo.

Finn stopped behind the long black car, checking the parking spot number against the label on the key fob the receptionist had given him. J-7.

"Perfect." He said the word out loud, sarcasm sliding into bitterness. He tried not to think of Jazz.

Even the fucking spot number looked like her name. For all he knew, this was the same limo she had rented for their last date.

He managed not to crush the fob or chuck it across the garage after unlocking the doors. The receptionist was already helping him out by letting him examine the car. He didn't want to get her in trouble. He didn't want to get *himself* in trouble, either.

Technically, Garrett had called Finn off the case, but there was no way he was walking away from it. Finn hadn't just become a private investigator because he was uniquely well suited to the job. He couldn't stand to leave a mystery unexplored. And Dante Lucerne was a complete mystery.

He was living with one of Garrett's closest friends, Elsa Sinclair. Someone had just broken into her house, and for whatever reason, she refused to call the cops.

Garrett was over-protective of the people he cared about. It was part of what Finn loved about the big guy. So Finn had been checking into Dante for Garrett's peace of mind. Trouble was, the things Finn uncovered weren't reassuring.

The only Dante Lucerne Finn could find that was a match for Elsa's new friend had died in a fire in London—in 1881.

Even after Finn let Garrett know his preliminary findings, Garrett told Finn to back off. Elsa didn't want anyone poking around in her life. From what Garrett had told Finn about the break-in, she should have been hiring private security to watch her place. Maybe even a bodyguard.

No, Finn wasn't walking away from this case. It was under his skin. He'd been feeling…something. He wasn't even sure what. But it was building. A creepy sensation in his guts, like something was coming. Something bad.

Normal private investigators knew to listen to their gut. Finn wasn't normal—he was psychic. He damn sure needed to listen to his intuition, and it was screaming at him that there was much more to this case than met the eye.

He had no idea why Elsa was being so stubborn about this. No wonder she and Jazz were best friends. But Elsa and Garrett were close, too.

If Elsa wanted to take chances with her safety, that was her choice. But Garrett was near enough to the line of fire that Finn refused to sit by and do nothing. He had to find out how dangerous the situation was —even if that meant crawling around inside the back of a limo and sifting through everything that had gone down in it over the last few weeks.

This was not going to be pleasant, even without dealing with his own associations with limos.

He remembered the pale gold dress that Jazz had been wearing when she picked him up for what had become their last date, the intricate way she'd put up her hair, knowing how much he loved undoing her work and watching the dark strands tumble down over her shoulders. He remembered that damned secretive smirk tugging at her lips while she tried to negotiate her compromise.

A night out on the town—as long as they stayed behind tinted windows. As long as they weren't seen together.

He hadn't been able to take it anymore. The sneaking around. Not telling their friends they were a couple. He had ended their relationship right there, in the back of that limo.

Fucking maudlin thoughts.

He had work to do.

He opened the door and climbed in, then slammed it behind him. He didn't bother re-locking anything. If anyone came across him while he was working, they would think he had nodded off. Sometimes people thought he was meditating. Whatever helped them feel at peace with their world.

Finn had found his own peace in accepting that the world held a few mysteries that couldn't be unraveled—like his psychic power of psychometry. And he was glad for the mystery. Otherwise, life would be boring.

He decided to stay sitting by the door, since it was likely either Elsa or Dante had touched that part of the limo while getting in. Finn ran his hands over the seat until he found a spot that felt natural to rest them. He closed his eyes and took a deep breath, then let it out slowly. He relaxed and let his mind go blank. His hands itched and his eyes began to tingle.

Showtime.

He pushed his awareness into the past, imagining time speeding backwards. When he opened his eyes again, he wasn't alone. Not exactly, anyway.

The memories of the most recent occupants played out like a movie viewed on high-speed rewind. Looked like a bunch of kids celebrating prom. It was about graduation time. He smiled and let out a brief laugh at their antics, watching as they became *less* riled up as their evening unfolded in reverse.

Finn kicked up the speed, watching the people flit in and out of the limo even faster. He cringed at the few dreaded pornographic encounters, looking away and clenching his jaw. That could have been him and Jazz, if she'd had her way. He could have let himself hold her one more time, kissed her, buried his hands in her hair…

Goddammit, he needed to focus.

He let out another slow breath, bringing his attention back to the limo. This was a more challenging read than most, given all the traffic. At least the memories he was looking for were only a week and a half old.

Finally, something caught his eye. A man shrouded in a black cape sitting in the very spot Finn occupied. Those were always the creepiest readings—when he saw things from the person's direct point of view. He paused the vision and switched to what he called his pop-out view. His perspective shifted, like he was centered up above the action. The entire limo was visible in front of him.

More slowly, he rewound the memory a few moments, till he could see the unmistakable mask the man wore. Yup, it was Dante. Finn rewound the memories to the moment when Elsa and Dante entered the limo, then let it play out—with sound.

Finn went over their conversation three times, listening as Elsa explained to Dante that she had somehow transported him from 1800s London to modern-day Florida.

Finn tried to let it sink in, but his mind kept balking.

Time travel. *Time travel?*

It seemed unbelievable. Then again, Finn was watching events from the past play out around him like the ultimate 3-D movie.

No. No way. There had to be some other explanation. Elsa was a novelist. She was probably doing some sort of cosplay to boost her creativity.

Finn hovered, looking down at the limo's interior as he tried to think things through, letting time spin forward at a somewhat less accelerated speed.

The door opened again.

A man slinked onto the seat. He had blond hair that was about shoulder length, tied back in a ponytail. He slid his hands over the seat, a little like Finn had a moment ago.

Scratch that, not at all like Finn had.

This guy was being creepy about it. Really creepy.

He closed his eyes and took a deep breath, then let it out slowly.

"Elsa…"

Finn wasn't sure he heard right, so he rewound the moment and played it again. It sure sounded like the creep had said Elsa's name. But who was this guy?

"Mr. Connelly?"

Words spoken in real-time battered into his vision, snapping him back to his normal perspective with a jolt. Finn shook his head, then glanced at the woman leaning into the limo.

"My boss is about to come back from lunch. Did you find what you needed?"

"Yeah."

Finn did his best to ignore her hopeful smile or the way she was obviously trying to give him a glimpse of her cleavage. She was sweet and pretty, but he wasn't up for starting a relationship. And he sure as hell didn't want anything casual.

He handed her the key fob as he exited the limo, being careful not to let their hands touch. Reading objects for a case was one thing— reading the thoughts her body was already betraying was another.

"Thanks. I appreciate your help." He gave her one last smile before heading to the exit.

There *was* more going on with this case than he realized. He needed to call Garrett. But first Finn had a little more digging to do.

—

Thank you so much for reading *The Summer Park Psychics* series! These characters have always felt so real to me, as if I'm slipping into an alternate universe when writing them. The friends are all together, but I have a feeling their stories are far from over. Wait till you see what happens with their kids.

In the meantime, there's some bold paranormal romance waiting for you in *The Forbidden Knights* series. Or if you'd like to try some Science Fiction Romance (set on familiar Earth), check out the first *Blades of Janus* novel or *The Department of Homeworld Security* novellas.

It's been a grand adventure. Thanks for joining my friends and I in Summer Park!

—

About the Author

USA Today Bestselling author Cassandra Chandler uses her vivid imagination to make the world more interesting, spawning the ideas she turns into her whimsical Science Fiction romcoms and darkly evocative Paranormal and Urban Fantasy Romances. Fast-paced and funny, lighthearted or dark, her stories will introduce you to characters you want to be friends with and worlds where you'd like to build a vacation home.

www.ingramcontent.com/pod-product-compliance
Lightning Source LLC
Chambersburg PA
CBHW070339030726
47504CB00001B/3